Hesed

Hesed

by

Maytee Aspuro y Gonzalez

Cavalier Press
2006

Hesed

Copyright © 2006 by Maytee Aspuro y Gonzalez

ISBN 0-9765664-5-1

0 9 8 7 6 5 4 3 2 1

Cover Concept by Maytee Aspuro y Gonzalez
Cover Design by Michelle M. De La Rosa

Published by Cavalier Press, LLP
P.O. Box 6437, Falls Church, VA 22040
Web site http://www.cavalierpress.com

Printed and bound in the United States of America

Acknowledgements

My gratitude to my brothers, Gil and R. Andre, my friends, and my teachers for accompanying me on my journey, to Catharine Liddicoat for making me a better writer, to Michelle M. De La Rosa for bringing *Hesed* to Cavalier Press and for her cover artwork, to Nene Adams and Joanna Sandsmark for their editorial expertise, to Kay Porter for ushering the novel through the publication process and finally, to my fellow seekers of all faiths who left their words for me to ponder.

In memory of
Acacia Emma Gonzalez y Garcia
my mother

And among His [God's] signs is this, He [God] created for you mates from among yourselves, that you may find rest in them, and He [God] has put love and mercy between you: verily there are signs in this for those who reflect.

-Qur'an, Ar-Rum, Surah 30:21

CHAPTER 1

The young priest walked pass the thrift shop, the counter restaurant, and the scattered taverns – all the familiar storefront landmarks of a neighborhood of aged tall buildings that carved a canyon of poverty and despair onto the Chicago asphalt streets and cracked cement sidewalks. Disheartened, she left the neighborhood community center. With the economic downturn, City Hall went into a fiscal retrenching mode. The day care program for elders was at risk. Partners and other caretakers were called to organize early and lobby for continuation of program funding.

She did not know how to answer the question of why God made humanity so fragile, or why the society God's creation fashioned was so unjust. The priest knew that within the weeks to come there would be similar meetings called to order by other groups seeking continuation of program funding for homeless shelters and food pantries, for after school programs and health clinics. The paradox she observed was that as unemployment grew and with it the need for these very services, society was less willing to give.

She felt the chill of the wet autumn night seep into her bones and muscles. Underneath her raincoat she was dressed in the standard Episcopalian priestly garb of black slacks and a black blouse with a white collar. She wished she had worn a sweater to stave off the cold.

The assailant swung an arm across the priest's neck and pushed her back into the alley. Her body was pressed against the assailant's. Stunned, for the first few heartbeats she had done nothing to resist. Returning her focus to the moment she knew she had to act quickly. With her right leg she kicked back against the assailant's shin. She heard the slip of metal. A knife was placed at her throat.

"Do that again and I'll cut you."

The priest was surprised by the voice. It was low and throaty, and a woman possessed it. Though it may have been illogical, she felt less at risk. Rape was not a motivation. She relaxed. If she was being robbed the sum of money she carried was little, and her identification and one lone credit card could be replaced.

Her cessation of resistance was noted by the owner of the voice. "That's better."

With a quick motion the priest was thrust against the brick wall of the local dry cleaners. She raised her hands to cushion the impact. The rough-hewn surface scraped her palms, breaking the skin. She bled.

The voice directed, "Turn around and keep your hands where I can see them."

The priest moved slowly. She would rather not see her assailant. She knew that being able to identify who would do her harm only put her at greater risk of harm. The priest purposely kept her eyes down. Only her own shoes entered her line of sight.

Nothing happened. Nothing was said, no direction given. The priest wondered if she was being played with. Why must her fear be the object of folly? She knew that in incidents such as these perceptions are altered. Time passed slowly, unbearably so. She would wait no longer no matter the consequences. The priest raised her head. As she did her eyes traveled across the black boots, black jeans, black T-shirt, black leather jacket and long black hair of the woman standing before her. Her gaze continued up until it took in the beauty of the woman's olive skin and dark features. The woman's eyes bridged the chasm of light and dark. Her eyes were a crystal sea blue. The priest found it difficult to believe that the owner of those eyes would have placed a switchblade to her throat and yet, she had.

The woman, perhaps no more than five years older than her victim, stared at the young priest. "Do I know you?" The woman's voice betrayed her crumbling air of intimidation.

The priest braced herself as the woman reached out with her knife-holding hand.

The woman's hand trembled. So too did the blade a few inches from the priest's cheek. The image of the priest swept across the woman's already confused consciousness. The priest was not very tall but she had a presence to her. Her short blond hair fell in wisps across her forehead and over her ears. Her eyes were emerald green, clear and intelligent. Brave given that they dared match the woman's own. The woman was not sure why she had taken the priest at knifepoint, or why she stood in the alleyway with her. She had to have had a reason. She looked about her in an effort to lessen her disorientation. She shook her head trying to throw off the throbbing pain in her temples. The woman saw the cross hanging around the priest's neck. She pointed to it.

"That's a lie."

The priest did not answer her.

The woman grabbed the cross and ripped it off the priest.

Reaching for her wallet the priest begged, "Please don't. Take my money, not the cross."

The woman observed the passions of the priest rise. She liked what she saw, a vivid unbridled spark of life. Whatever it was that the woman sought she now had a bit of it in her hand and she was not going to give it up. "Where is your God now?" she asked the priest with satisfaction.

"Hey Rev! You all right?"

The priest and her assailant both turned their attention to the source of the question. Three young men were crossing the street toward the alley. The woman looked back at the priest. She felt a haunting incompleteness she could not explain. She was not done with the priest. Whatever still needed to be would have to wait. The woman looked back down the alley cut short by a wooden fence. She ran towards the fence and hoisted herself on top of an industrial trash bin that stood adjacent to it. She took one final look back to the priest before scaling over the wood, securing an easy escape.

With anger and equal fascination the priest watched her assailant's flight. Her most precious possession had been taken. 'Where is your God now?' She knew the answer was not always certain. She took solace in the fact that on this night God remained in her heart. God was not a lie. Lie or not, her assailant had stolen her cross. The priest wondered why.

CHAPTER 2

The mid-morning sun shone a wedge of light through the industrial skylight. The woman lay on her bed, legs and arms tucked close in a fetal position. She felt the warmth of the sunlight upon her cheek. It was not welcomed. She felt feverish and if she could have moved without pain she would have claimed the cool October air by raising herself up and out onto the fire escape. Weak, she drifted back to sleep.

By noon her headache had subsided leaving only a mild irritating trace to remind her of her helplessness, of how she was a slave to her body's betrayals. She opened her eyes slowly, allowing them to adjust to the bright light. Her arms were held against her breast. She was a child seeking safety from haunting demons. A tear cut across her cheek. She knew there was no escaping her demons. They resided within her.

She felt in one closed hand a foreign weight. She stared at the hand ignorant of its content. Slowly, with a sense of foreboding, she opened the hand. Her eyes studied the gold cross and chain. They were not hers. She did not know them. She did not remember how she had gotten possession of them. She raised herself up to a sitting position and studied the cross and chain further. The chain's clasp was broken. The cross was very simple in line and form. It was not modern. It had the look of an antique.

The woman closed her eyes, seeking her last memory. The threads of the previous day came to her one by one. She wove them together in an attempt to finish a tapestry that would illustrate all she needed to know. She remembered she had helped work the Elysian Fields Pub. Feeling a rising pressure against her temples, she had left before bar time. She remembered nothing more. It was hard for her to ignore the growing pattern of blackouts.

She got up and moved across the open loft space to the tall, floor-to-ceiling windows that comprised the building's façade. The city had been awake for hours. The neighborhood went about its business, an organism of dependencies. The delivery truck in front of the mercado was being unloaded as both the young and old neighborhood residents entered the market to buy the essential foodstuffs to feed themselves and their families. On the corner, the newsstand vendor kept a watchful eye to prevent his inventory from mysteriously slipping under a patron's jacket. Jacob Levi, the local attorney, stood outside of his office smoking his pipe. Stepping out alongside of him, offering the elderly Jew a cup of coffee was Liza, his wife and office manager.

There were more Jacobs and Lizas. Instead of Jew, they were Moslem, Buddhist, Hindu and an assortment of Christian denominations including Catholic, Episcopalian, Baptist, Eastern Orthodox, Lutheran and Methodist. Instead of Polish, they were old neighborhood Italians, Irish and Greeks blending with new neighborhood African Americans, Asians, Eastern and Western Europeans, and Middle Easterns. The mix of occupations ranged the gamut – local merchants, factory laborers, municipal workers, low end service providers and the few professionals, like the woman, who refused to permanently leave, having been born in the neighborhood, having left to be educated but returning, pulled back by a force closer to a mystic's temperament than that of a modern urbanite.

She turned back into her loft. The expansive setting was created by the combination of limited dividers, high ceilings, and skylights bracketed by Cream City brick walls. The space was complemented with furnishings of simple line and form, not unlike the cross she held in her hand. She stood within her office amid a teak desk, credenza and computer table. Tall back-less bookshelves lined the loft wall. Before her was her one extravagance, a chef's kitchen with wood block island, and three tall stools to one side. To her right, a black steel bed, with adjacent teak night tables, a tall chest of drawers, and a freestanding mirror formed the bedroom. A series of oriental screens provided privacy. The living room was at one side of the loft entrance while the dining room was at the other. A few area rugs delineated the individual spaces, offering warmth. Her preference was to maximize the exposure of the well-polished oak floors.

Throughout the loft she had hung limited edition black and white photographs, original charcoal and pencil drawings, and limited edition prints of the female form. She had accented her space with a few selected tabletop sculptures and hand-made works of pottery.

This was her home. It was a sanctuary she consented to share with only a handful of friends. All but a few in the streets below were aware of its existence. The day was half-gone and she had work to do. She was relieved that the work could be done without leaving this space. But she also knew that she would have to eventually leave its protection and she wondered, once again gazing at the cross and chain, who was in more danger – she or those she encountered.

CHAPTER 3

The bars were closing. The street was scattered with the last nighthawks reeking of alcohol and cigarette smoke. Nicole Thera and her companion, Paige Manstead, walked down the street. Paige strutted, visibly claiming possession of the much taller Nicole. Nicole saw the young female priest approaching them. The priest paused; her gaze held them, her mien hardening. Nicole felt Paige's hold tighten. Paige wore a scowl. Nicole knew Paige had little patience for anything that hinted of religion.

As they passed underneath a streetlight Paige challenged the cleric. "What you looking at, Reverend?" she asked disdainfully.

The priest directed her response to Nicole, her tone a sharp clip. "Hello."

Paige interrupted the silence. With a mocking bow, she offered an introduction. "Nicki, have you met the good Reverend Elizabeth Kelly? The Reverend is the new priest at St. Ann's."

Nicole felt mastered by the young priest's eyes. She remained silent. Something felt terribly wrong but she did not know what.

Paige called Nicole from her passive stance. "Hey girl, look this way." Numb, Nicole did as she was asked. Paige seized her and gave her a sloppy, exaggerated kiss.

Reverend Kelly stepped away and then began moving ahead toward her destination. Nicole pulled herself apart from her companion and watched the priest take her leave.

"Hey, Nicki, if getting close to God turns you on, we'll have to hang around the church," Paige said sarcastically.

"Shut-up, Paige!" Nicole's temper showed itself.

Paige spoke with greater care. "What's with you?"

"Nothing. Let's go."

Paige placed her hands on her hips. "Gotta admit, the priest has balls to still be walking the streets this late at night."

Nicole had no point of reference. "What do you mean?"

"Hell girl, where have you been? Neighborhood line is she got mugged a couple of weeks ago. Bastard stole her grandmother's cross."

"Cross?"

"Yeah. Mugging a priest is low."

Nicole felt a consuming dread. "It was a man?"

"Guess so. She didn't call the cops. Must be that forgiveness of sins bullshit."

Nicole had had enough of Paige's disrespect for the cleric and the cleric's faith. "Do you mind?"

Paige said sincerely, "You know Nicki, I'm never gonna figure you out."

Nicole took a good hard look at Paige. She was right. Paige was incapable of understanding her. Paige was a good time, nothing more. She could never be more.

CHAPTER 4

With the approaching evening hour, the St. Ann's office activity gradually moderated to the sounds of an occasional telephone ring or individual walking past Reverend Kelly's office door. Employees, volunteers and those seeking services left the building for their respective homes. Those less fortunate relied on city shelters or self-constructed hovels. Within her office the Reverend completed a brief get-well note to a parishioner, signing her more commonly used name, Beth.

Beth stepped into Father David Bentley's office. "Good night David."

David looked up from his draft of Sunday's homily. "Beth, come in please."

Beth accepted the invitation.

David removed his wire-rimmed glasses. "Take a seat."

Beth did as suggested. She spoke with a disarming smile. "You're making me nervous."

David returned the smile. "Don't be. I just want to check in and see how you are doing."

"I'm fine, David."

"How is Mrs. Wesley?"

"The nurse thinks she will die soon. I've had a couple late nights reading to her. She gets frightened and it calms her."

"How late?" David leaned forward.

"Late." Beth tried to assuage his obvious concern. "David, don't worry. I've had my quota of muggings for the year."

David shifted back in his chair. "I would like you to stay in one piece."

"May God will it." With playful intent, Beth goaded the man whose ministry had been hewn to a practical and prudent purpose.

"Oh please! God gave you intelligence to know not to tempt danger."

"David, I was kidding." Having obtained the expected reaction Beth took David's temper in stride. "I am careful."

"All right. You are careful. How about pacing yourself? I know you are half my age and have more than twice the energy but burn out is real, and I don't need to hear from the Bishop that I drove you into an early grave."

"Aren't you being a little dramatic?"

"How much sleep did you get last night?"

Beth sidestepped the question with casual ease. "Enough for a woman half your age."

David scolded, "If it wasn't at least seven or eight hours, it wasn't enough. If you won't take care of yourself for your own sake, then do it for the people you are here to help. Hell, do it for me. I don't need any more stress."

David's tone struck a painfully tender cord in Beth. She looked down to her hands in discomfort. She liked David and wanted to be an asset to him. "I'll do better."

"Thank you," David said, closing the subject. "Now what are your plans for the evening?"

Beth looked back up to the caring man. "I'm staying in. There's a book I've been meaning to get to."

"Another of the German theologians?" David quipped gently.

Beth stood up. "No. A well respected American feminist theologian."

"So, when can I look forward to the next installment of our robust argument?"

Beth wished she could receive David's invitation more enthusiastically. "How about lunch next week sometime?"

"Can't wait." David reached for his glasses. "Goodnight, Beth."

"Goodnight, David."

Beth walked down the hall and then up the stairs to the third floor landing. Her apartment entrance was the first door to her left. Living in the church complex had its advantages. The briefest commute was one of them.

CHAPTER 5

Nicole had been standing in the shadows for hours, determined not to leave until she fulfilled her mission. She was acquainted with the routines of the church. She hoped that Reverend Kelly at some time of the day would enter the sanctuary without escort.

Nicole heard the door connecting the church offices to the sanctuary open. Her sight was keen to the entrance. The young priest entered the basilica through the transept, her task to set the altar for mass. Nicole moved quickly giving her fear no chance to turn her back to the safety of her anonymity. Undetected, she stood before the altar, waiting to be acknowledged.

Beth heard movement behind her. She turned to see who it was. The sight of the tall, dark-haired woman startled her. She felt a surge of fear, as well as anger. Beth spoke with a stern and measured voice. "What do you want?"

Nicole took the first step up to the altar. Defiant, Beth held her place on the third step. Nicole wore a black trench coat, her hands hidden in its pockets. She reached out her right hand and opened her palm to Beth. "Is this yours?"

Beth looked down, recognizing the gold cross and chain. She raised her unyielding gaze back to the stranger. "You know it is."

Nicole was penitent. "Did I hurt you?"

The priest was confused by what she saw in the other woman's eyes. She spoke less harshly. "The bruises have healed."

Struggling to manage her wavering voice, Nicole tried to explain. "I know you have no reason to believe me but I don't remember. My friend told me what happened to you. All I know is that I woke up with your cross in my hand."

Beth reached out and took possession of the chain and cross. She closed them protectively into her fist. She had given up hope of ever seeing them again. Her relief and gratitude was not conveyed.

Nicole's words were heartfelt. "I'm sorry."

Beth returned her gaze to her contrite assailant. She was not inclined to forgive. All she offered was silence.

The priest's disdain cut deeply into Nicole. She had hoped for some hint of absolution from the cleric. As Paige had pronounced, are not the religious in the business of forgiveness? Obviously they were human and subject to all human emotions. Nicole turned around and walked slowly down the nave towards the church's main entrance. Upon reaching the center doors she looked back. Beth stood firm, as cold and hard as the marble statues within the edifice. With a sigh Nicole exited feeling no better, and in some ways worse than when she entered, for where there had been hope there was now only a void.

Beth opened her hand and studied the cross and chain. The clasp had been repaired. There was no hint of the damage done.

CHAPTER 6

A man of average height and slender build stood at the Elysian Fields Pub entrance watching the mid-afternoon storm rage. Miguel Santo's Cuban ancestry had endowed him with striking, handsome features and a romantic outlook.

Nicole walked over and stood beside him. "This is one way to clean the streets."

Miguel shook his head. "You know I love you but there are times that you miss the magic."

"What's wrong with a little practicality?"

"That isn't what this neighborhood needs."

"Oh, tell me *viejo*, what does this neighborhood need?"

"Girl, I am not that old."

"Just showing respect to my elders."

"Bitch."

"Back at you."

"Hope. That's what this neighborhood needs," Miguel said thoughtfully.

"That's what everyone needs." Nicole felt her left hand begin to tremble. The tremor started to travel up her arm. She took hold of the appendage with her other arm and hugged it close to her body.

"I won't argue with you." Miguel returned his attention back to the city street. "Hey, isn't that the new priest?"

Nicole looked up. Her discomfort compounded. "Yeah."

"You would think the church could afford an umbrella. She's getting soaked."

"It's just another block."

Miguel sighed. "God, what's wrong with you lately? Have you forgotten how to care for your fellow man?"

"She's no man." Nicole reflected feeling an unexpected shyness.

"No, she's too damn cute." Miguel took a couple of steps out onto the sidewalk. Standing under the Elysian Fields canopy he called out, "Reverend! Come in out of the rain!"

Another wave of the rain swept across her. Beth hesitated. She had no reason not to accept the invitation. Subjected to the unceasing torrent, she welcomed any shelter.

Nicole backed into the pub, taking her place behind the bar.

Miguel motioned Beth inside. "Reverend, you picked a hell of a day to take a walk."

Beth stepped inside. She was surprised by what she saw. The Pub was exquisite. The blend of well polished deep hardwoods, brass light fixtures and accents, and simple green half curtains that provided privacy between the booths transported her back to Ireland – a country she had toured before entering seminary. Her gaze traveled to the bar. All fell away from her sight except for the woman standing behind it, washing glasses.

Miguel enjoyed watching the Reverend take in this unheralded haven. "Do you like it?"

Beth whispered, "Yes."

"This is only part of the Elysian Fields."

Beth turned her attention to the Latino man. "I never thought the Elysian Fields would be an English pub."

"Nicki and her Greeks." Miguel turned to Nicole. Seeing that the proprietress made no gesture of hospitality, he continued in his role as host. "There is a dance bar downstairs and a gourmet restaurant upstairs," he said to get a response from Nicole, but once again he was disappointed by her resolve to clean every glass behind the bar. He winked at Beth. "But don't trust me. The Garden is my baby."

"Yours?"

"I'm the chef and manager. Nicki keeps me around so she can have food service at all hours of the night. Isn't that right, Nicki?"

Nicole had no patience for Miguel's banter. A wineglass slipped from her hand and fell to the floor, breaking at her feet. "Damn it!"

"I should go." Beth began to move towards the door.

Miguel extended his hand. "Wait, Reverend."

Beth paused.

Miguel retrieved one of a half-dozen umbrellas stored in an antique oak coat tree. "Here, take this."

"Thank you but it's not necessary."

"Reverend, what's the point of getting wet? You can return the umbrella when you're done with it." Miguel offered a broad grin. "I know where to find you, you know."

Beth held the man with her gaze. His dark brown eyes were warm and gentle. She reached out and accepted the umbrella. "Thank you."

"You're welcome."

Beth went to the door. She paused and turned back to her guardian angel. "I don't know your name."

"Miguel."

Beth offered him her hand. "I'm Beth."

Miguel took her hand gratefully. "It's good to meet you, Beth."

"God bless."

Miguel watched Beth as she exited, passing before The Fields' glass pane window toward St. Ann's. "Never expected that," he said. He turned back to Nicole. "You okay back there?"

Nicole was down on one knee picking up the broken glass. She looked at her left hand. She had cut herself. "I'm fine. Don't you have something to cook?" She listened for a response. Instead she heard Miguel's footsteps cross The Pub and go to the stairs which led to The Garden. She hated herself. She hated her life.

CHAPTER 7

Sunday, prior to first service, dressed in full vestments, Beth opened the front doors of St. Ann's. She scanned the street, taking in a deep breath of the morning air. From afar, on the opposite side of the street, a figured turned the corner and walked in the direction of the church. With the diffused light of dawn and a lingering mist, the remote form was vaguely defined. Beth watched, feeling an affinity with the lonely specter.

No more than half a city block away the pedestrian's tall height, long black hair and dark clothing came into finer definition. Beth recognized Nicole. She noted that the woman walked with cautious deliberateness. What little she knew of Nicole led Beth to speculate that Nicole was returning to The Fields from a long night out.

Nicole passed in front of the church. As she reached the street corner she staggered. She stretched her hand out to a lamppost, taking hold, arresting her motion. She rested her forehead against the cool metal, steadying her weary body.

Beth waited for Nicole to continue on her path. There was no indication that Nicole was capable of taking another step. Beth grew more and more uneasy. Having waited long enough to satisfy her doubts, and certain that Nicole needed assistance, Beth crossed the street.

Beth remained a couple of paces away. Nicole's face had a gleaming film of perspiration. Her eyes were closed, her brow knit tight in tension. Beth spoke Nicole's name. Not given an answer, she tried again. "Nicole, can I help you?"

Nicole opened her eyes and turned her head. She focused upon the intruder to her silent pain-filled world. She recognized Beth. The young priest's vestments gave Beth an otherworldly appearance. She shifted her body leaning her back against the lamppost for much needed support. "You are a priest," s' said hoarsely. There was a hint of awe in her voice.

Beth was not expecting to be the subject of their meeting. Nicole ʼ to Beth's breast. "The *chi-rho*." She smiled. "You and I do have sor common. The Greek alphabet is beautiful, isn't it?"

The young cleric looked down at the gold emblem embr' chasuble. The *chi-rho* had always been a favorite monogram' Christ.

Nicole's distant voice interrupted Beth's thought' alpha and the omega … the beginning and the end.

expression changed. She was pensive. "Endings can be a beautiful thing. Endings can bring peace in a way nothing else can."

Beth's eye caught the sight of crimson blood on Nicole's hand. "Nicole, you're hurt."

Nicole followed Beth's gaze to her bleeding hand; the knuckles were scraped. She seemed surprised. "I am." She turned her palm up. "Doesn't hurt." She raised her hand to her head and rubbed her temple, leaving a stain of blood. "You know what hurts? Beginnings hurt. How do you begin again after everything has been taken away from you? It's not the same as the first time. The first time there's innocence and hope. Our naiveté gives us the courage to try. But, later when you learn the dirty truth, how do you …"

Mesmerized, Beth listened until Nicole's speech drifted to silence. "Nicole, let me help you."

Nicole shook her head. "Sometimes I wish it were true. I wish wearing Constantine's labarum could stop others from hurting me." Nicole referenced the *chi-rho*'s legendary role as the imperial standard that helped win the Battle of the Milvian Bridge in the early fourth century. "It would be so easy to just believe and go on with nothing to fear. Is it that way for you, Beth?"

Astonished by Nicole's naked confession, Beth wondered what manner of soul the woman harbored inside her. She felt compelled to answer. "No, it's not."

"Do you wish it would be?"

"Yes. But that's not the life we've been given."

Nicole's eyes brightened upon receiving Beth's answer. "We all have a story, don't we?"

"Yes." Beth thought of her own unspoken story, finding an unimaginable communion of understanding in the silence she shared with Nicole. Life was hard and her faith in God would never change that fact. Her faith could never sweep aside the impress of the people and events that had touched her.

"I think that, because of their stories, some people take from others." Nicole's voice grew more assured. "And I think some people give to others. You give."

"Don't you?"

"It's easy to write a check. It's hard to give …" Nicole jerked her head as f she had been struck. "Damn it!"

Beth reached out her hand.

"Don't!" Nicole looked down to her coat. "You'll get dirty if you touch "

Beth pulled her hand back.

Nicole glanced toward The Fields. "I'm safe there. It's the only place I am ." She turned back to Beth. "Thank you."

h was at a loss. "I haven't done anything."

"Sure you did. You crossed the street. Not every priest would do that for someone like me." Nicole stood straight, stepping away from the lamppost. "Good Sabbath, Reverend." She crossed the street, taking a diagonal route to The Fields' main entrance.

Beth stepped forward. She placed her hand upon the lamppost as she observed Nicole's journey come to an end at The Fields' doorstep. Only after Nicole entered The Fields did Beth turn back to the church, walking up the stairs in thought. She could not reconcile the many contradictions she had, in a brief period of time, witnessed in Nicole.

CHAPTER 8

Two weeks after Beth took her first step into the Elysian Fields, Nicole attended a community business association meeting at St. Ann's. She had no memory of her conversation with the young priest in front of St. Ann's. She dreaded seeing Beth in a public gathering. Beth was an incontestable reminder of her progressive deterioration. Nicole's resolve to move on with her life, disregarding recent indiscretions, had become difficult to maintain.

Nicole wondered if Beth had revealed her identity as the thief of the cross. More than one fitful night of sleep was haunted by dreams of public exposure. Each time she woke drenched in her own perspiration. The fear that she was losing everything that was precious to her began to consume her life, stealing what peace she had been able to claim in the years following her mother's death.

The church meeting-room tables were set end to end in the shape of a rectangle. Folding chairs lined the perimeter. David was speaking with Giovanni Sella, the owner of a small grocery store and deli, when he caught a glimpse of Nicole. Nicole saw David smile his usual warm welcome. Having no distractions to lead her elsewhere, Nicole approached him.

"David."

"Nicki, I haven't seen or heard much of you lately. Keeping a low profile?"

"Just taking my reputation underground."

David lowered his voice. "Anything I can do?"

David's intuitive powers never ceased to amaze Nicole. She steeled herself. She refused to expose her vulnerability, to see her weakness reflected back to her in David's eyes.

Receiving no answer to his inquiry David redirected the conversation. "How's business?"

"Good. The Garden is exceeding my projections."

"I'm not surprised. Eating a little closer to heaven is attractive." David's smile returned.

"Why do you have to bring heaven into it? The stars and the moon are more than enough."

"True, they're God's creation."

"So are drugs, alcohol, and sexually transmitted diseases."

Nicole had succeeded in wiping away David's smile. His eyes narrowed as if in pain from an all too brilliant light. "I can't argue with you, Nicki."

Nicole placed her hand on David's shoulder. "I'm sorry David, but you have to be willing to take as much as you give."

"You're right of course. I can take whatever you've got to dish out."

Nicole's remorse was replaced by pity. David felt the pain of the world to the depths of his core. She did not know how he lived with such an intimate experience of sorrow.

"Excuse me, Nicki." Nicole followed David's gaze as he called out Beth's name and waved her over. "Nicki, you haven't met our new Associate Priest."

Nicole turned. An all too familiar apprehension took hold of her. She was certain her nightmare of public censure was finally going to be realized. Her only solace was that she could stop hiding the truth of who she was becoming. There was great irony in the realization that she would gain relief in her final ruin. There could be no rehabilitation of her reputation after Beth exposed her.

David made the introductions. "Beth, I want you to meet Nicole Thera. Nicole owns the Elysian Fields, a club with a delightful restaurant."

Beth met Nicole's eyes. "I believe we've met."

Nicole struggled not to divert her gaze. "Yes, we have."

David was surprised. "Have you! Where?"

"Church," said Beth.

David seemed truly confused. "Church?"

"Nicole was the one who returned my cross."

David put his hand on Nicole's shoulder. "Beth told me a stranger returned it. Where on earth did you find it?"

Nicole felt like an incredible hypocrite. "David, you obviously don't know the whole story."

Beth interrupted, "Maybe we can continue this conversation later. It's time to start the meeting."

David looked at his watch. "You're right. I'd like to get home at a decent hour for once. I'll start rounding people up."

Nicole waited for Beth to turn to her. She spoke with pain-filled sincerity. "I'm sorry about how I behaved at The Fields. It couldn't have been pleasant for you to see me and I just didn't know what to say to you. I still don't."

Beth studied Nicole. She was struck with an improbable insight. She responded softly, "I haven't told anyone what really happened between us, and I don't intend to."

"But why?" Nicole did not trust the cleric.

"Because I believed you when you said you didn't remember. I'm not sure others will," said Beth, composing a response that Nicole could accept though, in fact, it was untrue. It was only in the present moment that Beth had been convinced.

David's voice calling the meeting to order disrupted the intimate exchange between the two. Without another word, Beth moved toward her seat next to David. Nicole sat at the far end of the room, more uncertain than ever.

The meeting concluded at 9:30 p.m. Nicole did not linger, as was her custom. Beth followed Nicole down the corridor to the exterior exit and called out her name. Nicole turned and waited for the young priest to reach her.

Beth suggested, "Don't you think you should wait ... Wouldn't it be safer if you walked with someone else?"

"It's not far." Nicole looked out into the night. "I know how to protect myself."

"Your knife?" Beth recalled Nicole's deft use of the weapon.

Nicole did not mask her surprise. "How did you know ..."

Beth's voice imparted a genuine awareness. "You really don't remember, do you?"

"What did I do to you?"

"Where's your knife?" Beth asked matter-of-factly.

Nicole removed her switchblade from the inside pocket of her jacket and held it in the palm of her hand. Beth took it. "How do I open it?"

Nicole retrieved the knife. She turned it to its side and placed her thumb over the switch. "Press here." The blade slipped out. The sound was familiar to Beth. Nicole pressed the switch a second time. The blade returned to its housing. Nicole offered the knife to Beth.

Beth felt the weight of the weapon. She pressed the switch. Once again the blade emerged. Beth studied the knife. It was the right shape and size. She decided it was the knife that had grazed her skin. She looked up and studied its owner with equal interest. "You grabbed me from behind and put this knife to my throat. Then you turned me around. You seemed confused. You asked if you knew me. You took an interest in my cross. You ripped it from my neck. I asked you not to take it and offered you my wallet. You didn't seem to want my money. When a few kids came our way, you ran down the alley and jumped over the fence."

Nicole took a step back and leaned against the wall

Beth observed Nicole with growing concern. "Has this happened to you before?"

Beth offered Nicole one piece of that night's many missing pieces of time. The blackouts did not happen often but when they did, her actions left her disgusted with herself. She usually found herself in a stranger's bed, or more rarely with a stranger in her own bed. She had woken up in the park sharing space with the local homeless. She had more than once found herself bloodied, with no trace of how the cuts and bruises were inflicted. The common denominators were sex and violence.

She had not returned to drinking. That one fact had been confirmed with Connor, her pub manager. Raised in a bar, receiving daily lessons on how people forfeited their souls as they plunged into alcoholism, and witnessing the stupid and at times unconscionable actions done under the influence, and accepting that she was no exception to alcohol's pitiless impact, she had ceased drinking after completing graduate school. Feeling insufferably exposed, Nicole hardened her heart. "I was drunk."

Beth remembered there was no scent of alcohol on Nicole's breath. The confusion she saw in Nicole was not drunkenness; it was of a different sort. "Then maybe you should consider not drinking."

"I'll take it under advisement." Nicole turned her head towards the door. Once again she looked out through the glass pane windows. "I'd better go." She wondered if the night could get any darker.

Beth closed the knife and handed it to Nicole. She tried one more time to reach the familiar stranger. "Nicole, if there is anything I can do."

Nicole's misplaced frustrations rose to the surface. "You've done enough."

Beth watched the solitary figure walk down the exterior stairs, across the street and down the block toward the Elysian Fields. The streetlights cast the figure as a shadow. There was the black of night and the artificial light. The opaque expanse embraced Nicole.

CHAPTER 9

Her day done and her apartment uninviting, Beth entered the basilica through the transept seeking a respite. She hoped she would have the sacred space to herself, as selfish as that thought might be. She had yet to acclimate herself to the lack of anonymity at St. Ann's. Parishioners were free to come to her at any time, requiring her to place her own need for worship and prayer aside.

To live beside the church gave her unprecedented access. In the brief period of her residence, she had formed the habit of leaving her apartment in the quiet of the night, seeking the refuge of the church. St. Ann's was mortar and stone, rafters of wood, stained glass, and murals; it was hard floors and smooth wood pews; it possessed a unique silence in the heart of the city; it was a world unto itself that claimed her. She felt welcomed and protected. When alone in the sanctuary, she knew a peace that escaped her both outside its doors and when shared within. As long as she was a priest, and known as a priest by those who entered this sacred space, she could not relax completely; she could not enter a state of contemplation that allowed the divine presence of God to enter her heart. She never shared this truth. It was one of many truths that remained unspoken. Her silence was a mark of her aloneness, an aloneness that rarely found relief outside of prayer.

A figure sat in a front pew at the far end of the right aisle. Beth was disappointed, even though she knew what she longed for given the time of day was unreasonable. She walked before the altar and bowed in reverence to the cross. She turned with the intent of finding a quiet space further in the heart of the nave. It was then that she recognized Nicole. The woman's countenance was reminiscent of their first meeting in the church, one of uncertainty and vulnerability. Nicole's enigmatic personality, her shift from violent thug, to remorseful penitent to practical businesswoman intrigued the young priest. Nicole rested her hands in her lap, the left hand trembling. The image was not one Beth could ignore. She chose to go to the woman who dominated her thoughts during the previous weeks.

Nicole looked up taking in Beth's gentle beauty. She then returned her gaze down to her lap. With her steady hand she took hold of the trembling other. "DTs. I guess I could use a drink."

Beth was not going to judge this woman. She discerned that Nicole would reject a conventional approach. "Our sacramental wine isn't very strong."

Nicole turned to the priest and offered a smile in gratitude. "Don't touch the stuff. Rumor has it that it's got a spirit in it."

Beth shared the smile. "Of a different sort."

Nicole looked up at the altar. "Do you really believe in transubstantiation or is it consubstantiation?"

"Not all Christians believe in one or the other. Some consider the Eucharist as symbolic, but others do believe that the Host and wine are changed during the ritual."

"So?"

"So what?" Beth questioned.

"What camp do you fall into? Or are you a symbolic transignification sort of gal?"

Beth did not expect a theological inquiry from Nicole, let alone one that reflected such an obvious command of knowledge. "I'm more the latter."

"Earthy. And that's okay for a priest?"

"Yes." Beth knew it was time to redirect the focus of their conversation. She gently placed her hand over Nicole's. "Is there anything I can do for you?"

Nicole removed her hand from Beth's touch. She spoke in a jagged diction. "It's all right if I just sit here, isn't it?"

"Of course."

Nicole could not withstand much more of the priest's caring. Her anger rose, engulfing whatever tenderness of self she had allowed in the prior moment. "You can go. I won't steal anything," she said bluntly.

Beth studied Nicole carefully. Her response was a sincere assurance. "I know."

Nicole bit her lower lip. She did not understand nor did she like her own volatility. Her tone was no longer harsh. "Beth, I don't want you to be my priest or Father Confessor."

Beth respected the request. She nodded. "All right." It was time for her to take her leave.

Nicole followed Beth's movement. She needed to complete her thought. "Beth?"

Beth paused and returned her attention to the woman who remained an enigma to her.

Nicole swallowed. "I could use a friend. If you allow yourself to have friends."

Beth stepped forward. She spoke reflexively. "Priests have to keep a ministerial distance from their parishioners."

"I don't think of you as a priest. I'm not a member of this church. Hell, I don't believe in your God."

Beth's confusion was apparent. "Then why do you come here?"

Nicole was left to confess the truth, or at least part of it. "I was hoping to see you. If you worked in a restaurant, I would have come for a cup of coffee and sat at a table I knew you were serving. No difference."

The young priest longed for friendship. However, she knew that the offer before her could undermine all semblance of order in her life. Nicole's unpredictability promised only complications. "I'll think about it." Uncomfortable with the prospect of sharing her space and time further, Beth exited toward her apartment.

CHAPTER 10

Nicole sat on one of the two benches outside of the Elysian Fields. In her hand she held background information relating to her latest consulting client. She could think of better ways to spend her day. At the same time she was grateful she had the luxury of working at home. She chose when and where she read the research. Cell phone technology gave her the freedom to take her calls while she remained connected to the neighborhood, her one constancy.

Jacob stepped outside of his office, pipe in hand. He smiled in recognition of her rare public appearance. Not one to let the opportunity slip away he crossed the street. At hearing distance, the elder cleared his throat.

Nicole looked up. "Good morning Jacob."

"I haven't seen you out for a while." The small man's voice was far larger than his body.

Nicole grinned. "Jacob, I've been out since I was fourteen."

"Yes, of course." He pointed to Nicole's papers. "Well, then, what are you reading?"

"Business."

"That's no good."

Nicole set the documents aside. "You're telling me."

"May I join you, Nicole?"

"Of course, Jacob. You know I could never turn you away."

"That's good. You, young lady, are one of the few women I can spend time with without hearing from Liza."

Nicole nodded over towards his office. "Don't be so sure." She waved to the matron.

Jacob turned. His wife stood at the office entrance with a cup of coffee in her hand. "God, how I love the woman." With youthful vigor Jacob blew Liza a kiss.

Nicole envied the man who had escaped Germany as a youth. Though he lost generations of his family at Auschwitz and Treblinka he did not turn his back on life, he did not seek pity, he lived, he relished life, he loved.

Jacob sat beside Nicole. "May I smoke?"

Nicole frowned. "Just stay down wind."

"Soon, a man will lose all his freedoms to the women in his life."

"Isn't it a matter of respect? I respect your right to burn that awful tobacco and swish the taste of it in your mouth, and you respect my right not to want to smell or inhale the smoke."

Jacob nodded toward the Elysian Fields. "You who own a tavern say this to me."

"You know very well that I don't spend that much time in The Fields."

He changed the subject to a topic of mutual appeal. "So, what have you been reading that is of interest?"

Nicole regretted her recent laxity in pursuing her studies. "Jacob, I honestly haven't had much time. Life has been complicated."

Jacob persisted. "Too complicated to read. I do not think so. You are my Nicole, are you not?"

"I read the Elie Wiesel play you recommended."

"Good. Now we have something to talk about. What did you think of it?"

"It reminded me of Job."

"Yes, I can see why it would."

"There is no answer. The one who hates God most ends up defending God."

"Of course he did."

"Why of course?" Nicole challenged. "Because there could be no meaning without God? I don't buy it."

Jacob was patient. "Nicole, we all need God."

"God is the only one who is left unaccountable. Saying I'm God and that's good enough to justify my actions is indefensible."

"Like Job, you are assuming you can understand."

"Like Job, I believe I am capable of understanding if someone would just explain it to me."

"You cannot explain away doubt, just as you cannot say magical words and give someone faith. If that was possible, I would have said the words to you and the rest of the lost souls I've met in my life."

Nicole bristled. "Is that what I am to you, a lost soul you are determined to save?"

Jacob placed his hand on Nicole's arm. "You are my girl. You do not need saving. You are smart, compassionate, and strong. The time will come when you will do the saving."

Nicole gentled. "Have I told you lately how much I love you?"

"No, I cannot say you have."

"Liza is lucky to have you."

"I do not know about that. I do know that I would die if I lost her. I pray to God every day that I will never know life without my Liza."

Nicole voiced a deeply felt appreciation. "You, sir, know love."

"I know I am nothing alone. You should consider sharing your life with another ..."

Nicole finished his sentence. "Woman. Jacob, after all these years you still stutter at the thought that the one thing we do have in common is that we both love women."

Jacob removed his pipe from his mouth. "Nicole, have you loved, really loved a woman?"

Nicole could not respond. The truth was far too painful. Her mentor knew her well. He was friend enough not to allow her to lie to herself. For that, she valued him above all others.

Jacob gestured with his pipe. "Now there is a woman who will someday steal a noble heart."

Nicole followed Jacob's eyes. They took her to the sight of Beth walking down the street towards them.

"Good morning, Reverend," Jacob said to the young priest.

Beth returned the greeting warmly. "Good morning, Jacob." She offered an equally warm greeting to his companion. "Nicole."

Nicole's contentment was swept away. She was chary in her greeting. "Good morning."

Jacob offered a spirited invitation. "Reverend, you should join us. We are having a theological discussion and I would welcome your opinion."

Beth was intrigued. "Oh?"

"Yes, Nicole did me the favor of reading Elie Wiesel's *The Trial of God*. Have you read it?"

"Yes, I have."

"Nicole was comparing it to Job."

Beth's gaze shifted from Jacob to Nicole. The latter averted her eyes. "I felt the same way when I read it."

"So we are in agreement," Jacob concluded.

Nicole found her tongue. "Jacob, the only thing we are in agreement of is that two stories in the Judaic tradition have been written that question God's veracity. We don't agree in what those stories mean, or if there can be a proof of Yahweh's existence."

Jacob said gaily, "Nicole, we know you and I do not agree. We have not heard from the Reverend."

Nicole interjected, "As a Christian, the Reverend's God is not Yahweh. We all know that the God of the Hebrew Bible is different from that of the Christian New Testament."

"Do we know that, Nicole? I think you are presumptuous," Jacob countered.

Nicole looked up to Beth. "What say you, Reverend?"

Beth was captivated by the exchange. She remembered Nicole's comment regarding the *chi-rho* and her questions when they spoke in the church. Nicole had demonstrated an unusual command of theological terms. Now Nicole argued the distinction between the Judaic Yahweh and the Christian

God. Nicole read Wiesel and she obviously had earned Jacob's respect, if not affection. The subject that commanded Beth was not theological, it was temporal. Beth looked to the two before her and smiled. "If we consider only the Gospels, I believe you could argue sufficient similarity."

"Ah ha!" Jacob exclaimed victoriously.

Nicole would not leave the argument alone. "Oh right! You pick and choose only parts of the canon that make you comfortable – a canon I might add that was closed by one Bishop writing a letter to calm the heretical waters of fourth century Christendom. Sorry, that is poor theology as far as I'm concerned."

"You see, Reverend, Nicole is brilliant in arguing her atheistic ways," Jacob explained.

"Jacob, I have told you a hundred times I am not an atheist! I just don't define the divine by your standards."

Beth found herself regretting that she was expected elsewhere. "I would really love to continue this discussion, but I have a committee meeting I need to get to."

Jacob quipped, "Meetings, the burden of the clergy. I am amazed your faith survives such tedium."

Beth smiled. "They are not all that bad."

"They are surely more challenging than Nicole's corporate consulting. She does not have anyone using God as a justification for their irrationality."

Nicole interjected, "Oh, don't be so sure."

Once again Beth found herself surprised by a new piece of information. "Consulting?"

Jacob reached over and pointed to the report lying on the bench. "Nicole is a very respected business consultant. The Elysian Fields is just her hobby."

"I didn't know."

Jacob's pride in Nicole was obvious. "She is a very talented young woman."

"Jacob, I'm sitting right here. You don't have to talk about me in the third person."

"You never talk about your good points," Jacob said, defending himself. He turned toward Beth. "Nicole revels in her rebellious reputation."

Nicole pleaded, "Jacob, will you stop."

Jacob laughed. "I apologize, Reverend."

"Why are you apologizing to the Reverend?"

"Because you are not being gracious to our new friend."

"Me? I give up!" Nicole leaned back against the bench, raising her hands in dramatic exasperation.

Beth laughed at the two. Theirs was a shared joyful irreverence. Her original assessment had been confirmed. There was an authentic affection between the two.

Jacob swept this hand toward Beth. "At least the good Reverend is being gracious in keeping her humor."

Nicole looked up to Beth. "And I'm very grateful," she said, her voice low and intimate

Beth held Nicole's gaze. She would wager Nicole was not necessarily referring to the present moment.

Jacob kept to the cordial spirit. "As you should be."

"I really must go."

"Join us again, Reverend." Jacob placed his hand on Nicole's shoulder. "I promise you the conversation is always lively."

"I have no doubt. Good-bye Jacob." Beth purposely caught and held Nicole's gaze. "Be well, Nicole."

"God be with you, Reverend," Jacob said, bestowing a blessing.

Nicole smiled a wordless farewell.

Jacob mused, "Yes, she deserves to win a noble heart."

CHAPTER 11

Nicole began reading on the bench outside of the Elysian Fields every mid-morning. Sometimes Jacob joined her. Other times he simply waved a greeting. On this particular morning he chewed on this pipe, apparently enjoying the lingering taste of menthol as he observed Beth approach the Elysian Fields. Jacob returned to his office granting the two women their public privacy.

Nicole was intent on the strategic plan. With a highlighter she marked the more relevant points. She did not sense the woman standing before her.

Beth waited hoping that Nicole would acknowledge her. After a half dozen heartbeats she resigned herself to her invisibility. She needed to speak up. "Good morning."

It had not been the gentle autumn weather or the comforting murmur of the neighborhood that had been the catalyst for Nicole's renewed habit of taking a break from her work by stepping out from her loft and sitting on one of the Elysian Fields benches, nor had it been the prospect of a challenging conversation with Jacob. It had been the hope of hearing that voice. She looked up to see Beth. It was Nicole's turn to be surprised. Beth was dressed in jeans, a white blouse and a short tan leather jacket. Nicole liked what she saw all the more. "Hello. You are out of uniform."

Beth looked down at herself, suddenly feeling quite self-conscious. "I guess I am. It's my day off."

"Monday, that makes sense."

"Are you working?"

Nicole looked down at the report. She lost all interest in it. Closing the cap on the highlighter for emphasis she announced, "It's nothing that can't wait."

"I enjoyed listening to you and Jacob."

"He's a good man."

"He seems to think well of you too."

"Well, I admit he has a blind spot when it comes to me."

Beth wondered what bound the two very disparate personalities. "Why is that?"

Nicole had long ago quit trying to explain the grace of Jacob. "Don't know."

The wind gusted. "It's really starting to feel like autumn."

Nicole quipped, "Just in time for Halloween. It'll keep the drag queens shivering in their heels while they go trick or treating."

"I could say something very crass to that," Beth said playfully.

"A perfect lead-in, now that I think of it. Sorry for the temptation, Reverend. I never thought you the type to pick up on the sordid side of life."

"Please call me Beth."

"If you call me Nicki." Nicole was charmed, and in turn she was charming. "Would you like some coffee or tea? I can show you The Garden."

"Yes, tea would be good."

The Garden was lit by natural light cutting through the same floor-to-ceiling windows that fringed Nicole's loft. An atrium jutted out at the rear. The view down was of asphalt rooftops. Looking up, Beth could see the distant downtown Chicago skyline. She imagined the skyline would be striking in the dark of night with an array of lights emanating from the buildings.

"Why don't you choose a table while I get the tea," said Nicole.

Beth chose to sit by the forward windows. She surveyed the dining room. The tables varied in size, with some seating two and others seating four. The tabletops were made of inlayed, soft, smooth tiles framed by a light, hardwood molding. The tile design consisted of a marble pattern bordering a sheet of solid mauve. At the heart of each table was a triangle the length of Beth's hand. The imagery was subtle yet definite in its statement. The chairs were black metal with an oval back sculpted to form a palm leaf motif. The carpet had a gentle green diamond pattern with a mauve four-leaf center. Free standing and hanging plants were placed throughout the restaurant, enough to earn the space its namesake without overwhelming. If Miguel's cooking was even passable, Beth could understand a patron's desire to come up to The Garden for a respite from the city.

Nicole returned with two mugs of tea. "Here you go."

"Thank you. Nicki, this is really a beautiful space. Was it here when you brought it?"

"My mother owned The Pub. I put my money into refurbishing it, and then I expanded down to The Fields dance club. I saved The Garden for last. I needed to make sure I had enough income to subsidize it until it turned a dollar. I give Miguel most of the credit. Actually, I don't know what I would do without the Three Musketeers."

"The Three Musketeers?"

"Miguel has The Garden; Connor, The Pub; and Tony, The Fields. They have been with me from the beginning of each phase."

"They must be loyal to you."

Nicole fell back to her self-deprecating humor. "The profit sharing doesn't hurt either."

Beth smiled at the joke. "And your consulting?"

Nicole sipped her tea. She did not often have occasion to speak of her work to those outside of her business world. "I'm a member of a consortium of consultants. There are twelve of us in total. We pool our resources to take care of administrative support. We each have a portfolio of clients. We have our specialties so we complement more than compete with each other. We offer each other technical support and we also swap referrals."

"Do you like it?"

"I'm good at it," Nicole admitted

Miguel approached, his manner genial. "Excuse me. Nicki, Kate is on the phone. She said it's important."

Nicole explained to Beth, "My lawyer. I'll be right back."

Beth watched as Nicole and Miguel walked into the kitchen.

Nicole picked up the wall phone. "Kate."

"Hey, girl. How about dinner tonight?"

Nicole's irritation carried in the punched phrasing of her words. "I thought this was important."

"Well, thanks."

Nicole purposely softened her voice. "Is something wrong?"

Kate kicked back. "You tell me."

Nicole's gaze settled upon the kitchen doors, her impatience building. "Kate, if there isn't anything else, I've got someone waiting."

After a few heartbeats of silence Kate's acerbic question crossed over the telephone. "Is she beautiful, Nicki?"

Nicole smiled knowing that if Kate could see Beth, a friendship might very well be lost in the here and now. "Of course."

Nicole heard the phone click as the connection was severed. She leaned her forehead against the wall.

Miguel went to her. "Everything okay?"

Nicole hung up the wall phone and turned to the chef. "Live for the day, Miguel. It's all we've got."

"Did you and Kate have a fight?"

"The usual. I don't want to go out and play. She'll get over it." Nicole took a deep breath. "There's more interesting company out there, and I'm not going to make Beth wait any longer."

"*Chica*, you be nice to the Reverend."

Nicole proceeded toward the dining room. "*Hombre*, I'm on my best behavior."

Beth marked Nicole's return by placing her tea mug down. "Is everything all right?"

"Other than that my lawyer, Kate, is a mother hen, no."

"You're friends?"

"Ever since college. Now, where were we?"

"You didn't answer my question. Do you like your work?"

"Yes, I like the work. Between my consulting and the Elysian Fields I can have the lifestyle I want. I work when I want. I do what I want."

Beth was silent. Nicole felt a growing discomfort, a sense of being judged. "You don't approve of me, do you?" she asked.

"Nicki, I try not to judge."

"But you are a priest."

"And ..."

"You're in the family values business."

Beth repeated the commonly known fact: "There is a significant presence of alcoholism in the lesbian and gay community."

"Yes, there is. That's what happens when a community is ghettoized. A bar is one of the few choices there is to safely meet your own kind."

"It's hard to think of this neighborhood as safe."

Nicole felt the press of guilt. "I wasn't drinking that night."

Beth's suspicion confirmed, she still had unanswered questions. "But ..."

"It was easier if you thought I became a mugger when I was drunk, then try to explain that I black out and don't remember what happens to me except that I seem to be doing some rather stupid things," Nicole confessed.

"Dangerous things," Beth emphasized.

"Yeah."

"Have you seen a doctor?"

Nicole shook her head. "No doctors."

"You have your reasons?"

Nicole settled her gaze on Beth. "Yes, I do."

"You're not going to tell me?"

"No."

Beth was confused. "Then why did you tell me the truth?"

Now Nicole was the uncertain one. "What do you mean?"

"Usually, people don't bring up a painful subject unless they are looking for something."

"I don't want anything from you," Nicole responded sharply.

Beth held her tongue.

Nicole took a breath, steadying her emotion. She was contrite. "I just wanted you to know the truth. If you are going to judge me, I rather it be based on fact, not fiction."

"I told you I try not to judge people."

"We all judge people."

From the day Nicole asked for her friendship, Beth had wondered why. What was it that Nicole saw in her that promised the possibility of friendship? "Then tell me, how do you judge me?"

"I don't know you well enough." Nicole wished to learn more about the woman seated before her. "Tell me, how does someone come around to deciding to be a priest?"

The question was familiar to Beth. Her response was well practiced. "It just happened. One day I was walking down the street and the thought came to me. It didn't seem so outrageous. It actually felt right. I was finishing my second year of college. I changed my degree from Education to Religious Studies, and then I went on to seminary."

"No offense, but it doesn't sound as profound as an on the road to Damascus experience. What felt right about it?"

"I had been taking philosophy and theology courses as electives. Studying the scriptures, their impact on the people of antiquity and throughout the ages, fascinated me."

"Doesn't that make you more of a scholar than a minister?"

"There must be a reason for studying. Mine is to help others find God and live a better life."

"Finding God doesn't guarantee a better life, and you can have a good life without God."

Beth took a careful swallow of her tea, giving herself time to formulate a response. "I believe if you have God you will have a better life, no matter what that life is. And I won't argue that there are good people living good lives without an apparent presence of God. It's just that for me, when I look at them and their actions, I'm the one who sees God even if they don't."

Nicole was impressed. "What did your family think of your decision?"

"My father was pleased." Beth was feeling her own rising discomfort. She wanted to redirect the conversation back to Nicole. "You said your mother owned The Pub."

"Yes, she died when I was in college. I used the proceeds from her life insurance policy to buy the building. The landlord was happy to get rid of it. The fool wasn't willing to invest in the neighborhood. He let everything go to hell, so I had the leverage I needed to negotiate a good price."

"Did the building go to hell, or to Tartarus?"

Nicole smiled.

"So you were destined to be a business woman," Beth said.

"I don't know about that. Life presents certain choices. I did what I felt was best at the time."

The two continued to talk, each carefully choosing what small pieces of their lives they were willing to share. Beth was the oldest child of two; her sister Marie was currently studying nursing in Atlanta. They were born and raised in Riverton, Iowa, a small town near the southwestern border of the state. Her father owned the local hardware store. Her mother stayed at home to care for the children while they were growing up, helped out at the store, and volunteered at their church and the library. She had died suddenly when Beth was nine.

Nicole was an only child. She never knew her father. Her mother had never talked about why he left, and early in life she decided she did not care. There were certain subjects that remained unspoken. Beth asked no further questions regarding Nicole's health. Nicole quickly realized that Beth was reticent regarding her mid-western rural upbringing. She simply stated she never felt she belonged, so she spent her time in the library, reading and learning about worlds beyond the cornfields and dairy farms.

Miguel stepped into The Garden serving area. "Reverend, are you staying for lunch?"

Beth looked over to Nicole.

"You're more than welcome."

"I wish I could but I have a load of errands to run," Beth said to Nicole. She turned to Miguel. "May I come back another day?"

"You must. And you don't have to sit with her if you don't want to." Miguel smiled as he pointed to the proprietress.

Beth assured, "I kind of like her company."

"There's no accounting for taste. Excuse me, but I've got soup on. See you soon, Reverend."

Beth allowed her thoughts to rest upon Nicole. It was pleasant to do so. "Nicki, thank you for the tea."

"Anytime. Hopefully, you'll be able to enjoy part of the day."

Beth's enthusiasm rose. "I am. I'm going to a lecture at U.C. this evening."

Nicole teased, "Can't get away from the theology."

"One reason I wanted to come to Chicago was to be close to the University."

"Can't blame you. They do bring in some of the best."

Beth decided to take a risk. "Would you be interested in joining me? It starts at 7:00. I plan to leave around 6:15."

Nicole was genuinely flattered. "Are you sure you want a heathen sitting beside you?"

Beth was pleased by the prospect. "If you're willing to sit next to a priest, I'm game."

"Where do you want to meet?'

"I can come here."

"Sounds like a plan."

Beth stood up. "I'd better go. See you tonight."

Nicole leaned back in her chair and absentmindedly tapped a spoon against her tea mug. She spoke to herself. "Good behavior, Nicole Isabel Thera. Good behavior."

CHAPTER 12

The two women walked from the Swift Lecture Hall into the heart of the University of Chicago Quadrangles. They made their way onto 58th Street walking east through the historic Hyde Park neighborhood toward the 59th Street metro station. The night was cool and clear.

Nicole continued her ribbing. "Remind me never to get into a theological discussion with you without doing my homework first."

"He was wrong!" said Beth, speaking of the lecturer they had heard at the University.

"Obviously," Nicole affirmed with mock seriousness.

"All I did was to point out a couple of inconsistencies in his argument."

"Quoting book and verse, no less. You can be fierce."

"I was respectful."

"So much for the benign religious."

Beth paused. "Benign?"

Nicole turned and slowly walked backwards. "Come on, admit it. The poor guy would have expected a skewering from someone like me, but not you."

Beth continued in step with her companion. "Appearances can be deceiving."

"I'll say."

Beth smiled sheepishly. "At least it wasn't boring. You weren't bored were you?"

"No, not at all. Now, as you were saying …"

Beth studied her new friend. She found no hint of insincerity. Assured, she continued. "The one thing that made Biblical studies in seminary so special was that I never knew what I was going to come up with. I would research the Greek and Hebrew word origins. I'd pour over all the commentators, from liberal to ultra-conservative. I'd try to see if there were parallel myths in pagan, Egyptian and other traditions that might have informed the pericope." She explained, "Pericopes are self-contained passages."

"Yes, I know." Nicole said gently.

Beth was apologetic. "Sorry, I try not to assume."

Nicole smiled. "Go on … I'm listening."

Beth's confidence in Nicole's interest grew. "I tended to come up with some unorthodox readings. Putting the pieces together and explaining them is like writing my own version of the story, with my own twist and turns. I get to emphasize what I think is theologically important. And the most exciting

part is I never know the ending – the theme or moral – until I'm done."
She paused and turned her attention to Nicole, who wore an irresistible grin.
"You're smiling at me."

Nicole would not deny the obvious. "Yes, I am."

Beth cocked her head aside in question. Nicole chose to satisfy the
younger woman's curiosity. "You shine when you talk about your studies."

Nicole's words disarmed Beth. She returned to the topic at hand. "My
studies gave me more latitude than doing sermons."

Nicole was intrigued by the distinction. "How so?"

"There are some things I wouldn't say in the pulpit. The congregation
would call me a heretic."

"Maybe. If they did you would be in good company."

"I don't think David would appreciate it."

"You don't know David. He appreciates having the dust and cobwebs
swept aside."

Beth was once again reminded that Nicole knew David in a way that
seemed beyond her. The two walked quietly.

Nicole observed Beth from the corner of her eye. Beth's passion had subsided. Nicole longed for its return. "So, do you miss your studies?"

Beth countered. "I haven't given them up. I don't plan ever stopping."
She fell back into her thoughts. She knew her answer was incomplete. "What
I do miss are my professors. I miss having someone to read my work and to
discuss my ideas with."

"How about David?"

"I don't feel he takes me seriously."

"Really?"

"He likes the argument. Sometimes it feels as if he really isn't listening to
me. Not that he means to make me feel so discounted. It's just his way."

Nicole juxtaposed David with Jacob. She agreed that David did not share
Jacob's openness. He tended to let her arguments hang in the air between
them without truly engaging in the debate. Jacob was always willing to lock
wits with her, working with her in search of new insight. "You still have the
pulpit."

"Nicki, like I said, it's not the same."

"Maybe the people sitting in the pews aren't a bunch of academics but
don't underestimate your congregation. They may be poor and they may be
struggling to survive the streets but that doesn't mean they don't know life. I
believe they know more about life than the better-educated people living in
their middle class neighborhoods. And isn't that what theology is all about
– making meaning out of life, finding the divine in the God-forsaken corners
of the world?"

Once again Nicole's words gave Beth pause. "David mentioned expanding our adult education program. I just don't know what to offer."

"You could always ask. Radical thought I know."

Beth had not yet achieved a sense of comfort with the congregation. "And if I get silence?"

"Put yourself in their place."

"That's the problem. I'm an alien on foreign soil."

Nicole knew enough about the small-town Iowan to realize that prior to her move to the city, Beth understood how it felt not to belong. Beth's empathy would serve her well as she reached out to the poor Chicago neighborhood that grappled with its own sense of alienation. "Oh, I think you have more in common with the people of this neighborhood than you know."

"How so?"

"Beth, that's something you will have to figure out for yourself."

"You're not being very helpful."

Nicole chose to change the subject and satisfy a lingering curiosity. "Can I ask you a question?"

"Sure."

"Why the uniform? It's not mandated outside of worship, is it?"

Beth had decided her manner of dress after considerable deliberation. "David always dresses as a priest, unless he's doing physical work. I didn't want a distinction between us." Beth hesitated expecting to be teased for her next statement. "I'm also young. What I wear does make a difference in how people see me. My clothes help set my authority in the church."

How Beth dressed did change how Nicole saw her. "That makes sense. You look younger and more approachable in your street clothes." Nicole withheld her other observation. Beth alluded to an otherwise well-hidden fragility, the source of which Nicole wanted to understand.

"So, tonight I'm not a priest to you?"

"I wouldn't say that. I can't forget you're a priest. That's a part of you, just like being the owner of the Elysian Fields is a part of me. Seeing you like this helps remind me that you are more than a priest. And, I think that's a good thing to remember."

CHAPTER 13

A third of The Pub was occupied with a casual lunch crowd. Connor Rowe tended the bar. The roguish Irishman sported red, short-cropped hair and a well-trimmed goatee. A few years older than Nicole, his fair face was speckled with freckles. He wore a black t-shirt firmly tucked into his blue jeans. Broad shouldered, with muscular arms and a slender waist, his was a virile presence. Beth walked into The Pub at noon. Connor recognized her from Miguel's description. It was also hard to miss the collar. Beth approached the bar. He attended to her immediately. "Welcome Reverend. My name is Connor. May I help you?"

Beth was grateful for the hospitality she experienced in The Fields. "I'm here for lunch."

"Pub menu or The Garden?"

"The Garden."

Connor smiled as he waved his hand toward the stairs. "You can go right up."

Beth mirrored his smile. "Thank you."

Connor picked up the house phone as Beth walked away.

Dressed in Chef's whites, Miguel was an impressive sight as he entered the dining room. He crossed his arms and tapped his foot as he met Beth. "So, you've finally decided to come back."

Beth sighed. "I needed a break from the office."

Miguel whispered in confidence, "Well, we are very discrete. We won't tell on you if you're playing hooky. Let me seat you."

He gave Beth an atrium table. "I've made a nice batch of turtle soup. I also have Jambalaya and Shrimp Creole. And if you're really hungry I can recommend the catfish, pan fried in lemon butter."

Beth laughed. "Am I still in Chicago?"

Miguel played with a Southern accent. "Child, you are now experiencing the best of New Orleans' French Quarter." He returned to his slight Latino inflection. "Gil will take your order. *Bon appetite.*"

Nicole was working in her office. The house extension rang. "Yes?"

It was Miguel. "How about lunch?"

"Not hungry. Maybe later."

"Too bad. I was hoping you might keep the Reverend company, and I don't mean David."

"I'm coming right down." Nicole smiled a broad free smile, one that she would not allow herself in the company of another. She suspected a conspiracy among the Musketeers when it came to keeping an eye out for Beth. Her positive disposition during Beth's previous visit to the Elysian Fields was a bit too obvious for Miguel not to repeatedly comment upon.

Nicole reached for her keys with her left hand. They slipped out, falling to the floor. "Damn it." Her hand began to tremble. "Son of a bitch! Not now." She leaned back against her chair. The tremors traveled through her left side. They were getting worse. "Please. Please don't." She begged her body not to fight her and allow her to regain control. The helplessness she felt was intolerable. She knew better than to try to stand up, so she waited.

Beth had completed her meal of soup and salad with fresh French bread and was sipping her coffee. She had hoped to see Nicole. She told herself that Nicole was a busy woman and could not be available at her whim.

Gil returned. "How about dessert?"

Beth was gracious. "I don't think so."

Gil pleasantly nudged. "You don't want to disappoint Miguel. We have a choice of bread pudding or pecan pie."

"I recommend the bread pudding." Nicole stepped to Gil's side.

Beth smiled. "Will you join me?"

Nicole turned to the waiter. "Gil, how about a bowl of the soup, bread and decaf for me and bread pudding ..." Nicole paused seeking confirmation from Beth. Beth nodded. "Bread pudding and some more coffee for Beth."

"Coming right up." Gil left the two women.

Nicole took a seat opposite her guest. "I'm sorry I couldn't come down earlier."

"Did you know I was here?"

"Oh yes, the network did a fine job of letting me know the minute you stepped into the door. Something came up while I was at my desk and I couldn't get away." Nicole excused the half-truth. "So what brings you to The Fields?"

Beth considered the woman across the table from her. She debated whether she should echo Nicole's words to her: 'She could use a friend.' Where Nicole came to the church to see her, Beth came to the Elysian Fields to see Nicole. Though she did not understand Nicole's motivation in seeking a friendship, she had come to appreciate Nicole's easy company, her intelligence and her humor, her ability and her desire to see Beth beyond Beth's identity as a cleric. "I needed a break."

"I don't think so," Nicole drolly remarked. "Breaks are not in your job description."

Beth's fatigue equaled her frustration. "David tells me to get away and then he turns around and gives me a list of a half-dozen assignments."

Nicole offered her own solution. "The key is leaving town."

"I wouldn't know where to go." Beth's limited financial resources also limited her options. "And I don't have a car. I use the church's."

Nicole formed a plan. "When is your next Sunday off?"

"A week from this coming Sunday, why?"

"I usually go up to Wisconsin for the day every October or November. I'm running late this year. The colors are past peak but it should still be nice. Are you interested?"

The prospect of leaving the city in Nicole's company for the day was tempting. "Yes, I'd like that."

"Good. I'll pick you up in front of the church at 7:30 a.m."

"Isn't that early?"

Nicole spoke with false indifference. "I want to make 11:30 mass."

Beth's reaction did not disappoint. "Mass?" She was incredulous. "We're going to church?"

"Don't worry, I haven't been struck dead yet."

Beth laughed lightly. "Jacob is right when he says you're incorrigible."

Nicole leaned forward, her curiosity aroused. Nicole's gaze captured and held their quarry. "When did Jacob say that?"

Beth smiled guiltily. "Changing the subject ..."

"Reverend, you should know that at this very moment your finesse is wanting," Nicole teased.

Beth kept to her evasion. "Nicki, there is a favor I need to ask you."

Nicole cheerfully granted Beth a reprieve. "Anything."

"You know the church hosts a Thanksgiving dinner for the neighborhood."

"And ..."

"We're always looking for some ovens to cook the turkeys. I was wondering if the Elysian Fields kitchen might be available."

Nicole scanned the dining room, imagining the bittersweet holiday. She gave her answer, suppressing the ire she felt against the Church, which she held responsible for much of the hardship endured by her patrons. "Beth, we serve a Thanksgiving buffet. There are a lot of people who don't have homes to go to for the holidays. It's our tradition."

Beth tried not to betray her disappointment. "I understand."

Nicole mused, "I could still cook two turkeys in the loft. It's been so long since I've put the ovens to any use I hope I still remember how to turn them on."

Beth brightened. "Thank you. The turkeys will be delivered to the church the Monday before ... "

"Don't worry about it. Consider the turkeys my donation to the cause."

"I'll subtract two from the order." Beth drew her hands together on the table, restraining a desire to reach out and take Nicole's hand. "Nicki, you're welcome to join us even if only for a little while."

Gil returned with coffee. "Your order will be up in a minute."

Nicole took advantage of the interruption to redirect the conversation.

CHAPTER 14

David joined Nicole in the left front pew of the church. Nicole glanced toward him for the briefest moment before casting her eyes back to the altar. "Thanks for seeing me."

David appeared apprehensive. "It's been a while, Nicki."

"She would come and sleep on this pew." Nicole looked down; her left hand stroked the worn wood. "There were times when this was the only place in the neighborhood where she felt safe."

"That's true, but she never did make her peace with the Church. I only wished I could have done more for her."

"You couldn't take away her demons. Nobody could. The hardest part was when she would go through an extended period of lucidity. I would always begin to hope. I knew better but I still would fall into the trap. It would break my heart that much more when she relapsed." Nicole took a deep breath. "David, I never thanked you for caring for her." She reached out and covered his hand with her own.

"I wanted to. She had a gentle soul."

"When she wasn't trying to tear the world apart." Once again Nicole paused to gather her thoughts. "David, there is something you need to know. Beth didn't tell you the whole truth about the night her cross was taken from her. I was the one who did it."

"What?" David's question was more a statement of disbelief.

Nicole felt a rising desperation she could not completely control. "David, I don't remember. I was working the bar. Next thing I know I was in my bed with a major hangover and Beth's cross in my hand. I hadn't been drinking. Not that night and not the other nights before and after that I've blacked out. It's happening more often. I'm frightened I'm becoming like my mother."

David maintained his composure. "Any more violence?"

Nicole removed her hand and crossed her arms. "Not that I know of but that isn't saying much."

"Have you seen a doctor?"

"I have an appointment tomorrow."

David took a moment to think. "Do you want me to go with you?"

"No ... thank you. But I may need your help depending on what I'm told."

"Of course."

Nicole took a deep breath. Her eyes traveled once again to the altar, continuing upward to the wooden sculpture of the crucified Jesus of Nazareth that hung on the wall before her. "David, a favor?"

"Yes?"

"Don't say anything to anyone, including Beth."

"If that's what you want." David kept a ministerial presence. "You know it might make it easier for her if she knew."

Nicole turned to him. "What do you mean?"

"Nicki, you're a hard enough nut to crack for someone like me who has known you half your life. You've confused her at best and frightened her at worst."

"She's not afraid of me." Nicole needed to believe their friendship had enabled Beth to overcome her initial wariness. "I want to wait until I know more."

"Don't wait too long."

Nicole walked a fine line. There were questions she wanted to pursue, however, she knew the man that sat beside her was Beth's ecclesiastical superior. "David?"

"Yes."

"There is something about her."

David hesitated. "Meaning?"

"I don't know. Why didn't she say something about what I did?"

"Have you talked about it?"

"A little. I first led her to believe I was drunk. I later fessed-up and told her about the black outs. She doesn't know about Mom."

"Why are you holding back? She can handle the truth."

Nicole leaned back against the pew. "Yeah, but who's to say that I can?"

CHAPTER 15

Nicole drove to the park after seeing her surgeon. It had been a week since her first doctor's appointment. A battery of priority tests followed. From the beginning, the source of her concerns was considered organic. She had found relief in that notion, but now organic was translated into tumor and there was little comfort in the diagnosis. Her surgeon wanted to perform the operation immediately. One desire prevented Nicole from entering the hospital – her plans to spend the day with Beth in Wisconsin. It was Thursday. Thanksgiving was a week away. She was scheduled to enter the hospital late Sunday. Her surgery would take place the following day.

It was mid-afternoon and the park was forlorn. She walked down the Lake Michigan shoreline. With each step she journeyed a little closer to her heart. With each step she felt the press of her life. She believed there were no guarantees in life. She believed that she was born without a promise of any kind except one – life. Life itself was a grace. She believed the life she had been given was hers to live to her best ability.

Since her mother's death she had slowly reopened long closed doors to living. All she had known since her early youth was survival. Survival did not allow for the passions. Survival did not allow the heart to feel. Now she walked and she felt the challenge of her very beliefs. She did not know if she was going to die young. She did not know if the following five days prior to her surgery would be her last. She only knew what the surgeon told her. The operation was delicate. One question would be answered on the operating table: Can the tumor be removed? A second question would be answered in the lab: Was the tumor malignant? The final question would be answered in recovery: Did the operation damage any adjacent tissues and impact her capacities?

Her tears began to find a way from her depths to the surface. She continued to walk even as the tears blinded her. Her body began to convulse independent of the tumor's influence. She hugged herself, relinquishing all remaining self-control. She conceded to the arbitrary winds of life. They took her down to her knees. In the aloneness of the park she surrendered. There would be no more pleas for her symptoms to leave her. There would be no prayer for a reprieve given that there was no God in her life. There was only the painful acceptance that this was her destiny. There was only the painful countenance of life. So she cried freely until her tears subsided. She looked up and out over the horizon. Returning back to her beliefs she knew that she wanted to live the next few days no different than she would have had she not known the intimate face of death.

Upon returning to the loft, she informed Jacob and Liza, Kate and The Fields' managers of her surgery.

CHAPTER 16

Beth waited in front of St. Ann's. She could see her breath in the crisp November air.

Nicole drove up in her two-year old Jeep Wrangler. She parked, reached over and opened the door. "Hi, jump in."

Beth liked the rugged sportiness of the vehicle. It suited Nicole. "Nice."

"I've got coffee and rolls complements of Miguel."

"This is good." Beth jumped in and threw her backpack onto the rear seat. "I brought an extra sweater just in case it gets cold."

Nicole smiled. "I checked the forecast. I hope you brought sunglasses. It's going to be a perfect day."

"Tell me, where are we going?"

"Holy Hill. Have you heard of it?"

"No."

"It's Catholic. Do you want a history lesson?"

"Yes, please."

"Good. Makes my homework worthwhile." Nicole pulled away from the curb and steered the Jeep towards the interstate highway. "Ready? There's a quiz afterwards."

Beth chuckled. "Hopefully you'll grade on a curve."

Nicole began reciting what she learned from her Internet reading the night before. "Holy Hill is northwest of Milwaukee on what's considered the highest point in southeastern Wisconsin. It had a history of attracting the religious or at least religious legends. The Discalced Carmelite Friars belong to the reform order of Carmelites begun by St. Teresa of Jesus and St. John of the Cross. Discalced means barefoot." She looked over to Beth. "You probably already knew that."

Beth smiled. "It came up in seminary once or twice."

"I'm still telling you the story."

"Trying to impress me?"

Nicki laughed. "Too late for that." She gathered her thoughts and continued the history lesson. "Their identity reflected the fact that the order placed greater emphasis on community and contemplation than the ancient Order Carmelites. The Discalced Carmelites came to Holy Hill from Bavaria at the invitation of the Archbishop sometime in 1906. I think that within the year there were seven men who slowly built a community. Between 1919 and 1931 they built the monastery, the shrine and replaced an older church with the current upper church. It was a minor seminary from the mid-30s to early 50s. In the mid-80s they reworked both the upper and lower churches. We are going to service in the main sanctuary. We can visit the Shrine of Mary and take a walk through the grounds where they have the life-sized Stations of the Cross carved in Bedford Stone. There's also a tower if you want to climb a whole bunch of steps to see a better view of the countryside." Nicole looked over to a Beth who was quietly opening the thermos and pouring a travel mug of coffee. "How does that sound?"

"Wonderful." Beth was curious. "Why do you go there every year?"

"My Mom would take me. She was raised in Cedarburg, a town on Lake Michigan about twenty miles north of downtown Milwaukee. Her Mom would take her every year. It's a tradition. I remember that no matter what was happening with my Mom, when we went to Holy Hill everything was okay. On that day, everything was always okay."

"Weren't they otherwise?"

Nicole knew it was time to share more of her history. "My Mom was mentally ill. It got pretty bad sometimes. You see that's why I never questioned my father leaving us."

This new facet of Nicole gave Beth pause. "I didn't know."

"She's a ghost nobody talks about. When she died a great weight was lifted from the neighborhood. She was high maintenance. When she was good she would give back, but I never felt the debt was paid. I don't think it ever can be.

"My Mom was smart ... very smart. She loved to read English literature. She read everything. Her critiques were fascinating. She could pick out the most subtle ..." Nicole quieted as a memory of sitting outside The Pub with her mother discussing George Eliot's *Middlemarch* came to mind. The memory shifted to a violent tantrum. A few days later her mother had ripped the Eliot book into pieces. Nicole's thoughts returned to the present. "I thought of her as one of those geniuses that could never find a place in the world. I often wondered if her illness was the price she paid for that genius."

There was an uncomfortable hush between them. Beth remembered Jacob's description of Nicole as brilliant. The young woman admitted she was good at what she did. How good was good? Maybe if the genius stayed in the family, the fear of the accompanying madness did, too.

Nicole breached the tension. "You see I'm like my Mom. I've been high maintenance all my life."

Confirmation of Beth's speculation had come within a heartbeat. Beth needed to shake it off. "That doesn't mean you're mentally ill. Nicki, I know we haven't spoken about your blackouts since you mentioned them to me. I've tried to respect your privacy, but don't you think you should see someone about it."

"It's been on my mind, Beth. Give me today. I want everything to be okay today."

"Promise you won't sweep your illness aside."

Nicole gave Beth her complete regard. "You have my word. Now pour me some coffee will you."

Beth allowed her eyes to rest upon the Wisconsin landscape of farmland and small towns. The interstate took them through Milwaukee. Given the early hour of the day Nicole chose not to take the bypass. For Beth's benefit they went through the heart of the city.

From Milwaukee they traveled west. After another thirty minutes, Nicole exited north unto a county highway. They soon left any trace of the suburban returning to the rural. As they neared the church, groves of trees paralleled the road. Most stood bare, their leaves long fallen. The ground was blanketed in hues of auburn, yellow and the crisp brown of decay. Beth imagined the greater beauty they had missed by a number of weeks. Neither spoke as Nicole casually maneuvered the Jeep through the winding road. Nicole would occasionally glance over to Beth. Beth's pleasure was self-evident.

Nicole was directed to park at the Shrine's lower parking lot. The two women had not spoken since entering the grounds. They left the Jeep and took the road leading to the upper church. Walking beside Beth, Nicole found herself wanting to take her companion's hand. Instead, she buried her own hands into her jacket pockets. Nicole shortened her normal stride to match Beth's lesser gait. Beth looked about intently. She had the immediate impression that she was in a special place. There were many others coming and going. There was a graceful purpose manifest in their conduct. Their movement led to the appearance of stillness in motion, as all present shifted from the noise of the world to the quiet of this sacred space.

Nicole motioned toward an exterior path. "We can walk up or go in there," she indicated the gift shop and restroom facility, "and take the elevator."

Wordlessly Beth led them toward the exterior steps. Content with the choice, Nicole followed. Upon reaching the top of the stairs Beth walked to the concrete parapet that enfolded the perimeter of the elevated plaza. The view of the Wisconsin landscape took her another measure within herself. She realized that in the city she had lost the ever-present childhood wonder of the magnificence and simplicity of creation. Nicole stood beside her with a reassuring reserve.

Beth spoke her heart. "It's beautiful."

Nicole echoed. "Yes, it is."

The tower bells announced the next service. Beth turned toward the church admiring its Romanesque façade. She walked along with the other worshippers. Nicole again followed, placidly coming to Beth's side. As they entered the main sanctuary Nicole took another glance toward her companion. Beth said nothing but the brightness of her eyes spoke as they scanned across the expanse of the aisles and nave, and ahead to the altar and apse. Beth walked forward toward the first few pews, which like a schoolroom's first row of desks remained sparsely occupied. Beth went to the front pew, and deliberately knelt upon one knee before the image of the Christ as she performed the sign of the cross. She stood and entered the pew. Nicole approached and looked up to the image of the crucified Jesus of Nazareth. As a gesture of respect she bowed her head before joining Beth. Beth lowered the knee rest, knelt and closed her eyes in prayer. Nicole sat back. The image of Beth was gently tugging at her heart. She found herself captivated by the young priest.

Nicole remembered when she first broke away from the church. Her disdain for anything religious was expressed at every opportunity. Her feeling of betrayal left no room for tolerance. She had named believers naïve at best and fools at worst. She had spat Marx's comment of religion being 'the opiate of the masses' out of context, with great relish and regularity. How time heals. There was no longer a need to damn others to find her peace.

The choir began singing a hymn. There was very little in terms of the liturgy that Nicole could repeat with sincere belief but that was not why she had come. She sought the spirit, the posture of humility. She sought the capacity of acceptance that what will come, will come. She did not need to believe in a higher power or divine plan. She did need to come to a place within herself that would take hold of goodness and not allow it to slip away from her in the fear and uncertainty of the moment.

The liturgy progressed to the Sign of Peace, the symbolic act of unity performed by the ecclesial community in preparation for receiving the Eucharist. Standing, Nicole and Beth turned to one another. For an awkward moment Nicole thought to extend her hand. Beth opened her arms and took Nicole into her embrace. Nicole felt the embrace viscerally. Beth whispered in her ear, "Peace be with you."

They tenderly separated. Nicole yearned for the peace Beth wished for her. She searched for it in the other woman's eyes, eyes she held dearly in her gaze. "Peace be with you, Beth." Nicole was rewarded with Beth's warm smile. A surge of sorrow shook the former to her core as they both allowed the moment to linger. It was only the voices and motion of the other worshippers exchanging the Sign of Peace that broke the spell between them. With an alternating, contradicting sense of relief and regret, Nicole turned to the elder gentleman to her left.

At the Eucharist, Nicole and Beth stepped out of the pew to allow the other worshippers an exit. They returned to their seats. Nicole watched as "the body of Christ" was offered to all Catholics wishing to receive it. Beth, in turn, observed Nicole.

The service ended in an hour's time. They exited allowing the silence between them to continue undisturbed. Once again Beth went to the parapet and looked out to the landscape. Nicole stood beside her as she had done throughout the visit. Beth could not remember being with anyone other than her grandmother who gave her such complete freedom. Without diverting her eyes from the horizon she took Nicole by the arm. Nicole was surprised by the gesture. Beth's voice trembled. "Thank you for bringing me here."

Nicole covered Beth's hand with her own. She did not trust herself to speak.

After the passing of a few minutes Beth looked at Nicole. "Where next?"

"The path to the Stations of the Cross. This way." Nicole stepped away. Self-conscious, she gently released herself from Beth.

They walked down from the hill, passing each of the Stations of the Cross. Beth spoke first. "Nicki, what does Christianity mean to you?"

Nicole remembered how her mother would stop at each station and impress upon her as a child the tragedy of the Passion. Her mother could never keep hold of the hope promised by Easter. Her worldview remained in the pain and torture of the crucifixion. Nicole believed in God as a child because her mother did. She also believed in the tooth fairy, Santa Claus and the Easter Bunny because her mother taught their stories. When her mother confessed that the latter three were a comforting fiction, she wondered why the line was drawn without the addition of the wise, fatherly, all-knowing, all-powerful divinity.

The only model she had known was the Creator who knew all, controlled all, and bestowed grace and judgment. It was a God she found to be capricious, a God she could never understand, let alone affirm. She had studied the Greek classics, philosophy, and theology in college trying to understand why humanity seemed intent on keeping a god, or the gods, real to them.

Her god – and given a choice her god was always a small "g" – was the source of the mystery of existence. Her god was the creative spark of life and the cessation of that spark in death. Her god was humanity's capacity for compassion and rage, for trust and fear, for love and hate. Her god flowed from her and to her during a passionate yet tender sexual union with another, as well as when she gently placed her hand over that of a friend. Her god allowed for tears of joy and sorrow, knowing that the line between pain and pleasure could be rather thin. Her god abounded in a shared silent gaze when there were no words to convey what was felt or understood – when silence was enough.

For her, god was all and all was god. She had found god in Beth, in the surrounding environs, in her own capacity to feel, to will, to breathe. Nicole knew all of this but she could not explain it anymore than Jacob could explain to her why he knew Yahweh. And she felt with equal certainty that Beth would not be able to truly explain why she knew her Christ.

Beth continued to walk, patiently waiting to see if Nicole would answer her question. Nicole seemed to be deep in thought and Beth was not going to bring her back prematurely.

Nicole returned to the question at hand: *What did Christianity mean to her?* "Beth, I look up at the cross and I see a man who died because he wanted to change the world. I believe he was frightened in the Garden of Gethsemane when he asked God to remove his cup from him, but also said he would accept God's decision. And I believe that on the cross when he cried out 'My God, My God, why have you forsaken me?', his heart was broken. I believe a group of people tried to create a movement based on that broken man's teachings, and during the centuries it has been twisted and turned to the point that it's sometimes hard to find the original message – to love God with all your heart and soul, and to love your neighbor as yourself."

Beth knew she should not be surprised by Nicole's response, but each time Nicole broached the theological it left her humbled. "I can't argue about the twists and turns. I experience them in the Episcopal Church."

"How can you stand it?" Nicole asked sincerely.

"Nicki, a church is as imperfect as the people who create it. You can't have a church if you demand perfection."

"That is one reason why I'll never have a church."

"What other reasons do you have?"

"Theology is the re-creation of life; it's not God who gives order and reason and meaning to our world, it's us, you and me."

"Can't we find that meaning together?"

"No. All that comes from trying to meld our disparate visions into a holistic whole is to taint our unique experiences of life. Authenticity is lost in trying to harness the mystery into a common language."

Beth was disappointed. "We are so different."

"Beth, I want life to be more than an empty expanse of time between birth and death. Don't think me callous. I haven't turned my back to the world. I've tried to step right into the eye of the storm, seeing the chaos and yet not losing a sense of place."

"Nicki, I think you prefer to be detached from the world. You have The Fields, you keep the world at arm's length."

"While you step right into the chaos with a faith that you will survive no matter what is thrown at you."

"My existence will not end with this life. It makes taking a risk less a risk for me than for you because you believe you have nothing after death. This life is your one chance."

"I don't want to see you get hurt."

"That from a woman who put a knife to my throat."

Nicole stopped abruptly. "You're right, Beth. I prefer the solitude of my loft to an ill advised attempt at creating a friendship with someone who will never be able to understand me."

"Nicki." Beth gestured toward Nicole. "I didn't mean to accuse you. My point is that I'm willing to take the chance of getting hurt because the rewards often exceed my greatest expectations. Like meeting and getting to know you."

"You have no idea who I am."

"We are getting to know one another, aren't we? I know a few things about you. I know that you came here today. Holy Hill means something to you. I know you are still linked to St. Ann's. You can't tell me you're not."

Nicole realized that Beth had failed to make the connection. Beth did not understand that the Hill and St. Ann's were both places she returned to because of the woman who gave her life, the woman who had left an indelible imprint upon her daughter's soul. "Beth, it's about my Mom. It's always been about her."

Beth looked down, feeling foolish. Now it was Nicole's turn to wait for the other's return to the moment. For Beth, her faith was always about her grandmother. Suddenly, she and Nicole did not seem to be so different. The chasm had been crossed. She spoke with true understanding. "Of course."

The clarity between them seemed palpable. Satisfied, Nicole began to walk down the path. Beth joined her. The comfortable silence renewed.

✢   ✢   ✢

They spent the balance of the day in a lighter mood. They brunched at a nearby restaurant, sharing stories of one's mother and the other's grandmother. Nicole purposely kept to the easier stories. Beth had no need to filter her telling. There was nothing about her grandmother she could not celebrate.

They returned to the city as the sun approached dusk. With reluctance, Beth stepped out of the Jeep. She turned and looked back to Nicole. "I had a wonderful time."

Nicole felt an all too familiar press of her heart. She was determined not to wince from the pain of what she feared was the pending loss of her life as she knew it. "Me too. It was a perfect day. Thank you for joining me."

Beth hesitated. "About Thanksgiving."

Nicole cut Beth short. "The turkeys will be delivered as promised."

"My invitation is still open."

"We'll see. Okay?"

Beth pursed her lips together and nodded. There was nothing more to be said. "Goodnight, Nicki."

"Goodnight, Beth."

Beth closed the Jeep door and stepped back onto the sidewalk. Nicole took one last look at the beautiful young woman. She wished there had been a way to steal a kiss. She would have been complete with a kiss. Instead, over-whelmed by loneliness, she drove away with her own salt tears falling upon her lips.

CHAPTER 17

Beth was in charge of managing all the incoming food deliveries to the St. Ann's community kitchen. With each entry, she looked up in anticipation of seeing Nicole. It was hard to explain why the enigmatic businesswoman meant so much to her.

Miguel dressed as a pilgrim and Peter Kilpatrick, the Elysian Fields' sixteen-year old kitchen assistant, walked down the entrance stairs carrying large covered serving dishes. Miguel, true to form, made a flamboyant entrance. "Happy Thanksgiving!"

Beth waited to see if Nicole was trailing behind the spectacle. She was disappointed. "Miguel, over in the kitchen." She followed him. "You look delightful."

"I was hoping for butch!" He laughed upon seeing Beth's reaction to his incongruous self-characterization. "Didn't mean to make you blush, Rev."

"Don't worry about me. I know a young woman priest is a target few can resist."

"Beth, you may be irresistible but it has nothing to do with your collar."

Beth's blush deepened. "Enough already."

Miguel set the serving dish down. "You've got to be kidding. We've got at least three more trips of food to get out of the van."

"What? I asked Nicki for two turkeys."

"And you got them, *chica* I've also got fresh baked rolls, salad, yams and pies. Oh and when you open these birds don't be surprised if you find Cuban black bean dressing. Got to put a little Latino culture into this white man's holiday."

"I can't wait to try it."

"I expect a complete critique next time you come to The Garden."

"Miguel," Beth asked, "do you know if Nicki plans to drop by?"

Miguel hesitated before answering. "No, can't say I do."

Beth cautiously proposed, "Maybe I'll come over after we finish up here."

"I'd better unload the food before it gets cold." Visibly uncomfortable, Miguel turned toward the entrance.

Beth shyly touched the chef's arm. "Miguel, will you be honest with me?"

After a heartbeat, he responded tentatively, "I'll do my best."

"Would I be out of place at The Garden today? I don't want to make Nicki uncomfortable."

"You're always welcomed." Miguel placed his hand over Beth's as an added confirmation.

Beth nodded.

"Got to get moving. I have a wild bunch to feed." Upon reaching the kitchen entrance Miguel paused and turned back. "Beth, don't come by The Garden tonight."

Beth studied the gentle man; his demeanor was one of regret. "I understand."

"No, Beth you don't. Nicki won't be there. She's going to be away for a while."

Nicole's absence was truly unexpected. "She didn't mention it."

"She isn't very talkative or haven't you noticed?"

"I've noticed. Did she say when she was coming back?"

"Not really. She left it kind of open. The Musketeers are used to keeping The Fields going when she's away."

Beth had little success in hiding her disappointment. "Thank you for saving me a trip."

"Don't thank me, Beth."

Beth gave Miguel a questioning look.

Clearly frustrated, Miguel thrust his hands into his pocket. "Damn it if I burn in hell for this. Beth, priests visit hospitals, don't they?"

Beth nodded.

"So, if you happen to go to Memorial to visit patients and you happen to notice Nicki's name on some list, you might decide to go visit her, right?"

Beth was only beginning to understand what Miguel was alluding to. She whispered, "Yes."

"I figure she'll be angry at first but then she'll be happy to have you with her."

"You think?"

"Yeah, I think."

Beth swallowed with difficulty. "Why is she ..."

"She'll have to tell you. Okay?" Miguel tried to calm the young priest's obvious fear. "Beth, it's Thanksgiving. There is reason to be thankful. Trust me on this."

"I will ... thank you, Miguel." Beth watched the chef as he went for a second load of food. The jovial spirit of the holiday slipped away from her.

Having ensured the meal preparations were under control, Beth searched for David. She found him in his office. "David, Nicki is in the hospital."

David stood up and circled his desk. "I know."

There was an accusation in Beth's tone. "Why didn't you tell me?"

"Beth, remember we must respect the confidentiality of those we minister to."

"Nicki and minister don't go together."

David was firm. "What does that change? She confided in me and asked me to respect her privacy. What would you have done?"

Beth took a seat. "I know you're right."

"How did you find out?"

Beth smiled. "Confidential source."

"How much do you know?"

"I'm tempted to pretend I know more than I do."

"Won't work. More devious people have tried to play me. You don't minister in the streets without learning a thing or two."

Beth admitted, "All I know is that she's at Memorial."

"Nicki will have to tell you the rest."

Beth tried to negotiate her sense of displacement. "David, Nicki said she didn't want me to be her priest. She wanted a friendship. But I'm confused. If I was her friend, she would have told me."

"Don't be so hard on her or yourself. She told only the people she had to to keep her life in order." David paused as a thought entered his mind. He smiled. "So, Miguel spilled it. Bless his compassionate heart. Thank God he doesn't have the same vows I do."

"So am I Nicki's friend?"

"You tell me. There is nothing that says you can't be. She is a part of the neighborhood community but not a congregant of this church. She and I go back to a time when she was, so that makes my relationship with her different from yours. She's not a bad friend to have although there are times she exasperates me. Beth, the question is, 'Are you a friend or a priest when you are with her?'"

"I never stop being a priest."

David shook his head disapprovingly. "What did they teach you in seminary? Beth, you better learn to draw your boundaries or you'll never have a life to call your own."

"David, I'm not any different than a doctor or a police officer. I don't forget what I am ... I don't forget everything I know just because I've taken my collar off."

"Fine. As long as you're not trying to save Nicki's soul."

David's counsel angered Beth. "I've never thought of myself in the business of saving souls, and even if I was, Nicki's soul doesn't need saving."

CHAPTER 18

In the ascending hospital elevator Beth realized she was still wearing her collar. She removed it and unbuttoned the first two buttons on her blouse, intent on being a civilian during her visit. She walked pass the Neurology 4 West nurses' station toward Nicole's room without checking in on the patient's status. She paused outside the open door uncertain of how she was going to explain herself. She knew all she could do was confess the truth. She cared.

She entered the single bed hospital room. It was dark except for a florescent light that hung on the wall over the bed. Nicole lay propped up at a 45° angle. Her head was bandaged. She was pale, her eyes bruised black. A book rested on her chest. Beth stood by the bed. Her eyes traveled across the body that seemed void of all life. Careful not to disturb the IVs, Beth took Nicole's hand into her own. She heard footsteps behind her.

"Still asleep?" The nurse's voice was kind.

Beth turned and acknowledged the caretaker. "Yes."

The nurse walked around Beth to the other side of the bed and checked the IVs. "She may not wake up for a while."

"I'm in no hurry."

The nurse smiled. "Reverend, you look younger without your collar."

"Special effects," Beth gently quipped. She should have known that anonymity was not hers to have.

"How well do you know Nicole?"

"We're friends. Why do you ask?"

"It's just the way she took the news. It was hard to gauge her. When a patient is as young as Nicole, I'm used to seeing a lot of anger. She's been very quiet. I'm hoping she shows some spirit. She's going to need it if she's going to walk again."

Beth's gaze returned to Nicole. She spoke in a hush. "I didn't know."

"Oh." The nurse was apologetic. "I assumed you checked the chart." After a brief silence she reported, "The tumor was contained and the biopsy was negative. The doctors are optimistic that they got it all. But when Nicole woke up her legs didn't respond to stimulation. By Tuesday she had gotten some feeling back. We're hoping the paralysis is only temporary."

Beth felt a heaviness against her chest. She was finding it hard to breathe.

The nurse walked to the foot of the bed. "So, is she a fighter?"

Beth repeated the question to herself. Was this confounding woman a fighter? She voiced the answer she needed to believe. "Yes, she is."

"Good. I've got to go. Call if you need anything."

"Thank you."

Beth wondered if Nicole would, in fact, fight. She seemed exceedingly vulnerable in her state. She returned Nicole's hand to the bed and reached out for the book. She noted that it was a collection of American poetry. She opened it to the bookmarked page, and saw a poem by Henry Wadsworth Longfellow titled *The Day is Done*. Once again Beth looked to the mystifying woman before her. She spoke aloud. "Longfellow, Nicki? I wouldn't have guessed." The young priest proceeded to read the poem to the sleeping patient.

"'The day is done, and the darkness
  Falls from the wings of Night,
As a feather is wafted downward
  From an eagle in his flight.

I see the lights of the village
  Gleam through the rain and the mist,
And a feeling of sadness comes o'er me
  That my soul cannot resist:

A feeling of sadness and longing,
  That is not akin to pain,
And resembles sorrow only
  As the mist resembles the rain.

Come, read to me some poem,
  Some simple and heartfelt lay,
That shall soothe this restless feeling,
  And banish the thoughts of day.

Not from the grand old masters,
  Not from the bards sublime,
Whose distant footsteps echo
  Through the corridors of Time.

For, like strains of martial music,
  Their mighty thoughts suggest
Life's endless toil and endeavor;
  And to-night I long for rest.

Read from some humbler poet,
  Whose songs gushed from his heart,
As showers from the clouds of summer,
  Or tears from the eyelids start;

Who, through long days of labor,
  And nights devoid of ease,
Still heard in his soul the music
  Of wonderful melodies.

Such songs have power to quiet
   The restless pulse of care,
And come like the benediction
   That follows after prayer.

Then read from the treasured volume
   The poem of thy choice,
And lend to the rhyme of the poet
   The beauty of thy voice.

And the night shall be filled with music,
   And the cares, that infest the day,
Shall fold their tents, like the Arabs,
   And as silently steal away.'"

Beth placed the book aside and then moved a nearby chair to Nicole's bedside. She sat down and reached into her blazer pocket removing a small velvet pouch. Within lay her Anglican Prayer beads. The use of a string of knots or beads to keep track of prayer was common to many religious traditions. A cross hung at the end of the beads. A large bead, the invitatory, separated the cross from the wheel of twenty-eight beads that were divided into four groups of seven called weeks. Between each week was a single bead, the cruciform. The placements of the four cruciforms formed a cross.

With one hand Beth gently explored the wooden beads with her fingertips until the string was draped across her palm. She silently completed her prayers while keeping hold of Nicole's hand. Time passed unmarked.

Beth felt Nicole's fingers move. She sat up in her chair, her eyes traveled from their intertwined hands to Nicole's face. Nicole's eyelids fluttered. Beth willed herself to remain silent. She had learned to allow patients to take the lead, consciousness was fragile and reentry into a harsh reality was not to be rushed. Nicole squeezed her hand tightly. Beth studied Nicole closely to see if she was in pain. A low moan escaped from the back of Nicole's throat. Beth stored her prayer beads into her pocket and stood up.

Nicole opened her eyes. It took a few heartbeats for her to focus. She was rewarded with the sight of a beautiful though concerned Beth.

Beth did not speak until Nicole returned her smile. "Hi."

Nicole scanned Beth. "You're out of uniform."

"I'm not on duty." Beth took a steadying breath. "You know how to keep a secret."

"Yeah. I also know how to wring Miguel's neck. He'd better watch his back once I'm on my feet again." Nicole realized what she had said. The despair she felt the days before returned. She briefly closed her eyes in an effort to stay her tears.

"I know Nicki. You'll walk again. You'll just have to work through it." Beth was breaking every rule in the book of chaplaincy. She did not know if

Nicole would walk again. She was not supposed to give false hope, but she did not care. "I hear the tumor was contained."

Nicole gathered her courage. "Yeah, I can no longer plead temporary insanity."

The two women's eyes met and held. After a few moments Nicole squeezed Beth's hand again.

Beth whispered, "What is it?"

"It's good to see you."

Beth pressed Nicole's hand reassuringly. "Why didn't you tell me?"

"I'm used to being on my own."

"I understand." Beth turned the subject to a hopeful future. "When do you start physical therapy?"

"What time is it?

Beth looked to her watch. "1:30"

"Today. Shouldn't you be home in your own bed?" Nicole admonished.

Beth lied. "I lost track of time."

Nicole released the younger woman's hand. "Go home, Beth."

Beth did not presume her return would be welcomed. "Would you like me to come back?"

"Why don't you give me some time?"

"Seeing you this way doesn't bother me."

"What if it bothers me?" Nicole asked sharply.

Beth was indignant. "You can't ask me to be your friend and then unilaterally decide to shut me out. It's not right."

Silence weighed heavy between the two strong souls. Nicole relented. "You can bail out if I get to be too much of a bear."

Beth smiled. "I'll keep that in mind."

Nicole excused Beth from her bedside for a second time. "Goodnight."

"Goodnight, Nicki." Beth waited as Nicole closed her eyes and drifted back to sleep.

CHAPTER 19

The following afternoon Beth was redirected from Nicole's hospital room to the Physical Therapy department. Two more inquiries led her to Nicole. At a distance, Beth observed Nicole from the back. Nicole was standing in between waist-high parallel bars. Her legs were braced with appliances made of leather and metal. She moved stiffly, nearly dragging her legs as she worked her way from the center toward the end of the expanse. Beth remained intentionally out of sight. She could hear Nicole grunt with each step forward as the physical therapist encouraged her. Nicole reached the end of the bars. With the therapist's help she turned around to attempt another length. She was drenched in perspiration. Beth was enthralled by Nicole's dogged expression.

There was something about this woman that captivated Beth. She had seen so much in Nicole in such a short period of time. Nicole was not an onion with layers. She was far too complex for that analogy. Beth wondered how removal of the tumor would change her, how many different facets of the Nicole she had come to know would survive. There was the woman of the night who toyed with violence, the business owner, the consultant, the philanthropist, the woman who defined the divine in her own terms without discounting other religious traditions, and the woman who did not have to be right but who did need to be true to herself, hold to her integrity, and live with dignity.

Beth found the same latter qualities in Jacob. She understood that was the foundation of Nicole's friendship with the neighborhood elder. She felt the connection she shared with Nicole differently. How, she could not articulate. From Nicole's first words to her, 'Do I know you?' Beth had both welcomed and feared the pronouncement coming true. To have someone else know her completely was a devastating prospect. She knew she withheld herself from Nicole and she wished she had the courage to let her defenses fall. Such a surrender was, at the least, imprudent because Nicole was impossible to anticipate. The more time Beth spent with Nicole the less she felt she could control their friendship. It was deepening in spite of her efforts to keep the other woman safely at arm's length. The danger of Nicole was that she unknowingly had the ability to break open Beth's soul, as she had done with the haunting question, 'Where is your God now?'" One could not be with Nicole without being true to one's nature. Nicole compelled the truth, and Beth's will was succumbing to the tender seduction that was Nicole.

"Damn it!" Nicole's cry and the sound of her fall pulled Beth from her reverie.

Beth stepped forward. The therapist caught Nicole, buffering the impact. He cradled her, slowly resting her completely onto the floor. "Are you hurt?"

Nicole had no patience for him. "No!"

"You've done enough. Let's get you back to your room."

"I'm going to walk!"

"Nicole, you can't do this all in one day." The therapist reached out to help her up.

"Mark, get your hands off me! I can get up by my damn self!".

He leaned back on his heels and waited. Nicole looked ahead. Someone was standing in front of her. She looked up. It was Beth. "Fuck!"

Beth bent down to her. "Nicki."

Nicole looked to the floor. "I told you I didn't want you to see me this way!"

"You were doing so good. You're just tired."

Nicole would have none of it. "I don't want your condescending pity!"

"Nicki, I'm trying to be your friend."

"I don't need your friendship."

Beth's anger rose. "That isn't what you said to me at St. Ann's. Or was that the tumor talking? When the doctors excised the tumor did they also excise our friendship?"

Nicole's frustration shredded her composure. "I want to walk."

"You will walk," Beth promised. "But it's going to take time. Let Mark help you." Beth looked over to the therapist. He smiled reassuringly to the young priest.

Nicole raised herself up on her elbows. "You're in uniform."

"I've got a couple of visits to do."

"Always the professional."

"Not when it comes to you."

"I thought David would have warned you about my corrupting influence."

"He did. I decided not to listen to him."

Bested, Nicole chuckled. "Go ahead. I'll see you later."

Beth looked over to Mark. He nodded, encouraging her to take her leave.

Beth placed her hand over Nicole's. "I'll be by your room later today." Beth stood up and left the facility. Walking down the hospital corridor she unwittingly found herself smiling.

Back in Physical Therapy, Nicole looked over to Mark. "Well, aren't you going to help me up?"

Mark laughed. "Remind me to call in the Reverend for all your PT sessions."

CHAPTER 20

Beth was in the midst of her second patient visit when her pager vibrated. She clipped the pager from her waist and read the phone number. It was David. After the conclusion of her visit, she went to the nearest telephone in the hospital corridor. David hesitated upon hearing her voice. He conveyed the message he had received from Beth's father Her grandmother had had a stroke. The prognosis was not good. David offered Beth one of the church's cars to drive home. She accepted the offer. She would return to the church immediately.

Beth walked down the corridor to the elevator getting out on the main floor. By rote she found herself at the hospital chapel. It was a small, quiet, dimly lit space that provided the repose that patients, staff and visitors were apt to seek out during the arduous days and nights of the hospital. She found it empty. She did not have the strength to move further into the space. She leaned against the back wall. Her hand went to the cross hanging around her neck. Given to her as a child, the delicate gold cross symbolized both her grandmother and God. In many ways she could not imagine one without the other. Beth felt weak; her strength had been taken from her.

Her grandmother had always been her champion. From her earliest memories Beth's earthly sense of belonging, of value, was found in her grandmother's arms – nowhere else. No one else had seen Beth for who she was. No one else had encouraged Beth to create a life for herself in spite of the obstacles set against her. She heard the sobs without being completely aware that they were her own. She slid down the wall, unable to sustain herself any longer.

Beth returned to Nicole's room. Entering she found Nicole asleep. She stepped up to the bed. Beth longed for Nicole's comfort. She could not ask for it. She wrote a brief note and placed it on the bed table. She left the room and walked down the desolate white washed corridors that smelled of illness and death. She was devoid of the hope that only a few hours before she was so certain of.

CHAPTER 21

Nicole woke slowly. Her muscles ached from the morning exertion. She looked down to her legs, foreign entities that no longer seemed a part of her. She would have them back. She would meld them seamlessly to her.

She had fallen asleep without seeing Beth. Her fatigue took her to a deep sleep. In her sleep she found contentment. She could dream of walking as effortlessly as she had done before the tumor-caused tremors claimed her equilibrium, before the surgical damage. She scanned her room. A note was prominently positioned on the table beside her. She assumed the writer and smiled.

Nicki,
    I've been called away. I should be back in a week.
Be well,
Beth

Nicole read the words repeatedly. Beth would not come to her today. The note was bereft of any emotion. There was no promise of a phone call. There was nothing but what needed to be said. Nicole closed her eyes and leaned her head back. She struggled to find grace in the moment. She was humbled, her self-pride doused by the antiseptic ink on paper.

CHAPTER 22

Beth entered The Pub. Connor waved her over to the bar. She approached and leaned against the bar as she waited for Connor to finish serving a patron. He greeted her warmly, "Welcome back."

"It's good to be back. How is she?"

Connor tossed a bar rag from one hand to another. "I'm waiting for her to get real angry. She's not there yet."

"I don't understand."

"When she's angry there's no holding Nicki back. I know she'll be okay when she throws the wheelchair out of the loft. She needs to decide she'd rather crawl across the room than sit in the fucker." Connor blushed realizing what he had said. He quickly apologized for his language. "Sorry."

Beth ignored the language she herself used on occasion. "Isn't that extreme?"

"Yes, but that's Nicki."

Beth glanced toward the stairs leading to The Garden. "I've never been to the loft."

"Just go up to The Garden. Keep going down the hall. You'll see another set of stairs. Go up. She usually keeps the door open. Walk right in."

"Thank you."

"Beth, don't be too easy on her. That's not what she needs right now."

Beth nodded, and followed Connor's instructions. She found the large oak door open. She stood on the threshold scanning the loft. It was splendid. Given the rest of the Elysian Fields, she was no longer surprised by the jewels Nicole possessed. The space was very much Nicole; it had an unassuming elegance even with the dining room table positioned against the wall, displaced by a set of parallel bars. The owner sat in a wheelchair behind her desk. Beth knocked on the door and walked in. "Hi."

Nicole looked up from her book. She offered a muted greeting. "Hello."

Beth forced a light spirit. "You're up."

"Sitting-up," Nicole clarified.

Beth pointed at the volume in Nicole's hands. "What are you reading?"

"Alice Cary." Nicole looked again to the poem. She chose to read it aloud. It would speak for her.

"'To Solitude
I am weary of the working.
   Weary of the long day's heat;

To thy comfortable bosom,
  Wilt thou take me, spirit sweet?

Weary of the long, blind struggle
  For a pathway bright and high,
Weary of the dimly dying
  Hopes that never quite all die.

Weary searching a bad cipher
  For a good that must be meant;
Discontent with being weary,
  Weary with my discontent.

I am weary of the trusting
  Where my trust but torment prove:
Wilt thou keep faith with me? wilt thou
Be true and tender love?

I am weary drifting, driving
  Like a helmless bark at sea;
Kindly, comfortable spirit,
  Wilt thou give thyself to me?

Give thy birds to sing me sonnets?
  Give thy winds my cheek to kiss?
And thy mossy rocks to stand for
  The memorials of our bliss?

I in reverence will hold thee,
  Never vexed with jealous ills,
Though thy wild and wimpling waters
Wind about a thousand hills.'"

Nicole fell silent and turned the wheelchair so she could look out the windows.

Beth did not know what to say. She simply spoke Nicole's name.

"Beth, don't mind me. I don't recommend Alice Cary after brain surgery. Now Sara Teasdale has potential." Nicole paged through the book and found the poem that she had found compelling. She had read it countless times since Beth left her alone in the hospital. "Here it is."

"'Since there is no escape, since at the end
  My body will be utterly destroyed,
This hand I love as I have loved a friend,
  This body I tended, wept with and enjoyed;
Since there is no escape even for me
  Who love life with a love too sharp to bear:
The scent of orchards in the rain, the sea

And hours alone too still and sure for prayer—
Since darkness waits for me, then all the more
Let me go down as waves sweep to the shore
    In pride, and let me sing with my last breath;
In these few hours of light I lift my head;
Life is my lover—I shall leave the dead
    If there is any way to baffle death.'"

Nicole looked up. What was she doing? She had before her the one person she had wanted to see more than any other during the previous five days, and now she was wallowing in her own self-pity. "You came back."

Beth was flustered by Nicole's abrupt shift in focus. "Yes, I'm sorry I didn't say good-bye."

"You left a note."

"I didn't want to wake you."

Nicole was solemn. "Beth, next time, wake me."

Beth owned up to her error. "I will."

Nicole repositioned her wheelchair to face her guest. "What was so important that you had to leave? David was absolutely worthless as a source."

Beth took a moment to collect herself. "May I sit down?"

"I'm sorry, yes."

Beth sat down. She held her hands before her. The last few words of the Teasdale poem echoed in her mind. *Life is my lover—I shall leave the dead / If there is any way to baffle death.*

Nicole watched Beth's mien shift as sadness swept over the younger woman. "Beth, what is it?"

Beth looked up. A single tear fell down her cheek. "My grandmother had a stroke. She died before I could see her."

Nicole was stunned. A battery of questions flashed through her mind. She spoke none of them. Nicole's eyes were drawn to the cross that hung around Beth's neck. Beth never went without her grandmother's gift. "I'm sorry."

Beth grieved. "She loved me. I loved her. And now she's gone."

"Is there anything I can do?"

Beth gestured toward Nicole's book. "Read another poem."

Nicole complied. They would mourn their individual losses together.

CHAPTER 23

Two days passed before Beth returned to the loft.

Miguel stood in front of Nicole's desk. "You have to eat."

Beth approached. "Hi."

"Tell her to eat."

Nicole retorted, "I am not Beth's Cocker Spaniel."

"More like a Doberman."

"How about a Black Lab?" Beth said brightly.

Miguel shook his head. "No. They have longer hair."

Nicole was not amused. "Bite me!"

Miguel feigned shock. "Nicki. Not in front of the priest."

"Have you had lunch?" Nicole asked Beth.

Beth was caught by the unexpected query. "It's been a busy day."

Nicole was triumphant. "Miguel there's your gal. Beth, do we have a lunch for you!"

"Will you share it with me?" asked Beth.

Miguel smiled. He knew he liked Beth for a reason. "You're right Nicki. She's my kind of gal."

Nicole raised her hands in defeat. "Fine! I'll eat."

"Bye, girls." Miguel strutted out of the loft.

The two women watched the Latino make his exit. Beth chuckled as she returned her attention to Nicole. Nicole's thinness troubled her.

Nicole smiled. "Hi."

"Hi again. You're a bit cranky."

"My P.T. came over this morning."

"How did it go?"

Nicole looked down to her legs and tapped both wheelchair arms with her hands. "Still here. I wanted to work longer. I'm not going to walk if I'm sitting in this chair all of the time."

Beth was pleased to learn the source of Nicole's frustration was not that she did not want to work but that she did. Beth nodded over to the lunch tray. "You need to get your strength back."

Nicole knew better than to renew the argument. "Soup or sandwich?"

"I'll take half the sandwich."

"There's mineral water in the 'fridge."

Beth retrieved two bottles. She returned and held them up. "No glasses?"

"Let's picnic."

Beth pulled a chair over to the tray. She had begun to feel quite comfortable in Nicole's space.

They lunched, speaking easily. Beth shared what she could of her day, always taking care not to break confidentiality. Fortunately the church, like any organization populated with humanity's own, gave her plenty of material to entertain Nicole. In turn, Nicole enjoyed being taken away from her world if only for a little while. She also confirmed that organizational dysfunction was alive and well in the religious community.

Nicole yawned.

Beth observed, "You're tired."

Nicole spoke with some satisfaction as a second yawn overtook her. "Morning workout, good food, good company."

"I can help you get into bed."

"I can do it myself," Nicole said tersely.

Beth remained calm. "I didn't say you couldn't."

"Can't stop being the priest, can you?"

Beth reached up and removed her collar. She held Nicole firmly in her gaze as she did so. Her voice did not waver. "I'll help you get into bed."

"I …" Nicole could not finish the thought. She could not tell Beth she loved her though in that moment she knew she did. She loved the young, strong, combative, compassionate cleric.

Beth said, "You what?"

"I could use your help." Nicole unlocked her wheelchair and guided it to her bed.

Beth stood up and followed. "Tell me what to do?"

"Just steady me when I stand up. I can do the rest."

"Okay."

Nicole locked her chair and managed to raise herself to her feet. Beth stood before her, taking her by the waist. Nicole placed her hands on Beth's shoulders for support. She looked down at the beautiful woman. Beth was determined in her task.

"Take a step back, Beth. I'll walk with you."

Beth met Nicole's eyes and nodded. She took a small step back.

Nicole stepped with her. "One more."

Again they stepped in unison. This gave Nicole enough distance from the wheelchair to turn and sit upon her bed. Beth moved with her, bending down, bracing Nicole.

"If you could help me lift my legs?"

Beth did so, as Nicole slid herself against the bed backboard. Beth reached over for the comforter and covered Nicole.

Nicole felt her fatigue more than she would willingly admit. "Thank you."

"Anything else?"

"I'm re-reading *The Iliad*. It's on my desk."

Beth secured the volume and placed it in Nicole's extended hand. "Wiesel, now Homer. You don't go for light reading."

"Never got enough of the Classics in college."

"Why the Classics?"

"Why the Bible, Beth? To find myself, to find meaning in the world. Personally, reading Homer makes more sense to me than reading the latest Harvard Business Review."

"I've noticed you read those, too."

"I have to make a living."

"Yes, you do. And, you do all right from what I can tell." Beth patted the bedcovers. "Rest."

Nicole spoke shyly, betraying her false stoicism as she did. "You know you're welcome here anytime."

Beth understood. "Is tomorrow too soon?"

"Not at all."

"Mid-morning?"

"Knowing Miguel he'll serve tea and crumpets."

Beth stepped away amused with the idea.

Nicole called out. "Beth."

The young woman paused.

"I'm getting used to seeing you without your collar."

Beth cocked her head, taking in the remark. "Good, 'cause you know I wasn't born with it on."

Nicole blushed. Her mind had flashed to a naked Beth, and the image seemed at that moment utterly sacrilegious.

CHAPTER 24

As dusk overtook the city, a woman equal to Nicole in age entered the loft after knocking lightly on the door. She immediately caught sight of Nicole in her wheelchair. She set down a large purse and a medium sized suitcase, and glanced over to the exercise bars before walking toward her friend.

Nicole did not hide her surprise. "Tess!"

Tess Talbert crossed her arms disapprovingly. "Still in the chair?"

Nicole volleyed back, "Sorry to disappoint you."

"I'll get over it."

"Glad to hear it. Why didn't you tell me you were coming?"

Tess relaxed. "I'm in town for a pre-holiday visit. I had to choose between you and my mother-in-law. It was a tough choice."

"How on earth did you choose?"

"I flipped a coin."

"I lost, huh?" Nicole grinned. "Stay where you are." She wheeled the chair to the side of the desk and locked it. Straining, she raised herself up. Nicole teetered on her feet. "I feel like a baby learning to take her first step."

Tess watched with concern. "Need help?"

"The crutches are over there." Nicole gestured toward a niche between two bookshelves.

Tess retrieved the crutches. Holding them with one hand, she embraced Nicole.

"Hey …"

"Shut up!"

Nicole realized that Tess was crying. "I'm going to be fine. I just need some time."

"I knew something was wrong. It's not like you to disappear from the face of the earth."

"You wouldn't have liked me, Tess. I didn't trust myself. The tumor was causing me to do things I wasn't very proud of."

Tess stepped back. "You still should have called before the God damn surgery."

"I didn't want to ruin your Thanksgiving."

Tess slapped Nicole in the arm. "Don't to it again."

Nicole raised one hand in oath. "I promise the next time I have brain surgery you'll be the first to know."

-|-　　-|-　　-|-

After dinner Nicole situated her wheelchair across from Tess, who sat on a love seat with her legs tucked underneath her, enjoying Nicole's best chardonnay. "What does Beth make of you?"

"I'm her favorite heathen."

"Heathen? Since when is it okay to call you a heathen?"

Nicole did not want to quibble. "Last time I looked I met the definition."

"You've never described yourself by what you're not."

"Come on, Tess. I'm not of the people of the book. No harm done."

"Nicki, you're not a murderer or pedophile either." Tess was keen. "There's a fricking stigma to being on the defensive. It isn't right."

Nicole latched onto the absurd. "Are you equating Christianity with pedophilia?"

"I'm serious. Be careful. You don't go around saying 'I'm not heterosexual'."

"I don't go around saying I'm a lesbian either."

"But you don't shy away from saying so if asked." Tess leaned forward.

"Because people know what a lesbian is. If I say I'm a materialistic pantheist, their eyes glaze over. They figure I'm a capitalist gone amuck, drumming and howling to the moon."

"You aren't?"

Nicole dropped her head in an exaggerated gesture of frustration.

Tess laughed and placed her hand on Nicole's head. "I still remember when you explained your beliefs to me."

Nicole looked up. "Yeah, that was a conversation to remember."

"Why you didn't just say you were a pagan was beyond me."

"That was Amelia's translation." Nicole referred to a fellow college student.

"It fit."

"It's incomplete." Nicole insisted, impatient with the ceaseless effort of explaining herself, even to her closest friends.

"So you said. You were a materialistic pantheist with … what was it?"

"A humanistic ethic, a.k.a. heathen."

"I love you."

Nicole gave Tess a puppyish look.

"Don't look at me like that."

"What?" Nicole played innocent.

"You're one of my dearest friends. What's wrong with saying so every once in a while?"

Nicole grew earnest. "I love you, too."

Tess placed her hand on Nicole's leg. "Nicki, don't lose yourself in someone else's dream for you, no matter how well meaning."

"Why so serious, Tess?"

"Friends like us have to stay in touch, keep each other grounded, otherwise we might lose sight of our ideals."

"That seems like a lopsided deal. I don't have much to offer you."

"You have no idea, do you? Nicki, you are the most courageous woman I know."

Nicole knew better. "You've got me mixed up with Amelia. Being a survivor doesn't equate with being courageous."

"In her own way, Amelia put us all to shame." Tess studied her wine glass. "She's gone now…" Silence enveloped the two friends. Nicole was attentive, patiently waiting for Tess to return to the moment. Tess raised her pensive eyes. "Nicki, I need to believe in the dreams we shared in college."

"Tess, you're living your dreams. I'm the one who walked away from hers."

"You've got a second chance. Don't throw it away," Tess entreated. "Don't make me watch you throw it away."

"Hey, I'm looking to you for inspiration. You're teaching the Classics, you've got a great love and two hellion kids."

With the mention of Tess's family, Nicole succeeded in mollifying her friend. Tess settled back on the love seat. "Speaking of which, there are a couple gifts in my bag. You'll have to call your goddaughter before the night is out and give her artistic creation an appropriate assessment."

Nicole laughed. "I'm in trouble, aren't I?"

CHAPTER 25

Beth waited outside the loft door. A woman Beth had never seen before opened the door. The woman was a couple of inches taller than Beth, with shoulder length curly brown hair, bright brown eyes, a pug nose, and full lips. She was attractive. What most caught Beth's attention was the fact that the woman was dressed in a robe and pajamas. Beth relied on her ministerial experience to overcome the awkwardness she felt. "Good morning."

The woman smiled broadly. "Good morning. You must be Beth. Nicki told me you were going to drop by." She waved Beth in. "I've got coffee on. Would you like some?"

Beth stepped into the loft. "Yes, thank you."

"Nicki's got first dibs on the bathtub. She should be out any minute." The woman went to the coffee brewer. "How do you take your coffee?"

"Black is fine."

"Black it is." The woman poured the coffee and handed the mug to Beth.

"Thank you." Beth wrapped her hands around the mug. "I'm sorry, I don't know your name."

"Oh, damn. So much for making a good first impression. I'm Tess. I'm an old college friend of Nicki's. I'm also still half asleep. We had a late night catching up."

"You don't live in Chicago?"

"I flew in from Ann Arbor." Tess's gaze shifted to the bathroom door. "I wanted to see how Nicki was coming along."

As if on cue Nicole rolled her wheelchair into the living space. "Hey! It's all yours."

"We've got company," said Tess.

Seeing Beth, Nicole smiled. "Watch out for Tess, Beth. She can't be trusted."

Tess walked toward Nicole. "Sweetheart, I haven't even started. I'm going to make sure Beth hears about your most scandalous acts of debauchery while we were in college."

"I was going through a phase," Nicole defended.

"A really long one, from what I can tell."

"Go take a shower. Your mother-in-law waits."

Tess turned to Beth. "Nicki promised me a night at The Pub. Kate will be there, too. I hope you can join us." Tess winked. "I promise I'll make it worth your while."

Beth glanced over to Nicole. Nicole's smile reassured her. "I'd love to."

Tess gently squeezed Nicole's shoulder as she passed her on the way to the bathroom.

Left alone, Nicole read an unspoken question in Beth's eyes. "Tess teaches Classics at the University of Michigan. We went to school together."

"She mentioned that." Beth tried not to be too obvious. "You're good friends?"

"I'm her daughter's godmother." A memory caused Nicole to laugh. "Tess badgered her poor Methodist preacher into changing the baptismal rite so I would agree to participate in the ceremony."

"Sounds like she was determined."

"Tess? Try bullheaded. The ceremony wasn't the hardest part. The hardest part was choosing a name with a Classical reference."

"Helen?" Beth offered an obvious choice.

"Oh no. Helen was beautiful, but to a Classicist she is at best morally suspect."

"What were her choices?"

"Clytemnestra killed Agamemnon. Electra wanted vengeance, and depending which poet you read, killed Clytemnestra. Medea killed her children. Phaedra was admirable but committed suicide when she got in the middle of Aphrodite's revenge against Hippolytus. Hecuba was noble but the Trojan War destroyed her life. Andromache saw her husband Hector killed by Achilles, and her young son smashed to the ground from the ramparts by the Greek victors. Antigone went against Creon, and committed suicide after being buried alive in a cave. Ismene drifted into anonymity. The pitiful list goes on forever."

"What did Tess choose?"

"Well, as the baby's godmother I thought I should have a say."

Beth saw the gleam in Nicole's eyes. "What did you suggest?"

Nicole grinned. "Bacchae."

Beth laughed. "Nicki, you didn't."

"What? To follow Dionysus, to find purity and joy in nature, to know happiness and beauty."

"To indulge in wine."

Nicole leaned forward. "I have one word for you – Eucharist."

Beth was game. "Nicki, what is your goddaughter's name?"

Nicole announced triumphantly. "Dion."

CHAPTER 26

Sitting at a table in The Pub, Kate Cabot cried foul. "Stop that!"

Tess and Nicole smiled at one another. Tess challenged, "What?"

"You damned well know what!" Kate directed her next comment to Beth, the only ally she could hope to muster. "They did that all through college. Ajax, Phaedra, Medea. Their code words for God knows what."

Tess defended herself and her fellow Classicist. "We were trying to get Kate to lift her nose out of her law books and get a little culture." She accused the attorney, "You didn't read one play all through grad school."

"I didn't see you reading any law books."

"Please." Tess dismissed the idea.

"So speaks the bourgeoisie."

"Dilettante."

Nicole leaned over to Beth, speaking low. "Philoctetes and Odysseus."

Beth smiled.

Kate turned a deep shade of red. "What now?"

Beth was sheepish. "I don't know but I have a feeling it was funny."

Kate glared at Nicole.

Nicole repeated her reference to the two combative characters in the play *Philoctetes* by Sophocles. "I just said, 'Philoctetes and Odysseus'"

Tess slapped Nicole. "I'd better have been Philoctetes."

"Who else?" Nicole granted Tess the more noble character.

"Ha!" Tess's voice traveled above the crowd.

"I hate you both!" Again, Kate turned to Beth, seeking a comrade. "Nicki was just barely sufferable on her own, but when the three Electra's got together she was beyond hope."

Tess laughed again. "I forgot about that."

"The three Electra's?" Beth directed her question to Nicole.

Nicole was content to listen. "It's Tess's story."

Beth looked across the table. "Tess?"

Tess clearly relished the telling. "Amelia and I were sitting in the school commons debating how Aeschylus, Sophocles, and Euripides portrayed Electra in their respective plays."

"Were they very different?"

"Nicki, I'm disappointed," Tess playfully chastised. "Haven't you given Beth a primer on the tragedies?"

Nicole was deliberate. "Tell the story, Tess."

"All right. Yes, the characterizations are very different. Anyway, Kate joined us while we waited for Nicki. Kate wouldn't have anything to do with us otherwise. Kate said God knows what condescending thing about our studies. It got Amelia's goat. So Amelia made up this whole explanation about the three Electra's with wonderful mythic embellishments. She was so good I even started to believe her.

"A half hour later, Nicki finally showed up. Kate decided she's was going to impress Nicki with what she had learned." Tess glanced over to a pouting Kate. "You were a peach." She turned anew to Beth. "Nicki's expression was priceless – a combination of stunned incredulousness and slowly bubbling suspicion. Kate went on and on about the three Electras. Finally, Nicki had enough and asked Kate if she was stoned."

Beth looked over to Kate.

Kate sulked, saying, "They were worse than the Fates."

"I think you mean the Furies," Nicole deadpanned.

"Damn you!"

Beth tried to console the outcast. "I don't think I would have known the difference."

"There! There! I am not alone!"

Tess needled, "So, ignorance is something to cheer?" She tried to isolate her target. "No offence, Beth."

"Bourgeoisie," Kate repeated.

"Dilettante," Tess responded on cue.

Nicole raised her eyes and gazed about. "I didn't realize The Pub had an echo."

Having met Tess, Beth was curious about the third member of the threesome. "Where is Amelia?"

The table quieted. Tess realized that Nicole had no intention of speaking. "She died a couple of years after grad school."

Nicole wore an impenetrable mask. Kate explained, "She knew. We all knew she would die young."

The mention of the young death took Beth by surprise. She wondered what kind of friendship Nicole allowed when the prospect of its loss was so imminent. "I'm sorry."

Tess attempted to sweep aside the wave of melancholy. "Amelia was the one who introduced me to Nicki. You, my friend, were a revelation."

Beth was intrigued. "How?"

"I'll tell you later when we can have a private moment. Right now, imagine our beautiful Nicki in her black leather. She had a reputation that would give Aphrodite reason to blush."

Kate said tartly, "You had nothing to worry about. You and Bruce were inseparable."

Tess shot back, "You're not a Greek."

Nicole burst out laughing.

Kate was furious. "There you go again with your inside jokes."

Beth whispered to Nicole. "What did Tess mean?"

Nicole responded in equal voice, "I can't explain in a sentence or two. I'll give you a rain check."

Beth smiled. "I accept."

Later in the evening, Tess and Beth stood by the bar retrieving fresh drinks.

Tess took advantage of the private moment. "Has Kate played nice?"

Beth was confused by the question. "Why wouldn't she?"

"The three Electra's. Kate has always wanted to have Nicki to herself. She never fit in when Nicki, Amelia and I were together. Kate and Nicki shared the bar and party scene. But even then, when Nicki was on the prowl, Kate didn't have a chance of keeping up."

Beth did not appreciate Tess's predatory description of Nicole. "I still don't understand what Kate would have against me. I'm not a rival."

"Oh, yes you are. Nicki is anything but one-dimensional. That means she has different kinds of friends and a whole lot of acquaintances. What irks Kate is that of all of Nicki's facets, the most important are her spiritual beliefs, as unconventional as they might be. Nothing else comes close. Not The Fields, not the consulting, not even her friends. The fact that you are a priest gives you a unique affinity with Nicki that Kate can't begin to have."

"But Nicki isn't a Christian. Believe me, she hasn't been shy about pointing out how different we are."

"Beth, you share the same passion. The fact that you differ in your approach is beside the point. You don't have to agree with Nicki. All she asks is that her view be respected as equal to your own."

"Kate can share that with Nicki."

"Kate? This is a woman who read *The Tao of Pooh* and *The Tea of Piglet* as a primer to Eastern spirituality."

Beth could not help but laugh. "How about you? I can tell that you two are close."

"We are. My interest has always been the philosophers. Nicki's has been the playwrights and poets. There is a difference."

"I really haven't known Nicki very long," Beth admitted. "There's a lot about her that I don't understand."

Tess smiled knowingly. "I expect that when I'm old and gray I'll still be trying to figure her out. It doesn't really matter. She's a good friend. It's nice to know that she'll set aside her books for me."

"You make her sound like a recluse."

"I bet if you ask her which she would choose, an evening with her books or one with her friends, the choice wouldn't come easy."

"You know her better than I do."

"Nicki covered my grad school reading list while sailing through her MBA. She knows the Greeks just about as well as I do. She studied the Romans and Jews, and when that wasn't enough she moved on to the early Christians. She's a hairsbreadth away from being a genius though she'll never admit it. I don't know anyone more hungry for learning. She would go crazy without her reading."

"I haven't really seen all of her library. It seems impressive."

"Beth, I can't help notice how Nicki is with you. I bet you can hold your own with her."

"I do all right."

"Thought so." Tess went back to her original subject. "Kate's smart. The woman knows her law. Nicki, with one business law course under her belt, listened to Kate talk about her class work and peppered her with questions trying to get a handle on a concept. Kate used Nicki to practice her legal arguments. Nicki had a knack of coming up with show stopping questions that Kate would rarely get from other students in her study group. I watched them. Their conversations tended to shift from the law to justice. They both care about getting beyond the theoretical and tackling the ethical consequences. More times than I can count the two ended up in a knock down, drag out fight."

"That must have been fun to watch."

"It was. Would you be surprised if I told you that Kate wanted to change the world and Nicki was intent on accepting the vulgarities of the legal system as an inevitable consequence of a humanly defined system?"

"Yes, I am."

"You don't agree with Nicki, do you?"

"I think if we embody the divine, which is what Nicki believes, then our charge is to define a law for humanity equal to God's law. That we fail is to our heartbreak as a global community."

"The Greeks do not need to love their gods, only to find a life worth living while subject to their capriciousness. The divine is as flawed as humanity. There isn't any hope for perfection on earth or in heaven. That's what makes Nicki a Greek. She'll never be an Idealist."

"I don't see her as being that cynical."

"To Nicki that isn't being cynical, it's being realistic. Given her life, I can't blame her for seeing the world the way she does."

Beth's gaze traveled to the table where Nicole and Kate sat conversing. "May I ask you a question?"

Tess nodded.

"I don't understand why Nicki didn't stay with the Classics if she loved studying them so much."

Tess followed Beth's gaze. "Her mother died."

"Why would her mother's death stop her?"

"There are some people who never shed their skin. As much as they try, the same old skin grows back, making the statement, 'this is what you are; don't forget it.'" Tess had Beth's complete attention. "If Nicki had gone on to grad school she would have had to conform to her professors, then she would have had to play the tenure game, and throughout all that time, she would have had to teach. If you haven't noticed, Nicki is a loner. She's the kind of loner who doesn't conform. She's the kind of loner who does everything she can to control her world. When her mother died she realized how much she was her mother's daughter. She built The Fields and her consulting career so that she could spend her time in the loft reading and learning about the Classics in her own way, in her own good time. She tolerates her public life because it is the means to her private life. Few people understand that about her."

"You think Kate doesn't."

"Kate knows how important Nicki's private life is to her. She just keeps waiting for Nicki to shed her skin."

Beth had come to understand the crucial distinction between Nicole's two friends. "And you don't."

"I didn't understand her at first. Amelia did. I think because in many ways they were the same. What separated them was that Amelia was fated to die young. She placed her hope in death. In death, she would be free of all the pain that she endured because of her body. Nicki, on the other hand, has been fated with the prospect that her one hope is to make peace with herself, because as far as she is concerned the only thing that waits for her in the grave is oblivion."

Beth turned to her wine. What Tess was telling her melded well with Beth's sense of Nicole.

Tess glanced at the wall clock. The evening would soon draw to a close. Unprompted, she continued in her storytelling. "During the first year of our undergraduate studies, if you asked me to describe Nicki, I would have painted a portrait of an intellectual who was somewhat shy. Nicki came to life when she talked about her studies. Early in the second year she fell in love and for a few months blossomed. She got hurt and something inside of her broke, or maybe she was already broken and the damage had gotten so bad that there was no way for the pieces to be put back into place. She started to go out with Kate more often. She used her beauty in a way she never had before. She had one goal – conquest. To be honest, it was rather ugly. There were two Nickis – the scholar and the night owl. Three months before we finished our undergraduate studies, Nicki's mother died. It was the one time Kate had better luck reaching her than Amelia or I did."

Beth speculated. "Is that when she stopped drinking?"

"No, she still drank. She changed her plans for grad school. She pulled a full load and kept The Pub going. Something else happened just as we all finished grad school. It was then that she stopped drinking. No one knows for sure what made her stop. I'm just glad she did."

"Why are you telling me all this?"

"Because Nicki wants your friendship and I don't want her to get hurt. I want you to know what you're getting yourself into. Nicki's not an easy friend to have, Beth, but I think she's more than worth the effort."

It was bar time when Nicole escorted Tess outside. A taxi waited to take Tess to her in-law's home. Tess paused and turned to Nicole. "You're my favorite Spartan woman. Don't forget that."

"I won't."

"You're going to get on your feet and stay healthy. Promise me, Nicki."

"I'll do my best."

Tess kicked a tire. "Get rid of this wheelchair."

"Soon. I just wanted to get your sympathy."

Tess went down on one knee. "I'm not angry at you for not telling me. Live, Nicki. Isn't that what we learned together?"

"One day at a time, Tess."

"How are you and Kate doing?"

"Never better." Nicole chuckled. "Couldn't you tell?"

"What does she think of Beth?"

"Cautious, I think."

"Has she figured it out yet?"

"What?"

Tess's countenance sharpened.

Nicole sighed. "Kate doesn't need to hear me say I'm falling in love with Beth."

"But she knows?"

Nicole was rueful. "I'm obviously not hiding it well."

"Amelia … Beth …"

"Don't." Nicole cut Tess short. Her friend was very close to crossing a forbidden line and both of them knew it.

"Be careful. You've gone through enough …"

"Poetic justice. What's happened with Beth … it serves me right."

"You don't believe in poetic justice."

"You and I are friends. Why can't I be a friend to Beth?"

"If we were talking about me, seeing in me what I see in you, I'd say you were wrong to think you can just be friends. But, you're not me. You've never followed the rules, so I'll just say maybe." Tess kissed Nicole on the cheek. "I love you."

"Love you, too."

Nicole watched as Tess entered the back of the cab. She would miss her.

CHAPTER 27

The early dusk of the winter evening and the lull of city activity were soothing. Nicole took each step with a blend of determination and gratitude. Each step made her feel triumphant and yet humble. She was getting better, stronger. Each step was proof. She kept walking, lost in this simplest of tasks. She looked up to the silhouette that was St. Ann's. The church had taken on new meaning, displacing difficult memories. The edifice was so much more to her. The church was animated by the people it housed, by the people who sought help from it, by the people who worshipped in it. But above all else, St. Ann's and Beth were inseparable.

She studied her watch. Beth might still be working. Nicole felt ready, confident that she would be whole again. It was time to share the extent of her progress with Beth. For weeks Nicole had hidden her renewed abilities from her friend. Beth had never observed Nicole's efforts on the parallel bars at the loft, or her efforts to walk up and down the Elysian Fields' stairs, or her first step out onto the street. Nicole, with the help of the Musketeers, kept the secret. For a moment Nicole imagined Beth's expression in seeing her friend standing before her, hearing Nicole simply state she walked over "just to say hello." As if the feat was nothing out of the ordinary, the feat once again having become ordinary.

Nicole entered through the main entrance of the basilica. Instead of shunning the sanctuary, she welcomed its ambiance. Walking up through the nave would give her the time she needed to transition from her world to Beth's. She opened the large wooden door with care. It seemed disrespectful to make more noise than necessary. She passed through into the space, her cane finding easy footing upon the marble floor. The interior doors at the right were propped open. She chose the route that bypassed a struggle with the heavy wood panels hanging on iron hinges. Entering the ambulatory she walked eagerly, joyfully though the effort had renewed her fatigue. For a moment she chose to pause and consider the space. It was then that she heard the sound, a muted sob. She looked ahead. A figure was kneeling before the altar. Nicole continued to walk slowly forward. With each step she was able to see the figure with greater clarity. When she neared half the distance to the altar she confirmed a growing apprehension. It was indeed Beth. Nicole stepped to the side, behind a pillar, away from sight. She felt an intruder. Beth seemed small and vulnerable without the vestments of the priesthood Her posture was markedly different from that of a priest. She did not stand in authority but was hunched over in defeat more than in humility. Nicole felt she was witness to a truth that was not meant to be shared, not with her, not with anyone but Beth's God.

The sound disturbed the sanctuary's silence once again, echoing within the walls that more commonly serve to raise up the voices of a choir, the music of an organ and the words of praise of a celebrant. Nicole took a step toward the priest but then, for a second time hesitated. Before her were the remnants of a broken spirit and she felt at a loss as to what to do. This was not the time for a proud entrance. She countered her first instinct and stepped back into the shadows. Weary, she looked about seeking a niche to rest in, a means to gather her strength. There was no ready outlet so she leaned against the wall and waited. Within her she parlayed a steady dialogue, a debate trying to define the right and the wrong of her paralysis. As the minutes passed she resolved to do nothing. The second-hand of her watch ticked away the time.

A quarter of an hour passed before Beth raised herself up, wiping her face with her sleeve. She sat back on her heels and looked up to what was to her a forbearing image of the Christ. She stood up holding her gaze upon the cross. After the passing of a half dozen heartbeats, she bowed and made her way across the transept towards her apartment while holding a crushed envelope firmly in her fist.

CHAPTER 28

The following morning Nicole walked down the corridor leading to the church offices. With the hectic activity of people moving past her she concentrated on each step. She dreaded the possibility of losing her balance and falling. She had done it often enough This was not the time for a failure no matter how minor it may be weighed against the difficulties that enter the church each and every day. She heard a familiar voice. Looking up from the floor of the aged building, which had garnered her attention with its patterns of scattered paint chips, her eyes caught hold of Beth walking toward her with Blair Davis, St. Ann's religious education director. They were both engaged in their conversation. Indifferent to her surroundings, Blair shifted to her right, moving in front of Beth in order to pass by Nicole. Nicole turned her body in unison with Beth's advance. The motion was quick and taxed her ability to keep her body and mind in synch. She was struck dumb.

It was then that Beth looked up, the momentum of her step taking her forward as her gaze met and held to Nicole's. Beth stopped and turned. Her eyes traveled down to Nicole's unbraced legs, and then back up to the bright blue eyes that claimed her regard. A smile slowly formed as she took in the meaning of Nicole's presence. She had no words that would do justice to her feelings. She moved forward and took Nicole into her embrace. Nicole bent down and carefully surrendered herself leaning upon Beth for support. Beth felt Nicole's physical dependency and increased the firmness of her hold, tactile assurance of her support. Beth breathed in Nicole's musk scent. It suited the tall woman. It drew Beth further into the other's world. The young priest whispered into Nicole's ear, "You've done it."

Nicole could not have imagined a greater reward for her tireless effort. "I wanted to surprise you."

As much as Beth did not want to release Nicole she knew she must. She did so carefully, taking a step back, her hands still holding Nicole's arms to ensure balance.

Nicole repeated the words she spoke in a dream. "It's a beautiful day for a walk."

Beth responded softly, "Nicki."

Nicole scanned the hallway. "You look busy."

Beth glanced at Blair who watched the women with interest. Beth returned her attention to Nicole. "I'm on my way to a meeting at the diocese."

"You better go."

"We need to celebrate."

Hopeful, Nicole proposed, "You could come to The Garden for dinner."

"That sounds wonderful but I have a couple appointments already scheduled. How about tea? I can drop by around eight."

"I'd like that."

Beth lingered. She did not want the world – her world – without Nicole to go on. This moment was too sweet, too complete to let go of easily.

Blair called out, "Beth, we'll be late."

Beth gently pressed Nicole's arms, a signal of her forthcoming release. Wordlessly she lifted her hands, stepped back and turned toward Blair. Nicole felt the loss. She took hold of her cane leaning upon it for much needed stability.

Blair waited until Beth was at her side. "Who do you think she'll be now that she's healthy?"

Beth responded with aplomb, "The woman she's always been."

Blair was not impressed. "And that is?"

Nicole watched the two women until they were out of sight. She decided to complete an intended task. She made her way to Beth's office. Upon reaching Beth's desk, Nicole removed her backpack. From it she retrieved a golden hair teddy bear and a card. She placed the teddy bear prominently at the center of Beth's computer keyboard. The card was propped beside it. It read:

Beth—

This little fella gives great hugs. Thought you might give him a home.
Nicki

CHAPTER 29

Dressed casually in jeans, a cream sweater, and a leather jacket, Beth entered The Pub. Connor waved a welcome and called out that Nicole was in The Garden. Beth smiled and made her way to the stairs. Finding the 'little fella' in her office had been a wonderful surprise. She did not know why Nicole had thought of the gift. She did know that she found herself holding the teddy bear for quite some time. His face could fairly be described as sad and yet it brought a smile to her and those who happened to see him during the course of the day. When she could no longer delay her work she gave the teddy bear a place of honor where she could see him by simply raising her eyes, which she found herself doing time and time again.

"What's a priest without a collar?" A woman's voice called out.

Beth paused and turned toward the speaker. It was the woman she had seen with Nicole during their first encounter after the theft of her cross. "Excuse me?"

Paige stepped forward within an arm's length of Beth. "Just asking a question, Father. What's a priest without a collar?"

It was obvious to Beth that the woman had been drinking. "You're a friend of Nicki's."

Paige spoke with bitter sarcasm. "Friend? I don't think so. The word I would use is whore. But who needs a whore when she's got a priest? Ain't that right, Father?"

Beth was determined to be patient. "I don't know what you're talking about."

"You must be very good. In giving comfort, I mean. Nicki's back on her feet and all. You know I thought she threw me out of her bed because of the tumor. And then I thought it was because she was crippled. But then it hit me." Paige slapped herself on the side of the head. Not too lightly. "It was the day we ran into you on the street. That was the last time she touched me. Now I know it's always been about sex but damn it was good sex." Paige emphasized each of the following three words. "Real ... good ... sex! But I don't need to tell you that do I, Father? Hell, you probably got her off her feet all over again."

Connor approached from the back of the bar. Having overheard the damage Paige's stiletto tongue was inflicting, he shouted, "Paige!"

Paige waved Connor away. "Connor, you're interrupting."

"Go home Paige."

"You don't have to protect the Father. She's a big girl. She knows how to take care of herself … and Nicki. Right, Father?"

Beth maintained an impassive expression. Paige did not take it well. "Don't look at me that way. You're no better than I am." Paige's taunts elicited no response. "Say something, bitch!"

Connor had enough. "That's it. Paige. You're out of here." He took Paige by the arm.

Paige jerked her arm free. "Don't touch me! A whore has got some dignity."

"Connor, don't," Beth quietly pleaded.

"Don't let her mess with you."

"She's not." Looking directly at Paige, Beth said, "Nicki is expecting me."

Beth weaved through the crowd as Connor's and Paige's voices drifted into the din of the room. She ascended the staircase in quick steps, pausing at the top. She was trembling. *'What is a priest without a collar?'* The taunt was familiar. It had haunted her dreams. How could a stranger come forward and challenge her with such precision? Beth took a deep breath. She spoke to calm herself. "Hold on. Just hold on."

Beth entered the restaurant. Peter was busing a table nearby. "Hi Peter."

"Hello, Reverend. She's over there." Peter pointed to an atrium table with the best view of the Chicago skyline.

"Thank you." With each step she took, Beth felt she was entering a world that was calling her with a greater generosity than the world she had left behind outside of the Elysian Fields. With each step her certainty of self was further compromised.

Nicole had been keeping a steady watch on The Garden's entrance. She saw Beth enter. The immediate sighting gave her enough time to use her cane to stand and steady herself.

Beth stopped a couple of paces from Nicole. "Hi."

"Hi."

"You didn't have to get up for me."

Nicole smiled. "Oh, yes, I did. What kind of host would I be if I didn't?"

Beth stood silent. Nicole felt there was reason to be concerned. "Is there something wrong?"

Beth took her seat. Nicole, disappointed by a lack of an embrace, did the same.

Beth would have preferred not to mention Paige but she feared Nicole might learn of their exchange from Connor. "I just had a few words with Paige."

Nicole had tried to carefully end their liaison. She had hoped her illness would provide the necessary rationale to temper the rejection. Paige had sulked. She had boasted that Nicole would change her mind. Paige had reckoned Nicole's insatiable libido would ultimately bring her back begging for release. Nicole knew she had been running out of time. Paige's eruption had come sooner than expected. "I hope she wasn't too tough on you. She can be toxic."

"She's jealous."

Nicole did not know how to maneuver the space between Beth and her. She saw land mines everywhere. "It has nothing to do with you."

"What is 'it'?" Beth's vehemence was hard to withstand.

Nicole attempted to dismiss the concern. "I'm not seeing her anymore."

Beth was persistent. "You were lovers?"

"No, that would be too generous of a description," said Nicole candidly.

"What was she to you?"

Nicole saw no reason to temper her answer. "Sex."

Beth spoke with an edge. "And you don't want sex anymore?"

"Beth, do we have to have this conversation?"

Beth's anger broke through. "I just want to know why I've been accused."

"We have never spoken of our lovers. I don't know why we have to start now."

"Maybe I didn't have anything to tell."

"And maybe as far as I was concerned, I didn't either."

Beth was grave. "Things have changed."

Nicole was struggling. "Because of Paige?"

"Assumptions are being made."

Nicole's confusion was replaced by a painful clarity, one she had no patience for. "To hell with assumptions."

"You may be able to afford your reputation, but that doesn't mean I can."

Nicole expected better from Beth. "It isn't a reputation we're talking about. We're talking about my life. Do you care that much about what other people think?"

"Nicki, I'm an Anglican priest."

Nicole was absolute. "I'm sorry, I thought you took the collar off when you became my friend."

Beth placed her hands flat on the table. She looked down. Beth was feeling the tear of her interior fabric. It had been gradually happening to her. As hard as she tried she could not stop it. She knew she and Nicole stood on the edge of a precipice. She did not want either of them to fall. She wanted to reach out for Nicole's hand. She wanted the friendship, the companionship and she knew her next words might shatter all possibilities between them. She moved her hands together, holding them before her. Her eyes focused on nothing else. She finally looked up to Nicole's intent gaze.

"Paige said some things. I guess she shook me up more than I thought."

Nicole gentled her voice. "What things?"

Beth leaned back. "It doesn't matter. She got what she wanted didn't she?"

"And what was that?"

Beth whispered fearfully, "To put a wedge between us."

"Only if we let her," Nicole reassured, taking control from Paige's shadow.

"I'm being foolish aren't I?"

Nicole needed to acknowledge her friend's distress. "I'm sorry she hurt you."

An image came to mind. Beth smiled. "That's okay. I've got a 'little fella' that gives great hugs."

With a sense of relief Nicole mirrored Beth's smile. In that moment she envied the 'little fella' more than she could say.

CHAPTER 30

Beth stood at The Garden entrance. Miguel was creating omelettes on demand at the brunch table. He waved Peter over. "Make sure the omelette doesn't burn. I'll be right back."

"I don't cook!" Peter protested.

"You've just been promoted." Miguel chuckled at Peter's youthful panic as he sauntered to meet Beth. He joyfully greeted the radiant young woman. "*Feliz Navidad!*"

She hugged Miguel. "Merry Christmas."

Miguel spoke wryly, "Reverend, what will people think? You could ruin my reputation."

"Miguel, I don't think that's possible." Beth looked about.

Miguel answered the unspoken question. "She's not down yet. Go on up."

Beth knocked on the open loft door. "Nicki?"

Nicole called out from behind the bedroom screens. "Beth, come on in. I'll be ready in a minute."

In her many visits to the loft, Beth had never had the opportunity to linger freely without observation. She had always wanted to explore Nicole's library of books. She gravitated toward the living room shelves. The books were arranged by subject: Ancient Greek and Roman History, Greek Poets, Greek Philosophy, Modern Philosophy, Mythology, Judaica, Christian History, Biblical Studies, World Religions, and Archeology. On the wall hung Nicole's diplomas – a bachelor in Classical Humanities, another in Philosophy and a third, her MBA.

It was impossible, given her reliance on her cane, for Nicole to approach without announcing herself. Beth turned and watched the other's cautious gait. Beth's heart stirred at the vision of Nicole. "Hi."

"Hi." Nicole felt breathless at the sight of Beth. "Santa came early and left a package for you on my desk."

"Nicki, I thought you said you didn't celebrate Christmas."

"I don't. It's from the Three Musketeers."

Beth walked past Nicole but not without touching her as she did. Upon the desk laid a small box and a sealed card. Beth opened the card first.

Beth-

When Nicki's happy we're happy. We've been very happy since you came into her life.

Merry Christmas.

With love,

Miguel, Connor, Tony

Each of the men had signed their name. Beth studied the individual signatures – Miguel's flowing strokes; Connor's matter of fact letter that neared print, and Tony's 'T' followed with a straight line with a sharp downward stroke for the 'y'.

Nicolè watched Beth with great interest. She had no idea what the card said, nor what gift awaited Beth in the small box.

Beth took a deep breath. Though she had gradually grown to appreciate their presence in the Elysian Fields, always welcoming and sometimes protective of her, she never expected this from the Musketeers. Beth took the present in hand and carefully untied the ribbon and wrapping, revealing a black felt jewelry box She took another deep breath before opening it, revealing two diamond stud earrings. They left her speechless.

Nicole waited patiently. She knew in Beth's silence that the woman had been deeply touched. Nicole went to Beth and peered over her shoulder. Nicole smiled upon seeing the earrings. The Musketeers had done well.

Beth spoke in a hush. "I don't know what to say."

"I'm sure you'll think of something."

"I'd like to wear them."

Nicole approved. "That will make the boys happy."

Beth looked up at Nicole.

Nicole felt Beth's amity. "What?"

"It's just that I'm very happy."

"And that's good, isn't it? How about brunch?"

The two women entered The Garden and made their way towards Nicole's reserved table. Miguel met them as they were about to be seated. He pointed up to the ceiling. "Mistletoe. Can't let it go to waste."

Beth leaned up to him and kissed him on the cheek. "Thank you."

Miguel objected. "Hey! Hey! Hey! What did I tell you about my reputation! I didn't mean you were supposed to kiss me. I'm going back to my omelettes. You two figure it out."

Nicole glared at Miguel. Beth smiled sheepishly. She did not wait for Nicole to cast a rebuttal. She stepped up to Nicole and kissed her lightly on the cheek. "Happy Holidays."

Nicole made a mental note to increase Miguel's Christmas bonus.

CHAPTER 31

Beth left Chicago mid-morning Christmas day. She had celebrated the 4:00 p.m. Christmas Eve service and midnight mass. David was scheduled to celebrate the Christmas day services. She drove through the sparse, snow-covered landscape, feeling very much a part of its desolation. She did not want to go home. She would have preferred to stay in Chicago. The warmth and joy of the previous day was slipping away from her. It was late in the afternoon when she arrived at her father's house in the heart of Riverton. Though she had a key, she chose to ring the doorbell and wait for admittance.

Frederick Kelly opened the door to his daughter. "Elizabeth."

To Beth her father was a constant figure in her life. A tall, slender, severe man with blond hair like her own, his body had a dried and lifeless appearance. "Father, how are you?" Beth entered as her father stepped back.

Frederick considered his daughter "You wouldn't know, would you?"

Beth regretted the truth of his words. "I'm sorry." They both paid a price for their strained relationship.

"It's all right. You are doing God's work and that is all that matters."

Beth hated this dismissal of their estrangement. "That isn't all that matters."

Frederick closed the door. "You are wrong, young lady. There is nothing more important than God."

Beth kept her day bag on her shoulder. "Father, I want to talk to you about your last letter."

"It's Christmas. Must we go directly to our unpleasantries? I said all that needed to be said."

Beth tried to apologize. "I was wrong to tell you so soon after grandmother's death."

"Leave your grandmother out of this." Frederick spoke with low-pitched harshness. "You want to leave the priesthood when you have only just begun. How can you expect me to give you my blessing?"

Beth stepped forward. "I have my reasons for leaving."

"Is your love for God any less?"

"No."

"Has your call to ministry changed?"

"No, Father."

Frederick moved to the living room. "Then tell me your reasons."

Beth followed. "I don't agree with the Church."

"You don't agree with the Church. Who are you to disagree?"

Beth attempted to appease. "Someday I may become a minister in another church. One with a more liberal view."

Frederick was unrelenting. "You don't shop for a faith like you do for a new pair of shoes. You take what God gives you."

"That's what I am trying to do," said Beth in a defeated whisper.

To the extent Beth's voice fell, Frederick's rose. "You still haven't told me why. What is so important that you would throw away your priesthood?"

Beth looked at the fireplace mantle. The familiar family photographs held court: her father with her mother on their wedding day, her grandmother, Beth as a young child with her sister Marie. She stood silent.

"Elizabeth, think long and hard. Make sure you understand the consequences of your actions. There won't be any going back."

"Yes, Father."

"Now, why don't you wash up. We have dinner reservations at the Inn."

Beth turned her gaze away from her father. She walked past him toward the front stairs, sensing no human warmth from him as she did. She so wanted to be deserving of his love. Placing her hand on the banister she considered the door. Taking her leave promised a life free of the suffocating press of her father's commands. She told herself he was her father. Nothing would ever change that. She looked up toward her childhood room. Making her decision, loathing herself for it, she took each of the stairs lifting a weight far greater than her youthful heart could bear.

Sitting upon her bed Beth delayed reentrance into her father's world. She remembered her grandmother's bitter self-recriminations for her son's misplaced piety. Beth's grandmother never understood Frederick. She made allowances for him until she could no longer deny the damage he was inflicting on her two grandchildren. She tried to temper the barren world of the young girls. Beth spent the greater portion of her childhood at her grandmother's house, in her grandmother's embrace. How Beth missed her. Her grandmother was the only mature love she and Marie could remember, their mother's memory having become too faint to comfort, yet salient enough for grief.

Her thoughts drifted to Marie. She missed her younger sister. Marie left Riverton right after high school and refused to return. Not even her grandmother's funeral was sufficient cause to bring her back. Marie could not forgive her father for his part in their loveless childhood, nor could Marie understand Beth's religious vocation. It smacked too close to Frederick's religious zeal.

Beth hoped Marie would one day meet Nicole. Both Marie and Nicole judged that life had betrayed them by promising what they deemed to be in reality a false god. And yet, unlike Marie, Nicole was able to conceive of the divine in life. Beth wished she could somehow give her sister the same confidence Nicole demonstrated in fashioning a faith of her own.

Frederick called up to her. Beth looked out the window. She wished it were snowing. Somehow it would be easier if she could take a walk in the falling snow.

CHAPTER 32

It was a frigid New Year's Eve. Nicole held court in a large circular booth in The Pub. The Three Musketeers were working to keep The Fields running smoothly on the busiest night of the year. The Fields offered patrons everything they might desire during a night on the town – excellent dining in The Garden, a robust pub atmosphere to enjoy conversation, and dancing in the Elysian Fields to hard throbbing music with an occasional slow romantic interlude.

There had just been a mass exodus of Nicole's party to the dance floor. Nicole and Kate remained behind.

Kate brushed back her short auburn hair and leaned back in the booth. "The night is young and I can't believe I'm ready for bed."

Nicole looked up to one of The Pub's antique timepieces. "Midnight isn't that far off."

Turning the subject to her latest conquest, Kate asked. "So what do you think of Angie?"

"Seems nice enough. Are you serious?"

"Who knows? Every time I think I'm close there comes a full moon and some nasty transformation."

"That could be interesting."

"I've had enough interesting women in my life, thank you. Speaking of which, I've heard Paige is no longer welcomed."

"I figured it was about time I take your advice."

"I don't think so. You've always taken pride in doing the opposite of what I counsel."

"Only in terms of women. Not your legal advice."

"How's Beth? I hear from the boys she's become a regular at The Garden."

Nicole assessed Kate's demeanor. Sensing no bitterness, she answered freely, "Good. The church has a New Year's Eve shindig going on."

"So I won't be seeing her tonight?"

"Nope. Anyway, I don't think it would be a good idea for her to be here. Appearances, you know? I told her I might drop by St. Ann's for a while."

Kate glanced at her watch. "It's almost midnight."

"Didn't I just say that?"

"Why are you here?"

"Beth understands I have friends."

Kate peered at Nicole. "I'm not talking about what Beth wants. Why don't you just admit the truth? Tell me, where would you rather be, here or at St. Ann's?"

"Kate, she's a friend."

"And I'm a friend. Which friend would you rather be with? You've never worried about hurting my feelings … why start now?"

Nicole felt the salvo. She held her tongue. Kate's jealously was misplaced. No matter how much she loved Beth, Nicole could not have her. Their terms of engagement were set. Theirs was an incomprehensible friendship, one Nicole refused to set aside. Nicole hoped, that by the Fates design, the day would come when a woman equal to Beth would enter her life and her bed. Nicole expected that with time she would let go of the impossible. For now, the impossible made her want to walk, it made Christmas Eve the best she ever had, and it made her impatient to go to where Beth waited for her.

Nicole slid out of the booth. "Let the gang know that I'll be back after midnight."

Nicole retrieved her coat from behind the bar and exited The Pub. She enjoyed the walk to St. Ann's. She took the church stairs down to the basement gathering room. There was a very good turnout. Congregants and guests were drinking coffee, cider and soft drinks, and eating a potluck buffet of snacks and desserts. Beth was at the far end of the room talking to a couple of teenage girls. She was dressed casually in a white blouse and blue slacks. Nicole stood back and enjoyed watching the young cleric in her world.

"Don't you have a bar to be at?" Mrs. Stephens spoke unkindly.

Nicole turned to the old woman who through the years had become one of St. Ann's conservative matriarchs. Nicole never considered a woman like Mrs. Stephens worth the effort of engagement. She knew the woman had a particular distaste for the Elysian Fields, and no argument from civil rights to Christian charity would win her over to toleration, let alone acceptance. Nicole chose to minimize their encounter. "Good evening, Mrs. Stephens."

"I would think a church gathering like this would be too pious for your kind."

"My kind?"

Mrs. Stephens seemed to be in quest of an argument. "A number of us in the church have expressed our concern that Reverend Kelly has been seen in your establishment on a regular basis."

Nicole was unapologetic. "I consider the Reverend a friend."

Mrs. Stephens turned her gaze towards Beth. "A woman in her position should be careful whom she calls a friend."

Nicole maintained her gaze upon Mrs. Stephens. "As careful as Jesus was with the prostitutes and tax collectors of his time?"

Mrs. Stephens snapped her head back to her adversary. "Don't be smart with me young lady. We are Episcopalians and only a year and a half ago the Lambeth Conference renewed our position that homosexual behavior is incompatible with Scripture."

"Is that a direct quote?"

"Yes, as a matter of fact it is."

"How about 'love your neighbor as yourself'? Do you know that quote?"

Beth had caught a glimpse of Mrs. Stephens with Nicole. She excused herself and moved quickly, hoping to intercept any verbal missiles. "Nicki, I'm glad you made it."

Ignoring Nicole's last comment, Mrs. Stephens turned to Beth with clear intent. "Reverend, I was just informing Ms. Thera of the 1998 Lambeth Conference resolution regarding homosexuality." Mrs. Stephens returned her attention to Nicole. "We of course are not without our mercy. We teach to love the sinner and not the sin."

Nicole echoed in a low controlled voice. "Sinner?"

"Yes, as Christians we realize that only a few of you have the necessary discipline to control your aberrant behavior. There is no reason to condemn you for your weakness."

Nicole looked at Beth. Mrs. Stephens followed suit. She zestfully posed her question to Beth. "Reverend, isn't this the teaching of the Church?"

Nicole waited for a response.

Beth struggled to find the right words to mitigate the damage. "Mrs. Stephens, many American bishops disagreed with the resolution. We have gay and lesbian congregants, and the church will ordain gay and lesbian priests."

Mrs. Stephens clarified. "Only if they are celibate. Isn't that true?"

Beth paused as the truth crushed her. "Yes."

"So as an Episcopalian priest you uphold our teachings that homosexual behavior is wrong, don't you?"

Beth looked from Mrs. Stephens to Nicole.

Mrs. Stephens pressed. "Reverend?"

Beth's voice begged forgiveness. "Nicki, I'm sorry."

Mrs. Stephens made no effort to hide her triumphant smile. Nicole stared at Beth in complete disbelief. It was one thing that Beth could never love her. It was another for Beth to see her in the same terms as that of the Church. Nicole did not trust herself. Her rage had overtaken her every nerve. She stepped back, turned and began to make her way out of the church basement.

Beth was in shock. In a matter of moments she allowed the most precious person in her life to be torn away from her. Mrs. Stephens was speaking but Beth did not hear her. Beth regained sufficient mindfulness to follow Nicole through the otherwise empty corridor. She called out to her as Nicole was at the church door exit. "Nicki, please don't go."

Nicole turned as Beth reached her. She raised her arm pointing back to where they had come from. "Is that what you think of me? How you see me?"

"Please don't."

"Damn it! How can you even stand being with me? The sinner! The aberrant!"

"Nicki, please …"

"Don't lie to me. Don't lie to yourself."

"You knew when you met me. I didn't hide myself."

"No, I didn't know, Beth. I really didn't know. There are enough clergy through all the ranks that buck the system, that try to change the archaic positions of the Church. Who aren't ashamed to say that they believe lesbians and gays are God's creation, and that our love has God's blessing."

The church bells began to chime midnight. Nicole looked up reflexively. At the strike of the bell she hated the Church. She hated the Church's unique ability to destroy souls.

Beth trembled. She did not know what to do. She felt caught in a trap of her own making.

Nicole returned her gaze to Beth. Nicole took a step forward and then another. With her momentum she pushed Beth against the wall. Nicole's hands rested upon the wall above each of Beth's shoulders, one holding her cane.

Beth remained still. She could only take in Nicole's hardened expression.

Nicole spoke harshly. "The ruse is over. You might as well know that I love you. I love you with all my heart and soul. And I am one of those poor bastards that can't control my love, my lust for you." Nicole took Beth's lips with her own. The kiss was rough, demanding; it accused, it begged, and it broke Nicole's heart.

Beth did not fight Nicole. She could not. She felt she deserved whatever Nicole chose to do with her. As Beth's body began to respond to the kiss, Nicole broke away. "Now Beth, you can hate me and we'll both know I deserve it."

Without another word Nicole pushed violently away. She thrust the church door open and walked down the stairs toward the Elysian Fields. Beth turned her head. With her gaze she followed Nicole's diminishing form until it disappeared around the corner. She closed her eyes and prayed, "Please help me."

Nicole stood outside the Elysian Fields. The New Year celebration was at full force. She could not face the revelry. She walked to the back entrance and up the stairs to the loft. She saw Peter as she traversed the second floor landing.

"Nicki, is everything all right?" He called out as he jogged to her.

Nicole kept her eyes averted. "I don't want anyone to know I'm back."

"Sure." Peter hesitated. "Is Beth okay?"

"Peter, please don't mention her name again."

Peter nervously shifted his weight from one foot to the other. His voice betrayed his bewilderment. "Nicki, I'm sorry."

Nicole raised her eyes up to meet the young man's compassionate gaze. There was nothing for her to say. "Goodnight, Peter."

"Goodnight, Nicki." He watched in silence as Nicole slowly walked up the stairs.

CHAPTER 33

Peter told Miguel of Nicole's homecoming only after they had closed the restaurant during the early morning hours of New Year's Day. Miguel shared what little was known with Connor and Tony. They all waited for Nicole to mention Beth's name. She did not. To their disappointment, Beth was not seen at the Elysian Fields. A new silence with its own melancholy permeated The Fields.

Two weeks later, Tony responded to a message from Nicole. He knocked at the open loft door as he entered. "Hey, you wanted to see me?"

Nicole was at her desk. "I'm leaving on Thursday. I'll be gone until February 10."

"A month? Where to?"

"I have an assignment in New York."

"Is that a good idea?"

"I just got a clean bill of health. I'm allowed to travel."

Tony crossed his arms. To Nicole, it was a familiar gesture of disapproval. "That isn't what I mean."

"Tony, I appreciate your concern. I need to get away for a while."

Tony's Italian charm was nowhere to be found. "But you're not running away?"

"Maybe I am. But I'll come home. I always do, don't I?"

"Nicki, what happened between you two?"

Nicole picked up her pen and held it with both hands. In her mind's eye she briefly revisited New Year's Eve. "Nothing I'm proud of."

"So it was you?" he said disdainfully.

Nicole met his gaze. "Isn't it always me?"

"That sucks. I miss her. We all do."

Nicole understood that the loss of Beth was not hers alone. "I know. With me gone maybe Miguel can convince her to come for lunch."

"She won't come back unless you're here to come back to."

For Beth's sake, Nicole attempted to contain the damage. "Tony, it was never like that. But you're probably right, she won't come back."

"Nicki, whatever happened – would an apology help?"

"I can't change who I am."

"Is that what it will take?"

"Yes."

Tony remained cool. "Anything else I need to know."

Nicole admired Tony's misdirected loyalties. "No, that's it. I'll touch base with you before I leave."

Tony nodded, turned and left the loft.

Nicole looked down to her desk, her airline ticket in front of her. She just had a conversation about Beth without mentioning Beth's name. She preferred that the reason for their break was not known. Though Nicole regretted the violence of her kiss, a part of her felt no remorse. It was not that she felt justified. She felt there had been nothing between them more honest.

CHAPTER 34

Nicole knew New York City well. It was a city rife in business consultants; as a Midwesterner, she took great professional satisfaction in being called in on an assignment. Lodging in an extended stay apartment on West 72nd Street, she was within walking distance of everything she might need, including a subway ride to her Wall Street client.

She found she was living at a slower pace than usual. In the evenings she walked, relishing the city scenes as she continued to rebuild her stamina. There had been, to date, only a few extreme winter days of snow and biting winds. On those days she took equal pleasure having a simple dinner at a local restaurant and enjoying quiet, uninterrupted hours in her apartment.

Nicole stepped out of Luzia's, a Portuguese restaurant on Amsterdam and 79th Street, arm in arm with Carrie Nolan. Carrie was a long-standing business associate and a woman Nicole valued as a friend. "I'll walk."

Carrie turned to Nicole, and placed her hands flat against Nicole's shoulders. Old enough to be Nicole's mother, she radiated a warm maternal concern. "Are you sure?"

"It's not far."

"You will take care of yourself?"

Nicole smiled. "I promise."

"I'm proud of you, you know."

Though rarely shown, Nicole never ceased craving the approval of those she admired. "I'll try not to disappoint you."

"Call me if you want to talk."

"I'm planning on keeping a low profile. I've had enough crises to last a lifetime."

Carrie raised a hand to Nicole's cheek. "Someday the right girl will find you and you won't know what hit you."

"Hey, I found her but then I learned she was married and had two beautiful daughters."

Carrie laughed. "We'll keep it our secret. I don't want John to get jealous."

Nicole embraced Carrie. "I love you."

Carrie held Nicole close. "I love you, too."

The two friends separated. Carrie watched Nicole as she walked away, relying less on her cane than when she first arrived in the city. "Be careful!"

Nicole raised her hand and gave Carrie a wave as she continued toward her apartment.

As she walked, Nicole's thoughts turned from the city she was about to leave to the city of her return. She reflected upon the events of New Year's Eve. The image of Mrs. Stephens squaring off with the unsuspecting Beth was a memory she was unable to erase. In retrospect, Beth seemed completely unprepared for the challenge, not knowing what had hit her. Mrs. Stephens had been giddy in her triumph, and Nicole knew that she had played a part in giving Mrs. Stephens her victory. Beth's words, "I'm sorry," were more a plea than a statement. It was a plea Nicole had chosen to ignore. Those two sincere words stayed with Nicole; so, too, did Beth's unrecognizable passivity. The formidable young cleric had been nowhere to be found.

Nicole would be going home the following morning and she was glad for it. She felt ready. As hard as it would be, she planned to keep her distance from St. Ann's. Her confession and the kiss could not be swept aside. Her actions had consequences. She had stripped all nuances from her relationship with Beth. All along, as her feelings for Beth had grown, the sole motivation for her silence had been to maintain the friendship she and Beth shared, a friendship she believed the truth had the power to destroy. A friendship she was certain her truth had destroyed.

Eight hundred miles away, Beth walked the city streets in thought. She needed to establish a space between herself and the Church. She felt the insidious consequences of betrayal. In her heart she felt her Church had betrayed the message of Jesus and she, in turn, had betrayed Nicole. The betrayals did not have to be. She did not have to accept the mantle of the Church. But she had. What she had convinced herself was not too great a price to pay for her vocation became a price that, in good conscience, she could not ask of another.

For Beth the price had always been minimal. She had carried throughout her young life an impregnable loneliness, a loneliness that she felt even as she laid her head on her grandmother's lap. The gap between the generations reminded her that she had a life to live that would take her beyond her father's arid house.

She sought an affinity to someone or something beyond herself. The Christ, as she had been taught as a child, was her salvation, her hope, a companion to mitigate the loneliness that permeated her life. In college only a few of her childhood religious teachings had survived scrutiny – teachings at the very heart of her faith. She believed in a first cause, a Creator. She believed in the power of love, and she continued to hold Jesus of Nazareth as the personification of the divine. Jesus was the bringer of a new worldview that could be had only if humanity remembered his teachings and acted to realize them.

Beth remembered Nicole's nutshell summarization of Christianity. Nicole's assessment was close to Beth's own beliefs. Whereas Nicole had rejected all, Beth never lost sight of the innocence. She refused to live a life that was not grounded in her faith. She fought dearly to hold to her faith. She looked to the miraculous child born, to the child who became a teacher destined to guide humanity to a better way of life. Why could not the faith expounded by the Church be as simple as the two great commandments: to love God and to love thy neighbor as thyself? Not that it would be any less profound. In fact, she believed doctrine and dogma ultimately derailed the best of the Christian faith. The arguments consumed the energies, muddied the focus across Christendom and between Christendom's institutions and those of other world religions.

David had spoken to Beth regarding Mrs. Stephens' account of the evening, an account the woman had proudly shared. Beth had affirmed the accuracy of the telling. She now recalled how quiet David had become. When he had spoken again it was to remind her of the prophetic role of the clergy. Nothing else had been said. It had been Beth's choice not to pursue the subject. She remained uncertain of what David would have had her do under the circumstances. She knew David would not tell her. It was for her to find her own way.

Standing at the street corner with a view of the Elysian Fields, Beth once again replayed her last encounter with Nicole. She wondered whether anything but Nicole's unbridled rage could have driven her to voice her feelings and to demand from Beth the still-haunting kiss. Beth wondered if there was any way their friendship could survive Nicole's raw truth.

CHAPTER 35

Nicole sat at her desk. Her chair turned toward the window, she enjoyed watching the late February snow as it fell gently onto the city streets. The moment of peace was interrupted by the house extension. "Good morning."

"Nicki, it's Connor. Jacob is here and he said you should bring your coat and come downstairs."

"Did he say why?"

"No." Connor paused. He spoke in a low voice. "Nicki, it's not like Jacob to come here on a Sunday. Hell, it's not like him to come in here at all."

"I'll be right down."

Nicole observed Jacob watching her walk down the stairs.

He smiled appreciatively. "You are walking well."

"Pretty soon no cane," Nicole was pleased to report. "With the snow and ice, it's safer to have a third leg."

Jacob offered his arm. "You can lean on me."

"Where are we going?"

"Church."

Nicole's tone carried a reproach. "Jacob."

Jacob was sanguine. "Reverend Kelly is going to preach on *hesed*."

"So?"

"Nicole, that can only mean the Book of Ruth."

Nicole continued to flex her resistance. "And ..."

"Don't take me for a fool. I have no doubt she will be speaking to you above all others and you must be present to hear."

Nicole felt a rising trepidation. "Jacob, what do you know?"

"Only what the whole neighborhood knows. You and Beth have not spoken to each other since New Year's Eve." Jacob solicited Connor's corroboration. "Is that not right, Connor?"

Connor hesitated. "Jacob, with all due respect, I'd rather not go there."

"No, you would not, would you?" Jacob directed his next comment to Nicole. "None of your friends are willing to speak up."

"Jacob, please don't interfere," said Nicole.

"Can you discard love so easily? Nicole, the love of a friend is no less precious than that of a lover. Give her a chance to apologize."

Nicole was wary. "What has she told you?"

"Nothing. But I do know David made the mistake of assuming your responsibility in this matter, and Beth did not take it well."

"Since when are you and David so close?"

"Nicole, the service is about to begin. If I, a Jew, am willing to go to that Christian conclave, the least you can do is come with me for moral support." Jacob waited, but Nicole gave no indication of joining him. He waved his hand and said, "Come. Put on your coat."

Nicole did not have the heart to argue with the gentle man. She proceeded to do as she was told. "What will Liza say?"

"My Liza knows as I do that you believe in good deeds. She will say that we have both done a *mitzvah* today and, she will be proud that I had you on my arm as we did."

The procession had begun by the time Nicole and Jacob entered the church. They stepped to the side, taking a seat near the rear. Nicole sat passively as the service progressed. She did not want to see Beth, the priest. It was too painful. Though she could choose not to open her eyes to Beth, she could not stop her ears. Beth's voice was strong and authoritative. It carried the grace of her god.

✤   ✤   ✤

Beth entered the pulpit. She looked out among the large congregation as she had done at the earlier service. There was no reason to expect to find Nicole. In the course of their friendship Nicole had not attended a service either she or David had led.

Beth looked down to the pages before her. She had never written a more personal homily and yet she knew that only one other person on this earth could hope to understand the nature, and the depth of its meaning. It would need to be enough that she knew, and that she found herself covertly sharing an intimate part of herself with the congregation.

"*Hesed* is a key covenantal term of the Hebrew Bible. *Hesed* is God's loving kindness, compassion and grace. In human terms, *hesed* is more than the loyalty that one can expect when in covenant with another person – it is that additional element which both establishes and sustains a covenant. It is more than ordinary human loyalty; it imitates the divine initiative that comes without being deserved.

"Verses 16 and 17 of the Book of Ruth are pure poetry. They, as a declaration of love, embody the Hebrew concept of an act of *hesed*. Nowhere in the Hebrew Bible is their simplicity and power surpassed. Elimelech, Naomi's husband, and Mahlon and Chilion, Naomi's sons and the husbands of Ruth and Orpah have died. Naomi directs her daughters-in-law to go back to their mother's house, to find husbands and have children. Orpah does so. But Ruth asks of Naomi 'Do not press me to leave you or to turn back from following you!' Ruth makes an explicit request to Naomi. Ruth asks Naomi to set aside all the arguments she has voiced, arguments located in her culture and to accept another possibility.

"Ruth, who had been defined in relationship to men, finally breaks tradition and acts as an individual, as a force in her own right. Pressed to separate from Naomi, she acts first physically and then in voice. She clings to Naomi. She speaks — and in her speech clearly demonstrates an understanding of the meaning of her action. 'Where you go, I will go; where you lodge, I will lodge; your people shall be my people, and your god my God.' The Anchor Bible translation is somewhat different than our Bible of reference. In the Anchor Bible the verse is translated as 'Your people become my people; Your God is now my God.' The latter translation gives a stronger sense of conversion from Ruth's Moabite tradition to Naomi's Hebrew tradition. The words 'become' and 'is now' provide a sense of motion, of movement from one idea to another. What is striking is that Ruth's marriage to one of Naomi's sons had been insufficient to elicit a conversion. Though Naomi used the term *hesed* in blessing her daughter-in-law for all the kindness she had demonstrated to her and the dead, it did not include the acceptance of Yahweh. If it had, Ruth's declaration would have been unnecessary.

"Ruth continues to press her desire to be with Naomi by invoking an oath. The oath is not taken lightly. Ruth speaks to a communal burial, 'where you die I will die — there will I be buried.' These words take the bond beyond the limitations of life unto the transcendent. The oath is completed with the invocation of Yahweh, 'May the LORD do thus and so to me, and more as well, if even death parts me from you!'

"Scripture states, 'When Naomi saw that she (Ruth) was determined to go with her, she said no more to her.' The argument ceases in silence. Commentators differ in interpreting Naomi's silence. Of all the interpretations, the one I prefer is that Naomi's silence should be taken as grateful acquiescence.

"Ruth acts contrary to what is culturally established as her first concern, that being to find a husband and to have children. Ruth confesses her devotion. It is not motivated by marriage and familial obligation, but by love. It is a love great enough to have her embrace not only Naomi, but also Naomi's god, Yahweh. As her name promises, Ruth is the personification of a 'companion,' one whose fidelity holds in both life and death. Later in the Book of Ruth, Ruth's decision to accompany Naomi is framed as another act of *hesed*, as an imitation of the divine initiative. Though seen as such, it can also be equally argued that hers was a consummate act of human love.

"The return of silence marks the end of this chapter of their lives. It marks closure to the question of who they are to one another now that there is no civil constructed bond — marriage — to hold them together. It is an ending made possible through mutual understanding. An understanding made possible by the exercise of voice and action, one not necessarily consistent with cultural expectations, but one that is seen as right under the hand of Yahweh.

"We all have the divine capacity to perform an act of *hesed*. The act may not be to give up one's way of life or one's God for another's but it may encompass a reconsideration of the culture we live in. An act of *hesed* can seem quite ordinary – as ordinary as a kiss – and yet in retrospect we come to know the act as a splendid gift.

"Not only should we consider our capacity to perform an act of *hesed* but we should also be attentive when such an act is placed at our feet so that we don't trample upon it. Not only did Ruth break free from convention, Naomi had to accept Ruth in that new light. We may feel compelled to hold to the past when in fact our truth has been reshaped and now carries a different face in the present.

"We should consider the actor in the light of God even if they are determined to remain in the shadows. We must have the courage to step out of the shadows if that is where we suddenly find ourselves to be. An act of *hesed* has the power to alter both the giver and receiver.

"There are those who must effuse their care and their gratitude and there is a place for such openness. However, an act of *hesed* is much quieter. It is realized in the living, in the being, in making the uncommon common. Imitating the divine initiative, it comes without being deserved, just as our first breath of life."

Beth's words, phrases, complete thoughts, her inflection, her pauses – they all iterated in Nicole's mind. Nicole's heart stilled at the mention of a kiss. How many women throughout the ages read the words of Ruth to Naomi and took solace that such words could be spoken between two women? Daughter-in-law to mother-in-law – could anything less romantic be presented? And yet the narrative fell away; it was simply one woman professing her love for the other. It was more than love, as Beth said. It was a gift undeserved. It was the imitation of the divine initiative. Nicole also considered Beth's assertion that the return to silence was a grateful acquiescence. Was silence Beth's proffered solution?

The service ended. Nicole gave no indication of leaving. Jacob placed his hand on her knee. She raised her eyes to him.

"She is quite the theologian, is she not, Nicole?"

Nicole nodded.

"She has a heart. I felt it breaking as she spoke."

Attempting to gather her errant thoughts, Nicole looked away in contemplation.

Jacob gave her a little more time before asking, "Are you ready to go?"

"Yes."

Jacob rose. Nicole looked up to him. "Jacob please understand – there is no Naomi or Ruth in our story."

"Of course not. There is only Beth and Nicole. The question is what act of *hesed* have you placed before her that she fears she has trampled?" Jacob smiled. "Could it have been a kiss?"

Nicole knew that a kiss given in anger could never be an act of *hesed*. Her kiss was not an act of kindness or compassion. If there was grace in the kiss, if Beth accepted the kiss as a gift, she was not looking to Nicole as the giver. She was looking to her God. "No, Jacob. It wasn't a kiss."

"Too bad."

"Jacob, even the mention of a kiss between us could destroy her vocation."

"Nicole, you are starting to sound like Naomi – so certain of what is right for Ruth that you would drive her away when what she wants more than anything, even her own God, is to be with you."

Nicole stood up. "Jacob, we are not sitting outside The Fields debating ideas and beliefs for the sake of raising each other's blood pressure. You are toying with Beth's life."

Jacob spoke contritely. "That is not how I meant my words. I do not wish to harm her or you. You know I love you."

Nicole smiled for the first time since entering the church. "I know. Just leave it to Sophia to dole out the wisdom."

Jacob walked toward the main entrance where Beth stood greeting exiting congregants. Nicole walked a few paces behind him.

"Well young lady, I must say you did not disappoint my high expectations."

Beth was pleasantly surprised. "Jacob, this is unexpected."

"I wanted to hear what the Christians have to say about our scripture."

David approached. "Jacob, this is a rare treat."

"David. You have a wise young associate. I hope you plan to keep her."

"Wouldn't have it any other way."

Jacob smiled. "Did you notice the feminist interpretation she gave the scripture? It would make a Rabbi proud."

"That's a compliment I've never elicited from you."

"We must bring God's words to life, not allow them to gather dust undisturbed."

Nicole stepped forward. All three turned to her. David spoke first. "Nicki. This is quite a day!"

Nicole tried to diminish the import of her presence. "Jacob asked me to come along for moral support."

David's banter not-so-subtly conveyed the truth. "And here I thought Beth's magnetism in the pulpit brought you in."

Nicole turned her attention to the young priest. She had no words.

Beth extended her hand. "It's good to see you."

Nicole took Beth's hand with her own. Still, she had no words. She squeezed Beth's hand and offered a smile. Jacob and David observed the exchange with equal interest. There were congregants waiting in line. Nicole held Beth's eyes with her own for a moment longer than necessary before moving on.

David leaned over and whispered in Beth's ear. "So, have you two resolved your differences?"

Nicole's silence left Beth disenchanted. "I don't think we can."

"That's not the impression I've just gotten. Where's your faith?"

Beth sighed. "That's a good question."

-¦-   -¦-   -¦-

Jacob and Nicole walked back to the Elysian Fields. Jacob paused and looked up to the constant snowfall. "Nicole, have you ever noticed that poets speak of rainfall as God's tears, but never a snowfall? And yet the only difference is the cold. Why is that?"

Nicole followed the elder's lead and looked up. "Jacob, I've never seen a tear in the shape of a snowflake."

"True. But I'm talking about God's tears."

When they reached Jacob's office, Connor ran out of The Pub and across the street. He called Nicole's name. His voice and demeanor were unsettling.

"Connor, what is it?"

"It's Peter. He was jumped last night after closing. His mother just called from Memorial. He was beaten badly. He's unconscious."

Jacob posited the less troubling motive. "Robbery?"

Connor was resolute. "No, Jacob. You know damn well it had nothing to do with robbery!"

Jacob lowered his eyes. "It is shameful."

"Yes, it is," Nicole said, sharing Jacob's disappointment in the human race. She calmly referred to Peter's mother. "How's Stephanie?"

"The strong Irish in her is keeping her together. But I don't think she should be alone."

"I'll go now. I'll call you from the hospital." Nicole held Jacob in her regard. "Jacob, thank you for what you tried to do today."

His bearing was dispirited. "I'm sorry I couldn't do more."

"Jacob, remember what Beth said about making the uncommon common. For a moment I believed again that the impossible was possible. I will never be able to thank you enough for that gift." She leaned over and kissed him upon the cheek. "You are the best of men, Jacob Levi."

CHAPTER 36

Peter floated in and out of consciousness. He had suffered a broken wrist and fractured ribs. Contusions and cuts covered his body, but the internal damage he had sustained was not life threatening. The doctors were confident that physically Peter would make a complete recovery.

Nicole visited the hospital daily. She sat beside Ms. Kilpatrick – Stephanie – mostly in silence. The two women had a great deal of respect for the each other. Nicole knew it had been hard for the young divorcee to accept her son's affectional orientation, but the woman loved her only son and wanted him to be happy.

Peter began to stir. Stephanie and Nicole quickly got to their feet and went to his bedside. Stephanie took her son's hand gently into her own, while Nicole stood at Stephanie's shoulder.

Peter's eyes fluttered open. "Mom."

"Hi, honey. I'm here."

Peter took in his surroundings. "Nicki. Hi."

"Hi, Peter. How are you feeling?"

"They ... banged me up good ... huh?"

"You're going to be all right," said Stephanie.

"They called me ... a fag ... kicked me ... and took my wallet."

Nicole had been waiting for this information. "Who, Peter?"

Peter closed his eyes in an apparent effort to remember. "Ty ... Mike ... and Phillip."

Stephanie looked at Nicole. "Do you know them?"

"Yes. I wouldn't have expected it from them. It might have been a gang initiation."

"They beat my son so they can belong to a gang?" Stephanie's temper rose. "They won't get away with it!"

"They won't if Peter is willing to press charges." Nicole knew the streets. Her desire to protect the boy set a cautionary tone. "Stephanie, it could get nasty if he does."

Peter countered, "And if I don't they'll do it again." The two women remained silent. Peter focused on his mother. "Mom, you've told me to be proud of who I am."

Stephanie turned again to Nicole. "I don't know if I should thank you or despise you for giving him his dignity."

Nicole smiled. "I didn't do it by myself."

"So we're both to blame."

Nicole looked over to the boy. "Peter, I think your Mom is trying to tell you that she's never been prouder of you. I know I haven't."

CHAPTER 37

Nicole entered The Pub. Without missing a step she called out to Connor, "Get Miguel down here, now!" She continued to the back storage room, returning to The Pub with a baseball bat in each hand. Miguel rushed down from The Garden. The specter of Nicole told him all he needed to know. Nicole tossed one of the bats to Miguel who caught it effortlessly. Nicole shared what she knew. "It was Mike, Phillip and Ty. They're usually playing basketball at the church gym around this time."

Beth was enjoying a quiet evening reading when she was startled by a loud banging on her apartment door. She heard Blair called out her name. Dressed in jeans and a sweatshirt, Beth opened her door to the uncharacteristically agitated woman.

"Thank God, you're here."

"What's wrong?"

"I was just closing up my office ... I looked out the window. I saw Nicole with some of the men from The Fields. They had baseball bats and were walking toward the basketball court. I'm afraid they're going to hurt the boys."

Having personally experienced Nicole's capacity for violence, Beth took the threat seriously. She simply could not imagine the reason for it. "Why would they hurt the boys?"

"There's been some talk among the kids that Ty and a couple other boys in the congregation were involved with Peter Kilpatrick's beating."

Beth's frustration broke to the surface. "Why didn't you say something before?" she said sharply.

Blair nervously wrung her hands. "I never thought something like this would happen."

"Damn it, Blair!" Beth grabbed her coat and ran down the stairs. "Call the police."

Beth ran into the churchyard. Nicole, Miguel, Tony and Connor backed Mike and Ty against a wall. Beth went to Miguel, who was closest to her. "Miguel, I don't know. what's happening here, but you can't beat those boys."

Dispassionate, Miguel continued without acknowledging Beth.

Mike shouted, "Rev, stop her!"

Beth saw Nicole grip the bat with both her hands. Beth called out Nicole's name as she ran to her. Nicole held her place. At Nicole's side, Beth spoke so only Nicole could hear her. "Nicki, please. You don't want to do this."

Nicole confronted Beth. "Don't I? There is something called street justice. Tell me Beth, how many more boys like Peter have to be sacrificed? How much longer do we have to be despised by old ladies and young thugs?"

Beth gently placed her hand on Nicole's arm. "Nicki, I'm sorry. I know I'm no better than they are. I know I'm worse. I'm supposed to be a moral example and I've been afraid to stand up for what I believe because of how great a price I may have to pay. I swear to you I'll do better. No matter what you decide to do, I'll do better. But Nicki, as much as I'll defend your right to be who you are, I'll condemn you for your vengeance. The cycle of hate and violence has to stop. You have to be strong enough not to be seduced by it."

Nicole heard every word. One phrase echoed in her head: 'stand up for what I believe.' Nicole looked down to Beth. "You'll hate me if I hurt them."

Beth's response was genuine. "I can never hate you."

Nicole walked up to Mike and swung the bat high over his head. It slammed the wall with a loud crack. He fell down to a fetal position, raising his hands to his head trying to protect himself. Nicole was disgusted. "You coward." She walked over to Ty. They stood eye to eye. Nicole's rage carried forth with every word she spoke. "Tell me, what did Peter ever do to you that you would want to kill him?"

The boy clenched his jaws. He responded slowly, defiantly accentuating each word. "He's no man."

Nicole challenged him. "What makes a man?"

The boy remained silent.

Nicole called out without diverting her gaze. "Tony, call the police. We'll keep these 'men' here until they arrive."

Tony pulled out his cell phone and dialed 9-1-1.

Nicole whispered to the boy. "I'm going to make sure you get tried as an adult. You're going to find out about manhood in jail. When they rape you, and they will, tell yourself that what's being done to you doesn't have anything to do with being a man." She paused to let Ty take in her promise. She saw his cheek quiver. "And if you come to believe that where you stick it doesn't have anything to do with being a man, then you'll know how wrong you were about Peter."

Ty spat at her. "Bitch."

Nicole raised her bat-holding arm and wiped the spittle off her face with her sleeve. Ty stepped back to avoid a graze from the bat. Nicole looked at the boy with a hard expression. "You're going to pray that we had beaten you and let you go because what's going to be done to you is going to happen again and again for a long, long time."

"I'll do it to them before they do it to me," Ty boasted.

"Maybe." Nicole could not help but pity Ty. He would use sex as violence, as a means to stake out his safe zone among a population of equally violent men. For Peter, still a virgin, sex promised an avenue of expressing his passion and love for another. Her sorrow deepened, knowing that Peter's decency and right to a life unharmed was challenged by youths like Ty who indiscriminately acted out society's worst intolerances.

Nicole took a step back. The others held their place. In the stillness, time was frozen. The sound of the police sirens broke through the silence. Tony called out, "They're here!"

Samuel Franklin got out of the first of three squad cars and approached Nicole and Ty.

In the police officer's presence, Ty rediscovered his bravado. He raised his arm and pointed his finger at Nicole. "That bitch tried to kill us!"

Samuel shouted back. "Shut up!"

"Hey, you gonna listen to some dyke instead of a brother?"

Nicole found Ty's evocation of race disingenuous given Mike's fair skin. She turned and walked to meet the officer. "Sam, those two bastards beat Peter Kilpatrick to within an inch of his life."

Samuel eyed the two teenaged boys. "I heard about Peter. We'll take care of it."

Nicole saw Samuel place his hand on his nightstick. "Sam, don't give their public defender anything to leverage."

Samuel nodded in understanding. "Kid gloves, Nicki. We'll leave it to their cell mates to show them prison hospitality."

"Then we understand each other. I'll be at the Elysian Fields if you need me."

"Nicki, I need to know … are you sure Peter will press charges?"

"He'll do the right thing."

"All right." Samuel lowered his voice. "There's something else."

"What is it, Sam?"

"Nicki, I know everyone in this churchyard. I know what I have in common with you and the guys from The Fields. I don't like what this means. The neighborhood doesn't need a war between the gays and the gangs."

Nicole was incredulous. "You don't want Peter to press charges?"

"No, don't get me wrong. I do. I just want you to be careful. I guarantee you this isn't over."

"I can take care of myself."

"Nicki, we go back a long way, don't we?"

"Yes Sam, we do."

"You're not alone in this. Let me know if there's anything I can do for you."

"I will." Nicole was grateful. "Thanks, Sam."

"Goodnight, Nicki."

Nicole walked away from Samuel and everyone else in the courtyard. She passed Samuel's brethren. It was good that the Chicago Police Department had a representative cadre of gay and lesbian officers. It gave her some hope that justice could be had.

Beth visually followed Nicole as she quit the scene. She wanted to go to her, but chose not to. She doubted Nicole would welcome her. In fact, she did not feel she deserved to be welcomed. She felt the untenable price her choices had caused her to pay.

CHAPTER 38

Beth stood outside of the Elysian Fields. She watched as a workman painted over an exterior wall vandalized with gang-related graffiti – a consequence of the arrest of Peter's assailants. In the two intervening weeks since the incident in the courtyard Beth debated who was in the best possible position to approach the other, she or Nicole. Given New Year's Eve, she realized that the burden was hers, and no matter what happened it would always be hers. She took a deep breath to settle her apprehension. She needed to steel herself for a rejection. She did not know how she would endure Nicole's rebuff were that the cup presented.

Working the bar, Connor noticed the young priest immediately. He caught her eye, greeting her with a smile, and motioned her upstairs. Beth was grateful for the familiar hospitality. Reaching the second floor landing she paused, her courage waning.

Miguel, holding a tray of food, approached her. "Reverend. What brings you here?"

Beth wanted to run away. It was not like Miguel to be so formal.

Miguel's heart went out to the young woman. It seemed to him that no matter how hard she tried she could not or would not allow herself a modicum of happiness. Beth's silence was a vestige of a moral breach that had no foothold in his life. "Beth, could you do me a favor and take this up to Nicki. Tell her to eat before the soup gets cold."

Beth glanced at the tray. She took hold of it as Miguel placed it in her reach. She looked up to Miguel with an immeasurable feeling of gratitude washing over her. "Thank you."

Miguel nodded. Beth walked down the corridor to the back stairs. Miguel called out her name as she reached the first step. The young woman turned to him. He said, "It's good to have you back."

Beth smiled. She suddenly understood what she had missed about the Elysian Fields – she felt that she belonged in this space.

Beth entered the loft through the opened door. Across the extent, Nicole sat at her desk. She sensed a presence and looked up from her work. Somehow, having Beth before her was not a complete surprise. Wordlessly, Beth walked toward Nicole.

"Hello," said Nicole.

Beth sighed. "Hi."

Nicole nodded at the tray.

"Miguel sent this up. You're not to let the soup get cold."

"I'll pretend it's gazpacho. You can put it over there." Nicole pointed to the kitchen island.

Beth did as requested and returned her attention to Nicole.

"Thank you," Nicole said tenderly.

A shy smile formed upon the nervous young woman.

Nicole pushed her chair back. "How are you?"

"Good." Beth answered too quickly, nodding as if trying to convince herself.

Nicole motioned to one of the two chairs across from her desk. Beth accepted the silent invitation and sat down. Nicole waited, playing with a pen in her hands.

Beth looked down. "Not good." She raised her eyes slowly. "I've missed you."

Nicole hesitated, and then leaned forward. "I've missed you, too."

"I'm sorry I let you down."

"I can be unforgiving. Even against my better judgment."

"I wish we could start over."

"I don't. I don't want to forget waking up to you beside me at the hospital or our day in Wisconsin or how I felt listening to your homily."

Beth did not hide her remorse. "Those are not our only memories."

"As much as I regret some of the things I've said and done … they are a part of me. If we are going to …" Nicole paused, taking care in choosing her words. "If we are going to be friends you have to know the darker side of me. The tumor didn't create my anger. It only prevented me from exercising my usual control."

"I wish you would forget some of the things I've said and done."

"You're young."

Beth's eyes flashed a challenge.

Nicole smiled and raised her hands up in defense. "Hey, I'm not that far ahead of you and I'm the first to admit that you've been a good influence on me."

Beth was not so sure. "Have I?"

"I swung the bat high, didn't I?"

"Would you have hit him?"

"I don't know. Something inside me snapped when I saw Peter in the hospital." Nicole relaxed back into her chair. "I hope you know that it meant a great deal to Peter when you visited him."

Beth felt a deep satisfaction. "He mentioned me? I'm glad."

"It wasn't just about what you represent. It was about who you are. If he wasn't gay, I'd swear he has a crush on you."

The two exchanged modest glances.

Nicole swept her hand across her desk. "Beth, I'm under a deadline with my client."

Beth reacted abruptly, standing up. "I understand. I'll go."

"Sweetheart, don't ..."

Beth cocked her head.

Nicole's unintended use of the endearment caused her to blush. "I didn't mean ..." With limited success Nicole set aside her discomfort and offered an explanation. "The report is due on their desk first thing Monday. If I stick to my work plan I'll have it done by Saturday night. If I hit a snag I still have Sunday." Beth crossed her arms. She wore an amused grin. Feeling very much the idiot Nicole stopped herself and tried to regroup. "What I'm trying to say is ... Beth would you like to get together on Monday?"

"What do you have in mind?"

"Don't know, but I'll think of something."

"I do like the idea."

"Why don't you come over at nine? I'll be waiting."

"Okay."

The two fell into an intimate, comfortable silence.

Nicole regretted what she was about to do. "I hate to send you away but ..."

"I'll let you get back to work."

"I'm glad you came."

"Me too." Beth turned and with a restored serenity headed for the front door.

CHAPTER 39

It was Saturday night and Nicole worked on the Executive Summary of her report. She never understood why she was called in on a consulting assignment like this one. They knew the problems. They knew what they needed to do to address them. They just did not listen to one another. No one had the courage to break through the corporate culture, or maybe they had tried and exhausted themselves in the effort. Top management was 'clueless' of their organization's reality. She heard this time and time again. It did not matter if she was scoping a pristine financial institution or a soot-worn manufacturer; she got paid an obscene amount of money to tell the CEOs that the senior managers were the greatest obstacles to survival, or to shifting from mediocre to best of class.

Early in her career, Nicole helped turn around a couple of struggling firms, not by playing nice, but by fearlessly challenging the status quo as more experienced consultants blanched. She judged her ability to directly face conflict as her mother's legacy. Nothing she addressed in the workplace came close to managing her mother's worst moments.

She enjoyed the luxury of being able to work as a consultant only as much as she wanted, and that meant six months out of the year. Although those six months were often comprised of twelve-hour days, a good third to half of them were spent away from home.

Home kept her grounded. She shared her life with families that lived on one sixth or less of her income. Nobody in the neighborhood knew how 'successful' she was in her other life and she liked it that way. She gave generously under the guise of the Elysian Fields – giving back to the neighborhood. The intangible debt she owed was great. For too many years the neighborhood had kept a watchful eye on her mother, had contacted Nicole to gather her mother up and take her home, and had cared for her mother when Nicole could not be found. During Nicole's rebellious years they granted her leniency, but not so much so that Nicole cut across all lines and boundaries without consequence. When all was said and done, they forgave her and welcomed her with open arms back into their embrace.

Nicole stood at the window, looking down at the streets. She raised her gaze up to the moon, the symbol of the mysteries. Its juxtaposition to the concrete and asphalt of the city always seemed askew to her, the elemental trying to get humanity to look up and recognize her. She thought that too much of western humanity's vision was directed down and forward. She strove to create a life that allowed time to pause and simply search the heavens.

Nicole remembered how, as a child of seven, she would come with a sincere belief in God to St. Ann's and kneel before the altar, looking up at the crucified Christ. Now as an adult she knew that children were sponges, taking in the world openly, with an innocent trust, if life had not already beaten their innocence out of them.

She could not believe in Beth's God. After struggling for years, wondering why she could not make the leap of faith, she realized that she was allowing others, outsiders, to define her. She realized she had to trust and honor her beliefs, to accept that they were indeed good enough. They were more than good enough. They were her truth, and required no justification.

There was no severing her self-image as a child with that of Beth kneeling before the altar. Being with Beth, Nicole found that she mourned who she could have been if she had not watched God die in her mother. When God had died in her mother, God had died in her as well.

Standing at the window high over the street, and yet so far below the moon and stars, Nicole remembered that the little girl too soon had to learn to play interference with her unstable mother. That little girl was so small, which meant two things to Nicole: she was vulnerable, and she was insignificant. She never again wanted to feel so exposed, so fearful, so inconsolably alone. She would never be small again. And so she lived her life in an upright posture, taking the force of the harshest winds unyieldingly.

Nicole recalled seeing Beth weeping before the altar. She looked up to the moon and the stars and knew how wrong she had been, that in proportion to the cosmos she was and would always be small – so very small – as small as Beth before her God.

CHAPTER 40

Nicole decided upon a day at the Art Institute. Beth was pleased with the choice. They explored the galleries, at times silently, at other times commenting on what they saw. Playful debates came to the forefront, accentuating their aesthetic differences. Nicole's eye for high contrast, dark paletted realism was countered by Beth's preferences for the more romantic, pastel paletted, Impressionistic canvases.

Nicole hoped for an opportune moment to broach the subject of New Year's Eve. She soon realized that there would never be such a moment. They were walking through the expansive Egyptian exhibit when Nicole chose to speak. "Beth, I was thinking about Ruth and Naomi."

Beth felt an immediate apprehension. Fearful of Nicole's next words, her response was a low, cautious, "Yes?"

"About Naomi's silence," Nicole said tentatively. "About the silence between them marking the close of a chapter in their lives." Nicole's resolve faltered. They continued walking in silence for a few steps before Nicole made a statement posed more as a question. "You believe that they understood each other well enough to go on without having to revisit their past?"

Beth understood that Nicole was not speaking of the Bible story. "I think it's best that way."

"To agree to disagree?"

Beth, in her own way, made a request. "Nicki, sometimes you must trust actions – they can speak louder than words."

"And sometimes actions tell you things that a person can't, for whatever reason, put into words."

Beth paused and waited for Nicole to meet her gaze. "You understand then?"

Nicole's response was honest and gentle. "I don't understand, really. But right now I don't feel I have to."

Nicole explored Beth's eyes for a heartbeat. She was uncertain of what lay behind them. Nicole realized that there were aspects of Beth still beyond her reach. Nicole took the next step continuing their journey. Beth joined her without comment.

Nicole was not satisfied. Keeping her eyes forward she closed the moment with one final and, for her, necessary statement. "Beth, someday I hope you will help me understand."

Beth looked over to Nicole's profile. She accepted the implicit. Someday Nicole would ask more from her. This was not the day. Beth prayed that when the day came, she would not disappoint Nicole a second time.

CHAPTER 41

Beth answered her office phone. "Reverend Kelly."

"Hi."

It took a moment for Beth to recognize Nicole's voice. "Hi. I didn't expect to hear from you for another hour."

Nicole had been in Washington D.C. on an assignment for two weeks. "My flight has been delayed."

"When will you get in? Can we still do a late dinner?"

"That would be nice, but I'm not scheduled to return until 9:30. How about a rain check?"

Beth looked over to Little Fella sitting beside her computer, sharing the sadness stitched on the teddy bear's face.

"Beth?"

"I'm here."

"How about tomorrow?"

Beth brightened. "Breakfast?"

Nicole laughed. "Can we make it lunch. I'd like to get some sleep."

"Meet you at The Garden at noon."

"Sure."

Beth reluctantly said, "I guess I should let you go."

"Oh yeah. Let me go so I can get back to the excitement of working in an airport," Nicole quipped.

Beth sympathized. "Are you miserable?"

"I'll be home soon."

"Nicki?"

"Yes?"

"I ..."

Nicole took a risk. "I've missed you too."

Beth smiled. "Tomorrow, lunch."

"Tomorrow, lunch." Silence fell between them. Nicole needed to find her way beyond her sweet sorrow. She whispered, carrying in tone what could not be said in word. "Sleep well."

"Be safe." Beth held on to the telephone, not wanting to end their connection. Resigned and torn, she placed the receiver down.

When the quiet night was disrupted by the sound of sirens, Beth awoke. She lay in bed listening, her eyes fixed upon the stream of moonlight crossing through her apartment window and touching the bare floor. The emergency was nearby. More sirens approached. They alternated between police and fire rescue. She realized that a chaplain's services might be needed. She dressed and quickly exited the church.

Beth was jolted. The night sky seemed to be ablaze. She knew by the flames' proximity that the Elysian Fields was on fire. She took a step forward and then another and then she broke into a run. The building was engulfed on all sides. She stopped at a police barricade.

One of the two officers looked over to her. He was tall, in his mid-forties. He spoke in an authoritative yet good-natured voice. "You can't come any closer. It's hell in there."

Beth identified herself. "I'm a priest at St. Ann's. Is there anything I can do?"

"Not right now, Reverend."

Seeking Nicole, Beth searched the faces of all the bystanders who had come out of their homes to watch. With each disappointment she felt a rising panic. Seeing no one else in the vicinity she addressed the officer. "Excuse me. The owner ... her name is Nicole Thera. She lives on the third floor. Do you know where she is?"

The officer spoke sadly. "I know Nicki. There's been no sign of her. Reverend, I hate to say it but ..." The officer turned to the fire. "Look at it. If she's not out now ... I can't see her living through that."

Beth's eyes were fixed upon the ever-rising flames. She had one remaining hope. "Nicki was flying back from Washington D.C. I know her flight was delayed. If her Jeep isn't in the back ..."

"Hold on." The officer went to his radio.

Beth waited as he made an inquiry. Both heard the answer from an officer on the other side of the building. "Affirmative. The Jeep is parked in the back lot."

The irony did not escape the officer. "Her flight wasn't late enough. I guess it's a good thing Nicki didn't have family."

Beth protested. "Nicki wasn't alone. She has friends."

"I know. It's going to be hard for them when they find out that this wasn't an accident."

"I don't understand."

"A witness reported that he saw a couple of guys throwing firebombs."

The two fell silent and continued to watch the flames. The officer turned to Beth. He did not know what else he could say. Beth looked at him and then walked away to the sidewalk curb where she sat down and watched as the walls of the Elysian Fields began to collapse onto themselves. She could not think. She could not feel.

CHAPTER 42

Beth sat against the pew, her legs pulled up to her chest. She hugged herself as if she were a child. The numbness of the shock left her as she shed silent tears. Though she sought the sanctuary, she found no solace within its walls. Nicole's death was one more loss in a life of short-lived happiness. The seemingly aimless death of the extraordinary woman, and the act of violence that took Nicole's life, left Beth's faith broken. Beth could not begin to locate the will of God, no matter how she labored in her search. Her appeal to God was met with a haunting interior silence. Beth had slowly grown deaf to God's voice, hearing only on occasion God's timbre. The now all-consuming silence irrefutably impressed God's divorce.

A figure entered the sanctuary and walked forward through the shadows. Garment bag hanging from one shoulder, laptop computer case on the other, she walked slowly down the nave, contrary to her habit of always taking a less conspicuous route. Each step evinced her hope, driven by a need. She turned to her left. Beth seemed so very small, as vulnerable, if not more so than she did the evening Nicole clandestinely observed her tears. Nicole bent down and placed her bags upon the marble floor. Beth raised her eyes. Nicole stood up tall, uncertain.

Beth took in the apparition. She would have sworn she was being tormented, but for the array of Nicole's things resting at her feet. Could it be true that she had not been home during the fire?

Beth whispered Nicole's name, fearful that her grief was playing the cruelest trick upon her mind.

Nicole answered the unspoken question. "I missed my connection in Detroit."

"You weren't home?" Beth needed to confirm the obvious. "Your Jeep was parked in the back."

"I took a cab to the airport." Nicole studied Beth. "I got back an hour ago. I needed to talk to the Fire Marshall and Police. I was told you were seen at the fire."

"I thought I lost you." Beth's words came as a hushed statement, one she needed to understand, their import having been driven deep within the silence of her, the place where loss is most felt.

"No." Nicole took the necessary steps to reach Beth. Beth in turn opened her arms in invitation. That only strengthened Nicole's resolve. She took Beth into her arms. Beth released a sob.

"Oh God! Nicki." The young woman trembled.

Nicole rested her head upon Beth's shoulder seeking her own comfort.

Beth felt the weight of Nicole upon her. Nicole's physical presence calmed her. Her thoughts turned to Nicole's well-being. "You must be tired."

Nicole nodded. She had no desire to speak.

Beth urged, "Come up to my apartment. You can rest."

Nicole's voice was dispassionate. "That might not be a good idea."

Beth pulled Nicole to arm's length in order to better gauge her. Nothing she saw changed her mind. "Don't argue with me on this. Please."

Nicole did not have the strength to fight. "All right."

"Come on." Beth waited for Nicole to stand. She followed, taking Nicole's hand. She picked up Nicole's computer case. Nicole reached for her garment bag. They walked wordlessly to Beth's apartment.

Beth led Nicole into her studio. Upon entering, Nicole paused, hesitating. Enough damage had been done in one day. She did not want Beth to get hurt. Still holding Nicole's hand, Beth squeezed it demanding her attention. "The bathroom is that way, if you want to freshen up."

Relieved to secure a moment of privacy, Nicole nodded and entered the bathroom. Beth placed Nicole's laptop beside her desk. She had never seen Nicole like this, not even in the hospital. There was a quietness to her. She seemed to take up very little space. The impressive, imposing Nicole had disappeared.

Beth walked to the front door and carefully closed and latched it. She quickly stripped out of her clothes and put on a pair of sweat pants and a sleeveless T-shirt. As Beth began to recapture her own sensibilities, she realized Nicole could very well be in shock. Concerned, she walked to the bathroom door and listened. She heard the splash of water. Somewhat relieved, she stepped back. She felt helpless in this divided space. She felt a growing need to hold Nicole, care for Nicole.

Within the bathroom Nicole hung her garment bag on the shower bar. She opened an outside compartment and removed her toiletry case. From another compartment she removed the sweat pants and pullover she slept in. She could not shake the sense that the world was moving in slow motion. Her senses seemed muted, dulled. She changed and placed her folded street clothes on top of the toilet seat. She stared in the mirror. Her hair was still short. She knew it would take over a year for it to regain its pre-operative length. There had been so many changes. She had tried her best to cope. Never did she imagine someone would fire bomb the Elysian Fields.

Practically speaking, she knew she was in good shape. She and her insurance agent had gone through an annual New Year policy update. She had also updated her business interruption plan. Copies of all her electronic files were backed up and in the Elysian Fields safe. If they did not survive, a second set of Zip-drive tapes was housed with her accountant. Financially, she would survive the loss intact. Ironically, she might even be in a stronger position. Her employees would not be so lucky. The Musketeers would be devastated. Peter would not have a job to return to once he got well.

The thoughts continued to swirl in her mind. They were too much for her. She was tired. She wanted the world to stop. Tears broke through the void. She felt disengaged from the mirror image. This was not the homecoming she had looked forward to. She heard Beth lock the apartment door. She could not stay in this room indefinitely. She ran water into the sink. She bent down, her hands clutching the sides of the sink. Were she alone, she would have allowed herself to collapse to the floor. She looked to the door. She would soon need to cross that threshold. Life would go on. Her hands cut into the water and raised the cool wetness to her face. It did not penetrate the numbness that had taken possession of her body.

Beth waited, sitting on the side of her bed. She heard the door open. Nicole stepped out, her garment bag in hand. She looked about, disorientated. Beth stood up and pointed to her closet door. "You can hang your bag on the hook."

Nicole's eyes followed Beth's hand to it. She mechanically completed the task, and then turned to Beth. She was feeling very lost in Beth's space.

Beth waited for some kind of sign from Nicole that would clue her as to what the proud, self-reliant woman would allow to be done for her. It struck Beth how vulnerable Nicole seemed. Beth decided to take a chance. She walked up to Nicole and gently took her hand.

Nicole looked down at all that was beauty and tenderness. Beth smiled reassuringly and guided her across the room. Nicole slid under the bedcovers Beth had raised up for her. The softness of the comforter enfolded her body. Beth walked to the door and turned off the overhead light. She then walked to her side of the bed and carefully got in, taking as little space as possible. Still sitting up, she turned to Nicole. "Is there anything I can do?"

Nicole looked over to Beth. She did not want Beth physically close and yet beyond her touch. She chose not to suppress her need. "Sleep close to me."

Beth nodded. There were so few words between them on this night. Beth turned toward her bedside table and switched off the last remaining light. She slid down into the bed and moved her body to Nicole's side, resting her head on Nicole's shoulder and wrapping her arm across Nicole's waist. Nicole felt stiff. Beth waited. Nicole took in a deep breath and exhaled. Beth felt Nicole relax. It was only then that she knew she had done the right thing in bringing Nicole into her bed.

It was morning when Beth heard a light knocking at her door. She opened her eyes. Her room was awash with sunlight. Nicole slept soundly. Beth carefully removed herself from Nicole's embrace.

She found David waiting on the other side of the door. "Good morning. I was wondering if you planned to work today."

Beth tried to clear the haze from her mind. "What time is it?"

"Ten."

"Oh, I'm sorry." Beth turned to look back at the reason for her absence. "We had a long night."

David peered in. "I know about the fire. I didn't realize Nicole was here."

"She got in late from Washington, D.C."

"Tell her she can stay in one of our guest rooms until she can make other arrangements."

"I will."

David was somewhat distant. "You know Beth, you have the authority to grant use of our guest rooms."

Beth recalled Nicole's state. "I didn't want her to be alone."

"I see. How is she?"

"I'm not sure."

"Well, she's your ministry for the day."

Beth bristled. "David, Nicki is not part of my ministry."

"She's not?"

Beth was adamant. "No, she's not. I'll touch base with you later today if that's all right?"

"Of course." David stepped back as Beth closed the door. She rested her head against the smooth hardwood. She was claiming her life as her own, just as she was becoming more and more uncertain of what her life was meant to be. She felt her fatigue and longed only for one thing, to return to Nicole's embrace.

Nicole stirred as Beth reentered the bed. "Who was that?"

"David. I'm taking the day off. Go back to sleep."

"I promised you lunch at The Gardens." Awareness cut through Nicole's consciousness. The memory of smoldering timbers flashed into her mind's eye. With it came a remembrance of her loss. She turned onto her side, her back to Beth.

Beth realized what Nicole had said and waited to see the effect. It came silently in the motion of a withdrawn body. Beth honored Nicole's movement by effortlessly releasing Nicole from her embrace and accepting Nicole's back not as a sign of rejection, but as a sign that the numbing shock was beginning to wear off. Beth wanted to reassure Nicole, but words did not belong between them, not yet. Nicole's withdrawal posed the question of how welcome a renewal of their physical connection would be. Beth held to Nicole's request, 'Sleep close to me.' Those words gave her the courage to rest side by side with Nicole. She slowly placed her arm over her companion.

Nicole closed her eyes. The effort could not hold back the images of the previous night. She compressed herself in body and soul. She felt as if she had been whiplashed back to her past where a fragile, worn thread held her together. She felt Beth fit her body to hers. The postures of their bodies made Nicole feel all the more vulnerable. She remembered lying in her hospital bed wondering how it would feel to be held. She found herself once again feeling battered, but this time Beth was not just holding her hand or placing a hand on her brow. Beth was holding her completely and all Nicole had to do was to surrender to it. Nicole held Beth's arm tight to her body. Though she had lost so much in the previous twelve hours, she had this one consolation. There might never again be a reason for Beth to be with her like this. This fleeting moment might be the consummation of their friendship, the ultimate physical intimacy they would ever be able to share.

Nicole hoped that in the days to come her tenets would serve her well. She hoped her rage would stay dormant in the maelstrom of hatred. She knew all too well the power of her rage; the capacity for it to consume all that was good in her. She pressed Beth all the closer to her. Nicole knew that with Beth beside her she would continue to swing the baseball bat high of the target to make a point but not to injure. She also knew that the community would be looking to her to see if, when, and how she swung the baseball bat against those who would do her and other lesbians and gay men harm.

Nicole continued to navigate her converging thoughts. Though the sun was shining through Beth's thin gauze curtains, Nicole felt darkness at the perimeter threatening to expand its domain. She felt Beth's embrace as a tangible counterpoint to the intangible thoughts and emotions. She knew she would need to balance the effect of the two once she consented to face the day. She was not ready to do so. Slowly she fell into a fitful sleep full of scattered, conflicting images of who she was and who she wanted to be in the world she had inherited.

It was impossible for Beth to know Nicole's thoughts. All she had were Nicole's physical cues. Twice Nicole pulled Beth closer to her. Twice Beth welcomed the gesture she took as a sign of her belonging.

Nicole awoke. She looked over to the table clock. The day was more than half over. Beth rested comfortably against her. Nicole could not remember the last time she slept in another woman's arms. Her routine was always to go to their place so she could leave at her leisure. It was far less complicated than trying to choreograph the other's exit from the loft. Going to the woman's place kept the loft hers. She did not share her home. Now, she ruefully thought, she did not have a home to share.

Nicole carefully released herself from Beth's embrace. She entered the bathroom. From there she made a few telephone calls from her cell phone. She then showered, allowing the waters to comfort her. Dressed in the same jeans and sweater she had worn the day before, she spied her shoes and took them in hand as she entered the studio and walked to Beth's desk chair. Compared to the apartments of women Nicole had known, Beth's was neither the smallest nor simplest. It was, however, one of the most anonymous. The space did not feel right to Nicole. No pictures of family, no incidentals that reflected Beth's interest outside of the books that lined her shelves. Sedate and formal, Nicole would be sad to live like Beth. She put on her shoes and coat and took her computer case in hand. She was going to leave a note but decided better of it. She sat on Beth's side of the bed.

Nicole's weight made Beth stir. Beth turned on her back. Her eyes focused on her guest. "Morning."

"Good afternoon," Nicole corrected. "I need to go to a meeting at Kate's office."

It took a moment for Beth to remember why Nicole was with her, as pleasant and natural as the reality of it was to her, and why Nicole would need to meet with her attorney. "How are you?"

"Better. It's past one and I have a lot I need to get done."

Beth sat up. "Will I see you later?"

"Can I call you? I'm good at what I do, but even I can't rebuild my life in a day."

Beth reached out and rested her hand on Nicole's arm. "David said you can stay in one of the church's guest rooms until you resettle."

"That would be good."

"I'll move your things next door. You can get the keys on your way out. Stop at the office."

Nicole was grateful for the hospitality. "Thank you."

"Thank David."

"No Beth, I'm thanking you … for everything." Nicole leaned over and kissed Beth on the cheek. "Got to go."

CHAPTER 43

Nicole looked up to the church tower clock. It was near midnight. She had had an arduous day. Still, the consensus was that she would be able to rebuild the Elysian Fields. The Fire Marshall and Police had opened a criminal investigation into the fire. They had evidence of multiple firebombs. If the Elysian Fields had been open, the death toll could have been horrific. Nicole assumed that if she had swung the baseball bat low, the attack would have happened during business hours. Instead, she was to be the only fatality.

Nicole walked up the interior stairs toward her room. Upon reaching Beth's apartment she paused. She was tempted to knock, but could not justify stealing a second night's sleep from Beth. She walked to the next room, keys in hand.

Beth had been listening for any sound that hinted of Nicole's return. She opened her door and stepped out into the corridor, relieved to confirm Nicole's arrival. "Hi."

Nicole was pleased to see Beth. "You're up late."

"I was about to say the same thing to you. How was your day?"

"Productive."

"And that's good?" Beth offered an affirming smile.

Nicole's strength resurfaced. "Yes, I don't do helpless very well."

"I know."

"Yes, you do, don't you?" Nicole harbored no regrets in having given Beth unprecedented access to her fragility.

"I can make some tea."

"An invitation?"

"Unless you're too tired."

"I'm wide awake."

"Come on then," said Beth happily.

Nicole put her keys into her pocket and walked back to Beth's apartment. Beth went to light the ancient gas stove. She glanced back to Nicole. "Make yourself comfortable."

Nicole sat down in Beth's desk chair. She had started her day in this room. It seemed so long ago.

With the water set to boil, Beth returned to Nicole. Beth observed how Nicole rested her hands on her lap as she waited patiently. Nicole had always demonstrated an admirable courtesy to those she interacted with. Her courtesy translated to a physical reserve when away from The Fields. Beth recalled how, during their museum visits, Nicole always held her hands behind her back or in her pockets, clearly acknowledging that she was a guest who was determined to trespass without disturbance, doing her utmost to be worthy of an invitation to return. "I don't know what I'm going to do with you."

Nicole was at a loss. "What do you mean?"

Beth stood before the woman whose entrancing blue eyes flashed a momentarily distress. "You could take off your coat."

Relieved, Nicole beamed. Hers was an uncensored confession. "I love your smile."

Beth held her gaze upon Nicole. She had thought of no one else throughout the day. She took Nicole's coat lapels with her hands, her intent to help Nicole remove the garment. Nicole in turn raised her head. Beth paused for a heartbeat; she was so close to Nicole, she breathed in Nicole's breath. Gently, Beth brushed her lips against Nicole's.

The kiss had been long wanted. Nicole closed her eyes and allowed the gentleness to master her. Beth raised herself up and took Nicole in her gaze once again. There were no words for her. She smiled and was rewarded with Nicole's own bright response. Nicole raised her hand to Beth's and released its hold upon her. She then reached up and cupped Beth's cheek. The softness of it surprised her. Her hand traveled to the back of Beth's neck. Nicole gently coaxed Beth back down to her. Their kiss was not as gentle. Nicole's hunger and passion rose. Beth responded in kind. Nicole felt a surge of desire in her body. She stood up.

Beth felt Nicole move to an upright position. She stepped back, stumbling. Nicole caught her by the waist, holding her close. Beth felt out of control. With it came fear. She placed her hand on Nicole's chest, pressing the woman away from her. "Nicki, please."

Nicole felt the pressure and pulled back. She was confused. "What is it?"

"I didn't mean to … please. I'm sorry."

Nicole's confusion heightened. She searched Beth's eyes. The young woman's fear was apparent.

Beth tried to regroup. "I don't know what I was thinking."

Nicole approved. "You weren't thinking. For a moment Beth, you weren't thinking."

"I can't, Nicki."

"You mean you won't."

"Nicki, please try to understand."

For Nicole there was only one question at issue. "Do you love me?"

Beth attempted to disavow her actions. "I care for you."

Nicole was no longer willing to give Beth room to vacillate. "That isn't what I asked you."

Beth searched Nicole's eyes, seeking mercy. "It would be wrong for me."

"To love me?"

Beth pressed her hands on Nicole's arms, demanding release. "Don't do this."

Nicole dropped her hands from Beth's waist and stepped away. Once again she reminded herself of the space in which she stood. She stood in Beth's space. She did not belong. The reasons were many. And yet, less than twenty-four hours before they had shared the same bed, sleeping in each other's arms. Had that been a cruel trick of her imagination? And the kiss – had she just imagined the kiss?

Nicole looked about her again. It was a hopelessly barren space, allowing no life. She needed to get away from it and the woman who pretended she could live in it. Nicole returned her gaze to Beth. Only one thing was left unsaid. "You'll never convince me that my loving you is wrong."

Nicole turned and walked toward the apartment door. She felt her rage break through. In her present state she did not trust herself. She clamped down on her tears as she left the studio. She went to the church guest room, retrieved her garment bag and exited the building. The loaned keys hung visibly in the door lock.

Beth stepped back as Nicole exited her apartment. The door was left ajar. She stared at the door and the breach of space that separated her from Nicole. She heard Nicole's movements: to the adjacent room, keys in the lock, door opened, steps within, a quick turnaround, a pause, the door closed, keys turned and then movement back toward her. Nicole's shadow swept across the open space and continued onward and away. The owner of the shadow did not come back to Beth. There was not even a momentary pause to reconsider. The sounds continued. Footsteps going down the stairs one after the other, each step more distant, less extant, until there was nothing more to hear.

For a moment Beth felt she was going mad. She wanted to go mad. How else could she continue? She felt hollow, as though her shell, made of layers of white granular chalk, was slowly disintegrating, falling to the floor. There was nothing within Beth to brace her, nothing without to stay her from the forces of life, to prevent her gradual ruin.

CHAPTER 44

Working at her computer, Beth felt a presence. She turned and scanned her office. Her stomach clenched with anxiety as she saw Miguel standing at the door. She got to her feet to welcome him. "Miguel. It's good to see you."

Miguel stood rigid. "I need to know what happened between you and Nicki," he said, clearly having no patience for insincere politeness.

Beth was taken aback by Miguel's confrontational tone. "What has Nicki told you?"

"Me? Nothing! She told Kate to forget about the Elysian Fields. She's selling the lot. Maybe the neighborhood will get a Starbucks or a new Walgreens."

"What does Nicki's decision have to do with me?"

"Two days ago we stayed late at Kate's working on a plan for a new Elysian Fields. By the time we broke up for the night we were all tired. Nobody was more tired than Nicki. She told us not to worry. Nothing was going to stop her from rebuilding. Yesterday everything changed. I think you're the only one who saw her."

"Miguel, you're making assumptions."

Miguel erupted. "Did you see Nicki?"

Although churning inside, Beth remained steady on the surface. "Yes."

"Tell me what you said to her!" Miguel demanded.

"You make it sound as if ..."

"She's gone, Beth. She's gone and she's not coming back!"

Miguel's news shattered Beth's composure. "What do you mean gone?"

"Exactly that. Kate is bound by her code of ethics to respect Nicki's privacy, but I'm not. I called her consortium's office. She took a long-term assignment in Philadelphia."

Beth looked down in thought, working the information in her mind. She raised her gaze hopefully. "That doesn't mean she's not coming back. She may want to earn extra money to help pay for expenses."

"That's not it! Money didn't drive her out of Chicago. The insurance coverage is more than enough and there are always plenty of assignments in the city to keep her going for months. She left the city to get away from ..." Miguel left the reason unspoken. "Haven't you figured that out yet? For Christ's sake, why do you think she took the New York job?"

"Because of New Year's Eve."

"Yes!"

Beth backtracked. "She said that?"

Miguel lost all patience. "Damn it! You just don't get it. Nicki doesn't say anything. You know her by what she does."

"Nicki does say things," Beth countered.

Miguel paused. He was contemptuous. "You're right. And when she does she means them. She means to let the Elysian Fields lie in an ash heap. And I don't like it!"

Beth spoke by rote. "Miguel, I believe there is a reason for everything."

"Then tell me why have I just lost one of the closest friends I've ever had in the world?" Miguel's anger turned to despair. His tears overtook him. Beth walked up to him and attempted to take him into her arms.

"Stay away from me!" He wrenched himself free from her. "God damn you to hell. I'm ashamed I thought you were too good for Nicki. Nicki deserves better than you."

There was nothing Beth could do, so she did nothing but stand and watch Miguel leave her in the hell he wished upon her.

CHAPTER 45

It had been a month to the day since the fire. Nicole had settled into her extended stay hotel room with relative ease. She worked. She allowed herself quiet time to think, to do nothing. She took advantage of free evenings and weekends to explore the city She kept in touch with Jacob and Tess. She arranged to travel by train to New York and spent a weekend with Carrie and her family. She spoke with Kate regularly to address the insurance settlement. A broker had been enlisted to market the property. There were a couple of interested parties. Nicole wanted to see an urban development that would contribute to the vitality of the neighborhood.

Her decision to sell the Elysian Fields lot was to be her final legacy. The breaking away from Chicago had been extraordinarily easy and that was unexpected. She had always felt that the neighborhood's hold would be enduring. The destruction of the Elysian Fields represented a severance from her past. As much as the Elysian Fields brought her comfort, it had also restrained her. She had tried to fulfill her debt, a debt the Elysian Fields represented. The neighborhood gave. It also took away. The account was now in balance.

Beth's rejection, for all the pain it caused her, did gift her with the reassurance that her capacity to love remained. It also confirmed that she would never ransom herself away. Beth could not love her. Nicole had convinced herself otherwise. She was wrong. The heart self-deceived was cruel unto itself.

Six months. She told herself she would give herself six months. Only then would she trust herself to reconnect. Kate had expressed her concern and asked at every opportunity if Nicole had contacted others in Chicago. Kate offered to share information about mutual friends and acquaintances, requested or not. Nicole consistently declined "going there." Kate's reprieve had its limits. Nicole knew the day would come when Kate would change tactics. Right now the dance between them carried a hint of grace.

CHAPTER 46

Beth waited in the lobby of the law offices of McDermott and Stanley. Located in the heart of downtown Chicago, the well-respected firm was known to hold an elite client list. It was also held in high regard for its pro bono work, championing individuals and causes that reflected its commitment to civil liberties. An administrative assistant guided Beth to Kate's office.

Kate greeted her unexpected guest with professional courtesy. "Reverend Kelly."

Kate's formality set the tone for their meeting. Beth took Kate's offered hand. "Thank you for seeing me."

"Please sit down." The attorney motioned toward a chair. "What can I do for you?"

Beth's threadbare courage was concealed under a cloak of direct inquiry. "I was hoping you could give me some information regarding Nicki."

Kate returned to her chair behind her desk. "You realize as an attorney I must respect my client's confidentiality, just as you must respect the confidentiality of those you minister to."

Beth hoped she could circumvent Kate's refusal. "I'm not here as a priest, and I didn't come to you because you are Nicki's attorney. I came to you because you are her friend. I just want to know if she's all right."

Kate spoke in a crisp diction, reflecting her simmering anger towards Beth. "That's a subjective notion."

Beth was on hostile ground and she knew it. "You're not going to help me, are you?"

Kate was terse. "I'm under very specific instructions. Nicki is both my client and my friend."

Beth grappled for leverage. "You can't believe running away from her life here in Chicago is the right thing for her to do?"

Beth had no idea of the caliber of woman she was dealing with. The litigator in Kate claimed the stage. "Your statement is rife with assumptions. It's your opinion Nicki is running away. It's your opinion that her life is tied to this city and it's your opinion you know what is right for her. Maybe Nicki's life is finally her own, free from her past. Beth, I'm not blind. Nicki never told me she loved you. She didn't have to. To her, you are a young, earnest, passionate woman with a ceaseless capacity for compassion and an optimistic ethos that struggles to survive in the harsh reality of the streets. But to her you also have your own pain. Nicki sensed it, but she could never figure out its source. I think, above all else, the one reason she felt a connection with you was that pain. I know she allowed you to be with her at her most helpless. I know she was overjoyed the day she was able to surprise you by walking to your church. I know she was devastated after New Year's Eve, and I know that devastation was eclipsed the day she called me to tell me she was leaving for Philadelphia. No one in my network has an explanation for why she changed her mind about rebuilding the Elysian Fields. I know she left my office to go to St. Ann's because David offered her a room. I know she did not see David that night. No one in my network saw or spoke to her. The only person who could have affected her so deeply is you and none of us felt, given your position, that we had the right to ask. I find it hard to believe that you've come to me for information when you're the only one other than Nicki who knows the truth."

Beth was overwhelmed. She looked down at her hands. Kate was wrong about only one thing. Miguel had not hesitated to demand her accountability. She took a deep breath and raised her eyes to Kate. "Will she accept any messages from me?"

Kate was emphatic. "No."

Beth stood up. "I've taken enough of your time. Thank you again for seeing me."

"Don't thank me, Beth. I agreed to speak to you because I wanted to see what on earth you were going to say to try to justify your actions."

Beth could not help but ask. "You don't think very much of me, do you?"

Kate got to her feet. "The worst I can say about you is that you're naïve and maybe selfish. I blame Nicki more than I do you. She knew better than to put her life on the line for you. A lot of innocent people are paying for Nicki's disappointment. I ultimately hold her accountable."

CHAPTER 47

Buyer and seller met at Chamberlain Development to complete the sale of the Elysian Fields property. Nicole finished signing the last of the portfolio of documents.

"Congratulations, Ms. Thera, you're a wealthy woman," announced Lance Griffith, the title company attorney.

Nicole looked at the pompous man. "Mr. Griffith, I was a wealthy woman before the fire and this sale."

Griffith coughed. "Yes, of course."

Nicole spoke to Kate. "If you don't need me for anything else I've got a plane to catch."

Jason Chamberlain, a distinguished developer in his late fifties and the buyer of the Elysian Fields lot, had not expected Nicole's immediate departure. "You're not staying? I was hoping to show you our latest plans and model. We've incorporated a number of your ideas."

Nicole packed her briefcase. "I appreciate the offer, but there is something I need to do before heading back to Boston."

"Boston? I thought you were in Philadelphia."

Nicole explained. "I finished my work there two weeks ago. I just started a new assignment."

Chamberlain asked, "So where is home?"

Nicole placed her hand on Kate's shoulder. "That is something I haven't decided yet."

Chamberlain had grown to admire the young businesswoman. Though negotiations were at times difficult, Nicole proved herself to be the consummate professional with an uncompromising vision "You are a true gypsy."

"This gypsy has her limits. I'm giving myself six months before I settle down. In the meantime I'm taking advantage of my assignments to explore some new cities."

"Well, that explains the option. Seems like taking some time to decide is a good plan. Best of luck, Nicole." Chamberlain offered his hand. "I'm sincere when I say I would welcome continuing our business relationship."

Nicole took the gentleman's hand warmly. "Thank you, Jason. Good luck to you too." Nicole turned to Kate. "I'll call you later this week."

Kate placed her hand over Nicole's. "Have a safe trip."

Nicole leaned down and kissed Kate on the cheek. "Thank you for taking good care of me."

CHAPTER 48

Standing before St. Ann's, Nicole knew there was no preparation for what she was about to do. David was expecting her. They had not talked, only exchanged email.

"Good night David." Beth paused when she realized he was not alone. "I'm sorry I didn't … "

Nicole turned to face the newcomer. Beth was dazed. She held on to the doorknob for support. Her eyes traveled to David. David remained a passive spectator. Beth was aware that David knew her routine of ending each workday by stopping by. He must have purposely taken no action to close his door, to bar her from entrance and discovery of Nicole.

Beth stepped backwards into the corridor. She still held Nicole in her gaze. Blair walked by and said, "Good night."

Beth turned, responding automatically. "Good night." She took advantage of the break away from Nicole and began her ascent to her apartment.

Nicole did not expect seeing Beth again would take so much out of her. Beth's bewilderment gave Nicole hope that Beth's emotion ran as deep as Nicole suspected.

David paused for Nicole. He spoke only after he had her attention. "What are you waiting for? We both know you didn't come just to see me."

Nicole took the stairs in twos. She held her position on the top landing. Leaning forward against the banister she watched Beth struggle to insert her key into the door lock. The young woman's hand trembled. She swore underneath her breath. "Damn it!" Beth wiped her eyes with her sleeve.

Nicole had Beth within her reach. She moved forward. Beth looked up. Nicole kept a few paces between them, and whispered Beth's name.

Hearing Nicole's voice, Beth cried out. "Damn you!" She stepped away from the door. "I gave up. I gave up all hope of ever seeing you again. I even went to Kate hoping I could get a message to you, but she said she couldn't take it. You shut me out."

Nicole spoke quietly. "I wouldn't have been able to handle the disappointment that came with every phone call or email or letter I got that wasn't from you."

Beth offered no absolution. "What about Miguel and the others?"

"It would have been too difficult not to have asked about you. I needed time to let you go."

Beth challenged. "Have you?"

Nicole was uncertain. She did not know if Beth was fighting for her to stay or leave. "I have to get on with my life."

"What are you going to do?"

"Catch my flight back to Boston. I promise I won't bother you again. I didn't want our last memory of each other to be … Beth, I just wanted to say goodbye and thank you for your friendship."

Beth was desperate for a return to a life that balanced faith and truth without requiring a choice of one over the other. "We can still be friends."

Nicole was unwavering. "No, we can't."

"Why not?"

"Because I have never been just your friend, and because of what I see in your eyes. I've caused you so much pain. I can't be with you knowing that."

"You're not the cause." Upon saying those words Beth knew that it was true. Nicole was far from the first cause of her torment. "You've brought me the only happiness I've ever known."

Nicole could not reconcile Beth's words to the woman who stood before her. Beth had become a sliver of the woman Nicole first met. "At what price? To go against your Church … your beliefs."

Beth cried, "You don't know what I believe!"

"Because you won't tell me." Nicole responded in a hush.

Beth trembled. "Every day." She paused trying to find the words. "With every day that passes I lose a little more of myself. I feel like I'm slipping away. There's nothing left of me. Nicki, I'm dying inside. I feel God dying alongside of me."

The haunting experience of a dying God was all too familiar to Nicole. She knew the brutality of such a loss. "But why, Beth?"

"You're asking me? You don't even believe … "

"I told you that in my own way I find the divine in life. I don't have your beliefs. I don't have to. That doesn't stop me from appreciating the gift that your beliefs are to you."

Beth was sardonic. "Gift? I'm suffocating. All I see and feel is … life is so goddamned tragic!"

"Beth, I believe we are ultimately alone. It's not as if we have been given a promise of anything more than that. Why should we expect more?"

Beth felt betrayed. "We have been promised more. I've been promised more. There has to be more. You don't understand."

Nicole tried valiantly to reach through the distorted space separating them. "You're right. I don't understand. Help me understand."

"I've been having a conversation with God all my life." Beth collided with her inner torment. "I can't anymore."

"Why not?"

Beth gave full release to her suffering. "Because I'm in love with you."

"You don't have to make a choice between me and God."

"The Church says different."

Nicole defended her right to have Beth in her life. "The Episcopal Church is not your God. You don't pray to the Church."

"I don't pray at all! I've lost God because of you. I've lost everything!" Beth took hold of her cross and ripped it off her neck. In one uninterrupted motion she threw it at Nicole.

Nicole turned away. She did not feel any contact with the cross. She returned her gaze to Beth, dumbfounded. There would be no more holding back. "Three months ago you said my love for you was wrong. Now you tell me that a consequence of my love is the very destruction of your life. I've been willing to take responsibility for a lot of things, but I won't take this on. I'm done, Beth. I've had it. I've stood back and said nothing about your Church. You're a scholar. You know that in this world right now there are Christians that disagree on a range of theological and social issues including whether the love between two women is to be blessed or cursed. I only know one thing in my life, and that is that no Creator would bless and then condemn its very creation. I don't know your God. To say that what is between us is not meant to be is a lie. You want me in your life, but you close yourself to any real intimacy. I don't know what bargain you're trying to make and with whom, but it isn't with the angels. If anything it's with the Devil himself. That bargain is not going to happen. There's no more playing safe. There is no more hiding behind the Church. Tell me, can you be in any greater hell than the one you're living in now?" Nicole's rage radiated between them.

Spent, Nicole whispered. "David knows how to contact me." She turned and took her leave.

Beth leaned against the wall. She closed her eyes and felt herself free fall into a relentless void.

CHAPTER 49

Tess waited at the Detroit airport. Nicole had arranged a brief visit during her layover. Tess waved upon seeing Nicole disembark from her Chicago flight. They embraced lovingly. "Hey gal, thanks for letting me know you were coming."

Nicole jabbed back, "The lady professor needs more than a week's notice?"

"The mother needs to make sure the father is home with their angelic children."

"I know Bruce loves having them to himself, so find something else to yell at me about."

Tess took a hard look at Nicole. "Are you sleeping?"

"Buy me a cup of coffee." Nicole took Tess's arm as they walked to an airport café.

"So, is it done? Did you sell The Fields?"

"All gone."

"Where am I supposed to go now when I visit Chicago?"

Nicole added Tess to the company of her friends who mourned the loss of The Fields and questioned the wisdom of not rebuilding. "You too, huh?"

Tess asked hopefully, "You still have the option?"

"Yes. Kate believes in slow bleeds."

Tess was skeptical. "You put the clause in to make nice with her?"

"And maybe for me," Nicole admitted. "It doesn't matter, the issue is now moot."

"You saw Beth?"

"Yes."

Tess paused, holding Nicole still. "How bad?"

"Bad. She loves me. The Church says she shouldn't. No winners. We're all losers as far as I'm concerned, including the Church."

"I swear, Nicki ..."

"Coffee, Tess."

The two women sat at a small table away from the constant human traffic of travelers. Their conversation took the form of a postmortem of Nicole's relationship with Beth.

"What?" Nicole found herself the recipient of one of Tess's ingenuous verbal raps.

Tess was artless. "I've always found it fascinating that someone who disavows the concept of God as articulated by the major religions owned a library that out-does just about anyone except a cleric or a scholar."

"I have to read something."

"Uh-huh. What did Beth think when she first came to the loft?"

"I think it was one of those defining moments when you realize that the book cover doesn't begin to give you a clue as to what lies on the pages inside."

"She told me the story of the first time she saw you and Jacob together."

"We only talked for a few minutes."

"It was enough to make her want to get to the truth of you."

"That's a hopeless cause."

"Tell me about it," Tess quipped.

Nicole narrowed her brow in response.

The reaction won from Nicole elicited Tess's smile. "You've said it yourself a thousand times – you are not easy."

"I know," said Nicole. "Beth and I didn't always talk religion, but those talks were an important part of our friendship. I used our arguments as a way of telling her about myself."

"Couldn't scare her away, huh?"

"She didn't heed the warnings."

"Neither did you. Remember … you and me outside The Fields?"

Nicole shared the same memory. Caution had been counseled early. "I didn't see any point in fighting myself anymore."

Tess reached out and covered her friend's hand. "Nicki, don't yell at me for asking …"

Nicole had come to trust the mercy in Tess's most difficult questions. "What?"

"From what you've told me about Beth, if something would have happened between you two, the rules would have been different. You would have been wrong to think that if the going got tough you could simply turn your back on her and walk away. If she had gone to you it wouldn't have been a one-night stand."

"That's the point, Tess. I never wanted her to be a one-night stand."

Tess tightened her hold on Nicole's hand. "But you must have known that in the long run nothing good was going to come from your friendship."

"You're wrong," said Nicole tenderly. "Good things did come from having Beth in my life."

Tess released Nicole's hand and leaned back in her chair.

Nicole wondered what her friend was thinking. "Tess?"

"You're right. You have changed. You're no longer a Van Gogh with bold heavy strokes of paint on your very human canvas. The brush strokes I see are subtler, nuanced. I have to give Beth credit for gentling you."

Nicole smiled. Only the closest of friends could see her so well.

Tess asked, "What now?"

Nicole took a deep breath, gathering in the vulnerability that hovered about her, replacing it with a confident air of resolved intention. "Accept and move on."

"Just like that?"

"Fate. Necessity. Chance. Doesn't really matter if at the end you find yourself standing in the same place. This is a good time to build a life somewhere new."

"So, you'll exercise a little free will in the face of Fate, Necessity and Chance?"

"I couldn't will Beth to …"

"To what?" Tess crossed her arms. "What did she do that you didn't foresee? It's ironic that you complain that Beth won't accept you for who you are, and at the same time you refuse to see her for who she is. This is not the first time she's disappointed you."

Nicole tensed.

Tess said gently, "Nicki, Beth is conflicted about her faith. You can't take that on for her."

"I know. I told her as much. All I can do is make it easier for both of us by walking away."

"Are you really making it easier for her? Don't you see that she wanted you to question and push her to the edge? She's drawn to you like a moth to a flame."

"That isn't reassuring."

"She can't touch the sun. She can touch you."

"And destroy herself in the process."

"I don't think so. One day she may learn to harmonize her faith with who she is, enjoying the light and warmth that comes with having a love in her life, without constantly being afraid of singeing herself."

"And what about me?" Nicole held Tess's gaze.

Tess shared her wish for Nicole. "You'll continue to learn to temper your extraordinary ability to sear away superficial insincerities and give the next woman that falls in love with you time to find her precious harmony. Nicki, you will have another love."

CHAPTER 50

"Good afternoon." Jacob's familiar voice carried gently to Beth's ear, as she sat working at her desk. She looked up from the church's latest financial report to the elder's welcoming presence.

"Jacob, hello." Beth stood up. Jacob raised his palm to her. "Sit. We don't need any formalities between us, do we?" He closed the door behind him.

Beth honored his request and returned to her chair, waiting for him to make himself comfortable.

Jacob went to one of the two chairs opposite Beth's desk. He kept his upright posture. "Nicole came to me late yesterday afternoon. She came to say good-bye." Jacob paused, studying Beth carefully. He continued. "Tell me Beth, have you spoken to David about your doubts?"

Beth could not ignore the direct question. She could, however, attempt to limit the damage. "What did Nicki tell you?"

"Do not be concerned. Nicole respected your privacy. Whatever she knows, she has kept to herself. I love the young woman for many reasons. Once is her integrity. I've watched her and I am amazed by who she has become. God has tested her time and time again. She has faltered. And yet somehow she has overcome the harshness of her life to find God's grace. Do you know what she believes, or do you only know her by what she does not believe?"

Beth realized she could not articulate Nicole's beliefs. "I'm not sure."

Jacob deliberately walked around the chair and sat down. "When Nicole was in college, one of her professors demanded that she stop defining herself by who she was not and find the words to describe who she was. It took some time for her to find those words. She came home to visit during a Spring break. We sat together and I listened. She told me she had four words – her four tenets she called them. She wanted to live by them, but she doubted she was strong enough to do so. Do you know what they are?"

Beth shook her head.

Jacob smiled. "Grace, humility, goodness and acceptance. Each day she says her prayer although she would never call it a prayer. Every day she prays that she may accept the grace of life with humility as she seeks goodness within herself and others. In those words you will find what our Nicole believes is the meaning of life. One simple sentence. What do you believe Beth?"

Beth took in Jacob's sincerity. The kind soul eased her fears. "To love God and to love my neighbor as myself."

"Yes, of course." Jacob leaned back in his chair. "The two great Christian commandments. Tell me, Beth, do you love yourself? You cannot love your neighbor as God would have you do unless you love yourself first."

"Jacob …"

"Beth, no manner of protest will impress me. I listened to you speak of Naomi and Ruth and I thought you may have finally understood the countenance of God's love. It can be both painful and astonishing. I know Nicole loves you. She does not speak of her love, but the woman she is when she stands beside you is nothing if not love personified. She has protected you even to her own detriment. Those who heard of Mrs. Stephens' boasting felt our hearts break for Nicole, but not for you."

Beth felt the cut of Jacob's last statement.

He went on. "I will speak only for myself. I expected more from you. I was more disappointed in you than I was angry with Mrs. Stephens. I told myself God had a reason for this. I could not imagine what it was. You see, I am but a man. Then I heard you speak of *hesed* and I was heartened. Yes, God had a reason. God needed to impress upon you the mercy we have the capacity to hold within ourselves. You needed to not only learn the lesson, but to share it with your congregation. And by doing so you healed the tear between you and Nicole.

"I knew you loved her, and I believed my own prayers for Nicole were heard and granted. I do not know what happened between you two after the fire. I know Nicole's love for you is constant in spite of the pain she feels. I know that she is doing her best to accept the grace of life with humility, seeking the goodness in herself and in you. She has decided that she must distance herself from you. Now that she has sold the Elysian Fields, she will not return. You are the only one who can bring her back. I do not doubt your love for her. I do, however, doubt your love for yourself. I doubt whether you will allow God to love you and give you the gift of Nicole. I shall be so bold to say, my dear Beth, that you are betraying God by listening to those too blind to see the truth – that love between two women is as holy as love between a man and a woman."

Beth silently shed a few involuntary tears. Jacob continued. "I say this because I am fond of you and I believe that you and Nicole can share with each other what I have shared with my Liza. We should all know that God loves us. We should not need proof, but some of us need a little more help than others. You and I are alike in that way. I tell you I have paid a high price for my life. It is a price I was able to bear because God gave me Liza."

Beth pleaded, "Jacob, please stop."

He nodded. "I have said enough." Jacob got up and walked to the door. He turned to the shattered priest. "Beth, talk to David. Let him help you. There will always be a place for you in the Christian world. It may simply not be at St. Ann's. And if I'm wrong you can always become a Reform Rabbi."

Beth laughed through her tears.

Jacob smiled again. "It is time I go home to my Liza. It is a good thing to have love such as hers." He stepped out of Beth's office closing the door behind him.

For the balance of her workday, Beth sat at her desk, eschewing her phone calls, hoping no one would come to her door. Jacob had, with the greatest simplicity, placed before her the ultimate challenge – to believe God had a plan for her that granted her love, reassuring her that God's mercy was hers to have.

She felt God too distant to trust that she had God's compassion. She feared she had earned the severe hand of God. She shed tears freely. She took hold of her prayer beads and tried to pray. Her inner voice continued to fail her; she had no words for her Creator. By the time the church offices closed and her colleagues left for the day, Beth was no more certain of God's plan for her. She was, however, sure that she could not continue in a Church that separated her from the love of God.

Beth walked out of her office toward her apartment. Reaching the upper stairs she searched for her cross. It was nowhere to be found. She sat on the stairs and wondered if the loss of the cross was a sign confirming her irreparable fracture from the Church.

She rose to her feet and entered her apartment. She paused. She stood at the scene of her denial of Nicole and of the holiness of Nicole's love. Disheartened, Beth turned around and walked out, leaving the church complex with no particular destination in mind.

CHAPTER 51

The previous days had shaken Beth to her core – first Nicole, then Jacob. Both challenging her to open her heart, to see herself as worthy of the place in the world she allowed herself to imagine only in her dreams.

Beth sat in David's office. As they spoke she felt her separation from him and St. Ann's. David shared his thoughts and feelings with compassionate, yet plainspoken directness. He had recognized Nicole's love for Beth. He admitted to Beth that he was skeptical of her feelings for Nicole, in part because of his own bias. He knew Beth's life would be far less complicated if she refrained from pursing a relationship, any kind of relationship, with Nicole. He reasoned that New Year's Eve might have been for the best. He, like Jacob, considered Beth's homily on *hesed* a watershed. He simply had to wait for the repercussions to manifest. The movement of the two women back into each other's lives, though cautious, was inevitable. In his eyes, they remained steadfast to one another.

David had suspected that Nicole's growing distance from him was an act of self-preservation. His position in the Church made it too perilous for Nicole to confide in him. Thus it was not what she said, but what remained unsaid that had fueled his suspicions. David raised the same unanswered questions to Beth. "What happened after the fire? What happened at your last meeting?" David also noted aloud that Beth was no longer wearing her cross. He wondered how deeply her faith had been shaken.

Beth had reached the conclusion that the loss of her cross was for the best. What it represented could never be recaptured. Mention of her lost cross caused Beth to finally voice the heartbreaking truth. "I need to leave the Church."

Beth waited patiently as David leaned back in his chair. He removed his glasses and rubbed his temple with his hand. David's was a dispirited mien. He spoke softly. "Yes, I know. I hate losing you. Beth, I do understand … you're too honest to live a lie and I agree, the Church isn't anywhere near changing enough so that you can stay." David studied the young cleric sitting across from him, a hint of animation returned to his demeanor. "Beth, the Episcopal Church isn't the only one in town. Give yourself the time you need. You are too talented. You have too much to give to let the Mrs. Stephens of the world rob you of your calling. I want to someday sit with you at the ecumenical table. Beth, if you can't come back to the ministry, I hope you can at least find your way back to wearing the cross with a sincere love for God."

Beth offered no reply.

"What are you going to do?" David said, putting an end to the uncomfortable silence.

Beth's plans addressed the most immediate family concerns. "I need to go back to Riverton and then Atlanta. I know it's asking a lot but I was wondering if I could borrow one of the cars."

"Of course." David cautiously voiced a third possible destination. "How about Boston?"

Beth considered the reference to Nicole. "I'll let you know. I have to take this one step at a time."

CHAPTER 52

Beth faced her father in the center of the living room of her childhood home. She had announced her intention of leaving the Church. He refused to accept her decision. He did not relent in voicing his objections, demanding from her an obedience she concluded he had no right to expect. Their emotions ran high. So, too, their voices.

Frederick's demands relayed the reasonable confusion felt by a man who had yet to receive an answer to the simplest of questions. "How many more times do we have to have this conversation? There must be something you are not telling me. What is so important that you would leave the Church?"

Beth realized that only the truth would end their conflict. Holding to her tenderest memory of Nicole, she spoke; her voice was remarkably calm. "The woman I love."

Frederick stared at his daughter. The meaning of what she said slowly seeped into his pores like poison. "Get out!"

Beth reached out. "Father, please listen to me."

Frederick was stone. "You are not my daughter."

Beth paused. She saw her father for the hard-hearted man he was. There could be no more allowances made. "I've forgotten what it feels like to have a father."

He was stunned by the savage simplicity of Beth's confession. "Are you determined to hurt me?"

Beth shook her head. "No, Father. I do want you to know what I've just realized. I have no choice to make. I never did. Whether you love me or not is your choice, not mine."

"Do you think I want to see you in hell? This woman ... she can't love you. Not the way I love you. She'll lead you to your ruin. I love you enough to try to stop you."

"Father ... I'm only starting to know how it feels to have a life of my own. I've been so afraid for so long. Why can't I be happy? I know Mom was happy ... why can't I?"

"There are things you know that your mother did not know. She did not give you life to have you turn your back on everything she believed in."

Beth grasped for what little she remembered of her mother. "She believed in love. She loved you and me and Marie. I only want what she had. I believe I've been given a chance to feel that kind of love, and I don't want to turn my back on it."

Frederick's words were cold. "You will regret this decision."

"Father …" Beth could not help but try one final time. "Please … will you give me your blessing?"

Silence fell between the two. Frederick kept a steady gaze upon his older daughter. His clenched jaw eased only enough for him to pronounce his answer. "No."

Her father's uncompromising utterance dashed Beth's lingering hopes for acceptance. "You really don't want me here, do you?"

Frederick said nothing.

Beth turned and walked to the front entrance. She opened the door and paused, her gaze meeting her father's. She suspected that this would be the last time she would have reason to see the man. She could not walk away without expressing a second, equally important truth. "Father … I will always love you."

Frederick spoke in an ache-filled whisper. "Good-bye, Elizabeth."

Beth waited a heartbeat, praying that her father's austere veneer would further break. It did not. She passed through the doorway out to an overcast day that had known only brief moments of sunlight.

From Riverton, Beth traveled to Atlanta. She called Marie while on the road. Given their frail relationship, her sister did not hide well her surprise when Beth proposed an impromptu visit. Beth received a cautious invitation to stay in Marie's small apartment near Georgia State University.

The two sisters sat on pillows on the floor of Marie's living room. Beth broached the subject of leaving the Church. Marie did not hesitate to express her bewilderment at Beth's decision. As much as Beth affirmed the constancy of her faith, she told Marie she simply did not belong in the Episcopal Church.

"Where do you belong, Beth?"

Beth was truthful. "I'm not sure. I want to stay in Chicago. I've contacted the University of Chicago about their Ph.D. program."

"Theology?"

Beth smiled. "Yes. That hasn't changed."

"What are you going to do with a Ph.D.?"

"Teach, or go back to the ministry with a denomination that will have me."

Marie shook her head in confusion. "Wait a minute. I thought you said you left the Church. Did they kick you out?"

"They would have."

Marie clearly had difficulty believing her Beth could have done anything to deserve such treatment. "Why?"

This was the moment Beth dreaded. "Because I fell in love with a woman."

Marie burst out laughing. "You're serious!"

"Yes." Beth felt slighted.

Marie tried to compose herself. "I'm sorry Beth. This is just too good. I thought I was the non-conformist in the family. You've got me beat hands down. So, what's her name?"

Beth looked down to her hands. "Nicole."

Marie chuckled. "I can't believe my big sister is making it with a woman. Dad will have a heart attack when you tell him."

"I'm not and he didn't."

"What?" Marie ducked her head, seeking a clear view of her sister.

Beth braced herself and met Marie's gaze. "I'm not with Nicki and Father didn't have a heart attack."

Marie felt a rare pride in her sister. "You told the old man?"

Beth nodded.

"What did he say?"

"I'm not his daughter."

"That's a relief." Marie paused. "I'm not helping, am I? Beth, I wish I could say I'm sorry, but I'm not. It's about time you got out from under his thumb."

Beth remained silent.

Marie's voice rose a notch. "And what do you mean you're not with Nicki?"

"It's a long story."

"I'm not going anywhere."

"You're not ..." Beth hesitated.

"I'm not what?"

"I didn't know how you would react. I was afraid you would feel the same way as Father." Marie's unrelenting scrutiny caused Beth to once again drop her eyes to her empty hands.

"Damn, that's an insulting thing to say."

Beth smiled to herself. Trusting the hint of sarcasm in Marie's voice she looked over to her younger sister.

Marie wore a broad grin. "Tell me about her, Beth."

CHAPTER 53

The telephone rang. Nicole marked her place in her new copy of Lucretius' *On the Nature of Things*. "Hello?"

"Ms. Thera, this is Andrew at the front desk. There is a Ms. Kelly to see you." Having received no response, Andrew restated his inquiry. "Ms. Thera?"

Nicole's mind raced. She scanned the suite. She needed to meet Beth on neutral territory. "Yes, Andrew. Could you ask her to wait for me in the restaurant? I'll be down in a few minutes."

"Of course," Andrew responded.

Nicole reset the telephone receiver onto its cradle. It had been three weeks since her return to Boston. Having heard no word from Beth, she had begun anew the effort to separate herself from the young woman. She stood before her desk, considering a small box that kept vigil for Beth. What lay in that box was the one symbol of hope Nicole refused to abandon. She picked up the box and dropped it in her blazer pocket.

In the lobby, Andrew turned to Beth and crisply conveyed Nicole's message. "Ms. Thera suggests you wait for her in our restaurant. It is down the corridor to your left."

Beth sat in a corner table. She felt the tepid air surround her. It brought no comfort. She sipped her tea trying to arrest her apprehension. She told herself that if she could withstand the force of her father, she could somehow find the means to confront the forthcoming Nicole. Her doubts rose with each passing tick of her watch.

"Hello." The long missed sound of Nicole's voice traveled to Beth's ear.

Beth broke away from her reverie. Nicole was stunning in jeans, a black sweater and gray blazer. Beth had never allowed herself to dwell on Nicole's beauty; now she felt she was drowning in it. "Hi."

Nicole sat down. She waited patiently for Beth to begin. Beth met Nicole's eyes for a heartbeat before shifting her gaze to her teacup.

"Good evening." Beth's waitress returned with a pot of decaffeinated coffee.

Nicole turned her attention to their waitress. "Hi, Sandy. You read my mind."

Sandy smiled. "Anything else?"

Nicole responded warmly, "No, thank you." She reconsidered. "Sandy, we could use some space."

The waitress lifted the coffeepot. "Sure. Just let me know when you're ready for a warm up."

Nicole reverted to her waiting posture.

Beth closed her eyes, gathering the threads of thought that threatened to unravel in chaos. She met Nicole's gaze. "Nicki, there is something I need to say to you."

"I'm listening."

"You were right about so much." Beth struggled to find the words. "I've left the priesthood."

Nicole leaned back. She was stunned by the reality that Beth had chosen to leave her vocation.

Beth continued. "I can't live a lie. I can't go against my vows. The only way I could have stayed was to remain without a love of my own and I don't believe that's what is meant for me. Not anymore." Beth looked away in thought. "Others can try to change the Church from within, but that's not my calling. I don't want to spend my energy trying to change the Episcopal Church when there is so much else I can do in another church that already accepts me for who I am."

Nicole wondered whether Beth appreciated the magnitude of her decision. "And you're willing to live with the consequences?"

Beth compressed the past three weeks into one declaration. "David is supportive. My father has disowned me, and my sister wants to meet you."

Nicole wondered what role Beth had cast for her. "Meet me? Why?"

Beth leaned forward in her chair, her confidence renewed. "Because I love you and I want to share my life with you."

Nicole was incredulous. "Just like that?"

Nicole's tone jettisoned any romantic notions of a blissful reunion Beth may have had. "No," she said meekly. She leaned back, taking hold of the table with her hands. Nicole remembered the gesture from times past. Beth steadied. She looked up again. "Nicki, I'm sorry. Please forgive me. If you can't love me … if I've destroyed what you felt for me …"

Nicole interrupted. "Sometimes I don't think I know you at all."

Beth released the table, reasserting herself. "You're wrong. There are things I need to tell you but Nicki, you do know me. There have been times that you have seen me better than I've seen myself."

Nicole reached into her pocket and retrieved the small box, placing it before Beth.

Beth was mystified.

"Open it."

Beth reached over and took it in hand. She hesitated, looking once again to Nicole for reassurance. Nicole smiled. Beth opened the box. Her eyes held to her gold cross and chain.

"It got tangled in my coat belt. I didn't realize I had it until I was getting into the taxi. It was the only thing I had of yours. I wasn't ready to give it up."

"I don't know what to say." Beth held the chain and cross in her hand. The weight of it was overwhelming. She was not prepared to consider all that it meant to her, not at that moment. She put the cross back into the box and closed the cover over it. "Thank you."

"Where are you staying?"

"I've got a bed waiting for me at the youth hostel."

"Stay with me. I have plenty of room."

Beth hesitated. "Nicki, I don't know what I can give you right now."

Nicole reached out and took Beth's hand. "Stay with me, Beth. It's the weekend. We'll take it easy."

Beth found sanctuary in Nicole's gentle countenance. "My things are in my car."

They talked past midnight. Beth opened herself to Nicole by telling one story after another of her life in Riverton. There was the story of a happy childhood that had crumbled after the shock of her mother's death. There was the story of how she and Marie were subjected to their father's unchecked piousness. He was certain that the loss of his wife was a reflection of a great wrong in their lives. Beth spoke of her daily escape to her grandmother's home, the slow painful estrangement from her sister as they each went on their separate paths; Marie's ultimate rejection of everything in Riverton, including Beth. Beth mentioned her father's letter, a letter written in response to Beth's confession that she was considering leaving the priesthood, a confession that was first spoken during her trip to Riverton for her grandmother's funeral. Beth described the nature of her Christmas visit to Iowa and Jacob's most recent visit. And finally, Beth recounted the final breach with her father and her reconnection with Marie.

They lay in Nicole's bed. Beth rested against Nicole as Nicole stroked Beth's hair, providing silent comfort. Nicole reckoned Beth's stories with what she knew or thought she knew about the young woman. Nicole now understood the trigger of that one unspoken night of Beth's tears. She had a sense of Beth's vulnerability on New Year's Eve, so soon after her confrontation with her father. Nicole could not pretend to understand or empathize completely. At the same time, the stories made it easier for Nicole to forgive past wrongs.

Nicole awoke, finding herself alone in bed. She whispered Beth's name. For a moment she doubted the previous evening. Beth's overnight bag resting on a chair reassured her.

Beth sat on the living room couch, her legs tucked underneath her. Nicole approached and sat across from Beth on the coffee table. She noted that Beth held the cross and chain in her hand. "Have you been up long?"

"A while." Beth was solemn. "Nicki, what are we going to do?"

"You mentioned staying in Chicago and studying at the U."

"But you sold The Fields."

"I can have my consulting home base almost anywhere I want. And there is something you don't know." Nicole waited for Beth's complete regard. "I have a six-month option to buy back into the development. There could be another Fields. Would you feel comfortable living so close to St. Ann's?"

"I'm not sure."

Nicole offered a compromise. "We could get a place in Hyde Park. You could walk to school."

"We?"

"I can't imagine living without you."

"Nicki, we're so different."

"Yes, isn't it wonderful? Tall and not. Dark and fair. Greek and Irish. Celtic music and Gregorian chants. German Expressionist and Impressionist. Italian and Indian food. Have I missed anything important?"

Beth held up her cross.

Nicole went down to one knee. "May I?" She took the cross from Beth's fingertips. She opened the clasp. "I know you have to make your peace with this cross and everything it means to you. I have a feeling it's not going to be easy, especially having a heathen like me in your life. It's bad enough for you as a theologian to love a woman, but a non-believer too? That's bold."

"I don't care."

"Oh, I think you will. You are too close to your God not to." Nicole secured the cross around Beth's neck. "Remember, I'm the one in the minority here, not you. Beth, I'm not going to change. And I don't ever want you to think that I would have you change." Nicole touched the cross. "Did I ever tell you that I've admired your faith? It's true to who you are. I would be happy to see you find your way back to a church just as long as you feel the value of who you are while you're in it."

Beth explored possibilities. "What if I decide to teach?"

"Academia? I'll manage if you remind me every once in a while that you love me."

"I do love you."

"There you go!"

"Nicki." Beth reached out hesitantly.

Nicole leaned forward and gently kissed Beth.

Beth trembled. "Nicki, I've never ... you'll be my first."

"I know."

Beth felt far too fragile. "I'm not ... "

Nicole understood. "When the time is right we'll both know it. Have faith."

CHAPTER 54 .

Beth stayed with Nicole for a week before returning to Chicago. David allowed her to remain at St. Ann's while she made arrangements for a new home. She met with her bishop. He too understood. He admitted that there were members of the clergy who were lesbian and gay and discreetly lived a complete life. Beth reaffirmed she would not make that choice for herself, nor for Nicole. She began the application process to the University of Chicago.

Nicole contacted Jason Chamberlain and Kate, informing both that she would be exercising her option on the Elysian Fields sale. Nicole's commitments kept her in Boston for the majority of the following two months. She flew to Chicago three times to meet with Jason and to consider the potential apartments and furniture Beth had chosen for them.

Nicole drove her Jeep back from Boston. The extent of her belongings remained limited. Living in hotels and extended stay apartments left her wanting for little. Since the fire, her purchases consisted solely of a limited wardrobe and books. The Philadelphia and Boston second-hand booksellers provided plenty of opportunities to hunt replacements of the books lost in the fire. Many of the books in her original library were out of print. Even if new editions were available, she had a particular appreciation for the look and feel of older volumes. In the passing months, she'd had the pleasure of making a few choice finds.

It was past eight in the evening when she arrived at her new home. She parked in the apartment's designated parking stall behind the building, a valuable commodity in the neighborhood. She sat in the Jeep knowing that upon entering the apartment she would be entering a new life, one that was no longer measured solely by her own needs and expectations. It was a life that also included Beth. Nicole would not sleep alone, awake alone, or come home to unshared space. She knew her aloneness would always be with her, but it was now tempered by her connection to another soul. Nicole's connection to Beth only grew stronger and with it Nicole's desire to be with Beth. The daily telephone calls and countless emails were insufficient recompense for their separation.

Nicole walked up the stairs with her garment bag, laptop case, and a small box of books under her arm. Their apartment rested on the second floor of the three-story brick building. The building had a musty smell to it, unlike the crisp, clean scent of The Fields. The difference was not unpleasant; it was another indication of the change in her life. Nicole chose to ring the doorbell instead of struggling with the keys Beth had sent her.

The door opened. A radiant Beth, wearing an infectious smile, stood on the other side of the doorway. "Hi."

Nicole found herself breathless. She returned the smile with a sigh. "Hi."

A number of heartbeats passed without motion. Nicole felt an intricate joy blend with the fatigue of her long drive. "Beth, do you think I might be able to come in?"

Beth was unmoved. "I've missed you."

Nicole echoed. "And I've missed you."

"Let me take that," Beth said, reaching out.

Nicole handed Beth the box and followed her inside. The apartment was large. In addition to the living room, dining room and remodeled kitchen, it had a sunroom, two full baths and two bedrooms – one to be used as a den. The floor was oak; oak moldings framed the floorboards as well as the ceilings. It had built-in bookshelves and a natural fireplace in the living room. The latter was one of the few amenities missing from the loft. The textured plaster walls were newly painted white. The apartment did not have the expansive, modern feel of the loft; it was classic Old Chicago.

Nicole scanned the room. The furniture she and Beth had chosen together rested comfortably in the space. They decided upon the Prairie style of simple lines and lighter woods. "I like this."

Beth was pleased. "It'll take time before it feels like a home."

"It's home, Beth." Nicole turned to the younger woman.

Beth felt a pull towards Nicole. She redirected her focus. "Hey, what's in this?"

"Books."

"I'll put them in the den." Beth left the room in search of the equilibrium that had suddenly abandoned her.

Nicole put her computer case and garment bag down. Her hand stroked a dining room chair. It was solid and so very real. She needed the reassurance that what was before her was not an illusion.

Beth returned. "Are you hungry?"

"No thanks. I've eaten."

"Thirsty?"

"I'm fine, Beth."

"Would you like a tour?"

Nicole nodded. Beth went to Nicole and shyly took her hand. Nicole followed as they toured the sunroom, kitchen and den. Upon reaching the bedroom, Nicole noted the lone mattress lying on the floor. Beth offered. "I talked to the store again today. The furniture should be delivered in about a week. We have to rough it until then."

"No problem," said Nicole softly.

Beth felt Nicole's distance. "Nicki, is everything all right?"

Nicole squeezed Beth's hand gently. "Yes. This is wonderful. I'm just tired and I could use a shower."

"Go ahead and wash up. I'll make some tea."

Nicole hesitated in releasing Beth. They both had been careful in their demonstrations of physical intimacy Their occasional kisses had been light and brief. They rarely had embraced outside of their shared bed. It was only in their bed that they had held to a constant embrace and a few accompanying words. Nicole would not break her promise. She would not ask more than Beth was willing to give. Nicole kept her word by remaining silent, both physically and verbally. In turn, Beth was uncertain of how to express her ever-growing longing for Nicole.

Nicole had maintained her celibacy after ending her liaison with Paige. Her focus was solely on Beth. She was unwilling to risk losing the possibility of Beth for the sake of a night's pleasure, even if it was with a stranger in a distant city. The cool waters of the shower calmed her physical need for sexual release. She braced herself for the extant loneliness of their unconsummated relationship.

Nicole entered the living room wearing a long white terry cloth robe. Her hair had grown to the length of her shoulders. Nicole wore her still wet hair combed back.

Beth waited on the couch with a mug of tea in hand. "Better?"

"Yes." Nicole sat in a chair across from Beth.

Beth set her mug aside and got up. Nicole followed the young woman's movement with her gaze. Beth took a small package from one of the bookshelves and knelt beside Nicole. "This is for you."

Nicole accepted the package without a word. She considered Beth's intent gaze for a moment and then returned her care to the package. The weight of it told her it was a book. She was curious what Beth chose for her Her answer came as she tore the brown paper, revealing an older, leather bound edition of *The Iliad*. Nicole opened the book and turned the pages one by one, allowing her fingertips to take up the sensation of the aged, somewhat rough pages. Nicole looked up to an attentive Beth. "Thank you."

Beth had watched Nicole's thoughtful consideration of the book. There was no doubt that she liked the gift. Still, Nicole's reserve was disconcerting. "Nicki?"

Nicole studied the book. "Yes?"

"I love you."

Nicole felt the immensity of Beth's statement. She closed the volume. She felt Beth's hand rest over her own. The gentle woman's voice came to her once again. "Nicki, please talk to me. Tell me what's wrong."

Nicole took a deep breath before raising her eyes. "You don't under-stand, do you?" Nicole paused. Beth cocked her head in consideration. Nicole continued. "I've never had this before. I've never lived with ... I've never loved like this before. I've never loved anyone the way I love you. I just feel very grateful ... I'm feeling very quiet inside. Telling you that I love you just doesn't feel like enough. Beth, I don't know what to do."

Beth understood and she knew what was to be done. She leaned forward and tentatively kissed Nicole. Nicole responded with equal caution. Beth did not withdraw. She continued to explore Nicole. Her hand traveled behind the other woman's neck, strengthening her embrace. After a moment Nicole pulled away. Beth leaned back, confused. "Nicki?"

Having felt her passion break though to the surface, fearful that soon nothing would stop her from taking Beth, Nicole reined in her desire. She struggled to find her voice. "I want you." She whispered. She did not have the courage to look Beth in the eye.

Beth smiled a bittersweet smile to herself. How she loved Nicole. How her heart broke for Nicole. "Your promise ..."

Nicole was apologetic. "I'm trying to keep that promise."

"Nicki." Now it was Beth who wrestled with the spoken language. "Nicki, you've kept your promise longer than you needed to. Longer than I wanted you to. I didn't know how to tell you. Nicki, please make me yours. Please make love to me."

Nicole did not understand the press in heart, why it was so painful to love Beth. Nicole was splintering apart. She was in the presence of the impossible and was humbled and awed by the very simplicity of it. Beth was hers, yet never would Beth be a possession. Beth's touch, Beth's smile, Beth's tears, Beth complete was a gift. Nicole recalled Beth's words.

We all have the divine capacity to perform an act of hesed ... it can be quite ordinary – as ordinary as a kiss ... we should be attentive when such an act is placed at our feet so that we don't trample upon it ... We may feel compelled to hold to the past when in fact our truth has been reshaped and now carries a different face in the present ... Imitating the divine initiative hesed comes without being deserved just as our first breath of life.'

Nicole moved forward. With modest hesitancy she kissed Beth. Beth met Nicole in her own gradual approach. Nicole's confidence grew as she brushed Beth's hungry lips. Her heart and breath quickened. With her arm she guided Beth to her. Nicole's desire burst free. She knew that on this night she would not be turned away.

Nicole stood up, taking Beth with her. Beth allowed Nicole to guide her body. Beth's hands unraveled the tie of Nicole's robe, freeing the terry cloth to fall to the sides. Beth stepped inside their folds. Nicole's nakedness was beauty unadorned. Beth felt Nicole's kisses begin to explore more than just lips and mouth; they traveled to cheek and ear and neck. Beth raised herself up, wanting to lessen the distance between them. Her body longed to meet

Nicole at the center of this shared journey. Beth's hand traveled to Nicole's back, pressing the woman closer to her.

Nicole found herself pulling Beth's shirt from her jeans. She explored the soft skin underneath. Not satisfied, Nicole's long practiced hands moved forward and released Beth's shirt buttons. Beth welcomed the exposure. More of her could now feel Nicole. They continued to seek each other out, inch-by-inch – returning to territories that promised pleasure.

Nicole's passion reached a breaking point, a place within her that abandoned the world as insignificant, a place that consumed her senses completely. She ushered Beth into the bedroom and onto the mattress. For a moment she considered the young woman, allowing Beth to speak to her in the midst of their silence. Beth reached up and stroked Nicole's cheek. A silent permission granted, Nicole returned to her. She lifted Beth up and unclasped her bra. With a gentle stroke Nicole swept Beth's shirt down from her shoulders and arms. She then guided Beth back down to the mattress. Nicole took Beth's bra straps and moved them forward. Beth was content to cooperate with the fluid motions. Soon she found herself laying on the mattress with Nicole leaning over her. Nicole renewed her explorations. Her lips traveled to Beth's breasts, taking one and then the other into her mouth, biting the nipples to bold hardness. Beth arched her back as the electric sensations traveled through her. Her hand rested behind Nicole's head, encouraging the exploration.

As much as Nicole hated to separate herself from Beth's sweetness, she raised herself up and with equal impatience and tenderness she stripped Beth from the waist down. Sitting back on her heels, Nicole took in the vision of the naked woman. Her Beth.

Beth sensed Nicole's observant eyes. She felt a momentary insecurity. She doubted if she could meet Nicole's standard. She doubted whether she was indeed a woman Nicole could desire.

"You are beautiful." Nicole said softly. Her hand made the ascent up Beth's leg to her hip. She moved her body over Beth like a gentle wave. The reward of flesh to flesh was overwhelming for both of them. Beth could not even consider words. Her body took dominion over her very existence.

Nicole returned to Beth's lips. Beth willingly met Nicole. She not only wanted Nicole, she trusted Nicole. She wove each of her hands into Nicole's and pressed with all her strength. Nicole returned an equal pressure. For a moment their bodies held still. Their joining was one of power. Neither overtook the other. They gave of themselves to the other. They relinquished the need to control, to protect themselves from harms that could be done. They accepted the other's surrender knowing the sacred covenant they were creating.

It was Nicole who first released her hold, giving Beth the right to lead them both. Beth's hands moved to Nicole's shoulders, traveling down to her breasts. She explored Nicole's supple flesh. Nicole bowed her head, keeping

Beth within her sight. Beth cocked her head up, seeking a kiss, which Nicole granted.

Nicole offered a restrained, tender passion as she explored Beth's most intimate folds and spaces. The more experienced woman's tentative touch was solicitous of her inexperienced partner. Beth allowed Nicole to carry her forward. She fixed her gaze upon Nicole's, holding it steadfastly, finding within Nicole's clear blue eyes a refuge from her fear.

Sensations provoked from Beth involuntary moans and stirrings, as she closed her eyes. She felt Nicole's explorations ease. She returned her gaze to Nicole anew, silently reassuring her lover to continue. Nicole listened, observed, and learned Beth's body. Beth's breaths quickened. Her hold upon Nicole tightened as her body neared release. Beth cried out as she climaxed. Nicole continued her rhythmic strokes until Beth pleaded for her to stop, the first words spoken by either of them in their passion. Beth buried her face into Nicole's shoulder. Nicole held Beth, wanting to safeguard the younger woman.

Beth whispered. "Hold me."

Nicole tightened her embrace. She lost all sense of time. She took in and became mesmerized by Beth's scent. She allowed her nerve endings to transmit to her consciousness the location of each drop of perspiration pressed between them as well as standing free upon her body. She lingered upon the taste of Beth infused on her tongue.

Beth's breathing abated and her body relaxed. Sensing these signs Nicole released her hold. Beth pleaded once again. "Don't let go."

Nicole murmured, "I'm here."

Beth felt silent tears fall. She could no longer keep her spirit encased protectively away from life's finer passions. Nicole had taken her outside to an unfathomable world. The immediacy of her life had never been more vividly experienced. Time passed unaccounted.

Beth allowed herself to feel emotions long chastened, feelings reproached as unbefitting. Her return was to herself – a self she had never completely experienced. Her return was to Nicole, a woman who had the capacity to create a safe haven for her. Beth eased her embrace. Nicole acquiesced. Beth kissed Nicole tenderly. She raised her hand and lightly traced Nicole's lips with her fingertips. Nicole felt a profound fragileness in Beth's gesture.

It was Beth's words that breached their shared silence. "I love you."

Nicole smiled. Her gaze delved deeply into Beth's inviting eyes. In their reflection she saw the grace of life. She accepted it, humbly so, knowing the pure goodness of it. "And I love you."

Beth's desire quieted. "Rest with me."

Beth turned to her side. Nicole followed suit, enfolding her lover's body with her own. Nicole reached back and draped a blanket over them. Beth felt the newness of their shared nakedness. Her hand went to her cross, and her fingers slowly enclosed it. She found the words of a simple silent prayer of gratitude rise from her heart.

Nicole kept watch. When Beth's hand went to the cross, Nicole felt an essential, shattering truth. She set aside what troubled her. Instead she focused on the fact that the searing betrayal of faith Beth had experienced did not cause Beth to segregate her sexuality into a ghetto devoid of her God. Nicole covered Beth's hand with her own. To hold Beth's hand was to accept the placement of the cross in Beth's life. Hand over hand, the cross at center, they drifted to sleep.

Agape

CHAPTER 55

Nicole awoke gradually. The feel of the space that held her was foreign. She pulled her mind from the depths of sleep, seeking the comfort that comes with the basic knowledge of one's locality. Her senses offered clues – the feel of the sheets, the smell of the room, and the bird songs slipping through to her consciousness. It was, however, the lingering taste in her mouth that brought forth the defining memory. Nicole reached out in search for the other woman. There had been a woman, this she now remembered. With the extension of her arm she sought flesh and blood. She met emptiness. Nicole's mind drifted to the remnants of a dream, a familiar dream that had sustained her for nearly a year, the dream of making love to Beth. The dream and the memory clashed. Their differences played against one another. The memory's setting was not the loft, but a mattress in a Hyde Park apartment. Nicole had not experienced Beth's reciprocation, instead falling asleep with the younger woman in her arms. The emotions were far deeper, more overpowering than she could have ever anticipated. Nicole opened her eyes to the sparse room. She lay alone. Her robe hung on a hook behind the door.

Beth stood in the sunroom holding a half empty mug of tea. She looked out to a dormant street. Even after a year in residence, the silence of Chicago still surprised her. The city was so large and active, to see it in repose conveyed an image of God's merciful hand soothingly encouraging creation to rest. Beth felt God's mercy for those beyond the pane glass, but not for she who stood within. In the name of God, she had denied Nicole. She had denied herself. The previous evening the denial had ended. They had physically joined, completing a minor odyssey.

Nicole's lovemaking had been passionate and tender. Beth had not been able to suppress her tears upon release. Descending back into her memory, she was not able to claim joy or peace, nor pain or despair. Beth had never before known the sheer physical hunger and abandon Nicole provoked in her. The juxtaposition of such a corporeal existence with her numinous sense of being was difficult for her to reconcile. Beth knew she was both women. Knowing herself more completely was not her greatest surprise. What she had not expected was to touch the sublime while in Nicole's embrace. For a reason that escaped her, the truth that Nicole's presence had brought into her life frightened her.

Nicole tied her robe around her as she left the bedroom. She walked through the hallway to the kitchen. Turning, she spied Beth. The young woman, dressed in gray sweatpants and a white tank top, stood motionless in the center of the sunroom. Nicole was relieved to see her. She longed for Beth and yet, Nicole hesitated to disturb her. She felt the distance separating them was far greater than the span of the living room. Nicole did not feel she had a right to trespass without invitation.

Beth closed her eyes. She felt the gentle weight of her cross upon her skin. The previous evening, as she had drifted into sleep, she had offered God a prayer of thanksgiving. She had longed for the presence of God through-out the night as an answer to her prayer. Contrary to all her desires, she had no sense of God's immediacy. During the prior evening, in the living room, kneeling beside Nicole, asking Nicole to make love to her, Beth had set aside the risk of losing God. Standing now with the sun warmly upon her face, she wished to believe no risk had been taken. She wished to believe God had been with her as she broke the rules of the Church. She wished to believe her sense of God's alienation had ended. Instead, she stood in God's sight, uncertain.

Beth opened her eyes. Reflected upon the windowpane was the image of Nicole. Nicole's presence reassured Beth. She smiled as she turned to her lover. "Good morning."

Nicole offered a gentle smile. "Good morning."

"Would you like some coffee?"

"It can wait. How are you?"

"Good. You?"

Nicole struggled with the physical distance. She felt an intolerable vulner-ability. "I love you."

Beth sensed Nicole's fragileness. It was the same fragileness that had found expression prior to their lovemaking. "And I love you."

Nicole matched Beth's gaze for a moment before feeling an unaccustomed shyness. She stepped back and turned into the kitchen. "I'll make coffee."

Beth approached, resting her tea mug on the oak banister that divided the living room from the kitchen. She watched Nicole as the woman stared at the cupboards.

Nicole did not know where to begin. She was a stranger in her own home. She felt a rising surge of undefined energy. It neared anger. She felt out of control and she did not like it. She could not choreograph the morning after with Beth as she had done with all but one other woman in her life. She was not sure she wanted to. At the same time she knew it would be easier if she could.

Nicole felt Beth take her hand. Beth offered, "Let me, until you get the lay of the land."

"This is hard," Nicole confessed.

"What?"

"What do I do now?"

"We're not talking about making coffee are we?"

"No." Nicole released Beth's hand and took a step away. She kept her back to Beth. "I've lost everything I've known. I'm going to have to apologize to Connor. He always said I lived a structured life. I told him he was wrong. But, he was right. I had the loft, The Fields, my lifestyle. They're all gone."

"You're rebuilding The Fields. And when it comes to the apartment you can move things around. Nothing is set in stone." Beth's words were met with silence. "Nicki, I'm not sure what you need ... what kind of lifestyle you want, but we can try to work it out."

Nicole turned back to Beth. "How would you feel if I left right now?"

Beth swallowed. "If that's what you want."

Nicole was incredulous. "Are you always going to be so easy?"

"Nicki, what's wrong?"

Nicole whispered, "I love you."

The insistent plea Beth heard embedded within Nicole's declaration was unexpected.

Nicole's voice trembled. "Damn it, Beth. I can't ..."

"You can't what?"

"Wake up to an empty bed. Not again."

"If I'm not with you, call me back. I'll come to you."

"All I have to do is call for you?"

Beth stood at Nicole's side. "Love me. Respect me." Beth reached up and stroked Nicole's cheek with the back of her hand. "Want me."

Nicole took Beth's hand with her own and placed a kiss upon its palm. Reassured, she raised her eyes. Her smile returned. "Where do you keep the coffee?"

"Nicki, are you sure it's coffee that you want?"

Nicole reached her arm around Beth's waist and pulled her close. Beth allowed herself to be taken.

Having guided Beth back to their bedroom, Nicole laid her body over her lover. She fought her desire. The strength of her physical need was over-whelming her. She could not keep herself from trembling.

Beth sensed Nicole's inner turmoil. "What is it?"

Nicole turned her head away, securing herself against Beth's shoulder.

Beth tightened her hold on Nicole. "Nicki, it's alright to let go."

Nicole's voice was hoarse. "I don't want to hurt you."

Beth turned and placed her lips near Nicole's ear. She spoke in a whisper. "You won't."

"You don't know what I'm capable of."

"But I want to." Beth stroked the back of Nicole's head. "I trust you, and I know myself well enough that I'll ask you to stop if you start to take me somewhere I don't want to go." Beth's assurances were met with silence. "Is this the 'lifestyle' you think you've lost? Give me a chance. I've always been a good student, especially when I want so desperately to learn." Beth waited. She felt Nicole's body tense, now motionless, it left Beth to wonder how such a dramatic physical change could be possible. "For the love of God, Nicki. I am yours."

Nicole raised herself up. Beth's gaze followed Nicole's every move. Whatever Nicole was feeling or thinking, it was beyond Beth's perception. Nicole opened her mouth as if to speak. She paused, and then took Beth's lower lip and bit gently down. She released her hold upon the soft flesh and raised her eyes to Beth's.

'For the love of God.' Nicole had not expected the specter of Beth's God to share their bed. The fact that Beth wore the cross did not prepare Nicole for Beth taking hold of the cross before falling asleep – her gesture to God. Contrary to her initial selfless resolve, Nicole did not want to share Beth. She had never shared a woman. She was determined she never would. Beth had to be hers completely. Nicole would make Beth hers. In their bed, Beth would experience Nicole's charismatic force and if Nicole had her way, that force would be the means to her greatest seduction. Nicole granted her resentment complete liberation. She damned the thief and made her claim. "Are you mine?" she asked.

Beth studied the intense woman. "Yes."

Nicole acted, having Beth's implicit trust. She took advantage of Beth's desire to please. Beth's youthful body responded completely to Nicole, and Nicole capitalized on every response. She kept an intent watch for all of Beth's reactions. No movement, no matter how subtle, escaped Nicole's keen observation. No sound that Beth gave voice to, no matter how muted, failed to be heard. For Nicole, taking possession of Beth was intoxicating.

Beth whispered Nicole's name as she held Nicole weakly, her breath slowing from the rapid pace Nicole had drawn from her. Nicole had driven Beth to her physical limit. Nicole felt a rising fear as she held Beth in her embrace. She felt the danger of her desire for Beth. She had not been good to women she desired far less than she desired Beth. She had the want, the hunger to take Beth yet again, and that part of her did not care how spent Beth was. She tried to rationalize her fear away. She had attempted to retreat from Beth, but Beth had encouraged her. Nicole found no solace in the fact that she had Beth's consent.

Nicole had convinced herself that her most fierce thoughts were caused by the tumor excised from her brain. She now knew that it was not true. The truth lay beyond their physical union, a truth that placed Beth's gentle soul at risk as Nicole pursued her all-consuming desire to triumph against her ethereal competitor. She had presumed an intimate safe haven for both of them. That safe haven did not exist. Her remorse rising, she removed herself from the younger woman before she did any measurable harm.

Nicole walked out onto the city street, leaving Beth sleeping in their bedroom. A light rain was falling, creating a dull, depressed atmosphere. She buried her hands into her black trench coat pockets as she made her way toward the lakefront.

The rain continued to fall. The rising wind blew unimpeded across the open lakefront. The raindrops cut like small cold blades across Nicole's face. Nicole did not care. She sat upon a park bench, her vision taking in the Lake Michigan waves crashing against the breakwater. Nicole wanted to be a wave. She wanted the force of her to hit an immovable object and be stopped, thrown back, prevented from washing away the shore, stealing the rich topsoil, severing the roots of growth.

The thought of returning to Beth was fraught with uncertainty. Nicole's inner ear heard Beth's voice, 'Love me. Respect me. Want me.' Nicole wondered if it could be so easy. She bowed her head and clasped her hands. How could she have lost herself in the span of less than a day? What had Beth stirred within her? She spoke the words that had guided her life since college. "May I accept the grace of life seeking goodness ..." Nicole faltered. Her heart ached. She looked at the roaring lake waves. Gathering her thoughts, she continued in a hushed voice. "Seeking goodness both within myself and within others." Nicole struggled to find the grace in the moment. She struggled to find the goodness within herself. She struggled to accept that her life had brought her to his time and place. She had not expected her destiny to be so unkind.

In the quiet of the apartment Beth lay beneath the deliciously cool sheets. A languid sensation coursed through her body. She could not recall ever feeling this free of tension. It seemed as if her muscles were liquid, maintaining their form only because of the skeleton they held fast to. Keeping her eyes closed and her body still, Beth could once again feel how she seemed to fit perfectly into the shape of Nicole's body. Nicole offered an astonishing desire. It had radiated from her, and Beth had felt the intensity of Nicole's heat to the level of a burn. There had been pain in the heat, but it was a seductive pain. With it came the pleasure of absolute abandonment of all restraint; of what Beth, for a lack of a better word, would have described as propriety.

To Beth, there was nothing indecent in Nicole's desire. It was, however, devoid of the civilized. It was base. It was fundamental, instinctual, feral. Nicole was insatiable. Beth knew that Nicole had wanted more from her than she had taken. Beth had wanted to give in return but Nicole was determined to have her way and had growled a low "No", as she had continued to explore Beth's body. In the present, the remembrance of Nicole's raw power caused Beth to shudder. Beth had been enthralled by Nicole's capacity to take her away from all thought. They had resided in a rapturous world of the body that did not involve the mind.

Her thoughts drifted to those moments in their past when she had witnessed Nicole at her most vulnerable. In Beth's judgment, Nicole consistently maintained an air of defiance. The thread of defiance was present when Nicole had first asked Beth for her friendship. The same thread had been present in Nicole during her hospital stay, as well as during Beth's first visit to the loft. At one time, Beth had believed that particular loft visit had provided a glimpse into Nicole's vulnerability. Later events had proved her wrong. The privilege of such an intimate insight was not to be hers until the Elysian Fields fire. It was only then that Beth had been exposed to Nicole's genuine defenselessness. It was Nicole's request to be held that had finally given Beth reason to believe that Nicole not only wanted her but, more importantly, needed her. That Nicole's need was physical had not seemed remarkable at the time.

Beth realized that during the previous evening, Nicole's vulnerability had been placed before her for only the second time. Nicole's confession that she did not know what to do defined the divide between Nicole, the woman of great intellectual capacity, and Nicole, the woman of great physical presence. Beth understood that when Nicole's intellect had reached its limit, when she could no longer use reason to cope, her body took dominion. After the fire, Nicole's physical needs overruled her determination to maintain a persona of strength and independence. Ultimately, Nicole could be known through her body. In a similar manner, during the previous evening, limited in her ability to verbally express her love, Nicole was stymied. Nicole was unable to act until Beth had engaged her body.

She considered their morning encounter. Nicole's behavior neared the irrational, a state of being unthinkable of Nicole, until Beth witnessed it. Nicole's initial distance, her confession of loss of all that was familiar, her momentary threat to reclaim her independence, her declaration of love, her spoken want for Beth, finally culminated in a physical yearning so great that it became clear to Beth that Nicole's precious control had been besieged. Once again, Nicole's vulnerability surfaced. Once again, Beth reached Nicole by physically engaging her. The sensation of Nicole's trembling body followed by Nicole's harness of all her energies in an act of sheer will left Beth in awe of her lover.

Beth was uncertain of what she had done to finally convince Nicole to allow herself to break free from her self-imposed restraints. Nicole's only words were those that prefaced their lovemaking. "Are you mine?" Beth knew that no one on earth could claim her as Nicole had. Beth hoped that some day Nicole would give to her as freely as she had given to Nicole. Beth suspected that for now, it was beyond Nicole to allow herself to be taken in like manner.

Beth was reading in the sunroom when Nicole entered the apartment. It was near five in the evening. Beth held her desire to go to Nicole in check. Instead, she watched her partner silently, content to follow Nicole's cue. Nicole stripped her coat off and hung it in the hall closet. She bent down, unlaced and removed her shoes, leaving them on the hall mat. She walked to the bathroom. Soon thereafter she returned toweling her hair dry.

Nicole rested the towel around her neck. She focused on Beth. "Hi."

Beth smiled. "Hi."

"I have some work to do."

"The den is all yours."

Nicole glanced toward the hall that led to her office. "Anything I should know?"

"I've set your laptop on the credenza and put your books away. The shelves are kind of bare but I figure you'll be filling them up soon enough. I left your papers alone. I wasn't sure how you wanted them organized in the lateral file."

"That it?"

"That's it."

"Thanks." Nicole turned away.

"Nicki?"

Nicole offered Beth her complete regard.

Beth stood up. "Nicki. I was wondering if it would be all right if I set up a space here in the sunroom for myself."

Nicole considered the space. It suited Beth. "The den for the sunroom?"

"Something like that."

In terms of space and privacy, the den met Nicole's needs. "I seem to have gotten the better deal."

The sunroom offered Beth a space awash with light, a space that offered solitude by the simple act of closing the glass paned French doors that separated it from the living room. "I think it's a fair trade."

Nicole swept her hand in a broad gesture. "It's all yours."

Beth was pleased to have the question resolved. "Thank you."

"Don't thank me, Beth. This is your home, too."

In the comfort of the den, Nicole delved into completing the final report for her client. She welcomed the diversion. Sitting on the park bench for over two hours, she had been able to calm her worst fears. In her mind's eye she froze the image of the waves crashing against the breakwater. That image would be her mainstay. She would recall it whenever she felt the danger of her darkness rising to the surface.

It was 7:00 p.m. and Beth saw no sign that Nicole would return to her. She went and stood by the den threshold. "Hey."

Nicole was immersed in her work. She spoke without breaking her focus. "Everything okay?"

"Thought you might be hungry."

"I'll grab a bite to eat later."

Beth wondered if she would soon lose Nicole again to the streets of Chicago. "Will you go out?"

Nicole looked up. "We have food?"

Bemused, Beth answered, "Yes. We have food."

"Don't know then. Depends on what I'm hungry for."

"Living over a restaurant did have its advantages, didn't it?"

"I'm spoiled rotten, aren't I?"

"You work hard for the privilege."

"It's still a privilege."

Beth felt a surge of pride in Nicole. Nicole had not been corrupted by her success. It was one of the reasons Beth loved her so. "I'll leave you to your work."

Nicole returned to her task. It seemed to her that instead of Miguel constantly questioning her about her eating, it would now be Beth. In the whirlwind of change, some things insisted on remaining the same.

Nicole made considerable progress in her report. She was pleased. By her desk clock it was past midnight. She had hit the zone, a state of complete mental focus. Time lost all meaning. Her analytical skills excelled. It was, for her, a creative force, one highly valued by her clients. It manifested itself in an ability to make connections between varied and at times disparate data, resulting in problem resolution strategies that were often quite novel, and usually very effective

Stretching, she felt the tension release from her muscles. She realized Beth had not bid her good night. Nicole was somewhat perplexed by this. She appreciated Beth's efforts to respect her work time but that did not have to translate to complete banishment. Having left her office, Nicole noticed a light in the living room. She found Beth asleep on the sofa, a book resting by her side. Beth had yet to learn that she would never be able to mimic Nicole's schedule. Nicole could only hope that Beth would quickly learn to live a schedule independent of her own.

Nicole knelt on one knee. She took Beth's book, noting the title, *Pastoral Care in Hospitals*. She leaned forward and placed a kiss upon Beth's forehead, whispering, "I love you." She waited patiently as Beth stirred.

Beth opened her eyes. Seeing Nicole, she smiled and sleepily said, "Hi."

"It's late. Come to bed."

Beth reached out for her partner. Nicole embraced Beth and then guided her to the bedroom. Nicole returned to the living room to turn off the light. She scanned the room. This was her home. She still did not know it. She looked back to the now empty sofa. It was the presence of Beth that made this foreign space bearable. Nicole knew she needed time to adjust; she had to give herself and Beth that time. She switched the light off, throwing the room into incomplete darkness. Streetlights shone through the sunroom windows. As long as there was not a citywide blackout, the apartment would always have a source of light.

Beth awoke gradually to the morning. She felt Nicole's arm around her waist. The closeness of Nicole brought Beth a tender comfort. It was during the silent moments between them that Beth renewed her commitment to their future together. Without the sense of safety and care, her passion would be unable to take flight.

Beth was seeking a foothold in the world. Like Nicole, much of what she knew had been left behind. The time that passed after she met with her father and her sister gave Beth the opportunity to begin rebuilding her life. It had been ten weeks since she went to Boston, where the first decisions had been made. Since then, Beth had spent her time divided between two significant tasks. First, she worked to create a home for Nicole and herself. With few exceptions, everything other than her clothes and her books were new. Also with few exceptions, Nicole paid for the furnishings with the insurance proceeds from the Elysian Fields fire.

Beth's second task was to enroll in the Religious Ethics Ph.D. program at the University of Chicago. Though Beth was ready to start anew, patience was demanded of her. It was too late to enter the fall semester. After researching available fellowships and speaking to the faculty, Beth realized that at best she would be able to formally enter graduate school in a year. Her savings could sustain her for no more than a few more months. Providence had placed an opportunity before her. She made a decision. Now, all that was left to do was to discuss it with Nicole.

Nicole's homecoming was not what Beth expected. She had anticipated a reconnection similar to their first night together in Boston. It was not meant to be. Touch replaced words. The language of the body took precedence, creating a new bond, a complement to their friendship. Of their first night and the following morning, Beth had no regrets. What was difficult was waiting for Nicole. Nicole, taking first to the city streets and then to her den, left Beth positioned outside of her world. Beth wanted entrance into Nicole's world. She prayed that unlike the University, she would find an easy admittance.

"Beth?" Nicole called out as she entered the kitchen.

"In here." Beth was sitting on the sunroom floor organizing an array of documents related to her education.

Nicole filled a mug with coffee before seeking out her elusive partner. "I'm glad to see furniture is optional."

Beth looked up to the tall woman, whose raven hair had grown after nearly a year to equal the length at their first meeting. "Are you being sarcastic?"

"Not at all. Mom used to yell at me for sitting on tables instead of chairs. Or taking to the floor when there was perfectly good furniture waiting to be used. She said that when I grew up and had my own place that I could do what I wanted."

"And so you can."

"Like I said." Nicole smiled.

Beth found Nicole's mirth infectious. "Do you have plans for the day?"

"Jason Chamberlain is expecting me. I'm going to be spending the next few months working on The Fields design."

"When do you need to go?"

"Breakfast, shower, go."

Beth looked down at her papers. They included her student loans from seminary.

Nicole noted a change in Beth. It was not for the better. "Something wrong?"

Beth moved a document from one pile to another. She spoke without looking at Nicole. "I was hoping we could talk."

Nicole bent down beside her lover. "Anything specific?"

"A few things."

"Want to talk now?"

"It can wait."

"You sure?"

Beth turned and placed a kiss upon Nicole's lips. "I'm sure."

Nicole raised her hand to Beth's cheek; it retained the heat from her coffee mug. Beth leaned into the warmth. Nicole hesitated to leave. Resigned to her workday, she said, "I'd better get going."

Beth followed Nicole with her eyes as she departed. Beth did not know how to begin.

Ready to start the day, Nicole took her briefcase in hand and walked toward the front hall. She called out to Beth, "I'm on my way."

Still shifting through her papers, Beth stood and entered the living room. "Will you be home for dinner?"

Nicole studied Beth. It was hard to believe that they were sharing their lives with one another. Something about Beth's question troubled Nicole.

She realized how little information she disclosed. She was not accustomed to accounting for her actions. "How about dinner at Salonika's?"

Beth was both pleased and disappointed. She would see Nicole for dinner, however she had hoped for a setting more private than the local Greek family restaurant.

"All right." Beth made a sincere effort to convey an enthusiasm she did not feel.

In her mind's eye, Nicole saw the frozen image of waves crashing against the lakeshore. She was dismayed by the warning it conveyed. Nicole set her briefcase down and walked to Beth, taking the young woman into her arms.

Beth had no chance to think. She was completely encased in Nicole's embrace. The feel of Nicole opened Beth to her loneliness and the sorrow that accompanied it. A small, involuntary cry escaped her. Beth held Nicole tightly, breathing in deeply Nicole's familiar, soothing, musk scent.

Nicole closed her eyes and allowed herself to feel Beth's need for her. "I'm sorry."

Speechless with emotion, Beth shook her head.

Nicole reached into her jacket pocket and retrieved her cell phone. She flipped it open and pressed the speed dial code for Jason's office. With her other arm she kept a firm hold on Beth. "Jason. It's Nicole. Can we reschedule for tomorrow?"

Beth waited as Nicole listened to Jason's response.

"No. Nothing's wrong. I want to spend some time with Beth … thank you for understanding. Nine o'clock … good. I'll see you then." Nicole pocketed the phone. She took a step back in order to have Beth completely in her vision. Seeing Beth's tearful eyes told Nicole all she needed to know. "Let's talk."

Nicole rested on the sofa with her legs stretched out. Beth lay couched against Nicole. She held Nicole's hand with her own as Nicole rested her free arm tenderly across Beth's chest. Nicole gave Beth time to gather her thoughts. "Where do you want to begin?"

Beth took a deep breath. Where did she want to begin? "We haven't talked about money. About sharing expenses."

Nicole cocked her head aside hoping to catch a glimpse of Beth's countenance. "Beth, you're not working and you have your school debt."

Beth noted Nicole's talent for being succinct. "Even if I'm accepted into the Ph.D. program, it's going to be a year before I can start my full-time studies. I'm going to be getting a job."

"What do you want to do?"

"Don't change the subject."

"I'm not. About expenses. What do you want to do?"

Beth continuously stroked Nicole's hand with her thumb, receiving comfort in being able to give comfort. "Fifty/fifty."

"What happens if I want to go out to dinner at an expensive restaurant or to a play or travel? Do I stop doing those things? Do I go alone? Do you come with me and just fall deeper into debt or do you accept them as gifts?"

Beth stilled. "I wouldn't mind if you went with friends or alone."

"I would."

"I could do a bigger share of the chores."

"Be my maid instead of my partner?" Nicole's words were terser than she intended.

Beth despaired. "Nicki, I'm trying ..."

Nicole spoke far more gently as she tightened her hold on Beth. "I fell in love with a minister. A lot comes with that. One thing that doesn't is money. The loft was about the same size as this apartment. I'm not paying any more for living space. I expect some incremental cost increases for utilities, for the Jeep." Nicole paused. She was being too businesslike. "You eat, I can't forget that." Nicole felt Beth relax. "And I expect you'll be calling Marie and making other long distance calls."

Beth now had a starting point to consider her household contribution. "If I cover the extra costs?"

"I'm not going to be counting pennies." Nicole did not want to dwell on their disparate incomes. She found society's focus on wealth destructive and had no intention on allowing a wealth-based merit system into their relationship.

"Help me." Beth's plea was for relief, for direction towards an answer she could not independently deduce. The issue was jointly theirs and neither one them could resolve it without the other.

Nicole needed to offer equitable terms. She wished she had had the presence of mind to anticipate this conversation. "You cover all your school costs, clothes and other personal incidentals. Plus, our shared telephone line, groceries, and you gas up the Jeep when it needs it."

"That's not enough."

"Cable."

Beth smiled to herself. If she did not consent soon to Nicole's terms, it promised to be an arduous conversation. "And cable."

Nicole patted Beth for emphasis. "We're not done yet. If you treat me to coffee and a scone at Mendici's, that equals my treating you to a night on the town. If we want to do something special like a vacation, we'll talk about how to manage our expenses before we finalize our plans."

Nicole waited for Beth's retort. None was forthcoming. Nicole feared she might have gone too far in her governance. She whispered Beth's name.

Beth leaned her head back, bending to the inevitable consequences of loving a woman who was financially more secure than she was. "Thank you."

Nicole was gratified. She allowed the silence between them to linger before speaking again. "Beth, you said 'things.'"

"Nicki, I've applied for two possible fellowships from the Divinity School." Beth sat up and turned to Nicole. "Either one would mean free tuition and a living stipend."

"They must be competitive."

"They are. If I get one, it'll become effective next fall. It would coincide with my formal admittance to the Ph.D. program. I have a year to wait."

"I thought you could still take courses between now and then as a special student?"

"I can." Beth paused. "I've had an offer. Pam Lathrop is the CPE supervisor at Memorial ..."

"CPE?"

"Clinical Pastoral Education. I sent Pam an application after I left St. Ann's, but it was past the interview process. One of their resident candidates decided at the last minute to take a position at a different hospital. Pam offered me the position."

Nicole recalled the title of the book she found Beth reading. "What does that mean?"

"I would be paid while I finish the nine additional months of training I need to be certified as a chaplain."

The requirement surprised Nicole. "Being an ordained minister isn't enough?"

"The training is intense. I had to do a quarter of CPE before I could graduate and be ordained. It was the most extraordinary part of my training. Some ministers aren't good in hospital settings. For others, there is nothing more rewarding."

"And for you?"

"Remember I told you when we first met that the reason for my studies was to help me help others find God and live a better life? I never felt I was doing more good than when I was working in the hospital."

Nicole took Beth's hand. "When do you start?"

"Next week."

"Anything else?"

Beth lowered her gaze to their intertwined hands. "I'll be working evenings and weekends."

"That will make two of us."

Beth leaned forward and rested against Nicole. "It may be hard for us to spend time together."

Nicole welcomed Beth back into her arms. "My schedule will be more flexible than yours. If you let me know your hours, I'll try to work around them."

"I know how much you value your freedom."

"Do you have any idea how much I value you?"

Beth smiled. "I do love you."

"So, what do you want to do with the day?"

Beth considered her list of outstanding errands. "There are still a few things we need to get for the apartment."

Nicole looked around. "The walls are bare, aren't they? What do you say to a gallery walk?"

"I don't know. Wouldn't it be safer if you surprised me?"

"But I was looking forward to the argument." Nicole chuckled. "Maybe we could set some ground rules."

"For instance?"

"Only female artists."

"Agreed."

"I get the den; you the sunroom."

Beth sat up. She protested. "The sunroom is all windows."

Nicole grinned. "So it is. You still have the option of pottery, glass, mobiles."

"If not the sunroom?" Beth interjected.

Nicole was enjoying herself. It took a bit of effort to maintain a measured facade. "Kitchen."

"Oh please!"

"Bedroom."

Beth was startled by the offer. "Bedroom?"

Nicole nodded. Beth was suspicious. "Who gets the living room?"

Nicole was firm. "The living room and dining room go together. We'll have to agree on the artwork or it's a no-go."

"You negotiate for a living, don't you?"

"It's part of the job. Pure strategy."

"You do it well."

"Thank you, but there's more."

Beth was wary. She drew out her question slowly. "What?"

"Vetoes. We each have two vetoes. If one of us chooses something the other absolutely doesn't want to live with, she can exercise a veto to prevent the acquisition."

"Acquisition? You really are sounding like a consultant."

"Sorry." Nicole wore a congenial smile. "I'll try to do better."·

Beth traced Nicole's smile with her fingertip. Nicole's playfulness was a rare treat. Beth found the joy in her partner beguiling. "Nicki?"

Nicole offered Beth an amused look. "Beth?"

Beth felt a physical longing. Suddenly the idea of leaving the apartment lost its appeal. She hesitated in being the initiator. Reflexively, she pushed herself up and away. "I need to shower."

Nicole kept hold of Beth's hand. Beth's gaze begged for disengagement. Nicole reluctantly granted Beth's tacit request.

-¦-   -¦-   -¦-

The gallery walk reaffirmed their aesthetic differences. Though Nicole did not outright exercise a veto, her cool reception to certain pieces that Beth pointed out dampened Beth's enthusiasm. Beth chose to reconsider the artworks, admittedly feeling no urgency to own them. At the forth gallery she was drawn to a landscape painted with her preferred palate. The artist's brush strokes were bold, compelling in the power they conveyed of both nature and to Beth, the force behind nature. She stood mesmerized exploring the burst of flora that bordered the image. At the heart of the canvas a mountain stream fed a distant valley. It was the juxtaposition of the unbridled force of nature with its balanced state of tranquility that captivated Beth, not much differently than how she received the seductive power and tenderness she found in Nicole. The image promised the serenity Beth longed for.

Nicole came to Beth at the gallery, standing behind her as she too found the canvas to her liking.

"This one." Beth stated with certainty. She turned and waited for Nicole's assessment.

"Where?" Nicole asked.

"Over our bed."

"Okay."

The decision came that easily.

They arrived home after dinner. Nicole followed Beth into their bedroom.

"Did you really like it?" Beth sought reassurance.

"Yes, really." Nicole was delighted by Beth's easy happiness. "Are you sure you didn't choose it for me?"

"No." Contrary to the day's evidence, Beth said, "Maybe our taste in art isn't as different as we thought?"

"I'll suspend my judgment until we finish the apartment."

Upon reaching the center of the room Beth happily whirled around to face Nicole. "It should look good with the furniture, once we have furniture."

"I'm glad you decided to wait."

"They won't sell it?"

Nicole crossed her arms. "Where were you when the clerk agreed to the two-week hold?"

"It really was lovely, wasn't it?"

"Yes, it was."

"I wish you had found something you liked."

"Beth, I bought my first serious piece of art when I was a sophomore in college. I spent years collecting the pieces I had in the loft. I've learned to be patient."

"In art and in books," Beth observed.

"Among other things."

"Yes, I've noticed."

The two women looked across the bedroom at one another. Beth had implied what previously had remained unspoken. "Nicki. You don't have to be so careful. I won't break."

Nicole's light mood was shattered. "I have to be careful. That is the point, isn't it?"

Beth approached Nicole. "What do you mean? I wanted you. I didn't want you to hold back."

"But I did." Nicole stiffened. "Beth, I did hold back."

Beth debated whether to ask Nicole how much of herself she had withheld, but deep inside Beth knew the answer. It had to have been a great deal to cause Nicole the level of distress she was obviously experiencing. Beth searched for a place of mutual safety. "Would you feel more comfortable if I grant you permission to be with me?"

"Beth, I told you. You don't know what I'm capable of."

"Yes, I do. Just yesterday, I was the woman in bed with you. I know exactly what you're capable of." A devastating thought cut through Beth. "Unless, I wasn't … "

Nicole saw the shadow fall over Beth. "It's not you."

"How can you say that? It is me."

"This isn't about sex."

"Then what?"

"I didn't expect to feel the way I do when I'm with you."

Beth was subdued. "How do you feel?"

Nicole hated confession. "Out of control."

"But you weren't."

"I was on a fine line."

Beth stepped forward. Nicole instinctively felt the danger and stepped back against the bedroom doorjamb. Beth stopped. "Nicki, I won't let you run away from me without a fight. And, you can't run away from yourself."

Beth waited. Nicole did not blink.

Beth approached a second time. She reached out and placed a comforting hand on an unyielding Nicole. Sensing Beth's touch, Nicole averted her eyes.

Beth spoke softly. "Do you have any idea how out of control I felt in your arms? Don't you realize you took me with you?" Beth raised her hand and guided Nicole's chin toward her. "Listen to me, Nicki. You weren't alone. There wasn't a moment that I didn't want to be with you."

There were thoughts and feelings Nicole was unprepared to share with Beth, thoughts and feelings that underlaid the intensity of her lovemaking, that related to motive. Bestowed with a conscience, she knew that no matter how she behaved, she was accountable for her intentions. To expose her intentions would be to destroy any hope for Beth's trust and love. Beth continued to interpret Nicole's admonitions as warnings of physical harm. That was not Nicole's fear. Nicole feared she would crush Beth's spirit.

If Nicole honored an archetype it was Sophia – wisdom. She had sought wisdom while sitting on the park bench. Her answer was simply to seek and hold to the goodness within herself and within others. Standing before her was all that was good. Goodness was seeking her out, calling Nicole to her. Beth was seeking Nicole and Nicole knew she did not have the strength of character to deny Beth. Beth would have her.

Nicole relented. Her posture relaxed.

Beth noted the change. Heartened, she leaned up and tenderly kissed Nicole. Nicole needed little encouragement to follow Beth's lead. Their kiss quickly grew in fervor. Beth's claim upon Nicole was not denied.

Having reached climax, Nicole leaned back and closed her eyes – a physical withdrawal from Beth. Beth had touched Nicole beyond the corporeal realm. Nicole was accustomed to physically opening herself up to other women, immersing herself in the sensations afforded the human body, allowing herself a total escape from all that might place meaning into the moment beyond the raw play of touch, taste, smell and unformed sounds. Nicole preferred the night, anonymous sex in darkness. The other woman did not need a name. The only personality acknowledged was a woman's willingness to participate in the physical encounter; her only value was her physical response. Anything more promised complications. No matter how clearly Nicole set the rules of engagement, inevitably claims were made, expectations for a relationship surfaced. Complications would come and dampen Nicole's desire. The body lying beside Nicole in the night would claim her right to have a name and all that came with the name. The body was no longer an instrument for Nicole to play. She became a human being with a soul.

Beth was first and foremost a soul. Nicole knew she could open her eyes to the light of day and recognize whom she was with and call her by her name – Elizabeth Ann Kelly. Loving Beth outside her bed had been both painful and easy. The pain from unrequited love had its noble element. Chaste love warranted no reassessment of what Nicole had been taught to hold true. There was love in the world. It was simply never to be hers.

Beth challenged Nicole's absolute conclusions. From Beth came words of love. From Beth came a desire that crossed the bounds of friendship though it remained firmly rooted in friendship. From Beth there was trust, not only that Nicole would do no harm to her body, but also that Nicole would do no harm to her heart. With Beth there were no known rules of engagement unless Nicole went back to 'Love me. Respect me. Want me.'

In having closed her eyes, in not returning to Beth, Nicole effected an evasion of all that Beth promised. A promise Nicole was not prepared to accept.

Beth waited for Nicole to return to her. Nicole did not return, but eased into sleep. The pleasure of making love to Nicole stayed with Beth. She was once again left to conjecture both the source of Nicole's fear and the relief of that fear. There was nothing in their lovemaking that frightened Beth. Nicole was characteristically intense, but also self-possessed. She eased Beth's insecurities by guiding Beth's novice hands with her own, and whispering words of instruction and affirmation. Beth relished her exploration of Nicole's body and her ability to solicit her lover's carnal responses.

Beth laid her body against Nicole's, resting her ear over her lover's heart. She fell asleep with Nicole's powerful heartbeat as a source of comfort.

CHAPTER 56

Nicole took to her office while Beth showered. By design she made herself an unobtrusive presence, giving her partner a mild morning to prepare for her first day at the hospital.

"I'll see you tonight." Beth called from the den door.

Nicole looked up from her computer screen. Beth was not dressed in what Nicole had always referred to as her uniform. Beth's Episcopalian priest garb was no longer part of Beth's identity; instead she donned a mandatory blue blazer. She was free to complement the blazer with her own wardrobe. For her first day she chose a long pastel flower patterned skirt and a white blouse open at the neck. Nicole had not missed Beth's priestly clothing until this moment. She got up from her chair and approached the chaplain-in-training. "I'm sure you'll do good."

"I hope so."

Nicole gave Beth a light kiss. "The patients are lucky to have you."

Beth smiled. "I love you."

"And I love you." Nicole understood that Beth's life, and in turn, her own, was about to change. A part of her wanted to keep Beth home, but another part of Nicole knew that if Beth stayed, she would not be the woman Nicole had fallen in love with. "Go on, Chaplain Kelly. You don't want to be late on your first day."

Nicole watched Beth leave the apartment. Beth turned and offered a final fragile smile before exiting. They had not spoken about Beth's position at the hospital except for that one day when Beth told Nicole of the offer. Nicole knew why she did not broach the subject. She was enjoying the temporary respite from Beth's religious profession. Nicole now wondered why Beth had been equally silent.

Beth walked toward the metro station. Nicole's voice echoed in her mind. 'Chaplain Kelly.' Nicole had not addressed her as Reverend. It had been months since Beth had heard the title in reference to herself. The disconnection she felt was unpalatable

Beth had given Nicole only a partial account of her meeting with her bishop. It was true that her bishop had been reluctant to see her go. It was also true that he alluded to other clerics living a life inconsistent with the rule of the Episcopal ministry. And finally, it was true that Beth had been firm that she would not hide away. What Beth had not told Nicole was that her bishop gave her a year to reconsider her decision. He did not ask her for a *Notice of Renunciation of the Ordained Ministry*. Unless the Church officially acted, Beth was still in the Church. Beth was still an Episcopalian priest.

Beth was guided into a private office by Reverend Pam Lathrop. Pam followed, closing the door behind her. The hazel-eyed United Church of Christ minister was in her mid-thirties. She wore her long blond hair down. A few inches taller than Beth, she carried her considerable weight easily. Dressed in a black skirt and blue blouse she projected a comfortable, approachable presence. Pam motioned for Beth to take one of two chairs in a sitting area. Beth did so, as Pam sat down across from her. Pam offered a warm welcome. "I can't tell you how blessed I feel to have you with us."

Beth mirrored Pam's sincerity. "I'm looking forward to the opportunity to work with you."

As Beth's CPE supervisor, Pam would act as a teacher, a guide, and a witness. "How have you been managing?"

"It's been hectic. Getting back into a routine is going to be good for me."

Pam laughed lightly. "We'll see how much of a routine you find here." She shifted in her chair. "Have you found a neighborhood church?"

Beth felt a pronounced discomfort. "I honestly haven't tried."

"I'm associated with the Hyde Park U.C.C. Baptist Church. It's a beautiful church and has a welcoming congregation. The door is always open."

"Thank you. I'll keep it in mind."

Pam must have sensed Beth's reluctance. "I hope you have maintained your spiritual practices. CPE is challenging. It's important to keep yourself spiritually grounded."

Beth had not kept to her prayers. She intentionally gave Pam a misleading answer. "Yes, of course."

"Beth, at our next meeting we will talk more specifically about your long-term goals. For now, I am curious about what you want to achieve during this first quarter."

"As I mentioned in my interview, I haven't worked much with those who are severely ill or dying. I would like to."

"There is the Oncology unit or I.C.U. We also have a palliative care unit where those imminently close to death are transferred. The nature of pastoral care is somewhat different with each of these units. Think about where you would like to focus this quarter, and then we'll talk assignments and a training plan for your complete residency."

Beth nodded.

"What else?" asked Pam.

Beth had considered the more difficult aspects of her first experience as a chaplain. "I've found that chaplaincy is different than working in a parish where I had a chance to get to know people outside of a medical situation. It's hard to know where to begin with a new patient, especially on a cold call. I'd like to find a greater comfort level."

"That's reasonable. Anything else?"

Beth looked down. Pam waited patiently. Beth took a deep breath to steady her rising emotion. She raised her gaze to Pam, a tear falling down her cheek. "I feel a distance from God I've never felt before. I want to be able to trust in God again. It may not be appropriate to use CPE for this, but I think being in an ecumenical spiritual community of chaplains will be helpful."

Pam reassured the less experienced cleric. "Beth, CPE has a number of purposes. One is to help you discern your calling. I believe you are in the right place."

CHAPTER 57

Jason Chamberlain sat at the head of the conference table. Nicole sat on one side alone. Across from her Miguel, Connor and Tony each took a chair. Jason glanced over to Nicole. Nicole knew that it was for her to begin.

Nicole assessed the Three Musketeers. Upon entering the conference room Connor was all warmth. He hugged Nicole and took a long look at her, finally asking, "How are you?" Miguel, in contrast, was all attitude. He shook Nicole's hand with an air of reluctance and kept a cool cadence to his voice. His trademark humor and irreverence were nowhere to be found. Miguel sat straight in his chair, his hands placed ahead of him, projecting a posture focused solely on business. Finally, Tony arrived, a tad rumpled and disconcerted. The mid-morning meeting was still too early for his liking. He was low energy and initially seemed disconnected from the proceedings. Nicole was saddened when she realized she had not missed the men. She thought it would have been otherwise. Still, having the Musketeers near was reassuring. She knew what she wanted to accomplish and she knew, given a choice, she wanted them by her side at the grand opening of the new Elysian Fields.

Nicole began. "I appreciate you coming in today." Nicole offered Tony a particular smile. "Jason and I are working on rebuilding the Elysian Fields. I want you three to come back and work in your previous positions. I will put you on the payroll on a part-time basis to work on the interior designs and in getting The Fields ready to open. Like our first time around together, you will have an opportunity to put your personal mark on your respective spaces in The Fields.

Connor sighed. "I've been waiting for this."

Miguel interjected, "Why should we? It was easy for you to throw The Fields and us away after the fire."

Connor turned to Miguel. "Hey man, we talked this out. Be fair."

Nicole had been waiting for the accusation. She glanced over at Tony. His attention was on his two fellow managers. The ensuing silence drew him to scan the room. His eyes met Nicole's. "Nicki. You know it was hard for us to lose The Fields, too."

Nicole responded softly. "I know."

"I've been working as a DJ and bartending. I had a couple of offers to manage but I just didn't want the hassle. I'm not sure I want to go back to running the show. I make less money now. A lot less money, but I don't have to worry about standing next to a trash heap where somebody threw all my dreams."

"If I let you down, I'm sorry."

Miguel burst out, "If you let us down! Yes, Nicki. You let us down. Not in the business. Damn the business. I thought we were friends."

Nicole kept her voice steady. "I won't make excuses. I did what I had to do to survive. I coped with my loss of Beth … of The Fields in my own way. I was obviously not the friend you needed me to be. You've all known me long enough to know what I can give. If you decide to come back to The Fields you come back under the same terms. The Fields is a business. I won't promise you I'll change. I don't know if I can. I don't know if I want to."

"Fair enough." Connor leaned forward. "Nicki, I'm in. I'll need a flexible schedule until you can put me on full time."

"I'm sure we can work it out."

"Nicki." Tony rocked his chair on its back legs. "If I don't want to stay, I go, no questions asked, no hard feelings?"

"You can give me as much notice as I gave you. No hard feelings."

Tony nodded in rhythm with the chair. "Okay."

Nicole turned to Miguel. The fiery Latino was far from placated. "You want an answer now?"

"No, you can get back to me. Is a week enough time?"

Miguel stood up. "If I don't call you, don't bother calling me."

"I understand."

Miguel made his exit without a further word.

Nicole watched him leave. Something told her he would be back. She felt he needed to make her and everyone else in the room aware of his hurt and anger. Nicole was prepared to take the public chastisement. It was a small price to pay given their history together.

Jason got up and closed the conference room door left open by Miguel. "We have a great deal to talk about."

The true business meeting could now begin.

The meeting concluded, Jason and Nicole bid farewell to Connor and Tony. The meeting had been productive. Connor was attentive from the beginning. As they discussed tangible issues, Tony's despondency was slowly replaced by a growing interest. Jason believed Nicole had reason to be hopeful. And yet, now separated from the Musketeers, her tenor was subdued

"Nicole, is something wrong?"

"I thought I would care more. I've done The Fields. Nothing in this development is new." Nicole gazed toward the door Connor and Tony exited.

"It is not just The Fields. We've added the rental units and the additional retail space. Our total square footage is three times what you had."

"I realize that Jason." Nicole returned to her chair. "You're a developer. It's a part of who you are. The Fields feels less personal. I'm duplicating a vision, not creating a new one."

"It was one hell of a vision that doesn't deserve to be thrown away." Jason sat down across from Nicole. "Have you changed your mind? Don't you want The Fields?"

Nicole nodded toward the door. "They want it more than I do. The Pub, The Garden and the dance club reflect Connor, Miguel and Tony's personalities. I was smart enough to give them the latitude to build their clientele."

"So you had nothing of yourself in The Fields?"

"That part of me is in the past." Nicole leaned forward. "Or maybe I just want it to be. When The Fields burned, I was able to walk away and look to new possibilities. Now my focus has been turned back."

"I don't understand. Why did you exercise your option?"

Nicole shook her head. "Habit. Before The Fields there was my mother's bar. Coming back to Chicago meant rebuilding the only home I've known."

"I thought you were creating a new home with Beth."

Nicole was rueful. "Don't ask me to make sense of this, Jason. I'll be the first to admit that I've made a mistake."

"What do you want to do?"

"Go on as planned."

Jason did not hesitate to renew his offer. "Nicole. I'm willing to buy you out."

Nicole leaned back with a bitter laugh. "And take the wrath of the Musketeers? I don't think so. I have a habit of finishing what I've started. I'm not about to change now."

"I think it's a high price to pay."

"This isn't just about me or the Musketeers. I've made a commitment to the community I intend to keep."

Nicole set aside her doubts. She would rebuild that part of her life inextricably linked to The Fields. By an act of sheer will the new Fields would symbolize a progeny freed of the demons that had possessed her progenitor.

CHAPTER 58

Beth stood in the stillness. From the sunroom threshold her eyes lingered on a teak jewelry box the length of her hand and about three inches in width and depth. It rested upon a double length two-shelf bookcase that held her library. The known contents of the box called to her. She took the box in hand and sat down, resting the wood on her lap. Her hands covered the box. She closed her eyes feeling her need grow. Within lay her Anglican Prayer beads.

Beth opened the box and removed the beads. She raised the cross and kissed it. She closed her eyes, holding the position, feeling the press of her lips upon the simple, warm wood. Beth lowered the cross and caressed it with her thumb cupping her right hand with her left. She prayed silently. "Blessed be the one, holy and living God. Glory to God forever and ever. Amen." She guided the cross with her hand until she held the invitatory. "Let the words of my mouth and the mediation of my heart be acceptable in your sight, O LORD, my strength and my redeemer." Her hand shifted until it held the beginning of the first week to the right. "I lift up my eyes to the hills; From where is my help to come? My help comes from the LORD, The maker of heaven and earth." She repeated this prayer for each of the seven beads in the week. Upon reaching the next cruciform her prayer altered. "Holy God, Holy and Mighty, Holy Immortal One, Have mercy upon me." She then proceeded to the next week, returning to her prayer for the week. Beth continued her prayers, traveling around the circle three times, an act symbolic of the Trinity. She completed her prayers.

The weight of the cross was a force in her hand. She felt broken. She felt an unbearable separation from God, a feeling she had defensively hidden away throughout the previous months. Her tears rose and for once she did not fight them. Beth cried, bowing her head down, resting her forehead against her raised hands as the beads cascaded down her arm. She prayed aloud, beseeching God to help her. As Beth's tears continued, so, too, did her prayers.

CHAPTER 59

Beth and Nicole sat at a small table in Medici's, a local restaurant catering to the University of Chicago students. The Sunday *Chicago Tribune* was split between them as each sipped her coffee. At a table beside them sat a young couple comprised of a man and a woman, and a little girl no older than three. The little girl screamed in delight. What caught her particular attention would be anyone's guess. Nicole looked over and smiled. "An opera singer in the making."

Beth was inspired by the child's spiky haircut. "Punk rock is a possibility."

"Can't see her dressed all in black."

"Look who's talking!"

"I thought you liked my color scheme?"

Beth always found Nicole's dress choices indicative of the woman's soul. "Black and white is not a color scheme. They're extremes in the spectrum with nothing in between."

"Green would suit her. Close to the color of your eyes."

Beth shifted her focus back to Nicole. "Nicki, have you thought of children? Of having a child?"

Nicole assessed Beth's question. It was apparent that this was not an easy query for her to make, nor would it be for Nicole to respond to. "Beth, I don't have the faith that it takes to bring a child into this world." Nicole gestured toward the newspaper. "Every day the world gets harsher. It's brutal. Too much can go wrong."

"You can't give up on life."

"I haven't. I'll let braver souls, like Tess, have the children. I'm fine watching from a distance."

Given Nicole's core belief in the goodness of humanity, Beth found it difficult to accept that she would be swayed by the harshness of the world. "Is that the only reason?"

"One way to guarantee I don't hurt a child is not to have a child."

Beth found the heartbreaking reason easier to reconcile with Nicole's life experience. "Who's to say you would?"

Nicole was unyielding. "Who's to say I won't?"

"Have you ever hurt a child?"

"I've never allowed myself to get close enough to do any harm."

"Nicki …"

Nicole interrupted. "Beth, I know where I come from. I know who I am. I know the rage I'm capable of. It's not worth the risk."

Having experienced Nicole's rage Beth knew better than to discount her partner's fear. The reality of Nicole's fear did not temper Beth's disappointment.

Nicole observed Beth as her gaze lingered on the little girl. "Beth, do you want a child?"

Beth looked over to Nicole. "Nicki, I never expected to have a love of my own, let alone a child."

Nicole reached over and placed her hand over Beth's. "Do you want a child?"

"We never discussed it."

"We are now. Do you want a little girl or boy of your own?"

Beth's gaze was drawn to the child once again. She spoke softly, giving voice to a new dream that had left an ache in her heart as she embraced Nicole's love for her. "Yes."

"Beth, I'm sorry."

"I don't blame you. And knowing how you feel, I can't ask you to consent to raising a child with me."

Nicole sat back. As young as a teenager she knew she would never conceive a child. She could not risk perpetuating the cruelty she had suffered at the hands of her unstable mother. The solution was easy. To her nothing was lost, but now a price was set. To deny parenthood was to deny Beth a child.

Beth reached out and took Nicole's withdrawn hand. "It may be for the best."

"How can you say that?"

"My childhood taught me a few things too. There are no guarantees."

Nicole held Beth's gaze. There was an underlying sincerity to her statement. Nicole would not pursue the subject further. She suspected that this one conversation was insufficient to temper Beth's desire. Nicole squeezed Beth's hand. Reassured, Beth leaned back and returned to her portion of the newspaper. Nicole did the same.

Beth completed reading an article about the latest court case addressing same-sex marriages. "Damn."

Nicole looked up from reading. "What?"

"Why don't the states just legalize civil unions?"

"Why does it matter?" Nicole said, unmoved.

Beth was astonished. "You're kidding, aren't you?"

This was a familiar argument to Nicole. She and Kate had sparred on the subject more than once. Nicole went on automatic pilot. "There is no reason for lesbians and gays to mimic marriage. Private industry is expanding fringe benefits to same-sex couples just to stay competitive. Outside of social security and tax disparities, most civil rights issues between two people can be addressed with the right legal papers. But that isn't why I object. There is an inherent bias against single people, period. Single people subsidize marriages and those who have children. I don't see why a caste system of couples and singles should be condoned by society."

Beth had never considered the disparity between singles and couples. It gave her brief pause. She chose to set it aside. "It's not just a civil rights issue. It's a public pronouncement of a commitment between two souls."

Nicole was well aware that Beth had sidestepped her argument. Nicole's eyes rested upon the cross hanging around her lover's neck. "Beth. Why don't you just admit, that to you, marriage is a breath away from a sacrament?"

Beth responded softly. "It is."

"I respect your beliefs. Please respect mine."

Beth felt a rising frustration. "You booked commitment celebrations at The Fields."

"Of course I did."

Beth was stern. "Good business."

Nicole tried not to smile. Her skills as a negotiator were at the forefront. She knew when an argument shifted from the factual and logical to the emotional, there was no point in arguing. Beth was transparent. Her only weapon was inferring, not too subtly, that Nicole was a hypocrite. "Yes, it was, but that isn't why I created The Fields and it isn't why I'm rebuilding. I want people, gay and straight, to have an inviting and safe place to go to meet friends, have a good meal, and dance. When they're in The Fields I don't care if they are celebrating a birthday, an anniversary or a bat mitzvah. Just as long as it's not the KKK's Annual White Sheet Awards ceremony."

Beth yielded. "I know." She had lost track of the argument. For the moment, she did not want to pursue the subject any further. Disheartened, she once again returned to the newspaper. In the course of a morning breakfast she learned that she and Nicole had two significant differences, and neither was inconsequential to Beth. Being with Nicole meant no blessing of their union before God, and no child. Beth's eyes stared at the newsprint. She could no longer read. She could only pretend to read.

CHAPTER 60

The hospital organized its Clinical Pastoral Education program by dividing the eight students into two groups of four. Each group met daily, Monday through Friday for ninety-minute discussions.

It was the Monday of the second week of CPE. With completion of the previous weeklong orientation, the chaplains were finally free to provide pastoral care. In addition to Beth, her group consisted of three divinity students: Luke Dale, a Baptist; Jamie Osborne, with the United Church of Christ; and Nathaniel Ethridge, a Methodist. The second group was comprised of two divinity students, Jerry Nystrom, a Lutheran, and Cynthia Bray, a Unitarian Universalist. Paul Lewis, a Catholic priest, and Christine Stuart, a Catholic lay minister, completed the second foursome.

Beth was impressed with the diversity of the students, although she noticed that non-Christian traditions were not represented. Pam and Anthony Stilton, the Associate CPE Supervisor, encouraged the students to meet in the Chaplains' Office before the workday began, to lunch together, and to close the day together, once again congregating in the Chaplains' Office.

Without hesitation the students chose to meet for lunch. A hospital cafeteria round table comfortably served the eight of them, so their lunches were often referred to as the Round Table. They conversed cautiously at first. Beth felt an ease with the students in her group not immediately shared with the other four. In her group, all their life stories had been shared. There was a place to begin a conversation.

She had felt some trepidation prior to sharing her life story. Acknowledging her relationship with Nicole was still new to her. Doing so in a religious community, no matter their commitment to receive one another with an open heart, infused her storytelling with an element of risk, of causing discomfort to those listening. She was forthcoming regarding her status with the Episcopal Church and the fact that she withheld the truth from Nicole. She also noted her break with her father and her reconciliation with her sister. Reflecting on the differences between sharing her story during her first CPE experience and this one, Beth realized that in the span of less than four years her life had been unimaginably altered. Her confidence that the change was for the better remained fragile, and she wondered whether her student peers had sensed the ambiguity she felt towards her life.

Beth had requested and was assigned the Oncology Unit. She would also share with Cynthia chaplaincy responsibilities for the hospital's two Intensive Care Units.

Cynthia's credentials were impressive. At age thirty-nine she left a successful nursing career to pursue the ministry, specifically chaplaincy. Her calling was not to take her away from a hospital setting, only to redefine her role within it.

Cynthia's affiliation with the Unitarian Universalist was comforting to Beth. Beth was well aware that the Unitarian Universalist Association was supportive of lesbians and gay men, to the point of approving ordination of lesbian and gay male clergy.

CHAPTER 61

Nicole left the den in search for a warm-up of her coffee. She spied Beth in the sunroom, where she sat motionless. But for her submissive posture, Nicole would have thought Beth intent upon something outside the panes of glass. Nicole kept watch waiting for some movement, some sign of life. Beth's uninterrupted stillness frightened Nicole. With Beth's back to her, it was impossible to study Beth's countenance.

Beth felt an unexpected hand on her shoulder. She jumped up from her seat, stood, and turned toward Nicole.

Nicole was taken aback. "I'm sorry. I didn't ..." Nicole's eyes caught sight of Beth's right hand. Beth held what to Nicole was a rosary. Nicole was confused.

Beth struggled for mental equilibrium. Her prayers had taken her to a private place not meant to be shared. She was unprepared for the jarring intrusion.

Nicole sought a quick retreat. "I was going to offer you a cup of tea."

"No. I'm fine. Thanks." Beth spoke in abrupt phrases.

"Beth." Nicole was at a loss. "I'm sorry I startled you."

Nicole stepped away. Beth looked down to her prayer beads. She wondered why she felt she should have been more careful to keep them from Nicole's view.

Nicole went to the kitchen and filled her coffee mug. She returned to the den and sat at her desk. She looked out toward the sunroom. It was hard for her to feel like an intruder in her own home; worse, to feel like an intruder in Beth's life.

CHAPTER 62

A number of chaplains sat in the Chaplain's lounge waiting for their small group sessions to begin.

Nathaniel entered. With uncharacteristic curtness, he said, "Turn on the TV."

Jerry looked up. "You could say please, brother."

Nathaniel's nervous demeanor caused Christine to reach for the remote control.

Nathaniel paced. "CNN. Channel 57."

Christine followed his instructions. Beth, Christine and Jerry sat in silence. Nathaniel continued to pace as a CNN reporter described the terrorist attack on the World Trade Center.

Nicole was working in the comfort of the den when the telephone ran. "Nicole Thera."

"Nicole. It's Brian Montgomery."

Nicole welcomed the call from her client. "Brian. How are you?"

"Do you have the television on?"

"No. Why?"

"Turn it on to CNN."

"Just a minute."

Nicole used her nearby remote control. She watched the video images from New York and listened to the commentators summarize what little was known. Two planes crashed into the World Trade Center within a matter of twenty minutes. It was no accident.

At the hospital the chaplains were mobilized to deal with the added stress felt by patients, family members and hospital staff due to the terrorist attack. The fear could not be easily arrested. People had family and friends in New York and Washington D.C. Others feared further attacks against United States citizens. Questions echoed throughout the hospital corridors. The first was simply a matter of identity. Who would do this? The second question cut through the temporal to the divine. Why? Why would someone do this? Why would God allow it to be done? The temporal question might someday be answered. The divine would challenge even the most devout.

Beth met Cindy at the ICU nurses' station. The sound of the televisions throughout all the patient rooms produced a cacophony of horror. A sickening trauma reverberated within the souls of those watching as the buildings crumbled. The estimated number of dead climbed. They included occupants and their rescuers in the World Trade Center, the planes in New York, Washington D.C. and Pennsylvania.

Cindy reported, "I called my brother, Frank. He said everyone in his office is in a state of shock. No one's working. They're all listening to the radio or watching TV. He said he tried to log on to CNN on the web but he keeps timing out because it's getting so many hits."

"I tried calling Nicki. Her private line was busy. I left her a voice mail."

"She travels for her work, doesn't she?"

"Yes, but she plans to be close to home until the Elysian Fields is rebuilt."

"Thank God for that."

Beth arrived home at the dinner hour. In the foyer were Nicole's garment bag and lap top computer case. "Nicki?"

From the den Nicole came to Beth. "Hey." She took Beth into an embrace, holding her dearly.

For a few moments Beth allowed herself the comfort of Nicole. "You're packed?"

"I'm going to D.C."

Beth pulled away. "What?"

"I've been getting calls from my clients all day."

"They've shut down air traffic."

Nicole's plans were set. "I'm driving."

Beth was incredulous. "You can't."

"It's safer than public transportation."

"Nicki, you can't go there. It's dangerous."

"Beth, my D.C. client had offices in the World Trade Center."

Beth paused for a moment. Her voice softened. "I'm sorry."

"I'll leave in the morning."

"No!"

"I have an obligation to my client."

"Not to get yourself killed! The terrorists are zealots. No one knows what they will do next."

"I know," Nicole said bitterly. "History keeps repeating itself, doesn't it?"

"What do you mean?"

"What people do in the name of God."

Beth shook her head. "This is evil."

"Yes it is. All too human. Souls fighting for their way of life."

"You can't condone what they've done."

"Of course I don't condone it. But that doesn't change the fact that the men who hijacked the planes had an incredible commitment to their cause. Just wait. They will be proclaimed martyrs."

Beth release Nicole. "They are not martyrs! Martyrs give up their own lives for a cause. They don't slaughter innocent people."

"To them it was a justifiable act of war."

"No, Nicki. We were not at war. Even if we were, in war there are rules."

Nicole knew better. "I wish that was true."

"How can you be so heartless?"

"Heartless?" Nicole protested.

"Have you been watching the news?"

The images of the collapsing towers were fused into Nicole's psyche. Had Beth not heard her? She had clients in the World Trade Center. Death had not come to strangers. Nicole knew the names and faces of more than one woman and man who in all likelihood were in the towers at the moment of impact. "Yes."

"It's tragic. Don't you feel it?"

Nicole felt her sorrow rise, a sorrow she had struggled to contain as reports of the ever-increasing death count progressed throughout the day. "Yes, I feel it. Today was tragic. Our country has finally had to face defeat on its own continent. It wouldn't have happened if we hadn't failed our moral duty."

"Don't." Beth's anger was acute.

"Open your eyes, Beth. The U.S. has intervened in foreign policy for generations. Our acts of self-interest don't just affect the powerful, they go to the hearts of the nations. The people bear the brunt of the pain. We exact a high price in our misguided campaigns to further our vision of a just and democratic society." Nicole was not finished. "Why do you think choosing death is a viable option? We have tried to strip these people of their dignity and their hope. What have they left to hold on to except their hatred of us? I blame the U.S. government more than I do the terrorists. We have done this to ourselves."

"How dare you! You have no idea of the pain people are feeling. You dismiss the death and destruction, and argue a reasonable cause. I don't give a damn about your easy political justifications. This isn't an amoral issue. What they did was immoral."

Beth hurt Nicole more deeply than she knew. Commentators and politicians alike, invited onto the broadcast airwaves to share their perspective of the crisis, had invoked morality and God with an easy conscious. Nicole saw Beth in her chaplain's blue jacket and she could no longer separate Beth from all the voices that had betrayed the public citizenry with their misguided rhetoric. Nicole had had enough. She wanted nothing to do with Beth's God and the morality ascribed to that God. She spoke in a frozen voice. "Tell me, Beth, what was the first cause?"

Beth was stunned into silence.

Nicole waited. She knew she had fired a missile that hit deep into Beth's faith. She knew it was unfair to enter a philosophical or theological debate in the near hours after the attack. As much as Nicole had contempt for the reality of hatred, hatred did exist. Hatred claimed the human heart as its abode. This day was testament of humanity's failure to arrest its greatest foe – itself. Nicole tasted the bitterness of that truth and she refused to pretend otherwise.

Beth was thrown into confusion. Nicole had asked the same question that Beth had heard repeatedly throughout the day, except she framed it in a way that accused God of immorality. Beth had no answer. She had come home longing for the safety and warmth Nicole had always promised her, if not by word, then by deed. Instead, the harshness of the day was compounded. "Go then." Beth walked to one side of Nicole and into the kitchen.

Nicole watched, taking no pleasure in what she had done. Nicole wanted nothing more than the silence that came with solitude. "I've changed my mind. I'm leaving tonight."

Driving the interstate, Nicole continued an on-going internal debate whether to call Beth. She understood Beth's fear, but only to a degree. Life must go on. The country was in a state of shock. Still, it could not afford to become despondent. She had her taste of destruction with the Elysian Fields fire. She had been financially prepared for the loss. She had her business recovery plan in order. But admittedly, she was not emotionally prepared for the devastation of all that had grounded her adult life. But because of the business recovery plan she had a reference point. She followed her own reasoned thinking, documented for just an occasion. She acted through the pain because if she hoped to survive she had no choice. Nicole was driving to D.C. because life went on. It did not matter if a business was fire bombed or the World Trade Center was destroyed. Life went on even as symbols crumbled.

Nicole's cell phone rang. She sighed. "Hello."

"Nicole. It's Brian."

Nicole set aside her disappointment. "Brian. What have you heard?"

"I don't know what I'm suppose to feel. We've accounted for five of our twelve employees. Right now there is no reason to believe the rest survived. Nicole, Carrie didn't make it."

Nicole had tried to prepare herself for the loss of her friend. "You sure?"

"I spoke to John. She was going into the office. We checked her electronic appointment calendar from our back up files. All her morning meetings were internal."

"How are John and the kids?"

"Devastated. Aren't we all?"

"I'm sorry, Brian."

"Are you still planning on driving out?"

"I'm on the road. I figured I might as well. I wasn't going to get any sleep tonight."

"Check in with me tomorrow."

"I'll call you mid-morning."

"God bless you."

"Take care, Brian."

CHAPTER 63

September 12, 2001

A message awaited Beth when she arrived home at the end of her workday.

"Beth, It's Nicki. I'm in Washington. I'm staying at The Jefferson. You can call my cell phone or call me at the hotel. The number is (202) 347-2200, Room 416. Beth. I'm sorry about the way we left things yesterday. It was a tough day for both of us. I love you. Be safe."

Beth listened to the recording with relief. She said a silent 'thank you' for Nicole's well being. In spite of this, Beth's anger did not subside. She was not ready to speak to Nicole.

CHAPTER 64

September 13, 2001- Noon

The chaplains met for lunch. The aftermath of the terrorist attack heightened their need for community. Their discussion had begun as a generic comparison of the individuals to whom they were providing pastoral care. Soon, the discussion shifted. The subject became the members of the Round Table.

Jamie, a second year seminary student, clarified a previous statement. "My point is, that in spite of our diversity, we are all Christians."

Cindy looked at the youngest member of the group. "Don't assume we all agree on what it means to be a Christian, or that our differences aren't important."

"Well, where do you want to start?" Jerry eagerly pursued the proposed forum for the exchange of ideas.

Nathaniel did not match Jerry's enthusiasm. "I'm not sure I want to." He garnered everyone's attention. His black skin glistened in the light with a sheen of perspiration. "I'm sorry, but I came here to learn to be a chaplain, not to get into theological debates."

Jerry was not deterred. "But isn't this a great opportunity to learn about each other's faiths? That is one of the reasons the CPE program tries to bring in diversity." By word and gesture Jerry had quickly exercised a birthright of leadership no one else was privy to. Each lunch gathering he purposely staked a generous claim on a portion of the table space in front of him, spreading his lunch items widely and storing his cafeteria tray at the center.

"I agree. Being able to articulate our faith can only help us in our ministry," Jamie said gently.

"How about when we disagree?" Luke raised his coffee cup to his lips as he waited for a response.

Jerry continued to advocate his vision for the Round Table rules of engagement. "Respect. The same respect we give the patients and their families and friends."

"As long as our respect doesn't end with Christianity," said Cindy.

"The atheists don't ask to see us." Jerry laughed. "That's why the hospital has that little question in the admittance form. 'Do you want the chaplains to stay the hell out of your room?'"

"Funny thing is how much we have in common with atheists," said Luke.

Jamie glanced his way. "I can understand you saying that about Jews and Muslims and Hindus, but what do we have in common with people who deny God?"

"For them there is no God, so life happens and you accept it and go on. For us, God has a wisdom beyond our understanding, so life happens and you accept it and go on."

Jerry offered a caveat. "If you believe in predestination."

"Since when? I believe in free will, and I still struggle to accept the wisdom of God."

Jerry swept his hair back, not making any effort to hide his frustration with the direction in which Luke was leading the conversation.

"God made a decision to give us free will and because of that, the World Trade Towers are destroyed, and I'm left to try to figure out why," said Luke.

Nathaniel's voice cut through the conversation. "Where's your faith?"

Jerry took advantage of the challenge. "Nathaniel's got a point. You are kidding yourself if you think you can reason your way into explaining what happened on Tuesday."

Paul's low, gentle voice provided a sense of calm. "I feel like we've been thrown back to the thirteenth century. Bonaventure versus Aquinas."

"Don't forget Augustine," said Jerry.

As a layperson, Christine's religious education did not compare to her peers. She leaned back overwhelmed. "Okay, I admit I'm fuzzy on the distinction."

Paul took the lead. "Bonaventure relied on traditional orthodoxy originally influenced by Plato. Plato acknowledged the existence of the divine and the incompleteness of the material world and our ability to know it. By the thirteenth century, the Crusades had opened up Western Europe to the East, including the works of Muslim and Jewish thinkers who had been commenting on the writings of Aristotle. Aristotle argued that mankind, with the information provided by the senses, could use reason to identify truths that held not only for the specific, but also, for the universal. So, relying on Aristotle, the argument was raised that we could use reason to better know God. That's Aquinas."

"Where's Augustine?"

"With Bonaventure."

"Augustine's argument was circular and left free will out of the equation. Contemporary theologians don't give it much merit," said Luke.

Paul continued, "But remember, as much as Aquinas tried to use reason in his theology, he was the first to admit that ultimately some things could only be known through God's grace."

"Like the existence of God." The table occupants' attention was drawn to Beth.

"Do you believe that is why your partner doesn't believe in God? She hasn't been given God's grace?" Jerry's comment was not well received by his peers. He was oblivious to the effect he was having.

Beth felt a rising defensiveness. "Nicki acknowledges the divine in all humanity."

Christine was curious. "How has she been dealing with the terrorist attack?"

"Nicki left for Washington D.C. Tuesday night to help a client who had offices in the World Trade Center. We haven't connected except by voice mail."

"How did she get to D.C.?" Cindy asked, impressed.

"She drove."

"If she finds the divine in all of us, does she believe we are inherently good?" asked Christine.

"We are good. But she also acknowledges that we are imperfect."

Jerry interjected, "That's the evil."

"But that isn't necessarily how I, as a Christian, define evil," Jamie argued.

"How do you define evil?" Christine asked, freely sharing her struggle to comprehend the nuance of faiths.

"Separation from God."

"God who is perfect," Jerry stated in triumph, having made his point.

Nathaniel attempted to be heard. "Adam and Eve. Before the fall ..."

"If they had been perfect there wouldn't have been a fall. We were made imperfect by God," Cindy said, trying to shake the foundation on which the argument stood.

"What you call imperfect, I call free will," said Luke.

Cindy remained constant. "I'm sorry but I take Genesis as symbolic. I read it as allegory, not history. Sin, and at its worst, evil, are part of the human condition."

"It's the Bible. The word of God." Nathaniel pressed his minority opinion.

His peers once again paused. It was Jamie who spoke first. "I hate to break up the fun. But it's one o'clock."

Beth and Cindy took their cafeteria trays in hand and rose to their feet. Cindy whispered to her companion, "If this is a taste of our ecumenical camaraderie, I might spend more of my lunch break in the library, away from the fray."

Beth smiled for the first time that day. "Don't be surprised if I'm sitting right beside you."

CHAPTER 65

September 13, 2001

Beth was called to Oncology to provide Holy Communion for an elderly Catholic patient – Roberto Chavez. At the nurses' station she solicited the assistance of one of the Catholic nurses. Catholic doctrine allowed a non-Catholic to recite the liturgy, but not to administer the Host.

Upon completing the ritual Beth thanked the nurse for her assistance as the latter returned to her duties. Roberto lay back against his bed and closed his eyes. Beth could see the furrows in his brow relax. She knew that it did not matter whether she was ordained or not, as an Episcopalian she would always need to seek out a Catholic to assist in offering communion to a Catholic. Still, she mourned the loss of her priesthood. The power, the grace of the sacrament was a mystery she could never reason. Beth felt the loss of not attending a service, of not participating in communion after she left St. Ann's.

Beth closed Roberto's bed curtain before leaving him to rest.

"You really believe that will help?" a gravel voice said to Beth.

"Excuse me?" Beth gave the thin male patient whose bed was next to Roberto's her consideration. The patient was in his mid-forties. His salt and pepper hair was disheveled. He wore his blue and white vertical patterned pajama top open, revealing his yellowed skin and pronounced ribs.

"Praying. Do you really think someone's listening?" The patient pointed to Roberto's curtained bed.

Beth looked over the bed headboard where the patient's name was listed – Michael Briggs. "Yes, I do."

"God mustn't think much of us then."

"What makes you say so?"

"A lot of unanswered prayers." He smiled wryly.

Beth was emotionally drained. She attempted to gracefully separate herself from the patient. "Is there anything I can do for you?"

The man laughed cynically. "I've got inoperable cancer. What on earth could you do for me?"

"I'm sorry."

Michael reacted to her sympathy with contempt. "Why are you sorry? You don't know me."

Beth deflected his angry question away from herself. "Are you in pain?"

"At least I'm going to die soon. Not like all the poor bastards that are living in this God-forsaken place."

Beth was tired, too tired not to engage. "God hasn't forsaken us."

"Is that all you got, a religious cliché? Go on praying and see what good it does you ... or me. Tell you what, Reverend ... come back in a few weeks. This bed'll be empty and I'll be dead and buried. That'll be my proof that I'm right and you're wrong."

"Excuse me." Beth felt a strangling darkness surround her. She did not have the strength to stand against it. She stepped out and walked down the corridor until she was clear of the patient's sight. She stopped and leaned her back against the wall. She closed her eyes and bowed her head. She prayed. "Please. Where are you?"

CHAPTER 66

September 13, 2001 – Evening

The apartment was unlit. Beth sat on the sunroom couch staring out the window, seeing nothing. The telephone's ringing intruded upon her much desired seclusion. She got up and walked to the living room where the cordless phone rested.

"Hello."

"Hi."

Beth recognized Nicole's voice. Her greeting was devoid of warmth. "Nicki."

Nicole spoke cautiously, "How are you?"

"It's been a hard week." Beth paused, trying to muster a grain of concern. "How's D.C.?"

"Tense. People are afraid. They're also grieving. How is it at the hospital?"

"The same."

"I may not be able to come home for a couple of weeks."

"I didn't expect you would," Beth said coolly.

Nicole heeded Beth's reserve. "Beth. I'm sorry. Tuesday wasn't the time to say the things I said."

Bitterly, Beth cast Nicole's apology aside. "But you still believe what you said was true?"

Nicole realized Beth was not going to allow them to move beyond their disagreement with ease. "Yes." Beth offered Nicole no response. Against her better judgment, Nicole attempted to explain herself. "Beth, I don't condemn religion, only how some people pervert it for their own purposes. And like I said, Tuesday wasn't about religion, it was about foreign policy."

"Nicki. I don't have much time. I'm going to a prayer service tonight."

"I understand." Nicole attempted to shift their conversation toward the mundane, seeking comfort in the ordinary course of living. "Do you have plans for the weekend?"

"I don't have much free time. I'm on duty Saturday."

Nicole found Beth's remoteness disheartening. Dejected, she chose to end the conversation. She would not presume her welcome given all the evidence to the contrary. "I won't keep you any longer." Nicole paused for a heartbeat. "I love you, Beth."

Beth could not echo the sentiment. "Take care, Nicki."

Nicole waited for the words that did not come. She held the telephone receiver with diminishing hope. All anticipation ended when she heard a click at the other end of the line. Beth's severance of their connection rent Nicole's heart. Nicole helplessly set the receiver down. She would return to her work. The importance of her work was the only reason she had to lift herself up from the rubble of a world one step closer to total annihilation.

CHAPTER 67

September 14, 2001 – Noon

Beth and Cindy joined the other chaplains at the Round Table. Cindy whispered to Luke. "So, what's the subject of the day?"

Luke responded, "Heresies."

"Jerry must have read a book," said Cindy.

Luke laughed.

Beth ate quietly, listening to the variety of heresies her fellow chaplains identified and commented upon.

"It all started with the Trinity," Jerry said, continuing his unelected leadership role.

"I hate to correct you, Jerry, but the first heresy had nothing to do with the Trinity." Paul placed a gauntlet before the young seminarian.

"Oh?"

"The first heresy was between Christ and the Jews. The issue was the Law."

Luke was poised for an argument. "Paul is right. That was the crux of St. Paul's ministry to the Gentiles. Did the converts have to become Jews before they could follow the teachings of the Messiah?"

"Fine. Then it was the Trinity," Jerry asserted.

"Wrong." Jamie comfortably argued the facts of history. "It was the Gnostics and the Marcions. That led to the creation of the Canon and the 'symbol of faith.'"

"The Apostles' Creed?" asked Christine.

"Yes," said Jamie.

Nathaniel joined in. "After that Novatian challenged Cyprian about readmission of the lapsed to the Church, and it was at that same time that Arius argued that the Word was not God. The Council of Nicea decided both issues."

"And that wasn't until 325," said Luke.

"And from then on the Trinity dominated the heresies until Luther." Jerry seemed determined to win a point.

"Hold it," Cindy protested. "You're missing two heretics that are close to my heart. Wycliffe and Hus both preceded Luther in arguing the primacy of Scripture."

"Yes, and Wycliffe also disagreed with the doctrine of transubstantiation." Jamie looked over to Paul. "Sorry, Paul."

Paul waved his hand dismissively. "We are all heretics. It's just a matter of perspective."

Jerry's dominancy had been arrested with glee by the Round Table. Not to be thwarted, he altered the focus to the one who had yet to speak. "Beth. You haven't said anything."

Cindy, who sat to Beth's right, placed her hand on Beth's arm. Beth looked up. Cindy nodded over to Jerry. Jerry goaded, "Living with Nicole. What's your opinion?"

Beth had yet to understand why Jerry chose to make her a target. She tried not to engage, but he did not make it easy. No matter Beth's current feelings toward her partner, she would not allow anyone to denigrate Nicole, especially when they did it out of ignorance. "Jerry, have you opened a dictionary lately?"

"Why do you ask?"

"Because you seem to think Nicole is a heretic. A heretic is someone who dissents from an established church's accepted doctrine or belief. Since Nicole isn't in the Church, she can't be described as a heretic. I, on the other hand, am a heretic because even though in my heart I am still an Episcopalian, I don't agree with the Episcopal Church's position on homosexuality and I hope one day I'll speak out, without hesitation, against it." Beth leaned forward. "You would also be wrong to call Nicole a pagan because that is technically defined as a follower of a polytheistic religion, or someone who has little or no religion or whose primary cares are for the sensual and for material goods. Nicole is not polytheistic. She has a faith she believes in profoundly and though I can swear to her ability to make the most of the sensual pleasures in life, she does not, in spite of her wealth, dwell on material belongings. Now if you call Nicole a heathen, you might be close, because a heathen is defined as an unconverted member of a people or nation who does not acknowledge the God of the Bible, which Nicole admits she is. The only problem is that Nicole takes exception to the secondary definition of a heathen as an uncivilized or irreligious person. No one who has met Nicole would describe her as uncivilized and like I already said, she is a woman of deep faith. Got that?"

Beth's succinct lesson left Jerry speechless. She had never spoken with such vehemence at the Round Table. He leaned back against his chair. The other chaplains struggled to suppress their smiles.

Beth did not wait for an answer. Having lost her appetite, she stood up, taking her cafeteria tray. Christine joined her.

"Sending Jerry back to the dictionary was great," said Christine.

"Why shouldn't I? Nicki did the same thing to me."

"She did?"

Beth laughed lightly. "Yes. Why else would I have the definitions down so pat?"

"Because you looked them up yourself?"

"There is always a reason behind the learning." Beth knew that in her life with Nicole that fact would forever be true.

Christine paused at the dish collection area. "Beth, I have to admit that I really don't know much about Christianity other than Catholicism. I'm starting to enjoy the Round Table … hearing all the different Christian perspectives. I can understand how we've come to believe differently. What I don't understand, and I do want to, is Nicole's faith. How does she describe it?"

Beth placed her tray down on the kitchen conveyor belt. "She doesn't really. When push comes to shove she'll say she's a materialistic pantheist. Few people understand what that means and I know that, for Nicki, it's still an incomplete statement."

"Materialistic?"

"In terms of the soul. She doesn't see her existence beyond life as she knows it."

"No afterlife?"

"No afterlife," said Beth.

"Then where does she find her hope?"

"In the good. In spite of everything, she still can see the good."

"How on earth did you two get together?"

In the mirror that was Christine's eyes, Beth had a glimpse of how incredible her life with Nicole could seem to others. She smiled. "That's a long story."

The chaplains walked back to their units. Christine chose to once again broach the subject of Nicole. "Beth, what attracted you to Nicole?"

Beth considered all that was Nicole. Her tone carried the gentle regard she held for her lover. "Nicki is smart and caring. She's intense and gentle. She's strong and on rare occasions she's even strong enough to let me see her when she's vulnerable. She hasn't asked anything from me except respect."

Christine asked, "Why wouldn't you respect her?"

Beth saw in Christine a vision of the world that could only be found in the exceptional souls of those who understood that humanity was comprised not of strangers, but of brothers and sisters. "That's a good question."

CHAPTER 68

September 15, 2001

Beth had a relatively quiet day alone at the hospital. During the evening she walked through the university campus. She found the grounds beautiful and intoxicating. Theological scholarship at U.C. awaited her. She looked forward. In a year's time she, too, would be a student.

Even though she had not actively participated in The Round Table discussions, Beth was fascinated with the broad scope of subjects chosen and the opinions revealed by her fellow chaplains. The previous day's joint rebuff of Jerry gave her hope that the playing field could become comfortable for all participants.

No one had been able to explain Jerry's behavior toward her. From what she could gather he was a capable chaplain. She hesitated in considering intolerance as the cause. However, she was not willing to discount the possibility without first researching the Lutheran-Missouri Synod position toward homosexuality. As she discovered, the Synod's position was clear. Homosexuality was a sin, one sin among the many sins of humanity. It was the Church's intent to uphold the teachings of Christian Scripture. The Church argued that homosexuality was a distortion of God's intention of having man and woman live in marriage. Still, the Church's position included a statement that it must resist any reaction of persecution and ostracism. If Jerry was a good Missouri Synod Lutheran, Beth was right to expect nothing less than courtesy.

The thought of whether to propose the subject of homosexuality at a Round Table discussion passed through her mind. She wondered how her peers would address the subject when it lay bare before them; when she sat present, an embodiment of what many called a sin. Jerry's denomination was not the only one at the table that took exception to full inclusion of homosexuals in the Church.

The juxtaposition of Jerry and Nicole was telling. It sometimes seemed Nicole disagreed with every position Beth took, but at least she tried her best to do so respectfully. Instead of sweeping Beth's arguments aside, Nicole challenged them directly. Nicole was also apt to further her study of opposing positions, open to the potential that within them lay an insight of merit. Jerry, Beth suspected, was quick to close or ignore a book that disturbed him – contrary to Nicole's effort to seek the book out and, with extraordinary skill, attempt to integrate the knowledge it held with the store of knowledge she already possessed.

CHAPTER 69

September 16, 2001 – Chicago

    Beth sipped her coffee in the sunroom. Work had filled her days, distracting her from Nicole's absence. She had this day to herself. Nicole was somewhere in Washington. It had been more than two days since they spoke Given the reception Nicole had received when she called, Beth could not fault her for not calling or sending an email. Beth reached for the telephone.

CHAPTER 70

September 16, 2001 – Washington D.C.

Brian Montgomery had insisted that Nicole take the day off. He had encouraged her to get away from the city. After a valiant protest Nicole had relented. She had decided to drive to Shenandoah National Park. The park was a treasure, one she had escaped to on numerous occasions when her D.C. consulting assignments allowed.

Nicole parked the Jeep. She swung her backpack over her shoulder and took to the trail. Her reward upon reaching the isolated trail's end would be a magnificent waterfall, ninety feet in height.

As she hiked, she began to feel the first hint of a headache. Unfortunately, the fresh air did not soothe the pulsating pain. In fact, she felt it intensifying. She reached the waterfall with a sense of relief. She would rest, eat, and hope for physical renewal. She lay against a tree with a clear view of the stream of water falling into the base pool before flowing down further into the valley. The arrested power reminded her of the Lake Michigan shoreline. The waters fell long and hard; yet survived intact, within the embrace of an essence similar to itself and yet unique in its own right.

Nicole closed her eyes and allowed the sounds of the waterfall to carry her away from her pain. The transition to a union with Beth had its difficult moments, and yet, Nicole's longing was for Chicago, Hyde Park, the apartment, Beth – all that meant home.

Thirsty she opened her eyes and reached for her water bottle. A wave of nausea struck her. "Damn." She was physically worsening. She felt numbness traveling down her left arm and hand. These symptoms were new to her. The headache sharpened. She involuntarily raised her right hand to her head, dropping her water bottle in the process.

CHAPTER 71

September 17, 2001 – Washington D.C.

Nicole lay in her private hospital room. She was enjoying the relative quiet of the late morning. All the ordered tests completed, her doctors were able to diagnose her condition and take the necessary steps to stabilize her health. She felt good.

The bedside telephone rang. "Nicole Thera."

"Nicki. It's Kate."

"Hey."

"How are you feeling?"

"Better. I'm going to be released later today."

As holder of Nicole's medical durable power of attorney, hospital staff had informed Kate of Nicole's admittance. However, given Nicole's lucidity, doctors had no cause to make Kate privy to Nicole's final evaluation. "Is that a good idea?"

"I told you I was admitted for observation. Nothing more."

"They could keep you another day and make sure they got your medication right this time."

Nicole smiled to herself. "Are you in the mood for a malpractice suit?"

"Pro bono."

"Down, tiger!"

Kate renewed an equally important subject. "Have you spoken to Beth?"

"Not yet."

"Will you please tell me again why you haven't called her?"

"I've got my reasons."

"She's a big girl. She can handle this. For God's sake she was with you after your surgery."

"Beth has enough to deal with at the hospital right now. If it was serious I would tell her."

"On the other hand, since your diagnosis isn't serious ... "

"Kate!"

"Nicki!"

Nicole reverted to an old plea. "Be a friend, will you?"

"I am, or haven't you noticed?"

Nicole gave Kate her due. With Nicole's return to Chicago, Kate had been on remarkably good behavior. She had eased up on her not too subtle critiques and had shown sincere warmth toward Beth. "I've noticed."

"When are you coming home?"

"I'm hoping to leave next Thursday. I'm making a quick stop to see Tess. I'll be home by Friday."

"Damned if you're driving," said Kate.

"I'm not leaving the Jeep here indefinitely."

"Arrangements can be made."

"Getting a flight is still near impossible," Nicole rationalized. "My doctors agreed it would be okay as long as I don't have a reoccurrence of my symptoms."

"Same doctors who gave you your original prescription?"

"Which worked fine for ten months. Give them some credit."

"All right." Kate sighed in resignation. "Now, don't give me any more reasons to worry about you."

"Wouldn't think of it."

"Good. Call me tomorrow."

"Will do."

"And Nicki."

"Yeah."

"Call Beth."

Nicole returned the telephone receiver to its cradle. She would wait until she was discharged to call home.

CHAPTER 72

September 17, 2001 – Evening

Beth sat at Nicole's desk, holding her prayer beads in her right hand. Their personal line rang. Beth pushed the button on Nicole's desk phone and picked up the receiver. "Hello."

"Hi.".

"Nicki. Where have you been? I tried your cell phone and kept on being told it was either out of the calling zone or not in service. I spoke to your hotel's desk clerk. All he would tell me was that you were seen leaving yesterday morning."

"I'm sorry. I took a drive to Shenandoah National Park. I knew I was out of the calling zone and turned the cell phone off. I forgot to turn it back on."

"Why didn't you call last night?"

"By the time I got your message it was late," Nicole lied.

"Next time wake me."

"Hopefully there won't be a next time."

Beth leaned back in Nicole's desk chair, feeling Nicole's comforting presence where there had been growing restlessness. "Are things better in D.C.?"

"Not really. I went to Shenandoah because Brian Montgomery, the V.P. of Operations, insisted I take the day off. It's not going to be better here for quite a while, and it will never be the same."

Beth closed her eyes, imagining her partner. She spoke tenderly. "Nicki, I love you. You can be maddening, but I still love you."

Nicole bowed her head, humbly accepting the grace of having Beth in her life. "Don't stop. I need you, Beth."

"When are you coming home?"

"Depends. I might be able to drive home on Thursday. If I do, I can stay only for a few days before flying back East."

"New York?"

"Boston is also a possibility."

Beth anticipated Nicole's extended absences. Contrary to her resolve to be supportive, her voice carried an admonishing tone. "Nicki."

"Beth, I have to do this. Not all my clients have their business continuation plans in order. They are fighting for survival. And even those that weren't directly hurt by the attack are doing everything they can to catch up before something else happens."

Beth sobered. "Do you think the attacks will continue?"

"I don't know." Nicole felt she was living in a different dimension. The issues she was addressing with her clients went beyond the pale of her management experience. "If someone had told me a week ago that terrorists were going to highjack and fly two commercial airplanes into the World Trade Center towers, I would have asked what movie script they had been reading."

"It is all so fantastic," Beth echoed. "I still find it hard to believe."

Nicole longed for Beth. "I miss you."

"I miss you, too." Beth yearned to replace her mind's image of Nicole with flesh and blood. "Come home, Nicki."

"Count on me for dinner Friday night."

"Promise."

"I'll do my best, Beth."

"I love you, Nicki. I'll see you Friday."

Setting the telephone down, Nicole looked out her hotel window to the Washington D.C. cityscape. Her life continued to change in unimaginable ways. She was no different than the men and women who, having no choice, strove to recapture a sense of normality in their lives in spite of the all-encompassing uncertainty they were experiencing. The anonymity of being just one more person in the city, just another person in the country had been swept away. A common identity was coalescing under the pressure of a common enemy – fear. Nothing in her worldview gave her reason to be optimistic. She narrowed her vision, focusing upon a limited geography, the landscape that encompassed Chicago, Ann Arbor, Washington D.C., Boston, and to her heartbreak, New York. Her ability to make a difference was limited. Her efforts would be reserved to helping those she held dear.

CHAPTER 73

September 21, 2001

Nicole arrived in Chicago by late Friday morning. With Beth working at the hospital she took advantage of her free time to go to Chamberlain Development. Jason entered the design department. Nicole stood beside his son, Alex, and the development's primary architect, Laura Morales. "Nicole, do you think you might be able to give me a few minutes?"

"I don't know, Jason. Alex and Laura have me under a tight timeline."

"I think we can spare you for a few minutes," quipped Alex.

Jason responded in kind. "That is very generous of you, son."

Nicole and Jason walked down the corridor toward his office. Jason placed his hand on Nicole's arm. "How are you feeling?"

"Good."

"You gave me quite a scare. Have you thought of slowing down?"

"You may not believe me but I have."

"Well, your pace puts the rest of us to shame."

"Jason, in all due modesty, I'm good at what I do. I don't put in as many hours as some people may think."

"So, I've imagined all the twelve hour days you've worked on the development."

"The truth is, right now I'm not ready to go home."

Jason paused. "I'm sorry."

"No." Nicole shook her head. "It's not like that. Beth is working until 4:30. And there is something I need to tell her. I'm working up the courage."

"Your health scare?"

"There is something else." Nicole proceeded down the hall.

"Well, I'm confident you'll get through it. You are one of the most daring women I've ever known."

"Thank you, but taking risks in the business world doesn't compare to the personal."

"I wasn't thinking of your business acumen. Beth is a lovely young woman. Loving someone with a religious vocation must have its own unique challenges."

"Loving Beth is the easiest thing I've ever done, and it's also the hardest. There is nothing superficial about her. Her faith is deeper than anything I can fathom."

"Then you can be confident that whatever you need to say to her, she'll have her faith to help her."

"May I ask you a personal question?"

"Of course. This seems to have become a personal conversation after all." They had reached Jason's office. "Come in."

"You loved your wife?"

Jason walked around to his desk chair. He motioned for Nicole to take a seat opposite him. "Very much."

Nicole sat in one of the two available chairs. "It must have been difficult to lose her?"

Jason's countenance grew serious. "Maggie's breast cancer was in its advanced stages when she was diagnosed. Chemo may have brought her a few months more, but that wasn't how she wanted to live or die. So, the doctors managed her pain. I gave Alex the run of the shop, and Maggie and I spent her remaining four months together. Every day I lost a little bit of her and every day I got a little bit more of her. I wasn't prepared for her death. Nothing could prepare me for that last breath she took." Jason looked away, out his office window. "I cried. I didn't stop crying until after her funeral. It's been seven years and I still cry for her. Maggie was so alive. She begged me to live on." He smiled. "She asked only one favor and that was that I wouldn't end up with a woman my daughter's age for at least two years after her death. After that she said all bets were off and she wouldn't feel I had tarnished her dignity by going off with a filly."

"You haven't remarried."

Jason reached for a photograph frame from his desk and offered it to Nicole. "Her name is Katherine. She's five years younger than I am. Maggie would approve. We've known each other for three years now. Katherine's divorced and doesn't want to remarry. I'm happy to have her. I would like the ring but I can do without it."

Nicole studied the photograph of the attractive woman. "She's lovely." She returned the photograph to Jason.

Jason looked at the photograph thoughtfully, and then returned it to its place on his desk. "Now tell me. Why do you ask?"

Nicole had followed Jason's gaze out the window. She wondered how differently they saw the world on the other size of the pane. She wondered how the loss of a loved one tinted the survivor's vision. "I can't seem to get a grasp on the future."

"Then don't. Maggie proved to me that the only future you need is the next breath you take."

For Nicole there was a crucial difference between herself and Margaret Chamberlain. "She knew. I don't."

"We all know, we just don't know when. I may be presumptuous, but I think you have an opportunity to turn your illness into an asset. Maggie told me she experienced life more vividly once she came to accept her diagnosis. In some ways, the closer she came to death the more alive she felt. Nicole, by saying this to you I don't mean to infer that you would be right to live expecting your imminent death. You can still learn the lesson and have a very long life."

Nicole leaned forward in her chair. "Jason. You've misunderstood. I'm not frightened for myself."

CHAPTER 74

September 21, 2001

It was mid-afternoon and Nicole wanted to make one more connection before returning home. She had called Jacob to set a coffee date. With Liza's blessing, they walked to the neighborhood diner together. Given the time of day there were few customers. They chose a secluded booth.

Jacob removed his pipe and tobacco bag from his pocket. Nicole pointed to the 'No-Smoking' sign. Jacob grimaced and returned the tobacco bag to his pocket. He then placed the pipe between his lips, clearly enjoying the familiar comfort the instrument gave him. They spoke casually.

Nicole gave an accounting of her inopportune interruption of Beth at prayer.

"Are you sure they weren't Anglican prayer beads?" asked Jacob.

"Never heard of them. How does a Jew know so much about Christians?"

Jacob laughed. "You seem concerned. Why?"

"I don't know."

"Yes, you do."

Nicole raised her coffee cup and took a swallow. What in fact did disturb her about that moment? "It was all so unexpected. Beth's reaction was so strong."

"She was in deep prayer."

"I can't share that with her."

The truth resonated between Jacob and Nicole. "No. I suppose you cannot. Nicole, Beth is very faithful to God. She loves God in a way you will never be able to understand."

"She loves her God." Nicole qualified.

Jacob leaned forward over the table and slapped Nicole's arm. "Don't make me ashamed of you."

"What?"

"Do not be jealous of Beth's love for God. If you take that love from her you will make her far less the woman she is. Beth will not be the woman you have grown to love."

"I know."

"No, you don't."

Nicole glared at Jacob.

Jacob echoed, "You do not know, Nicole."

"I have reverence for life."

"You have no God. When you speak of the divine you speak of the sacredness in all of us. It is the beauty of God's creation and I will not argue with your vision. But it is divinity on an equal plane with your self. That is not Beth's God. Hers, as mine, is a higher power. God is beyond and greater than Beth. Beth prays to God. What she prays, I do not know. Nor do you, I might add. So do not presume. Prayer is too intimate an act to reason. If you must know, ask her."

Nicole set her coffee cup down with a clatter. "I didn't expect this."

"Then you are a fool." Jacob waited for Nicole's retort. It did not come. He gentled. "You told me yourself, Beth did not leave her faith. She left the Church. I believe without her church she needs her faith more than ever. Of course she prays. That is who she is. There is nothing to prevent you from talking to her about her prayer. Tell me, have you ever told Beth of your prayer? Do you still say it?"

"I say it, but it's not a prayer in the same sense as Beth's prayers."

"Does Beth know you say it?"

"I've never …" Nicole's voice drifted to silence. She did not share what Jacob called her prayer. To Nicole the words were a challenge to uphold her moral ideals. They were not a call to a god.

"So, you resent her prayer said privately, quietly, when she thought you were in the den and yet as you sat in the den you could have very well been saying your own prayer without her knowledge."

"I do not resent that she prays … Jacob, I feel a distance between us."

"Do not blame God. I believe you are more comfortable with Beth as a scholar than as a priest. Beth, the scholar, allows you to maintain an academic distance to her theology."

To her chagrin, Nicole accepted Jacob's assessment. "Do you and Liza … do you have conversations with her like you do with me?"

"It is different. There is no embarrassment."

"I'm not embarrassed."

Jacob placed his hand over Nicole's. "I do not mean to hurt you."

"Jacob. Tell me. What is the difference?"

"The godless people I have met are pale to me. There is a dullness. If I mention God they give me a perplexed look. They think I am ridiculously disillusioned. Maybe, just a dupe. I ask them what is meaningful to them. They speak of the material. I cannot help but feel they are not experiencing life to the fullest. I do not mention God again because I have seen their hesitation and I prefer to avoid it. With Liza, and the members of Temple, praise to God slips from the tongue as naturally as water flowing down a mountain spring. With you, my Nicole, I stand at the river's edge, never carried upon it. You speak of the divine and I can see that it is an august divinity you have found.

But, it is still not my personal God. I speak to you about theology. I am more comfortable speaking to Beth about God."

"So, there is nothing I can do."

"You have a lovely home. It was Liza who mentioned to me as we came home from our dinner with you and Beth that she saw no cross other than the one Beth wore. It surprised her. And I admit, it surprised me as well."

"Beth has never mentioned it."

"No doubt, out of respect to your beliefs."

"Jacob, she knows I accept her faith."

"Do you affirm it?" challenged Jacob.

"Yes."

"How often?"

"Jacob." Nicole was in no mood to account for her acts of affirmation.

"I am serious, Nicole. Have you attended service with her?"

"When we went to Holy Hill."

Jacob discounted the effort. "A Catholic service where she could not partake of the Eucharist. It has been a year, has it not?"

"She hasn't asked me to join her."

"Must she ask? Haven't you done things for Beth simply because it makes her happy?"

"Yes."

"Why must Beth's faith be different? What would gratify her more than having you beside her when she worships? It is not as if you are being any less true to your own beliefs. I am not talking about conversion. I am simply talking about sharing. Nicole, for heaven's sake, Beth has left the Church. Can you not conceive how shaken she must feel?"

Nicole hated to admit Beth's reluctance to confide in her. "She doesn't talk to me about leaving the Church."

"And it is more comfortable for you this way. You don't have to feel the irrational responsibility of taking her away from St. Ann's."

Nicole's anger surfaced. "It was her choice!"

"Does that make it any less painful for her?" Jacob snapped back.

Nicole was stymied. She fell into a thoughtful silence.

Jacob sipped his coffee. "Nicole, do you know the word *yada*?"

"No."

"It is Hebrew. It is used in the Torah to express all manner of knowing. At times it refers to a child not being able to distinguish between good and evil. It is used to describe the knowledge of a wise man, knowledge gained by experience as well as contemplative perception. It describes the most intimate acquaintances and it describes knowing in terms of the marriage bed. And finally, it is used in one's relation to the divine, in our acquaintance with God. There is a knowing that is yours to have. You are not a child. You know the difference between right and wrong. You can know Beth both as an intimate and in the marriage bed."

Nicole smiled internally at Jacob's reference to the marriage bed.

"You must trust Beth. You must open yourself up like a book and allow her to read you. Better yet, you must read of yourself to her. You cannot protect Beth. You are wrong to believe you can. You must share with her your hopes and fears, your joys and sorrows. If she is who you believe her to be, she will welcome the intimacy … the truth. Your truth may break her heart but it is a pain that she will feel only because she loves you. It is a heartbreak that will bring you closer to one another."

"Is that what Liza gives you?"

"Liza." Jacob smiled as he always did when speaking of his beloved wife. "My Liza is very patient. When we first met I would give her only a word here and there. With time I was able to put words together and share a thought. More time and I told her brief stories, more pictures, snapshots, of what I had seen, what I still see in my mind's eye. And then the merciful day came when I could share complete chapters of my story with her. Often crying in her lap, as if I were a babe. My Liza listened. She held me. She cried with me as I cursed God and she cried with me as I begged for God to return to me."

Jacob looked down. He was visibly moved. Nicole took his hand allowing the old man the time he needed to compose himself.

"*Yada.*" Jacob nodded his head, refocusing on the original lesson. "Yes, we were talking about *yada*. Nicole, you have lived a life with an open mind, heart and spirit. You have wisdom. *Yada* will come to you if you pause and contemplate, giving time and space for questions to be formed and answers to come forth. But you must understand that there is a knowing that is beyond you. You will never know God. And because of that, there is a part of Beth that will always be out of your reach. It is something you cannot share. It is a loss that I am grateful I have not suffered with Liza."

Nicole had a question Jacob's lesson did not answer. "What if one day I fall asleep in Beth's arms and never wake up?"

Jacob's voice rose. "I thought the doctors said you have recovered well."

"They did."

Jacob sighed in relief. He refocused on Nicole's question. "You cannot stop loving – which is, my child, living – because of the inevitable loss."

"How can you stand it?" Nicole looked away. Peace was elusive. "I find myself wanting to cry every time I hold Beth. And when we make love – I feel desperate."

"Nicole, give Beth your tears."

"She's going through a lot right now. I don't want her to worry about me."

Jacob's life with Liza had taught him well. "You are wrong to think she does not worry about you. How could she not?"

CHAPTER 75

September 21, 2001 – Evening

Nicole leaned against her desk. It was good to be home. The day had been filled to the brim and she had yet to see Beth. Nicole closed her eyes. She felt the renewal of her health and took pleasure in it. She had admittedly begun to take her health for granted. Shenandoah impressed upon her the enormity of her mistake

She reopened her eyes and looked at the wall of shelving only partially populated with books. The task of rebuilding her library was, during these trying times, one of her few pleasures. She considered the seven new volumes she had purchased that afternoon.

In loving Beth, Nicole yearned to understand her. To understand Beth, Nicole knew she needed to understand Beth's faith. Given the lingering tension caused by September 11th, Nicole hesitated in broaching the subject. During her undergraduate studies, Nicole had studied the Hebrew Bible, Christian New Testament, and to a lesser extent, Christian History. She possessed only cursory knowledge of the theological development of various Christian dogmas. She now sought a greater understanding of Christian theology, one that would enable her to pose reasonable questions.

She heard the front door open. Nicole called out Beth's name. Beth was closing the door as Nicole entered the hallway. After several uninterrupted steps Nicole took Beth into an embrace.

Beth happily drowned in the sensual union. It had been too long since she had felt Nicole's strength enveloping her.

Beth laughed gently. "Hi."

Nicole felt her rising emotions, emotions kept at bay in her solitude. She was not prepared for another separation.

Beth released Nicole. Her partner kept a firm hold of her, causing Beth to feel a kernel of concern. She sought her own interior stillness. She felt the steady rise and fall of Nicole's breath. She heard Nicole's silence. Given the reassurance of touch, she doubted Nicole's silence was a conscious withholding. Beth had been in the midst of this particular silence, indicative of Nicole's vulnerability, only twice before. She renewed her hold upon her partner. After an extended moment she chose to temper the troubling spell Nicole's silence had cast. She whispered in Nicole's ear, "I've missed you."

Nicole sighed. She gradually relaxed her muscles, countering her overwhelming physical need for Beth. Her voice was hoarse. "I've missed you, too."

Separating, Beth raised her hand and traced the line of Nicole's jaw. "Nicki, how about a late dinner?"

Nicole nodded. There was no smile. For Beth, the time for patience had passed. She took Nicole's lips with her own, demanding all that Nicole had to give. Nicole broke her internal tethers. She swung Beth around against the wall, demanding, in turn, all that Beth had to give. It had been too long for both of them.

Nicole took command of their lovemaking. Their clothes were quickly stripped as she led Beth into the bedroom. Lying beside Beth the vital kinetic force of Nicole shifted dramatically, from mastery to solicitousness. Nicole calmed.

Beth welcomed the familiar weight of Nicole upon her. Nicole softened and successively diminished her kisses. They became feather light as her lips brushed Beth's, as she rose up and away, before returning anew to make a further claim. Beth attempted to follow Nicole's flight, but Nicole used the back of her hand to stroke Beth's cheek, soothing Beth to repose. They had journeyed to a mutually shared tranquility. Beth watched as Nicole's patient gaze studied her. She felt as if Nicole was memorizing her, nothing escaping Nicole's observation. With a sense of relief Beth marked the moment when Nicole offered her a modest smile. Beth reflected the smile back tenfold in radiance.

"Elizabeth Ann Kelly, I love you," Nicole said with a resonant voice.

Beth had never heard Nicole call her by her full name. The fusion of Nicole's gaze with her words left Beth, for a moment, speechless. She struggled for an appropriate response. "I love you, Nicole Isabel Thera." She took a quick breath in and then released it with a restored calm. "I've wanted you home. I've wanted us here together with the world left outside." Beth traced Nicole's lips with her fingers. "These past few weeks have been so hard. I don't want the world to take you away from me. I don't want the world to come between us."

Nicole understood. With understanding came the closing of a door within her, the door she had fought all that she was to open. What lay behind the door had just been uninvited. What Nicole was prepared to show Beth was unwelcome. The world had become fearful, touching the quick in a way that could not be denied. Beth wanted none of it in the private realm they shared. Nicole closed the door shut. She would not speak of Shenandoah. She would not be unburdened of her fear of losing Beth to God.

"I'm here and I'm yours. Nothing is going to change that," said Nicole.

Her doubts exposed, Beth said, "Make me believe you."

Nicole was given an invitation; at one time the invitation had dominated her desire. On this day, the invitation meant far less to her. Though making love was an extraordinary element of their union, it paled in comparison to the grace of simply having Beth in her life. Nicole accepted Beth's invitation. She would make Beth believe her. Not a further word was spoken.

After climaxing, Beth held Nicole tight. Nicole felt Beth's hands on her back, demanding the press of her body, an assurance to ease the pronounced vulnerability felt in the moment of complete physical release. Nicole buried her face in the crook of the younger woman's neck. As Beth's breathing subsided to an undisturbed rhythm, Nicole strode to re-tether her own emotions.

For Nicole, being with Beth had not been a disguised effort to impress her power and control. Nicole had not demanded anything from her lover, but only gave her what she desired. Though both the means and the end may have been the same to Beth, Nicole experienced their lovemaking differently. In place of strength, Nicole felt acutely exposed. As Beth was being overtaken by her sensations, Nicole acknowledged the unconditional trust Beth placed in her. She understood the nature of surrender; how unsafe a bedroom could become, not only for her lover, but also for herself. Their bedroom had become a perilous place, and it frightened Nicole to a degree long forgotten.

Nicole felt Beth's demand for her touch subside as Beth's taut muscles eased and the press of her hands lifted. Nicole was not prepared to accept Beth's reciprocation. She felt the door within her threatening to burst open, contrary to all her efforts to keep its bolt in place. She needed time. She shifted, migrating her body down, resting her head against Beth's breast, laying a hand over Beth's abdomen, lying still, seeking comfort.

Beth felt Nicole's movement. Nicole's placement was new to her. She stroked her partner's hair as she waited for Nicole to come back to her. There were kisses to be given, words to be spoken, but Nicole remained as she was. Beth was touched again by this newness in her experience of Nicole. She accepted it without understanding it. She draped her arms around Nicole as Nicole drifted toward sleep.

CHAPTER 76

October 2001

Nicole observed a continual, gradual dulling of Beth's spirit. There was little she felt she could do but offer Beth a safe haven. Determined to minimize her travel, Nicole worked as much as she could through phone, email and fax.

Their conversations were limited. Beth remained reticent regarding her chaplaincy. Nicole did not discuss her work, inseparable from the September 11th attack.

Nicole took solace in their physical joining. There were moments after their lovemaking when she felt she had drawn Beth closer to the surface, up from her fathomless depths. Those moments were fleeting, as Beth withdrew again to an interior life that excluded Nicole, an interior life that excluded the world.

These new terms of engagement were trying for Nicole. She relied on her other connections in order to maintain her equilibrium. Tess remained a dear confidant. She had Jacob. Jason was becoming a friend. Each touched one aspect of Nicole's life: Tess, the heart; Jacob, the spirit; and Jason, the mind of the entrepreneur.

Beth was relieved to have Nicole's acquiesce to her unspoken need for silence. The apartment was her refuge, contingent on Nicole's cooperation. Outside of Nicole's den the television and radio remained mute.

Everyone at the hospital had an opinion about current events and was not shy to voice it. Beth soon found herself withdrawing once again from the Round Table discussions. Though Jerry was on far better behavior, her initial enthusiasm had deadened.

God remained distant. Beth felt the void more so in the company of the chaplains. Each day during morning report they rotated the responsibility of leading a short devotion. The selections others chose expressed their faith with a sincerity that she could not, in her heart, equal. She struggled to meet her assignment of presenting her theological statement. What she had written felt dry, spiritless. Her prayers came with difficulty. Her hope for the return of her faith slipped away. She felt a mounting loneliness.

Beth spent much of her time reading in the sunroom. She eschewed the newspapers and news magazines. Her only proactive encounter with ideas was her books, books on subjects she chose. The books did not ask her questions she was not prepared to address. If an author placed a painful question before her, she had the power to ignore the challenge. The author was not in a position to demand recognition.

Nicole asked little, and Beth was grateful. Beth's ability to give to Nicole was reduced to their bed. Only in their lovemaking was Beth's generosity to Nicole unaltered. She was desperate to feel and Nicole was the only one who could make her feel anything other than the alienation and loneliness that dominated her life. Nicole had the power to carry Beth beyond all thought to the pure sensual nature of her physical being.

CHAPTER 77

October 9, 2001

Beth and Nicole sat at the dining room table, eating a late afternoon meal. Beth had the night shift at the hospital. She attempted to give Nicole a smidgen of conversation to compensate for the dearth of communion between them. "I spoke yesterday to the brother of a man whose surgery didn't go well. The brother had to decide whether to terminate life support."

Nicole looked up from her plate. "The patient didn't leave written instructions?"

"No. The brother told me that the patient was frightened and didn't want to face the possibility."

"What did you say to the brother?"

"I asked him if he had spoken to his brother about what he would have wanted. He said he knew his brother wouldn't want to be left in a vegetative state to be cared for in a nursing home for the rest of his life … he asked me to tell him what to do. He said he was a good Christian. He didn't want to be a murderer."

"How did you respond?"

"I told him I couldn't tell him what to do. That he should think of what his brother would want. I said because his brother didn't leave instructions, the decision was no longer just about what his brother wanted, it was also about what he could live with."

Nicole nodded. She returned her attention to her food, moving the vegetables about with her fork. Beth watched her. She could see Nicole was holding back. "Nicki?"

"Yes."

"What are you thinking?"

Nicole was sure. "If the patient wants to die he should die. It doesn't matter what the brother believes."

Beth demurred, saying, "You can't discount the survivors."

"I'm not. My heart goes out to the brother, but that doesn't change the fact that the patient should be removed from life support. Everyone has the right to choose the quality of their death."

Beth challenged, "How about the quality of their life?"

"I wish we could choose the quality of our lives carte blanche. We choose how we will live, given what life places at our feet, whether we are intelligent or challenged, physically complete or disabled. If my operation had gone badly, I wouldn't want someone else's values to interfere with my wishes."

They had never spoken of Nicole's instructions. Kate continued to hold Nicole's medical power of attorney. Beth asked, "You would have chosen death?"

"If I couldn't live a meaningful life, yes."

"What if you are depressed? Doesn't society have a responsibility to value your life, to place more meaning in your life than you are capable of?"

Nicole leaned forward in her chair. "It amazes me that our society is finally starting to recognized the cruelty of keeping someone alive when all they have to experience is physical pain, but that the same generosity isn't afforded those who are in horrendous emotional pain. It's arrogance to believe that we are any more adept in curing mental anguish."

"The mentally ill do not have the capacity to choose," said Beth.

"Who determines mental illness? What is illness to us may be ecstasy to another. Think of Pentecost. Who are we to judge?"

"Oh, no, you don't." Beth forcefully placed her napkin to the side. "Don't you throw a religious experience into the same category as mental illness!"

Nicole kept a measured cadence to her voice. "Only to the extent that it's not understood. We grant tolerance to the mystic. Who is to say that the homeless man praising Jesus isn't a modern day prophet? If God tells him to lie in wait and take the angel Gabriel's hand when offered, who is to say the angel isn't right there with him calling him to heaven? We draw the line based on what feels comfortable. Why? Because there is no fact involved outside the reality of the person feeling what they feel. This isn't cancer. You can't point to an X-ray that shows a malignancy, but doctors pretend that it is the same."

"So, if the day comes and you choose to die, that's it. I have no say in it?"

Nicole refused to waver. "No, you don't. On the other hand, when it comes to your life, you have the right to make the choice that is true to you."

"So you would let me go if I asked you to?"

Nicole paused. She did not want to concede the loss. True, she felt Beth slipping away from her, but she hoped that with time Beth would return. The prospect of losing Beth, with no expectation of return, was untenable. Yet Nicole knew from experience that the choice was not hers. "Yes."

"Every life has value." Beth could not accept Nicole's leniency.

"And every life will come to an end. Medicine and religion haven't conquered death."

"It's not right to take your own life."

"We're not talking about suicide. Not that it would matter if we were."

"No one should play God."

"God?" Nicole questioned Beth's choice of authority.

"Yes. God!" Beth seethed. "God is in this conversation."

Nicole labored to contain the intensifying storm within her, keeping a steady countenance. "I'm glad I can count on Kate to act on my behalf."

Beth did not register her exclusion in Nicole's statement. Her heart had shifted away from the speculative. "I'm glad my mother didn't choose death when she got sick."

"Well, my mother did and I didn't judge her for it."

Beth was startled by Nicole's revelation. Nicole's emotions were near the surface, threatening to break free. In addition to Nicole's undeniable anger, Beth could see tears glistening in her eyes.

Nicole stood up. "I need some fresh air." She went to the front closet, grabbed her coat, and made an abrupt exit.

Beth watched helplessly as Nicole closed the door behind her.

CHAPTER 78

October 9, 2001

Beth's pager sounded. She turned toward the nightstand and reached for the light switch. As she took the pager in hand, she could hear the code being called over the public address system. She wrote the I.C.U. room number on the slip of paper located on the nightstand just for that purpose. She then called the switchboard obtaining the patient's name, confirming the patient's room number and confirming that she was on her way. The time was near midnight.

She got out of bed and began to dress. The patient, Agnes Hanson, was familiar. The 72-year-old mother of five had undergone double bypass heart surgery two days before. She had been in good spirits, in part because of a steady stream of family visitors.

Beth entered the I.C.U. Determining the code location was not an issue. Hospital personnel surrounded the patient's bedside, overflowing to the common area. Beth walked to the code site, making sure she was within the sight of Debra Berry, the attending nurse. Debra approached her. "Beth, the family has been called. Could you meet them at Emergency?"

"What happened?"

"We're not sure. They were working on her respiratory tube when she started bleeding. They do the procedure all the time. Things like this aren't supposed to happen." Debra's voice trembled. "Beth, it doesn't look good."

Beth's eyes traveled back toward Agnes. Her hospital robe had been stripped down to the waist. Ten staff members from various disciplines were present to assist the attending doctor as needed. Beth thought it was a blessing that Agnes was not aware of her surroundings. She would have been mortified by her public exposure.

Ninety minutes later, Beth walked back through the I.C.U. double doors to the elevator. She pressed the 'up' button to return to the Chaplain's night room. As she waited, she recalled all the challenges she had faced within the brief period of time since she had received notice of the code: family members who refused to face the death of their matriarch, a doctor vehemently against continuing life support measures and a nurse – Debra – who had been taken to the edge of her emotional limits by having to retell the events that had led to Agnes' medical crisis to one family member after another as they arrived.

After an hour, with permission from Agnes' oldest daughter, all efforts to revive Agnes were stopped. Agnes died at 1:16 a.m.

The staff had dressed Agnes with a fresh gown and combed her hair. They did everything they could to restore Agnes' dignity before family members came to her bedside to begin their farewells and to have Beth conduct a brief memorial service. Afterwards, Beth escorted the family members out of the I.C.U. and returned to Agnes' bedside to enter a record of her pastoral visit in the chart.

Beth was exhausted. She leaned her head against the wall. The thought came to her, *Who ministers to the minister?* She struggled to keep her emotions in check. She returned to her room and quickly stripped her clothes off. Slipping into the bed, Beth pulled the crisp sheet and blanket over her as her body entered the fetal position. She was overwhelmed by a sense of complete emptiness. As she had ministered to others, beseeching God to touch them and comfort them, she felt nothing but her relentless sorrow. Within her she traveled a bleak wasteland. Prayer had failed her. Without the presence of God, her aloneness had become excruciating. And so she cried.

CHAPTER 79

October 10, 2001 – Morning

The fire burned, log upon log flamed in yellows, blues, and occasional whites. At the fire's bed lay the red carbon coal of wood nearing its complete annihilation. Nicole allowed her mind to enter the flames. Mesmerized, her thoughts ceased; intellect was in respite and she knew deep within her, that she was witness to both legacy and destiny. One day her life would end and by her wish she would be cremated, her matter to be transformed by fire to the remnants of bone and ash. She did not want imprisonment in an urn. She wanted to be taken up by the wind and scattered to every corner of the earth.

She came from the molten fires of an evolving earth, and she would return to it. It was right; it was just to return to her origins. She did not know how to speak to Beth of such things. Beth clung to union, to continuance, to a life beyond life. Beth, Nicole suspected, believed that by sheer sincerity and force of will she could bring Nicole's soul to her, keep her safe, and intimately close. Beth was prepared to argue before her God to forgive Nicole's failure to embrace the ineffable truth of the divine Creator, to argue for a dispensation for Nicole, to be by grace allowed a place in heaven. Nicole found that frame of Christianity romantic, contrary to her own Classical temperament.

She recalled the words attributed to the early nineteenth century dramatist Georg Büchnor, arguing that life is not a means but an end, 'for development is the end of life, life itself is development, therefore life itself is an end.' Here lay a critical difference between her beliefs and Beth's faith. To Nicole life was the end. To Beth it was the means.

The fire continued to burn, and the ash to gather. Nicole's heart ached for Beth. At that moment she doubted she could reach her. The chasm between them was growing wider. For Nicole to speak her truth was to cast doubt upon Beth's faith, and Nicole did not want to cause Beth any deeper pain. Love was not enough. Nicole had no capacity to comfort Beth without tainting her own integrity. To attempt, by offering a nonjudgmental ear, was destined to failure, for Beth knew Nicole well enough to understand skepticism resided behind the silence – respectful but unyielding skepticism.

Beth would not come to Nicole, and Nicole could not go to Beth for comfort. Nicole struggled to find grace in their truth. Her gaze continued to linger upon the flames. How could her vision of this particular fire, a fire with a finite ending, warm Beth when Beth did not recognize its existence?

Nicole heard a key in the front door lock. She looked out of the sunroom windows. It was daybreak. She had lost track of time. Beth entered the apartment. Nicole gently called out, "Hi."

Beth looked over to the living room. She was surprised to see Nicole sitting on the floor, leaning against one of their two tall back chairs in front of the fireplace. "Hi." Beth put her coat away. "You're up early."

"I haven't been to bed yet."

"I didn't realize you were under deadline."

"I'm not."

Beth approached and sat in the chair across from Nicole. "I wish you hadn't left."

Nicole returned her gaze to the fire. After a few moments Beth urged, "Please don't shut me out."

Nicole tried to surmount her fatigue. "I'm not," she said.

Beth did not believe her. She did not have the stamina to pretend. "This was a mistake."

"What?" said Nicole, shifting her gaze to Beth, her uncertainty evident.

"Living together so soon." Exhausted and seeking relief from the ever-present sense of estrangement that engulfed her life, Beth persisted. "I can get a place of my own through the hospital's housing services."

"No." Nicole's whisper carried an equal denial as it did a plea.

The two sat in silence.

Nicole broached the stillness. "Beth, I'm sorry about yesterday. There were far better ways to tell you about my mother."

"I can't talk to you," said Beth dejectedly.

"Why not?" Nicole was unable to reason their disjunction.

"Because you don't believe …" Beth stumbled on her thoughts. She was left to wonder what she believed.

"We could before." Setting aside Jacob's counsel, Nicole quietly protested.

"Things have changed. I've changed. Every time I look at you, I'm impressed by the fact that you believe that the most important thing in my life is a fallacy."

"I've never … "

"No, you haven't. I'm grateful that you've never called me a blithering idiot."

"Beth, where is this coming from?"

"Nicki, I'm tired. Can we talk about this later?" Beth stood up.

Nicole reached out to Beth, taking her hand.

Beth exploded. "Don't touch me!" Her violence was fed by her despair, a despair that had threatened to break through the surface for more days than she could count, and now achieved its deliverance. Her fury left Beth shaken. She fell into a helpless silence.

Nicole recoiled. The two women were confused, reluctant combatants conquered by the fatigue of wars fought within their interior landscapes. Nicole yielded. She had become inured to the caustic forces of unsubstantiated accusations. No more. Safety came through separation. She had her proof in the quiddity of her solitary existence. She felt she had no recourse. "I can arrange to give you some space."

Beth was surprised by Nicole's quick shift from reluctance to willing acceptance of a separation. The transformation of Beth's spoken proposition to concrete reality left her fearful. She did not want to lose Nicole. She spoke hesitantly, "What do you mean?"

"I have a number of clients on hold."

Beth struggled to find some semblance of order in a world that had gone out of control. "How long would you be gone?"

"As long as you need."

"Will you come home on the weekends?"

"If you want me to. Think about it and let me know."

Beth referred to practical considerations as a ruse to keep Nicole close. "What about your work on The Fields?"

"The interior design is just about done. Jason and I can work through fax and email. The Musketeers can take up the slack."

All the disparate demands in Beth's life had gradually coalesced to form an insurmountable challenge. Even though she was the first to suggest a separation, Beth was not willing to take responsibility for this one last inevitable loss. "Do what you think is best." She withdrew to the bedroom.

Nicole watched Beth disappear from her sight. She did not accept Beth's justification that it was their divergent faiths that had caused their crisis. Their friendship had prospered in the light of their differences. Nicole felt tried and convicted of an unnamed crime – her sentence: abandonment.

CHAPTER 80

October 10, 2001

While Beth slept, Nicole spent the morning hours connecting with her clients and arranging her itinerary. She would fly out Friday morning. She could have delayed her flight to Sunday, but saw no reason to remain in the apartment any longer than necessary. She slept on the den couch during most of the afternoon and then, without a word to Beth, left to work at Chamberlain's. From the sunroom, Beth watched Nicole depart.

It was past midnight when Beth heard Nicole enter the apartment. Having left the bedroom door open, she listened intently to Nicole's movements. She heard the den door close. It was then that she knew Nicole would not join her. Beth understood it was she who had banished Nicole; still, she had hoped Nicole would have challenged her, as she had done many times in the past, and attempted a reunion.

Beth drifted into a fitful sleep. She awoke to the sound of her alarm and quietly readied for the hospital. Before leaving, she carefully opened the den door. Nicole slept soundly on the couch. Beth chose not to disturb her. It was Beth's hope that by evening they would each be in a better place to find their way back to one another.

A note from Nicole awaited Beth at the evening hour.

Beth-

I'll be at Chamberlain's until late. I'm leaving in the morning. My itinerary is attached.

Be well,

Nicki

CHAPTER 81

October 23, 2001 – Noon

"Forgiveness." Jamie dropped her food tray down on the table. The contents rattled about on impact. She spoke with uncharacteristic severity. "I want to talk about forgiveness."

Jamie had been in good spirits at the morning report. Beth surmised that Jamie's upset must have been caused during the course of her morning pastoral visits. If she chose, Jamie would be able to confidentially share the experience with her small group. It was evident she did not want to wait for relief. After a shared silence, Jerry cautiously took the lead. "Divine forgiveness or human forgiveness?"

"Let's keep Scripture out of it."

Nathaniel was surprised by Jamie's request. "What do you mean?"

The young student was adamant. "For once, let's just talk without one reference to Scripture or a catechism."

Jerry tried to enforce the unspoken ground rules. "Jamie, this is a forum for us to express our religious beliefs."

Jamie leaned back, clearly angry. "Fine. Forget it."

Paul offered a starting point. "The Forgiveness Institute acknowledged a variety of sources in reaching its model of forgiveness. They included religious tradition, philosophy, and psychology."

Luke edged carefully toward the topic. "I can't conceive living a human life without forgiveness. Isn't the only alternative hate? And that'll destroy us."

"As a people we are obviously not doing a good job of forgiving one another," Cindy observed.

"Damn right." Jamie spoke to her food.

"I think forgiveness is misunderstood and that's why it's so hard. People think it means unconditional love."

"But it is unconditional," Nathaniel asserted. "I don't mean you don't hold the person accountable for their actions, you do. But you can't see forgiveness as something you do for yourself even though in the long run it will only help you."

Luke spoke with greater confidence. "You have to be able to forgive without expecting a 'thank you' from the one you've forgiven."

Nathaniel built on Luke's thought. "You have to be able to forgive even if you'll never see the person who hurt you again. How many people have had to deal with unresolved issues with someone who died? The anger can consume them. The anger comes not only because they were hurt, but because the confrontation they always dreamed of never happened."

"That's common in childhood abuse cases. Once the child grows to adulthood there's no chance to go back and say 'look what you've done to me'," Cindy added.

Christine went further. "But there is more to it with childhood abuse. There is the need to confirm that the abuse really happened. That it isn't just a nightmare. That they're not crazy."

"That. kind of confrontation probably wouldn't result in forgiveness," Jerry said.

"How do you know?" Christine challenged.

Luke defended Jerry's position. "Because it is a confrontation and nothing good can come from it."

"Luke, I think you misunderstand what is meant by confrontation," said Paul. "We are not talking about accusations or attacks. You have to confront the wrong. You have to define it. You have to attempt to understand its nature before you can address it."

"Paul, the hurt isn't an impersonal 'it'. The hurt can't be separated from the human being that caused it. Sometimes there is no way you can understand the why of the hurt. All you can do is accept that it exists for what it is."

"I agree. And I don't necessarily mean understanding why the person hurt you, that is assuming there was a conscious motivation. I mean confronting what the hurt means to you."

"There is the risk of rationalizing to the point of making forgiveness pointless," Luke warned.

"Why don't we take a real life example?" Beth did not believe the abstract nature of the conversation was helping Jamie. She wanted to put a human face into the forum. The chaplains gave their silent assent. "I'll use myself. My father has ended our relationship. It wasn't much of a relationship to begin with, but I still thought of myself as his daughter. When I told him I was leaving the priesthood he demanded to know the reason. When I told him I had fallen in love with Nicki, he said I wasn't his daughter. I realized that my father was never really a father to me. At least not the kind of father I believe we all deserve. It hurt to face that fact. I had to ask myself if something was wrong with me that I didn't merit his love. I had to deal with the possibility that not having a real father was a punishment. Then I looked at a group of little children playing in the park, and I knew there was nothing a child could do to deserve not to be loved. I came to the point of believing that I did deserve love. His love. The love of my sister, Marie. Nicki's love. Like Paul said, I had to confront my father and the harm he did so I could understand the hurt I felt. I had to understand why the hurt went so deep. Then I needed to look at my father as less than a monster, because all I could feel at the time was that only a monster could reject his daughter the way he rejected me. But the truth is, when I think of him, all I see is a lonely, bitter old man who loved his wife and let his love die with her. He never forgave God." Beth paused and gave Jamie a small smile. "Sorry, but I can't tell this story without mentioning God. When my mother died, my father couldn't find any consolation. Instead of rejecting God as some people do, he placed God into the center of his life. To my father, God is to be feared, and it's not the awe of Yahweh. I mean the fear that comes close to hate. It's the kind of fear that makes you look constantly over your shoulder. That's who my father is and I can't change him. So, I forgave him instead and I moved on and left him to the life he's chosen for himself. I needed to forgive him so I could live my life the way I believe God intends me to. So I could let Nicki love me, and so I could love Nicki the way she deserves to be loved."

"Why don't you blame God for the death of your mother and your father's rejection? Why do you still love God after everything you've gone through?" Jamie struggled to keep her voice measured.

Beth was caught. She did not want to lie to Jamie. "I want to believe in the primacy of love. I need to believe in God's grace."

Paul broke the silence that enveloped the table. "Amen."

"Let it be," said Christine.

CHAPTER 82

October 25, 2001 – Evening

Beth listened to Nicole's voice message:

Beth-

> *It's Nicki. I'm flying in tomorrow afternoon. I hope … I hope life is better. I'll see you soon.*

They had exchanged only a few impersonal emails during the previous two weeks. During that time, Nicole had not given Beth an indication of when she planned to return to Chicago. Her imminent return was unexpected.

CHAPTER 83

October 26, 2001 – Evening

Beth entered the apartment.

Fearful, Nicole was waiting on the living room couch. She stood up. "Hi."

Beth removed her coat and draped it over the banister. "How was your flight?"

"Good." Nicole slowly stepped forward.

"How long are you staying?" The question sounded severe, which was not Beth's intention.

Nicole paused. She would approach no further. "Sunday. I was hoping we could spend some time together."

"You didn't give me much notice. I already have plans made for the weekend."

Nicole had prepared herself for the worse possible reception. She was determined to accept whatever Beth was willing to give her. Her response was genuine. "I understand."

Beth took in the sight of Nicole standing in the living room with her arms behind her, her feet planted in an open stance. "I'm going to get out of these clothes. I'm having dinner with Cindy."

Nicole watched as Beth disappeared from her sight. She remained at heart uncertain. Time spent in the company of men and women, who in a crisis held to each other, sharing their tears and laughter, had rekindled Nicole's desire to construct a life with Beth. For two weeks she had waited for some hint from Beth that she would be welcomed. When none came, she set aside what disappointment and anger may have held her back and decided to come home. The only solace she could take was that Beth did not ask her to leave. She removed herself to the den. She had delayed unpacking. Somewhere deep within her, Nicole had held the unrealistic hope that Beth would invite her back into their bedroom.

Cindy and Beth met for dinner at a Hyde Park neighborhood restaurant. They shared a side booth. Though they worked closely together, it was difficult in their hectic schedules to relax and talk to one another. They had found that they truly enjoyed each other's company. Occasional shared dinners strengthened their growing friendship.

Cindy inquired, "Have you heard from Nicole?"

Beth had withheld sharing the difficulties she and Nicole were experiencing. "She flew in today."

Cindy was surprised. "Then why are you here with me?"

Beth remained silent.

"You should have canceled. I would have understood."

"She gave me no notice." Beth was compelled to defend her actions although she did not stand accused. "We are not in a relationship of one. Nicki can't come and go as she pleases without accepting the consequences."

Cindy offered a careful response. "That isn't how you've described her in the past."

"We don't talk anymore. I can't talk to her about what's important to me without getting into an argument."

Cindy explored gently. "Your faith? Your work?"

"Yes." Beth looked away.

After allowing Beth a moment of uninterrupted thought, Cindy recalled Beth back to their conversation. "Did you talk when you first met?"

Beth returned her gaze to Cindy. "Yes. All the time."

"What did you talk about?"

"Everything."

"Did you agree?"

Beth flashed back in her memory to their constant debates. "No."

"Then I don't understand. What's changed?"

Beth hesitated. Her voice was low and pained. "I'm not a priest anymore."

Cindy paused, holding her question until Beth met her gaze. "Beth, you don't blame Nicole for the loss of your priesthood, do you?"

The question so simply posed could not be set aside. Who was responsible for the loss of her priesthood? Did Beth lay the responsibility on the doorstep of a misguided Church? Did she hold God responsible? Or did Beth look to Nicole? It was Nicole who had earned her love and given her reason to set aside the oppressive mantle of her vocation. Beth's ensuing crisis of faith was inseparable from Nicole. Beth did not answer.

Cindy continued to pursue the truth. "Are you sure Nicole is the one holding back?"

After bidding Cindy goodnight, Beth walked home alone. Her thoughts lingered on their conversation. Cindy had not shied from asking difficult questions. Beth knew Cindy had indeed become a friend; only a friend would care enough to take the risk to probe, to challenge and, if necessary, to offend.

It was a clear and warm night for late October. The street traffic was steady. Singles, couples, and groups of friends made their way throughout the

Hyde Park neighborhood. Beth could hear their voices and their laughter; she watched them as they walked side by side, some holding hands. She missed Nicole. She knew Nicole was waiting for her.

Upon arriving home Beth found Nicole sitting in front of the hearth. A healthy fire burned.

Nicole looked up. "Hi. Have a good time?"

"Yes."

"You and Cindy seem to be building a nice friendship."

"She has an ulterior motive. She's trying to convince me to become a U.U."

"As a lay person or a minister?"

Beth was surprised by the ease with which Nicole broached the notion that she would return to a formal church ministry. "She's taking it slow. Just as a church member."

"Any possibility?"

"The U.C.C. has a better chance with me."

Nicole weighed what she knew about the Unitarians Universalist and the United Church of Christ. "I could see how hard it would be to go from High Church to a church with minimal ritual. Have you talked to Pam?"

"A little." Beth turned away as she hung her coat in the closet.

Nicole returned her gaze to the fire.

Beth approached. She leaned against the high-backed chair opposite Nicole. "What do you see in the fire?"

Nicole answered wistfully, "Eternity."

Beth felt a tug in her heart for Nicole.

"Do you know the meaning of *temenos*?" Nicole's tender voice called Beth closer to her.

"It's Greek, isn't it? A sanctuary ... a sacred place where people go to be in union with the divine."

"It has Classical origins. It was a constructed space. I was thinking whether I have a *temenos*. In the loft, if I was alone, and if it was quiet ... I stopped looking outside myself. I'd look in and touch the stillness. It's the closest feeling of peace I know, and for me that's divine."

Beth was attentive.

"Now it's the apartment." Nicole looked at Beth. "Sometimes it's here in front of the fire. Most of the time it's the den. I never thanked you for giving me the den."

"I knew you needed a space of your own." Beth wanted to reach out and bridge the expanse that separated them. "Do you have plans for tomorrow?"

"I called Jason. He has plenty of work for me to do. I'll spend the day with him. Kate and I are getting together for a late dinner." Nicole offered an apology. "I shouldn't have assumed that you would be free."

"Sunday?"

"All taken care of." Nicole offered Beth her complete attention. "Beth, really, I'm fine. I understand your life shouldn't revolve around my whims."

Beth did not know how to rescind her chastisement of Nicole without losing face, without compromising a point she felt was important to make. Nicole did not have the right to dictate the terms of their relationship.

Nicole seemed to have recovered well. She, in turn, was struggling with the fact that Nicole was in Chicago for the weekend and they would not be sharing any significant time together. Harder still was suppressing Nicole's impetuousness. Nicole was usually structured, living a life of self-control. The moments she would break free simply enraptured Beth, who regretted any reining in of Nicole's rare spontaneity.

Beth's fatigue subdued her. "I've had a long day. I'm going to bed."

"Good night, Beth." Beth's weariness had not escaped Nicole's notice.

Beth felt Nicole's sincere warmth. She wanted to invite Nicole to join her. She knew that it was in her power to undo what had been done. But before she did, there were truths she needed to consider with greater honesty. "Good night."

CHAPTER 84

October 28, 2001

Beth heard the sound of Nicole in the kitchen. The nightstand clock read 6:20 a.m. The previous day she had seen Nicole for only a brief shared cup of coffee in the morning. On this day she did not want a repetition of such a limited encounter.

"Nicki?" Beth stood at the kitchen threshold.

Nicole was dressed in jeans and a sweater. She paused from her task of pouring a pot of coffee into a large thermos. "Beth, I'm sorry if I woke you."

"You didn't. Nicki, it's early."

"I'll be on my way in a little while. I wanted to make sure I had plenty of time before my flight."

"When do you leave?"

"Eight tonight."

Behind Nicole, through the kitchen window, Beth's vision took in the sight of the trees, their foliage changing in response to the crisp October air, the leaves falling freely. Her eyes traveled back to the thermos. She deduced Nicole's destination. "You're going to the Hill."

Nicole placed the empty coffee decanter down and began to cap the thermos. "Yes."

"Why ..." Beth stopped herself from asking the question. She knew why Nicole had not invited her. The answer was obvious. Beth had done everything she could to dissuade Nicole from seeking her out. "Would you like some company?"

Nicole was sincerely surprised by the offer. "I thought you had plans?"

Beth repeated her offer. Her voice was gentle. "Nicki, would you like me to come with you?"

Nicole smiled. "Yes, I would."

"Good. I'll get dressed."

As Nicole watched Beth return to the bedroom, she wondered what the day would bring.

Nicole drove the Wrangler with Beth sitting by her side. They traveled through Wisconsin in silence. Occasionally, Nicole glanced over to Beth, who seemed intent on enjoying the countryside. She remembered their first trip to Holy Hill. Like this, silence dominated. Then, it was a comfortable silence.

Nicole wanted to believe their current hush was rooted in comfort and not in discord.

Beth reached for the thermos. "Coffee?"

"I'll share."

Beth poured and handed the thermos cup to Nicole. Nicole sipped the coffee, keeping her eyes on the road.

Beth turned and watched Nicole in profile. She searched for the beginning of a conversation. "The Round Table was at it again this week."

Beth waited as Nicole took another sip of coffee before returning the cup to her. "What subject did they take on this time?"

"Free will."

"What were the positions?"

"We have it complete. We don't. We do, but God may choose to intervene."

"Who were the haves?"

"Luke, Cindy, and Jamie."

"Have not?"

"Jerry."

"Bless the Lutherans."

"Missouri Synod Lutherans."

"Not to split hairs. If you ask me he sounds like he belongs to the Reform Church ... and those who believe we have free will but can still be subject to God?"

"Everyone else."

Nicole looked over to Beth. "Including you?"

"I believe in the grace of God."

"Yes, you do," said Nicole.

Beth accepted Nicole's comment as a mere statement of fact. There was no judgment.

Nicole chose to continue the exchange. "One thing I just don't get."

"Only one?" Beth teased.

"Okay. One of many. What image of God do you have if you believe God has a chosen elect that will be saved while everyone else is passed up for salvation? Where is God's unbounded love?"

"It's not my image."

"I know. I don't mean to be harsh but the doctrine of the elect and predestination seems to be tailor made for a society where a ruling class wants to convince the oppressed that the status quo is divinely ordained. Or worse, it's for those afraid to take responsibility for their lives."

"He is sincere ... Jerry."

"I'm sure he is. That's what makes it even harder to understand."

"What do you think about those who believe God can choose to intervene in our free will?"

Nicole looked over to Beth and smiled. "They believe in the grace of God." Nicole returned her gaze back to the road. "They're more optimistic than I could ever hope to be."

"Why optimistic?"

"Petitionary and intercessory prayer."

"God's grace is not dependent on prayer."

"True, but to believe you can petition God, and that God may not only hear you but act on your behalf – that's faith."

"You've prayed."

"When I was a kid. Before I knew the things I now know."

Beth tried to envision Nicole as a child. It did not come easily. "I wish I had known you then."

Again, Nicole turned her gaze towards Beth. For a moment, she held Beth's eyes with her own and felt the intimacy that had recently eluded them. "So do I." Nicole felt a rise of emotion. She turned her gaze to the safer landscape ahead. "Do you believe God has answered any of your prayers?"

Beth knew she sat beside the living proof that her prayers had indeed been heard, although the answer was not what she would ever have imagined. "Yes."

"It couldn't have just been happenstance?"

"No. It couldn't."

As they neared their destination Beth surveyed the church on the hill. She had not entered a church, any church, since she left St. Ann's. The hospital chapel and the sunroom were where she worshiped, sustaining her as she struggled in doubt. She knew this church, and vividly recalled the interior. The Catholic church had the distinction of being the only place of worship that she had shared, side by side, with Nicole. Ironically, it was a place that neither one of them could call their spiritual home.

Beth joined the congregants in reciting the Penitential Rite. As she confessed to God and those present of her sins, she felt a breaching of the numbness that had been dominating her spiritual life. From that moment through the Kryrie, Gloria, the Readings, the Blessing and the Eucharist Prayers, the breach opened ever wider. She kept her eyes upon the Christ over the altar. She sought out the Christ. She felt the Christ near, but still beyond her reach.

The celebrant led the congregation in the Lord's Prayer. Nicole listened to Beth's gentle voice as she prayed. Beth's eyes were closed, her head bowed. Ever more strongly, Nicole felt in this public yet sacred space, the renewal of their intimacy.

The celebrant raised his hands up and prayed, garnering both Beth and Nicole's attention. He then looked to the congregation. "The peace of the LORD be with you always."

The congregation responded. "And also with you."

"Let us offer each other the Sign of Peace."

Nicole remained facing forward, her hands held firmly to the pew. Beth turned to her. She perceived Nicole's hesitancy. She placed her hand over Nicole's. "Peace be with you, Nicki."

Nicole felt Beth's touch. It had been so unbearably long since she felt Beth's warmth. Nicole turned her hand upward, taking Beth's. She looked at Beth, who waited patiently for her. She could not say what she felt, so she said what was expected. "Peace be with you, Beth."

Beth squeezed Nicole's hand and smiled, holding her place for a heartbeat before turning to greet the other worshippers. Nicole watched Beth. The younger woman's motion seemed to momentarily slow, entering a different plane of existence before the spell cast shattered and she was returned to real time. Taking a moment to collect her thoughts, Nicole then offered the Sign of Peace to those beside her.

As the congregants received communion, Beth and Nicole fell back into their own thoughts. Beth was relieved that, as a non-Catholic, participation in the Eucharist was prohibited. On this day the decision was not hers. She felt too spiritually distanced from God to partake in Holy Communion. Unable to put words to her feelings, she was left to blink her tears away.

Nicole could see her mother in her mind's eye. The woman, lucid and healthy, reached out to Nicole. Nicole looked down to her hands. A flash of memory struck her – her hands were red and raw, beaten for what offense she could not remember. Nicole did not have the wherewithal to accept her mother's invitation.

After the service they wordlessly took to the path of the Stations of the Cross. Beth chose this space to ask a forbidding question. "Nicki, how did your mother die?"

Nicole paused. She turned her gaze back to the station they had just passed. Jesus carried the cross, a crown of thorns upon his head. "It was late January. She died from exposure at the foot of St. Ann's stairs."

Beth spoke her next question more as a thought. "Why didn't she go in?"

"The doors were locked. It didn't matter. She had her keys in her pocket. She was only a block away from The Pub. In her illness … I think she was trying to make a point. I've never been sure what it might have been."

"I'm sorry."

"I was relieved. A part of me was relieved when she died. I wouldn't have to worry about the suicide attempts, or the hysterical phone calls, or the neighbors telling me what damage she had caused. But at the same time, I … I never got a chance to say good-bye. I couldn't remember the last time I had told her I loved her." Nicole turned back to Beth. "What kind of daughter does that make me?"

"Very human," Beth said faintly.

Nicole confessed, "I didn't want to be with her."

"You were protecting yourself."

"I should have been with her."

"You were young."

"I was in college!" Nicole avowed. Nicole's emotions were dangerously close to slipping through her tenuous hold. She looked away from Beth in an attempt to refocus. Beth had raised the one subject Nicole did not want to discuss on this day. This day was meant to celebrate the good of her life with her mother. She did not want any further reminders of the darkness. She looked down to her gloved hands. The gloves were not enough to conceal the wounds so recently remembered. Nicole buried her hands into her coat pockets.

Beth had no salve for Nicole's self-recrimination. She wished for Nicole the ability to seek reconciliation. As a priest, Beth had performed *The Reconciliation of a Penitent* to those who came to her seeking absolution. Beth silently offered Nicole a blessing from the rite. 'May Almighty God in mercy receive your confession of sorrow and of faith, strengthen you in all goodness, and by the power of the Holy Spirit keep you in eternal life. Amen.'

Nicole took a step forward. "Let's walk."

Beth understood the subject was now closed. She had been given her answer. She had been given more than the simple facts of Nicole's mother's death. She had witnessed the guilt of a daughter who wrongly considered herself an accomplice to a death characterized as a suicide – a choice, not the outcome of mental illness.

As they reached the foot of the hill Beth whispered, "Nicki, look." Beth pointed into the woods. There stood a mature doe.

Nicole spied the doe. In all her visits to the church she had never seen a deer. She held still. The doe caught Nicole's gaze, matching Nicole's stillness. Neither diverted their fix upon the other. A group of children ran down the path, laughing as they threw fallen leaves up in the air and at one another. The doe, startled, bolted. Nicole watched the doe's flight to safety. She turned to Beth. "Thank you."

Beth was uncertain of the root of Nicole's gratitude, but she accepted it with a smile. They continued their walk.

Beth noticed that Nicole checked her watch as they reached the car park. "We have plenty of time."

"I should have ordered a cab before we left."

"I'll take you to the airport."

"It's a reimbursable expense."

Beth wondered why Nicole made it so hard. "Let me. I want to."

Nicole had no reasonable argument. "Hungry?"

Beth knew her offer had been accepted. "Yes, please."

Having stopped at the apartment for Nicole's luggage, Beth drove them both to the airport. Nicole got out of the Jeep. She tilted the passenger seat forward and reached back for her computer case and garment bag, placing them over her shoulders. She leaned back into the Jeep, the better to see Beth. "Thanks for the ride."

Beth debated whether to get out. But for the Sign of Peace, they had not touched all weekend. She did not know how to begin to reach out to Nicole, not even in the simplest way. "Please take care of yourself."

"I will."

"Nicki. When will you come home?"

"A couple of weeks if that's okay?"

Beth realized Nicole was asking permission to return. "Yes, of course. If you let me know ahead of time, I'll try to keep the weekend free."

"I'd like that." Nicole looked about at the heavy traffic. "Beth, I need to go. Security takes forever."

"I know."

"I'll miss you." Nicole closed the door and quickly made her way into the terminal.

Beth was taken unawares. Nicole left her no opportunity to respond. Beth unbuckled her seat belt and opened the Jeep door. She got out to follow Nicole.

A National Guard officer yelled. "Hey! No unattended cars. You'll be towed in a second."

Beth stopped. Nicole was out of sight. Beth looked at the guard. She understood he was doing his job. She gave him a friendly wave as she returned to the Jeep. Beth had erred in her caution and regretted it deeply.

CHAPTER 85

November 1, 2001

An administrative assistant entered Nicole's office. "Nicole, Brian had this package couriered over from Washington for you."

Nicole thanked the assistant as she accepted the large manila envelope. She opened it. Inside, a note from Brian was paper-clipped to a Federal Express envelope.

> *Nicole-*
> *John Nolan asked that I make sure you receive this today.*
> *Brian*
> *P.S.: If I don't speak to you, have a Happy Birthday!*

Nicole got up from her chair and closed the door to her office, one of three reserved for visiting consultants. The late afternoon sun cut across the hardwood. Looking through the large picturesque windows, she could see the sun hovering over the horizon, the beginning of a spectacular sunset.

Nicole returned to her desk and opened the Fed Ex package. Within lay a small card and wrapped in brown paper, what she surmised to be a book. She read the card.

> *Dearest Nicole-*
> *I hope this finds you and Beth well. The girls send their regards. It meant a great deal to them to see you at their mother's memorial service.*
> *I've been slowly going through Carrie's things. I found the enclosed. She meant to give it to you today.*
> *I hope we can get together next time you're in New York.*
> *Happy Birthday. Live life to the fullest.*
> *Love,*
> *John*

Nicole placed John's letter aside. Her gaze rested upon the package. Throughout the day, Carrie's memory had dominated Nicole's thoughts. From the moment she awakened and realized that for the first time in six years, Carrie would not be sharing the day with her, Carrie's ghost became her companion. For the first time in six years, Carrie's ridiculous gift would not threaten to publicly embarrass her. She would not see the glee in Carrie's eyes or hear her uncensored laughter. It was Carrie's irreverence that made their first two shared birthdays memorable. As their friendship deepened, Carrie had changed her tactics. There were always two gifts, one to mortify and one to enlighten. The latter was always a book, and Nicole knew Carrie took the task of choosing the volume seriously. It was always a book that Carrie had read during the previous year, one that impressed or touched her. The gift was always a reflection of Carrie's spirit. Nicole was never disappointed.

Nicole unwrapped the package. Jean Shinoda Bolen's *Ring of Power: Symbols and Themes, Love vs Power in Wagner's Ring Cycle and in Us, A Jungian Feminist Perspective* awaited her. Nicole opened the cover to the title page. It was there that she found a message in Carrie's flowing script.

> *Nicki—*
>
> *There is a challenge in this book to see oneself for who you are, accepting the reasons why you are, and having the courage to become who you are meant to become. I pray that you find the truth I found. It is a truth about love and power. It is a truth that can set you free.*
> *Love,*
> *Carrie*

Nicole's fingertips rested below Carrie's name. Unto her hand fell a tear, then another. Nicole's tears continued to fall freely as her sorrow quaked, threatening the foundation of her sensibilities. She could no longer master her emotions, and that brought her perilously close to the darkness that she had kept at bay ever since the merciful day she had risen above the grief of her mother's death.

Her workday done, Nicole left the office and walked to her hotel. She was greeted by the hotel desk clerk. "Good evening, Ms. Thera."

Nicole reasserted her resolute persona. "Hello, Andrew. Any messages?"

"Ms. Kelly."

Hopeful, Nicole, asked, "She called?"

"No. She's waiting for you in the lounge."

Beth sat on a large leather chair, next to a side table and standing lamp. She kept a watchful eye on the lounge entrance, not knowing when to expect Nicole's return. She was prepared to spend the evening in wait. She held her prayer beads in her hand. She had sought the solace of prayer during her flight to Boston, and feared she would need their comfort if her wait extended through the night. Beth saw Nicole turn toward the lounge. She pocketed the beads and reached for a small gift-wrapped package resting on the table.

As much as Nicole had longed for Beth to contact her, having Beth so near seemed impossible. Nicole approached. She purposely kept herself a few paces away. "Hello."

Beth stood and smiled nervously. "Hi."

Nicole waited. Beth realized the silence was still hers to break. She offered the gift to Nicole. "Happy birthday, Nicki."

Nicole's eyes rested on Beth's extended hand and the small box it held. She placed her briefcase and John's Fed Ex package down on the floor. Straightening up, she hesitantly took possession of the gift. She studied it; having no idea what Beth could offer her. Slowly, she unwrapped the gift, placing the paper down on the side table. The revealed black felt box promised any number of possibilities. She mentally steeled herself, and then opened it. A sterling silver Celtic pendant with a silver necklace was waiting. Nicole knew the pattern well – two circles intertwined, one above the other; the higher symbolizing the spirit, the lower the earth. At the center was a line, erect, symbolizing humanity joining both. Nicole took the pendant in her hand. This was the first time Beth had so clearly acknowledged the non-Christian roots of Nicole's beliefs. She smiled because she knew that this particular design was also the *vesica piscis*, a replica of the cover of the Chalice Well in Glastonbury. The early Celtic Christians had appropriated the pagan symbol and made it their own.

Beth stepped forward. "Nicki."

"It's beautiful." Nicole raised her eyes to Beth. "Thank you."

"Did you have plans for the night?"

Nicole returned her gaze to the pendant. "I was going to stay in and wait to see if you would call me."

Beth's heart ached at Nicole's unguarded frankness and the uncertainty it revealed. She placed her hand over Nicole's. "What would you like to do?"

Nicole was emotionally spent. "I'd like to go up and order room service." Nicole looked over to Beth's overnight bag. "How long can you stay?"

"Saturday. I have to be at the hospital by four-thirty."

"Two nights."

"I wish it could be more."

Nicole took hold of Beth's hand. "Let's go up."

Upon entering Nicole's accommodations, Beth realized that it was the same suite that Nicole had stayed in when Beth had last visited her in Boston. The suite was indicative of Nicole's effort to maintain the familiar. Nicole kept her things in the same place It was as if Beth had never left three months before.

Nicole released Beth's hand. "Why don't you settle in?"

In one fluid motion Beth placed her luggage on the floor and reclaimed Nicole's hand with her own. Nicole paused. Beth acted out of her own need. She went to Nicole and kissed her. Nicole stiffened in response to the unexpected press of Beth against her. Recovering her wits, she took Beth into a hesitant embrace, her hands falling lightly against the younger woman's back.

Beth did not withhold her passion. Nicole felt as if she was being split apart. She did not want to disappoint Beth, but she also felt ill-prepared to feel the emotions that Beth had the power to call forth.

Beth's kisses traveled to Nicole's neck. Nicole felt a light bite. The sensation drew her eyes shut as she exposed herself further to her lover.

Beth craved to give Nicole all that she had withheld during the previous weeks. She whispered, "I'm yours, Nicki," hoping the words would convey all that remained unspoken, the apology too painful to voice.

Nicole's self control was slipping away from her. She rested her forehead upon Beth's shoulder. Beth knew the gesture. It was the closest act of surrender Nicole ever allowed. Beth took Nicole by the hand and led her to the bedroom. Nicole followed passively. Upon reaching the bed Beth stripped Nicole of her coat, letting it drop at their feet. She continued the process of undressing Nicole, offering reassuring kisses as she alternately removed her own clothes.

Beth slipped under the bed covers, guiding Nicole to lie over her. The warmth of Beth's flesh stirred Nicole. She was with Beth; being with Beth was tenderness and care, more than passion. Nicole stroked Beth's hair aside. Nicole's eyes followed her hand's continuous gesture.

Beth studied Nicole, cognizant of her distance. Beth wanted to call Nicole to her, but chose to set aside her own needs as well as the needs she ascribed to her partner. She decided instead to follow wherever Nicole chose to take her.

Nicole returned her gaze to Beth. She did not know how to love Beth. She did not know how to keep her fear at bay. She did not know how to cross the bridge. In her mind the bridge was suspended over a chasm by a fragile cord. She did not believe she could survive falling into the precipice again. Nicole kissed Beth lightly and then pulled herself down resting her head upon Beth's breast, her hand over Beth's belly.

Beth understood Nicole's posture. She understood Nicole did not want a night of lovemaking. Beth laid her arms protectively over Nicole. Once again Beth's expectations were not realized. She closed her eyes and spoke a silent prayer for Nicole and for herself. Soon, she fell into a deep sleep.

Beth awoke in the middle of the night. The steady weight against her body had been removed. She wrapped herself in a blanket and went to the living room threshold. Robed, Nicole sat on the couch, hugging her legs close to her, her back to Beth.

Beth debated whether to respect Nicole's privacy and return to bed or to place herself within Nicole's reach. Beth knew that given Nicole's current vulnerability she had to temper her presence. Still, Beth had come to Boston with a purpose she had yet to realize.

Nicole recalled her birthday a year past. Beth's beauty, compassion and intelligence had intrigued her. Beth had seemed unreachable. Nicole had been certain of the limits and was determined to live with the constraints, grateful that friendship might be a possibility. A few days prior to her birthday they had enjoyed tea at The Garden and attended a lecture at the university.

November brought the trip to Wisconsin and her operation. November was the beginning of a love Nicole could never master. It was neither for her to master Beth nor for Nicole to master herself. It was for Nicole to live life unimpeded. It was for Nicole to begin to live those words that guided her life. To accept, not countermand. To accept, not hold at arm's length, to accept without doubt.

If Beth had maintained her distance, all that Nicole knew would have been affirmed. Now around her neck hung the Celtic pendant. She need only close her eyes and be still to feel its weight against her skin.

Nicole felt a blanket sweep across her arm. Beth silently made a place for herself near Nicole. Nicole adjusted her legs, inviting Beth to lie against her. Beth shifted to the familiar repose. A comfortable silence settled between them.

Beth covered Nicole's embracing arm with her hand. "Nicki?"

Nicole tightened her hold. "I'm here."

"I'm sorry I sent you away."

"I'm good at leaving," Nicole confessed. "It was easier than staying."

"I haven't been fair to you." Beth was tentative. "So much has happened. It's been hard. Harder than I thought it would be."

"Us?"

"Leaving the Church. Not having a church. I've been spending more time in the hospital chapel. It's helped a little."

"Good."

"It's also been hard at the hospital. I knew I would have some bad days but September 11th seemed to make every day harder to get through. I couldn't answer the questions. I didn't know how to get through the anger and depression people felt. I've felt there was nothing I could say or do to help the patients and families or the staff. The night before I suggested we separate I lost a patient in ICU. I watched the doctors try to revive her. It was ugly. No one should be touched the way she was touched. I was angry at you. We had just argued about DNRs and removing life support." Beth leaned her head back. "I thought I was strong. I thought my faith would always help me."

Nicole looked down to better see Beth. "I wish you had told me."

"I know. But, you handled the tragedy so well. I resented the fact that your faith in life wasn't shaken. September 11th just confirmed everything you believed."

Nicole was reeling inside. She found it difficult to believe that she was a model of strength to Beth. Had she camouflaged the truth so well, or was Beth incapable of or simply not wanting to see Nicole's truth? "I've had my bad days, too."

"I want you to come home."

Nicole said nothing. She did not know what kind of home she was returning to, what kind of home she had the heart to create.

Beth sat up straight. "Do you want to come home?"

Nicole searched Beth's eyes, seeking the familiar, gentle warmth that had the power to coax her from her cold protective shell. "Yes."

"There is a get-together for the student chaplains and their families next Friday night. I'll understand if you'd rather not."

It could be Nicole's introduction to the Round Table. "I'll see what I can do."

The following morning Nicole sat on Beth's side of the bed. "Good morning."

Beth opened her eyes. Nicole was fully dressed. "Hi," said Beth. "You leaving?"

"It's still a work day for me. I'll try to get back early. I'll let the front desk know to give you a key. It's going to be a beautiful day. You can do some exploring."

"Okay."

"If I can juggle my schedule, would you like to meet me for lunch?"

"I'd like that."

"I'll call you around ten." Nicole leaned down and kissed Beth lightly. Her Celtic pendant swept over Beth's cross. "I'm sorry I wasn't better company last night. I am glad you came."

"Me, too." The simple, easy waking assured Beth that she was right to come to Boston.

CHAPTER 86

November 3, 2001

Beth and Nicole walked out of the hotel lobby hand in hand. The doorman took Beth's overnight bag and waved a taxi over.

Nicole had grown progressively distant throughout the day. Beth felt that though the distance between them had narrowed in the previous two days, there was still a persistent span that separated them. When words had failed her, Beth tried to reach across to Nicole by engaging her body. Nicole had followed Beth's gentle seduction during the previous evening, and had made love to Beth with a fragileness of spirit that did not escape Beth. After taking Beth to climax, Nicole had retreated, lying on her side, her back to Beth. Beth had been powerless. Nicole would not open herself up any further. Beth had chosen to lie against Nicole, asking no more of her. What sense of rejection she had felt was tempered when Nicole had reached back and taken Beth's hand in her own, moving it forward, holding it close to her heart.

The doorman waited. Beth released Nicole's hand and stepped forward. Upon reaching the cab door, she turned and looked back toward her partner. Beth would not repeat her mistake. She retraced her steps, taking Nicole in a complete embrace. Overwhelmed, Nicole held Beth gingerly. Beth spoke the words she had withheld, for no just reason, from Nicole, "I love you"

Nicole tightened her hold for a moment before releasing Beth. They separated sufficiently to be able to see each other fully. Nicole begged patience. "Beth ... "

Beth cupped Nicole's face with her hand. "Come home as soon as you can."

Nicole nodded.

Without further delay Beth turned and entered the cab. The doorman closed the door behind her. Nicole watched as the cab drove away, out of sight.

CHAPTER 87

November 9, 2001

Nicole arranged to see Jacob upon her arrival in Chicago. Though feeling better, as much as she tried, she could not find her footing.

Jacob listened attentively. "Is there more?"

Nicole confessed, "I haven't been able to tell her that I love her."

"I don't understand."

"Since she pulled back from me … when I look at her, when I touch her, I feel … all I feel is my love for her, but I can't …"

"And you feel your fear. Is that not true? You are frightened."

Nicole gave Jacob her complete regard. "Yes."

Jacob patted Nicole's hand. "When you are young, when love is young you believe nothing will come close to your love, but you are wrong. So very wrong. The love deepens, and this new love is both familiar and new. What I believe you are feeling is a deepening of your love for Beth." Jacob bit down on his pipe. "How can that be, you may ask? She has already consumed you. What more can you give? How much more is there to receive? My Nicole, the depth of your heart has no limit. I believe Beth will take you places within yourself that you do not even know exist. There is a risk. Beth is as human as you are. She will make mistakes. And when she does, you may be hurt. And the hurt will be deeper than any you have ever known. This pain you have carried with you. Beth is one source of this pain. You must trust her. You must trust yourself. I have had this pain. I promise you, you will not regret it."

"Liza?"

"Yes. Except I must confess that I have hurt her more than she could ever hurt me. Why she stays with me I do not know, but she does. She is always with me, no matter how big the fool I become. She is my lifeline when I get lost on the sea. She brings me back. I may be an old man, good for nothing, but I know love because Liza's lesson cannot be forgotten."

CHAPTER 88

November 9, 2001 – Evening

"Who is that?" The strikingly beautiful woman at the door had diverted Jerry's attention.

Beth and Pam turned to look. Nicole stood at the threshold.

Jerry mused, "Wonder if she belongs to anyone?"

Pam turned to Beth and smiled.

"Excuse me." Beth went to Nicole and took her into an embrace.

Nicole held tight.

Beth whispered, "I've missed you."

"I hope I'm not too late. I dropped my things off at the apartment first."

The women separated. "How was your flight?"

Nicole placed her hand on Beth's cheek. "I love you."

It did not matter that Beth was certain of Nicole's love. Beth felt at times that Nicole's love and God's love came to her the same way – independent of her effort. Nicole's simple words had not been voiced in weeks, and Beth had yet to understand why. She did know that Nicole was struggling and until she finished wrestling with the angels she would not speak. The smile, the gesture, the incomparable three words had marked an ending and a new beginning. Beth felt the new beginning taking hold of her, shattering all doubts she harbored. Nicole belonged to her.

Beth embraced Nicole completely. Nicole was well aware of what she had done and Beth's recognition of the same. Nicole whispered in her lover's ear, "I think we're making a scene."

"I don't care."

"Yes, but I think I'm feeling a strong dose of envy in the air. You want these people to like me, don't you?"

Beth laughed and stepped back. "Come on. There's someone I want you to meet." She led Nicole to Cindy.

Later in the evening, Beth noticed a gathering had formed in a far corner of the room. She returned to her conversation with Christine and her husband, Gary. Christine noticed the gathering as well. "I wonder what's going on?"

Luke approached the threesome. "Beth, you might want to play referee between Nicole and our resident scholar."

Beth was not overly concerned. "What are they talking about?"

"DNRs and removal of life-support."

"Nicki can hold her own."

Luke smiled. "She's not the one I'm worried about."

"Come on, Beth. Let's at least watch," said Christine.

Beth relented. "Oh, right. But I'm not interfering."

Beth led the contingent. The other students and family members parted, creating a path to give her free access to the contest. Beth maintained a discreet distance.

Jerry was querying Nicole. "Beth mentioned you like to read the Greeks. Are they your authority?"

Nicole could not believe someone as condescending as Jerry would aspire to become a chaplain. "I don't particularly need to reference other philosophers to justify my beliefs, but as long as you mentioned the Classics, it's a good place to start."

"I have limited use for them."

"You do?"

"Their arguments are flawed."

Nicole was dubious. She wagered Jerry's offhanded nod toward Greek philosophy was indicative of nothing more than a superficial knowledge. She was looking forward to exploring the subject. "Which arguments, specifically?"

"The Cynics had no reverence for life. They felt death was a reasonable choice."

Nicole went to the foundation of Jerry's argument. "And it isn't?"

"No. Human beings shouldn't take a shortcut to eternity."

"But the Cynics didn't believe in an afterlife. They weren't taking a shortcut to anything but ceasing to exist."

Jerry was disdainful. "That's nihilism."

"Wasn't it the Stoics and not the Cynics who argued that death could be a rational decision? The Cynics' position was more an issue of being able to live life according to nature."

"You're right about the Stoics, but the Cynics still applied *logos* to determine whether they were living a worthwhile life."

"Yes, you're right." Nicole waited for Jerry's next move. He made none so she decided to take the lead. "What other arguments do you discount?"

Jerry would not be maneuvered. He responded with his own question. "How about you? What argument can you make?"

"I can't say I'm convinced by Plato's reasons for sanctioning the choice of death. I mean, I'm not going to choose death because the *polis* orders me to. And because of intolerable shame or devastating misfortune? Depends on the devastating misfortune. Complete loss of my ability to live independently might qualify. Then there's Aristotle's denial of choice because of our civic duty to the state to stay alive. What if the civic duty gets redefined to be a quick and inexpensive death? Problem there ... anyway, I'm not much for the wholesale sacrifice of individual free will to the benefit of the state. I agree with most of what the Cynics believed and I don't find them that incompatible with the Epicureans. The problem I have with the Stoics is their belief in predestination. It makes me wonder if Martin Luther read them."

Beth suppressed a laugh as Nicole linked Jerry's Lutheran tradition to her own Classical roots.

Nicole continued. "Still, they left a loophole. I mean, the Stoics argued that taking one's life might simply be one's destiny. If you don't mind a shift to the Romans, I personally hold to Cicero. In *Tusculan Disputations* he wrote that life is a preparation for death. I think its amazing that it was only thirty years ago that a modern like Elizabeth Kübler-Ross shook up the medical profession when she wrote the same thing in her groundbreaking death work."

Beth leaned over to Cindy, who had moved to her side, and whispered, "Should I rescue Jerry?"

Cindy responded with an equally hushed, "I'll never forgive you if you do."

Nicole paused.

The ensuing silence jarred Jerry from his effort to keep up with her argument. He lacked confidence in his own knowledge to offer a response.

Nicole chose to bring the subject back to a Christian reference. "Jerry, I'm confused. With the strong influence of Neo-Platonism on Christian theology, I'd have thought you would find merit in Plotinus' writings."

Jerry looked nauseous. "What do you mean?"

"He argued that no one could rationally decide to kill oneself. He also argued that a good soul should always decide to remain in the body. It's interesting that he didn't have to rely on the Pythagorean argument that to kill oneself was an act against God. I agree with Plotinus that to choose death can't be a rational act. I wouldn't want it to be. It's an act of the human will that takes into account reason, emotion and faith, so the choice is never completely rational. The problem with the issue of voluntary death is that the civic powers feel they have an obligation to intervene. I don't know if Seneca's perspective that death is the ultimate choice of a free man will ever be something our society can come to terms with," Nicole offered a satisfied smile. "What do you think, Jerry?"

Beth could see that Jerry was drowning. He could not match Nicole's mastery of the subject. Beth, well aware of Nicole's gifted, near genius intellect, was not completely surprised by Nicole taking Jerry and all the others listening on a whirlwind tour of Classical philosophy. Still, Beth was impressed by the relative ease with which Nicole had done so with a subject far from common social discourse. Beth was proud, so very proud, of Nicole. And she had to admit that within the span of a few minutes, she had come to a new appreciation for Nicole's position on an individual's right to choose death, even though Beth still dissented on certain specific points.

Jerry found his voice. It was fueled by hurt pride. "I can't argue with you. Anyone who discounts God is too far removed from this forum to be of any value."

Nicole felt the insult. Her response was tempered. "In your opinion."

"I can see why it's so hard for Beth to tolerate your godless arrogance."

The room stilled.

Nicolè did not know how much truth there was in it Jerry's brutal verbal assault and she did not care. In that moment, rational thought was hard to come by; still, she would not engage in the verbal violence. "Excuse me. I had a long flight from Boston. I think it's best if I call it a night."

Nicole walked away from both Jerry and Beth. Jerry looked around. His gaze crossed paths with Beth's. Hers was a mask-like expression. She maintained the connection until the self-created pariah turned away.

CHAPTER 89

November 10, 2001

Two hours had passed before Nicole returned to the apartment. She stood outside the door. There was a life within the apartment she ached for, yet equally feared. She felt the fine double-edged blade of joy and sorrow, a blade honed more sharply as the distance between her and Beth was abolished.

Beth entered the living room from the kitchen as Nicole closed the door. "Nicki?"

Nicole needed to break the tension quickly. "All I can say is if Jerry is going to be one of the elect, he better hope God has a storehouse of grace to go around."

Beth spoke before fully comprehending the humor behind Nicole's words. "I didn't say ... "

Nicole smiled broadly. "Don't you think I know that?" Nicole removed her coat. "I admit it took a couple of blocks before I remembered what a jerk Jerry is. Did he get out of the room alive?"

Beth grinned. "Barely."

"You didn't hit him or anything?"

Beth laughed. "No."

Nicole hung her coat in the hall closet. "By the way, how did I do?"

"I was impressed."

If it was possible, Nicole's smile grew brighter. "I've got to be the best heathen I can be when I'm with your crowd."

Beth was about to protest before she gave it a second thought. "They are my crowd, aren't they?"

"Yes, they are." Nicole looked about. "Well, I better unpack."

"I put your laptop case in the den and your garment bag in the bed-room."

Nicole gave Beth her consideration. Beth's invitation was evident; so, too, was Nicole's acceptance. "Thank you."

Beth took a step forward. "Nicki, are we okay?"

At that moment, Nicole had no doubt. "Yes Beth, we are."

"I want ..." Beth faltered in expressing her need.

"What is it?"

"I want to make love to you."

Nicole went to Beth, taking her hands in her own. "And I want you to make love to me. I want you to take me with you and if it seems as if I'm drifting away from you, I want you to call me back. Whatever you do, don't let me slip away from you. Keep me with you from the beginning until the end. Do it, Beth. Do it for me."

Beth acted upon Nicole's permission, guiding her to their bedroom, leading their lovemaking.

"Nicki," Beth gently called to her lover.

Beth's touch had Nicole on the edge of bliss. Nicole moaned as the pleasure neared pain.

"Say my name." Beth stopped all motion increasing Nicole's sweet torture. "Nicki, say my name."

Nicole felt Beth's voice pull her back. She complied, her own voice hoarse. "Beth."

"That's right. Stay with me, Nicki." Beth renewed the intimate strokes.

Nicole reached out with her hand, and held Beth's idle forearm. Without further coaching, Nicole whispered Beth's name. The tension within her body tightened to a degree she would have once sworn impossible to bear. Again, she voiced Beth's name. The break came. Nicole's self-control shattered in her complete physical release. Her body shuddered as she cried out Beth's name.

Beth felt Nicole's viselike grip on her arm. She held steady as Nicole's body convulsed in spasms. As Nicole calmed, Beth shifted, blanketing Nicole's body with her own, offering herself as a comforting shield. Nicole's hands fluttered on Beth's back.

"I love you, Nicki."

There were the words. Nicole began to cry. These were not easy tears. They came from the past with full, unrestrained force. They had been bound for all of her adult life, refused any mode of expression. Nicole cried deeply, her will surrendering to the demanding flow of emotion.

Beth had never been witness to Nicole's free tears. Her suspicions of the depth of Nicole's unexpressed sorrow were confirmed. She held Nicole until the tears subsided and she drifted to sleep.

Beth awoke to find herself alone in bed. The table clock read 2:28 a.m. She listened for a hint of Nicole's whereabouts. She heard nothing. Sitting up, she could see a sliver of light in the hall. Beth followed the light to its origin.

The den door was ajar. Beth used her hand to open it further. Nicole's desk lamp provided the dim light. Nicole stood at the corner window looking out into the night.

"Nicki." Beth entered the room.

Nicole turned her head slightly in response to Beth's voice. She gathered her thoughts. "I've been having a reoccurring dream, more like a nightmare. I was a ghost standing at the foot of our bed. I kept watch while you and I lay in bed. You were holding me like you always do. You woke up and leaned over and kissed me on the cheek. You must have sensed something was wrong. I must have been cold. I wasn't breathing. I had died. I died in your arms. It was the sweetest death I could have ever imagined, but then I saw what it did to you. I don't know how to live with that dream. I don't know how to live with the truth that the closer we become, the more painful it will be when that day comes."

Beth struggled to compose herself. She spoke softly. "Has your diagnosis changed?"

Nicole saw the fear in Beth. She renewed her decision not to speak of Shenandoah. "No."

Beth offered God a silent thank you. She approached Nicole, pausing less than an arm's length from her. "I could be first."

Nicole was taken aback. She shook her head in defiance. "No."

There was a part of Beth that understood Nicole's fear all too well. "My mother was thirty-one when she died of ovarian cancer. Her mother – my maternal grandmother – died young of cancer, too. I have the genetic trait that puts me at a high risk."

Nicole was wrenched from her own path onto Beth's. She turned to Beth, maintaining a steady tone. "You never said anything."

"Nicki, you believe in fate. I believe in God. Either way we can't change our destinies. We can only fight for them. I want to grow old with you. I want to love you as your hair turns salt and pepper and you wear your first pair of glasses and you move just a little slower so it's easier for me to keep up with you. But I don't know how long I'm going to … you've been ill and I know someday your illness might come back, but I can't stop loving you because of the possibility of a reoccurrence. I can't stop loving you because it will break my heart to have you leave me or for me to leave you."

Nicole searched Beth's eyes, seeing in them a conviction to the future that had the power to shelter her worst fears. "I will always love you."

"I need you, Nicki. Please, don't ever forget that."

"I'm scheduled to fly back to Boston on Sunday. I can call and postpone my flight."

Beth was touched by Nicole's offer, but she knew Nicole had to live her life fearlessly. "You have a job to do."

"There are more important things … "

"You made a commitment."

"Yes." Nicole was fierce. "To you."

Beth felt the force of Nicole's uncompromising nature. She felt the grace of having Nicole's love. "If your dream is true, you're going to die here in my arms, not in Boston."

Nicole had met her match. "So are you saying that as a matter of self-preservation I should go?"

"Whatever it takes."

Nicole had not dwelled on Beth's mother's death. The fact now loomed as a risk, a threat. "How often do you see your doctor?"

"Every year in late spring. She's thorough."

"Test results?"

"All negative."

"Marie?"

"She's fine. She's less at risk. She doesn't have the genetic mutation."

Nicole reached out and took Beth's hand, then repeated her earlier question. "Why didn't you tell me?"

Beth intertwined their fingers. "In the scheme of things, it just wasn't high on my list."

"Why tell me now?"

"Because we're not as different as you may think. You told me once you didn't believe that we were promised more than the life we were given – the here and now. You were right; accepting the finite isn't the hard part. Finding hope, finding meaning in life in spite of the finite is."

Nicole would need time alone to weigh what she had learned with who she believed Beth to be. "And so you have your calling."

Beth stepped closer, embracing Nicole. "And I have you."

CHAPTER 90

November 22, 2001

Nicole and Beth had chosen to enjoy a quiet, private Thanksgiving. They lay on the couch reading. It had become a habit they developed without words. If Nicole wanted to be alone she would read in the den. If Beth sought solitude, she would be found in the sunroom. If they longed for the other, they would rest on the living room couch, an unspoken invitation to the other to join her. Tonight, Nicole was the first to take up residence on the couch.

Beth had been reading the Psalms. She closed her Bible and shifted her body towards Nicole. Beth placed her hand over the pages of Nicole's open book.

Nicole wore a false frown. "I was in the middle of a sentence."

Beth waited. With one hand Nicole raised the book away. Beth leaned forward and kissed her. She laid her head against Nicole's chest, seeking her lover's heartbeat.

Nicole kissed the top of Beth's head and laid her book down. She then reached for Beth's Bible and took careful possession of it, placing it on top of her own book. "One thing I admire about the ancient Greeks was their concept of hospitality. They would feed and bathe visitors, total strangers, not requiring them to disclose their name. And it wasn't uncommon for a host to give a visitor a gift to take with them. The belief was that someday their roles would be reversed and the host would enjoy the hospitality of the visitor."

"It's too bad we lost that custom."

"It's made me think about the whole concept of gift giving."

"In what way?"

"I was thinking about the exchange of rings."

Beth raised herself up, her gaze intent. It took all of Nicole's self control to maintain their constant eye contact.

Nicole continued. "It doesn't necessarily have to be equated with ownership. There are many rituals in history similar in form, but the underlying meaning is different. And there is nothing to say that two people couldn't chose to imbue an old form with new meaning if they were of the same mind."

"I would agree."

"What if you exchanged gifts with someone else?"

Beth proceeded cautiously. "Rings?"

"Rings," Nicole confirmed. She searched for a common ground. "What would that mean to you?"

"With a friend or more than a friend?"

"A friend and more." Nicole offered a muted smile. "Much more."

Beth searched for words that remained within the temporal realm. "It would mean that I was true to her, that I would not live my life without consideration of her. That I loved her in a way that I don't have the words to express, so I've given her a symbol, a ring, without beginning or end, complete unto itself."

"The ring. Would it be elaborate or simple?"

"A gold band."

Nicole braced herself. "Would the exchange need to be public?"

Beth would not ask that of Nicole. "It could be private. Just the two of us."

Nicole searched Beth's countenance for assurance. She needed to be certain. "Are you sure that would be enough?"

"Yes, Nicki. It would."

Nicole looked away toward the fireplace. "It's something to think about."

"If and when … you'll know." Beth rested back on Nicole's chest. She decided to take advantage of Nicole's open mood. "Nicki, I'd like a Christmas tree." Beth waited for Nicole's yelp.

Nicole stroked Beth's hair. "Where do you want to put it?"

Beth looked up. She wondered when the real Nicole Thera had been kidnapped and replaced by the woman in her arms. Beth still doubted. She knew there would be no debate if she chose the sunroom, although that was not her preference. She decided to risk all. "By the fireplace."

"That should work. We'll have to move the chairs."

"Cindy and I were thinking of going tree shopping together. Want to come with us?"

Nicole scoffed playfully. "I'll pass. Christmas and everything that goes with it is yours. Okay?"

Beth was relieved. The Nicole she knew had not gone too far away. "Are you sure about this?"

"No decorations in the den and I'll be a happy heathen."

Beth laid her head back on Nicole's chest. She loved her 'happy heathen.' Given their unforeseen discussion of rings, Beth chose not to renew the subject of gifts. Nicole held firm their first Christmas. In spite of their conversation, Beth did not expect this year to be any different.

CHAPTER 91

December 13, 2001

Nicole searched out Tess. The Detroit airport, like all others in the country, had changed their security protocols, making it more difficult to locate those waiting for travelers. She was about ready to call Tess on her cell phone when she felt a tap on her shoulder. Turning, Nicole received an enthusiastic embrace, and laughed, relieved.

Tess said playfully, "We have to stop meeting like this."

Nicole considered the woman she embraced. "I like the idea of tarnishing your reputable reputation."

Tess warned, "We are not alone."

"We are in the middle of an airport."

Tess swung around, keeping her arm around Nicole's waist. Nicole's seven-year-old goddaughter stood hugging a stuffed tiger toy. Nicole knew happiness. "I swear Tess, one of these days I'm taking her home with me and no ransom will be enough to get me to give her up."

"She insisted on coming when she found out you were going to be on a layover. I left Jack in daycare. I figured the National Guard deserved a break."

Nicole chuckled. She took a few strides narrowing the space between her and Dion. She knelt on one knee and opened her arms. Dion needed no further invitation. She ran and flung herself into Nicole's arms. Nicole cried on impact. "Whoa!"

Dion laughed.

"Let me look at you." Nicole held the child at arm's length. "You are getting to be such a big girl. Does your mama let you drive yet?"

Dion shook her head. "No."

Tess put her hand on Nicole's shoulder. "Don't encourage her. She'll ask her father the minute we get home and you know how Bruce is."

"I see you brought Stripes." Nicole referred to the toy she had given to Dion on her last birthday. "Has he been a good boy?"

Dion nodded. "Yes."

"Good. I'm glad he's kept his promise."

"He's happy to see you." Dion offered Stripes to Nicole.

Nicole took possession of the tiger. "Oh. Oh. I just heard his tummy growl. Do you think he might be hungry?"

Dion looked up to her mother with questioning eyes.

"Honey, are you ready for lunch?" asked Tess.

"Stripes is."

"Well, we don't want Stripes to get too hungry," Tess explained to Nicole. "He gets cranky."

"That's decided." Nicole gathered Dion in her arms and stood up. "Your mama will lead the way."

"If the food here was only half as good as Miguel's cooking I'd be happy. I really wish you had more than a couple of hours."

"Flights don't come easy. Let's go. I expect to be properly spoiled by my two best girl friends."

Having their lunch served, Dion sat in Nicole's arms, sharing her god-mother's turkey sandwich and fruit cup. Stripes had sentry duty. He was placed at the center of the table facing Dion. Dion found Nicole's necklace worth an inspection. She reached out and traced the pendant with her finger-tips, exploring its contours.

Tess leaned forward. "What are you wearing around your neck?"

"It's a birthday gift from Beth."

"It's Christian."

"It's pagan."

"It's also Christian."

"The pagans had this symbol way before the Christians." Nicole looked down. Dion had it firmly in her small fist and was tugging. Nicole placed her hand over the child's to stay her effort. "This one's Celtic."

Her tone leaving no doubt of her disapproval Tess asked, "How many times have you told me you're not a pagan?"

"Tess ..."

"Don't Tess me! Nicki, I don't have to tell you how powerful symbols can be. Don't you find it a bit incongruous to be wearing a symbol that says nothing about who you are? Beth couldn't get you something Greek?"

"Will you stop? Give her credit for trying."

"She's not trying hard enough. Why not an Alpha and Omega or ..."

Nicole had taken possession of Dion's hand. She kissed it, appeasing the child. "Tess, we're good." Nicole looked up catching her friend's intense gaze. "Really."

Tess sighed. "You're not just saying that so I won't sic Stripes on you?"

"Like you wouldn't see through the lie."

"You do look good."

"Like I said." Nicole offered Dion a grape. "Come on sweetheart. I know you like these."

Tess smiled as Dion docilely took the offered fruit. "How do you do it?"

"What?" Nicole asked.

"What?" Tess mimicked lightheartedly. "That." She pointed to her daughter. "Did you sprinkle her with fairy dust when I wasn't looking?"

Nicole laughed as she glanced down to Tess's – at times – rebellious daughter. "I told you, she's my girl."

"Speaking of your girls, how's Beth?"

Nicole grew serious. "She has good days and not-so-good days."

"How is she dealing with the holidays?"

"She's getting a Christmas tree. That's a positive sign."

Tess shook her head in disbelief. "Nicole Thera, the things you do for love."

"Hey, the tree is her responsibility." Nicole was determined to hold Beth to their bargain. "I'm exempt from all holiday related duties."

"Are you exchanging gifts?"

Nicole gave a sly smile. "It's not her birthday."

Tess drew out Nicole's name. "Nicki."

Nicole focused on Dion. "Hey, we better eat up. My flight leaves in an hour."

CHAPTER 92

December 15, 2001

Nicole felt as if she was being watched. She looked up from her desk.

Beth stood at the den entrance. "Hi"

"Hello." Nicole leaned back lazily in her chair. "You're holding up the door frame quite nicely."

"Thank you." Beth wore a disarming smile. "I need a favor."

"Why are alarms going off in my head?" Nicole absentmindedly tapped her pen against the desk.

"I don't know."

"It might be the smile you're wearing."

Beth reminded, "You like my smile."

"Yes, I do."

"I need help with the tree."

Nicole offered her own reminder. "I thought we had a deal."

"Just one thing. I'm having a hard time reaching the top of the tree to put on the star."

"You want me to hold you up?"

"Or you could put the star on?"

"I'd rather hold you up," Nicole teased.

"I'll make it up to you."

Nicole was beguiled. "How?"

"Name it."

Nicole admonished, "Beth, you're taking a big risk here."

"Will you help me?" Beth was unfazed.

Nicole got to her feet. "Lead me to the tree."

Beth placed her hand over Nicole's heart as Nicole reached her. "What do you want in return?"

"I'll take a rain check. I'm sure something will come up."

Beth took Nicole's hand and led her to the living room. She had stored the unused decorations and empty boxes. All the furniture was in place except for the kitchen step stool awaiting Nicole. They paused before the eight-foot pine. Nicole had to admit it was beautifully adorned. The balance of the room was modestly decorated; Beth had exercised tasteful restraint. Nicole approved. All that remained to complete the tree was the star, which lay on the fireplace mantle. Beth offered the decoration to Nicole. Nicole took advantage of the step stool and quickly rested the star on the tree, plugging it to a nearby light cord.

"How's that."

"Perfect."

Nicole stepped down.

"Nicki, wait here for a minute."

Nicole suppressed a protest as Beth returned the step stool to the kitchen and darkened the nearby room lights. She then went to the back of the tree and plugged in the master light cord. The tree shone. Beth walked to the sunroom threshold to capture a broad view of the tree and the fireplace. Nicki basked in Beth's delight.

"It's beautiful."

"You really like it?"

Nicole walked over to Beth and gave her a gentle kiss. "You've done good."

Beth's eyes turned from Nicole back to the tree. "Thank you."

"Anything else I can do?"

"No. I'm just going to sit here for a while."

"Okay."

Nicole left the room as Beth made herself comfortable on the living room couch. Within a few minutes Nicole returned. Beth followed Nicole with her eyes. She said nothing as Nicole slid herself behind Beth on the couch. With a clear view of the tree, Beth rested against Nicole. She knew no greater happiness.

CHAPTER 93

December 24, 2001

Nicole and Beth walked home hand in hand after enjoying a quiet dinner. Nicole noted that Beth had grown introspective. She squeezed her partner's hand. "Beth, what is it?"

In spite of Nicole's immutable support, Beth debated whether to make her request. She did not want to threaten the only recently achieved equilibrium in their shared lives. "Would you mind very much if I leave the apartment for a few hours tonight?"

Nicole knew there could only be one reason for Beth's request. "Midnight Mass?"

"Yes."

"Where?"

"St Paul's."

Nicole considered her options. She could not deny the request. The only remaining question was whether to accompany Beth. Jacob's challenge was in the forefront of her mind. "May I come with you?"

"Would you?" Beth was pleasantly surprised.

"I want to be with you tonight."

Beth reverted to their gentle banter, easing the tension within her. "And you'll go to Mass to do it?"

Nicole kissed Beth's gloved hand. "Go figure."

St. Paul's and the Redeemer Episcopal Church on Dorchester Street was walking distance from the apartment. Beth took her Book of Common Prayer with her. It was a gift given to her by her home congregation on the occasion of her ordination. Six months had passed since she had worshiped in an Episcopal Church; her only formal worship experience during that time had been her visit to the Hill with Nicole.

Nicole held her hand as they entered the edifice. Beth chose a place to sit mid-point from the altar, at the edge of the center aisle. This would allow the least amount of inconvenience when Nicole excused herself from communion. Upon entering the pew, Nicole released Beth's hand. Beth lowered the kneeler and knelt in prayer. She sought her own words of adoration, praise and thanksgiving but found her well dry. She looked up to the Christ and silently recited Psalm 121.

I lift up my eyes to the hills;
from where is my help to come?

My help comes from the LORD,
the maker of heaven and earth.

He will not let your foot be moved;
he who keeps you will not slumber.
He who keeps Israel
will neither slumber nor sleep:

The LORD is your keeper;
the LORD is your shade at your right hand,
The sun shall not strike you by day,
nor the moon by night.

The LORD will keep you from all evil;
he will keep your life.
The Lord will keep your going out and your coming in,
from this time on and forevermore.

The celebrant entered in procession, followed by an assistant priest and a deacon. Beth admired their chasubles, flowing beautifully as they walked. All the garments that she had once worn to celebrate the Divine Liturgy were carefully packed and kept out of sight. She worshiped, unable to keep herself spiritually from the altar, placing herself in the role of celebrant. Though the Catholic liturgy was similar to the Episcopal, Beth felt a renewed intimacy here at St. Paul's that had eluded her at Holy Hill.

At The Peace, Beth and Nicole turned to one another. Beth leaned forward and kissed Nicole gently on the lips. "Peace, Nicki."

"Peace, my love." Nicole was hopeful for Beth's sake.

As the service continued, Beth silently recited the Eucharistic Prayer. In her mind she raised the Host and the chalice. She broke the bread. She offered both the Body and Blood of Christ to the communicants.

As communion commenced, Beth stood. Nicole stepped out of the pew as Beth and the other worshippers proceeded to the front of the church. Nicole watched Beth's every step.

Beth received the Sacraments in both kinds. She followed the Host as the priest placed it in her hands. She lifted the Host into her mouth, and felt its light weight upon her tongue. She stepped to the Deacon who offered the chalice. She drank the wine. The taste was a blend of sweet and bitter. Beth walked back to the pew feeling an incessant heartbreak. She knelt in prayer. The words of adoration, praise and thanksgiving still would not come.

Nicole's gaze rested upon Beth as she prayed. Throughout the service, Nicole felt as if Beth had left herself exposed to potential harm, although Nicole had no name for that harm. All Nicole wanted to do was protect Beth but she knew that the battle was not hers to fight. The conflict was between

Beth and the Church, mediated by Beth's God. The conflict was located so deep within Beth that Nicole knew she had no hope of mapping its topography.

Beth's stillness was interrupted by brief movement. Nicole leaned forward in concern. Beth was in tears. Nicole did not hesitate; she knelt beside Beth and placed her arm around Beth's shoulder, coaxing her devastated partner to her.

Beth allowed herself to be guided into Nicole's arms. Her tears continued as Nicole held her in a tender embrace.

Nicole looked to the image of Jesus of Nazareth on the cross, to Beth's Christ. Where was God's perfect love? Where was the agape? Where was the love this Church's namesake had preached in Chapter Thirteen of his first letter to the Corinthians? Where was the patient, kind love, the love that is not resentful, the love that rejoices in the truth? Where was the greatest of virtues?

Nicole could not fathom how a god would allow a child of its creation, a child who longed to love and dedicate herself to its service, the pain of estrangement that Beth clearly felt. Nicole could not fathom how a god would allow Beth to be rejected by the very institution that professed to live in Christ.

All Nicole wanted was for Beth to heal. There seemed to be no respite for Beth, no oasis to quench her thirst and sustain her on her journey. The one place where Nicole thought Beth should find rest and the affirming waters of life – the Church – had left her in the parched desert, and barred her from finding shade under its roof or access to its well. The Church had forced Beth to choose between her priesthood and her unsullied love for Nicole. Nicole had set aside her anger toward the Church. However, she still wished the day would come when the Church would recognize in shame the damage it had done when it wrongly claimed the Gospels condemned this child of its God. Whatever hope Nicole had held that Beth neared healing was shattered.

CHAPTER 94

December 25, 2001

Beth awoke with Nicole sleeping soundly beside her. Beth kissed Nicole lightly on the cheek before getting out of bed. As coffee brewed, she walked into the sun-drenched living room. The previous evening had ended quietly. Nicole had held Beth close as they walked home. Few words were exchanged. Beth had been grateful for Nicole's silence and her ability to console without words. Beth would not have known how to respond to even the gentlest query. Her heart was still tender to the touch. Her fragility lingered.

Underneath the Christmas tree was a set of large packages. These were new to Beth. She bent down for a closer look. Beth read her name on an envelope that rested on top of the larger package. She debated whether to wait for Nicole to awaken, but her curiosity was far too great to delay. She went down to her knees and removed the card from its sleeve. The cover had a simple gold cross, within Nicole's handwriting.

> *Beth-*
> > *To celebrate your Savior.*
> *Love, Nicki*

Beth re-read the card, not understanding. She put the card aside and rested her hands upon the first package, gliding them to each end. She began the process of separating the paper at the edges. She lifted the paper over and back revealing a teakwood box. Beth took in a breath and held it. She had seen similar boxes before, and knew what they were meant to protect. Her hand went to the simple swing latch that held the box closed. She released it with her thumb, then moved her hands to each side of the box and raised the cover. Her expectations were realized. Resting firmly in place within a cut felt cloth interior were a gold plated sterling silver chalice and matching ciborium. To the side lay a paten. Beth softly breathed Nicole's name.

Beth's eyes went to the chalice. She raised the chalice from its resting place. It had an onyx node and was set off with semi-precious stones. The base had palm leaves marking the four directions. Four identical grape and wheat designs had been engraved in a one-inch ribbon that wrapped the cup. Beth raised the chalice to eye level. Knowing she would never celebrate an Episcopalian Mass again she felt a profound sadness. She returned the chalice to its place then shifted her focus to the ciborium. She took it in hand. The cover had a raised emblem of the Holy Spirit. She lifted the cover from the cup. Within was a complete supply of Priest Hosts.

Beth returned the ciborium to its place and shifted her focus to the second, smaller package – certain of its contents. She carefully unwrapped the packages, finding a matching teakwood box with a similar latch. She opened the box to find a set of crystal cruets with a gold plated tray, beside the cruets – a full set of Mass linens. Beth's fingers went to the finely woven cloth. It was delicate and soft to the touch. Underneath the cover, held by elastic straps, was a simple wooden cross.

Beth fell back upon her heels, stunned. The message behind Nicole's words was clear to her. Nicole's acknowledgement of Beth's Christian faith had never been more unqualified. Nicole had reaffirmed God's place in Beth's heart. Beth bowed her head and cried openly.

Nicole had been watching Beth from the front foyer. Beth was so intent on the gifts that Nicole remained undetected. Nicole was satisfied to watch Beth's careful exploration of the two packages. The care and reverence Beth showed for the chalice and ciborium gave Nicole hope that she had not made a mistake. Beth's tears the previous evening had left Nicole doubting whether her gesture would be welcomed. Nicole's doubts spiked at the sight of Beth's renewed tears. Nicole went to Beth, falling to her knees beside her. Knowing she was the cause of Beth's weeping, Nicole hesitated offering any touch, fearful of rejection.

"Will you speak to me if I swear my intentions were good?" Nicole waited.

Beth's tears subsided. Her gaze remained fixed upon the chalice.

Nicole looked from Beth to the chalice and back to Beth.

"You're a scholar and a chaplain but you're also a priest. I thought ..." Nicole grasped at words to explain herself. "I know the Mass is supposed to be celebrated in a community ... "

Beth turned and pressed her fingers to Nicole's lips. "It's all right. I'm all right."

Nicole took Beth's hand and placed a kiss upon its palm. "I'm sorry."

"You have no reason to be." Beth wondered if she could ever love Nicole more than she did at that very moment. She felt a sudden regret. "Nicki, I didn't get you anything."

"That's what birthdays are for. I just didn't want to wait until July."

With a faint smile, Beth reached out and touched Nicole's Celtic pendant.

CHAPTER 95

December 31, 2001

The two-story lobby of Chamberlain Development was filled with guests. Jason had brought friends, family, employees and business associates together to celebrate the New Year. The affair was casual, with abundant food and drink.

Nicole approached Trevor Benware, a photographer Jason often contracted to document his developments. Nicole took the nervous little man aside. "Beth has noticed your overenthusiastic photography."

"I was being careful," said Trevor.

"Not careful enough. She asked me to come over here and slap you upside the head."

"I thought she was a priest."

"That's why I'm doing the slapping. Do you have what you need?"

"No!" Trevor clamored in frustration. "You haven't set the pose for me. Figure something out."

Nicole would have an end to the farce. "Follow me."

Trevor stood grounded in place. "What are you going to do?"

"I'm going to introduce you, and you are going to beg for one more photo to submit to your photography class professor and when you take the damn picture you'll have the pose we agreed on."

"Nicole, I've been a professional photographer for years. I teach photography."

"We are lying," said Nicole. "Ly-ing. It goes with deception. Take the damn photo and if Andrea doesn't like it you're going to hear from me."

Trevor was sullen. "Threatening someone who is doing you a favor isn't a good strategy."

"Neither is getting Beth so distracted that she had to send me over to you."

The photographer said proudly, "I'm taking the photo to show my students how it can be done in a crowded situation."

"Fine." Nicole led Trevor back to Beth.

Now that Nicole had bribed the photographer with one photo to set Beth free from his constant flash, Beth was able to enjoy the party. Connor was a charming companion. Alex joined them as Nicole slipped away to mingle.

Connor had a sheepish smile on his face as Beth described the monumental effort it had taken for her and Cindy to carry the Christmas tree into the apartment.

Connor laughed. "You must have really wanted that tree to go through all that even after Nicki's speech."

Beth was puzzled. "What speech?"

"The annual holocaust of trees speech." Connor paused for Beth to affirm Nicole's annual tirade. Beth's blank look conveyed an unexpected ignorance. "Nicki didn't give you the speech about what a waste it was to have millions of trees cut for the sake of a ritual that had nothing to do with the religious origin of Christmas?" Connor switched to a false academic persona. "Most people don't realize that seventeenth century German Christians appropriated the pagan fertility symbol of the tree and made it a symbol of rebirth appropriate to the celebration of the Christ's birth."

"No."

"My God, Beth." Connor laughed heartily. "Nicki must really love you."

Beth wondered what Connor's assessment would be if she told him about the gifts Nicole had given her.

Nicole noted the time on a wall clock – thirty minutes to midnight. She surveyed the room. Beth was being well entertained by Connor and Alex. Seeking a respite, Nicole wove through the crowd to the cloakroom. Retrieving her long, black leather coat, she wrapped it around her shoulders as she stepped out to the plaza. Others in attendance had not claimed the space, the cold being a sufficient deterrent.

Lampposts styled in the fashion of gaslights bordered the marble plaza. Nicole stood by one of the lampposts, a circle of light cast at her feet.

The New Year, the artificial mark of a new beginning; Nicole wondered why the human need to draw a line and jump over it existed. For her, New Year's Eve was a rite of passage too generic to have meaning. Still, what would she leave behind were she to step across the timeline? The year 2001 had begun painfully with the near brutal kiss seized from Beth, accompanied by the confession of a love she did not understand and was only now reconciling herself to. It was a year of leaving and returning, a year of destruction – the loss of the Elysian Fields, a year of grief – of loss that could not be reconstructed. She missed Carrie. She still privately mourned her friend and her business associates.

Never would Nicole have divined the events of·the past twelve months. She knew it was foolhardy to try to divine the next twelve. Change did not come by forced resolutions, at least not in the free world. There was no ritual beyond the ridiculous hats, the noisemakers and the alcohol. She had come to want none of it. She wanted dignity, silence and sobriety. She wanted ritual that touched the soul not numbed it. Letting go of Father Time was easy. She never knew him. Embracing the newborn child was unrealistic. The child would be fashioned by the inherited world, not the other way around.

Nicole breathed in the frigid air and found it sweeter than what she had stepped away from. It might be harsh, but it was real, unconditioned. Nicole was feeling very much alone. It was not terrible – her aloneness. She had been without her aloneness for too long. In recent months, she had been able to carve fragments of time for herself, but nothing extensive. How could she explain that the only sympathy she missed was her own? She awoke each day with a yearning for solitude that conflicted with her life, a life of recovery: recovery of her health, recovery of The Fields, recovery of the operations of business clients, and most importantly, recovery of Beth.

In a few turns of the minute hand, the year 2002 would begin. Jason called out to the crowd to fill their champagne glasses. Beth declined Connor's offer to secure a glass for her, and scanned the crowd looking for Nicole. Inquiries led her toward the plaza. She spied a tall, lone figure outside. Donning her coat, Beth sought Nicole's company. Behind her Beth could hear the countdown. "Ten, nine, eight …" Nicole was unmoved by the commotion.

In Beth's heart, she knew that Nicole was far away from her, gone to a place where no one was given admittance. Beth knew Nicole was in her realm, connected to life in her own unique way. Nicole required no church. She uttered no prayers. But where she stood was sacred ground, a holy place the nature of which Beth could only speculate. She could never feel it as Nicole felt it.

"Six, five, four …"

Beth understood the sense of loss Nicole hinted at in not being a part of her Christian faith. Nicole could never share Beth's God or voice a prayer. Beth, in turn, felt the same separation from Nicole. There was a place within Nicole that Beth would never know, though she longed to. She consoled herself with the knowledge that this truth was not only for Nicole, it was for everyone. The crucial difference was Beth's love for Nicole – a love that transcended human bounds. It reflected the divine. Because of this, Beth's distance from Nicole left her reaching into a void in the hope of seeing a glimmer of Nicole's inimitable light, the light that defined Nicole's faith, the light that illumed Nicole's soul.

"Three, two, one …" The voices surged along with the noisemakers' laughter and shouts.

Beth approached Nicole and took her hand. Nicole felt the familiar sensation, which lifted her from her thoughts. She turned toward its source.

Beth smiled. "Happy New Year, Nicki."

Nicole's attention was drawn to the sounds emanating from the party crowd. Awareness of time and place renewed. She returned her gaze to Beth. Nicole's expression remained solemn.

Beth feared Nicole was near tears. She did not know what circumstances had brought Nicole to the plaza, or what had altered Nicole's earlier casual demeanor to the contemplative. Beth knew what was required in order to claim Nicole. Beth raised her free hand to her lover's cheek. Nicole leaned down. Whether Beth was guiding Nicole or Nicole was guiding Beth was uncertain. The gradual motion toward one another was consummated with a kiss that was hesitant, cautious, fearful. It was tender. It was mutual. It was everything their first kiss was not. It did not mark an ending or a beginning; the kiss marked a continuation. The kiss did not cease in the plaza. It was renewed as they both found union and release in their bed. Nor did the kiss cease as they fell asleep in each other's arms, for its memory lingered in the givers' respective dreams.

CHAPTER 96

February 22, 2002

The Alderman's welcoming speech had gone on for ten minutes. "Damn the politicians." Miguel jumped up and down trying to keep warm.

"Watch your language," Beth playfully chastised.

"Beth! *Chica*, it's good to see you." Miguel gave Beth a bear hug.

"I've missed you, too."

"Hey, is there more of that to go around?" Tony stepped up.

"Hi, good looking." Beth welcomed the handsome Italian.

"Give us a kiss." Miguel stepped into Tony's open arms.

While Tony protested, Connor came and stood beside Beth. "We don't see enough of you."

Beth turned. "Hey."

Connor gave Beth a gentle embrace. "How are you?"

"Good."

"Where's Nicki? Didn't you come together?"

"She's fogged-in in New York."

"You've got to be kidding. I thought she was going to fly back yesterday."

"Something came up and she stayed an extra day."

Connor released Beth. "It doesn't seem fair. She worked so hard to rebuild and now she's missing the Grand Opening."

"She may still make it." Beth took Connor's arm, leaning against him, gathering his warmth. "She's staying at LaGuardia hoping to get a flight."

"Well, well, well. They let the riffraff out." Kate joined the group.

"You shouldn't speak about Beth that way," Connor quipped.

"I wasn't," said Kate. She turned to Beth. "Nicki called me. I've been appointed to keep an eye on you. I think she's afraid this shabby crowd will offend your finer sensibilities."

"Really." Beth was amused.

"It could be the other way around. I'm not sure." Kate winked.

Connor chimed in. "There you go again."

"People," said Miguel. "Jason is about to speak."

Jason stood behind the portable lectern.

"Good evening. My name is Jason Chamberlain and I am the co-developer of the Chamberlain House-Elysian Fields project. Since it's cold out here and warm inside, I'm going to keep this short. First, thank you for coming and joining us in this celebration. The neighborhood experienced a great loss with the Elysian Fields fire. It could have disheartened the residents if recovery had not been done right. One woman was determined to make sure that the wound would be healed. She wasn't willing to sell this property to just the highest bidder. She worked hard to ensure that the new building would serve the community. Unfortunately, Nicole Thera's flight from New York was cancelled. We spoke on the phone just a little while ago. She wanted me to thank everyone who has been a part of the rebuilding, with a special nod to our architect, Laura Morales, and to our project manager, a young man I am proud to call my son, Alex Chamberlain. She also wanted me to thank the people of the neighborhood and the broader community for their support. Working with Nicole has been an extraordinary experience for me. Her vision has been bold. She demanded only the best, and that is what we have here. The best quality craftsmanship. The best management. We have brought you affordable housing, retail outlets that will fill existing gaps, and a return of the Elysian Fields. We plan to be here for a long time. We plan to contribute to this neighborhood. We will live and breathe this neighborhood's tradition of embracing diversity. We will show courtesy, we will conduct business fairly, we will set the standard high and with our success – and I am certain we will be successful – we will become a magnet for more entrepreneurs to invest in this very special neighborhood so that it remains a viable home for this and generations to come."

The crowd applauded.

Jason continued. "It is customary to cut a ribbon to mark our new beginning. Since Nicole isn't here, I want to ask Elizabeth Kelly, Nicole's partner in life, to join me."

Beth had not been warned.

Miguel bent down to Beth's ear. "I think he said your name."

Connor turned to Beth as she released her hold of him. "Make Nicki proud."

Beth gave Connor her full regard, and then walked up to Jason. Jason wore a brilliant smile. He extended an oversized ceremonial scissor to Beth. "Let's do this."

Beth took the scissor with one hand and allowed Jason to position her for the photographers. Jason prompted, "Ready." Beth nodded. "Well then, for Nicole."

"For Nicki."

They cut the ribbon. Photographs were taken. Jason hugged Beth and then turned to Katherine, Alex, and Laura who stood nearby, and warmly embraced them. The Musketeers and Kate congratulated Beth for a job well done. With a general feeling of joviality, everyone streamed into the building to enjoy food and drink, compliments of Chamberlain Development.

Beth entered The Pub.

"Beth."

She turned toward the sound of the voice to see a well-dressed man approach her.

"Hello, my name is Brian Montgomery. My company is a client of Nicole's."

"Brian, yes, Nicki has mentioned your name." Beth offered the gentleman her hand. "It's a pleasure to meet you. Nicki didn't tell me you were going to be in Chicago."

Brian took Beth's hand in salutation. "She didn't know. I wanted to surprise her. Can I buy you a drink?"

"I'll take a cup of tea."

"Tea?"

"Chamomile. Connor keeps a supply behind the bar."

Brian was on his second pint of ale. Beth suspected he might have had one or two more before they met. He was in high spirits. "I can't tell you what it meant to have Nicole in Washington after September 11th. She was such a calming influence. Some of our employees were desperate to get out of the city, and here was Nicole, driving all night to get in. Everyone has a calling."

Beth smiled at the religious reference. It never surprised her how people tried to incorporate her vocation into a conversation.

"Do you know that once she got back on her feet after the fire, she contacted every one of her clients and reemphasized, no, insisted that we update our business recovery plans. We were two-thirds into the process on September 11th. Nicole must have been inundated with requests. Lucky for us she is loyal. For Carrie's sake, she would have crawled to D.C. or New York, if it would have helped."

"Carrie?" Beth's interest was piqued by the unfamiliar name.

"Carrie Nolan." Brian restated the name as if it should have been familiar to Beth.

"I'm sorry … "

"Nicole never mentioned Carrie?"

Beth mined her memory. "I think they had dinner together while Nicki was in Boston last summer."

Brian looked away, gathering his thoughts. "They loved each other dearly. Carrie joked that if she were single, ten years younger and gay, she would have been Nicole's lover. You see, Carrie was wonderfully insane. Quite a counterpart to Nicole's impeccable professionalism." Brian laughed as a memory came to mind. He leaned forward engaged in his own storytelling. "We brought in our out-of-town managers for Nicole's presentation. Carrie was stationed in New York."

Beth's fear rose. "The World Trade Center."

"Yes. In addition to our D.C. headquarters, we have offices in Boston, San Francisco, London, and Sydney. Carrie sabotaged Nicole's presentation.

I have no idea how she did it. Nicole took it in stride as we laughed at the bogus slides Carrie had loaded on Nicole's computer. Then Carrie got up and demanded we proceed with the work without further delay. She argued that if Nicole Thera's computer could be compromised, anything was possible. God love her, she was right. They both were."

Brian took another generous swallow of his drink. "You know, I said you and Jason had changed Nicole. And, you have. But I really think it was Carrie's death and what happened to Nicole in Shenandoah that is making her rethink her career. Thank God it was only her medication that needed to be adjusted. I don't care what Nicole said. I still say it was the stress of that week that made her ill."

As soon as she could separate herself from Brian without being discourteous Beth sought Kate out. There were no formalities. "We need to talk."

Kate could see something was wrong. She excused herself from the woman she was speaking to.

Beth waited only long enough to ensure their privacy. "What happened in Shenandoah?"

Kate took a hard look at Beth and made a decision. "Last September during Nicki's first weekend in D.C. she drove down to Shenandoah for the day. She hiked one of trails. She got sick. The symptoms were serious and she lost consciousness."

"Did someone find her?"

"No." Kate proceeded to give Beth a complete accounting of the incident. "I can't give you a reason why she kept this from you. I tried to convince her to talk to you but she refused."

"We had a disagreement before she left for D.C." Beth gave Kate an appreciative smile. "Kate, you've broken confidentiality."

Kate smirked. "Nicki can sue me."

It was near 2:00 a.m. when Beth returned home to the empty apartment. She longed for Nicole. She went into the den and sat in Nicole's chair. Across from her stood Nicole's wall of books. Nicole had made substantial progress in renewing her library. Nicole duplicated the same, meticulous topical organization she had created in the loft. Beth's eyes gravitated toward, what was to her memory, a new collection. A variety of books on the subject of Christian History lined two-thirds of a shelf. They complimented, not duplicated, her collection. Beth smiled in appreciation. She continued to glance at the library, and identified a second new collection. The titles caused her to shiver; they were all related to death. The variety of the titles reflected Nicole's humanist perspective: philosophy, psychology, theology, history, medicine, non-fiction, and fiction. Beth was drawn to them. She got to her feet and walked to the shelf. Her fingers traced the volume titles. She chose *A Noble Death*. The cover expanded the title: *Suicide & Martyrdom Among Christians and Jews in Antiquity*. She turned to the contents page. 'The Death of Socrates and Its Legacy' chapter caught her interest. She paged forward to and through the chapter catching the section headings. Plato, Aristotle, Cynics, Epicureans … Beth had found the source of the lesson on Greek perspectives of death that Nicole had so succinctly given Jerry. She closed the book and held it close to her.

CHAPTER 97

February 23, 2002

It was ten in the morning when Nicole arrived in the quiet apartment. Having spent the night at the airport, all she wanted was to be home. She put her gear down. There was no sign of Beth. She walked to the bedroom, where Beth lay sleeping. Nicole smiled to herself. The Grand Opening must have been a success. Nicole slipped out of her clothes and into bed, easing herself behind Beth's body. Beth stirred.

"Hi." Nicole grazed the back of her fingers against her partner's cheek. "I didn't expect to find you still asleep."

Beth turned onto her back. She found it hard to believe that Nicole was with her. All that she learned the night before had left her to wonder why Nicole had chosen to stay in their relationship after Beth's rejection. Beth raised her fingertips and traced Nicole's lips.

Nicole had learned the fragility that lay behind Beth's gesture. She waited, giving Beth the time she obviously needed. She saw a tear slip from Beth's eye. The time for silence ceased. "What is it?"

"You came back to me."

"Always."

"Were you ever going to tell me about Carrie's death and what happened to you at Shenandoah?"

Nicole was stunned. "How …"

"Brian was at the opening. He wanted to surprise you. We had a drink together. He talked about Carrie and what she meant to you. How proud she would have been to see The Fields rebuilt. He also mentioned Shenandoah. I got Kate to fill in what she knew."

"I didn't know Carrie was killed until after I left Chicago. I left on such a bad note and things didn't get any easier between us as the week passed that when I got sick, I just fell back on Kate for help. She is still named as my medical P.O.A."

Nicole waited for a chastisement. It did not come.

"I never understood how important your work could be." Beth paused in thought. There was much she wanted to learn. "You lost others, didn't you?"

"Four that I worked closely with. More that I knew in passing."

"My God." Beth looked away. Her heart ached.

Nicole took Beth's hand. "When I came home, you seemed to want to keep everything about September 11th at arm's length. I didn't know what to do. I didn't know if I should try to reach out to you. I was afraid that in need-ing you I was being selfish, so I decided to say nothing."

Composing herself, Beth returned her gaze to Nicole. "Shenandoah?"

"I'm fine. I just needed my medication to be adjusted. I swear to you I've done everything I've been told to do to take care of myself."

"Is there anything else you haven't told me?"

Nicole knew there was a great deal that remained unsaid and this was her first true opportunity to tell Beth. "Yes."

"Nicki?"

"Beth, I'm tired. Later today, I promise, I'll answer every one of your questions. I was up most of the night. Right now I just want to get some rest."

"Your word?"

Nicole gave Beth a gentle kiss. Nicole asked, "Will you stay with me until I fall asleep?"

"I'm not going anywhere."

Nicole shifted to the side, taking Beth into a complete embrace with her body. Nicole was not sure exactly what she would tell Beth upon awakening. For now she spoke her one truth. "I love you."

Beth depended on Nicole's words and touch to buttress her waning con-fidence. She expected to be tested when they spoke. "I love you, Nicki."

CHAPTER 98

February 23, 2002 – Evening

For Nicole the meaning of life had been clarified to the simplest forms – love, relationship, connection. She understood that contemporary culture did not support her choice. The values of Western society promoted speed, accumulation of material objects, not contemplation and simplicity. As she explored death, sudden death, death as a slow deterioration that allows an individual to document the journey, or death by choice in terms of martyrdom and suicide, she refined and deepened her commitment to life. Her source was not a god or a religion, though sacred writings were included in her exploration. As had always been her way, she sought out knowledge from those who preceded her. Either in books or in conversation with respected individuals, she searched. She then looked within, integrating what she learned. She worked hard to ally heart, mind and soul, all for the purpose of living a meaningful life. As she lay alone in bed, she felt she had just begun to live a more aware life, a good life. By act and deed, she had begun to share herself with Beth. She knew she could do more. She knew the time had come for words.

Nicole entered the kitchen in search of a cup of tea. She saw Beth reading on the living room couch. "Hey."

"How did you sleep?" Beth closed her book.

"Good. Want some tea?"

"Please."

Nicole had set the stage. They would talk. She brought two mugs of tea, handing one to Beth. Instead of lying beside her, Nicole shifted the living room table aside and sat on the floor, resting her back against the couch. Beth placed her hand on Nicole's shoulder. Nicole sipped her tea, gathering her thoughts, trying to decide where to begin.

"There is a wonderful waterfall in Shenandoah that you can reach by a footpath. When I reached the falls, I lay against a tree and watched the water crash down to the pond. I thought of you as the pond, a body of water that could contain and absorb my most powerful and volatile forces. You've brought a calmness to my life that I just can't explain.

"I started to feel ill. When the pain got bad … I thought I might be dying. I thought that it wasn't unjust because I had you in my life, even if only for a brief time. I didn't feel cheated, but I hated leaving you behind knowing that I hadn't given you everything I felt you deserved from me. I realized I needed to tell Jacob that we had two things in common. I could finally swear that I loved a woman. So, the first was that we both loved women. The second was that Jacob couldn't imagine life without Liza, and I couldn't imagine life without you.

"When I came home I meant to tell you what had happened. I also had a confession to make, but I couldn't. Not after you asked that we keep the world from coming between us." Nicole fell silent.

"Nicki, what did you intend to confess to me?"

Nicole placed her mug down on the living room table. She clasped her hands together as she spoke. "I thought I knew what is was to love you. Our first night together was wonderful, but it broke me open in a way I didn't expect. It was far easier to love you from a safe distance. You know I've been with other women. I've known passion and I've known tenderness, but except for my first, I haven't known what it is to trust. I've always been in control. I've always wanted to possess.

"From the day we first spoke in St. Ann's, when I returned your cross to you, I told myself that you were different. It was wrong to want to possess and control you. I wanted your friendship. And then the day came when I wanted your love. I never wanted you to be anything less than you are. But Beth, when I made love to you I got frightened. Being with you scared me out of my wits. A part of me didn't want you so close. I knew you could hurt me if I let you in. And at the same time, I wanted to let you in.

"I knew that I was always at risk of losing you. I didn't have to worry about another woman. It was easy to dismiss that fear because I knew you would never have consented to be with me if you didn't love me. I also knew how much you valued fidelity. I was afraid because I realized that you would always love God more. I couldn't compete with your faith, though for a while I thought I could. I thought I had to if I was going to keep you. I felt God was in our bed that first night and every night since. I've felt God was always in between us. I felt God was a ready thief and I resented it.

"Before I left D.C. I promised myself, and you, although you didn't know it, that I would accept that in the grace of having you in my life I had to accept that I would always be second to God and that didn't make your love for me any less of a gift. I came home ready to love you."

Nicole paused and took a deep breath. "September 11th. I couldn't help you deal with the aftermath. I wanted to, but you were so distant with me, and I didn't know why. I tried to not ask for any more than you were able to give me, but I was frustrated. I felt every time I got close something created a breach between us and it was always rooted in the fact that our beliefs were so different.

"I also had my own grief and you couldn't see it. Carrie and I didn't see each other that often, but when we did," Nicole smiled to herself, "the time apart melted away and we picked up where we had left off. Carrie was this beautiful, Irish, Roman Catholic mother of two wonderful, grown daughters, and wife to a quiet, generous man who relished Carrie's spirit. But first, she was her own woman. She had a great capacity for life. She was a great friend. My birthday has always been the most important day of the year for me. Not that it has always been the happiest. Carrie knew this. We would make an effort to meet for lunch or dinner. I could usually schedule an east coast client – D.C., Boston or New York. Carrie would find an excuse to fly to whatever city I was in.

"Carrie's spirit isn't gone. It lives on in John's love for her and in her two daughters. It lives on inside me. My birthday was so hard. I missed Carrie and I didn't have a clue of what was happening with us. I was ready to accept the fact that I wasn't ever going to find a love I could sustain. I surely didn't deserve you. But, there you were."

Nicole shifted and turned around to face Beth. "I once accused you of closing yourself to any real intimacy. I had to heed my own words. John sent me a gift Carrie had already chosen for me before September 11th. I received it by courier on my birthday right as I was leaving the office for the day. It was the Fed Ex package I had in my hand when I met you in the hotel lobby. It was a book by Jean Shinoda Bolen. It wasn't enough for Carrie to give me a gift. She gave it with a challenge. I've been trying to live up to the challenge ever since."

Beth felt the loss of never having met Carrie. Few individuals earned Nicole's admiration, fewer less who were readily able to influence her. "What was the challenge?"

"To look inside and name all the memories that drive me, and to decide if I'm going to allow the control they've had over me to continue. All my life I've been I afraid of being left alone. I've chosen to keep a part of myself from those I love, a preemptive strike to being abandoned. I don't want to live that way any more. I don't want to hide myself from you. I'm trying my best not to."

"I'm sorry I made it so difficult."

"Don't. It wasn't you. How could we have ever predicted all that has happened to us these past six months?

Beth took Nicole's hand. "Tell me more about Carrie …"

CHAPTER 99

February 27, 2002

The two women spent the evening comfortably together and yet, to Nicole, Beth felt distant. Beth retreated to the kitchen. She ran water to wash the dishes.

Nicole carried the dinner plates from the dining room. "You've been quiet."

Beth did not look up from the running water. She had been staring at the stream, mesmerized. She questioned Nicole's ability to understand what she faced each and every day at the hospital. She struggled to find a starting point for sharing. "There was a death in the unit today."

Nicole waited. Beth's ongoing silence prompted further inquiry. "Was there something special about it?"

"Every death is special," Beth whispered.

Nicole set the plates beside Beth. She wondered what she had to do to assure Beth that she could confide in her, that she had finally learned that events in the hospital were not fodder for political or moral arguments. "Tell me about it."

Beth kept her focus down and away from Nicole. Nicole decided to give Beth time. She walked back to the dining room for the remaining dishes.

Upon hearing Nicole's return, with her gaze firmly fixed upon the dishes, Beth began her story. "He ... I met him on Tuesday. He was given a few days to live. His doctor moved him from the I.C.U to palliative care. He was in his mid-60s. By the look of him you wouldn't have known ... he didn't seem frail. He was sitting up. He held an oxygen mask in his hand. Every five or six breaths he would move it to his mouth and take a breath. I came to his bedside first. I passed his wife who sat in a chair not far from his bed. I asked him what I ask every patient. 'Is there anything I can do for you?' He spoke quietly. He asked me to pray for him. I then asked him what he wanted me to pray for. He said that I should pray that he could breathe a little easier. He looked me straight in the eye. There was something. I don't know. I'm not sure why but I asked him if he knew he was dying. He said, 'Yes.' I now understood that he wanted to breathe easier until death came for him. We spoke a little more. Every few breaths he would pause and use the oxygen mask. He mentioned his wife and his kids. How good they had been to him. How he hadn't always been good to them. When we finally prayed, I took his hand in mine. I made sure I mentioned his gratitude in the prayer. Usually I invite family members to join us in prayer. This time I didn't. It was just us two. There wasn't enough space in the room for anyone else. I felt that, and I didn't even consider questioning it. He listened to the prayer and when I finished, he echoed my 'Amen.' He then squeezed my hand. I knew there wasn't anything more for me to do for him. Afterwards, I went to his wife. She had been shedding silent tears. I knelt down to her and took her hand. She thanked me and asked if I would come back the next day. I promised I would. When I went back, the patient was alone. He was unconscious. The oxygen mask was fitted over his mouth. He was having trouble breathing. I stood by his bed. I wanted to pray for him but I didn't have a prayer, so I silently said the Our Father. I sat in the same chair his wife had been sitting in and kept watch over him. I sat there for at least a half hour. During that time, the nurse came in and checked his IV. She didn't say a word. I'm glad she didn't because I didn't want any voices in the room. Today I went in. The room had been cleared. There was no sign of him. I was told he died in the middle of the night."

Nicole went to Beth and took her into her arms. Beth held Nicole tightly, droplets of water falling from her hands to the floor, others absorbed by Nicole's blouse.

"It's okay to cry."

Given permission, Beth released the sorrow the desolate death had left in her. On this night, she would find her solace in Nicole's arms.

CHAPTER 100

March 2, 2002

Nicole sat in the dining room enjoying a late breakfast. Beth had worked the night shift at the hospital. She had only now awakened from taking a nap. Beth wandered from the sunroom to the bedroom, back to the living room, and then to Nicole. "Nicki. Have you seen the book I was reading?"

Nicole feigned disinterest. "Where did you last have it?"

"The living room Thursday night. Remember, you and me on the couch?"

Nicole smiled. "We weren't reading."

Beth reflected the smile. "I gave it the college try until you interrupted me."

"My fault?"

"You didn't take it to the den, did you?"

"Why would I?"

Beth started walking toward the den. "I'll go look."

Nicole called out after her. "Beth! Den mine. Sunroom yours."

Beth called back. "I won't disturb anything."

With great satisfaction and a growing childlike sense of anticipation, Nicole raised her coffee cup to her lips.

The den was dark except for two new track lights installed on the ceiling illuminating the wall behind Nicole's desk. On that wall hung a portrait. It was an original pencil and charcoal drawing of Nicole standing behind Beth, holding her in an embrace. The portrait captured them waist high. Nicole was the secondary subject. Beth's figure dominated the portrait. The gaze in Nicole's eyes enhanced the focus upon Beth. Nicole's gaze was only for Beth. Beth leaned against Nicole; her head slightly tilted back, a gentle smile on her face. Around her neck, visible from her open blouse hung her grandmother's cross.

Beth entered the dining room. Nicole, looking down, scanned the *Tribune's* entertainment section. She asked, "Find the book?"

Beth's voice was subdued. "Didn't look."

Without raising her eyes, Nicole swept aside the newspaper sections that lay on the table to reveal the volume. "Then, this must be it."

"The portrait?"

Nicole finally looked up. "You going to exercise a veto?"

"No."

"Good." Nicole went back to reading the paper.

Beth maintained her place for a few heartbeats before she turned and made her way once again to the den. Nicole gave Beth a few moments of privacy. Beth stood inside the den threshold. Nicole came behind her, taking her partner in an embrace much like the one the portrait captured.

Beth was stymied. "How was it done?"

"Remember New Year's Eve when Trevor was taking all those pictures? Now you know why."

"Trevor did this?"

"No." Nicole pointed to the signature. "Andrea Trovasky. I commissioned Andrea. She worked from the photos and a couple of sittings."

Beth leaned back. "I wouldn't be able to talk you into hanging it in the bedroom?"

Nicole was gentle. "No. But you have visiting rights."

Beth turned around to face Nicole. "Who are you?"

Nicole took Beth's hand and placed it against her own heart. "You know me, Beth. I'm the woman that loves you."

CHAPTER 101

March 2, 2002 – Evening

In their bed Beth lay draped across Nicole's body. "Why don't you believe in our souls?"

Although it was not unusual for them to talk of the ethereal or the divine after making love, Nicole still found herself surprised by the question. "I believe in our souls."

"Not that they will live on."

"No one has ever given me an argument I could accept."

Beth recently read a short volume that had captured her imagination. "Would you be open to a fourth century woman thinker?"

Nicole encouraged with a smile. "Try me."

"Macrina the Younger. She was the sister of Basil the Great and Gregory of Nyssa. Gregory wrote about a conversation he had with Macrina. Scholars disagree whether the ideas are Macrina's or Gregory's. I like thinking they were hers. I won't try to put the ideas in her words. I remember as I read the account thinking that she was way ahead of her time. She used the atomic theory."

"Which came from Democritus, a Greek."

Beth playfully slapped Nicole. "Yes."

Nicole took possession of Beth's hand as a safety precaution.

"Her argument made me think of DNA."

"I'm intrigued."

Beth looked up to affirm Nicole's sincerity. "What if our souls were made up of atoms that we couldn't detect? What if the substance of our souls could permeate our bodies and fuse with our material without losing its identity? And when we die, what if the soul releases itself from the material and reforms as a separate entity, each division holding sufficient knowledge of the whole to recreate it? She used the analogy of mixing paint and then being able to separate the tints to their original form."

"Where does it go, the soul?"

"To God."

Nicole recalled an appropriate analogy. "If I were a Hindu I would say *moksha* had taken place."

"I don't know what that means," Beth admitted, having reconciled herself to Nicole's greater knowledge of world religions.

"The higher Self, what you might call the soul – the atman – unifies with the absolute – Brahman. Hindus believe that can only happen if one lives the correct way of life – dharma. Because we don't get it right the first time, or second time, or however many times are necessary, the soul comes back to continue the process until it reaches nirvana. Macrina doesn't seem to think coming back is necessary."

"We go to God without losing our identity."

"I would think that our souls must be able to code the changes they experience in their own nature. Does she believe the soul can change?"

"She said that the soul will go back to the original divine nature. Corrupted souls are first healed by experiencing the purifying force of fire."

"Universal salvation after her own version of purgatory. She's more generous than a lot of Christian theologians. The concept would make sense to a Hindu if the soul did record its changes. If the soul's DNA code was altered by the material experience and it took that knowledge with it."

Beth felt a mounting frustration. "You keep saying what you think a Hindu would think. You're not a Hindu. What do you think?"

Nicole raised Beth's hand, kissing the palm in a consoling gesture. "I think I might want to read what Gregory wrote."

"There is so much we don't know. There is so much we haven't thought to dream. You could open yourself up to some wonderful possibilities if you only let yourself … "

"Beth," Nicole interrupted, not wanting Beth's train of thought to cause a preventable derailment between them. "There are so many possibilities for our souls. The greatest thinkers have tried to understand the mysteries. A theory … a belief may touch you in a way no other does and for you it becomes the truth. I haven't the faith or sheer will to take on any one belief."

Beth raised herself up to better meet Nicole's eyes. "But our souls, Nicki. Us."

Nicole felt Beth's intensity. It demanded more than Nicole could give and it broke her heart to disappoint. "An eternity with you would be bliss. It isn't that I wouldn't want it if I knew I could have it. It's just that I don't know anything. I really don't know a damn thing."

Beth struggled to reconcile the Nicole she knew with the Nicole presented before her. Nicole never ceased searching. She could articulate the beliefs and myths of cultures throughout the ages and yet Nicole professed to know nothing. Nicole juxtaposed to so many who truly knew little and yet were certain in their belief; those who held for dear life to their doctrine and dogma because any assertion contrary threatened to crumble their precarious foundation.

It saddened Beth that as an adult Nicole had never stood in a faith community. Though her faith was primarily between her and her God, Beth was not alone as a Christian. To know that her faith was etched in the hearts and minds of women and men for two millennia brought Beth comfort.

Nicole was a woman who knew no God, believed in no future for their souls, remained isolated in her conviction. Beth did not want to see Nicole's life through that stark looking glass. If she could, she would break it, take a shard of glass in her hand, raise it to Nicole's eyes, and point to the fragments that remained on the floor to prove to Nicole that the image they reflect, in part or whole, was the same. That she was but one shard, Beth another, and the whole was God's universe. They were united even in their separate fragments by the omnipotent force that created them and gave them the capacity to reflect within themselves, the divine. Nicole's beloved divine. Beth would do this act of violence to bring Nicole to her if she could, but she could not. Nicole persevered in her claim that in spite of seeing the world in its diversity, in spite of the enormity of her knowledge, she knew nothing and thus, Beth felt Nicole remained beyond her reach.

Beth's thoughts returned to the present moment. "Nicki, you never will know for certain."

"Maybe when I die." Nicole offered Beth a fragile smile. Beth again lay to rest upon Nicole. Nicole wrapped her arms around Beth. "I'm sorry."

CHAPTER 102

March 12, 2002

Dressed in a fashionable, multi-colored, patterned skirt and a lavender blouse, Beth stood by the sunroom windows. The early evening hours were no longer cloaked in darkness. Sunlight was a universal impetus, driving Chicago residents to make more of the after dinner hours – to go out to play and explore. On this weekday, Nicole proposed an early dinner at a new restaurant that had garnered rave reviews from the *Tribune* food critic.

They had entered a new phase in their relationship. Beth could not mark the specific day or time when the transition from separate to shared lives came to an end. Being together had become a natural state to both of them. Beth discovered to her delight that more and more, Nicole's latent romanticism was rising to the surface on its own accord. Nicole's gestures could be as stunning as the portrait. They could also be simple and unassuming. The easy touch, the muted smile, the declaration of love that began every morning and closed every evening. It did not take long for Beth to deduce that Nicole yearned for and relished the return of those same small gestures. For Beth, being able to express her affection without reservation was an extraordinary freedom. She cherished knowing that her slightest effort had a disproportionate power to touch Nicole.

Nicole entered the living room dressed in black slacks, a black turtleneck sweater and a black dress blazer of mid-thigh length. She took Beth's breath away.

"Nicki. You look … "

Nicole smiled. She grasped Beth's hand to lead her to the door. "Time to go."

Beth tugged in resistance. "A kiss."

Nicole was happy to comply. Beth surrendered to Nicole's embrace and the sensuous kiss that followed.

Nicole stepped back. "Hi."

"Hi."

"We have six o'clock reservations."

"Where is this restaurant?"

"Downtown. Oh, I almost forgot. Pam called. She wants you to pick up some books at her church and bring them to the hospital in the morning. They should be at the church office."

Beth saw no reason to interrupt their evening. "It can wait. I'll go in the morning."

"We have time. Come on. I'm still trying to get her to like me."

Beth paused, concerned. "She likes you. What makes you think she doesn't?"

"Don't know. Just a feeling." Nicole looked at her watch. "Time is a-wasting."

Beth set the issue of Pam aside. She would revisit it on another day. "Lead on."

Nicole drove the Jeep to the front of the church, parking in a space reserved by two yellow cones.

Beth chided. "Breaking the law in front of a church. Not good, Nicki."

"I'll go in with you." Nicole grinned, very much a rascal.

Pam walked out of the main church entrance and remained standing on the top of the stairs. She was dressed in full vestments. "Hello, you two."

Beth had failed to ascertain the discrepancy between Nicole's instructions and Pam's presence. "What's the occasion?"

"A friend asked me to perform a special ceremony." Pam turned to Nicole. Beth followed Pam's gaze. Nicole stood aside in silence.

"Nicki?"

Nicole looked shyly to Beth. "I thought you would want a blessing of our union."

Beth was dumbfounded. She searched Nicole's eyes for the joke, but all she found was pure sincerity. That she hoped one day to find acceptance for her love of Nicole in the Church was an unspoken dream. The reality of the Episcopal Church's position, coupled with Nicole's beliefs, were overwhelming obstacles Beth never thought could be surmounted. She now found herself standing in front of a church of Christ. The Church welcomed her and her love for another woman. Not only welcomed, but was ready to bless her love before God. And to her astonishment, standing in front of the church was Nicole, ready to share the blessing with her. All manner of Beth's self-distancing was devastated. Beth felt the love of God. She was awed. She was humbled. Beth burst into tears. Nicole took Beth into her arms. On this day, in regards to Beth's faith, Nicole was certain she did right.

Pam watched the couple with great joy. She wondered if Nicole had a complete understanding and appreciation of the gift she was giving Beth. She spoke to the tearful young woman as she walked down the steps of the church. "I hope you're not wearing any mascara. I've had some brides end up looking like a raccoon."

Beth could not help but laugh. Pam offered her a few tissues.

Beth took them gratefully. "Thank you."

"Ministers have to be prepared. Now, are you two ready?"

Led by Pam, Beth and Nicole walked hand in hand through the church. Beth knelt before the altar. She looked up to a still standing Nicole. Wordlessly, Nicole knelt beside her. Pam proceeded with the blessing.

"Beth and Nicole, on this day, in this place you are performing an act of faith. In exchanging vows you are pronouncing to each other and to your God and to your mystery, respectively, that your faith will endure the challenges placed before you. You shall walk your paths not only as individuals, but also as two people in holy union. Come to each other with honesty, courage and above all else, love. Look to create a shared life measured by compassion and goodness. Have mercy when weakness is revealed. Hold wisdom high in regard, seeking guidance as the unknown makes itself known, at times with startling effect. Cherish the gifts of one another. Know joy intimately. Be intimate with joy. Always keep the spirit of this moment close to your tender hearts. Beth and Nicole, will you exchange symbols of your love and commitment to one another?"

Nicole reached into her pocket and opened a black felt jewelry box that held two gold bands. She took the rings into one hand as she returned the box into her pocket with the other. Nicole raised the rings up to Pam. "Yes."

Pam took the rings and placed them in the palm of her left hand. With her right hand she made the sign of the cross over the rings. "Ever-loving God, who having loved us, love us still. In this hour, bless these rings, symbols of the bond confessed by your children, in your sight. May the love of Jesus flow through these rings as a current of compassion, devotion, healing and life. In the name of Jesus Christ, your son, our Lord. Amen."

Pam handed one ring to each of the two women. "Nicole."

Nicole took Beth's hand and gently placed the ring upon her finger. She had chosen the poem *Today* by Jones Very to speak for her.

"Elizabeth Ann Kelly ...

'I live but in the present – where art thou?
Hast thou a home in some past, future year?
I call to thee from every leafy bough,
But thou art far away and canst not hear.

Each flower lifts up its red or yellow head,
And nods to thee as thou art passing by:
Hurry not on, but stay thine anxious tread,
And thou shalt live with me, for there am I.

The stream that murmurs by thee – heed its voice,
Nor stop thine ear; 'tis I that bid it flow;
And thou with its glad waters shalt rejoice,
And of the life I live within them know.

And hill, and grove, and flowers, and running stream,
When thou dost live with them shall look more fair;
And thou awake as from a cheating dream,
The life today with me and mine to share'

"Beth, my heart is yours. I pledge my life to you. Till death do we part."

Beth held Nicole's hand. She had, prior to Nicole's acrid denial of marriage and union ceremonies, allowed herself to wonder what words she would say to Nicole were their union to be blessed. To speak before God, Beth wanted words found in the Bible. She wanted words that would celebrate their love, words that would fall easily into Nicole's heart. Beth found those verses and visited them often. She recited, with only a minor variation, from the Song of Solomon, as she placed the ring on Nicole's finger.

"Nicole Isabel Thera ...
'I am my beloved's,
    and [her] desire is for me.

Come, my beloved,
    let us go forth into the fields,
    and lodge in the villages;
let us go out early to the vineyards,
    and see whether the vines have budded,
whether the grape blossoms have opened
    and the pomegranates are in bloom.
There I will give you my love.
The mandrakes give forth fragrance,
    and over our doors are all choice fruits,
new as well as old,
    which I have laid up for you ...

If I met you outside, I would kiss you,
    and no one would despise me.
I would lead you and bring you
    into the house of my mother,
    and into the chamber of the one who bore me.
I would give you spiced wine to drink,
    the juice of my pomegranates.
O that [your] left hand were under my head,
    and that [your] right hand embraced me!"

"Nicki. I love you. Death will never part us."

Nicole smiled. With a fingertip, she captured a tear falling from the corner of Beth's eye.

Pam watched the delicate physical exchange between the two women.

Nicole and Beth, hands held, turned to the minister.

"May the LORD bless you and keep you: May the LORD make a light shine upon you, and be gracious to you; and May the LORD grant you wisdom, and give you peace. Amen."

Beth echoed, "Amen."

"You may kiss," said Pam.

The two women kissed. It was a fragile kiss, light and tender. Upon separation, Beth rested against Nicole's shoulder. Nicole held Beth, looking over to Pam. The two women exchanged a knowing understanding of Beth's need for a gentle transition.

It was Pam who spoke first. "So, what are your plans for the evening?"

Beth leaned back. Her eyes did not stray from Nicole's. "Nicki is taking me out to dinner."

"Well, actually we don't have dinner reservations."

"We don't?"

Nicole beamed. The rascal reappeared. "I was hoping for pizza in front of the fireplace."

CHAPTER 103

March 20, 2002

Nicole's propensity to rely on restaurants for meals had been tempered by Beth's culinary skills. Nicole freely offered her talents as a chef's assistant. On this particular evening, the roles were reversed as Beth carefully chopped a green pepper.

Nicole, standing at the stove, looked over her shoulder. "Don't make them too small."

"I don't believe we are doing this."

"Have faith."

"Oh, no you don't." Beth exchanged a smile with Nicole. She peered over. "What spices do you use?"

"The usual. Oregano, rosemary, thyme, pepper, cumin …"

"Cumin? Since when do you use cumin for Italian?"

"Don't be so narrow-minded. I'm the one who taught you to use it in black beans."

"Right. Cuban, not Italian."

The chef exercised her prerogative not to be held accountable to the kitchen help. "How are those peppers?"

"Done with the green. Working on the red."

Nicole removed a wok out of the cupboard.

Beth could not restrain herself. "Hold it."

"What?" In light of her unorthodox methods Nicole was all innocence.

"A wok? You're going to use a wok?"

"You never used a wok?"

"To make Chinese, not spaghetti sauce."

"You agreed that I would chef tonight." Nicole continued with her preparations. "How are you doing with the mushrooms?"

"I'm still on the peppers."

"Maybe you should focus on the peppers and not the wok."

Beth returned to her work, swallowing a smile.

Nicole placed the wok on the burner and turned on the flame. "Can I ask you a question?"

"As long as it's not about the peppers," said Beth.

"I was reading the catechism in your Book of Common Prayer."

Beth placed her knife down and turned around, leaning against the counter. "The catechism?"

"It's a short read, nothing to the Catholic catechism."

"I know."

"I'm sure I read it as a kid. I didn't remember it and I was curious."

"Only you." Beth shook her head in loving disbelief of her partner.

"Got to love me, don't you!" Nicole turned to Beth with a wide grin.

Beth playfully warned, "Don't go there."

"No, wouldn't want to do that." Nicole shifted to a more tempered tone. "Seriously."

"Yes."

"Reading it as an adult … Beth, I'm probably going to inadvertently say something that might offend you so I'm going to apologize now before I get into this."

Beth was game. "Go ahead."

"If I take the catechism symbolically, and that's the only way I can, it can be quite attractive. Putting what I read into my terms … if God is the source of creation and we are a part of it; if sin is possible because of our imperfection, if sin is distorting our relationship to the source, and if prayer is responding to the source by thought and by deed with or without word – these beliefs don't differ from my own. If I consider the Trinity as a model where God is the Creator beyond all understanding, the Son the ideal we should strive to become and the Holy Spirit the revelation of the divine within each one of us … I can understand that too. And finally, if the sacraments are a ritual to make manifest the beliefs of the community, to help cut through the noise in the world and to express a common bond – well, that has been a part of the human condition from the beginning of time. Why, Beth? Why the Episcopal Church? Why not the Lutheran – in spite of Jerry – or the Baptist or Methodist or the United Church of Christ? They must be more similar than dissimilar. They all originated from the Reformation's questioning of the Catholic Church. Isn't it just more an issue of form than content?"

Beth listened carefully. Nicole's question was valid. "You can't ignore tradition."

"But that was Luther's argument against the Catholic Church. If I read my history right, Luther argued that the authority of Christianity was to be found in the Scriptures, not tradition. Wasn't the Word at the heart of the Reformation? Didn't Zwingli look to church documents only through the first four centuries of the Common Era? Wasn't the truth, for him, to be found in primitive Christianity?"

"You have been reading." Beth commented with appreciation.

"I'm trying to understand."

"Why now?"

"It hasn't been just now."

Beth granted Nicole's point. "Where are your Greeks?"

"Still with me, strong as ever. Need I remind you of Plato and Aristotle's impact on the development of early Christian theology?"

"No, it's better if you don't," Beth said in jest.

"Beth, sometimes I feel we're on opposite sides of the moon, not because it's where we belong but because tradition has led us to believe it is."

"Nicki, the Christian faith may all stand on the same side of the moon, but in some fundamental ways you and I do not. I've accepted that."

"There are parallels."

"You don't believe in God," Beth asserted strongly.

Nicole response was subdued. "Not your God. No, I don't."

"To you, Jesus is a wise teacher, not the Christ. To you, life ends with death. I believe in the soul everlasting."

Nicole realized that she had failed to reach Beth. She wanted nothing more than to extricate her self from the conversation. "And if that wasn't bad enough, I use a wok to make spaghetti sauce."

"Exactly." Beth smiled.

"You'd better get back to those peppers." Nicole turned around, facing the stove.

She heard Beth quip, "You know, I love you in spite of your heathen ways."

Nicole took a deep breath. She had surveyed Christian history and theology looking for common ground. She wanted to temper the disappointment she saw in Beth whenever they reached a theological impasse. She wanted to reassure Beth, and admittedly herself, that if they tried they could find a language of faith that would speak to them equally. Her months of study had been for naught. Although she could see aspects of her faith in the metaphors, in the myths of Christianity, Beth could not.

CHAPTER 104

March 25, 2002

Nicole sat outside of the Elysian Fields. The mild winter was slipping into an equally mild spring. Nicole had delegated more responsibility to the Musketeers, lessening the need to come to The Fields. Laura had designed a sun-drenched office with full bath for her on the third floor. It was about a third the size of the original loft, and had a private stairway to The Fields complex. There was an open-plan adjoining loft apartment that was currently leased with a 60-day notice provision. Nicole and Jason agreed that Nicole always had first right to that specific apartment. Combined with her office, the loft exceeded her original living space in the first Fields.

The design had been finalized in October when she and Beth were having difficulties. Nicole decided then that if Hyde Park was not her future she would return to The Fields, recreating her life as best she could. It may have been for this reason, more than any other, that Nicole preferred working in her den in the Hyde Park apartment. Whenever she had looked over to the door adjoining the office to the loft, she was reminded of her doubt and fear of losing Beth. The feeling was bittersweet because, at the same time, she knew that she and Beth were living a life of promise. They were moving closer, not farther away from one another.

Nicole watched Jacob walk across the street, his steps deliberate. She remembered the countless times he had taken to the street. In years past, he had moved with far more ease. Her Jacob was getting older. Still, he came to her to sit quietly and watch the neighborhood as well as to spar with words, which ever the spirit moved them to do at the time. Jacob sat down on one of the three new benches installed outside of The Fields. He slowly took out his pipe and tobacco case. Nicole bit her tongue. She was grateful to be able to return to the common practice of sharing an afternoon respite with him.

Jacob filled his pipe with tobacco. "So, you come and sit. Don't you know it's cold outside? Too cold for an old man like me."

Nicole did not take his chastisement seriously. "I have confidence in Liza. She usually bundles you up pretty well."

"She has enough to worry about."

"You didn't have to come."

Jacob gestured across the street with his pipe. "How could I not? I sit in my office and watch you. It's as if you were calling me over. What am I to do?"

Nicole put her hand on Jacob's shoulder. "Thank you for coming. There is something I want to tell you."

"Good or bad?"

"Good. Very good, I think."

"I could use some good news. What do you have to tell me?"

"I love Beth."

"Tell me something I do not know."

"We exchanged rings." Nicole removed her glove to show him.

Jacob looked over. He was unimpressed. This surprised Nicole. "Beth and I had a blessing of our union," she explained further.

"A blessing?" Jacob spoke his words heavily.

"I arranged for Reverend Lathrop – Pam, Beth's CPE Supervisor – to perform a small ceremony at the church she is associated with."

"You did this in a church?"

"Yes. It was just the three of us, otherwise you and Liza would have been invited."

"I don't care about not being invited," Jacob snapped.

This hurt Nicole. "Jacob, it was important to Beth to have the blessing. You were the one who told me to be more aware of her needs. I tried to give her … "

Jacob interrupted, saying, "Hopefully, neither one of you will regret your decision." He smacked his pipe against the bench arm.

Nicole pulled away, shifting to better see him. "Why are you saying this?"

"You will hurt her."

"You say that as if it's inevitable."

"It is." Jacob had never spoken more harshly to Nicole. "You have the power to destroy her."

"For the love of …"

"For the love of what, Nicole? God? There is no such love in your heart."

Nicole held her temper. There was something decidedly awry. "What's wrong? What is going on here?"

"Nothing." Jacob sighed sadly. "I just prayed you wouldn't do this."

"Do what?"

He raised his eyes, meeting Nicole's. "You have bound yourself to Beth in such a way that she will not be able to escape the harm you do."

"Jacob, I admit I have hurt her in the past, but not out of willful intent. I've had to learn how to love her. You were right about that. I admit it. But you can't condemn me for my past mistakes."

"So, she swore herself to you in the sight of God. Who did you swear to?"

"Beth. My oath is to Beth."

"Easily broken."

In a measured voice, Nicole said, "No, it is not. Until Beth, I have never given my word to any woman."

"You are as blind as a newborn infant. You think you see the world, but all you see is the mist. The truth lies outside your ability to see."

"Beth is happy."

"Is she? That isn't what you have told me."

"She is happy with me. I can't give her back the Church. I'm not responsible for what she's going through. That struggle is beyond me."

"You are wrong!" Jacob shouted. He shook with anger. "One can be loved by you and still be hurt by you. Have you no idea of how deeply your skepticism has challenged my faith?"

Nicole realized they were not talking about Beth. "Jacob."

"I have never shared this, not even with Liza. I love you, child, as if you were my own daughter. I have watched you blossom with each passing year. From your confusion has come clarity, but it is not the clarity I wished for you. You took a path away from me and I was left to question how this could be. You are so honest and sincere and I have no room to belittle you in my anger."

"Anger?"

"Yes. You have angered me more times than I can count, because my God is trivialized in your eyes. Your beautiful, intelligent, compassionate eyes have no reverence for my beliefs. As they have no reverence for Beth's." Jacob sadly patted his hand on Nicole's leg. "Oh, you respect our faith and the moral and spiritual lessons you can gleam from them, but much, if not almost all, is left on the threshing room floor as chaff. My nourishment is lifted up by the wind and carried away. You do not need my nourishment or Beth's. You, Nicole, do not need us to hold to your beliefs, but I need you to prove to myself that there is goodness and from that goodness God's benevolence. When I look to you, child, I see the greatest irony – you, who give me faith in God, deny God. You can see neither the impenetrable darkness, nor a brilliant light to call you to God. How must Beth feel? With her heart broken as it is, I can see how Beth has lost God." Jacob paused and took a breath, his stamina insufficient to sustain uninterrupted speech. He continued mercilessly. "You are an accursed presence. You are the greatest challenge to God that Beth could have ever invited into her life."

Nicole was stunned by Jacob's assessment. It redefined her relationship to him, as well as to Beth. "I've never intended to hurt you."

"Of course not. That is why you are so dangerous. You are not like the eighteenth century Rationalist who attacked religious beliefs, offending Jews and Christians alike. I could then allow my self-righteous anger to rise up against you, and discard your opinions. You offer an insidious, measured respect."

"Jacob," Nicole protested. She stood up. "Don't you know there was a time that I wanted to believe, that I wanted to go to synagogue with you and Liza, or to Mass again with my mother, not just as a guest but as someone who belonged in the faith? Don't you think I've wanted you to understand what I believe, and how I feel, so you could put it on an even plane with your own faith? Don't you think it's hard for me to be alone? But that is who I am. I've accepted it."

"We are all alone."

"No, you're not. You told me yourself, Liza shares your faith. You are a Jew. You have a history, a community, and a personal God." Nicole tried to harness her disappointment. "Damn it. I didn't expect this from you. All this time I thought you approved of Beth being in my life. I feel as if I don't know you. I don't know us."

"I have always told you what I believed you could tolerate."

Nicole's grief turned to anger. "Is there anything else you've held back for my own good?"

Jacob shook his head remorsefully. "No. I am just sorry I did not see the truth sooner. I failed in my responsibility to God. I should not have waited to speak."

Nicole stepped back as if she had been slapped. She did not know how to reconcile herself to this man whom she loved. He sat on the bench exposed, frail and vulnerable. She would do him no more harm. "I'm sorry, Jacob. I'm sorry I've disappointed you. I'm sorry I've hurt you. I will never hurt you again."

Jacob gave no response. If she felt it could have helped, Nicole would have fallen on her knees and pleaded with him to show her a way back to him. But to her dismay, she believed there was a grain of truth in his condemnation. She could not defend herself with complete confidence. She was not innocent. She walked away, leaving the man alone.

Jacob watched Nicole from the corner of his eye. He could not give her his full regard. It was only as she walked back into the Elysian Fields that he raised his head. He then looked over, across the street to his office. He did not have the strength to return to Liza.

CHAPTER 105

March 27, 2002

Sitting in a booth in The Pub, Kate had been giving Nicole a humorous blow-by-blow account of her latest first date. "Okay, that's it!"

"What?" Nicole raised her eyes from her salad.

"You're not listening to me."

"Oh, yes, I am. You were admiring the color of her eyes and the way she smiled."

"I hate you."

"Join the club."

Kate paused in concern. "How are you and Beth?"

"Good." Nicole saw Kate's doubt. "Really."

"Then who hates you?"

"Not hate." Nicole threw her fork down on the plate and leaned back. "It's Jacob."

"What? He adores you."

"He said I'm the greatest challenge to Beth's faith."

"I don't believe that."

"Jacob said it's not anything I've said or done. It's the fact that I can live without a god. Before I left for Boston in October, Beth said some of the same things."

"That was a while ago. You told me she admitted her anger had more to do with her own feelings than anything you may have done."

"How can she love me if every time she looks at me ... if I'm antithetical to all she values?"

"Now I'm getting angry. Different beliefs do not equate to different values. When it comes to Beth, no one can question your morality."

Nicole set aside the leading qualifier. Kate pulled no punches. "Yeah, well you're a lawyer. Your judgment is suspect."

"Go to hell."

"Don't believe in it so you'll have to show me the way."

Kate picked up her napkin and folded it as she spoke. "Nicki, why is it enough for you?"

"What?" Nicole knew her friend's nervous habit of engaging a napkin when she was uncomfortable.

"Life. A beginning and an end. Why do we have the capacity to imagine more if we can't have it?"

The topic of faith was rare between the two friends. "Why can't we hold all our dreams in our hands?" Nicole whispered.

Kate was sincere. "I can understand why it might be hard for Beth to come to you." She opened and then began to refold her napkin. "You are so damned honest. It's disarming."

"I was reading Jung. One thing that he wrote that I could agree with was that the goal of life is death, and that to be afraid of death is to stop living. I knew that before I read it. I want my life to end with a noble death. I'm grateful for my life. There has been a great deal of pain and confusion, but I've also had love: Jacob and Liza's, my mother's as hard of a love as that was, the love of my friends and Beth's love. What more can anyone ask for? I have to admit the closer I get to Beth, the harder it is to accept the simplicity of death. There have been moments between us that leave me dumb in awe. I can't put words to it. I wish with all my heart that I will never lose the possibility of feeling so intimately bound to another human being, but that wish isn't enough to make me put a god into the scenario so I can tell myself that death really isn't death. Kate, if my love for Beth doesn't make me believe in her kind of god, nothing will. I think Beth understands that and I think it hurts her."

"Because she wants you to know what she knows?"

"Because I'm incapable of knowing what she knows. Jacob was right about that."

Kate was given a rare access to Nicole. "What else did Jacob say?"

"It doesn't matter."

"I think it does."

Nicole weighed whether to continue. Kate's most biting comments were no longer part of their usual intercourse. "He said he wished he had spoken to me sooner. He said he wished he had been able to stop our commitment ceremony."

"Damn!" Kate tried to console. "He didn't mean it."

"He did. Believe me."

"I'm sorry. What are you going to do?"

"What can I do? I've made my vow to Beth and nothing is going to change that. Jacob has to accept me for who I am. I'll give him as much time as he needs to reconsider."

"What did Beth say?"

Nicole braced herself for a reproof. "I haven't told her."

Kate dropped her head on the table in mock disgust. Raising herself up she peered at Nicole. "Haven't we been through this before?"

Nicole leaned forward as she argued her case. "Do you really think this is the best time to tell Beth that one of the most important people in my life disapproves of our blessing? Don't you think she is having a hard enough time with God as it is?"

"You can't keep this from her for very long."

"I know." Nicole looked down to her plate. She picked up her fork. She knew there was no avoiding the bleak collision of forces in her life.

CHAPTER 106

March 29, 2002 – Good Friday

Beth knocked on the den door, which stood ajar, and opened it further. Nicole looked up from her book. "Nicki, I need a favor."

"Anything."

"Don't ask me to explain, but can you stay in the den for the next hour?"

Nicole was perplexed by Beth's request. She chose to honor it. "All right."

"Thanks." Beth closed the door.

Beth entered the dining room. She dimmed the lights and cleared the table of all the chairs. She covered the table with an altar linen. Carefully, she continued the process of making ready for the celebration of the Divine Liturgy. She stepped back from the altar and glanced over to the closed den door. Beth then went to the living room to change her dress.

Beth approached the altar and bowed her head, "Be with me, dear LORD." She stood in silence seeking the peace of God. She raised her head and opened her eyes. She stepped to the altar and began the Mass. "Blessed be our God. For ever and ever. Amen ..."

She read the Old Testament lesson: Isaiah 52:13-53:12, followed by Psalm 22:1-11.

"'My God, my God, why have you forsaken me?
  Why are you so far from helping me,
  from the words of my groaning?
 O my God, I cry by day, but you do not answer;
  and by night, but find no rest.

Yet you are the holy,
  enthroned on the praises of Israel.
In you our ancestors trusted;
  they trusted, and you delivered them.
To you they cried and were saved;
  in you they trusted, and were not put to shame.

But I am a worm, and not human;
  scorned by others, all despised by the people.
All who see me mock at me,
  they make mouths at me, they

shake their heads;
"Commit your cause to the LORD;
   let him deliver –
   let him rescue the one in whom he delights!"

Yet it was you who took me from the womb,
   you kept me safe on my mother's breast.
On you I was cast from my birth;
   and since my mother bore me
   you have been my God.
Do not be far from me,
   for trouble is near,
   and there is no one to help.'"

She then read the Epistle: Hebrews 10: 1-25. She announced the Gospel, "The Passion of our Lord Jesus Christ according to John." She then read John 19:1-37. She continued with the Solemn Collects. Beth stepped to the living room. She lit two candles, carried them forward and placed one on each side of the altar. She stepped away a second time and entered again, holding the cross. She set it upon the center of the altar, and recited the Anthem.

As she continued, Beth felt a rising emotion. The words slowly began to take hold of her. The Passion made a deep incursion into her heart. It became difficult to turn the pages of her Book of Common Prayer. She continued with the Confession of Sin. She closed her eyes and recited the Lord's Prayer, her hands raised in praise.

Beth lowered her hands and held them together before her. She stood in silence. She could have ended the service. When she began she had been uncertain whether she would continue with Communion. She had consecrated the Host and wine the night before, as it is tradition not to perform The Great Thanksgiving and the Breaking of Bread on Good Friday.

Beth opened her eyes to the altar. One lone Host rested on the paten. Wine had been poured into the chalice.

"The Body of our Lord Jesus Christ, which was given for thee, preserved thy body and soul unto everlasting life. Take and eat this in remembrance that Christ died for thee, and feed on him in thy heart by faith, with thanksgiving."

With trembling hands Beth raised the Host. Her head bowed as she took it into her mouth. Her sorrow consumed her. It was not only hers. She shared it with the Christ. She placed her hands on the altar for support. She did not fight the assault but surrendered herself to it. Her tears flowed. She spoke the following words as she cried.

"The Blood of our Lord Jesus Christ, which was shed for thee, preserve thy body and soul unto everlasting life. Drink this in remembrance that Christ's Blood was shed for thee, and be thankful."

Beth raised the chalice and drank the wine. She felt the wine travel through her. She felt its warmth. The elusive warmth did not escape her; it stayed with her; it consoled her.

Beth placed the chalice back onto the altar. Her tears would not be arrested. She did not concern herself with discovery. She was standing in the presence of God and nothing else mattered. She was not alone.

Nicole looked up from her reading to check the time. Ninety minutes had passed since Beth had made her request. Nicole closed her book and went to her CD player, turning the volume off. She listened to the sounds of the evening, and heard nothing from the other side of the den door.

Nicole entered the dining room. Her eyes scanned the chairs placed against the wall. She paused at the sight of the table set for Mass. A cross lay at the horizontal head. At center were the chalice and the paten; at one side the ciborium. Evenly placed lighted candlesticks stood at the forefront, all resting on fine linen. Nicole had envisioned the setting. The impact of its tangible presence was far greater than she had thought possible. The dining room table was transformed into a sacred altar.

She walked into the living room and paused at its center. Beth sat on the sunroom couch, her legs tucked underneath her. Looking at the reflection upon the sunroom windows, she could see that Beth was dressed in a simple black cassock alb with a knotted cotton rope cincture around her waist. Around her neck hung a black stole with the Celtic cross embroidered in metallic gold. Nicole could not define the feelings the image provoked. Before her was the image of Beth as she first knew her, the woman that she grew to love contrary to her better judgment. Before her was the woman who had gone into hiding during the past months, whether she had been lying dormant or forcibly suppressed, Nicole was unable to discern. Nicole saw the woman Beth needed to be. Somehow Beth needed to return to the part of her vocation she had left behind at St. Ann's. Nicole did not know how this could come to pass. She only knew that it had to be, whatever the price.

Nicole approached. She took her place beside Beth and saw what the glass' reflection had failed to reveal – Beth's tears.

Nicole longed to be recognized. "Beth."

Beth spoke, keeping her gaze out toward the night. "You said I was a scholar, a chaplain and a priest. You were right. In my heart I will never stop being a priest."

"Maybe you were not meant to leave the Church."

"I haven't." Beth turned to Nicole. "There's something I haven't told you."

Nicole's fear of losing Beth to God found a foothold.

"Nicki, the Church hasn't taken away my priesthood. My bishop gave me a year to decide. I declined until he asked me to do it as a courtesy to him."

Nicole knew better. "But you didn't do it as a courtesy to him."

"At first …" Beth needed to be completely honest. "No, I didn't. It was always for me. I really didn't know what I was giving up. My bishop knew I needed to leave the door open so I could come to this day. I can't go on the way I've been. I need a church. I don't want to feel like an outcast when I celebrate the Eucharist. And I want to celebrate the Eucharist. I want to be ordained in the Church. I still need some time, but I'm going to talk to Pam. I want to start attending her church." Beth reached out and took Nicole's hand, stroking Nicole's gold band with her thumb. "I know we'll be welcomed."

Nicole's eyes had followed Beth's hand. She now raised her gaze back to Beth's downcast eyes. With her right hand, Nicole raised Beth's chin. She searched for a confirming glimmer of hope. "Are you sure?"

"Yes. The Episcopal Church made the decision for me. I just couldn't leave until I understood."

"Understood what?"

"Why I didn't want to leave. Leaving meant I wasn't good enough to serve God. It meant God rejected my love. I tried to love God but it hurt so much … I felt forsaken. The distance between us seemed impossible."

"What made it better?"

"You did." Beth continued to hold Nicole's hand. "Our blessing was the beginning. And then when we talked about the Episcopal catechism I realized you were right. My core Episcopal beliefs are shared by most Christian denominations. I was holding on to form, not content."

Nicole looked over Beth's shoulder toward the dining room. "Did you celebrate the Mass?"

"Yes. I can't explain. Please believe me when I tell you that I've been touched by the love of God."

Nicole could not, nor did she want to deny the palpable vigor in Beth's appeal. "I believe you."

"There is one thing I need you to know. I've forgiven the Episcopal Church for what it's done to me and what it keeps on doing to women and men like me. I hope you can forgive it, too."

"Beth, there is nothing for me to forgive. I'm not a part of the Church. It can't hurt me the way it has hurt you."

Beth was confronted once again with the fact that the woman she loved was the most complex human being she had ever met. "Will I ever understand you?"

"Trust me. I am sincere in my respect for your faith."

"That's not what I mean." Beth leaned over and kissed Nicole. "I love you."

CHAPTER 107

April 27, 2002

Pam's four-year-old daughter, Sarah, was running around the picnic blanket giggling. Nicole stood a couple paces aside. "Pam, does she ever get tired?"

Pam sat on the blanket along with Beth. "Give her an hour."

"I'm exhausted just watching her."

Tom, Pam's husband, performed the duties of master chef, grilling hamburgers and hot dogs. Matthew, their eight-year-old, played the role of chef's assistant.

Nicole took Sarah by her pant's waist and lifted her up. Sarah hung on a horizontal plane. Nicole swung her from side to side. She called back to Pam, "You don't need to work out. Just lift and release. Lift and release." With each phrase Nicole lifted Sarah up and then lowered her again.

"Mama! Mama!" Sarah squealed in delight.

Beth could not believe Nicole with the children, nor could Pam. Pam glanced over to Beth. "You never told me Nicole was so good with kids."

"Nicki is full of surprises."

Nicole now had Sarah by her ankles. "Sarah, how do you like an upside down world?"

Sarah laughed even louder. With a quick motion, Nicole took Sarah by the waist and lifted her up, cradling her. "How's this?"

Sarah took Nicole by the neck and held tight. Nicole looked into Sarah's clear blue eyes, and was reminded of Dion. She felt the child's innocent joy. It reached deep into her. She wondered if she had ever known such joy as a child. Sarah quieted. In response, Nicole held Sarah closer. She held in her arms unconditional trust. Nicole acted upon her desire to kiss the girl on the forehead.

Beth noticed the silence and looked over to see what was amiss. What she saw moved her deeply – the strength of Nicole juxtaposed with the vulnerability of Sarah. She saw something in Nicole's tender embrace of the child that she believed, until that moment, had always been reserved for her alone.

"If Sarah were older, I'd say you have competition," Pam whispered.

Beth wondered if it could be true. Was Nicole falling in love?

-∤-　　-∤-　　-∤-

The evening picnic was a success. Nicole and Beth walked silently hand in hand, home from the lakefront. Upon reaching their apartment, Nicole placed the picnic basket on the kitchen counter and walked into her den. Beth withheld any comment regarding Nicole shirking her dishwashing duties.

Hours passed. Nicole remained in her den. Beth waited in the living room, hoping Nicole would choose to come to her. Disappointed, she used the only legitimate reason she had to interrupt. Standing at the den threshold, she saw Nicole in profile, sitting in one of the two tall back chairs. The side table lamp and the portrait lights were lit. Her desk was clear. Her computer was turned off. Nothing lay on the side table to indicate any task had been taken up. "Nicki. I'm going to bed."

Beth received no response. She entered the den and knelt beside Nicole, placing her hand on her partner's arm. She spoke softly. "Nicki."

Nicole turned to Beth.

"Nicki, it's late. Why don't we go to bed?" Beth asked gently.

Nicole surfaced from wherever she had been, and smiled. "In a little while."

"I'll be waiting." Beth kissed Nicole on the cheek before leaving.

Nicole entered their bed within the half hour. Beth welcomed her. "Hi."

Nicole lay alongside Beth and kissed her tenderly. She then shifted and rested her ear over Beth's heart. She draped her arm around her lover's waist. Beth had come to know this rare posture as an indication of Nicole at her most troubled.

Nicole spoke with no apparent distress. "Pam and Tom have done a great job with Matthew and Sarah."

"Yes, they have."

"They're happy kids."

"Pam keeps saying that she's dreading the teen years."

"Tess says the same thing about Dion and Jack. Pam and Tom ...they don't seem to be overly protective."

"No. But they are careful."

Nicole fell back into silence. As much as Beth wanted to lead the conversation, she chose to wait for Nicole to find her way.

"Something happened when I was playing with Sarah. I don't know, Beth." Nicole paused for a breath. "If I was ever that alive and innocent, I don't remember it. I felt it through her. Everything I knew fell away as unimportant, and it was just Sarah and making sure she was safe and healthy and happy. All her wild and crazy energy just stopped, and she got quiet and touched my cheek as if for that one moment I was the only thing between her and the world, and she trusted me to keep holding her in my arms."

"They can do that to you, especially when they're Sarah's age."

"You spent time with the kids when you were at St. Ann's."

"Yes, and during my internship at St. Michael's."

"After you finish your studies ... "

Beth stroked Nicole's hair. "Yes?"

"We'll have been together for a while ... a child. Beth, I could love your child."

Beth heard Nicole's fragile profession. It was not a mere consent to a child. It was a sincere desire and once again, Beth was left to wonder why the change? First, no union ceremony, and then she had found herself kneeling side by side with Nicole, exchanging rings in a church, being given the blessing of Christ and God. She had wanted a child for herself and for Nicole, but Nicole had been clear. The risk of a child was too great for her to take. Nicole's previous honesty could not be argued with. Having a child was a risk. The world could be a brutal place. Having a child with intention took great faith in oneself, if one was partnered, in one's mate, in the child yet born and for Beth, in God. Having a child reflected a belief that God's creation was good. That whatever came to be had a purpose, a purpose often beyond human reason.

Nicole laid upon Beth's heart asking for a child and Beth knew that this was the only way they could have ever chosen to become more than a couple, to become a family. Beth had to allow Nicole to find the heart to love. For Nicole, heart translated to courage. Nicole needed to find the courage to love her. That had been confessed. Nicole now needed a greater courage to expand the circle and include a third. One thing had not changed. Nicole was not asking to bear the child. Beth understood that limit remained. But, Nicole would love her child. 'Her child' – for Beth that sentiment was unacceptable.

"Nicki, come here." Beth coaxed Nicole up.

Nicole raised herself and hovered over Beth, as was her custom. Beth swept Nicole's hair to the side. "The child will always be ours, not mine. It's the only way it can be for us."

Nicole offered a whimsical smile. "Maybe we can find some Greek donor sperm."

Beth laughed. "A Greek with blue eyes."

CHAPTER 108

May 2, 2002

The two women sat across from one another at the dining room table, a Scrabble game between them. Beth was scoring high words. Nicole struggled to keep pace.

Beth finished the latest tally. "Want to know the score?"

"Nope."

"One thing I like about this game is the combination of knowledge and skill that is required to win." Beth was enjoying herself at Nicole's expense.

"There is still the luck of the draw."

"Yes, but if you really know words you can work with just about any letter."

"Give me chess. Chess is pure strategy. Luck is never an element."

Beth smiled as she set down her next word.

"You keep this up and I'll never play with you again," Nicole playfully warned.

"Are you sure you're not letting me win?"

"Yes!"

Beth had to wonder. "How can you be so illiterate?"

Nicole looked up from her letters; letters that refused to form anything more than a simple four-letter word. "Thank you for that. I can't spell. I admit it."

"The multi-talented Nicole Thera? Now I know the truth." Beth laughed.

"Now that you know the truth, do you still love me?"

Beth picked her replacement letters. "I love you more."

"Maybe we could play a game of chess later?"

"There isn't a competitive bone in your body, is there?"

Nicole smiled guiltily.

The telephone rang. "I'll get it," said Beth.

Nicole continued to play with her letters.

Beth walked to the living room and picked up the receiver. "Hello?"

A woman's voice said, "May I speak to Beth?"

"Speaking."

"Beth, this is Doctor Lorenz. Is this a good time?"

Beth looked at Nicole, intent on the Scrabble board. "Yes."

"Your test results have come back. I need you to come in for a follow-up exam."

"Is it ..." Beth pressed down her fear. She felt fine. There was no reason to believe she was ill.

"Beth, you have always asked me to be honest with you. I'm concerned, but there isn't cause for alarm. Given your family history I want to be sure everything is in order."

Beth held her gaze upon Nicole. "When?"

"I'll have my office call you in the morning. It should only take a few days before we get you in."

"Have your office page me. I'll be on the hospital floor most of the day."

"Do you have any questions?"

She had a store of questions, but it was not the time to ask. "I'll wait until I see you."

"All right. Good night, Beth."

"Thank you for calling." Beth lay the phone down on its cradle.

Nicole looked up. "Who was that?"

"The hospital. I asked the Nurses' Station to give me an update on a patient I've been counseling."

Nicole could see that Beth was troubled. "Bad news?"

Beth returned to her chair. "Don't know yet. The first tests were inconclusive. They need to do more."

Nicole offered what little comfort she could. "I hope the new test results are good."

Beth met Nicole's compassionate gaze. "So do I."

CHAPTER 109

May 14, 2002 – Morning

Beth walked out of Dr. Lorenz's office. She paused, uncertain. She chose to retrace her steps down the corridor to the connecting walkway that joined the medical professional office building to the hospital. Beth thought she had been ready to hear Dr. Lorenz say the two words that had haunted her much of her life – ovarian cancer. She had been wrong.

Deep in thought, Beth continued her journey through the hospital. The surroundings were diffused, no more than shadows and muffled sounds. What, she wondered, had her mother felt when she had received her diagnosis? What had she done? Had she been alone or had her father been with her? How had they consoled one another?

She entered the chapel. She would have the silence, the solitude she urgently needed. Beth reached into her pocket and removed her prayer beads. She raised the cross to her lips, closing her eyes as she did. She had spent countless hours praying for the strength to accept her diagnosis. She could ask God for no more. Given her diagnosis, her prayer changed. It was not enough for her to accept her destiny. Beth rested her forehead against her hands. She was facing the cruel consequences of her choices. She had allowed Nicole in her life knowing that this day would, in all probability, come. She had kept the truth from Nicole until after their relationship had been consummated.

"LORD, hear my prayer."

The memory of Nicole, the night before, taking her aside into an alley as they walked home from dinner and kissing her passionately "just because" swept across Beth's mind. Nicole's brilliant smile had been ample compensation for the teasing Beth's blush had solicited.

Nicole was happy. She was at peace. Beth knew that by day's end her life with Nicole would be forever changed. Nicole would be forever changed.

Beth struggled to return to her prayer. "Have mercy and grant me your compassion."

Her thoughts were interrupted once again. She remembered their first morning together in Hyde Park, how Nicole had revealed her fragile heart, confessing that never again did she want to wake to a lonely bed. Beth had given Nicole a promise that day. She would come to Nicole if called. She had asked in return for Nicole's love, respect and desire. Nicole had given Beth all that she had asked for and more. Beth feared the day would soon come that she would break her promise, that her cancer would prevent her from heeding Nicole's call.

Beth choked her next words, as she began to cry. "I am lost without you, dear LORD. Guide me to you."

She heard Nicole's request after her return from Boston. *Whatever you do, don't let me slip away from you. Keep me with you from the beginning until the end. Do it, Beth. Do it for me.'*

Beth's prayer was no longer to God. She beseeched Nicole, "Forgive me."

CHAPTER 110

May 14, 2002 – Evening

Beth entered the apartment. "Nicki?"

"In the den."

Beth leaned against the den doorjamb. "Hi."

Nicole looked up from her computer. "Hi."

"Will you be working late?"

Nicole smiled. "Make me an offer."

"You and me. A walk after dinner."

Sheepishly, Nicole asked, "Miss me, do you?"

Beth adored Nicole when she was playful. She memorized the moment; fearful she would never know another like it again. "Very much."

"I'm all yours."

The two walked by the lakefront to the murmur of the calm Lake Michigan waters washing up on the shoreline. "Here." Beth sat on a park bench.

Settled beside Beth, Nicole led the conversation. "What is it, Beth?"

Beth took hold of Nicole's hand, focusing on it. "I went for my annual check-up. My blood test worried my doctor. I had to go back for additional tests." Beth looked up.

Nicole knew Beth had an agenda. Beth was transparent, but only to a point. Beth's calmness did not hide the fear Nicole saw in her eyes. Nicole voiced the diagnosis first. "Cancer?"

"Ovarian. My family history … "

"Where is the tumor?"

"My right ovary."

Nicole stood and walked a few paces away from Beth. Beth followed her with her eyes. Nicole spoke with her back still to Beth. "When did you find out?"

"The final lab results came in today."

Nicole turned around. "What's next?"

"I need to meet with a surgeon. If the cancer hasn't gone beyond my ovary we can try just removing the one, but I do have a high risk of reoccurrence. It may be safer to have both removed now. If the cancer has staged, the surgery could include a hysterectomy, and I would need chemo."

"When?"

"I'm not sure. The surgery should be scheduled in about a week."

Nicole took a step forward. Having the facts, she could see Beth again. "How are you?"

Beth continued with the task-related details. "I need to call Marie tonight. She might want to fly in from Atlanta."

"Your father?"

"No."

Nicole looked away, trying to subdue her rising emotions. After a brief pause she asked, "Anyone else?"

"Pam. I'll tell her in the morning. She'll have to adjust my schedule at the hospital. At least I'm only going to miss the last week of CPE"

Silence took its place between them as they held each in the other's gaze. The reality of the conversation began to own Nicole. She spoke softly. "Beth, do you realize what you just told me?"

Beth stood up and went to Nicole. "Nicki, I won't mention God's will and my needing to learn to bend myself to it. I won't tell you that I've been struggling and that I spent the better part of the last few days in the hospital chapel praying to have the faith to accept my diagnosis. I'm just going to tell you that I'm determined to accept the grace of life with humility, seeking goodness both within myself and within others."

Beth offered Nicole her faith, fragile yet resilient. She melded her faith into Nicole's own tenets, hoping to remind Nicole of where their beliefs crossed paths.

"I wish you had told me. You shouldn't have waited alone."

"I needed time. I thought you, better than anyone, would understand. Anyway, I'm not alone. I've never been alone."

Nicole reached out and touched Beth's cross. She accepted that Beth's faith, her triune God was, and would always be, a part of their shared lives. Nicole could not displace Beth's God and as this moment once again affirmed, Beth's God took precedence over her. Beth went to God first and her second. Accepting Beth's love in the context of Beth's faith had been and continued to be humbling. God had Beth's divine love. Nicole had Beth's earthly love. It was hard at times, but Nicole willed herself to see the good, the balance in Beth's loves. Nicole's will trembled.

Nicole looked up from the cross. She could not consider the loss of Beth. To touch the possibility would be to enter despair beyond grief. Without a word, Nicole took Beth into her arms.

CHAPTER 111

May 15, 2002 – Morning

"No! I've tried, Kate." Nicole vehemently opposed any suggestion that she further indulge Beth's faith. "I've tried. From our first days in the apartment I knew I didn't want to share Beth with her God. I didn't want God between us. I wanted to steal her away and I thought that by giving her those things God couldn't give her, I would.

"Do you have any ideal how hard it was to accept that everything I gave Beth, to her, ultimately came from God? The more I loved her, the more God loved her. Do you have any idea how hard it was to accept that? Beth will never be completely mine. I had to learn to share her. If I didn't, she and I didn't have a future. If I tried to squelch her faith, if I tried to make her choose between us, I would destroy her. Don't you know I knew that! I could love her, make love to her, take her away from the world, but only for a brief moment in time, and never once were we alone. Beth can't live without her God and I didn't want to live without Beth. I relented. I finally came to a place where I agreed to the terms. I accepted the terms, Kate, but only because I still had Beth in my life. The terms have changed. Where is the love of God now? Where is the love of God in cancer?"

Kate had cleared her calendar and driven to the Elysian Fields immediately after Nicole had called with Beth's news. She stood before Nicole's desk trying to find a way to reach her friend. "Nicki, Beth needs both you and her faith. Now, more than ever."

"Don't tell me that, Kate. I went down on my knees for her. I've played nice with the ministers and chaplains. I've bitten my tongue, again and again. I redefined my integrity. She tells me this is the will of God, and that she has to learn to bend to it. Well, I don't have to bend to anything! There is no God, Kate!" Nicole slammed her fist on the desk. "There is no God! I won't pretend. I won't stand beside her and pretend."

"You can't let her go through this alone."

"She's not alone. She's got God!"

Kate sat down across from Nicole. "Nicki, please tell me you weren't like this when she told you."

Nicole stood up. "No. I wasn't like this. I was calm. I asked all the right questions. And then I looked at her and I couldn't speak. All I could do was hold her."

Kate looked relieved. "She's been having annual check-ups. The chances that they caught the cancer early are good."

Nicole walked away and stood in front of the windows looking out at the cityscape. Kate waited as the minutes ticked away. Nicole finally spoke Her violent emotions were checked, replaced by sorrow. "She wanted a child. I just told her ... I just told her I would share her child. Why did I tell her? Why now?"

Kate stood and walked to her friend. "Nicki, maybe Beth needed to know that you would have loved her child. Maybe that was the point, for both of you to know how far you have grown together. That in spite of everything you would choose to bring a child into this world."

Never had Kate so openly supported Nicole's relationship with Beth. The irony of the moment did not escape her. She would never have anticipated that a catalyst to the resolution of their past clashes would be her lover's fight for life.

Nicole recalled how she had guided Beth back to the apartment after being told of the diagnosis. Beth had phoned Marie. Afterwards, she had changed into her nightclothes and slipped into bed. Nicole had followed, and they had lain side-by-side. Wordlessly, Beth had turned to Nicole, taking a firm hold of Nicole's shirt, anchoring herself as she shed silent tears.

Recollecting past conversations, it was only now that Nicole grasped the full extent of Beth's revelations. Beth's early experiences were those of a love-less childhood. Nicole had assigned the cause to Beth's father, but for Beth, a loveless childhood was the consequence of her mother's early death.

By not having a child, Beth had saved her child the inconsolable grief that formed her as no other life experience had. By remaining childless, Beth would do no harm – just as Nicole was determined to do no harm. The reasons differed, but their solutions were the same.

Nicole was left to wonder why, in spite of her willingness to acquiesce to a childless relationship, Beth was equally drawn to the path that risked per-petuating the cycle of a mother's early death and a child left behind. How did Beth's faith inform her choice? What role, if any, did Nicole play in inform-ing Beth's choice? The evidence that, in some ways, Beth's reticent nature equaled, if not exceeded, her own, humbled Nicole. Beth's contention that, in some ways, she and Nicole were not so different, had never been truer. Nicole wanted time. Insight came sparingly and at a high cost.

Nicole was determined not to repeat past mistakes. A familiar accusatory specter entered her mind.

"Nicki," said Kate, calling Nicole back to the present.

Nicole turned to Kate, but her thoughts were on Beth. "She's so young."

"So are you. The threat of cancer hasn't been foreign to either of you. Nicki, remember you told me that at Shenandoah you had accepted your death? That you would have died grateful for your life even though it was short lived. What's to say Beth doesn't experience her life in the same way? She wanted to give, and she has, as a priest and a chaplain. She has the love of her friends. She has never been closer to Marie. After all the pain of leaving her church, she still has God. And Nicki, she has you. You said your only regret at Shenandoah was that you hadn't been able to give Beth everything she deserved from you. Look at what you've done since then! I've watched you. I'm so proud of you. I'm so proud of how much you've given Beth. Beth has never been happier. If the absolute worst happens and she accepts it as the will of God, you have to stand by her in every way. So help me, if you don't, I'll find hell, take you there myself and make sure you never leave it."

"You won't have to. I'm already feeling the fire."

"Why are you being so hard on yourself? I haven't seen you like this since ..." Kate grabbed Nicole's arm and pulled her so that they faced each other. "It isn't the same."

"She's sick and I can't help her."

Kate repeated, "Nicki, it isn't the same."

Nicole looked away.

Kate's memory vividly brought the past to the present. "Beth knows. You've told her. I know you have."

Nicole pulled her arm free. "Yes, she knows. I tell her every day."

"This is not like your Mom. This is nothing like your Mom."

Nicole returned her gaze to the cityscape. "My Mom, Amelia, Carrie ..." She looked down to the building across the street. "Jacob."

"If you had given up when your Mom died, you would never have become the woman you are, and Beth would never have come into your life. I know what it did to you. I was there. I'm here now and I'm telling you that you can't let this destroy you. You can't shut down again."

Nicole kept her eyes forward. "I don't think I can get through this alone."

"I'm here, Nicki. Just tell me what you need and you'll have it."

CHAPTER 112

May 15, 2002 – Afternoon

Beth returned to the apartment after an abbreviated workday. She sat in the den, her gaze rested upon the portrait. Pam had agreed to inform Beth's peer chaplains of her illness during the afternoon small group sessions, and had encouraged Beth to care for herself, taking whatever time off she needed prior to her surgery. Beth preferred to continue her work schedule. The alternative was to dwell on what was ultimately beyond her control. Cancer was not the only challenge she faced. The telephone rang, interrupting her thoughts. She picked up Nicole's desk phone. "Hello."

"Beth, it's Kate."

Beth responded automatically. "Kate, Nicki's not here."

"I know. Nicki called me." Kate was clearly struggling to find the right words. "I'm sorry."

Beth deflected the sympathy. "How is she?" Beth's concerns for Nicole were compounded during the course of the previous evening and their morning waking. There was an obvious war raging inside Nicole. Even as she held Beth, Beth felt her partner had never been more remote, containing her emotions.

"I don't know what to say."

"Confidentiality." With gentle whimsy, Beth noted the on-going defining limitations of her relationship with Kate.

"No, it's not that. I've only seen Nicki like this once before and it's hard to know what she's feeling, or what she'll do." Kate shifted the conversation back to who, at the moment, was her primary concern. "Is there anything I can do for you?"

"No thank you, Kate. I just have to wait."

"Nicki authorized me to take care of your legal needs: Medical Durable Power of Attorney, Power of Attorney, and Will. Do you have them done?"

"No."

"You work in a hospital. You know how important they are."

Beth agreed that the task was not optional. "When can you see me?"

"Anytime. I'll open up my calendar for you."

"Tomorrow morning?"

"Nine o'clock."

"That'll work."

Kate's tone shifted from that of a caring friend to that of an accomplished professional. "Beth, in spite of my friendship with Nicki, as your attorney I will keep your decisions in confidence."

"I know."

"Now, I'm speaking as Nicki's friend. Whom you choose to name as your representative is your decision; it must be someone who knows you well and whom you literally trust with your life. If you don't choose Nicki, she needs to be told. If you do name her, you must talk to her before you go into the hospital. She can't read your wishes on a piece of paper. You must discuss them with her until you're certain she understands, accepts, and is capable of giving you what you want. There can be no doubt."

"I understand." Beth recognized the fine line that Kate walked as she upheld her standard of professional ethics while, to the best of her ability; she safeguarded Nicole from unnecessary harm.

"Good. I'll see you tomorrow at nine."

"Thank you, Kate." Beth set the telephone receiver down. She wondered what Kate had meant about having "only seen Nicki like this once before." Beth's fear for Nicole escalated.

CHAPTER 113

May 20, 2002 – Monday Afternoon

Marie's plane arrived at Midway Airport late on Saturday. Beth waited for her at the gate. Marie's composure crumbled at the sight of her sister. As she held Marie, Beth said a silent thank you to Nicole for insisting that the two sisters have a private reunion.

It was now the evening before Beth's surgery. Legs crossed, Marie sat on the living room couch. The younger Kelly shared her sister's beautiful features, though Marie was a couple of inches taller and wore her richer strawberry blond hair longer.

The previous night, Beth and Marie had joined Nicole and friends at The Fields for dinner. Under orders from Nicole to have a good time, their friends had done their best to keep a lighthearted mood. To Marie's delight, the Musketeers had made Beth the brunt of their merciless ribbing. Though Nicole had smiled throughout the festivities, she said few words.

Marie called to her sister, who was in the kitchen, "Is Nicole always so talkative?"

Beth entered the living room and took her place on the opposite side of the couch, well aware of the source of her sister's muted sarcasm. "You'll be surprised. This isn't the best time."

Marie's gaze lay gently upon her sister. "No regrets?"

"Some. I could have made our life together easier for Nicki."

"I've watched her with you. She loves you. I can tell."

Beth smiled. "There isn't a day she doesn't say so."

"I've got a feeling two women together don't have to work as hard at being romantic."

"That a comment on Joe?"

Marie smiled at the mention of her boyfriend. "He's got potential."

Seeing the grin on Marie's face, Beth laughed lightly.

"Joe offered to come to Chicago with me."

Beth would have welcomed meeting the young man who had won Marie's affection. "And you said no because … "

"I'm already sharing you with Nicole. Is there anything I can do for her while you're in the hospital?"

"Give her plenty of space, especially if the news isn't good."

"Beth …" Marie leaned over and laid her head upon Beth's lap.

Beth welcomed the intimacy. She stroked her sister's hair. When they were children she would often comfort Marie in just this way.

Marie concluded without much deliberation, "I think Nicole for Dad was a good trade."

"I wish it didn't have to be that way."

"You can't change the old man."

"I know."

Marie reached up and took Beth's hand. "I don't remember Mom very well."

"It's hard to keep the memories from slipping away." Beth recalled how her mother would hold her and Marie. "We were so young when she died. Grandmother was good in telling me stories about our life with her. You take after Mom more than I do. There was a bit of a rebel in her."

"I miss Grandma, too. I'm sorry I didn't go to her funeral."

"Maybe we could drive down together some time and visit the cemetery."

Marie hesitated. "We don't have to see Dad, do we?"

"No," Beth promised. "Just the two of us."

"I'd like that." The two sisters fell into a comfortable silence. Marie was the first to speak. "Beth ... We will live to grow old together."

Beth looked down at her younger sibling. "I want to believe that."

Marie sat up. "No! That's not good enough. I need to know that we both have a future."

Beth realized that Marie's fear went beyond her own immediate health concern. Beth knew her illness did not bode well for Marie's future. Life had never felt more precarious. "Hey ... listen to me. You're young ..."

"So are you."

"We both knew I had a higher risk."

"When it comes down to it, your risk isn't that much higher than my own. Remember, you're talking to a nurse."

"I'm talking to my little sister." Beth saw the tears that welled into Marie's eyes. "I lost you once. I really don't want to lose you again."

Marie reached out and took Beth into her arms. "Then fight to stay."

"I am. Believe me, I am." Beth wished she could give Marie some tangible reassurance. She could not. So, she held her sister tightly, taking solace in their renewed closeness.

Later, responding to the doorbell, Beth opened the apartment door to Kate. "Hi, come on in."

Kate entered the front foyer. Marie approached. Kate greeted her. "Hi, kid. You ready?"

"Any time."

Kate looked around, clearly seeking Nicole. "Where is she?"

"She went to the park. She said you would know where to find her."

"I know the place. I'll bring her home in a little while."

"Kate." Beth steadied herself. "Please take care of her."

"I'm doing my best."

"Thank you."

Kate turned toward the opened door. She paused and looked over to Beth. "Beth, have I ever told you I liked you?"

Beth smiled. "No, you haven't."

"I do. You're the best thing that has ever happened to Nicki. I hope you realize that."

Beth had long wondered if Kate approved of their match. She felt a particular satisfaction in confirming that Nicole's prickly friend had accepted her. "Don't take too long. Nicki and I have some things to talk about."

A ten-minute walk from the apartment, Nicole sat on a park bench, cell phone in hand. Tess was on the line. "I should be there with you."

"Kate is riding shotgun. She's picking up Marie for a stay-over so Beth and I can have the night alone."

"How are you?"

Nicole felt more comfortable focusing on Beth's need. She tried to sweep aside her friend's concern. "You know me. I'll get through this."

"Remember who you're talking to."

Nicole sighed. "Tess ... I thought I was so smart. I wasn't going to lose a young love. Look at me now."

"Nicki, you told me they caught the cancer early and Beth agreed to a radical approach to prevent a reoccurrence. She's fighting to stay alive."

Nicole closed her eyes. "Tell me, what's my great flaw? Where's my hubris?" They both returned to the familiar stage of the tragedians. It was a place to argue the vulgarities of life at an objective distance.

"Don't look to Oedipus. Hecuba lost everything. The hardships were simply beyond her control."

"Doesn't work. Hecuba lost everything to war – man against man. This is the body turning against itself."

"Hey, between the two of us I'm the one with the Ph.D."

"And I'm the one who had a brain tumor."

Tess continued her search for an appropriate analogy. "The play has changed. If anyone is Oedipus, it's Beth. You're Antigone. You're the one who will keep the promise."

Nicole placed herself in the role of Antigone, who gave her brother Polyneices a sacred burial. "To bury Beth."

"If it comes to that, then yes. Nicki, I'll understand if you hang up on me for saying this but you didn't bury Amelia. You've got a second chance. Don't throw it away."

An uncomfortable silence held between the two women. "Tess ..." Nicole's voice was breaking with emotion.

"I'm here," Tess reassured.

"Do me a favor."

"Anything."

"Tell me what Bruce and the kids are up to. Just talk to me about how ridiculously normal life in Ann Arbor is right now."

Tess granted Nicole her request, telling tales of Dion's and Jack's most recent escapades.

Having bid Tess a goodnight, Nicole watched the lake waters and listened to the gentle waves washing against the shoreline. She knew she faced an incomprehensible mystery. For Nicole, God was and would always be the mystery of life. To come to terms with the mystery, with God, was a constant struggle. She engaged that mystery privately, without using the word God. To name the mystery God was to convey an understanding to those who would hear her speak far different from her intent.

Unlike Beth, she did not know if she was guided by the mystery. She did not know if the mystery had any expectations of her. Nor had she a sense that the mystery loved her. Though she did not know its nature, she did know that the mystery existed. She knew, that for reasons beyond her comprehension, she had the capacity to contemplate the mystery. And so she did. Nicole knew that her life would be incomplete were God not a constant, indecipherable companion.

Nicole hesitated to refer to God because to look to the heavens and allow the name of God to slip from her tongue could be interpreted to mean that she believed in the mystery in a way that granted the possibility of a response from its source. Nicole could not fathom the mystery as a sentient essence, which would, in turn, know her and believe in her.

It was hard enough for Nicole to accept that there were people in this world who saw more in her than she saw in herself. She had hesitated with them as well: with Jacob and Liza until their constancy won her trust, with Tess until their talks proved that their love for the Classics reflected a mutually held ethic strong enough to carry them through the most difficult storms, with Kate until their friendship was tested by the despair that consumed Nicole after her mother's death, and with Beth until Beth's love mastered her. Nicole did not understand their confidence in her. She did not understand how they could be so sure of her, and yet, each in their own way believed in her.

Nicole's greatest uncertainty resided between her and God. How could Nicole reach out or reach in and touch God, and believe in God? How could she trust in God when she did not know God and would never know God?

There lay the key. She knew she had yet to trust God, as she had learned to trust Jacob, Liza, Tess, Kate, and Beth. She knew that her lack of trust was a function of not directly experiencing, not physically sensing God as she did the latter five. She knew that her lack of trust was a function of her inability to sense the infinite within the finite, the finite being miraculous enough to leave her awed. In this moment, all that she could do was trust and respond to the divine that she sensed in life itself.

This evening, Nicole was bereft of the faith she once held as a child, faith in what stood beyond the mystery, faith that God was Beth's God and Jacob's God, not her enigma. She remained a woman who contemplated God without knowing God. She remained a woman who loved a woman who loved God. In her hour of need she would soon reach out and touch Beth. Her act of holding Beth, the divine she found in Beth, was the closest Nicole could come to God. In her hour of need, holding Beth would be her prayer.

Kate approached Nicole. She sat down beside her. "How're you doing?"

Nicole sighed. "I wish I smoked or drank."

"Do you really think it would help?"

"No. But at least I could fall back on a cliché."

"There are other cliché's to choose from."

"Not now, Kate. After I know, one way or another." The prospect of hearing the most difficult news caused Nicole to shudder. "Then I might fall back on the cliché of a wailing banshee ... just don't come near me then. I won't be responsible for my actions."

"Have you two talked?"

"A little. We'll talk tonight." Nicole was impatient for time alone with Beth. "Thanks for putting Marie up for the night."

"We'll meet you at the hospital."

"Remember it's 7 a.m., not p.m."

"Did I know that?" Kate gave Nicole a friendly shove. "I figure I'll get some good stories about when Beth was a kid in the bargain."

Nicole smiled. "I hadn't thought of that. I need to take Marie out for a private lunch."

"You'll have the chance while Beth recovers."

Nicole looked at Kate. "Thank you for that."

"Marie seems nice enough."

"I like watching the two of them together. It's like watching you with Tracy." Nicole referred to Kate's younger sister.

"That's now. You should have seen us when we were growing up. We had love/hate down to a science. It was different with Adam and Cal. Having older brothers was cool and it was nice knowing they kept an eye on their little sisters."

"Until you wanted to start dating."

Kate laughed out loud. "They didn't like the competition!"

Nicole wrapped her arm around Kate. "You're incorrigible."

They fell back into a comfortable silence, the kind of silence that could only be shared with friends who have walked through the uncertain, opaque mist of life together.

Nicole spoke softly. "Beth has been so calm. She's taking care of us more than we are taking care of her."

"It's who she is. She isn't going to change now."

Nicole turned toward Kate. "But I want to help her."

"You'll figure it out. You both will."

CHAPTER 114

May 20, 2002 – Evening

In the bedroom Beth packed her things while Nicole read on the living room couch. Her task near complete, Beth paused. Her gaze shifted to the door. She thought of Nicole. She held all that Nicole was to her close to her heart. She had tried to be strong during the intervening days between Dr. Lorenz's first phone call and this day. She had tried to come to terms with her mother's legacy, a life engendered with a predisposition to a young death. She thought she had surrendered herself to the finite, but that was before St. Ann's, before Nicole. The life she had fashioned imploded in response to the weight of truth: the truth of the Episcopal Church that denied her, and the truth of Nicole's disbelief that had driven a wedge between Beth and God only because Beth had failed to accept Nicole as a grace from God. Beth assumed her father would claim Beth's cancer was divine retribution for leaving the Church, and for loving Nicole. Beth wondered if that was true, then what great, unforgivable acts had her mother and her grandmother committed to offend God?

Beth held Nicole close to her heart. She was grateful that in the previous year, her life had been stripped down to its purest core. If her life was to be short lived, at least it would be an honest life, a life that had known a great love. She wanted to know Nicole's love in all its forms, forms yet to become, forms that would be shared with time as they aged, as life challenged them, as she gave birth to their child, and they parented the child. Before Nicole, Beth had stifled her dreams. With Nicole, the dreams slowly manifested themselves and found footing in her life. Love, partnership, a promise of family – these were primary. There was also her vocation, which had found new depth of meaning in her ministry as a chaplain. And finally, with receipt of an academic fellowship, she looked forward to her studies.

Why was she given so much to have it all placed at risk before the harsh reality of cancer? Was it so she would die knowing she was worthy of God's love – that as Jacob had told her, she needed "a little more help than others." She had needed proof, so she was given Nicole to know how deep and abiding love could be, how the impossible could be possible. She was given a brief time in her vocation to be a valued instrument of God. She was given the University fellowship to set aside any lingering doubts of the merit of her scholarship.

Beth held Nicole close to her heart. She did not want to let go. She did not want to die. God help her, she did not want to be released from her earthly life. It would have been easier before Nicole. In her arid life at St Ann's, a young death would have been difficult, but it would not have come close to what she was now fighting within herself. Beth held Nicole close to her heart knowing that she had to let go. She prayed that God would have mercy on her and help her let go of all the blessings that had been bestowed.

Beth turned her gaze to her Bible. She took it in hand, lifted it up and placed a kiss upon it. "LORD, have mercy upon my soul. Give me the strength and wisdom to endure. Amen." She set the Bible in her overnight bag. For a second time Beth shifted her gaze toward the door. Beyond waited Nicole. There were things that she still needed to say to Nicole. The need for God's mercy was immediate.

She walked into the living room and accepted Nicole's unspoken invitation. Nicole put her book aside as Beth claimed her place, resting her body over her partner's. Nicole held Beth gently.

Beth took comfort in their ability to share silence even though she knew it was necessary for her to break it. "Nicki, I saw Kate this morning and signed my legal papers. Thank you for making the arrangements."

"You're welcome."

"I've named you my primary representative and Marie my secondary on everything."

Nicole stroked Beth's hair.

"Nicki, if things go badly during the operation or afterwards – if the time comes that there is no hope – let me go. I know I've argued the point with you. My feelings have changed a bit. I've seen too many extraordinary precautions taken at the hospital. I trust that you'll fight for my life and, if it's my time, I trust that you'll fight for my death."

Nicole closed her eyes. She gathered all her strength to maintain her composure. She could not find her voice. She placed a kiss upon Beth's head.

Beth continued, "I talked to Marie. She understands my wishes. You won't have to decide alone if you don't want to." Beth paused. She heard Nicole's heartbeat and felt the rise and fall of Nicole's breath. "Nicki?"

"I'm here."

"Writing my will, I realized how little I own. I left you everything except my grandmother's cross. I want Marie to have it."

Nicole could not conceive of parting with the cross. It had always been Beth to her. She would, however, honor Beth's wishes.

"I'd like to be buried beside my mother in Riverton. I want to be holding my prayer beads."

Again, Nicole was losing a symbol of Beth's faith. "Your father … are you sure you don't want to call him?"

"If I'm not his daughter healthy, I'm not his daughter sick. I've seen what happens when estranged families are forced to deal with each other in a hospital. It won't take long before either you or Marie goes after my father ... and with reason. You don't need that. I don't want it."

Nicole resorted to another kiss.

"I could never have imagined you. I could never have prayed for you to come into my life. My God, having you in my life changed everything. I love God more because you came into my life. I know it didn't always seem that way, but it's true." Beth reached out and took Nicole's hand. She kissed it tenderly, and went on, "Nicki, I didn't expect this so soon. I think I always knew I would get sick, like my Mom, but I honestly thought I would have more time. I thought we would have more time." Beth bit her lip, trying to hold back her tears. "I wanted to give you a child. I'm so sorry. I should have told you when I first met you. You shouldn't have to deal with my illness."

Nicole had reached her limit. She took Beth by her arms and raised her up as she leaned her own body forward. "Stop this!" Nicole's stern gaze held Beth's. Beth looked away. "Look at me, Beth." Nicole accentuated each word as she repeated her command. "Look. At. Me."

Beth complied. There was one final gift Beth wanted from Nicole. Her fingertips traced Nicole's mouth, bidding the anger away, seeking Nicole's more tender passion. Trembling, Beth leaned forward and kissed Nicole. The trembling kiss grew more needy. Beth's longing had surfaced.

Nicole braced herself. Beth would have her. She would have Beth. On this night of fear, all that words failed to convey would be expressed through touch.

CHAPTER 115

May 21, 2002 – Morning

They entered the same day surgery admitting area of the hospital. Nicole carried Beth's overnight bag. Beth paused. "I'd like to stop at the chapel first." Nicole nodded and allowed Beth to lead them forward.

Beth entered the chapel. There were four small pews on each side of a center aisle, and at the forefront, an altar. On the wall behind the altar were the symbols of the major faiths: the Celtic cross of Christianity; the Mogen David of Judaism; the star and crescent of Islam; the Sanskrit characters which were pronounced Ohm, the Hindu symbol of ultimate reality; the Yin-Yang of the Tao; and the Eight-Spoked Wheel representing the Eight-Fold path of Buddhism.

Beth went to a second row pew and knelt. Nicole remained standing in the back. For a moment, she released her steadfast gaze from Beth and scanned the chapel, knowing that it had been Beth's spiritual home for the previous nine months. This was the space, more than any other, where Beth went to be with God. It was a gentle space, the lighting muted, placed outside a quiet corridor of the hospital. It was as welcoming to as many as it could possibility be without becoming so generic that it held no hint of the sacred. Nicole liked the space.

She placed Beth's overnight bag down on the floor and stood erect, her hands clasped before her. She closed her eyes and bowed her head to the infinite, to all that surpassed human understanding, to the force of creation, to the source of the divine she found in every living being. She felt the pulse of her own life course through her veins and with each breath moved closer to a stillness within her that stripped away all that was nonessential. She felt her strength and her vulnerability, her love and her fear. She felt Beth's spirit. She knew she was both alone and part of a shared universe, inexplicably linked.

Beth completed her prayer. She sought courage to face the truth and to accept it gracefully. She sought compassion for those she loved, and who loved her. When Beth turned back, she saw Nicole standing, head bowed, eyes closed, in complete stillness. To Beth it was a posture of prayer and yet she knew Nicole did not pray. Beth was deeply stirred by the image. She wished she understood what she was seeing.

As Beth approached her, Nicole opened her eyes and offered a small smile. Beth placed her hand over Nicole's heart. "I need you to do something for me."

"Anything."

"They won't let me wear my cross and ring in surgery. Keep them for me."

"Of course."

Beth raised her hands behind her neck and unclasped her cross. She took Nicole's hand. Nicole opened her palm to Beth. Beth placed the cross and chain upon it. She then removed her gold band and placed it over the cross. She closed Nicole's palm and covered it with her own hand. Beth kissed Nicole's hand. She looked up and said the words spoken less often than those of love but which were of equal importance. "Thank you, Nicki. Thank you for everything you've given me."

"Beth ..." Nicole fought any suggestion of a good-bye.

"It's time." Beth closed the moment between them.

The same day surgery area was comprised of a honeycomb configuration of patient rooms. Nicole and Kate stood outside of Beth's glass-enclosed room, giving Beth and Marie time alone.

"So, did you get any good stories about Beth?" asked Nicole.

"A few. We were up half the night talking. How about you two? Did you talk?"

"Yes."

Kate caught sight of an approaching crowd. She exclaimed too loudly, "My God, it's a choir!"

Nicole followed Kate's gaze.

Led by Pam, the chaplains, all in their blue blazers, were approaching. Pam maintained her dignity in spite of the fact that everyone in the surrounding area was following the pseudo-choir's procession. "Good morning, Nicole."

"Morning, Pam. I don't think you've met," Nicole quirked her head toward her tactless companion and spoke drolly, "my friend, Kate."

Kate ignored Nicole's introduction. She exchanged greeting with Pam, then continued whimsically. "Are you going to sing to Beth? If you are, I have a pretty good voice."

Nicole quipped, "Don't listen to her. What she calls singing most people think of as cats in heat."

Pam laughed. "I'm glad to see you're in good spirits."

"Better than crying," Kate said soberly.

Pam explained to Nicole, "We thought we would offer a prayer."

"Of course. Go right in."

Through the open door the chaplains entered Beth's room, congregating around her bed. Their spirits were warm and uplifting.

Kate turned to Nicole. "You coming in?"

"Go ahead. I need a minute."

For a moment Kate carefully studied her friend. She then entered Beth's room.

Having a measure of privacy, Nicole lifted Beth's ring, and cross and chain from her blazer pocket. She studied the symbols as they rested in her palm. She did not fight the surge of emotion, but felt it freely. Her love and fear bound together. She strung the ring to the chain, and then secured the chain around her neck. The ring and cross fell together beside her Celtic pendant, which hung independently on its own silver chain.

Nicole heard Pam's voice. "Let us pray."

Nicole turned toward the room entrance. The occupants had joined hands. She walked in and stood a few paces to the side, keeping a clear view of Beth, who lay in bed, one hand holding Marie's, the other, Pam's. Nicole did not hear the words of the prayer. She heard nothing. The world had stopped and she stood alone with Beth.

"Amen."

Beth opened her eyes, immediately capturing Nicole's gaze and holding it.

"I'm sorry to interrupt, but Surgery is on its way," Beth's nurse announced.

The chaplains exited in a well-ordered procession, hovering outside, intending to wait until Beth was transported away. Kate squeezed Beth's hand and silently stepped out. Marie kissed her sister and spoke a word of love before following Kate to the door. It was only then that Nicole returned to Beth's bedside. She took Beth's hand, sharing it with the prayer beads.

Beth noticed the cross. She reached out and touched it. She smiled. "What are people going to think?"

"There goes my reputation."

"Could you hold these for me until I get back from surgery?" Beth allowed the prayer beads to slip into Nicole's grasp.

"We really are going to confuse people." Nicole offered a fragile smile. She raised her free hand to Beth's brow, sweeping a wisp of hair aside. "I have one regret."

Beth looked thoughtfully at Nicole. She could not begin to guess what Nicole was feeling, what they had not spoken of the night before.

Nicole spoke intimately. "I regret that I couldn't love you as perfectly as God loves you."

Beth released a small cry. "Nicki."

Nicole kissed Beth lightly on the forehead, and then peered over to the door. "Oh good. Now everyone is going to say the heathen made you cry."

Beth laughed quietly, composing herself, grateful for the blessing of humor in the moment. "Nicki, you know the concept of Christians seeking to become the bride of Christ?"

"Yes."

"Do you know how it applies to marriage?"

Nicole was uncertain of Beth's reference. "In Paul's writings?"

"… And St. John Chrysostom. The love of two joined souls creates the experience of becoming one with another without losing oneself, without being destroyed. God gave us this so we could have a better understanding of what our union with God would ultimately be. Every time you've made love to me, I've known the perfect love of God. I've never separated that love from you."

Nicole never expected the honor Beth bestowed upon her. Having no words equal to the moment, her answer was a kiss.

The surgical transport team arrived at Beth's door. Nicole stepped out of the room as Beth was placed on a gurney. She gave Beth one final kiss before Beth was wheeled away to surgery. Pam stood beside Nicole. "Pam, I understand the theology of redemptive suffering. Tell me, knowing Beth, what could she possibly have done to deserve this?"

"It may not be Beth who needs to learn the lesson."

Nicole took a hard look at Pam. Pam placed a consoling hand over Nicole's arm. "Nor you. Many of us have been touched by Beth's illness."

A half-hour later Jerry entered the chapel. Nicole looked over to the man that sat beside her. Had she attempted to guess the person's identity, Jerry would never have come to mind. His eyes rested upon his own hands. She returned her gaze to the front of the chapel.

Jerry broke the silence. "Beth comes here often."

Nicole responded in a hushed voice. "Yes, I know."

"Makes me feel closer to her," Jerry confessed. "I envied her. When all the chaplains sat together at lunch … "

Nicole gave Jerry a sharp glance. She did not want the chaplain to trespass upon Beth's confidentiality a second time.

Jerry met Nicole's gaze unflinchingly and said, "She is poised and articulate. She sees and senses things others don't always pick up on. She digs deep and takes us along for the ride. And all I can think about is 'she's so young.' How can someone so young know life and God the way she does? She didn't talk about you in intimate terms, just generalities, but there was no question that your beliefs differed from hers. I refused to believe you two could make a relationship work. I had it in my mind that it was a lie, that Beth was lying either to us or to herself. Then you came to the reception. The minute you walked in it was obvious that everything Beth had told us was true. Actually, if anything, she had been modest in her description of you. The way you embraced each other … do you have any idea of how your love for her radiates from you?" Jerry paused. Companioned only by Nicole's silence, he confessed, "I was stupid. I thought I could knock you down a notch or two, but instead you took me down. You gave me enough chances to admit I didn't have a clue of what I was talking about, but my pride kept on getting in the way until I completely humiliated myself by attacking you and betraying Beth. I apologized to her."

"She told me."

"I never apologized to you. Nicole, I hope you can forgive me."

"I let go of that night a long time ago." Nicole could see that Jerry needed more from her. "I accept your apology."

Jerry offered Nicole a shy smile. "Thank you." He stood up. "I know you don't put much merit into it, but Beth is in my prayers."

Nicole was sincere. "Thank you."

Jerry's smile broadened. He turned away and exited the chapel, leaving Nicole once again to her own thoughts. Jerry's words were in the forefront. 'How can someone so young know life and God the way she does?' Of all that Jerry had said, it was his question, complete with his appreciation of Beth, which touched her heart.

CHAPTER 116

May 21, 2002 – Morning

Dr. Nash, Beth's surgeon, entered the surgical waiting area. Seeing him, Kate reached out to Nicole. Nicole looked up to see Nash, then stood and met him in the middle of the room. Kate stayed a pace behind. Marie joined Nicole. Connor and Pam stood close enough to hear, but distant enough not to intrude.

"Beth went through the operation very well. We got to the tumor early. We removed both her ovaries, as agreed. I won't know more until we get all the lab results, but I believe the cancer was localized. There was no hint that it had metastasized. Under the circumstance, the news couldn't be better."

Nicole stood silent, struggling to take in the meaning of Nash's assessment.

Marie asked, "When can we see her?"

"A couple of hours." Nash looked over to Nicole. "Dr. Lorenz and I will stop by later and talk to both you and Beth."

Nicole nodded.

Nash reached out and took Nicole's hand. "I have every reason to believe Beth is going to be fine."

"Thank you." Nicole squeezed the surgeon's hand. He smiled then took his leave.

Nicole turned and walked toward the corner of the room where she had been waiting. She looked out the window to the overcast sky and wondered why the sun was not shining. They had prepared for the worst possible news. For the moment they had received a reprieve. Both she and Beth would leave the hospital with the overwhelming grace of life still theirs. Nicole began to cry, tears of unexpressed sorrow, tears of relief, tears of joy. They burst through the well-constructed internal fortress she had built in order to survive.

Marie, through her own tears of relief, helplessly watched the trembling Nicole. Marie turned to Kate for guidance. Kate raised her hand to stay Marie in place, and then walked over to Nicole, placing herself as a sentry between Nicole and the others. Kate knew her role. Nicole's tears would not be interrupted.

A few hours later Marie and Nicole entered the surgical recovery unit. Nicole allowed Marie first access to Beth.

Marie walked through the unit and to Beth's bed without hesitation. "Beth."

Beth smiled at her younger sibling. "Hey."

"You did good, sis."

"I wasn't alone."

"Makes me proud to be in the medical profession."

Nicole smiled with a renewed sense of relief. She understood the meaning of Beth's comment to be far different than Marie's interpretation.

"I love you." Marie leaned over and kissed the pale Beth on her forehead.

"I love you, too." Beth's low, throaty voice betrayed the lingering effect of the anesthesia and the on-going effect of the painkillers she had been given.

"We can only stay a few minutes. First visit rules. You know the drill. But I'll see you after they move you into your room."

"Okay."

"There is someone else here to see you." Marie turned toward Nicole. Nicole's presence had not escaped Beth. Marie stepped away offering complete privacy.

Nicole took Beth's hand. "Hi."

"Hi. You look tired."

"I still haven't learned to do helpless very well."

"Tears?"

"Yes."

"Tell me later?"

"Everything. I promise." Nicole honored Beth's deflection of focus away from her own fragile state.

Beth said with appreciation, "You've changed, Nicole Isabel Thera."

"Because I love you, Elizabeth Ann Kelly."

"I'm going to get well."

"Yes, you are." Nicole touched a tear falling from Beth's eye with her fingertips.

Beth leaned her face against Nicole's hand. "We have more time."

"Yes, we do."

The attending nurse approached. Nicole looked over to him, and then returned her gaze to Beth. "Have to go. I'll see you later."

"Nicki?"

Nicole heard a muted plea in Beth's call. "Yes?"

"In the chapel." Beth could not continue with her thought because she did not have words to phrase it.

"What about the chapel?"

"Did you like it?"

"Yes, I did." Nicole waited, expecting more from Beth.

The nurse gently interrupted. "I'm sorry. But there are things I need to do."

Nicole's gaze did not waver. "Okay?"

Beth nodded. Nicole kissed her and walked with Marie back to the waiting area.

CHAPTER 117

June 5, 2002 – Noon

"Hi." Beth entered Nicole's office in the Elysian Fields.

Nicole looked up from her work. She was surprised to see the still healing Beth. "Hi. What brings you here?"

"Cindy and I are having lunch."

"You could have brought her up."

"Connor is keeping an eye on her for me. Can we talk?"

Nicole got up from her desk and went to her partner, giving her a gentle kiss. "Something wrong?"

"I got a call from Liza today. You haven't been by to visit Jacob."

Nicole closed her office door. "No, I haven't."

"Why?"

"Jacob ... I'm not welcome." Nicole walked over to the window where she had a view of Jacob's office.

Beth did not trespass on Nicole's physical space. "What happened between you two?"

"I hurt him."

Beth could not imagine Nicole's offence. "How?"

Nicole turned toward Beth. "The same way I hurt you."

Beth was mystified. "How do you hurt me?"

"I challenge your faith."

"I told you having you in my life has strengthened my faith," Beth implored. "After everything that we have gone through this past year, how can you doubt me?"

"Jacob said ... "

Beth was firm. "If my Christianity and Jacob's Hebrew faith can't stand up against your beliefs or any other belief that is different, then it's not a faith worth having. It's not a faith at all. Whatever Jacob said to you about me, about us, he was wrong. And the truth is he had no right to interfere."

Nicole would not allow Jacob to be discounted. "He's been with me through everything."

"I know how much you love him, but don't let that cloud your judgment." Beth had received Liza's blessing to share the reason behind Jacob's harsh behavior. She still hoped to save herself the confession. Nicole was unmoved. Feeling she had no choice, Beth spoke reluctantly, "Nicki, Jacob was fighting depression when he spoke to you."

Nicole shook her head. "Not Jacob."

Beth took a step forward. "Liza told me that from the first day she met Jacob he has had episodes of clinical depression. His boyhood was a nightmare. He has never been able to completely leave it behind."

"But, I've known him all my life and I ... "

"You were already dealing with your mother's mental illness. He didn't want you to know. The depression didn't come often, but when it did, Liza would lie to you and tell you he was on an extended business trip. There was no reason for you to question her or him."

Nicole returned her gaze out the window, towards Jacob's office. "How is he?"

"Better, but he misses you. He doesn't know how to apologize to you."

"I'll take care of it."

Beth went to Nicole. "We should invite him and Liza over for dinner."

Nicole took Beth's hand. "Thank you."

"I love him, too, you know."

Beth left Nicole and returned to her role as Cindy's host. Having completed a tour of The Fields, the two friends were seated at a window table in The Garden. Cindy looked around. "This is Nicole's? I'm impressed."

"It's nice, isn't it?"

"So, the Elysian Fields is where you two fell in love?"

Beth looked out the window. "I'm not sure exactly where and when that happened. Somewhere between St. Ann's and here."

"Have you gone back ... to the church?"

"No. I know it's around the corner, but for me it could be the other side of world. I remember when The Fields burned and I thought Nicki was inside. That was the beginning of the end of my priesthood."

"What was the end?"

"I'm not there, yet, but I will be soon."

"Good afternoon." With two menus in hand, Gil greeted the women.

"Hi, Gil."

"Good to see you, Beth." Gil handed a menu to each of the women. "Would you like to order something to drink right away?"

"Could I have Chamomile tea to start?"

Cindy completed the order. "And I'll have coffee."

"I'll be back in a minute." Gil stepped away.

Beth smiled as she watched Gil leave. Many of Nicole's employees had returned to The Fields when it reopened. The continuity was comforting.

"Now, you said over the phone there was something you wanted to talk about," said Cindy.

Beth returned her attention to her friend. "Yes, there is ... Nicki and I stopped at the hospital chapel before I was admitted. I saw something there that I've never seen before."

Cindy was attentive. "What?"

"Nicki. When I finished my prayers I turned to see her standing in the back. She was so still. She was at peace. She wasn't searching. She had found what she was looking for, if only for a moment. Since then I've tried to remember other times that have come close to that moment. I remember coming home and finding her sitting alone in front of the fireplace mesmerized by the flames. I'm sure there have been more, I just couldn't see them for what they were."

"What were they?"

"Nicki reminded me that the Episcopal catechism describes prayer as responding to our Creator by thought and deed, with or without words. Nicki was praying. I fought her when she tried to describe prayer in her own terms because what prayer means to me is different than what it means to her."

Cindy smiled knowingly. "Beth, I struggle to see others in their faith just like you do. Sometimes I feel the Unitarian Universalist's diversity is both a blessing and a curse. The blessing is to see all the traditions included in our circle of faith. For me the flame of our symbol, the chalice, is hope eternal that one day our diverse faiths will live in peace. The curse is that it's difficult to find a mode of worship that is meaningful to everyone who comes to us. And then there are seekers like Nicole who don't fit any of the labels we offer: humanist, deist, theist or whatever. She is just there with her beliefs and there is no denying that they are profoundly sacred to her. From what you've told me, I wonder if Nicole wasn't born two centuries too early. I can see her as a desert Mother searching for that elusive wisdom."

Beth was fascinated by Cindy's portrayal of Nicole. "That's how I've described her to you?"

"Of course. Her need for solitude, her knowledge of myth, religion and philosophy, her insatiable search for meaning in life. There has to be a source to her strength. Her illness. The fire. September 11th and the death of her friend. Your illness. She didn't lose faith in the world during all that time. Just one of those things could have shaken her beliefs. All of them together ..."

Images of Nicole at her most vulnerable were at the forefront of Beth's mind. "Nicki's not invincible."

"Exactly. She's tapped into something that she can't describe to our satisfaction but that to her is no less the source of her belief in life than God is to us. We get jaded because we live in a country that is founded on the Judaic-Christian tradition. I guarantee you our view of faith would be different if we spent any amount of time in the East or Africa."

CHAPTER 118

June 5, 2002 – Afternoon

Nicole sat on a bench outside The Fields, waiting for Jacob. She was determined, if necessary, to spend the balance of the day in her silent call to him. Jacob could not hide from her. Nicole smiled to herself. She knew Liza would give Jacob only so much latitude before she threw him out into the street. It was a good forty minutes before the door opened and Jacob stepped out onto the sidewalk. He looked to his left and his right. Nicole wondered whether he was weighing potential escape routes. To Nicole's advantage there was no escaping Liza. Somber in countenance, he slowly made his way to Nicole, who kept a close watch. Jacob did not seem too concerned about traffic. Nicole restrained every impulse to chaperon his crossing. Jacob stepped up to the sidewalk and stood before her. Nicole offered a warm smile. Jacob took his seat beside her. Nervously, he pulled his tobacco case and pipe from his pocket.

Nicole kept her eyes forward. "I'm having a birthday party for Beth at The Pub. It would mean a great deal to her if you and Liza came."

Jacob kept his gaze focused on his tobacco case. "How is she?"

"Good. She's looking forward to starting school in September."

"Thank God."

Nicole smiled hopefully.

Jacob spoke with regret. "I didn't know she was ill. If I had, I would have gone to see her."

"I know. I should have gotten word to you. Liza explained everything to Beth … I'm sorry you felt you had to keep the truth from me."

Jacob raised his eyes. "Your mother. She caused you such heartache. I did not want you to fear that I would do the same. God forgive me for what I said to you."

Nicole looked at him. "I don't know about God, but I don't think there's anything to forgive."

Jacob turned to her. "Nicole, what I said was a lie. I blamed you for my loss of faith. That was not right."

"You were ill."

"Tell me I did not hurt you."

"You hurt me as deeply as anyone could."

Jacob sighed sadly and dropped his eyes back down to his hands.

"I forgive you for wrongly believing you were fighting to save Beth's soul and maybe even my own." Nicole took Jacob's hand. "Understand me, you old Jew. You will have your Day of Atonement. God gave you that day for a reason. But in the meantime you have to accept the fact that the hurt never stopped me from loving you. I will always sit on this bench and wait for you to come to me because I know that you will always come to me because you have always come to me. I know every time you cross that street it is an act of love. I know that nothing I've done in the past or will do in the future will change your love for me."

A tear traveled down Jacob's cheek. Nicole gave the blessed man's hand a squeeze. She waited for him to compose himself.

"Nicole."

"Yes, Jacob."

He used his pipe to gently tap Nicole's hand. "I like your ring."

"So do I." Nicole's relief was tangible.

Jacob looked up to Nicole. "Was Beth pleased?"

"Yes."

"What did you say to her during the ceremony?"

"I recited a poem by Jones Very."

"And what did she say to you?"

"Verses from Song of Songs."

"It is a passionate book. I am not surprised she chose it." Jacob smiled. "Nicole, it was a good thing you did."

"I'm glad you think so."

"Are you happy, Nicole?"

Nicole recalled the sight of Beth entering her office that very day. "Yes. It's a good life, Jacob."

"I sometimes forget."

"Sometimes it's hard to remember."

"It is a gift – life." Jacob looked across the street to where Liza waited for him.

"The grace of life."

"Yes Nicole, it is your grace of life."

They fell into a gentle silence. Still holding hands they watched the neighborhood's movement.

Learning of Jacob's depression charged Nicole's mind with a series of questions. "Jacob. How do you get through the darkness when it comes?"

"The darkness. I don't see that the darkness is with me until it is too late. Until God is lost to me, and Liza is a faint presence calling me to her. Liza takes care of me. My doctors are good. They listen. They prescribe medicine to help me. They all stand by me until I can see the light again. If it were not for them, I would give up. I would fall asleep praying never to wake again."

"Like my mother."

"I would watch your mother in fear that the day would come that Liza could not reach me and bring me back to her. And I know Liza watched with the fear that I would slip away from her embrace, never to return. My Liza's greatest fear was that like you, no matter how hard she tried to save a life she loved, she would have to live with the sorrow of losing that life. It is a sorrow you know too well."

Nicole looked across the street to where she knew Liza was working. She had never realized they shared such an arduously learned knowledge. "I would like to talk to Liza about my sorrow, if that would be all right with you?"

"Yes." Jacob patted Nicole's hand. "I believe she would welcome you with open arms."

"Jacob. There is no other way for Liza."

"You are right. She and Beth have that in common."

CHAPTER 119

June 5, 2002 – Evening

Beth sat in one of the two tall-backed chairs in the den. Only the portrait was illuminated. Beth's private visits to the den were always driven by an ardent need to feel closer to Nicole. Until this day, to her, all that was Nicole could be found in the den. Her computer and files represented her work, her books – her passion for ideas, and the portrait – her love. Beth searched for the Nicole she saw standing in the chapel, and could not find her.

Beth's thoughts traveled back in time, remembering the moments that she knew, in retrospect, defined the woman standing in the chapel: the first conversation between she, Nicole, and Jacob, complete with Nicole's rebuttal to being called an atheist, her assertion that she did not define the divine by Jacob's standards; the conversation she had enjoyed with Nicole after attending a lecture at U.C. when Nicole shared her definition of theology as making meaning out of life, as finding the divine in the God-forsaken corners of the world; being in Nicole's loft and asking her why she read the Classics and learning that for Nicole the Classics were a means to find her self; watching Nicole sitting by the fire, seeing eternity within its flames; listening to Nicole as she described having a *temenos* in her life, and finally, witnessing Nicole's attempt to link her faith with the Episcopal catechism, an attempt to stand on the same side of the moon with Beth.

The Nicole who had stood New Year's Eve in the plaza touching the ineffable, oblivious to the frigid night; the Nicole who had sat alone in her den struggling to reconcile her commitment to never hurt a child as she had been hurt, with her newly surfaced unerring impulse to safeguard a child within her arms and see the child prosper to maturity; the Nicole who stood within the walls of the chapel in silent contemplation was a woman of faith, deep abiding faith.

What humbled Beth was that Nicole held her faith without feeling compelled to belittle the faiths of others. Nicole did her utmost to respect what lay at the core of all traditions. She was uncompromising, but only in her effort to bring to the forefront the truth of tradition. She spoke with such brutal frankness and knowledge that it hurt, because the truth hurt. So Nicole saw Jesus of Nazareth as portrayed in the Gospel of Mark, the very human Jesus who called out to his God in spiritual torment, begging to understand why he had been forsaken. Nicole demanded recognition that the Church and the faith were not necessarily one. She sourced the Anglican thirty-nine Articles of Religion and used them to argue her point that the content of much of Protestant theology was fundamentally similar and points of diversion were more a matter of form. Nicole did all this and still honored the cross, still gifted the chalice, and was still willing to bend to her knees as Beth's companion.

Against Jerry's derision, Beth had cause to defend Nicole as a woman of faith. Her defense had been one isolated event, removed from Nicole. Beth was ashamed to admit she had never affirmed Nicole's faith with the same conviction that Nicole had affirmed hers. Beth was ashamed of her failure to acknowledge that Nicole lived and breathed her faith in all that she did and that in doing so no distinction could be made between her and Beth, who was sworn to live her life in Christ.

When she arrived home, Nicole sought Beth out. She was surprised to find her in the den. Nicole wordlessly sat opposite Beth; her eyes followed her partner's gaze to the portrait. Nicole interrupted the silence after allowing a few moments to pass. "You haven't visited here recently."

"I have. When you're not home. I come here when I want to feel closer to you."

Nicole was concerned. "Have I been far away?"

Beth's gaze traveled to Nicole's pendant. "I have a confession to make about your Celtic pendant. It's a *vesica piscis*."

Nicole smiled. "I know."

Beth knew better than to be surprised. "For how long?"

"Since the day you gave it to me. I liked the idea that you might see your faith in me."

Beth was humbled. "Nicki, I know when you gave me the chalice you didn't have mixed motives. You were acknowledging my beliefs without qualification. I gave you the *vesica piscis* The fact that it was a Pagan Celtic symbol was only part of the reason why I chose it."

"It's a part of you that I share. It's a symbol of our similarities." So expert was Nicole in framing the world in order to minimize her alienation that she took no notice of the effort. "It's how I accepted it."

Beth paused, gathering her thoughts. "Can you honestly tell me that why I gave you the pendant doesn't matter to you?"

"You gave it to me because you love me." Nicole could not believe that within a handful of hours two of the most important people in her life had broached the same subject. "Beth, you once told me that even when you are with people who live their lives without an apparent presence of God, you still see God in them, even if they don't. I've always taken comfort that, as exasperating as I can be to you, you have never stopped seeing me in the light of your faith."

"I've disappointed you. I know I have."

"I'm not easy."

"Cindy asked me if there was any book that came close to scripture for you. I told her I didn't know. I didn't know because I've never asked you."

"I don't." Nicole tried to ease Beth's self-directed censure. "Feel better?"

"No. I have never tried to see the world through your eyes. We always begin our conversations with Christianity, never the Greeks."

"It's easier for me if I set a point of reference, so I say the Greeks." Nicole leaned forward. "Remember my conversation with Jerry on voluntary death?"

The memory drew a smile from Beth. "Hard to forget."

"Do you remember how I went from one philosopher to another to another? There wasn't agreement. The one thing they shared was their search. They wanted to understand the world and they sought it through knowledge with the ultimate hope of achieving wisdom. Beth, look at my library." Nicole gestured toward the bookshelves. "My faith is woven into all those words and more. My faith is defined and redefined by each passing day as I experience life. So is yours. The difference is you approach life from the base of Christianity and I don't."

Beth turned her eyes from the library back to Nicole. "I've seen you pray."

"Have you?"

"Yes. More than once."

Nicole was intrigued. "And who have I prayed to?"

"The divine."

"How do you know this?"

"You told me. You respond by thought and by deed, with and without words, to your divine."

Nicole was pleased. "Yes, I do."

Beth continued confidently. "You experience life as a grace."

"I try to."

"And you try to live your life in humility."

Nicole nodded.

"And what is most important to you is the good. To be good and to find the good in others no matter how hard that can be – even if you are facing the men who killed Carrie."

The mention of Carrie was still difficult. Nicole's voice was pained. "Yes."

"I have learned so much from you."

"And you've been one of my best teachers."

Beth protested, "How can you say that?"

"Because it's true." Nicole was determined to win the argument. "When you got ill, Kate reminded me of who I had been in the past. She told me what she saw in me now. I have changed. I didn't change because I read one more book; not even Carrie's book was that powerful. I changed because I saw something in you I couldn't explain. I still can't explain what I see in you. It is my divine, as I knew it before I met you, and more. It was strong enough to break open my heart so I would love again. It was strong enough to feed my courage to take risks I never thought I would ever take. When I am with you, I feel like I'm standing in the eye of a storm, in the midst of eternity. And even though it can be at times terrifying, I'm in a place of calm."

CHAPTER 120

July 6, 2002

The friends sat around a large pub table. Invitees included Kate, Jacob, Liza, the Musketeers and their dates, Pam, Tom and many of Beth's CPE peers and their partners and dates. Beth picked up Kate's card next. She opened it to a caricature of a stork with a baby hanging on a cloth swing held by its beak. Beth opened the card.

> *Dear Beth,*
>
> *Wishing you a happy birthday. My gift to you is yours to redeem at your pleasure – no expiration date. It will be my privilege to provide free legal services toward the adoption of your child.*
>
> *Love,*
>
> *Kate*

Beth looked at the uncertain attorney, sitting across the table from her. Beth got to her feet and went to Kate. Kate stood up to meet her. Beth took Kate into a warm embrace, and did not let go.

"Hey!" Nicole called out, having observed the exchange. "What on earth could she have written to deserve that?"

Still holding Beth, Kate looked over to Nicole. "None of your damn business. What's the matter, you jealous?"

"In your dreams."

Beth slowly released Kate. She waited for the attorney, now far more relaxed, to meet her gaze. "Thank you." Beth turned, keeping one arm around Nicole's friend. She spoke to Nicole. "We'll talk later."

"By the way, what did you give Beth?" Kate asked.

Nicole shrugged. "She got her present on Christmas Day."

Beth looked up to Kate. "We're going to Ireland."

"Show off!"

After their friends had gone home, Beth rested against Nicole in one of The Pub booths. Beth held their plane tickets in hand. "I never thought you'd take time off."

"There's a new kind of normal out in the world. I needed to help my clients get on good footing to deal with it."

"Nicki? There is something Brian said at The Fields grand opening." Beth turned her head and looked up. "He said you were rethinking your career."

Nicole met Beth's gaze. "He did?"

"Yes, he did." Beth shifted, separating herself from Nicole's embrace. "What do you want to do?"

Beth's illness had given Nicole reason to rethink her priorities. "I want to slow down."

"Could The Fields be enough?"

"Do you want me to stop consulting?"

"I want you to be happy and I don't want you to think we can't step down our lifestyle."

Nicole smiled with unabashed satisfaction.

"What?" Beth wondered what had engendered Nicole's reaction. Her offer had been serious.

"Beth, we're living at a fraction of what I can afford, especially since you've been working at the hospital. Now with your fellowship that's not going to change."

"I didn't realize." Beth had never pursued concrete knowledge of Nicole's wealth. "If we're doing so well, why are you working so hard?"

"Because I'm good at what I do."

"But that doesn't mean ... "

"You're right." Nicole did not need to hear Beth's argument to concede to her position.

Beth gave Nicole a suspicious glance.

Nicole laughed. "I love you."

"Don't change the subject."

Nicole knew of no better time to broach an outstanding question. "Jason has made me an offer. Actually two offers."

"What are they?"

"The first is to buy the Elysian Fields."

"You would sell?"

"I never really wanted to rebuild."

The confession surprised Beth. "Why not?"

"Because it was the past and I wanted the future." Nicole touched the oak table in front of her. "Sitting here, I'm happy I did rebuild. I forgot I like being a bar owner."

"The Fields is not just a bar." Beth could not hide her own preference. "So, you're not going to sell?"

"It's staying in the family."

"What was Jason's second offer?"

"An office at Chamberlain Development."

Beth doubted Nicole would surrender her independence. "You would work for him?"

"Not exactly." Nicole took Beth's hand, intertwining their fingers as she spoke. "He wants to retire soon and spend more time with Katherine. Alex is an excellent project manager. That's what he enjoys. He doesn't want to take over the management of the company. Laura is a rising star in urban architecture and Jason knows she wants and deserves more authority in choosing her work. So Jason would sell Chamberlain to the three of us."

"Do you want to be a developer?"

"Saying yes would mean that I would be one of the three making the final decisions. I wouldn't be spending my time trying to convince top management that good business means not losing sight of the people in their organization, their customers and the public in general. It would mean that I could work to revitalize other marginalized neighborhoods. And it would mean, that for the most part, I would be coming home to you every night. I told Jason I would talk to you and that I would give him my decision after we come back from Ireland."

CHAPTER 121

July 23, 2002

Hand in hand, Beth and Nicole approached the offices of the Diocese of Chicago. Beth paused. "Would you rather wait here or inside?"

"Here is good."

"It won't take long." Beth slipped her hand free.

Nicole kept an unwavering watch upon Beth until she disappeared through the large entrance door. Nicole understood that Beth needed to complete her task alone. Nicole was torn. She wanted to stand beside Beth. There was no loving Beth without the desire to safeguard her spirit. At the same time, she did not want to witness Beth's renunciation. Her role in Beth's loss would forever be with Nicole.

An assistant guided Beth into the bishop's office. Bishop Stratford awaited her. David Bentley and Reverend Monica Parker stood with him. The bishop approached Beth, offering her his hand. "Beth."

"Bishop Stratford."

"I hope your recovery has been going well."

"Yes. Thank you."

"Is Nicole with you?"

Beth felt Nicole was indeed with her. "She's waiting for me outside."

"I'm sorry it has to be this way."

"I know you are. Thank you again for your patience and understanding."

The bishop turned toward David. "I believe you two know each other."

David stepped up to his former Associate Pastor. "Hello."

Beth embraced David. "Thank you for being here."

David was his usual matter-of-fact self. "I hope Nicki realizes what you have given up for her."

"David, I'm not doing this for Nicki."

"Then, it's the right decision." David released Beth.

Reverend Parker offered her hand. "Reverend Kelly, I am Reverend Monica Parker."

Beth took Reverend Parker's hand. "Thank you for acting as a witness."

Reverend Parker nodded.

Bishop Stratford took his place in the open space of his expansive office. With the motion of his hand he directed David to his left and Reverend Parker to his right. Beth approached and stood before her bishop.

The bishop allowed a moment for all to settle in their place. He bowed his head slightly. All others followed suit. "May we act with wisdom, mercy and compassion, through our Lord, Jesus Christ. Amen."

"Amen"

"Reverend Kelly, please proceed."

Beth handed the bishop a letter. She spoke with a steady voice, one that conveyed her certitude. "I, Reverend Elizabeth Ann Kelly, declare in writing to the Ecclesiastical Authority of the Diocese of Chicago, my renunciation of the ordained ministry of this Church and my desire to be removed therefrom."

Bishop Stratford opened the letter and read it. He closed the letter and took a long look at Beth. He then completed the Declaration of Removal, reading from a small card held in his hand.

"I, Bishop James Stratford, Bishop of the Diocese of Chicago, in accordance with Title III Canon 18 of the Constitution and Canons of the Episcopal Church of the United States of America, am satisfied that the resignation and renunciation of the ministry by Reverend Elizabeth Ann Kelly is a voluntary act, and for causes assigned or known, which do not affect her moral character. With the advise and consent of the Standing Committee of the Diocese of Chicago, as of this date, I do accept the resignation and renunciation of the ministry of the Church as made to me in writing on this date by Reverend Kelly.

"Reverend Kelly is, therefore, deposed from the ministry, released from its obligations, and deprived of the right to exercise the gifts and spiritual authority as a Minister of God's Word and Sacraments conferred in Ordination. This sentence is pronounced in the presence of two presbyters of the Diocese of Chicago."

After the ceremony had concluded Beth walked out into the fresh air. Her renunciation marked an ending. It also marked a new beginning. She had not left Christianity. She knew there was a Christian church in her future, one that would welcome her without asking her to deny a part of herself. With appropriate preparation, she would be ordained again.

Beth saw Nicole sitting on the stairs across the grounds. Nicole turned her head and caught Beth's gaze, then stood up and waited. The image of Nicole moved Beth. Beth could see the elegance of Nicole's spirit. She recalled the woman she had met nearly two years prior. Contrary to Beth's original impression of the rebel, Nicole had, by her unwavering vision of life as a grace to be cherished, given Beth hope that she could also experience the beauty of life in its greatest depth and breadth.

It was a hope that had slipped away from her when, as a teenager, she had begun to understand her mother's legacy. For Beth, from that moment of understanding, the finite nature of individual human existence became her constant companion – a companion that restrained all desire for more than a life of giving. To have more only to have it taken from her in her youth was beyond Beth's strength, as she stood alone. It was not, however, beyond her strength as she stood beside Nicole. Once again, Jacob's words rang true. Like him, she needed 'a little more help than others' to know God's love. And what was it that Nicole reflected, if not God's love?

Still, her companion – the knowledge of the finite – returned to her and demanded its due. She gave it. To her surprise, the price was not what she had expected; the early call to God did not come, but a mature life would not be hers without a price. Though the surgery excised her cancer, it also excised her ability to bear a child. Her mother's legacy to her would end with her. Though her loss took residence in Beth's heart, she consoled herself with the knowledge that there would be no opportunity for her daughter to share her fear. Beth's loss pressed within her heart along with the other losses of her life, including the loss she experienced on this day.

As much as Beth experienced what to her were the inevitable losses subscribed to humanity, she held to her faith. To be with Nicole was to live life with a promise of a future. Nicole's illness had been a not-too-subtle confirmation that the finite touches others young. To be with Nicole was to have the privilege of intimately sharing knowledge of the finite with her life partner. Beth was beginning to understand that if she opened herself to a different form of expression, she could also share with Nicole the knowledge of the infinite.

Beth took one step after another towards her future. It was still a fragile future for both of them, but it was a future that she would not deny. With each step she felt the love of God. Through all the trials in her life she had never been alone. She would never be alone. And if the day came that she once again doubted, she would look to Nicole to remind her of the perfect love of God. If the day came that Nicole was not with her, she would simply remember one glance, one word, one touch Nicole had given her, and once again God's perfect love would be hers.

Emet

CHAPTER 122

March 2003

Nicole and Alex Chamberlain listened intently as Laura Morales presented her argument for a new multi-use development in the heart of one of Chicago's more depressed neighborhoods, a neighborhood she grew up in and one that was familiar to both Nicole and Alex. The architect was passionate. Her presentation was well reasoned, supported by strong economic and demographic data and an ingenious design for the preservation, renovation and expansion of the majority of buildings situated on one street block.

The project exceeded the maximum level of risk that the new partners had previously agreed to. Nicole was certain that she could easily justify a negative vote. She peppered Laura with a series of questions to unequivocally establish all the reasons against the endeavor.

Laura patiently answered Nicole's questions. That Nicole's scrutiny was relentless was no surprise, she had demonstrated her exacting standards during the Elysian Fields project.

Nicole was not alone in her challenges. Alex identified the logistical construction problems they would face and took every opportunity to oppose Laura's preservation strategy. Over three hours passed before the partners grew silent.

"Do you have any more questions?" Laura finally asked.

Nicole sat comfortably in her chair, studying the young architect. "Laura, I appreciate all the hard work you did to pull this together."

"Thank you," Laura replied warily.

Nicole continued, "I wish you had spoken to me sooner."

"I second the motion." Alex said with the slightest hint of acridity.

"We could have helped you. I think our questions proved that you've missed more than one issue that could make or break this project."

Laura bristled. "I didn't want to waste your time."

"You need to remember what it means to be in a partnership," said Alex. "If we can't lean on each other we are going to fail. At the very least we deserved to be informed of how you were spending your time."

"I did most of the work on my own time," Laura said.

"That was a mistake, too," Nicole interjected. "This project may be a labor of love but it redirected your focus away from the work we've been doing on our other projects. I noticed the change in you. I just couldn't figure out what was wrong."

"We can't be afraid to do important work," Laura insisted. "I didn't become part of this partnership to do small renovation projects."

Alex shifted forward in his chair. "Laura, we need time to learn to work together. My father held the Elysian Fields project together for us. We don't have him doing that anymore. We have to do it for ourselves. Starting with a project as big as The Fields or as big as the one you are now proposing would have been stupid. I don't do stupid."

"You do conservative!" The architect had lost her patience.

Nicole checked her desire to reprove the brash woman. "A good attribute for Alex to have to balance your risk-taking tendencies. I guess I'm supposed to supply the reasoned perspective and try to help all of us find a compromise we can live with."

Laura stated defiantly, "You're against this project."

"It's high risk, Laura. It's more than you have ever done, but it is also well in your reach. You've proven that to me today. The question is whether it's within the reach of CMT Development." Nicole turned to the man who would manage the construction. "Alex, what do you think? Are we ready?"

Alex studied the model that sat in the middle of the table. "We can do this. But, I'm telling you the price tag is going to drain every penny we have. We won't be able to afford any mistakes."

Nicole caught a rare glimpse of animation in Alex's eyes. She could see he wanted to be convinced. He also needed someone else to take the burden of fiscal responsibility from his shoulders. Jason had counseled Nicole that as the third partner her role would be to orchestrate the commercial administration that neither Laura nor his son had the aptitude and stomach for. "Alex, I joined CMT to make a difference. I don't want to play it safe. I'm not worried. We can afford failure."

Alex picked up a small plastic fir from the model and slapped it from one hand to the other and back again, indifferent to Laura's steely gaze. "How much failure?"

Nicole had reviewed their financial status before the meeting. "Given our cash flow, maybe three projects standing completely idle."

"What's the chance of that?" Alex placed the fir back in place.

Nicole measured her partners. "With you two, none. We can mitigate the risk by taking a phased approach," she said, offering a compromise. "Housing first. Retail second. It'll give us time to line up tenants." She turned her attention to Laura. "I'll agree to this project on the condition that we can secure economic development funding to cover one-quarter of the budget."

"I can agree to those terms plus one more," said Alex "Laura, you have to trust us. Nicole and I want to succeed just as much as you do. This project is everything CMT stands for. You shouldn't have held back on us. I need your promise that you will keep us in the loop for now on."

The tide had turned so quickly that Laura was left momentarily speechless. "That's it? A phased approach. We get grant funding and I talk to you about what I'm doing until you can't stand having me in the room any longer."

"That's what I heard." Nicole tapped her pen against the table. "What I haven't heard is your answer."

Laura smiled for the first time. "How soon can we start?"

"I'll call Kate right after this meeting to start drafting the options to purchase. And I want to go over your city and federal development grant research."

"Then, damn it, this meeting is over. We have a project," Laura declared with obvious delight.

"Hold it!" Alex halted the architect's elation. "There is one thing we forgot."

"What?" Laura demanded.

Alex smiled. "A name. This project needs a name."

"I had the Elysian Fields." Nicole was ready to acquiesce to her partners' decision. However, she did have a name in mind. She wanted to honor Laura and knew that the young architect was too modest to suggest a namesake. "Alex, if you're willing to wait for our next project how about the 'Morales Standard'?"

Laura turned her gaze from Alex to Nicole. She asked. "Why 'Standard'?"

"You're the one who taught me that a standard is an upright support or support structure. This project is meant to support the neighborhood."

Laura leaned closer to the model, reverently placing a fingertip upon the roof of the main structure. She turned her eyes to Nicole. "I like that."

"Good, now that we have a name may I start making my phone calls?"

"Thank you." Laura directed her next comment to Alex. "I promise you won't regret this."

CHAPTER 123

April 2003

Nicole cut a swath through the presumed Christian believers walking on the University of Chicago campus. Each step took Nicole closer to what had become a dispiriting destination. Nicole felt the looming risk of yielding to the institutional precepts of the University, and in turn, the Church. To her dismay, they were precepts channeled by Beth, a very human, young woman wanting to find herself valued by those who, less than a year before, were only names scribed on a faculty list. Nicole paused and leaned against a large oak tree, her gaze resting upon Swift Hall – the School of Divinity. At this time of day she could usually find Beth in her office.

Nicole had opened her world to new forces. Each informed her, and a number enjoined her once freely exercised will. In less than three years her life had been transformed. The only tangible remnant of what she had created, of her response to her terrible loneliness, was the Elysian Fields. Change came, she told herself in retrospect, because her life was no longer terrible.

Walking on the well-landscaped grounds, the beauty of the school did not escape her. Her own love for knowledge was stirred. Where beauty failed was the image that laid the foundation for, and which continued to be, the subject of learning – a man crucified on a cross. To Nicole, the brutal image had become vulgar and not worthy of her praise. She checked her disgust. If she were willing to turn away from Beth's love, the sacrifice, and the God she was told demanded the selfless act to redeem humanity's sin, would have no place in her life. There was no dramatic irony; she knew how the whims of the Fates touched her. She had consented, though her tolerance had grown paper-thin.

Nicole envied the image and the myth for one reason alone. Though to her the landscape was ill-used, a wasteland, to her lover the most recent eight months in academic residence was a boon. The one heart that Nicole gave herself to was a heart that held to the image and the myth. Beth had stepped away from their shared life in Hyde Park and taken shelter within the University. This academic, theological collective offered an invitation Nicole reluctantly had accepted, restricting her participation to one of a disinterested escort.

✢   ✢   ✢

At a distance, within Swift Hall, Beth sat with her chair turned toward the large arched window that faced the heart of the quadrangle of buildings. She watched campus life, feeling a quiet wonder. From a distance she spied Nicole and smiled. Her partner would soon be at her door.

Her days took Beth away from their Hyde Park apartment. Although the journey to Swift Hall and the Divinity School was brief, the minor distance did not begin to explain the monumental transition she felt. The patch of secularity she shared with Nicole had been supplanted.

The school year had brought a personal renewal. Given an unexpected opportunity to teach an undergraduate introductory course in religious studies, she had discovered that she enjoyed working with the students, exploring with them a multitude of religious themes.

In her own studies, Beth continued to explore the theological and ethical import of suffering – the focus of her dissertation. Her studies did not approach the emotionally charged atmosphere of her work at the hospital. She was academically engaged, far from overwhelmed. She had the luxury of time to complete her assignments, to independently pursue her academic interests, and to occasionally volunteer as a chaplain. The latter helped her keep a pulse on what her calling, at its core, always meant to her – binding her scholarship to practical ministry.

In her home, Beth enjoyed both solitude and companionship. Beth's days began and ended with Nicole's gentle kiss and words of love. Nicole's presence steadied Beth. Beth blossomed in the ring of safety that Nicole created for her. Lying in her lover's embrace, she clung to the harmony unique to their relationship, the miracle that blended discordant notes into a melodious song. She knew that she possessed the love of a remarkable woman Not a day passed that Beth did not thank God for her partner. It was because of their shared intimacies that Beth was certain there had been a change, not necessarily for the better.

Beth heard a knock on the door. She turned her chair to greet her visitor. She smiled upon seeing the breathtakingly beautiful woman. "Hey."

"Will you be long? I thought I'd walk you home."

Beth looked at the wall clock. It was past six, the end of her office hours. She scanned her desk. There was nothing that needed her immediate attention. Even if there was, she did not want to keep Nicole waiting. "Give me a minute."

"I'll be outside." Nicole exited.

Beth stored a few papers in her briefcase. She stepped out of her office and locked the door. Nicole extended her hand. Without a word Beth went to her; standing toe-to-toe she took the offered hand and leaned forward. Nicole met Beth in a kiss. She sensed Beth's hesitancy. Nicole knew she had been distant and that her distance had dampened Beth's spirit.

Nicole took Beth by the waist, gently guiding her closer. Beth fought an inner battle. She felt Nicole's touch as a tactile promise, one that offered to relieve her growing loneliness, but she still felt a need to be cautious. She stepped back, seeking from Nicole some sign that her lover was willing and able to give more than she had in recent weeks. Beth was met by Nicole's enigmatic silence. She rested her forehead against Nicole's chest.

Nicole embraced Beth. After a few moments, she whispered, "Let's go home."

Arriving at their apartment, the two women held to their custom; Beth prepared dinner with Nicole's assistance. They sat across from one another at their dining room table, eating in silence. Nicole went to the kitchen and retrieved a coffee carafe. Returning to the dining room she refilled her coffee cup. "One of the extra parking spaces has opened up. I told Ben we would take it."

Beth was surprised. "You want a second car?"

Nicole filled Beth's cup. "It would be for you."

"Nicki, I can walk or metro just about anywhere I need to go. And there's always a cab around when I can't." Beth stood up and began removing the dinner plates.

Nicole watched, taking Beth's retreat from the table as a sign of disapproval. "Being a two-car family is not really aligned to your values, is it?"

"Not when we do fine without, no." Beth walked to the kitchen.

Nicole followed, carafe in hand. "What if I told you I hate knowing that you're out there exposed to the weather?"

Beth argued, "I would still walk to school."

Nicole set the carafe in the coffee brewer and leaned against the counter. "And what if I told you I'm being selfish. With the new project I expect I'll be working longer hours. If you had your own car it would be easier for you to meet me for lunch or dinner."

Beth debated whether the expense of a car was worth a few more convenient meals with Nicole.

Not receiving an immediate reply, Nicole looked down uneasily. "I'll just have to make an effort to come home."

Beth watched as a shadow crossed over Nicole's face. She knew in her heart that there was more behind Nicole's silence. She could not begin to guess what was left unsaid. Without trying to charm, without her playful cajoling, Nicole retreated to the den.

Beth worked on her studies for the majority of the evening. Satisfied with her progress she closed her books and sought out Nicole. She stood by the open den door and glanced up to their portrait; reliving the moment when she had first seen the artwork – her wonder and overwhelming joy. Beth knocked lightly.

Nicole was standing at the window. She greeted Beth warmly. "Hey."

"I'm going to bed."

"Finished?"

"No. The rest can wait. I was wondering if you might be free for lunch tomorrow?"

"I should be."

"I miss The Fields."

"I'll let Miguel know to expect us."

"The best table?"

Nicole smiled. "Nothing less for you."

"Thank you." Beth approached. "You would think I would learn." She placed her hand over Nicole's heart. "You will never cease to surprise me. God forbid if I thought you wanted to spend more time with me."

Beth's reference to God triggered Nicole's disfavor. Privately acknowledging she was being overly sensitive, Nicole set the feeling aside. "How about a used, late model car with good gas mileage. Nothing too fancy."

Beth smiled guiltily. "A little sporty would be good."

Nicole laughed. "You pick."

"I'll start thinking about it."

"Good."

Their gazes settled fondly upon one another. Beth broke the spell, shyly looking down. "Good night, Nicki."

"Beth?" Nicole waited for Beth to raise her eyes. "Would you like some company?"

The unexpected surge of emotion caused Beth not to trust her voice. She nodded.

Nicole leaned forward and kissed Beth. The tenderness of the kiss was fleeting. It soon gathered heat. They guided each other to their bed. Their lovemaking was intense. Beth buried her face into Nicole's shoulder biting down as she climaxed. Nicole was unfazed by the wound. As Beth's mouth released Nicole's flesh, she tried to supplant what pain she had caused with the balm of a kiss. Beth leaned back, spent both physically and emotionally. She did not have the presence of mind to hide her tears. Nicole kissed Beth's tears as they drew slowly down her cheeks, tasting the salt. Beth pulled Nicole into an embrace, whispering, "Hold me."

Nicole heard Beth's desperation and was frightened by it. She feared she was on the verge of witnessing the once strong weave of their friendship, now frayed, finally sundered. She feared that in spite of her vigilance, Beth was becoming aware of her feigned serenity. Their union was weak at the best of times, and tattered at the worst. Nicole spoke, her voice unsteady. "I love you."

Beth left Nicole sleeping. She stood at the den door. She knew she would always be a visitor to this space. The den belonged to Nicole. The two years they had lived in Hyde Park had not changed Nicole's need for privacy. Beth took solace in the fact that she was always a welcomed visitor. Nicole never denied her entry, never closed the door to her.

Nicole had not slept in the den since early in their move to Hyde Park. Those difficult months had forced them to make the choice of either fighting to keep their union or to surrender to their differences. The lessons learned had been painful. On occasion Beth still wondered how she and Nicole had sustained their balance.

Beth switched the portrait light on. Her eyes followed each pencil and charcoal line that formed Nicole, black upon white, the shades graded to create an image, not illusion. Andrea's rendering of Nicole was true. The artist had captured not only Nicole's beauty but also her spirit. There was Nicole's love for Beth, simply drawn, appropriate to Nicole's Classical sensibilities. Nicole had placed herself in the frame but deliberately remained in the background. She was a counterpoint to Beth, an intentional supporting character. For the first time in their relationship, the image disturbed Beth.

Nicole's priorities had gradually changed. Beth remembered how attentive Nicole had been during their time in Ireland. Beth had been left with no cares. All that had needed to be done, Nicole had done. For two weeks it had been only she and Nicole driving through the countryside, staying at different Bed and Breakfast establishments, visiting museums, archeological sites, churches, walking mile upon mile, and sleeping in during the two lone days of rain.

Nicole's lovemaking had eased to a tenderness that Beth found irresistible. At the time, Beth had suspected her illness was a contributing factor. Nicole's touch had been feather light yet it somehow traveled deeply into Beth. Every day that had passed, Beth felt as if she was literally falling in love again, without understanding how that could be possible.

Upon their return to Chicago, Beth had no doubt that Nicole would decide to accept Jason Chamberlain's offer. The decision had been soon made. To Beth's astonishment, Nicole had decreased the amount of hours she worked. She had expanded her delegation to the Musketeers. She had split time between CMT, The Fields and the den. She had tailored her schedule to Beth's. Beth took the decision and the restructuring of Nicole's work life as proof that Nicole's motives went no further than her need to establish a lifestyle that would allow their relationship to thrive.

Nicole's joys had always been quiet with rare outbursts of delight. As the school year began, Beth had rejoiced in Nicole's new optimism. Nicole's smiles came more easily. Beth was witness to Nicole's ever growing enjoyment of their home, and to Nicole's rediscovery of Chicago's greatest assets: memberships in the Art Institute and the Museum of Contemporary Art, season tickets to The Steppenwolf and About Face Theatre, and long walks by the lakeshore. From Beth's perspective, Nicole had succeeded in fashioning the slower life she had yearned for.

In the previous two months Beth had been given reason to be concerned. She had observed a gradual change in Nicole, a change so nuanced that it would escape a lesser intimate. That all had been well between them, left Beth puzzled by the return of Nicole's reticence. Beth wondered if Nicole was aware of her progressive movement inward.

Nicole had grown quieter. She had seemed to need a greater degree of solitude. Though they had still discussed theology and philosophy, Beth felt that Nicole had, by design, removed herself from a wider dialogue. Nicole seemed to have been rejecting the farther reaches of a world made of a series of concentric circles; the outer rings had fallen away from her immediate interest. She slowly had isolated herself even as the economy struggled and the international political climate forecasted war. The Nicole Beth knew best would have engaged, not disengaged.

Nicole had fashioned an intimate life. Not only was her attentiveness directed toward Beth, but Jacob, Liza, Tess, and Kate also felt the benefit. So, too, did The Fields and CMT. Chicago was more than enough for Nicole and that caused Beth pause. If only she could feel confident that the change in Nicole was for the better.

A part of Nicole had always been hidden; it was Beth's privilege to have Nicole share with her what others did not see. Jacob and Tess also knew Nicole in ways others would never know her. That had not changed. What differed was that along with the bare, raw, honesty that Nicole placed before Beth, there was an accompanying sadness. The ability to see the world through Nicole's eyes was the ability to face pain without wincing. If Nicole kept herself removed, Beth surmised, it might be her way to lessen the influx of truth. There was a new sobriety in Nicole that was fed by an undercurrent Beth could not source, nor could she identify the grievous truth traveling upon it.

There was a hesitation in Nicole that was new to Beth. It signaled a frag- ileness not of a singular moment. Nicole's fragileness had taken residence within her. Beth judged Nicole's retreat a protective tactic, and had waited for Nicole to come to her, as inevitably she did. To date, Beth's expectations had been disappointed. Her only recourse was to continue her vigil. She needed to trust Nicole. She needed to trust that their intimate union could not exist without their love and commitment to one another. She held to their love- making as a sign that all would be well. More than her trust in Nicole and her trust in the sanctity of their intimacy, Beth placed her trust in God's wisdom and mercy.

In the warmth of their bed, Nicole awoke to a soundless night. She was alone. The clock read 1:46 a.m. She left her bed. From the front foyer she saw the light of Beth's small desk lamp. Beth was sitting on the sunroom couch. She sat in stillness, her head slightly bowed. Nicole interpreted the posture and returned to the bedroom leaving Beth to her prayers.

Nicole breakfasted at the dining room table while reviewing the Morales Standard cost projections. She kept an attentive ear to the sounds emanating from the bedroom.

Dressed in oversized sweatpants and tank top, Beth approached, reaching for the coffee cup Nicole held in her hand. "May I?"

Nicole granted the cup to Beth.

Beth took a generous sip of the rich brew. She returned the cup to Nicole. She leaned down and gave her lover a deep kiss causing Nicole to nearly spill the contents of the cup. Releasing Nicole, Beth held her partner unceasingly in her gaze. "Thank you." With her left hand Beth grazed Nicole's cheek before turning and walking toward the kitchen in search of her breakfast.

CHAPTER 124

April 2003

Nicole and Beth lay together on the living room couch, reading. Nicole placed her book to the side and closed her eyes, keeping a hand near Beth's heart.

Beth noted the gesture and leaned her head back. "Are you falling asleep?"

"No, I'm with you." Nicole's languid voice carried to Beth's ear.

"You've been quiet."

The younger woman's observation described nothing more than the natural order, its insight no greater than if Beth had mentioned Nicole's height or that Nicole's eyes, now reopened and considering Beth with a glint of amusement, were blue.

Beth raised herself up and turned toward her partner. She qualified her statement, saying, "More than usual."

"I'm fine."

"You would tell me if there was something wrong?"

Beth's pensive countenance caused Nicole to weigh her next words. Her response had the power to take them down a difficult road she preferred not to tread. She donned a puckish mask. "Maybe I should gear up and work harder. You would worry less if I wasn't so lazy."

Beth smiled. "You call your life lazy?"

Nicole shrugged. "It's all relative, isn't it?"

Beth was not satisfied. She pursued a more pressing question, proposing her own conclusion. "Are you happy? Do you miss the faster pace?"

"I was kidding!" Nicole objected, purposely ignoring Beth's first question and focusing on the latter.

Beth gave Nicole an exaggerated, studied look.

Nicole chuckled.

"Okay." Accepting that on this night she would receive no further insight from Nicole, Beth settled back against her partner and returned to her book.

Nicole released a nervous breath, grateful for the reprieve.

Beth read, 'Go and pray to the LORD to command some struggle to be stirred up in you, for the soul is mature only in battles ...'

She stared at the words. There was no moving beyond them. She looked up from her book, a collection of sayings from the early Monastics, and studied Nicole, who continued to lay with her eyes closed, keeping to her mental solitude. She wondered if Nicole had invited her current struggle or if it was God's grace. It was hard for Beth to reconcile herself to the divine role of suffering. Nicole remained defiant; nothing kept her from God more than that one question, 'Why the pain?' Beth could freely confess that her greatest growth came through the redemptive power of suffering. That her pain had merit was a belief that had slipped away from her more than once. Not until she had walked through the fire and looked back could she bow to God in gratitude – not only for the relief of her pain but also for the awareness of how her pain had molded her, leaving her purer in spirit.

Beth wanted to lift away whatever was pressing down Nicole's spirit. She was tempted to suggest that Nicole take a trip, placing herself in a different environment. Maybe then she would gain the perspective that eluded her. Beth meditated on another saying.

'In some, temptation arises in the place where you dwell in the desert; do not leave that place in time of temptation. For if you leave it then, no matter where you go, you will find the same temptation waiting for you.'

Replacing temptation with suffering, Beth knew Nicole might find temporary relief were she to leave Chicago, but that upon her return the struggle would still be waiting for her.

CHAPTER 125

April 2003

The three partners stood in front of a red brick warehouse that would anchor the Morales Standard development.

Alex proposed for the second time, "Why not tear it down?"

Laura patiently repeated her assessment. "It's solid and the cost of a full demolition will make the risk prohibitive."

"Not that it isn't now," Alex quipped.

Nicole turned around, surveying the surrounding neighborhood. Walk-up apartment buildings stood side-by-side across the street. A little girl walked out of one and sat at the foot of the stairs.

Alex's sarcasm was at full throttle. "Wonder what the cockroach population count is?"

"I'll do a census and let you know," said Laura dryly.

Nicole found herself intrigued by the girl. She was no more than seven years old with short curly brown hair. Nicole could not see the color of her eyes. She imagined them to be dark. The girl was dressed simply in jeans and a clean white sweater.

Alex turned to Nicole. "Come on Nicki, it's your turn to tell us to stop behaving like children."

"You're not behaving like any child I can see right now." Nicole reluctantly turned her gaze away from the girl. "I think you two are the epitome of systematic organizational dysfunctional behavior and I know better than to try to do anything about it."

At a disadvantage, Alex fulfilled Nicole's expectations of systematic organizational dysfunctional behavior by seeking out an ally where there had, only a moment before, been an antagonist. "Laura, have we just been insulted?"

The architect found her good humor restored. "I'm not sure."

Alex complained half-heartedly, "I hate when the consultant in her comes out."

Laura stepped to Nicole's side. "Do you want to meet the little girl?"

"Do you know her?" Nicole expressed her interest freely.

"Her name is Nastasia Varnavsky." Laura waved to the child.

The girl smiled and waved back.

Nicole could not place the ethnicity of Natasia's fine features. "What nationality is she?"

"Russian Jew."

"She's beautiful."

"So was her mother."

"Was?"

"Tasi lives with her grandmother."

"What happened to her parents?"

"Irina died of an overdose before HIV did its worst to her. Thank God she got infected after Tasi was born."

"What about Tasi's father?"

"Irina wasn't sure who Tasi's father was. It would have taken more than a couple of DNA tests to figure it out."

"Was the O.D. an accident?"

"Who knows? She was so lost at that point. She did everything that would give a mother nightmares. I don't know how Yeva managed."

"Irina's mother?"

"Nice woman. Tough. Old world. She was always good to me when I was growing up." Laura hoped to see the stories of other neighborhood residents changed by the development. "So, do you want to meet Tasi?"

"Sure, why not?" Nicole followed Laura across the street.

CHAPTER 126

April 13, 2003 – Sunday

The morning began with Beth's gentle seduction. In the midst of intensifying intimacies, Nicole pulled back from Beth and sat upon her heels, confused and ashamed.

Beth was confused in her own right as Nicole slipped away from her touch, their lovemaking unexpectedly aborted.

"Nicki?" Beth sat up. "Nicki, what is it?"

Nicole had collapsed inside herself. The familiar turned ugly, no longer reassuring, no longer promising a life beyond threadbare dreams woven to form a mundane blanket. The blanket cloaked over Nicole's shoulders weighed heavily without giving comfort. Wrapping the blanket around her trembling body did nothing to stay the chill in her heart. There was nothing for her to give. Beth placed her hand over Nicole's.

Nicole shunned the connection. "Please don't."

Beth removed her touch.

Nicole wondered if this is was how her mother had felt. She was held to Beth's gaze. "I'm sorry. Beth, I'm tired."

Beth asked nothing more from her. "Why don't you sleep in? I'll stop for rolls on the way home from church. We can have a quiet afternoon."

Alone in the apartment, Nicole lay in bed, her thoughts fixed upon Beth. Nicole willed herself out of bed. She chose to follow their Sunday morning routine. She showered and dressed. Soon she was walking down the church corridor that led to Beth's Sunday school classroom. Nicole was early. She sat in the back. A child-sized, armless wooden chair offered an optimal means to observe the activity in the classroom draw to a close. It was an uncommon perspective for her. The perspective left much above Nicole, the proportions a truer gauge of her stature in the world. Nicole traveled slowly, gently into her thoughts; she felt a growing quiet.

Beth was relieved to see Nicole. Nicole's morning withdrawal had been disconcerting. Beth felt as if she had been thrown into a dark thicket; any movement placed her at risk of being scratched by the sharp woody spines obscured from her sight. "Hi."

Beth's inviting voice called to Nicole. She looked up to her life partner, taken anew by her beauty. "Didn't John Hick say that in a world of religious pluralism, Christianity should consider shifting to a theology where God is at the center?" Nicole goaded Beth playfully with a sophisticated counter-argument to the lesson Beth had shared with the students.

Beth responded in kind. "Don't start with me. These are eight and nine-year olds. Let them know a personal God before they try to imagine a cosmic divinity."

Nicole remained unconvinced. "Kids have great imaginations. You shouldn't underestimate them." She smiled broadly. "Anyway, it was just a question."

Beth knew best how to express her displeasure. "No Mendici's scone for you."

"Ouch! I looked forward to it all week."

"Come on." Beth reached out. Nicole pouted. Beth relented. "Okay, you get your scone."

Nicole took Beth's offered hand. "Can we sit here for a moment?"

"Sure." Beth took an equally small chair and positioned it across from Nicole before taking her seat.

"The world looks different from down here. The kids are so little. Always looking up to the adults. I can still remember how that felt."

"With your height I don't think it was that long before people were looking you in the eye." For a brief moment, Beth caught sight of a young Nicole and her lonely childhood. "Remember, they have their friends. Maybe that's one thing that makes them hold on to each other the way they do. They see each other in a way they don't see adults."

"I met a little girl during our site visit Tuesday. She's about a year and a half younger than Dion. Looks completely different." Nicole spun her finger. "Curly dark brown hair, bronze skin, and the deepest, darkest eyes I've ever seen. She was sitting outside watching us. I don't think she has many friends. Laura knew her and made the introductions. When I walk in here I can feel the mischievous spirit of the kids. Tasi is … cautious. Even with Laura, whom she's known all her life."

"It's not the best neighborhood."

"It's definitely not Hyde Park." Nicole scanned the classroom, focusing on the posted artwork drawn by young hands, reflecting minds that still see people in colors of green and purple. Nicole's thoughts returned to Natasia. "Tasi only has her grandmother. I hope that by the time she grows up she's known enough happiness to lay aside her reserve."

"I think I know why she's stayed with you," said Beth softly.

"Yeah." Nicole looked toward her attentive partner. "We've gone through a lot, haven't we?"

"Yes, we have."

"Beth, do you ever think about what a child of ours would have been like – a little girl or boy that was both your Irish and my Greek mutt and still new, unique in her or his own way?"

Beth was taken by surprise. "Nicki ..."

"It feels so unfair, so terribly wrong. If there is a God, it is one more reason to damn the Creator. To give me these feelings when having my heart's desire is impossible. This morning, making love to you became what it wasn't. It wasn't creating a baby. It would never be." Nicole paused as she neared her hard confession. She spoke deliberately. "By entering your life I took away your chance ... "

Beth raised her hand and placed her fingers against Nicole's lips. "Don't."

Nicole removed Beth's hand with her own. "It's true."

"I can't have a child." Beth's heart ached. She had found her answer and would not accept any challenge, especially one from Nicole.

"When you could, we couldn't," Nicole said, unrelentingly.

Beth's passion spiked. "You listen to me. Our love does not need a child to be sanctified. No love does. You cannot tell me that infertile couples are less in God's eyes. They are meant for another purpose."

Nicole held her tongue.

Beth calmed as the tick of the classroom clock marked the passing of time. "Nicki, whether I had met you or not, I can't imagine that I would have had a child before the cancer. It came too early in my life. And you seem to forget that I fell in love with you. I have only loved you. No one has ever come close to touching my heart the way you have, the way you still do. Why are you focusing on what we don't have instead of what we do have?"

Nicole leaned back, still keeping her hand intertwined with Beth's. "I never expected to feel the way I do. Makes me wonder why."

"I don't know why. I do know it isn't because you are meant to feel unworthy of me or ..." Beth paused, and altered her argument. "Nicki, did you ever think that you feel what you feel because you are worthy? I know we don't agree about the reason for suffering but maybe what you're feeling is because you are meant to become a Nicole you can't even imagine. I still remember the day you told me you didn't have the faith to bring a child into this world. I know you believed every word you said to me. My heart broke that day. Not just because you didn't want to share a child with me but because you confessed you didn't have faith in the future."

"I'm sorry."

"Don't be. We will have a child. Remember, I've got a lawyer with very good connections just waiting for my phone call. And I promise you, I'm going to remind you of this conversation when it's your turn to do the middle of the night feedings and changing."

A small laugh escaped Nicole.

"Nicki, I see her in this room …"

"Do you?"

Beth smiled. "Oh, yeah. When the end of class draws near she'll begin to look up at the clock counting the minutes until you come for us. Nicki, we will be ushering a life to her destiny. She may not be Irish or Greek, but we will teach her, her first words and her first steps and all the other firsts. She will be ours in every way. I promise you … and with a little grace she'll forgive us both for being imperfect parents."

Nicole set aside the disturbing thought of her daughter in a Christian classroom and embraced Beth's light spirit. "You know how to give a gal confidence."

"You do believe me, don't you?"

Nicole reached out and cupped Beth's face. "I'll remind you of this conversation when she rebels and goes out dating some overly tattooed, pierced wanna-be guitar player."

"I'm glad you left the gender unspecified."

Nicole stood up. "She'll have to find her way just like her mothers did."

Beth looked up to her tall, graceful lover, allowing the sexual attraction she felt to master her. The intensity was very different from her dull adolescent years. "I never thought about it much when I was growing up."

"You didn't? You must have had crushes." Nicole held out her hand.

Beth accepted it. "They went both ways."

Nicole was given a new insight into Beth. "The door was wide open for you, then."

"Yes, it was."

Nicole was stunned by the implication. "You didn't have to leave the Church. You could have waited."

Beth saw how her revelation troubled Nicole. "For someone else? A man? No, Nicki, I couldn't have stayed an Anglican." Beth spoke with a lighter tone. "Come on." She tugged on Nicole's jacket. "You can have two scones at Mendici's."

Nicole allowed herself to be moved.

Beth smiled. "Scones are good, yes?"

At home, after their brunch, Beth was determined to give Nicole a quiet day. She relieved Nicole of all errands, and assumed Nicole would spend the day in solitude. She was mistaken. It was not long after returning to the apartment that Nicole sought Beth out, and seduced her into an afternoon of blissful lovemaking.

After the dinner dishes were washed, knowing she had monopolized Beth's day, Nicole chose to read in the den, leaving Beth to her work.

Nicole's thoughts lingered upon death, which came in many forms. She had faced death. Death in the form of a tumor was unexpected. She had always assumed death would come in a more familiar guise.

Nicole knew death presented a different specter to her partner. Beth understood death to be an unwanted, threatening companion early in life. Death by association, by heredity haunted Beth, cinched her hope in its fist until it had materialized in the form of cancer. Surviving the first threat ironically lessoned death's paralyzing effect upon her. Beth embraced a new vision of life that was not as certain of loss. Beth continued to give. She was now more willing to receive.

Death of the soul was a different disease all together. Nicole compared such a death to her mother's dementia. Death of the soul was often a slow insidious process where the afflicted was unaware of the depth of their loss. When death of the soul was complete, death of the corporeal was inconsequential. The nightmare, the great horror, was when the mind, in a brief moment of lucidity, became aware of the soul's wound and was powerless to prevent further damage. The nightmare was compounded when the afflicted understood that even if one sought out a physician, ultimately there was nothing anyone could do to help. What little Nicole knew of Irina Varnavsky led her to believe that young Natasia's mother experienced her soul's death long before HIV infected her.

Nicole feared the death of her soul. Like Beth, a trigger resided in her genetic pool, an imprecise locale. Unlike Beth, there was no test to measure the probability of illness.

Nicole found insanity standing side-by-side with death. Although they were not bound together, they could be close intimates. By focusing on the final junction from life – death – she overlooked an equally treacherous facet of existence, a facet that leads to a spiritual death. Like death, insanity came in different, unexpected forms. In Nicole's life her mother would always be the ruling example. Her mother had been a woman whose violent assessment of life contradicted the acknowledged, if not true, status quo. A minority of one, her mindset had been deemed toxic, a bane to those who had known her.

Insanity came in a different form. A broad. stroke so vast that it encompassed more than one society. Insanity came in a form so powerful, individuals of reasonable intelligence embraced the irrational. Nicole reread the words of Karl Marx published in the book she held. Marx was kinder to religion than Nicole would now willingly grant the conceptual ordering of beliefs in the supernatural. Marx argued, "Religious suffering is at the same time an expression of real suffering and a protest against real suffering. Religion is the sigh of the oppressed creature, the sentiment of a heartless world, and the soul of the soulless conditions. It is the opium of the people." The last seven notorious words, the conception of religion as an addictive drug that pacifies pain, dwarfed Marx's thesis of class inequities. Nicole turned back one page. "Religion is indeed man's self-consciousness and self-awareness so long as he has not found himself or has lost himself again." Was it insane to knowingly lose oneself?

Nicole's bitterness reframed religion as a stepchild of insanity. Legitimized not by merit but by the mass number too cowardly to stare unblinkingly at life and at death. A minority of one, Nicole was held accountable for her failure to turn her eyes away from humanity's harsh and cruel nature.

Nicole's thoughts turned to Beth, who remained in the sunroom with her studies. There was a more personal insanity: what one chose to do for love. Such abandonment of reason, such a romantic surrender to emotion, could captivate and arrest even the most resilient soul. Love was an intoxicating force. The mind ceased to care or went against caring because nothing in life could better mitigate an individual's existential loneliness.

What happened when love failed? What happened when love lost its power over the mind? What happened when the madness came in clear view and the soul was threatened? What could a woman do when she was near losing herself, becoming someone beyond recognition of her ideal? What possessed humanity to continue under such circumstances?

For many the answer was a child. It did not matter how much Nicole loved Beth, they could never create a new life together. There would never be a child with Beth's emerald eyes and compassionate smile. There would never be a blend of Irish and Greek. There would never be a continuation of their union. Creation together could never be because of their gender. Separate, creation for Beth could never be because of her cancer. And Nicole knew that it was her choice to deny creation through her own body. Gender, illness, and history collided into and stifled hope.

Nicole wanted to shed that particular hope with her skin and would do so if she could. She would plunge her hand into her body and rip her disappointment out if only it was possible to isolate and hold it in her grasp. The pain was diffused, molecules traveling through arteries and veins to the tips of her fingers and the center point of her gut. The pain expanded, taking every millimeter of space. During the early morning hours, the pain had won. Now, at the evening hour, she experienced a reprieve. The question remained, 'for how long?'

As night fell, Beth observed Nicole shift to the living room couch to read, offering an unspoken invitation. Beth soon joined Nicole. Bookless, she took comfort in the sound of Nicole's heartbeat against her ear. Time was marked with the beat of her lover's heart and each page turned. Beth's thoughts returned to the morning. Nicole's yearning to create a life through their love echoed Beth's desire. Making love with Nicole had always been an act of union. To also be an act of creation was beyond physical possibility. Beth's impossible desire to have a child from their union was a bittersweet testament of her love, her trust, her respect, and her joy in giving herself completely to Nicole.

Beth's fears were checked by the immediate deliverance she experienced in their physical intimacy. There was no moment between them that demanded greater courage from them both.

CHAPTER 127

April 29, 2003 — Tuesday

Unbeknownst to Nicole, she and Tasi were being scrutinized through the apartment building's glass door. Yeva Varnavsky opened the door. She used a cane in her left hand to support her weakened legs. Short and full-bodied, possessing a cool bearing, she was a substantial, imposing presence.

Hearing the door open, Nicole and Tasi paused in their conversation and turned to see who was exiting the apartment building.

"Bobe," said Tasi cautiously to her grandmother.

Nicole stood up. "Mrs. Varnavsky."

"So, you know my name." Mrs. Varnavsky spoke critically.

Nicole realized she was facing a formidable woman. For the sake of Tasi she held to courtesy. "Yes ma'am. My name is Nicole Thera."

The elderly woman challenged Nicole, pointing to Tasi with her cane. "What is it that you want with my granddaughter?"

Tasi stood beside Nicole, discreetly taking the tall woman's hand.

Reassured by Tasi's gesture, Nicole kept her poise. "I hope to be Tasi's friend."

"Why should I believe you?"

"You have no reason to," Nicole conceded. She presented her one reference. "Laura Morales introduced me to Tasi. If I ask her, I'm sure she'll vouch for my character."

"Laura was my daughter's friend," admitted Mrs. Varnavsky.

"Yes, I know." There would be no pretense between them. Nicole offered her sympathy, alluding to Irina's death with discretion. "I'm sorry for your loss. Your daughter's struggles must have been difficult for you."

"What do you know of my daughter?"

"Only what Laura thought might help me understand you granddaughter's circumstances."

Mrs. Varnavsky seemed impressed by Nicole's unassuming dignity in the face of her less than hospitable greeting. "How do you know Laura?"

Nicole knew she had made a minor inroad into Mrs. Varnavsky's defenses. "I'm her business partner."

"So, you are here because of the construction?"

"Yes, ma'am. We have a field meeting every Tuesday."

Mrs. Varnavsky's suspicions were aroused. "And you, with your important business, have time to spend with a little girl?"

Nicole looked down and gently squeezed Tasi's hand. Tasi met her gaze and smiled hopefully. "Seeing Tasi is the highlight of my day."

Mrs. Varnavsky set aside her reservations for the moment. "Come upstairs. I wish to talk to you and this is not the place for it."

-:-   -:-   -:-

Nicole waited patiently as Mrs. Varnavsky guided Tasi to her room. She took inventory of the well-kept apartment. The aged furniture did not show the scratches and dents expected in a family household. The upholstery of the chairs and couch was worn smooth and shiny, a testament to their age. The colors were subdued. Overall, the atmosphere was sober. There was no hint of a child's influence. Nicole was left to wonder if Tasi's bedroom was in keeping with the rest of the apartment or if she was allowed a space to nurture her imagination and youthful energies.

Mrs. Varnavsky returned to the living room. Nicole stood before her; a statuesque beauty dressed with impeccable elegance, a woman who easily addressed an older generation with respect. The elderly woman observed, "It is a dangerous world. One cannot be too careful, especially with a child."

"I agree. That is one reason I visit with Tasi in clear sight of the neighborhood."

Mrs. Varnavsky would not be so easily appeased. "Have Laura call me."

"I will." Nicole did not think her interview would be so brief. She waited for a new round of questions.

Mrs. Varnavsky's gaze fell on the gold band Nicole wore on her left ring finger. "Do you have a special man in your life?"

Nicole deflected the obvious query to her martial status. "Yes, I do. His name is Jacob and he is like a father to me."

Mrs. Varnavsky set aside her original query and pursued Nicole's response further. "Your father is not alive?"

"I never knew him."

"Your mother?"

"She died when I was in college."

"I'm sorry. Do you have brothers or sisters?"

"No."

"Natasia has me and her uncle, Aaron. I don't have much to give her, but I keep her safe and warm. I cook her good food and I read to her every night. I am not enough for her."

Nicole attempted to protest but Mrs. Varnavsky raised her hand.

"I am not enough and it was you who showed this to me. Natasia is a sweet child. She does not know how honest words can hurt. She told me about a beautiful woman who shared her milk and apple with her. I give her milk every day. Her eyes have not been as bright for me as they have been for you. I thought she had a pretend friend. She is a lonely child at times. When you did not come last Tuesday, I knew you were real."

Mrs. Varnavsky sat down in an oversize chair. "She did not come upstairs. She stayed outside waiting for you until I came and called her to dinner. I don't know why you want to spend time with my granddaughter, but I will allow it if you give me your promise never to hurt her and that you will not walk away when you grow tired of her. She is not a toy."

Nicole stepped forward, standing before the older woman. "The construction project is scheduled to last another two years. I don't know what I will do afterwards. I may have reason to leave Chicago."

"You tell Natasia that you will go away. Do not let her think you will be her friend after the work is done."

Nicole had learned much from her time with Dion. She knew the little girl was far too young to understand. "She won't accept that."

"You are right. She will pretend that you will stay." The grandmother leaned back, her body tired, her soul worn. "And when you leave she will miss you. It will be a good lesson for her. She will learn to respect the truth. She will learn that people don't always stay."

"She knows that lesson already."

"She knows mothers die." Mrs. Varnavsky's mien saddened. "It is a different lesson."

Nicole understood that in spite of Mrs. Varnavsky's terms, she was on the verge of making a commitment with potentially far reaching ramifications. She doubted herself. "Maybe I shouldn't keep seeing her."

The woman's face was expressionless. "I will tell my granddaughter that I did not like you and asked you to go away. She will blame me, not you."

Nicole glanced toward Tasi's bedroom. The thought of never seeing the little girl again prompted a surge of unexpected emotion. Nicole was not prepared to walk away. There was no logic in the matter. She had alternatives. Her relationship with Dion was close, though geographically distant If being with a child was important to her, she could always spend more time in Ann Arbor. A promise to this child would complicate an already full life. Still, given Beth's schedule, Nicole's visits with Tasi were not an inconvenience to either herself or Beth. Nicole had spoken the truth; spending time with the child was the highlight of her day. "Mrs. Varnavsky, do you have any other conditions if I keep seeing your granddaughter?"

Mrs. Varnavsky paused in thought. "Natasia eats only good food. Milk and fruit is good. No sweets. No gifts without my permission. You will not buy her love. I do not want to teach her to want more than she has. It would be good if you try to see her at least once a week."

The terms were easy to manage. However, Nicole could foresee times when her responsibilities to Beth and CMT would conflict with her visits to the Varnavsky's. "Sometimes my business obligations may get in the way."

Mrs. Varnavsky was unfazed. "You call her then."

Nicole nodded.

The elderly woman sat forward, leaning on her cane. "And you. What do you want?"

Nicole had what she wanted. She paused in thought, considering the future. "When it gets cold may I come to your apartment?"

"Yes."

"And may I take Tasi to the library some day and help her pick out some books to read?"

"The library?" Mrs. Varnavsky nodded. "Yes. That would be good."

"If I think of anything else, I'll talk to you."

"Very well."

Nicole might have been able to excuse herself from the interview, taking her leave without broaching the subject of Beth, but she knew better than to trifle with Mrs. Varnavsky. If a rebuff was imminent, better for all involved that it happened now. Nicole raised her left hand. "Mrs. Varnavsky, I think you want to know about this."

She remained dispassionate.

"I have a life partner. Her name is Beth."

Mrs. Varnavsky repeated the name slowly. "Beth?"

"Yes, ma'am."

"What kind of person is your partner?"

"Beth is the finest soul I've ever known." Nicole allowed Beth's resume to speak for her. "She is studying at the University of Chicago for her Ph.D. in Religious Ethics. She was an Episcopalian priest. She left the Church after she met me. She has worked as a chaplain at Memorial Hospital and still volunteers there during her free time."

Mrs. Varnavsky addressed the obvious. "She is very much a Christian."

Nicole could not help but smile. "Yes, she is."

"And what does she think about Jews?"

"Beth has great respect for your faith. She respects all faiths."

Mrs. Varnavsky pointed at Nicole. "And what do you think about Jews?"

The question struck Nicole as quite stupid. "Jacob is a Jew."

"I did not ask you that." Her tongue was sharp and demanding.

Nicole reminded herself that she was a stranger to the woman. She spoke carefully. "I feel a closer affinity with your faith than I do Christianity."

Nicole's profession surprised Mrs. Varnavsky. "You are not Christian?"

"I have my own personal faith."

"I will not have you teaching Nastasia heathen ways," she said truculently.

Nicole felt the all too common disappointment of being judged godless. There was no excuse for Mrs. Varnavsky's arrogance. For Tasi's sake, Nicole kept her temper. For the sake of her own pride she kept an upright posture. "I would not presume to have that right."

Mrs. Varnavsky's next words came carefully, as if she was pursuing what she suspected was an equally, if not more sensitive subject. "So, your partner is a woman. Were you afraid I would not approve of you? You thought I was prejudiced."

Nicole never presented herself first as a lesbian. She believed that if affectional orientation was inconsequential there was no reason to publicly announce the fact. In turn, if a conversation crossed to the personal, she believed she had not only the right, but the obligation to be as equally open and clear about her relationships with whomever she was speaking to. "I would have preferred that you got to know me first, but since you asked I wasn't going to mislead you. I apologize."

"Don't apologize. I did not say you were wrong to think I would judge you."

For the second time in their brief meeting, Nicole tasted the acerbic bite of Mrs. Varnavsky's callous interrogation. Nicole clenched her jaw. The subtle sign of arrested tension did not go unnoticed.

Mrs. Varnavsky persisted in her challenge. "Did you think now that Nastasia has feelings for you, I would consent to you seeing her in spite of the fact I know about your ways?"

Nicole did not give a damn what the old woman thought. Mrs. Varnavsky was one more ignorant, obstinate, obstructionist to human understanding. She had the power to cause Tasi irreparable harm by indoctrinating the child in her prejudicial thinking. Nicole focused on Tasi and the power she could have to change one impressionable mind by being a model of human diversity embodied. "I would never use Tasi against you. I never expected I'd grow to care for her the way I do."

"So, you," Mrs. Varnavsky pronounced the next word heavily, "*care* for my granddaughter?"

"Yes."

"She is not your child."

"I know."

The grandmother stuck again with an accusation that carried a warning against misguided motivations. "She will never be your child."

"I know that, too." Nicole caught a glimpse of the elderly woman's fear of being displaced. She saw Mrs. Varnavsky for what she was – aged and poor, proud and protective. Nicole chose to give the old woman a glimpse of a dream that would forever be bound to an agonizing disappointment. "At one time Beth and I thought we would have a baby. Now, we hope to adopt after Beth finishes graduate school."

Mrs. Varnavsky was thrown off balance. She sat perplexed. "Why not have one of your own?"

"I won't. I have my reasons."

"What reasons?"

Mrs. Varnavsky continued to try to dictate the terms of engagement. Nicole faced another choice – either she answered truthfully or she walked away. "My mother was mentally ill. I'm frightened that I might one day become like her. No child deserves that legacy from their parent."

Mrs. Varnavsky was given reason to pause. She gently inquired, "Have you been ill?"

"Not in that way. A couple of years ago I had surgery for a benign brain tumor."

"You have had quite a life, Nicole."

Mrs. Varnavsky's use of her name swept aside Nicole's frustration and simmering anger. Recognition in the simplest form was all she ever desired, not to be invisible, or to be denigrated when seen. "Everyone has their story."

"Is there a reason why Beth will not have a child?" asked Mrs. Varnavsky with sincere compassion

"She was ill." For the first time in Mrs. Varnavsky's presence, Nicole found it difficult to meet the older woman's piercing gaze. "She cannot have children."

"Beth likes children?"

"She adores them." Nicole smiled sadly.

Mrs. Varnavsky nodded in understanding. "Someday I would like to meet her."

Nicole found the implied acceptance gratifying. "I'd like that."

"Is there anything else you need to tell me?"

"No, ma'am."

Mrs. Varnavsky stood up from the couch. "Well then. You should say good-bye to Natasia. Let her know you will see her next week."

"Thank you."

"Nicole, don't give me a reason to regret my decision."

Nicole heard a request, not a demand. In her career, she had never experienced a more arduous interview. It was fitting. Never had the stakes been higher. "I'll do my best not to disappoint you, or Tasi."

Mrs. Varnavsky had the last word. "We will see."

CHAPTER 128

May 16, 2003 – Friday

In The Pub, Nicole sat at a table along with Beth, Kate and Allison Polland, Kate's latest girlfriend. This was Allison's introduction to The Fields. Nicole had been amused to learn from Kate that Allison had qualms, not about meeting her, but about meeting Beth. Nicole appreciated anew how her partner's religious vocation could be a barrier to creating friendships. Nicole did not tell Beth of Allison's reluctance, confident that by simply being herself Beth would win Allison's regard.

Beth finished telling a story of a young imp of a boy in her Sunday school class who took to mimicking everyone around him with uncanny precision. Though Beth found the boy entertaining, she had encouraged him to embrace his own voice and his own identity, teaching a subtle lesson while she attempted to rein in his antics.

Allison sipped her second glass of wine. "Any children in your future?"

Beth reached under the table and took Nicole's hand. "We want to adopt."

"No turkey baster for you?" Allison repeated the common joke.

Beth turned to Nicole, who averted her gaze. Beth continued to speak for them. "I can't have children."

"Oh, I'm sorry." Ill at ease, Allison glanced toward Kate. Kate's expression was humorless. Allison considered Nicole. "And …"

Kate diverted the conversation. "I can use another wine."

Nicole got to her feet. "Let me. Beth, Allison, the same?" Her offer accepted, Nicole went to the bar. "Two Zinfandels, a Melo and a Guinness."

The order of a Guinness jarred Connor out of his methodical bartending. He looked over to the booth. Troubled, he spoke in a low, uncompromising voice. "I'm out of Guinness, Nicki."

Nicole debated whether to press the issue. Looking back at the table she knew that if she returned with the Guinness, the evening would derail. Her reckless impulse was reined in by the knowledge that she could not drink in the presence of Beth and Kate without offering an explanation. Explaining herself was the last thing she wanted to do. Friends and lovers made for a complicated life. She was ready to barter for a less complicated life. "No Guinness. Can you take the drinks to the table? I'm going to my office for a few minutes."

Connor served the drinks. Beth gave him an inquisitive look. Connor answered the unspoken question. "Nicki will be in her office for a little while."

Kate announced to Allison, "Come on, we're going dancing."

"Isn't that rude?" asked Allison.

Kate stood up. "No. I'm family. I'm allowed."

Allison reluctantly followed Kate down to The Fields' dance floor leaving a sober Beth alone with her glass of wine. Beth turned her gaze to the staircase leading to Nicole's office. A decision made, she got up and followed her lover's footsteps.

Beth entered the office. Nicole sat on the couch. She sighed. "I'm sorry."

"Kate and Allison are dancing."

Nicole nodded.

"Nicki, talk to me. You hardly said a word all night."

"It's been a tough week. I'm just tired."

Beth stepped forward and sat on the coffee table, opposite Nicole. "You're lying."

There was no retreat. Nicole offered a fraction of her thoughts. "I can't help remembering ..."

"What, Nicki?"

Nicole alluded to Beth's surgery. "It will be a year this Wednesday."

For Beth, her surgery seemed to reside in another lifetime. "We don't talk much about our illnesses, do we?"

"No reason to dwell on the past."

"I don't think I will ever have a Thanksgiving that I don't remember spending the night beside your hospital bed. I hardly knew you, but that didn't change the fact that I was afraid for you. I didn't know how you would handle the possibility of not being able to walk again."

"We didn't have to find out." Nicole tapped her feet on the floor; pleased by the motion she tried not to take for granted.

"Thank God." Beth was heartened by the minor rise in Nicole's mood. "Your tumor explained so much. The fact that you didn't tell me ... I realized just how much you kept to yourself. I also realized that it was all right to come to you. You would talk to me."

Nicole understood that was her cue. Sometimes she wished she could place Beth's hand over her heart and just let Beth feel what she felt. Instead, she was left to struggle with words. "This was supposed to be an easier year. Hasn't felt that way."

"I know."

"Do you?"

"We've made choices that have changed both our lives. It only stands to reason that we would need time to adjust. You've had a year at CMT and I've had a year at school. Our lives should get easier now."

Nicole smiled. "You are an optimist. I have the new project and you still have to get through your qualifying exams, not to mention your dissertation."

"And then we'll take a short break before adding a little girl to our lives. Piece of cake, Thera."

"Is that right, Kelly?"

"It's a life worth living, Nicki." Beth took Nicole's hand. "I have to believe I was given a second chance for a reason. We both were."

Nicole glided her free hand around Beth's waist and pulled the younger woman to her as she turned her body to rest across the couch. Beth happily followed the easy movement. Her reward was to find herself lying over Nicole's body. "Hi there."

"Hello."

"You beckoned?"

"No. You did."

Beth played with Nicole's top shirt button. "I have you exactly where I want you."

Nicole grinned. "And what, pray tell, will you do with me now that you have me?"

Beth smiled. Nicole's eyes glistened invitingly. Sometimes they were so easy with one another. The moments were unheralded. They could not be summoned or enticed. They were rooted in their sincere caring for one another, a consequence of a love affair that arose from an ardent friendship. Beth kissed Nicole. She could feel Nicole pull her closer. The kiss caused the world to slip away into the recesses of Beth's mind. The moment allowed for only the two kindred sprits, hers and Nicole's. It was this astonishing union that compensated for the uncertainties and the labors of their relationship. Beth broke free of the kiss. Her breath quickened. "I hope Kate and Allison don't wait for us."

CHAPTER 129

May 24, 2003 – Saturday

Preparing for her afternoon flight, Beth laid her garment bag on the bed. Nicole stood at the threshold keeping silent vigil. With the semester at an end, Beth hoped to devote herself to spoiling Nicole. She disliked the timing of the conference and retreat. She paused in her task. "I don't want to go."

Nicole walked into the room. She went to the top of Beth's dresser. Resting easily in his watchful perch was Little Fella. Nicole had always liked the teddy bear's sad face. At first sight he magically brought a smile to her; it was a power he still possessed. Holding him to her ear, she pretended to hear a secret. "What? I'll ask her."

Beth smiled.

"Your little guy wants to go with you."

"Does he?"

Nicole was grave. "He's afraid he'll get in the way."

Beth stepped up, taking the bear's paw. "That's impossible."

"I'd feel better if he was with you, making sure you're safe."

Beth heard Nicole's own wish in the statement. "I've got space in my backpack for him."

Nicole made the bear jump happily.

Beth laughed.

Nicole gave Little Fella to Beth to hold.

Beth wondered, "Who will keep an eye on you?"

"Jacob and Liza have invited me for Shabbat dinner. And Tess has always been a good chaperon."

Beth placed Little Fella on the bed and retrieved her clothes from her dresser. "Nicki, maybe we can get away for a few days when I get back."

"I thought you were going to start at the hospital right away?"

"Pam only needs me to cover for the other chaplains while they're on vacation. The rest of my schedule is flexible."

Nicole lay on the bed near the garment bag. "With the new project just starting it's going to be hard to take more than a long weekend."

Beth paused in her packing. "I'll take as many as you can give me."

Seeing her lover's radiating need, Nicole's response was immediate. "I'll start planning my calendar."

✛   ✛   ✛

After sharing lunch Nicole insisted on escorting Beth to the airport, seeing her off at the security gates. Beth embraced Nicole. "I'm going to miss you."

Nicole memorized the feel of Beth against her body. "Get some rest."

"I don't know about that. I may have slept without you in the past, but I was always in my own bed."

Nicole released her lover. "You forgot the hospital."

"I was heavily sedated and you were in the room with me."

Point made, Nicole took Beth's hand, holding it close to her heart. "You'll be fine."

Beth quipped, "You can't wait to have two weeks without me."

Nicole returned the volley. "If only I can get you on the plane, or at least past security."

"Give Tess my love."

"I will."

"Maybe I could call?" Beth asked.

Nicole set herself against Beth's pining. "We had an agreement. This is supposed to be a retreat, a time away from everything and everybody, including me."

"What kind of peace do you think I'm going to have if all I can think about is you?"

Nicole had no defense against Beth's wry wisdom. "Call me."

Pleased, Beth leaned forward and gently kissed Nicole. "Are you going to let go of my hand?"

Nicole glanced down. She sobered. "Come back to me."

All levity was swept aside. "I will. I promise." Beth released Nicole and slung her backpack over her shoulder. "I love you."

"I love you, too." Nicole stood her place, unmoved, watching Beth go through security. Beth took one final look toward Nicole and smiled. Nicole smiled through her loneliness.

CHAPTER 130

May 31, 2003 – Saturday

Beth was one of a handful of conference participants who traveled the ninety-minute route north from Minneapolis for an extended retreat at St. John's Abbey, a Benedictine monastery. The community resided on 2,400 acres including woods, lakes, and a wildlife refuge.

Beth walked a well-worn lakeside path from the monastery to a small open stone chapel. She wondered what Nicole would have thought of Benedict of Nursia, the sixth century monk given credit for writing the Rule of Benedict, a small volume that she carried in her backpack. Undoubtedly, Nicole would have taken exception to Benedict's destruction of a pagan temple dedicated to Apollo and the subsequent building of the monastery of Monte Cassino upon the confiscated land. Beth could not argue that the greatness of one religion was often built on the subjugated vision of another. It was at Monte Cassino that Benedict was said to have written the Rule.

Sitting against a tree, Beth read the seventh chapter. The topic – humility. Benedict's counsel was to model ones actions on the sayings of Jesus, not ones own will, and to be patient and obedient to God in the face of difficulties and contradictions, even injustice. Beth meditated upon a quote from Psalm 66: 'For you, O God, have tested us; you have tried us as silver is tried. You brought us into the net; you laid burdens on our back.'

Beth marked her place. Once again her thoughts returned to Nicole. Nicole named humility as one of her four prime tenets. Beth felt an affinity with her partner's faith. After the conference, her assessment seemed far less incongruous than it might have once been. The four days in Minneapolis had been a whirlwind of activity. The massive catalogue of sessions offered the opportunity to sample an extraordinary array of religious perspectives. Never was the diversity of Christendom more apparent. Beth purposely chose sessions that promised to challenge her biases. She learned in counterpoint to her core beliefs. Growth came with engagement, with dialogue.

She left Minneapolis with two problems dominating her thoughts. The first was modern Christology. Beth wondered if Nicole would be surprised to learn that there were Christians who found no more of the Godhead within the personality of Jesus as they did within any of God's other creations. Jesus of Nazareth was placed before her as a historical man. The same individual was brought forth by the Homoousians as Christ Jesus, consubstantial with God the Father. Could two perspectives diverge any farther? Returning to the

Hebrew Bible, the messiah – anointed one – was the common reference to a king. Isaiah never used the term. Still, he was the prophet who spoke of the Davidic descendent who would restore Israel and bring peace to the world. The conceptual construction of the Christ was extraordinary. The translation of the Hebrew term messiah to the Greek Christ did not begin to explain the religious metamorphosis.

Closer to Beth's interest and her work for her dissertation were the soteriological arguments that could not be extricated from the perception of Jesus' personality. The doctrine of salvation presented Jesus as suffering for the sins of humanity. That begged the question of whether Jesus was sufficiently man to have suffered. Broadly, the argument was that if God is the entity imagined by humanity, suffering was nothing more than an awareness of the universal condition. What meaning then could be implied in the crucifixion? What power did Jesus' words in the Gospel of Mark carry if he was not human complete? What obedience to God did Jesus demonstrate in the Garden of Gethsemane if his acquiesce was to an aspect of his self? On the cross what did Jesus' last words, his cry to God mean if he was both speaker and listener?

Who then was Jesus to Beth? What did she mean when she referred to the Christ? Obedience, humility, reverence for the Creator, all this Beth found in Jesus. When Beth struggled to find God she raised her gaze to the Christ, the messiah, the man who tried to restore Israel and bring peace to the world. He had trusted God and at death, according to Mark, he was uncertain. In spite of his cry, Beth had no doubt that Jesus never stopped loving God.

The second problem was her paradox – a reasonable woman of the nascent twenty-first century drawn to the illogical. The ritual and the liturgy of High Church were forces that kept company with Nicole's mystery. The power of ritual lay in the void, in the unknown; it reached into the deepest emotional and spiritual crevices of Beth's being. Beth had yet to find the means to explain the elemental importance of being a celebrant, of the priesthood she had forfeited when she left the Anglican Church. She longed for her ordination in the United Church of Christ, and the ability to be a celebrant once again.

As a guest of the Benedictine monks Beth participated in Morning, Noon, Eucharist and Evening Prayer. The juxtaposition of the exhilarating conference with her contemplative days at St. John's brought Beth to a third consideration – the role of Christianity in the world, more specifically her calling. For Beth, a Christian was less a person who bound herself to doctrine and more one who lived an ethic that strove to realize the greater good. A minister was an individual who attended the needs of others, whether motivated by religious or secular beliefs. Her Ph.D. work in Religious Ethics was concerned with the meaning of religion for both an individual and a society, with a focus on the problems of justice and the common good. Beth faced moral problems as a priest, equally so as a chaplain. Much of her ethical concerns targeted human suffering. There were never easy answers. She searched for a framework to guide her in the future, a framework she could offer others as they navigated the treacherous currents of life.

Beth returned to her room after Evening Prayer. Her roommate, Rachel Baynes, read in bed. Beth had first met Rachel, an ordained United Church of Christ minister, in January when they had both enrolled in the same advance course at the University. Older by three years, Rachel was poised and confident, and quite unsentimental about her faith. She worked for a shelter for abused women and their children.

The two women were excellent roommates. When sharing space, courtesy ruled. They could be quiet with one another, but also enjoyed conversation.

Rachel looked up from her book and offered Beth a warm smile.

Beth turned her back to Rachel, maintaining as much of her modesty as she could without using the bathroom to change. Rachel watched unobserved as Beth traded her sweater and jeans for sweatpants and tank top.

The trip was their first opportunity to share an uninterrupted period of time with each other. Beth's focus remained within the realm of her vocation; she chose not to discuss her life with Nicole.

Beth sat on her bed with her knees raised, leaning against the wall, which served as a headboard.

Rachel set her book aside. "How was your day?"

"Good."

"You disappeared after lunch."

"I took a walk by the lake."

Rachel had come to understand Beth's priorities. "No people?"

"No people," said Beth. "I can't remember the last time I was alone in nature like that."

"We still have four more days. Enjoy the quiet while you can."

St. John's had made an indelible impression upon Beth. "A place like this ... the pendulum swings toward an awareness of a religious life more than a secular one. I feel ... it's stronger here than at U.C."

"Not a surprise. U.C. is in the middle of Chicago and it doesn't have a bunch of monks walking around." Juxtaposing one against the other, Rachel showed a definite preference. "I like being on campus. It's a break from the rest of the city without completely leaving its wonderful energy."

"Is that why you keep taking classes?"

"The shelter doesn't always give God much space and once you're ordained going to church is never the same. The aura of being a minister, you know?"

"I know," Beth responded collegially. With the subject of the shelter raised, Beth chose to pursue her curiosity. "Rach, when you're working with the women and kids in the shelter ... do they talk about God?"

"If they do, it's always on their terms. It isn't that much different than your work in a hospital. I'm there for the residents. It's up to them to take up the invitation. If they don't I still have things I can try to do for them."

"It can't be easy."

"I see battered and abused women. I see kids that have had to grow up way too fast. I swear Beth, sometimes it's hard to like men."

Beth did not condone the broad condemnation. "You can't judge all men because of what you see. Women hurt children, too."

"I know," Rachel conceded. She also reiterated two aspects of her identity that contributed to her sense of safety. "It does make me grateful that I'm gay and an adult."

Beth imagined a different grace. "I think going home to a compassionate, gentle man can be equally, if not more healing than going home to a woman."

"Point taken." Rachel was well acquainted with Beth's ability to argue, broadening a perspective without negating the original proposition. She carried the subject forward. "I think one difference between the shelter and a hospital is that the root of the problems is different. Most of the women choose to have a relationship with the guy that ends up beating them. If they aren't raped, they decide to have kids or are just careless. Many of them don't have the kind of education they need to get a decent job. They blame themselves. They have so much to account for, blaming God sounds hollow. Some do get angry enough that they blame God for what has happened to them. What if they were born into a different life circumstance? What if they hadn't been abused? The kids must wonder why they were destined to be smacked around, left hungry and shuttled from one place to another until they landed in a shelter."

Beth had worked with women and children who, if not abused, were in harrowing circumstances when admitted to the hospital. "Some of the people in the hospital are coming from the same place. Others can't even point to something extreme. They're accountable. They are in the hospital because they smoked, drank or ate themselves into it."

Rachel drew an analogy. "There are also those that wake up one day feeling things are not right. They go to their doctor and end up getting a dire diagnosis. It didn't matter that they did all the right things. That's the kids for me. Some shut down. They go so deep inside themselves I don't know how to reach them. They keep waiting for the next blow. They want to trust but everything in their lives has taught them not to. They believe that sooner or later they will be betrayed. Some kids want to be loved so badly that they'll stay close to their abuser. They'll take a beating just to have human contact. They have a warped sense of love that might never be made straight again."

Beth stared at her hands, focusing on her commitment ring.

After a few moments Rachel called Beth from her contemplation. "Beth?"

Beth looked at Rachel. "I was thinking of someone I know. Her life wasn't exactly the same but there are similarities."

"How's she doing?"

"Good."

"Does she have kids?"

"Not yet." Beth smiled. "She wants to."

Rachel was pleased. "It takes a special kind of courage to personally know how terrible life can be for a child and still want to bring a child into the world. When I really think about it ... it's frightening knowing that abused kids are apt to model their behavior on their mother or the guys who abuse them. The victim and the aggressor. They're both lousy. I've seen too many examples of the intergenerational transmission of violence."

"It must be hard for you."

"It would be impossible if I didn't know that there were other stories. There are adults who were abused as children who would first cut off their hand before ever hurting a child. Still, even their stories can be heartbreaking. I've met more than one adult who harbors such a deep, simmering anger ... they are so frightened of continuing the cycle of violence that they refuse to have anything to do with a child. They will never be an abuser, but at the same time, they will never be a parent. What really gives me hope is that I've met the angels. The abused kids who grow up to be extraordinary parents and advocates for children's rights."

Beth took comfort in Rachel's final observation. "I've seen my friend with kids. I think she's one of the angels. She just doesn't know it yet."

The two women shared a smile. After a moment Rachel continued the conversation. "Beth, may I ask you a personal question?"

Beth nodded.

"Before, at the hotel ... I couldn't help but notice your scar." Rachel paused, giving Beth a moment to anticipate her question. "What happened?"

Beth looked down at her body. "Ovarian cancer." She raised her gaze with equal sorrow and gratitude. "The doctors caught it early."

"Damn, I never thought ..." Rachel paused. A few heartbeats passed before she posed a second question. "How long have you been cancer free?"

"A year."

"Was it one or both ..."

Beth cut Rachel's question short. "One, but I had the surgeon remove both ovaries as a precaution."

Again, Rachel's usual confidence was arrested by Beth's unaffected admission. Her composure was compromised. "Isn't that extreme?"

Beth relied on the facts to establish her case. "My family history was against me."

"Your mother?"

"And grandmother."

Rachel tried to measure Beth's loss. "Did you want children?"

Thoughtful, Beth answered in a hush. "Yes, I did. When we got together, Nicki and I decided to wait until I finished school. The timing didn't work out."

"I'm sorry. Will Nicole ..."

"No." Beth rushed her answer. Flustered, she clenched her jaw. Silence hung uncomfortably. Beth wanted to explain. She could not without breaching Nicole's privacy. She offered an inadequate justification. "She has her reasons."

Rachel diverted the focus from the specific to the general. "I have to admit its stories like yours that make me wonder why God made the world the way it is. Good people can't have children. People who would be better without do. And the possibility of shifting the kids from one to the other becomes impossible because the adoption system locks out those with bad medical histories."

Rachel's sweeping statement gave Beth reason to pause. "There are ways. I have a friend who is a lawyer."

Rachel was uncertain. "Would you buy a baby?"

Beth bristled at the suggestion. "All adoptions cost money."

"That's true. I guess if you want something enough you'll do whatever you have to, to make it happen."

The easy spirit in the room slipped away. Beth quieted. What was she willing to do to have a child?

Rachel said regretfully, "I'm sorry, Beth. This is a retreat. You didn't need me to bring ..."

"It's all right." Beth sought no apology. In fact, she was grateful. "I don't have too many people in my life I can talk to about what my choices mean to me."

Rachel smiled. "I'll take that as a compliment."

Beth considered the woman. Their brief conversation had both disturbed and calmed her. "It's meant to be."

CHAPTER 131

June 2003

Tess, carrying a paper bag, entered Nicole's office in The Fields.

Nicole looked up from her work. "There you are." She stood, stowing an array of papers into her briefcase. "We're going to be late."

"Nicki, who is Tasi?"

Nicole paused. She was ready to slap whomever had spoiled her surprise. "Where did you hear that name?"

Tess raised the paper bag. "Miguel. He sent me over here with three pints of milk and some really nice looking strawberries."

"What did he say?"

"He said Tasi was the new love in your life."

Nicole smiled wryly. "I guess she is."

Tess suspected Nicole's whimsy was at play. "What are you not telling me?" She swung the bag from side to side. "What's this for?"

"Tasi is seven years old." Nicole noted Tess's amused expression. "Well it's nice to see that you believe me."

"So, you're not dragging me along just to see the new development."

Nicole took Tess's hand and pulled her out of the room. "Come on, you get to meet Tasi after the construction meeting."

Later than afternoon, Tess followed Nicole out of a construction site trailer. Nicole carried the snack bag. They crossed the street to where Tasi sat on a stoop. Tasi stood up and walk to the curb where she waited. As Nicole approached, Tasi opened her arms. Nicole took her into an embrace, lifting the child.

Nicole kissed Tasi on the cheek. "Missed you."

Tasi looked over to Tess, silently assessing the stranger.

Nicole did the introductions. "Tasi, I want you to meet a friend of mine who is visiting for a few days. This is Tess. Tess, this is Nastasia."

Tess brightly greeted the child. "Hi."

"Hi," Tasi responded quietly.

Nicole beamed. "She's beautiful, isn't she?"

"Yes," agreed Tess wholeheartedly.

"And Tasi is good with her numbers. And she speaks both Hebrew and English. Isn't that right."

Tasi nodded.

"Well, I'm impressed," said Tess.

As always, Nicole gave Tasi the option of choosing where they would visit. "Outside or inside?"

Tasi took possession of the snack bag. "Outside."

"Okay." Nicole walked to the stoop and placed the girl down gently. She sat beside the child. "Let's see what Miguel has for us."

The following day, Tess exited The Fields front entrance and found Nicole sitting alone on a bench.

"Hey."

"Hey back to you."

"Connor told me you were here. Your cell phone is off. That becoming a new habit?"

"I just needed some quiet time."

"You've never been one to completely shut the world out." Nicole gave Tess a disbelieving look. "All right, you have, but I'm not used to being included among the banished." She sat down and patted Nicole's thigh. "So, I've meant to ask, how are you surviving temporary bachelorette-hood?"

"Bachelorette-hood?" Nicole's gaze turned toward the street. "Three days, two hours and ..." She looked down at her watch. "... twenty minutes before Beth's plane lands."

Tess's voice betrayed her concern. "You look a little tired."

"I miss the loft."

Tess seemed uncertain whether Nicole had changed the subject. "It was a beautiful space."

"It was mine. Everything about it was me. I could be comfortable in it alone."

Tess clearly understood. "And the apartment is about you and Beth."

"Yeah. Too many reminders of her."

"I swear you two are still newlyweds."

"I'm thinking of shifting some of my work time from my CMT office to The Fields. I've spoken to Alex and Laura and they're fine with the idea."

"You do miss The Fields," Tess observed thoughtfully.

"I want to spend more time with Jacob and Liza."

"I know they would be happy to have you back here."

Nicole fell silent, her gaze holding to the façade of the Levi Law Office across the street. She felt a trace of a once familiar melancholy.

"Nicki," Tess said softly, "is there something else?"

Nicole wanted to break her sense of isolation, to have one other human being understand what she was feeling. "In Ireland, Beth and I stayed at a B&B in a small coastal village. One evening we got a blanket from the innkeeper and trekked down to an isolated cove. The waters lapped the shore and the sky was painted with brilliant hues of amber, ochre and violet. For a good hour we didn't say anything to each other. I had the softness of Beth's body against mine. I felt the steady movement of her breathing. She stroked my hand with her thumb, the way she does, not realizing she's doing it. For that piece of time it was just Beth and me, and we were able to keep the world at bay. The world couldn't touch us. Everything that separated us fell away. I can't remember a day since then that I've felt the same way about us. I miss her, Tess."

"I don't understand. Beth is ridiculously in love with you."

"She's gone back to a world I can't share. The church ... school ... it's a world we both know I don't belong in."

Tess shifted towards Nicole. "Has someone said something to you?"

Nicole would not inventory the cause of her sorrow – the occasions when she had heard Beth's choice of an unbelieving partner questioned, both by direct query or allusion. She and Beth were a couple whom many people who were associated with the University and Beth's church could not comfortably place in their rigidly structured minds. She had witnessed Beth's struggle to account for her, giving the questions merit they did not deserve. She set the cause aside and focused on the effect. "That old feeling has come back with a vengeance. I'm standing outside looking into a home; a fire is burning in the hearth. I place my bare hand against the glass pane." Nicole raised her hand demonstrating the gesture. "I feel the cold separation." Nicole dropped her hand unto her lap. "Now it's worse because Beth is standing in front of the fireplace surround by familiar faces and I can't go to her. She won't invite me in."

Tess studied her friend closely. "You're wrong."

Sadly, Nicole replied, "No, I'm not. Tess, she's got a spiritual home again. She's doing great at school. She's scheduled to be ordained in less than a year. She's living in a world that has helped her rebuild her faith. She's gotten her confidence back. Her God hasn't forsaken her." Nicole turned a piercing gaze toward her companion. "Tess, she's never been in a stronger position to realize her calling."

"You're missing one very important fact. Beth's faith may not have survived if you hadn't been with her when she left the Anglican Church."

"Maybe." Nicole did not dismiss the importance of the past. She also did not presume that the past set an unalterable course for the future. "I had a reason to be with her while she was in transition. She's not in transition anymore."

"So, you think she'll just set you aside?"

"Not so blatantly. We're different and I have to accept that."

"Okay, I grant that your relationship may be changing. I would think you would want to spend more time with Beth. Why not shift operations to your den?"

The question took Nicole too close to the truth. "Can we stop talking now?"

Tess knew Nicole's patterns. "Are you looking for reasons to be away from Beth?"

"I want her to be happy." Nicole's passion rose. "Can we just leave it at that? Please, Tess."

"No, Nicki. I can't leave it at that. What makes you think spending more time at The Fields will make Beth happy?"

Nicole's trembling emotions stuttered to the surface. "I need ... I need to be away from her."

"Hey ..." Tess had driven Nicole to her limit. She tried to ease the resulting tumult. "You're worrying me."

"How do you think I feel?" Nicole asked.

"I don't know. Tell me."

"I was never this lonely when I was alone."

Tess took Nicole's hand. "How long have you been feeling like this?"

"I don't know." Nicole combed her free hand through her hair. "I'm having a hard time remembering how it felt not to feel like this."

"Talk to Beth."

"I've tried."

"Try again," Tess insisted.

Nicole judged Tess's simplistic direction naïve. "How do I tell Beth that I find little joy in our life together? Don't you know what that will do to her?"

"It'll give her a chance to do something about it."

"Tess, she can't stop being who she is. We've been through that. I can't ... I won't ask her to put me first."

"Nicki, what are you going to do?" asked Tess fearfully.

"Maybe take a lesson from my past."

"Meaning what?" Nicole did not answer. Tess squeezed her despondent friend's hand. "Nicki, listen to me. I know what you're capable of. You left the life you had before Beth for a reason. If you go back it will destroy you."

Nicole saw a different future for herself. "Tess, it depends what part of my previous life I go back to. I think I'll save myself."

CHAPTER 132

June 2003

Beth and Rachel disembarked from their plane and walked quietly toward baggage claim. Rachel spied a waiting Nicole. She reached out and touched Beth's arm. She motioned to the left. "Your ride."

Beth followed Rachel's gesture, seeing Nicole. She paused, wanting a final private word. "Rach, it was good to spend time with you."

Rachel narrowed the distance between them, creating an intimate space. "Let's not be strangers over the summer. I'll call you."

"Give me a few days to settle back in." Beth glanced toward Nicole. "I need to go."

"Beth, I'd like to think we're friends. If you ever need someone to talk to, I'm a good listener." Rachel's words drifted into the din of the airport terminal.

Having no reasonable response, Beth embraced Rachel as her answer. It had been a long two weeks. During the final days, Rachel's obvious attraction to her, as well as her own unexpected welcoming of that attraction had unsettled Beth's moral universe. "Thank you." She broke free and walked to Nicole.

Nicole watched the two women. She had met Rachel on a number of occasions throughout the school year. Rachel had earned Beth's admiration. Beth described Rachel as intelligent and dedicated to her social justice ministry. Unfortunately for Nicole, Rachel kept in-step with the majority of Beth's university friends. She was cool with Nicole, never offering more than a cursory exchange of greetings.

Nicole opened her arms to Beth. "Hi."

Beth entered Nicole's warm embrace. She held tightly to the familiar feel and smell of her partner. She desperately needed Nicole to anchor their shared world. They gently separated.

Nicole noted Beth's fatigue. "Hey. Problems sleeping?"

Beth knew better than to deny her weariness. "Told you."

"Did Little Fella lose his magic?"

"He's not the same as having you."

Nicole wrapped her arm around Beth's shoulder and guided her toward the baggage claim area. "Well, you have me now."

Beth leaned into Nicole's body as they walked. "How's Tess?"

"Good." Nicole beamed with pride. "We have a second portrait of me compliments of Dion. I think I might frame it."

The mention of the child abruptly buckled Beth's composure. She paused and turned away, releasing Nicole. She caught sight of Rachel as she was greeted by an older woman, whom Beth assumed to be Rachel's mother – another reminder of a mother-daughter family unit. Beth felt mocked by her dreams, which had been recast to nothing more substantial than the illusions of a guileless innocent. Beth was no innocent and yet, she had been sure, so sure that she was meant to know the love a mother feels for her daughter. She needed to find a way to mend the breach, and to reclaim hope.

Nicole followed Beth's gaze. "Everything all right?"

Beth shook her head in an effort to discard her haunting thoughts. "I want to go home."

Confused, Nicole suppressed her desire to take Beth's hand. "Sure." They walked down the airport corridor. The resurgence of the distance between them was, to Nicole, inexplicable. It was this baffling facet of their growing estrangement that assailed her dwindling optimism.

At the close of the evening Nicole lay on the couch reading. Beth sat at her desk in the sunroom.

Beth's prayer for a child remained unanswered, neither fulfilled nor denied. That God would grant her prayer was never in greater doubt. Using her laptop computer she searched the Internet for information regarding Illinois adoption services. Beth focused on the health requirements of the adoptive parents. She doubted that either she or Nicole would meet the standard. That, along with the fact that they were a same-sex couple, led her to believe adoption was improbable. Her only hope was Nicole's financial resources. A private adoption might be feasible although the costs, by her calculations, could reach $100,000 if they had to pay for the mother's living and medical expenses throughout her pregnancy.

Beth wanted to set the doubt aside. She wanted to know if Nicole's financial resources could engage the right forces to overcome the obvious barriers to their adoption of a child.

Beth turned off her computer. She went to Nicole and sat on the edge of the couch. Nicole closed her book, giving Beth her complete attention.

Beth kept her hands in her lap. Her voice was tentative. "Nicki, I want you to do something for me."

All of Nicole senses warned caution. She abandoned herself to Beth's obvious need. "All right."

Beth looked down. Her emotions surged, threatening her composure.

"Beth, whatever it is, tell me," tenderly urged Nicole.

Beth took a deep breath and then raised her gaze to find and hold to Nicole's. "I'd like to meet with Kate and her law firm's adoption attorney."

Nicole was disconcerted by the implication of the request. "You want to start the process now?"

"No," Beth corrected. "I want to ask them if we should even bother trying."

"Beth ..." Nicole's mind was a tangle of disconsonant thoughts.

"Nicki ..." Beth owed Nicole an explanation. "I was told our medical histories might make it impossible for us to adopt. I've done some research. It may be true."

Nicole set aside her concerns and focused on Beth. "I'll call Kate in the morning."

"Thank you." Beth stood up.

Nicole reached out and took Beth's hand. "Beth, let's take this one step at a time."

Given the speaker, it was hollow assurance. "I'm going for a walk. I'll be back in a little while."

Nicole released Beth's hand. She swung her legs down, sitting upright. She watched her partner's departure. She could no longer withstand her unresolved, every rising desperation; she sought release from the imbroglio of their shared lives. "Beth!"

Beth turned back to Nicole and cried out, "How much more am I supposed to give up for ..." She could not complete the damning statement.

Nicole finished the thought in her mind. Responsibility had been placed at her feet. She answered. "You don't. You have always had a choice."

Beth saw in Nicole the fierce, enduring truth of their union. It came with a price. Beth had no response. She picked up her keys from the foyer banister and left the apartment.

CHAPTER 133

June 2003

Ann Cabot, Nicole's administrative assistant at CMT, informed her that she had a call from Kate. Nicole debated whether to delay the expected unpleasantness. A week had passed since she and Beth had met with Kate and her fellow attorney, Elaine Miles. Nicole bore the burden of not immediately consenting to a private adoption scheme. In the passing days, Beth found reasons to be away from home during the evening hours; avoidance was her response to her disappointment.

Nicole picked up the phone receiver. "Kate, what's up?"

Kate was impatient. "Nicki, what have you and Beth decided about the adoption?"

Nicole closed her eyes and concentrated on keeping her temper to a low simmer. "What do you mean?"

"You haven't reconsidered?"

"What do I have to reconsider? My medical record? Beth's?"

"You have options," said Kate sharply.

Nicole countered angrily, "A little girl to the highest bidder? Pretty soon we will be buying and selling children on E-bay."

Kate continued her advocacy on Beth's behalf. "So you'll deny Beth a child because cutting a check for a baby offends your finer sensibilities."

"You don't think the idea of going around the system offends Beth?"

"Not enough to stop her from the adoption. We were all in the conference room together. She was looking to you to bail her out. She wanted you to tell her it was all right. You gave her nothing. Not a goddamned bit of hope to hold on to."

Nicole snapped, "I have never been nor will I ever be Beth's moral authority."

"Damned lucky for her."

"Did you ever think that the process might be valid? Beth and I both have a long time to go before hitting the five-year mark. I didn't have cancer, but she did. What good does it do to leave a child parentless before they're ten years old?"

"Is that your moral objection? What might happen? Christ, your morality is so fluid, you pick and choose when and how to apply it."

"I will not buy a baby," Nicole said deliberately, striving to end the argument.

"Fine!" An exasperated Kate turned to the only other alternative. "If you are so against this then have a baby. There is nothing medically stopping you."

The proposal stunned Nicole. She took a moment before responding. "Kate, you know better than to suggest ..."

Kate's voice was charged with indignation. "I'm suggesting. We both know Beth won't, no matter how much she may want you to give her what she was willing to give you. Nicki, you are such a hypocrite."

"Do you have anything else to say to me?"

"I would if I thought it would make a difference," spat Kate.

"Then this conversation is over." Nicole set the phone down. She got up and walked to the window. She stared blankly, her rage making any reasonable thought impossible.

Nicole drove to the construction site with Kate's accusations echoing in her ear. The field meeting was a welcomed distraction. Focusing on her work helped Nicole transition from a hypothetical child that was disrupting her life, to a living child who, without effort, brought her joy.

Upon arriving at the construction trailer, Nicole received a message that Mrs. Varnavsky had called her office. Tasi was ailing with a cold and would not be waiting for her outside. Nicole was to go to the apartment. Nicole liked neither the fact that Tasi was ill nor the probability of an abbreviated visit.

Mrs. Varnavsky opened the door to Nicole. "Come in. Tasi is waiting for you."

"How is she?"

"Her fever has fallen. She refuses to sleep until she sees you. Try to have her drink some juice. I set a glass beside her bed."

Nicole entered the child's bedroom. "Hey."

Tasi extended her arms. Nicole went to the child, sitting on the side of the bed. Tasi embraced Nicole, her hold weaker than Nicole was accustomed to. "I don't feel good."

"I know, sweetheart." Tasi's open display of affection was common. The bald sense of the little girl's vulnerability was new to Nicole. She was frightened for Tasi. "You're going to be all right." Her words served to assure her just as much as the child.

The dinner hour had long passed. Nicole remained at Tasi's bedside watching the child sleep. Mrs. Varnavsky entered the bedroom. She placed her hand on Nicole's shoulder. "It's late."

Nicole stood up and followed the elderly woman to the living room. "I'm sorry. I didn't mean to overstay my welcome."

"Did I say you did?"

"No, ma'am."

"You have been good for Tasi."

"She's been good for me. Mrs. Varnavsky, may I ask you a question?"

Mrs. Varnavsky took to her chair. "Sit down. You are making me nervous."

Nicole did as instructed. "Do you think it's wrong to adopt a child if you've been seriously ill and there's a chance that you might be ill again?"

Mrs. Varnavsky was thoughtful. "There are no guarantees for any child."

"It's one thing when you don't know. It's another when you do."

She leaned forward. "Do you know, Nicole?"

"Beth and I talked to a lawyer who specializes in family law. It won't be easy for us to adopt. I can understand why the process is so difficult." Nicole glanced toward Tasi's bedroom. "If Tasi or Tess's children needed a home, I would want every assurance that they would be well taken care of."

Seeing Nicole's sadness, Mrs. Varnavsky offered the young woman she had grown to respect a modicum of hope. "I think if you really want a child, you would not let others discourage you."

Nicole purposely gave Tasi's grandmother access to her troubled soul. "It's hard to know what's the right thing to do. It's hard when your heart tells you one thing and everything you know about the world tells you something completely different."

"I think that is why God gave us a heart. That is why we speak of brave hearts. Such hearts change the world. Sometimes in very small ways. Sometimes in very grand, unimaginable ways."

Nicole humbly assessed herself. "I've never considered myself a brave heart."

"If you ask Tasi, she would say differently."

Nicole smiled gratefully. "I can't measure my fitness to be a parent by Tasi. I'm not her mother. I haven't taken on that responsibility."

"No, you have not," Mrs. Varnavsky confirmed. "That was not our agreement."

"Tasi hasn't met Beth. If I lost Beth … Tasi wouldn't be affected."

"You are wrong. She would see your hurt and feel for you just as I would."

"Sometimes our losses are not as unexpected as we lead others to believe," Nicole said in a hush. "If I'm honest with myself … my relationship with Beth is very fragile."

Mrs. Varnavsky listened closely. "Nicole, will you do me a favor?" she asked sympathetically.

Nicole wished to please. "If I can."

Mrs. Varnavsky reached out and took her hand. "Call me Yeva."

CHAPTER 134

July 2003

Nicole sat on the bench with her legs nestled under her body. Jacob sat beside her, keeping the distance between them minimal. He placed his hand on her knee.

Nicole turned her gaze to the gentle man. With caring eyes, he waited for her patiently. She answered the unspoken inquiry. "I met a little girl. Her name is Nastasia. She's seven years old. I've been spending my Tuesday evenings with her and her grandmother, Yeva. They live across from the new development. I want to arrange for them to have an apartment at The Standard. I'm sure they will qualify for the low-income housing program."

Jacob gave his blessing. "That would be a good thing for you to do."

"Beth doesn't know much about Tasi or Yeva." Nicole drew a clear line for Jacob, preempting any assumption that her partner shared her commitment to the Varnavsky's. "Jacob, even though I've had Dion in my life since the day she was born, we don't see each other that often. Having a child in my life like Tasi is new to me."

"Are you worried?" Not receiving an answer, Jacob tried to quell his ward's misgivings. "Nicole, you are good with children. It is adults you have no patience for."

"I wish I could show Tasi The Fields." Nicole mused. "It's not a place for a little girl."

"And why not?" Jacob challenged. "Invite her and her grandmother to brunch."

Nicole considered. Having Jacob's approval, she gingerly called forth into her mind's eye the image of sharing a meal in The Garden with those she loved. "Would you and Liza join us?"

CHAPTER 135

July 2003

The following Sunday Beth accompanied Rachel to Rachel's church, St. Chrysostom's, for the 10:00 a.m. service. Rachel was the consummate host during the after-service coffee reception. She introduced Beth to many of the parishioners, never leaving her side. Beth enjoyed the anonymity that came with worshiping where her ecclesiastical history was unknown. To those she met, she was simply a friend of Rachel's, a student at the University. Time passed too quickly during this particular morning. Beth regretted leaving. She announced her intentions during a lull in the conversation. "Rach, it's getting late."

"Let me buy you lunch," said Rachel.

Beth was expected elsewhere. "I should go."

"You don't want to." Rachel stepped closer, establishing an intimate space shared only by the two. She whispered, "I can tell."

Beth raised her hand to touch Rachel. She arrested the motion. "Nicki is hosting a lunch with her friends."

"Can't be any fun spending time with people you have nothing in common with."

Those people were Jacob and Liza. Nicole was introducing them to Mrs. Varnavsky and Tasi. Beth contended with her competing interests.

"Beth." Rachel took her companion's hand. She spoke with unassailable confidence. "You want to be with me."

Beth acknowledged the inevitable compromises required of a life bound to another. "I can't always have what I want."

Rachel was unwavering. "Today you can. Just say yes to me and no to Nicole."

Beth and Rachel lunched at a small Indian restaurant located a fifteen-minute walk from the church. After the initial strain caused by Rachel's invitation and Beth's hesitant acceptance, they slipped into an amicable conversation. Rachel exiled the subjects of Nicole and fidelity to the nether lands of her conscious as she did her best to earn Beth's affections.

Sitting across the restaurant table from Rachel, Beth felt Nicole's presence. Her partner would have liked the restaurant and the quirky waiter that attended them. She would have liked the walk through the neighborhood.

Beth juxtaposed Rachel to Nicole. She considered Rachel a very attractive woman. And yet, what drew her to Rachel was Rachel's obvious infatuation. Beth was flattered. She had never seriously dated anyone, including Nicole. Her relationship with Nicole was borne from a friendship in crisis.

Rachel's attentiveness also carried Beth away from the harsher facts of her life – none harsher than the truth she associated with Tasi. Meeting Tasi meant facing the child that Nicole was growing to love unconditionally. Tasi had displaced the dream of having a child of their own. If it were not for Tasi, Beth felt she might have a chance of convincing Nicole, in spite of the risks and costs, to immediately pursue adoption. Nicole wanted Beth to meet Tasi. She wanted to close the circle, creating what Beth felt to be nothing more than an artificial family, a poor substitute to a greater grace. She wanted no part of the child and the end to a dream that she represented.

As they walked back to her car, Beth could see St. Chrysostom in the distance. She recalled sharing with Nicole its namesake's belief that the marriage bed was a path to understanding one's union with God. She focused on the cross perched on top of the church. The cross presented a challenge to bear her truth bravely, to bow her head before God in obedience, not to deflect responsibility. Beth felt a surging shame. She had blamed a child for her own childlessness. She had begrudged Nicole for taking a vulnerable little girl into her heart. She had refused to heed Nicole's argument.

Nicole had argued a cautious vision that promised an honorable approach toward their destined parenthood. Nicole had not denied their dream. She had suggested a pause, a wait to ensure their respective health, to wait four more years, not two. They would proceed with an aggressive adoption only after they both were five years free of disease. Nicole had promised she would not allow the expense to prevent them from adopting a baby. It was not the money. It was the need to ensure that their child would have a future with two parents. She wanted their child to know the life Dion and Jack shared with Tess and Bruce. She did not want their child to live with the bone-deep loneliness she saw in Tasi. Characteristically, Nicole's arguments were reasoned and brutally honest.

Beth knew that even with a four-year wait and Nicole's financial resources; their ability to adopt was questionable. She rued that it was always easier to blame Nicole than the ineffable first cause. She owed Nicole an apology.

"Beth, everything all right?" Rachel's query interrupted Beth's reverie. She buried her hands in her jacket pockets, knowingly mimicking her partner's self-protective habit. It was Nicole's hand, not Rachel's that she wished held hers. "Just thinking."

"Want to share?"

"It's just hard sometimes to figure out why life is what it is."

Rachel kept to an insouciant manner. "No offense, but with the life you've had I thought you already knew that."

"Sometimes I need to be reminded."

Rachel paused, taking Beth by the arm. "If you insist. I'm here to remind you that we owe it to ourselves to find happiness wherever we can. Life isn't always as dignified as we wish it were. Sometimes we have to do things that go against our higher virtues. Beth, I haven't been shy about my feelings for you …"

"Rach. Don't." Beth pulled away.

Rachel continued her campaign. "Beth, first loves are not always meant to be lasting. Most aren't. They're meant to get you started in the right direction. Believe me, I'm grateful Nicole entered your life. If she hadn't I wouldn't be standing here with you now. I just don't believe she can give you what you need and want. I don't think she has for quite some time."

Beth defended her partner, feeling a rising regret, knowing that Rachel's impressions were based on the dark canvas she had painted. "It isn't because she hasn't tried."

Rachel altered her bearing to a tender regard, presenting a passiveness that instinctually drew Beth's compassion. She quieted her voice. "Doesn't that prove my point? With me you can have a life that isn't split in two. We can be together both here in the world and there," she said, gesturing toward St. Chrysostom, "in the Church. Beth, I'm asking you to give me a chance to prove to you that you can be happy with me." Rachel leaned down and gently kissed Beth, gathering confidence when Beth did not push her away.

For a moment, Beth forgot everything outside the immediate moment. She had wondered what it would feel like to kiss Rachel, and now she was. Rachel offered an enticing gentleness that quickly grew in fervor. Rachel coaxed Beth's mouth open, jarring Beth away from the vague, insubstantial yearning of an isolated heart to the cold hard consequences of what she was inviting by her indiscriminate behavior. She stepped back abruptly. "No."

Rachel stepped forward, unwilling to surrender their engagement. "Beth."

"No, Rachel!" A rarely seen anger took full possession of the younger woman.

Denied, Rachel retaliated. "Are you angry at me or at yourself?"

The question had merit. "I'm going home." Beth continued to walk towards her car.

Rachel acted quickly, jogging after Beth, catching her as she was opening her car door. Rachel took hold of the door. "Beth, I'm sorry. Look. Take as much time as you need. I'm willing to wait."

"For what, Rachel?" Beth damned the moment. No one was to blame more than her. "I'm in a committed relationship. Just because Nicki and I aren't legally married doesn't make my vow to her any less sacred."

"Are you sure?"

"Yes!" Beth was weary of defending her relationship.

"Okay … okay …" Rachel recovered her tactful nature. "Beth, we can still be friends. I gave it my best shot. I needed to try. Please understand, I couldn't live with myself if I hadn't."

Beth dismissed Rachel's apology. There was a poverty of sincerity between them. They were conspiring thieves in the midst of an act of larceny, one penitent, the other defiant. "All right."

Rachel sighed. "Are we still on for Tuesday dinner?"

Beth hurriedly accommodated Rachel's request. "I'll see you then."

Nicole drove back to The Fields after delivering Tasi and Yeva to their apartment. She was not ready to return to Hyde Park.

To her relief, Yeva had approved of The Fields. Connor and Miguel had been attentive gentlemen. In spite of Jacob insisting on telling a few stories of Nicole's brash childhood, he and Liza were the best references she could have hoped for. In turn, Tasi had charmed the Levis and The Fields' employees with her youthful jubilance.

Nicole's guests had briefly remarked upon Beth's absence. Though Beth had given no reason when she spoke to Connor, the consensus was that church or hospital business had kept her away. Only Nicole knew that Beth had spent the morning with Rachel at St. Chrysostom's and that she was not on-call at the hospital.

The fact that Beth had chosen not to call her was the latest sign of their troubled relationship. Beth had changed. Nicole attributed the cause to Beth's time spent in Minnesota and their subsequent adoption inquiry. She reluctantly acknowledged that Rachel was a force to be reckoned with. The more time Beth spent with Rachel, the less effort Beth made to address their growing estrangement. As June drifted into July, the couple had become no more than strangers living under the same roof. Beth kept her distance. Their bed had become a cold place, lacking the tender union that had always helped the two women transcend their differences.

Beth's cross-town drive concluded at The Fields. The Sunday brunch crowd filled The Pub. From behind the bar Connor called out to her as she crossed the room. "Hi, Irish."

Beth was subdued. "Is Nicki here?"

Connor prepared a Bloody Mary with an expert's negligent ease. "Are you going to liberate her?"

"From what?"

"Don't know. Her door is closed. It's becoming a new habit. I thought you might enlighten me."

"Sorry." Beth could guess the reason, and regretted her role as a contributing cause. "You haven't checked in on her?"

"I know better."

Beth contemplated the uninviting private staircase.

"You have always been the exception."

Beth walked up the stairs and knocked lightly before opening the door office. She found Nicole sitting on the floor, leaning against the couch, a book in her hand. "Hi."

Nicole looked up. Seeing Beth left her disconcerted. "Hello."

"You're not answering your cell phone."

"I turned it off. I figured you'd call Connor if you needed to get word to me."

Beth closed the door. She deserved Nicole's reproof. She approached and knelt beside Nicole. "May I?" Beth reached out and turned her partner's hand to better read the title of the book: *A Confession and other Religious Writings* by Leo Tolstoy. "I haven't read this. Is it good?"

"Too early to tell."

"We haven't talked books lately."

Nicole cited an often thought justification of minimal consolation. "I figured with school and your friends you get plenty of conversation."

"Not with your perspective." Beth acknowledged the obvious difference yet, in her assessment, parity between Nicole and her student peers.

"We always end up arguing," said Nicole with listless resignation.

In the light of an encroaching loss, Beth's determination resettled over the uncertain terrain. She would reclaim Nicole. They would prevail over the apparent hardships suffered in their relationship. Theirs was a bond not of bold but of nuanced giving and receiving. Simple conciliatory gestures marked their commitment to one another. Such gestures had the power to heal, to vanquish their terrible insecurities. "I know it's a couple months off, but we have a guest scholar next school year. He is a religious progressive. I think you might like him. In late August he's giving a lecture based on his book. There'll be a reception afterwards."

"Beth." Nicole was in no mood to pretend to feign an accord or to be held to a promise she had no intention of keeping. "U.C. is your place, not mine."

Beth fought calmly for a reconciliation. "You used to want to come with me."

Nicole was not immune to Beth's solicitude. She missed her lover's kindness. "What's the book about?"

"Religion in a post-modern world."

Nicole waved her book slightly. "He couldn't write about Tolstoy or Hume?"

Beth smiled knowingly. "Something closer to the Stoics?"

"Anyone who doesn't propose to know the truth with a capital 'T'."

"I don't think he talks about truth with a capital 'T'. That's why you might like him."

Nicole would not discount the scholar without a fair hearing. "What's his name?"

"Lawrence Elliott."

"Let me know when and I'll put it on my calendar."

Sensing Nicole's warming receptivity Beth placed her hand gently over her partner's. "Connor mentioned that you've been closing the door up here more often."

Nicole glanced toward the office entrance. "I guess I have."

"Are you stepping away from the world for a while?"

Nicole's words came thoughtfully. "I've never felt the world more."

Beth heard the acute fatigue that had taken residence in Nicole's voice. "Haven't you?"

Nicole cast her eyes down. She focused on Beth's hand. Nicole placed her thumb over Beth's gold band. She spoke in a fragile whisper. "Elizabeth."

Beth heard her formal name so rarely that when spoken she could not help but feel jarred away from the familiar. When Nicole spoke her name complete it meant one of two things – either Nicole was playfully chastising her, or Nicole was renewing her vow. When the latter, Beth knew that Nicole had reached a place where language failed her. She could do nothing but revert to the code they had built between them in the course of their relationship. "Nicki, I'm sorry."

Nicole looked up. There was no need for elaboration. She was certain, by Beth's remorseful countenance, that they understood each other. "Why?"

Beth spoke a private truth. "I needed to be somewhere else."

Nicole swallowed her first response. She needed Beth. She lied, "I understand." She then spoke truthfully. "You were missed."

Beth was grateful for the implied pardon. "So, how did the lunch go?"

"A good time was had by all." Nicole smiled. "Liza and Yeva hit it off. Jacob was Jacob. And Tasi said Miguel's strawberry pancakes were the best she ever had."

"Did you get Yeva's stamp of approval?"

"I think so."

"I'm glad." Nicole's glistening crystalline eyes drew Beth to close the distance between them. She leaned forward and tenderly kissed Nicole. Their kiss displaced the morning memory of Rachel. There was no comparison. The poor substitute had no station in Beth's life when set beside the authentic. "What am I tasting?"

"Chicken livers." Nicole quipped as she felt happiness edge near.

"Oh no, there's something sweet on the tip of my tongue."

"I shared some of Tasi's pancakes."

"That's it." Beth returned to Nicole, capturing her lips in a longer, deeper kiss. Separating, a breathless Beth shifted her body over Nicole's lap. "Nicole Isabel Thera, I love you."

CHAPTER 136

July 2003

Nicole waited on the bench outside The Fields. Jacob and Liza turned the street corner. Nicole stood up. Liza tugged on Jacob's sleeve. The elderly couple stopped.

Nicole crossed the street and took Jacob in an embrace.

The unexpected gesture was cause for concern. "My girl, is everything all right?"

"Yes Jacob, everything is fine." Nicole released him and kissed Liza on the cheek. "Good morning."

"Good morning." The matron smiled.

"I need a favor."

"And what might that be?" asked Jacob.

"With Tasi in my life I want to learn more about what it means to be a Jew. How it touches your daily lives. Books can only take me so far. I can't think of two better teachers."

Liza spoke for the two. "Of course, child. We would be happy to help." She turned to her husband. "Won't we, Jacob?"

Jacob stood quietly. Nicole turned to him deferentially. "You have my word that I will be respectful of your traditions."

"Why would we worry?" asked Liza. "You have shared many Shabbat meals with us and you have never misbehaved."

Again, Nicole turned to Jacob. "Jacob, is it all right?"

"Yes Nicole, it is a good thing," said Jacob.

Nicole's smile returned. "Thank you."

Jacob struggled to maintain an unaffected composure. "I have a few early appointments. Let us talk this afternoon."

"Good." Nicole kissed him on the cheek. "I love you." She looked over to Liza. "I love you, both."

"Go on before you make Liza cry," Jacob admonished.

"Yes sir." Nicole placed her hands in her pockets and twirled around as she happily returned to The Fields.

CHAPTER 137

August 2003

Nicole and Tess sat side-by-side, watching Dion and Jack playing in a park sandbox. Tess took hold of Nicole's arm. "Finally, I have you all to myself. It's not good when a mother is jealous of her daughter."

"For shame," Nicole playfully admonished.

"I know. Especially when loving you is something we have in common. I can't help thinking you came here to spend time with the kids."

"Don't I always?" Nicole's gaze fell gently on the children. "They're growing up so fast. I love watching Jack with Bruce."

"Two peas in a pod," Tess agreed with undisguised pride. She then spoke of her daughter with a hint of exasperation. "Dion, on the other hand, can be such an independent cuss. I think it's her godmother's influence."

Nicole visibly pouted in response to the critique.

Tess chuckled. She pointed to her daughter. "Look at her, Nicki. There she is in that sandbox digging away. Jack is happy with his little shovel. He gets under the surface, but only so far. Dion is like you. She keeps digging. If she had a bulldozer she'd use it. She's never satisfied. If it's hidden out of sight, she'll work to uncover it. Most people are like Jack. You and my beautiful daughter are the rare fearless type. Uncovering the truth is worth the effort no matter how painful."

"And you, my friend, are not shy in asking what truth I've uncovered."

Tess continued, "I can't ignore the obvious. You haven't mentioned Beth since you arrived."

"When she's not working at the hospital, she's researching her dissertation at the University."

"I thought Beth wanted to take advantage of her summer break and spend more time with you."

"It hasn't happened."

"Why didn't she come with you?"

"Dion's birthday came at a convenient time. I had reason to be here while she stayed at Hyde Park and made an appearance at the annual University picnic."

"A picnic that partners are invited to?"

"She's more comfortable going without me."

"She said that?" Tess was indignant for her friend's sake.

Nicole had readily excused herself from the event. "She doesn't have to. After a year it's obvious. Like you said Tess, I'm not one to run away from the truth. Being at the University has brought to the forefront the part of Beth that needs acceptance and approval. Right now she needs her professors to approve of her and her work."

"And of you?"

"Yes. And that doesn't come easily."

"She's always been proud of you."

"When we're at The Fields or with friends outside of her religious establishment. Tess, she honestly doesn't see this side of herself."

"Call her on it."

"What do I say to her?" Nicole's voice rose, and then ebbed. "If I can have my friends, why can't she have hers?"

"Last time I looked none of us made Beth unwelcome."

"I'll bide my time."

"Nicki, we've talked about this. How long can you hold on? You have to be practical. Even on a fast track, Beth has at least three more years before she graduates."

"It's been a tough summer. I feel like I've been riding a roller coaster," said Nicole gravely. "After your last visit we got better for a little while and then the Robinson controversy shifted Beth's mood all over again." Nicole referred to Reverend V. Gene Robinson, an openly gay man, in a committed relationship with his partner Mark Andrew. Reverend Robinson had been selected to serve as bishop of the diocese of New Hampshire. The international uproar triggered by the United States Episcopal Church's General Convention's ratification of his appointment caused the Archbishop of Canterbury to call a summit of world Anglican Church leaders in the hopes of avoiding a split within the Church.

Tess had followed the controversy with interest. "Beth was always on my mind when I was reading about the schism. How does she feel about it?"

"How do you think she feels about it? She left the Church before she came to me in Boston. At the time she didn't know if I wanted her in my life."

"Do you think she would have gone back to the Church if you had said no?"

Nicole understood that Beth's actions hinged on her perceived obligation to God to be truthful, never more so than when in distress. "Beth said she couldn't have gone back. She couldn't break her vows. She couldn't live a dishonest life."

"Robinson did."

Nicole was no fan of Reverend Robinson. "Makes me wonder how he can preach integrity and truth. I don't see his breach with the Church as being any different than a Catholic priest that marries or has a sexual relationship on the side. Neither situation has anything to do with heterosexuality or homosexual-ity. The Church they've given their vow to demands certain behavior. If they take the vow, they have given conscious assent to the doctrine of the Church. No one forced them to join the Church, let alone become ordained."

Tess's assessment was not as concrete. "Liberal church and gay rights groups disagree."

"They have an agenda and this is one time they're reframing the issue to serve their own purposes. I don't like it when the religious right plays the political game. And I really don't like it when the liberal left falls down to the lowest moral common denominator in response."

"So Beth feels Robinson is wrong."

"She said she and Robinson obviously understood their vows differently. He can turn the Episcopal Church upside down on its head and she still won't judge him. She said Robinson is answerable to God, not her. I don't think she's been able to reconcile herself to the fact that she left the Church while Robinson has stayed on, as a Bishop no less."

"Nicki, there's one thing I've never understood. Why did Beth enter the Church in the first place?"

In many ways, Nicole thought Beth's choice had reflected a conscious annulling of what, to others, could have been natural alternatives. The Church offered the spiritual context to give and more importantly, Nicole assessed, to receive. The Church as a path to God promised Beth unconditional love if only she opened her heart to the divine. In the most intimate crevice of her soul, Beth did not brave the world well. She had lost love: her mother's and grandmother's to death, her father's to grief and only recently, after years of estrangement, had she come to once again know her sister's love. With the undeniable evidence of cancer's presence in her preceding generations, she also believed she was granted a limited time on earth. That Beth loved Nicole was a remarkable feat of faith. Nicole tried not to lose sight of Beth's journey and how that journey touched both their lives. "I think she never expected to fall in love. I know she believed she was destined to die young."

"So she's finding out how complicated life can be when you don't live with one foot already in the grave."

"More complicated than you know. We probably won't be adopting a child."

Tess stilled for a heartbeat. Her gaze traveled from Nicole to her children, and back to Nicole. Her voice carried a heartbreaking ache. "Why not?"

In contrast to Tess, Nicole kept a cool mien. "Our health issues make us high risk parents."

"When did this come up?"

"Right after Beth came back from Minnesota. It's going to take time for her to accept the fact that she won't have a little girl of her own."

"There's nothing Kate and the other lawyers can do?"

"There is. I'm not sure I want to bend the law just shy of breaking."

"Nicki, I know you. I listened to you and Kate arguing all through grad school. You'll take justice over the law. Respect for the law isn't stopping you. The truth, Nicki," Tess demanded.

"What happens if one or both of us gets sick again?" Nicole neared a precipice.

Tess's skepticism was keen. "Bruce and I will raise your child like our own daughter."

Nicole debated whether to end the conversation and save herself from a freefall. If only she could lighten the burden of her isolation. To do so, she needed to confess. "I'm not sure Beth and I have a future ... together."

"Sweetheart ..."

Nicole could not check her tears. "I love her, Tess. It's just not enough. It doesn't matter how hard I try. I can't make us work."

CHAPTER 138

August 29, 2003 – Friday

Lawrence Elliott's lecture and subsequent reception was well attended. Nicole recognized many of those present: professors and students with their respective partners, as well as city church leaders from a cross-section of denominations. Nicole went to the serving table to retrieve a glass of wine for Beth. Rachel approached, her wineglass not yet half empty. "Nicole, I haven't seen you at one of these for some time now."

Nicole did her best to be congenial. "Beth guaranteed that I would like Lawrence."

"Did you?" Rachel asked in a patronizing tone.

Nicole would not be condescended to. "I'm glad I came, if that's what you're asking me."

"He's passionate about religion." Rachel sipped her wine. "Is that what you find attractive? I know Beth can be very passionate."

Nicole was wary. She remained silent.

Rachel traced the rim of her wineglass with the tip of her finger. "The last time I was in your apartment Beth told me that Hyde Park is very different from the loft you had at the Elysian Fields. I don't know how you could do better than the bedroom you have now."

Nicole clenched her jaw as she considered a response. "Rachel, be careful. You don't know who you're dealing with."

Rachel's belligerence stepped out from the shelter of social decorum, her parlor antics dismissed by Nicole's straightforwardness. "Am I supposed to be intimidated? Nicole, don't flatter yourself."

"I wasn't talking about me." Nicole had had enough of the woman. She stepped away and delivered the refreshed wineglass into Beth's grateful hands. After a few minutes, Nicole discreetly excused herself from the small clutch of friends. She sought refuge through a pair of French doors leading to an open balcony. Standing outside, underneath the stars, alone with her thoughts, she focused on reining in her anger, setting Rachel's dirty insinuations aside.

"Ah, this is better." Lawrence Elliott stepped onto the balcony. He smiled. "Gets hard to breathe in there after a while."

Nicole recognized Lawrence with a nod.

Lawrence stood a couple of inches shorter than Nicole. He was dressed in a rich, blue, linen blazer, a white shirt open at the neck and freshly pressed black slacks. His hair, a blend of brown, red and gray, and his equally colorful beard had been recently trimmed. His eyes were bright brown. He fit the model of a casual professor. Lawrence reached into the inside pocket of his blazer and retrieved a pack of cigarettes. He removed a cigarette and held it in one hand as he searched for his lighter in an exterior blazer pocket. The upside-down pack of cigarettes threatened to spill its contents. He caught this error in time and placed the pack back in its original position. The motions were awkward, whether caused by a natural clumsiness or nervousness, Nicole could not tell.

"Says something about me that I come out here for fresh air and then take one of these out." He raised the cigarette. "Do you mind?"

Nicole returned his courtesy in kind. "No problem."

Lawrence nodded in the direction of the reception. "Rather an exclusive crowd." With sincere modesty, he measured himself against his colleagues. "I'll always be a professor from a small, less prestigious college. Makes it hard to walk onto a campus like this."

"Even if you are the guest of honor?" Nicole ventured.

"Especially when I am the guest of honor. There is always one half-wit wanting to flaunt their intellectual calisthenics at my expense."

Nicole knew the feeling well. Her sympathy went only so far. "Isn't that the price you pay as an author? By definition the text is recreated at every reading."

"Yes." Lawrence seemed to welcome the candid challenge. "But that doesn't mean an engagement should be without civility."

"Civility," Nicole echoed. "Around here, that can seem like the Holy Grail."

Lawrence lit his cigarette. "I noticed you were quiet."

"I'm not one of them." Nicole tried to preempt any assumptions he might form because of her presence. "My partner is a doctoral student."

Lawrence cocked his head. "Which one?"

"Elizabeth Kelly."

"Beth?"

"Yes."

Lawrence smiled. "I like her."

Nicole mirrored his smile. "So do I."

"You must if you're willing to put up with the bombast." Lawrence raised his cigarette to his mouth and inhaled deeply. "So, you had no interest in my lecture?"

"Actually, I did," Nicole corrected affably. "No offense, but I'm feeling a bit overexposed to Christianity."

"Oh." Unflappable, Lawrence observed with an amused glint in his eye, "You really aren't one of us."

"Ask just about anyone in the room and they will freely comment on my solipsism."

"That doesn't sound so bad to me. You still leave room for revelation."

"Not if you're a materialist."

"Really?" Lawrence appraised Nicole's open demeanor. "Something about you struck me as more spiritualistic."

"Close. I consider myself a pantheist with the heart of a transcendentalist and the outlook of a pragmatic." Nicole offered Lawrence a devilish grin.

Lawrence laughed. "No wonder they don't know what to do with you."

"They leave me to Beth."

"I admit I'm disappointed. For a moment I was hoping you were Wiccan. That would have really riled a few of my distinguished colleagues."

"You don't seem to take them seriously."

Lawrence sobered. "I take them very seriously. I'm here as proof of their openness to my liberal post-modern bent. I do fear that at their core, many on faculty are conservatives hedging their bets against the inevitable changes in society." He savored the acrid taste of his cigarette and considered Nicole. "I don't sound anymore sincere to you than they do, do I?"

"They're sincere. That's what disturbs me," Nicole confessed. "I'm just glad they stay in their little world. A lot of energy is spent keeping appearances. No real harm done."

"You're wrong. They ... we are not as isolated as you think. We teach the men and women with a religious vocation who go out from academia into the parishes and social justice programs. They preach homilies and sermons, they testify at government hearings, they mobilize people. Don't underestimate how far reaching our theologians can be."

"We have different perspectives." Nicole discounted the self-importance of many religious activists.

Lawrence's quick response betrayed his agitation. "Meaning what?"

Nicole was succinct in demarcating their worldviews. "You're Christian. I'm not."

"But not all Christians are alike," Lawrence protested.

"Variations of a theme, but still the same theme," Nicole insisted.

"Even Beth?"

"Yes."

Lawrence applauded. "Then that makes you all the more remarkable."

Nicole shook her head, deflecting the praise. "No, I'm not."

Having been given insight into Nicole, Lawrence offered his story in recompense. "My ex-wife and I couldn't come to terms. I refused to embrace any specific denomination. She was ... is Lutheran. She held to her dogma as if her life depended on it."

"Maybe it did," Nicole observed, knowing dogma to be the lifeblood of many believers.

"It's that kind of rigidity that is at the root of our social ills."

"No one wants to live in an assault zone all their lives. I appreciate the need to be able to live in peace. Isn't that why people gravitate to certain congregations? To be among like spirits, if only for an hour out of every week. The rest of the time you have to make your way through a minefield of differing ideologies – your post-modern world."

"It's not my post-modern world. Where do you go to be with others that believe like you do?" he asked with unrestrained curiosity.

"I don't."

"Must be lonely."

The personal observation was unexpected. Inexplicably, Nicole felt safe in Lawrence's company. She answered without reservation. "Sometimes it is. I … I'm use to it. To be honest, there is a part of me that wants nothing more than to be left alone."

"And I am interrupting your retreat? I apologize," Lawrence said sincerely.

"Don't. There is another part of me that enjoys a good conversation."

"I'm flattered." Lawrence returned to impersonal ground. "What did you think of my thesis?"

Nicole had given Lawrence's lecture some thought. "I believe that circumstances shape us, but ultimately how we act is a matter of free will. Your soft determinism muddies the waters unnecessarily. It's a philosophy that substitutes God for cause and effect, trying to reason what is ultimately irrational."

Lawrence was completely engaged. "And what do you consider ultimately irrational?"

"The belief that we can know the first cause."

"I would think wanting to know the first cause would be very rational."

"Wanting to know is human," said Nicole, making, what to her, was a critical distinction. "Believing that we can know it is a whole other matter. I used to be a business consultant. I walked into environments where a unique culture had developed during the course of an organization's history. I came with only a cursory knowledge, one that was admittedly tainted by whomever hired and briefed me. It didn't take long for me to identify the underlying beliefs and values that made the place tick and to identify the barriers those beliefs and values raised against a different reality, one not steeped in the past but truer to the present. The organization operated at a mythic level and if you asked how they came to be who they were, they would attempt to explain by retracing their steps, as if logic could lead them to their place of origin. They never reached that place because it did not exist. There was no isolated, finite, exclusive force, no one simple answer. In my experience, there is always the blending of an incalculable number of variables. Members of the organization, those that lived viscerally in the environment and had a stake of making sense of it, sometimes tried to argue a rational formula that would account for each hue in their spectrum. Even if they could achieve some semblance of an explanation, doing so still did not explain the why, the one why. And the truth was that trying to explain it was a fruitless exercise. It's an exercise in vanity no different than much of philosophical and theological exposition."

Lawrence was impressed by the thoroughness of Nicole's observations. "You take no prisoners, do you?"

"Maybe because in my own way I am like them. I'm searching. They just don't see me. They never will see me because I stand on a plane they refuse to acknowledge, let alone explore. They fear that if they do they won't be able to return to their own plane without the possibility that what they bring back with them will cause a tremor that will dislodge their once sure footing."

"A loss of faith due to a resolve you've weakened," said Lawrence.

Nicole refused to accept either the power or the responsibility inferred. "I have done nothing but speak what I believe to be the truth."

"There is nothing more threatening than the truth, especially when it is reflected back to you with sincerity."

"If I'm right that there was a trace of the post-modernist in your speech, then you believe, like I do, that there isn't necessarily one truth."

"One human truth, no. One divine truth, yes."

"That brings us back to where we started," Nicole concluded.

His cigarette burned to the filter, Lawrence studied it, disappointed. "Well, I better get back in there before they send a posse for me. The price of being the guest of honor."

"Being *persona non grata* has its pluses."

"I would never think of you in that way."

"You don't know me." Nicole smiled brightly. "Give me a chance to earn my reputation."

Lawrence laughed.

Beth entered the balcony, relieved to find Nicole in pleasant company. "Hello."

Nicole reached out her hand. Beth accepted the unspoken invitation.

Lawrence turned to his first companion. "I am at a disadvantage. I don't know your name."

Nicole was happy to oblige. "Nicole Thera."

Lawrence addressed Beth. "I have been enjoying Nicole's insightful critique of my soft determinism."

"Have you?" Beth glanced up to her lover.

Lawrence continued to linger. "Nicole, you said you were a business consultant. What do you do now that you are not in that profession?"

"I'm an entrepreneur."

"You are well versed in philosophy."

"I did my undergraduate studies in Classical humanities and philosophy."

"I teach undergraduates. Not one of them could conceive of a pragmatic transcendentalist pantheist."

"I read," Nicole deadpanned.

"Undoubtedly." Lawrence directed himself to Beth. "I would imagine having a partner with a similar interest is an advantage."

Witnessing Lawrence's appreciation of her partner, Beth followed their conversation with pleasure. "Similar interest? Yes. Similar beliefs is something I wouldn't know about."

Lawrence extended his hand. "I hope to see you again, Nicole."

Nicole accepted Lawrence's hand in a firm handshake. "Beth has a habit of bringing me along to these things."

"Good. Call me Larry. I reserve Lawrence for those who run in my profession's pretentious circle. You are obviously not one of them." Larry turned to Beth. "Goodnight, Beth. I'll see you in class."

Beth waited until Larry was out of sight. "I came to see if you were all right."

Nicole found herself to be in an excellent mood. "I'm good."

"You like it better out here."

"It can get claustrophobic in there."

"I'd like to think you were having a good time."

"I liked Larry. That counts for something," Nicole said good naturedly.

"It's a first." Beth's words were far more tart than she intended.

Nicole was jolted by Beth's critical tone. She released her partner's hand. "Don't you think you're being a little bit unfair?"

More than one voice asking Nicole's whereabouts resounded in Beth's inner ear. "No, I'm not. I really wish you would give my friends a chance."

"I have. It's been a year, Beth. I realize not all your friends are going to be like Cindy and Pam. I'm all right with that."

"So it's their fault?" Beth's tone conveyed her frustration.

"We're different. We haven't found a common ground. Maybe it's because Cindy and Pam are out in the real world and not in this insulated environment."

Beth countered defensively, "Now you're the one who is being unfair. Many of the people in that room have active ministries. You know Rachel works for a woman's shelter."

Mention of Rachel left Nicole cold. "I don't embrace others as easily as you do."

"What does that mean?" Beth felt her judgment was being assailed.

"It means that I haven't had the same experience with your school friends as I've had with Cindy and Pam. When you got sick they proved to me that they not only cared about you, they cared about me."

"Who do you think I've relied on for support during my first year here? Don't they get credit for that or do I have to be dying before the help I get counts for anything?"

Nicole's thoughts were arrested by the allusion to Beth's death. She had no tolerance for the all-too-real possibility. Their argument carried no merit in comparison. Her resolve collapsed. "You're right. You're in the best position to judge."

Nicole's shift took Beth by surprise. She studied her, at times, obstinate partner, trying to understand what had caused the abrupt change. Confused, she quietly asked, "Are you going inside?"

"Give me a few minutes," Nicole begged dully.

Beth felt something grievously wrong had just happened. "Nicki …"

"Beth, I'm a grown-up. I can take care of myself." Nicole dismissed her partner. "Go be with your friends."

CHAPTER 139

August 31, 2003 – Sunday

Nicole was asleep on the couch in her Fields office. Her desk lamp and a side lamp lit the room. A bottle of Jack Daniels and a shot glass rested on the coffee table. She had taken both from the bar hours before. A light knocking at the door awakened her. She glanced at a nearby table clock. It was past closing. She chose to ignore whoever was at the door. She closed her eyes. She then heard the door open and someone approach. After a moment Nicole opened her eyes to Connor. He was crouching down by the coffee table. He held the shot glass and sniffed it. She knew it carried no scent of alcohol.

Connor teetered the glass. "Not a drop."

Nicole closed her eyes again and shook her head slightly. "No."

"Call Beth." Connor's voice carried through the darkness.

Nicole opened her eyes again, focusing on Beth's self-appointed guardian angel. "And say what?"

"That you've come close to this." He tapped the bottle's pouring spout with the glass.

"We've never talked about it."

"You're kidding?"

"No." Nicole sat up. "Beth just takes it for granted that I don't drink."

Connor was incredulous. "She never asked why?"

"No."

"Christ, Nicki."

"What? It's not as if I'm a recovering alcoholic. I just don't drink."

Connor leaned back bracing himself with the flat of his hand as he sat down. "Don't you think the reasons are important?"

"Beth is insightful enough to figure it out."

"Did you ever consider that she might get it wrong or at least that she might not get all of it right?"

What Connor did not realize was that Nicole allowed him to erroneously believe he knew why she had stopped drinking. The real reason was one she did not want to share with him or Beth. "She could ask me if she really wanted to know."

"Why is it so hard for you to admit that you don't drink because you're scared."

Only touching the edge of truth, Nicole responded with practiced ease. "It's not hard to admit. It's who I am. It's what I do ... or don't do."

Connor pressed. "Why did you take the bottle?"

Nicole turned her gaze toward the bottle in question, studying anew its familiar contours, and the label that dressed it. "I stared at the damn thing for a good hour. Something to think about."

"Instead of what?"

"What I was feeling before I picked it up. It could make the feeling go away."

"You know better than that."

"I didn't say forever." Nicole leaned back against the couch. "Just for a couple of hours. False courage."

"Courage to do what?"

Nicole did not answer.

Connor yielded to her silence and changed the subject. "Why is Kate angry at you?"

Nicole had no incentive to equivocate. Sooner or later Connor would pry the truth from Kate. "Beth and I met with her and a Family Law attorney a while back. Because of our medical histories adopting is a long shot, at best."

"Nicki, I'm sorry." After a few moments thought, Connor asked, "Why would Kate be angry? As much as she had her heart set on being a godmother ... "

"Godmother?" Nicole interrupted.

"You're Dion's," Connor stated as ample argument.

"That assumes a baptism."

"So?"

"Dion is not my child. The decision was Tess's."

Nicole's intimation seemed to trouble Connor. "You wouldn't have baptized your child?"

"Beth and I haven't spoken about it," Nicole admitted.

"Do you really believe Beth wouldn't have wanted the baby baptized?"

"I have no doubt she would have." Nicole stood up. "It doesn't matter. The issue is moot."

Connor followed Nicole with his gaze. "You still haven't told me why Kate is angry."

"I could try to circumvent the adoption system."

"You won't?"

"No, I won't." Nicole braced herself for another bevy of criticism.

"Why not?"

Disappointed to have her expectations so quickly realized, her retort was sharp. "Not you, too?"

"Hey, ease up." Connor tried to calm Nicole's edgy temper. "I'm just trying to understand. I know you. It isn't the money."

"I'd sell The Fields to have a baby." Nicole sighed. "I think Beth and I should wait another four years."

Connor clearly weighed the importance of the number in his mind. "Beth's cancer?"

"Yeah." Nicole allowed another partial truth.

"What does she say?"

"She isn't saying much of anything to me right now."

"Where is she tonight?"

"By now, home. She spent the evening with her friend Rachel. She didn't miss me." Nicole turned her gaze toward the windows. She wondered if Beth was sleeping in their bed or waiting up for her. Given the time, she thought the former.

Connor tried for a pleasant turn to their conversation. "Changing the subject, how's Tasi?"

"Good." Nicole smiled.

"When will I get to see her again?"

"Gee, Con," Nicole jibed, "I didn't realize you had a soft spot for little girls."

"I don't. I just like seeing what she does to you."

"And what's that?"

Connor took pleasure in the telling. "You are the gentlest woman I know when you're with children. You also let the little kid in you come out and I'd like to see more of that."

Nicole was too tired to censure her response. "My relationship with Tasi isn't universally endearing."

"Has Tasi anything to do with what's going on?"

"To Beth, Tasi is just a kid hanging around the development."

"Even I know better than that."

"I've stopped trying to introduce Beth to Tasi and Yeva. I don't need to complicate my life any more than it already is."

"It's not like you're having a clandestine affair."

Nicole quieted. An impenetrable curtain fell behind her eyes as Connor's attempt at humor was painfully received. She continued to hope there was no ground for a charge of infidelity.

In response to Nicole's silence Connor gallantly tried to extricate both of them from the conversation. "Hey, I'm hungry. Want to raid the kitchen with me? We can reorganize the freezer."

Nicole smiled as she remembered a time early in The Garden's history when she had stood in the corner of the kitchen watching Miguel blow-drying dozens of frozen eggs before the Sunday brunch crowd arrived. "Lead on."

CHAPTER 140

September 23, 2003 – Tuesday

Larry Elliot knocked at Beth's open office door. "May I come in?"

Grading student papers, Beth welcomed the interruption. "Of course."

"I need a break from my over-zealous students." Larry sat down across from Beth's desk. "You, of course, are not one of them."

Beth knew Larry well enough to know that his sometimes nipping remarks were directed with clear, purposeful intention. She braced herself. Her warmth slipped away, displaced by a guarded mien.

"You may not have yet noticed, but I loathe unrealized potential in my classroom. I must say, Beth, you are not who I expected. The other professors who have worked with you led me to believe that I would find a much more engaged student than I have had in my class. Have I said or done anything to make you hesitate to speak up?"

Larry's conciliatory question brought no comfort. Beth kept to her reserve. "No, not at all. I just haven't had anything to add to the conversation."

"I find that hard to believe. Your eyes say a great deal."

"Some of the other students are so sure."

"Not all."

"Not when you're done with them, no," said Beth. Larry's Socratic style of teaching, coupled with his wit, left more than one seminar student in a state of total perplexity by class end. A few had responded unwisely, with undisguised rancor. Such a response had only proved his point; they were poor candidates to function in a post-modern world. Not one to pander to his students' self-drawn aspirations of sublimity, he hit them harder with his questions, pushing them to and beyond their limits. To date, Beth had been spared.

Larry laughed. "I find it amusing that even advanced students struggle with the most fundamental questions. What is religion? Does religion have a place in the contemporary world? Is secularism a natural progression, the evolution from superstition to rational thought?" A self-satisfied smile reflected Larry's good humor in the pursuit of truth. "How they bristle when I lump them with the superstitious."

"It's not easy to sit still while your life's vocation is being chopped to cinders."

"Am I doing that?" Larry referred to the spiritual biography assignment completed by all his students. "I was impressed by your reason for study. You

are a practical theologian. It did make me wonder why you are pursuing a
Ph.D. Wouldn't CPE supervision be a closer match?"

"I haven't ruled that out."

"Then why spend five or more years of your life here?"

Beth kept an unfelt calm in her voice. "You don't think I belong in the
Ph.D. program?"

"Doesn't matter what I think. I don't know you. I'm gleaning my observation from your biography and your class participation." He changed tactics,
tapping a very different resource. "What does Nicole think?"

"She's never questioned my desire to go to school."

"Not surprising, given her obvious passion for learning. I can't tell you
how refreshing it was to simply have her tell me that she reads."

Beth smiled, relieved that the subject had shifted away from her. "She had
a wonderful library."

"Had?"

"Two years ago there was a fire. She lost everything she owned."

"I would hate to lose my books. I carry them with me from place to place.
I don't care if I never open them again. They're a part of me."

"You and Nicki would get along."

"Oh, I'm sure of it. I liked her the minute we met." Larry returned to his
objective. "She's practical, like you. Her beliefs need to mean something in
the present day. I should invite her to come to our class to speak about her
pantheistic beliefs."

Beth did not like the idea. She squashed the proposition without having
to address her own discomfort. "I don't think that would go well."

"Why?"

"She really is private about her beliefs. She has a few good friends whom
she feels comfortable talking to. Otherwise, she can be reticent."

"I noticed Nicole spent most of the evening of my reception on the balcony."

"She doesn't have much patience for my world."

"I can't blame her." Larry shifted into his lecturer mode. "Christendom is
getting better at interfaith dialogue, but that dialogue presumes membership
in a mainstream faith community. We are missing the mass of people that the
Church inappropriately groups as secular. Secular is equated with unchurched,
and every time I meet someone like Nicole I'm reminded that unchurched
does not mean godless. They either left the Church because the Church closed
their doors to them or seeing the writing on the wall, they voluntarily removed
themselves from the congregation."

Beth confidently clarified her partner's proximity to Christendom. "Nicki
doesn't see herself as unchurched. Anything that references the Church as
the norm has placed her in a relationship she does not recognize. And Nicki

doesn't refer to God. To her life is a mystery. She doesn't have a need to go beyond that one truth."

Larry chuckled. "She floored me when she described herself as a pragmatic transcendentalist pantheist. That after telling me she was a materialist and a solipsist."

"They're not mutually exclusive."

"No, they're not. I couldn't make Nicole up if I tried. I'm not that imaginative. Your partner is an original." Larry leaned forward. "Beth, I know some of the students in my class aren't apt to celebrate Nicole's faith. I find that sad because they're missing out on an opportunity to expand their view of the world. You could be Nicole's surrogate. I don't mean that you would speak for her, but you do know her and when one of your peers says something bordering on the asinine, I would appreciate it if you would offer your insight in light of what you've learned in being in a relationship with someone whose faith falls so far beyond the Christian norm."

Beth felt her inadequacy. "Larry, I can't do that. I can only speak for myself."

Larry leaned back. "I admit I'm disappointed."

"It's not because I don't want to, it's because Nicki's faith is beyond my imagination. I see her through my faith, not hers. I can't pretend otherwise."

"You can't see the world through Nicole's eyes?"

"No, I can't. And if you ask her, she'll tell you that she can't see the world through mine. That's not what we need from each other."

"If you don't share a mutual vision, then what binds you to each other?" asked Larry.

The answer was remarkably simple. "I need Nicki to support my search."

"And she does?"

"Yes. Sometimes reluctantly."

"That does not sound good."

"Lately, it hasn't been."

He stood up. "You've made your point. I was wrong to expect you to speak for anyone other than yourself. It's not your job to advocate for Nicole's place in the world. That's not your ministry. Anyway, I'm sure she's capable of defending herself quite nicely. But Beth, starting next class I do expect you to speak for yourself. Your written work demonstrates a unique point of view I want discussed in my classroom. You are a doctoral student. Start acting like it."

Beth was hit with two direct missiles. They left her dumbstruck. Her answer was a slight nod of the head, holding Larry's gaze as she did. Larry turned and exited without further comment.

CHAPTER 141

September 23, 2003 – Tuesday

Jacob and Nicole sat together outside The Fields keeping quiet company. Jacob watched as the clouds traveled to the east, casting shadows across the street.

"Nicole." He waited for her to look at him. "For weeks now you have sat on this bench without saying more than a few words to me. I think there is something you want to tell me. And yet, every day I go back to Liza and disappoint her saying 'Not today. Our girl still keeps us away.'"

"I'm fine." Nicole set aside his concern.

"You're fine," Jacob echoed as a challenge. "After all these years you think we do not sense when you are troubled? Liza iş concerned. So am I."

"I have a few things on my mind," Nicole confessed.

"You cannot talk to us about these things?"

"I need some time."

Jacob invoked a trusted ally's perspective. "What does Beth say?"

"About what?"

"These things that are troubling you."

"They're troubling her, too," Nicole said carefully.

Jacob's questioning became more exacting. "Your worry, it is about Beth?"

"Jacob, please."

"Tell me." He said sternly.

"Yes."

"Is she ill?"

"No."

Jacob chided Nicole. "Do not play a game of hide and seek with me. If Beth is well, what troubles you?"

Nicole was not in a state of mind to appease Jacob through calculated assurances. She struggled, not knowing where to begin. She decided to focus on the elemental. "She's changed. It's been very subtle. It's a small word here and there. The comments seemed so inconsequential; I felt it would be petty to argue. When I've gone to functions at the University, she's been more obvious in distancing herself from me. There is a part of her that wants me with her, but there is another part of her ... she needed me once. I believe that with all my heart. I know she was sincere and true to me from the beginning. I can't fault her for growing and becoming more confident. She wants something from me that I can't give her."

"What?"

"I can't let her God into my life."

Jacob was confused. "She honors your faith."

Nicole was self-deprecating. "What faith, Jacob? What do I have that I can give her?"

Jacob took her hand. "Don't talk such foolishness."

"You've challenged me since I was a little girl. I thought you would agree with Beth."

"No, I questioned you because you were a child and I wanted you to become a woman that was not satisfied with easy answers. I wanted you to dig deep, to go beyond the superficial, and touch the soul of life. You are stubborn, but you are also brave. You came back to me time and time again and answered my challenges. Your answers were not mine. They were not your mother's or David's. You have your unique wisdom. It is a good belief."

"I don't know anymore." Nicole's voice trembled. "What I believe keeps Beth at a distance, and every day that distance only grows greater."

"So, are you telling me you are going to convert to Christianity to keep Beth?"

Nicole shook her head. "No."

"I did not think so." Jacob patted her hand.

A brief silence ensued. Jacob kept a steady gaze on Nicole, entreating her by his steadfast presence to speak on. Nicole willed away a perceived advancing darkness by focusing on the mundane life passing before her on the city streets. "Beth has become close friends with Rachel."

"I know the name. Beth has spoken of her. Rachel is from the University?"

"Yes."

"For Beth to make a new friend, that is a good thing, is it not?"

"I met Rachel. If she isn't already in love with Beth, she's well on her way."

Jacob outwardly remained unaffected. "Beth is a wonderful young woman. What matters is who she loves, not who loves her."

Nicole turned to him, her eyes fierce. "Exactly. It doesn't matter how much I love her. What matters is who Beth loves."

The world slipped away, leaving Jacob and Nicole alone. "Are you saying she loves this other woman?" Jacob asked, disbelief in his voice.

"She probably would if I didn't stand in the way." Nicole tempered her accusation, looking down to her hands. She twisted her gold band nervously. "I think she would be happier if she shared her life with someone with like beliefs. She didn't know what she was giving up in choosing to be with me. Now that she knows, I can't blame her for wanting a complete relationship."

She looked up. "Jacob, she's shut me out. We can't talk to each other anymore – at least not about the important things in life. I see her everyday and I've never been lonelier. The only thing that is holding us together is our physical relationship and I'm finding it hard to respond to her. She took me beyond sex with a stranger. What am I suppose to do now that she's becoming a stranger to me?"

"Give her time. Her studies have excited her. She is enthusiastic in being with teachers and students like her. She still comes home to you."

"She comes to the apartment. That doesn't mean she comes home to me. All she thinks about is school and her volunteer work. I can understand why I'm not a priority."

"No." Jacob's tone was severe. "There is no condoning one partner's neglect of another. You are busy with business. If you can find time for her …"

Nicole cut Jacob off. "She doesn't need any more pressure."

"And what about you?" Jacob demanded.

Nicole took his hand in her own. "Like I said, I'm fine."

"You remember our talk. No matter how ill I have been, Liza never forgot to take care of herself. She went to others to help her and to help me."

"I remember," said Nicole soothingly.

"What are you going to do?"

"I don't know."

"Nicole, listen to me." Jacob tightened his hold on her hand. "Do what you must to be true to yourself."

"How high the price, Jacob?"

"As high as it must be. There is no other way for you."

Nicole doubted her ability to live up to the man's expectations. "Promise me that you will be here for me?"

Jacob looked pained. "You know Liza and I will hold you up."

CHAPTER 142

September 27, 2003 – Saturday

Beth worked at her desk. Nicole approached and laid her hands on Beth's shoulders. Beth leaned back against the chair, placing a hand over Nicole's.

"You've been at it all day. How about I take you out to dinner?"

"Sure. I need about another hour."

"Okay." Nicole let her hands slip away.

Beth turned, observing Nicole as she stepped to the window. "Nicki, I've been meaning to tell you. Rachel has invited me to St. Louis for a long weekend. A college friend of hers is getting married. I'd like to go."

Nicole looked across the room. "When?"

"We would leave Friday, October 31 and come back Sunday night, November 2."

Nicole barely checked her disappointment. She nodded and returned her gaze to the street.

Beth waited. She expected more from Nicole. Nicole's silence was a marker of discontent. Beth did not have the stamina to leave the unspoken undisturbed. "I thought we could celebrate your birthday before I left."

Mention of her birthday magnified the affront. Beth remembered. Nicole's sense of exclusion triggered her anger. Her anger overwhelmed all her other emotions, including her love. Nicole had her proof. There was a limit to her love for Beth. Beth had set her aside. Nicole stood alone, far removed. She returned to a place she thought she had conquered – a lonely place bereft of another soul. She had lied to herself. Their separation was not semantical, purely a misunderstanding caused by a failure to communicate. It was intentional. It was brutally human. Nicole felt the heartbreaking effect of being in the apartment. "I need some space. I'm going for a drive."

Wordlessly, Beth watched Nicole exit. She had wondered if Nicole would care about the trip. She had her answer. She knew better than to ask Nicole if she was all right. She was not. What Nicole felt could not be ignored or resolved by a drive. Beth would give Nicole time. Upon her return, Beth would rescind the idea of going with Rachel to St. Louis.

CHAPTER 143

September 27, 2003 – Saturday

The sight of the sedan crashing into the Jeep came too quickly for Nicole to respond. The force of metal against metal, flesh against metal was immediate and merciless. All motion stopped. With a disorientated sense of place, Nicole leaned her head against the headrest. She could feel her blood seeping from her forehead and nose. She experienced a subtle darkening of her sight, the inner apertures shutting. Not wanting to fight for the light, she kept her eyes closed. She had no curiosity. She cared not what meaning the diffused sounds carried. She was pinned by metal. She felt wetness in her jeans. Whether she wet herself or she was bleeding was beyond her ability to ascertain.

She was drifting away from the material, beyond sensations of pain. She was drifting away from life. She did not fret letting go. She wanted to be free of her pain, the pain present prior to impact. If she died, the rising pain would end. Pain was as finite as life.

Her thoughts returned to what they were only a few moments before impact. She had done what little she could to usher Beth back to her faith. She had acknowledged that the cross would always have a place in Beth's heart. She was a silent, ever present witness as Beth returned to the Church. She could do no more, though she had tried. Beth had multiple faith communities. She stayed in touch with the hospital chaplains. She had her church and she had the University. The only constant in her life that did not have Christianity in its identity was her partner. Nicole could slip away; she could embrace death easily knowing that her departure would present Beth with an opportunity to complete her life without the tension of Nicole's antithetical beliefs. Beth could have everything without breaking her vow.

Nicole was grateful that she had kept silent, held her confusion and associated anger away from Beth. Beth would miss her, but Beth would go on and find solace in her Christ, her God. Beth would have a good life, compliments of Nicole's bequest. A fair trade Nicole would be released to oblivion, to the peace of the finite end, and Beth would go on to continue her ministry and one day love again. Nicole weighed life against death. She could still fight. She chose not to, deciding death was the better way.

Kate, still Nicole's emergency contact, had received a call from the police. She relayed a message from the police to the Hyde Park apartment. She now waited for Beth in the emergency room. Upon seeing Beth arrive, Kate stood up. "Nicki is going to be all right."

"I want to see her," Beth demanded

"They took her for an MRI. It's just a precaution. They want to keep her overnight for observation."

"What happened?"

"Sit down first."

Beth did as told.

Kate joined her. "An on-coming car crossed the median and hit Nicki head-on. Thank God for seat belts and air bags. The police said she could have been badly hurt without them."

Beth asked, "What about the driver of the other car?"

"She was an older woman."

"Was?" Beth began to comprehend the enormity of the collision. "She died?"

"On impact," Kate confirmed. "It was bad, Beth. The Jeep is totaled."

Beth's thoughts were with her partner. "Did Nicki say anything?"

"Not really."

Beth looked toward the curtained rooms, imagining Nicole lying injured.

Kate spoke Beth's name, interrupting her thoughts. Beth returned her gaze to Kate.

"Don't go by me," said Kate. "Nicki and I haven't been on the best of terms lately."

Beth could guess the reason why. She set aside the discord raised by their aborted adoption. "How did she look?"

Kate's troubled aspect conveyed more than her words. "I think she's still in shock."

Given permission by the attending nurse, Beth entered Nicole's curtained bed site. She stood at the foot of the bed. Nicole lay with her eyes closed. She wore a square bandage on the left side of her forehead. Beth approached. She took gentle hold of her partner's hand. Nicole opened her eyes.

Beth's emotions resonated in the tone of her whisper. "Thank God you're alive."

Nicole stiffened. She wondered what gratitude those who knew the driver of the other car would have reason to express.

Beth's eyes glistened with tears. "How are you feeling?"

"Headache. I've had worse," said Nicole indifferently.

"Your leg?" Beth glanced down Nicole's body.

Nicole's answers continued, devoid of emotion. "Thirty-seven stitches. Nothing's broken. I'm going to have to pull my cane out of storage."

"Kate said a car crossed over and hit you."

"I was in the wrong place at the wrong time. I didn't see her coming."

"You're going to be all right," Beth said, needing the assurance of the open declaration.

Nicole felt Beth's hand tremble. Unable to find the grace in having survived to feel Beth's touch, the sensation did not move her. "It wasn't my time."

CHAPTER 144

October 7, 2003 – Tuesday

Nicole waited patiently outside of the Varnavsky's apartment. Yeva opened the door and commanded, "Come in where I can see you." Nicole stepped inside. Yeva raised her hand to Nicole's bandaged forehead. "That does not look good."

"I wear it for sympathy," quipped Nicole.

"I'm not impressed."

"No, ma'am."

Yeva grew serious. "You look tired."

Nicole was suffering from an uncommon bout of insomnia since the accident. "A little. It's been a long day. I can't stay too late. Beth expects me at a University thing."

The older woman soured.

"I'm sorry, Yeva." Nicole's voice carried a plea for understanding. "It's important to Beth. Things have been … difficult. I was hoping I could drop by over the weekend. I owe Tasi some quality time."

Pleased with Nicole's plans, Yeva informed her, "She's waiting for you in her bedroom."

Nicole wondered what Tasi had done to be banished to her room. "What did she do?"

"She's been good. I told her I wanted to see you alone first."

"So you could yell at me privately?"

"I wanted to see the looks of you." Yeva walked toward the kitchen. "How did I know the sight of you wouldn't scare the child?"

Nicole followed. "Always protecting Tasi, huh?"

Yeva paused. "Nicole, you're limping."

Nicole tapped her left thigh with the flat of her hand. "My leg got hurt in the accident. I have a few stitches and bruises. I left my cane in the car. I was afraid you'd beat me with it."

Yeva's expression betrayed a growing discomfort. "Nicole, why did you think I would be angry?"

"I missed a Tuesday."

"You were hurt," Yeva admonished. "You must take care of yourself."

"The best medicine for me is waiting in the next room." Nicole cocked her head toward Tasi's bedroom.

Yeva waved Nicole away. "Go on with you."

Nicole happily complied.

After dinner, Nicole reluctantly left Tasi and Yeva. Driving to Hyde Park and the prospect of another University reception brought her no comfort. She parked her new Wrangler at the apartment and walked to Swift Hall. The lecture had ended. Nicole entered the reception area, and paused at the sight of Beth and Rachel gathered together with a number of other attendees. She observed the two women. Rachel turned toward Nicole. She held Nicole's gaze for a moment. She broke off the match, placed her hand on Beth's shoulder, lean forward and whispered in her ear. Beth laughed lightly, playfully wrapping her arm around Rachel's waist and nudging her with her body. Beth released her companion and returned her attention to the others while Rachel once again turned her gaze toward Nicole. She wore a self-satisfied smile.

Nicole stepped out of the room. She walked the corridor, taking the stairs out to the courtyard. There she stood alone. Beth had done nothing wrong. The exchange with Rachel was reasonable between any two good friends. With her own friends, Nicole showed her affection without apology. The difference was that Tess was not in love with her. Rachel was in love with Beth. She was making her claim, and had thrown down the gauntlet. Nicole wondered how Beth could not know what, to Nicole, was so apparent. A darker thought edged into her mind. If Beth knew, she was, by her gentle receptivity, encouraging Rachel's advances. The thought was incongruous to the woman she had made love to the night before, feeling Beth's taut need for her touch, hearing Beth's words of love that still quivered with fear, an aftereffect of the car accident.

Beth entered the apartment followed by Nicole. They had not spoken walking home. Beth removed her coat, hanging it on the coat tree. Nicole continued into the living room. Beth turned to Nicole, her frustration spilling over into her words. "Why did you bother coming if all you were going to do was stand outside?"

Nicole was not about to explain herself. "Because you wanted me to be with you."

"It's not worth it." Beth's voice rose. "I can't enjoy myself when I know being with me and my friends makes you miserable."

"Beth, it's not about you."

"It is, Nicki," Beth insisted. "It's about who I choose to work with, who my teachers are … it's about who I call my friends."

Nicole demanded her due. "And who you've chosen as your lover."

"Yes." Beth stepped closer. "It's very much about that, too."

"You must get tired of making excuses for me."

"I can't make excuses for you. There is no excuse for you." Beth's words were harsh and uncompromising.

Nicole heard Beth's anger and more. She heard the accompanying truth that she embarrassed Beth. Nicole froze. She stood horribly alone, undefended as Beth's words denigrated her. Alone, without Beth as an ally, Nicole had reached her limit. To apologize would be to negate all that she was for the sake of keeping a conditional love. Nicole touched destitution. No profession of love could compensate for the unworthiness she felt. Never had she suspected that by Beth she would know betrayal. Where rage once resided there was only inconsolable sorrow. She had lost the fight for Beth's heart. Beth belonged to a different people, to a creed that Nicole could never recite. On this night, after day after day of struggle, the outcome was clear. They were wrong. Both of them had been wrong to believe that they could share a place in a world hostile to Nicole. Beth cared too much for the world that affirmed her place in eternity. Beth could not live in the Episcopal Church because it denied her. Beth could not be with Nicole because, though Nicole did not deny her, neither did she affirm her. And Beth needed to be affirmed, as Nicole did.

Beth helplessly observed the change in Nicole. Nicole's muscles tightened. Beth prepared herself for Nicole's rage, which she had only experienced on a few occasions. She knew the time had come. She had crossed the line. But Nicole's body changed. Her knees broke their lock and her shoulders slumped. Nicole's formidable presence deflated. Her bright, piercing blue eyes dulled.

In the silence, Beth's last words hung. They were not crushed. They were not smacked back in anger. They established a dominion and remained unchallenged.

Nicole stood before her; never having been anyone other than the woman Beth knew her to be. Nicole's soul had not changed, except that the passion was gone. Nicole stood before her, wounded by Beth's careless honesty.

Nicole made one final appeal. "I can't do this alone."

Beth hesitated. "What?"

"Us." Nicole found and held Beth's eyes with her own.

Beth had her chance. She could take responsibility. She could avow her role in their estrangement. She could look into the mirror of Nicole's gaze and see herself as a contributing factor. She could admit that the burden of their unraveling relationship was not Nicole's alone. To do so was to see more than her will allowed. Beth's heart hardened. "Don't put this on me. You're alone Nicki because you want to be … because you've always been alone. This isn't about me. It's about you."

Nicole did not answer.

Beth hated what she saw in Nicole. Hated that they had been driven to this point in time, and yet, Beth would not rescind her words. What was done was done and could not be undone. Unable to bear the silence, unable to bear the evidence of Nicole's injury, Beth stepped away to their bedroom.

Nicole's eyes followed Beth's departure. Her hand went unconsciously to her pendant. Feeling the coolness of the metal Nicole closed her fist around it. She ripped the chain from her neck and held it in her palm, staring at the *vesica piscis* – the symbol that she had once believed merged her and Beth's beliefs. The symbol was just another lie. She closed her fist on the pendant. Like dry ice, the metal burned her; keeping hold was no longer possible. She threw the pendant and chain into the cold fireplace. She scanned the room. The colors, shapes and forms caused a dizzying disorientation. Nicole walked out of the apartment, stopping halfway down the building hallway. She leaned her back against the wall. She was conscious of her breathing. It seemed as if she could breathe unabated for the first time since having left for the reception.

The morning birdsongs serenaded Beth as she awoke the lone occupant of their bed. She was not surprised Nicole had chosen not to join her. She got out of bed and quietly made her way to the den. She found the den empty with no sign that Nicole had slept there. "Nicki?" Beth's call garnered no response.

CHAPTER 145

October 8, 2003 – Wednesday

Terri Aberg, the CMT leasing manager, arrived at her office at 7:00 a.m. "Terri."

With a start, she turned to find Nicole sitting in a corner chair. "What!"

"Hey, it's all right." Nicole tried to calm the frightened woman

"You scared the hell out me!" Terri angrily barked.

"Sorry."

"What time did you get here?"

"Early," Nicole answered wearily.

Terri responded with characteristic sarcasm. "Obviously."

"I couldn't sleep."

Terri dropped her briefcase on her desk and plopped into her chair. "That explains why you look like hell."

"Thanks."

"Sorry. I'm usually more respectful to the owners after I've had my second cup of coffee."

Nicole stood up. The gesture signaled that it was time to talk business. Terri sat up straight. "Nicole, what can I do for you?"

"I've decided to exercise my option to lease the loft beside the Elysian Fields office. Would you contact the tenant and let him know?"

Terri quieted. "Of course. He has sixty days to vacate, right?"

Nicole walked to the door. "Tell him I'll cover his last two month's rent if he moves by the end of this month."

"Will do."

Nicole began to step away.

Terri called to her. Nicole paused as Terri asked, "The lease … should I draft it for your sole signature?"

"Yes. Thank you."

Terri respectfully stood up. "Is there anything else I can do for you?"

Nicole could not tolerate her employee's sympathy, no matter how well intentioned. "Just get me the loft."

Nicole returned to her office and sat at her desk. Beth's photograph rested in front of her. They had taken a risk; failure was probable, some had thought inevitable. The time had come to release them both from their

sincere, misguided promises. Nicole methodically began making the necessary arrangements to return to the life she'd had before meeting Beth. In business, Nicole always believed in amputation over slow, partial cuts. She did not like indecisiveness. She had no patience for the unknown. Transitions needed to be managed and kept as brief as possible. She applied her philosophy to her personal life, determined to make the severe cut quickly. She did not want any more sleepless nights in her Fields office.

Her left hand began to tremble. Her eyes fixed upon the discordant movements. Her doctor had reassured her that the tremors signaled neither a return of her tumor, nor were they symptomatic of an undiagnosed injury from the car accident. What she was experiencing was caused by stress and fatigue. She had been counseled to make the necessary life changes and had now begun the process of doing so.

Nicole stored Beth's photograph in the bottom drawer of her credenza. She leaned back in her chair and closed her eyes. She brought forth the loft in her mind's eye. Laura had designed the space for her. She would have it. Three weeks at best, sixty days at worst. No longer would her *temenos* be limited to a segregated space in Hyde Park.

CHAPTER 146

October 8, 2003 – Wednesday Afternoon

Kate barged into Nicole's office, where Laura and Nicole were sitting at a meeting table. Kate set aside all decorum. "I want to talk to you. Now!"

Ann, Nicole's administrative assistant followed behind Kate. Flustered, she apologized. "I'm sorry."

Nicole looked from Kate to Ann. "It's all right." She turned to Laura. "Would you excuse us?"

Laura stood. "We can finish this later."

"Thank you." Nicole felt her acute exhaustion. She had hoped for a better closing to her workday.

Laura followed Ann out of the office.

Nicole stood and faced Kate, bracing herself for an uncompromising assault. "I said I would call you."

Kate was beside herself. "You send me an email telling me you left Beth and you expect me to wait for a phone call? What the hell were you thinking?"

Nicole emotionally distanced herself from Kate's radiating anger. "Regarding my expectation that you would wait for the call, or in my decision to leave Beth?"

"Beth! God damn it!" Kate's outburst elicited no response. "Who is she?"

"What?" The accusation sparked Nicole's anger.

"You heard me!"

"Don't cross the line, Kate."

"Something you've never done," said Kate bitterly.

Nicole's defense harkened back to their nascent friendship. "I have never pretended to be someone I'm not."

"You're right. You've always been the good fuck."

Nicole would not subject herself to Kate's warped history lesson. "We're done here."

"Well, I'm not! Did you ever see what you did to other women as the ugly thing it was?"

"What do you want from me?" Nicole demanded. "After all these years what can I possibly say to you?"

"Not a damned thing." Kate remained truculent.

Unwilling to discount their friendship, Nicole tried to bridge the divide. "Kate, you know who I was. I don't think you know who I've become."

"Don't flatter yourself, Nicki. You haven't changed. What you're doing to Beth proves it."

"There isn't another woman." Nicole hated having to answer Kate's indictment.

Kate renewed her charge. "Just back alley, anonymous sex."

Nicole saw Kate with painful clarity. "When did we stop being friends?"

"You never deserved Beth."

"I know that!" Nicole grabbed a vase that rested at the center of the meeting table and threw it against the wall. Silence overtook the room. Nicole stood trembling.

Ann entered. She stopped at the image of the two women frozen in place. Nicole motioned for Ann to leave. She did, closing the door behind her.

Nicole remained unmoving. There was no hint of the self-possessed woman who, at one time, had indiscriminately traded lovers.

Kate seemed confused by what she saw in Nicole. She tempered her tone. "Go back to Beth."

Nicole was unyielding. "That's not an option."

Kate walked to the door. "Do you want a new lawyer?"

Nicole clenched her fist as she sensed the beginning of a tremor. "Might be best."

"If you want to stay with my firm I'll give you a couple of names to choose from."

"Do it." Another decision made, one Nicole had not expected.

CHAPTER 147

October 8, 2003 — Wednesday Evening

Beth came home from school. She sensed that Nicole had returned. She walked from the living room through the kitchen and then into the bedroom. Looking about, she recognized a change but could not define it. She went to the den. Nicole's desk was cleared. She stepped in and turned to the bookshelves. A number of the shelves were bare.

She cried, "No ..."

Beth ran to the bedroom opening Nicole's dresser drawers. Many were empty. She went to the closet. Half of Nicole's clothes had been cleared. Beth stepped back, away from the evidence, clearly in sight, of Nicole's departure.

She frantically searched the apartment looking for a note. She found none. She went to the sunroom and turned on her computer. As she waited to access her email she picked up the phone. There was no voice mail. She reset the receiver and stared at the computer screen as it went through its start-up routine.

Beth spoke her plea; it was nothing less than a prayer. "Nicki, don't do this. Please, don't do this." With her computer ready, she impatiently accessed their joint email account. There was no message from Nicole. Beth's mind raced. Her gaze shifted to the living room, to the space where she had stood at cross points with Nicole. She recalled her pitiless words. The memory triggered a dry heave of her stomach. Overwrought, she took a number of shallow breaths in an attempt to calm her nausea.

Beth leaned back against the chair. She tried to find some reason to hope that Nicole was not leaving their relationship. She latched on to Nicole's past behavior. Nicole, when most confused or angry, left the source of her turmoil to find her equilibrium. Beth told herself this was no different. Nicole needed time alone. She would come back. She always came back.

Beth debated how best to reach out to Nicole. Fearful of an outright rejection she chose to send an email. Her tears fell upon the keyboard as she typed. She kept her message limited to what she believed was essential.

Nicki —
> *I'm sorry.*
> *Please call me.*
> *I love you,*
Beth

Beth sent the email to Nicole's office. She would wait. She would give Nicole time.

CHAPTER 148

October 9, 2003 – Thursday

Jacob and Liza turned the street corner and walked the last city block to their law office.

"Husband." Liza paused. Her countenance grew serious.

Jacob turned to her and swallowed whatever quip he had in response to her call. His gaze followed his wife's across the street to a bench in front of the Elysian Fields. There sat Nicole, wearing her long black autumn coat. Huddled, her posture recalled her mother. The sight of Nicole frightened him, as he knew it frightened Liza. "God in heaven." Impatiently he led Liza across the street.

Jacob stopped, paralyzed. He had never seen Nicole more disheveled. She rocked slightly, her arms pressed across her abdomen. Liza sat beside her. She observed Nicole for a moment debating what best to do. Touch could be dangerous. She chose soft words to measure Nicole's receptivity. "Child, what has happened?"

Nicole continued to rock, deaf to Liza's question.

Jacob's anger shook him from his stupor. "I know who has done this to her."

"Old man, be still." Liza carefully reached out and placed her hand on Nicole's arm. "Nicole, look at me. It is Liza. Girl, look at me when I talk to you. Where are your manners?"

The older woman's gentle reproach cut through Nicole's murky thoughts. Nicole paused and turned her head slowly toward the matron. "I can't."

"Child, what can you not do?" Liza said, encouraging Nicole to continue. She caught sight of Nicole's eyes. They were glazed.

"Pretend. I don't belong. I'll never belong."

"Belong where?"

"With Beth." A tear fell from the corner of Nicole's eye. "Jacob was right. I was wrong to believe she could love me. How can she? She's ashamed of me."

Nicole was describing a stranger, not the Beth Liza loved. "She said this to you?"

"No excuse for me." Nicole paused. "I can't be what Beth wants me to be."

"Shush, girl," said Liza. "You don't have to be anything for anybody. You can be yourself."

"I wanted her love. She ..." Nicole's thought drifted incomplete into the murmur of the cityscape.

"Listen to me," Liza said to her with steely determination. "You are loved."

Nicole shook her head. "How can you love me? I'm not a Jew."

For one of the few times in her life with Nicole, Liza was left at a loss. She looked to her husband. Jacob was pale. The years of banter between he and Nicole – the coaxing, the cajoling – all took on a dark destructive edge. They were reframed into a constant assault upon Nicole's beliefs. It was terrible because the assault had been committed by someone she loved, respected, and sought approval from. Liza had tried to counsel her husband not to be so aggressive, to give an inch. He had done so, but now it did not seem enough. The humor was lost in the same void that Nicole had fallen into.

Faced with silence, Nicole apparently had her answer. "I didn't want to believe that, but it's true isn't it? Beth is like Jacob that way. It's because I don't know God. Liza, I don't ... I can't help it. Am I supposed to lie?"

Liza was near tears. "No, Nicole. You do not lie. You tell the truth. It is the right thing to do."

"Liza, I'm always going to be alone, aren't I?"

"You are not alone. I'm here. Jacob is here." Liza glanced at her heartsick husband.

Nicole did not acknowledge Jacob's presence. She looked down and rocked.

Liza feared she would lose Nicole to her disorientation. "Child, how long have you been sitting here?"

"Couldn't sleep. Haven't slept in days."

"Where are you staying?" Liza placed her hand on Nicole's brow. "Jacob, she has a fever."

Nicole arrested her motion. "Liza, I'm cold."

"Nicole, you must go inside."

"I don't want to be alone." The statement was reminiscent of Nicole as a youth, who on rare occasions when facing her mother's most abusive episodes would take herself to the Levi's doorstep seeking a safe house for the night.

"We will stay with you. Where are your keys?" Liza reached into Nicole's coat pocket. It was empty. She directed Jacob. "Her other pocket?"

Jacob bent down and retrieved Nicole's keys.

Nicole raised her head. Her eyes held to her mentor. "Jacob."

The old man found his voice. "Yes, my girl."

"I'm sorry I've been a disappointment to you."

Jacob was left speechless by the innocent, vulnerable child he saw within Nicole.

"Come now you two. We are going inside." Liza took Nicole's arm and guided the younger woman to her feet. "Come now, child. We will keep the others away. I promise, we will not ask questions, but we will also listen if you wish to talk."

They led Nicole to her office. Liza had Nicole lie down on the couch. She retrieved a pillow and blankets from the bathroom closet. Sitting on the edge of the couch, she tucked the blankets around Nicole's body. Nicole closed her eyes and began to slip towards sleep. Liza turned to Jacob. "Darling, will you go and see if there is someone in the kitchen? Bring back some hot tea."

Jacob kept a steadfast watch. Liza stood up and guided her husband to the door. Jacob declared, "Beth hurt her."

Liza was not ready to discount Beth so easily. "It must have been a terrible mistake."

"Nicole told me. I did not want to believe this was possible. I told you all these days she has been too quiet."

"Nicole has been quiet before. It is her way. It has never meant this."

Jacob's gaze went to the sleeping woman. He wanted to be with her. However, he knew he had other obligations. "I have appointments today."

"I will stay with her."

Jacob took his wife's hand, cradling it tenderly in his own. "Liza, Nicole is not our daughter but ..."

Liza saved Jacob the asking. "My dear, I cannot tell you the day and time when it happened. Maybe it was when she first came to us to escape her mother's violence, maybe it was at her mother's funeral, maybe it was just a moment ago when we saw her across the street and knew we had to go to her, but Nicole is our daughter. Now, be an angel and get us some tea."

It was mid-afternoon when Jacob escorted his final client of the day out of his law office. He locked the door, crossed the street and entered The Fields; walking up to Nicole's office without a glance at Connor, whom he could sense was watching him. He knocked lightly before entering. Nicole was asleep on the couch. Liza sat in a nearby chair. She stood up to greet her husband. "She's just fallen asleep again."

"How is she?"

"She has not slept since Tuesday when she left Beth."

That Nicole had initiated the separation was unexpected. "She left Beth? Why?"

Liza's brief conversation with Nicole had garnered limited information. Liza was careful to keep to her promise to listen, and not solicit an accounting of what had driven Nicole to such a fractured state. "Nicole will not say."

"There has to be a reason," Jacob insisted. "Something happened."

"Give Nicole time. She has made herself ill. We must help her get well. Then she may choose to speak to us."

Jacob scanned the room. "She can't live here, like this."

"She will have the next-door apartment in a month. She is paying the tenant to move out quickly."

Jacob did not like the idea of using the office as an interim residence. "Our girl should stay with us."

Tired, Liza sighed. "I have asked Nicole. She said 'no'."

"The child has not changed in all the years we have known her. She still refuses help."

"That is not true. She was waiting for us. She needs us, Jacob. I think she also needs a place of her own, even if it is only this office." Liza placed her hand on Jacob's arm. "Darling, I know it is hard for you to see her like this. You must be strong for her. She needs you now more than ever."

Liza's fatigue did not escape Jacob. "Why don't you go home? I will wait until she wakes."

Liza consented only because she believed Jacob would have greater success with Nicole if they were left alone. "Have Miguel bring a tray of food for your dinner. I have spoken to him and Connor. I also called Alex Chamberlain."

"What did you tell him?" Jacob was determined to safeguard Nicole's privacy.

"The truth. Nicole is ill and would not be coming to the office for the day. He was not surprised. He said she did not look well when she left their offices yesterday."

Jacob sat forward in his chair as Nicole began to stir from her sleep.

"Jacob," said Nicole, her voice hoarse. She gazed around.

Jacob assumed she wanted her other caretaker, desiring a gentler interview.

"Where's Liza?"

"I sent her home," he said quietly.

Nicole looked out of the windows. "What time is it?"

Jacob glanced at his watch. "7:15. How are you feeling?"

"Better." Nicole was embarrassed. "I'm sorry about this morning."

"Do not apologize. You and I must talk, but first you should eat something. I will call the kitchen."

"Not right now. I had soup for lunch."

Jacob set down his terms. "Before I leave, you will eat."

Nicole conceded. "Yes, sir."

"Now tell me what happened?"

Nicole sat up, leaning against the corner of the couch. She kept to the simplest truth. "Tuesday night I realized I needed to leave Beth."

Jacob's tone conveyed his doubt. "You decided?"

"Yes." Nicole's straightforward gaze was meant to stifle any further challenge.

Jacob was unconvinced "Beth had nothing to do with your decision?"

"We talked."

"What did she say?"

Nicole looked away.

Receiving no answer, Jacob continued to probe. "This morning you said Beth was ashamed of you. Did she say those words to you?"

"No, sir," Nicole answered.

"Nicole." Jacob's paternal insistence commanded an explanation.

Nicole returned her gaze back to her beloved mentor. "Jacob, you want me to be true to myself. That's what I'm trying to do." Her voice strengthened. "I see the divine in all of us: you, me, Liza, Beth. But that doesn't mean I don't also see our imperfections. We have all made mistakes. I need to believe there is grace in life. I need to place myself under a humble light so that I can accept that what was taken from me was lost for a reason. And in the most painful times, if I am to have a chance in saving my soul, I need to be merciful. I need to find the good. What Beth said to me doesn't matter. What matters is why she said what she did. She's unhappy and her unhappiness springs from our life together. When she's not with me, she's happy. She's happy in school. She's happy in church. She's happy with her friends."

He stood up. "Why do you protect her?"

"Jacob, you're not listening to me."

He stepped beside the couch, purposely looming over Nicole. "Do you remember this morning?"

"Yes," Nicole obediently replied.

"All of it?" Jacob demanded.

Nicole nodded.

"Do you think I am so old that I did not hear you or that I have forgotten what you said?"

"I was exhausted," Nicole said, clearly trying to justify her actions.

Jacob sat on the edge of the couch. Angered, he placed his hands on each side of Nicole's face and held her still. "Your love for Beth will not make you a Christian, nor will your love for Liza and me make you a Jew. Listen to me, my girl. You have always been a child of God. Not Beth's God. Not my God. You belong to your God. It is time you accept that your faith is equal to ours. It is more demanding because you must stand alone if you are to stand before God truthfully. We have spoken of this before. The *hesed* of God demands only one thing and that is for you to always … always stand before God in truth. You deserve and have God's steadfast love. As the beautiful child you were and as the beautiful woman you have become. Do you believe me?"

Nicole had no response. She closed her eyes and wept.

Jacob kissed her on the forehead and gathered her into his arms. "Tears. Good."

CHAPTER 149

October 14, 2003 — Tuesday Noon

Beth entered The Pub. A week had passed since Nicole left Hyde Park. Seeing Connor, she approached the bar at the far corner. Connor finished serving a patron before going to her. "Beth, what can I do for you?"

She noted the formality. "Is Nicki in?"

"Yes, but I don't think it would be a good idea for you to see her."

Beth would not be sent away. "Don't you think Nicki's the best judge of that?"

"Talk to Liza," Connor said sharply.

"Why?" The mention of Liza troubled Beth. "I don't understand."

Connor kept a closed expression. "She and Jacob have been taking care of Nicki. Nicki won't let anyone else close to her except to talk business."

Beth looked over to the stairs as she gathered her thoughts. "What about Kate?"

"I'm not sure they're friends anymore."

"My God …" Beth found the report staggering.

"Beth, I think I deserve to know. What is going on?"

Beth's thoughts were with Nicole. "We've been growing apart."

"I don't get it."

"Connor, I do love her."

"Does she have any reason to doubt that?" Connor asked with a hint of suspicion.

Beth had never known Connor to be so cold toward her. Unwilling to answer Beth turned toward the entrance. She could see the Levi Law Office through the glass pane windows. "I need to talk to Jacob."

Connor reached out across the bar and took hold of the young woman's arm. "Beth, go to Liza first."

Connor's vehemence gave Beth pause. "Is Jacob all right?"

The bartender released this grip. "You know that except for Liza, there is no one in the world that Jacob loves more than Nicki."

"I know."

"He can't stand seeing her hurt."

Beth understood. "He blames me, doesn't he?"

"I don't know about blame. I know that he dragged me aside and read me the riot act when I asked him why Nicki moved back to The Fields. In all the years I've know him that was the first time I've ever heard Jacob raise his voice to anyone."

Beth stepped away. "I'd better go."

Connor called out as Beth reached the door. "Talk to Liza."

The time was past six in the evening when Beth pressed the Levi's intercom button. She responded to Liza's query by identifying herself and asking permission to enter. The door buzzer sounded. Beth entered and walked up the flight of stairs to the Levi's second floor apartment. Liza opened the door as she arrived. "Beth."

Beth set aside all formalities. "Liza, I went to see Nicki at The Fields. Connor told me I should talk to you first."

"Yes. Come in." Liza gestured for Beth to enter. Her husband stood beside the fireplace mantle. Jacob followed Beth's progress with a hard expression.

Beth shyly greeted him. "Jacob, how are you?"

Jacob did not answer her. He turned his disapproving gaze towards Liza.

Liza broke the silence. "Please sit down."

"No!" Jacob protested in a low harsh voice. "She is not welcome in my home."

Beth was not prepared for the hostile reception. Desperate for information, she arrested her desire to run away. Her unsteady voice reflected her inner turmoil. "I just … I came to see if Nicki was all right."

Liza offered a succinct report. "We saw her on Thursday. She had not slept in days. She stayed out half the night waiting for us on the bench. She needed to sleep and to eat … and to have someone to talk to. We visit her every day. She is better. She is working again. She is also making arrangements to move into the loft next to her office."

"Nicki's taking the loft?" Beth said in disbelief.

"She had an option. The tenant agreed to move at the end of the month."

"That's less than three weeks … where is Nicki living now?"

"In her office. She will not stay with us. She wants her privacy."

"I need to see her," said Beth. She had been wrong to wait for Nicole's return. Her patience had served them badly.

"You will not!" Jacob shouted.

"Jacob," said Liza, begging her husband to be merciful.

"No! Do not ask me to hold my tongue. Do not ask me to stand here as witness to your insane civility. How much longer will you be silent? What good has silence done?" He turned sharply to Beth, taking a step forward. "You hurt my girl. Tell me, when did Nicole not show you and your faith respect? When did she ever make you feel unworthy? When has she ignored your needs? She could have tried to convince you to leave the Church completely. Did she? No. She held the door open for you, inviting you to return. She shared her vows with you, willingly allowing a blessing that went against her beliefs. She supported you when you wanted to work as a chaplain and she encouraged you to return to your studies. When in the name of God did Nicole not place you first?"

Beth remained silent. She could not begin to answer Jacob.

He continued is a softer, anguished voice. "How did you choose to thank her? You took her gifts and changed them to entitlements. What she gave freely became an obligation. You stood back and watched others belittle what you knew Nicole held close to her heart. Have you no idea of what you have done?"

Liza went to Jacob, resting her hand on his arm as a calming gesture.

He looked at his wife. Tears welled in his eyes.

"Husband, I do understand," Liza whispered.

"She hurt my girl," Jacob answered in an equal whisper.

"Beth didn't realize."

"She should have."

"Darling, why don't you go to your study?"

"No." He pulled away. "I'll take a walk."

Releasing her hold, Liza gently encouraged him. "You do that."

Jacob avoided Beth's gaze as he went to the door and put on his coat.

Beth felt unfairly judged. "Jacob, won't you give me a chance to explain? You can't judge me only by what Nicki told you."

He responded in a tremulous voice, "May the day come that my Nicole thinks of you and rends her clothes." Jacob cited the Jewish tradition of expressing grief for the dead by tearing one's garments. "She must mourn you before she can live again."

"Jacob, don't ..." pleaded Liza.

"Say it is not true!" he demanded combatively.

Liza remained silent, and turned to Beth, her regret apparent.

Beth understood the enormity of the sentence Jacob had pronounced upon her, and that Liza, a reluctant juror, had concurred with. Jacob's bitterness seared through all of Beth's defenses. She believed the Levis to be just. Their lives were testament to their honorable conviction to speak the truth, to never do harm, to never stand mute in the face of injustice. That she would be the subject of their witness crushed her spirit. She responded to her accuser, keeping her eyes cast down. "You're being unfair."

Jacob answered sadly, "You have learned nothing in your years with Nicole." His last words were reserved for his wife. "Tell her what Nicole told us."

Beth raised her gaze as Jacob exited the apartment. Liza stepped to the door and rested her forehead against the hardwood. The moment passed. She gathered her strength and turned to Beth.

"What did Jacob mean?" Beth asked.

Liza toppled Beth's expectations. "Nicole blames herself, not you."

CHAPTER 150

October 15, 2003 – Wednesday

Nicole stood by The Pub entrance. Jacob walked from his office to her. He paused beside their usual bench, and tapped the back of it with his pipe. "Are you not going to sit?"

Six days had passed since he had found her on that bench half out of her mind. Nicole hesitated in returning to it. "Did I frighten you?"

"Yes, you did."

Nicole stepped forward. "I frightened myself." .

The mentor attempted to guide his student. "Where is the grace in your fear?"

"I don't know."

"With time you will find the grace. Now be kind to an old man and sit with me."

Nicole joined Jacob. "Liza told me that Beth came to see her yesterday. She said Connor sent Beth to her because the two of you have been taking care of me."

"That is true."

"It couldn't have been easy for Beth."

"She managed."

Nicole studied Jacob's tense profile. "I don't want you and Liza to feel you have to choose between us."

"Do not be concerned about that."

"Jacob, Beth loves you and I know you love her."

Jacob turned to Nicole, his tone severe. "I have the right to feel what I feel, Nicole."

Nicole saw in Jacob's anger his love for her. She would not admonish him. Instead, she kissed him on the cheek. "I'm tired. I'm going in."

"Stay here." Jacob took her hand. "I have been thinking about you."

Nicole waited.

"That you search and have never stopped searching is testament that you have never stopped believing that there is more to life than what your senses show you, what your mind contemplates, and what your heart feels. You, my Nicole, have spoken often enough of the mystery. It is the mystery that you believe in. For you, the mystery is God's abode."

Nicole's toleration for any reference to God was as fine as the threads of a spider's web. "God is dangerous. I prefer the mystery. I don't want to make one and the other the same."

"You have not always felt this way." Jacob clearly grieved the loss of Nicole's liberality.

"I have," Nicole corrected. "I have also learned my lesson. I made the mistake of letting others believe that they understood me. All that has come from my silence is that what I believe is reframed to fit into beliefs that are more theirs than my own."

"No one owns God."

"And yet in our world people shamelessly claim that their god is the only right God. Jacob, we're gone through this a hundred times. Don't speak of God to me. I haven't changed my opinion. The world will be destroyed in the name of God. Humanity has come so close. One of these days we will succeed in destroying creation in the name of the Creator. The greatest atrocity is what we have done to love. It is nothing more than folly."

Jacob was thoughtful. "That is what you think of my love for you? Liza's love for you?"

The question broke Nicole's composure. She could not afford to lose her belief in their love. "No, sir."

"I will debate God with you, my girl, but I will not debate love. There is no life worth living shut away from human warmth and love. Maybe I am the fool. Am I wrong to believe you love me?"

"Jacob. I didn't mean …" Shamed, Nicole fell silent.

"Nicole, you have your truth. Your truth is driven by a unique love for life. We live in a world frightened of truth, and so love gets lost in the silent deceptions. They, I think, are more damaging than shameless lies because they pretend to a goodness they do not possess. People do not take responsibility for the truth."

"Whose truth?" It was a sincere question. There was no jockeying for position within the context of a philosophical or theological argument.

"Yes, I know." Jacob smiled. "You have yours and I have mine."

Nicole had not seen Jacob's smile for too long. She mirrored his smile. "You, Jacob Israel Levi, are a post-modern."

Jacob sobered. "Take responsibility, Nicole. Do not hide behind relativism. You must admit that Beth hurt you. I agree that you allowed the hurt. I agree that you hurt yourself by doing so. For your love of Beth …" Jacob painfully acknowledged his role, "For your love of me, you have stepped away from who you are. It is true; I wanted you to believe as I do. I have been your witness. As your witness, God has humbled me. I have learned that I have no right to your soul. You must become who you want to be, who you must be, not who I want you to be. If I love you, I must step aside. If I don't, I truly do not love."

Nicole had waited her lifetime for Jacob's unconditional affirmation. She checked her tears and focused on his message. "So truth is more important than love?"

"No," Jacob clarified, "because truth is purer when given with love."

"It's love that tempers truth, then?"

"No, it does not temper it." Jacob looked into the depths of Nicole's eyes. "Love allows truth in the face of fear and loss. It is a difficult love. I swear to you that it does exist."

Nicole had every reason to believe him. "Is that the lesson of the day?"

"It is."

"All right. I'll take it with me. I really am tired. I'll see you tomorrow." Nicole stood up.

Jacob followed her with his gaze. "Rest well, my girl."

CHAPTER 151

October 21, 2003 – Tuesday

Two weeks passed without a word from Nicole. Though Liza had been comforting after Jacob had left the apartment, Beth hesitated in relying on the Levis for information regarding Nicole. She felt that she had two other sources outside of the Musketeers. Though Tess had always been warm toward her, Beth felt Kate would be more forthcoming. Through an exchange of emails with Kate, Beth confirmed that Kate and Nicole's friendship had suffered a serious blow. Kate refused to elaborate on the context of their disagreement. Beth assumed she had been the catalyst. Without an ally, Beth remained isolated, left to do nothing except wait.

Beth logged on to their joint bank account. It was nearing the end of the month and she was uncertain of how she would financially manage the apartment.

The account balance surprised her. She scrolled down the transaction lines to investigate. She found two unexpected entries. The first was a $10,000 deposit, the second an early rent payment. She leaned back and studied the screen, trying to decipher Nicole's intentions. She sat up and accessed their joint credit card account. There were no unusual transactions. In fact, Nicole had not charged to the account since leaving the apartment. Beth was aware Nicole held other credit cards that she used for business.

The majority of their monthly bills were on automatic payment. Beth deposited her fellowship payments into her savings account and completed a transfer to the checking account once a month equal to the bills they agreed she was responsible for. Together they wrote few checks. Though Beth held the checkbook, electronic banking made that fact almost inconsequential. It was Nicole who had ensured there were always sufficient funds.

Beth leaned back again, both relieved and disturbed – relieved that in the short-term she did not have to be concerned about her expenses, and equally disturbed, because accepting Nicole's financial support had always been difficult. In the past Nicole's unwavering generosity and insistence had caused Beth to reconcile herself to the fact that she would not be an equal monetary contributor to their household. She now felt it was wrong for her to continue the arrangement during their separation.

CHAPTER 152

November 1, 2003 – Saturday

Beth entered The Pub. She hesitated at the door, uncertain. Uncomfortably, under Connor's watchful gaze, she proceeded up the private stairs to Nicole's office. The door was closed. She looked down to the door handle, debating what she should do next. She took hold and turned. The door was unlocked. She entered the office, closing the door behind her. Only the desk lamp illuminated the room. The adjoining door to Nicole's loft was ajar. A ray of light cut a path on the floor. Beth went to the door. Again she paused, uncertain. She took a steadying breath and then knocked.

"Come," Nicole called.

Beth pushed the door open and stepped in. A light over the kitchen island marked the immediate space. More light came from the living room. The loft took her breath away. She felt both a deep sadness and a stirring appreciation for what she saw. She was taken back in time. Though the furnishings were different than Nicole's first loft, the teak, black leather, and black metal that filled the space were familiar. Nicole had gone back to her aesthetic roots. The polished hardwood floor was covered with patterned rugs; the Cream City brick walls radiated gentle warmth. A few limited edition black and white photographs were hung on the walls. The balance of the walls remained bare. The number of bookshelves were only a fraction of those found in the old loft, both a reflection of a library still in progress and the fact that many volumes had been left behind at Hyde Park. A striking fireplace bordered by black marble tile drew her eye to the far corner of the living room. At the opposite corner, in the unfurnished dining room, lay a stack of flattened cardboard boxes, evidence that the process of moving into the loft remained incomplete.

The space was everything that the old loft had been and more. Standing in the space, Beth realized how exacting the design was to Nicole's taste. Beth's eyes scanned back to the door adjoining Nicole's office. It struck her that the space was not an accident, but a premeditated design. She traveled in her memory, trying to align the timeline of their life together with the rebuilding of The Fields. It had been during their turbulent first months of residence in Hyde Park. She understood that Nicole had left nothing to chance, planning for what may have seemed at that time the probable end to their relationship.

Nicole sat at the window seat; book in hand. She was dressed in blue jeans and a white sweatshirt. Shoeless, she wore thick gray wool socks. Nicole could not define the approaching figure. Whoever it was, he or she was too diminutive to be any of the Musketeers. She marked her place and closed her book.

Beth stepped into the light.

Nicole swung her legs down on the floor. She spoke as she placed Beth's image in her mind. "Hello."

"Hi," Beth responded shyly. Nicole stood up. Beth marked a change. Nicole had lost weight – weight she could not afford to lose. There was more that Beth could not define. "Liza told me it would be best if I gave you some time."

"I know," Nicole answered softly.

"How are you?"

Nicole looked around. She was searching for an answer but had none. She hugged her book close to her and confessed, "I've been spending most of my time alone. The quiet has been good."

Beth felt her presence was a mistake. "I've intruded."

"It's all right," Nicole reassured.

"Nicki, I know this isn't the right time or place, but we need to talk about our arrangements."

Nicole's eyes narrowed. "I'll set up a time with you for later next week."

Beth had hoped for an earlier meeting. She chose to honor Nicole's request without comment. "I should go." She stepped back and turned, walking to the open door. She paused, standing in profile to Nicole, and looked back. Nicole stood poised, yet fragile. "Happy birthday, Nicki."

Nicole recalled a different birthday two years before when Beth had traveled to Boston to be with her. Beth's gesture seemed as sincere on this day as it was then. "Thank you, Beth."

Beth retraced her steps through the office and down the stairs before turning toward the back exit. Connor called out her name. Though desperate to leave, Beth changed her route.

"What did you say to Nicki?" Connor demanded

Resentful of the question, Beth's retort was uncharacteristically blunt. "Why do you want to know?"

Connor's voice remained steady. "Was she all right seeing you?"

Beth calmed. "I think so."

"Here." Connor took Beth by the arm and guided her to a quiet corner. "You know Nicki has always gone off by herself to try to figure things out. Beth, this time she wasn't strong enough. I don't know if this is the way she's always been or if it is something new. None of us – me, Miguel, Tony – we don't know how worried we should be. Jacob and Liza keep beating us off with a stick saying we should leave her alone, but I don't like it."

"Connor." Beth understood and appreciated his concern. "Nicki can get very quiet. You have to give her time."

"So you're not worried?"

"I'm not sure I'm the right person to ask."

Connor studied the younger woman for a moment, and then asked, "Beth, why did you leave Nicki?"

"She said that?" Beth asked in disbelief.

"No. You know her better than that." Connor's unflinching gaze gave credence to his statement. "I've got a good memory. Nicki will protect you to her dying breath. I also know she wouldn't be this hurt if your separation was her idea."

Nicole's loyalty had proved steadfast. Beth felt the grace of loving a woman who, in spite of her sorrow, had kept to her moral tenets. "I didn't leave Nicki. There was just this moment between us when we both knew we couldn't go on, at least not the way we were."

"But why?"

Beth had touched only the edge of her apologia. She could not go further. "I can't ..."

"You can't what?"

"I'm not as strong as she is."

"Beth, Nicki just got stomped on and she isn't getting back up," Connor said impatiently.

Beth needed to believe differently. "She will."

"How can you be so sure?"

"Because she's a survivor." Beth thought of Jacob's accusations. "Because she did the only thing she could do; she left me and everything I stand for."

Connor was dumbfounded. "This had to do with the Church?"

"Yes."

Crestfallen, Connor looked down.

Beth gave him a moment. "Connor?"

"She's never going to find what she's looking for. God, it's not fair!" He looked to Beth. "I have to get back to work. Take care of yourself, Irish."

CHAPTER 153

November 6, 2003 – Thursday

Beth let herself into The Fields using her master key. She walked up the stairs to The Garden. The sliding glass entrance door was open. The morning sun shone gently through the windowpanes, refracting the colors of the rainbow. "Nicki?"

Nicole entered through the kitchen door. "Good morning. Coffee or tea?"

"Tea."

"I have a table set." She pointed. "I'll be right back."

Beth took a seat at the table. It was set with warm muffins, two glasses of orange juice, fresh whipped butter and English cream.

Nicole entered with a decanter of coffee and a small teapot. "Thank you for agreeing to meet here."

"I don't have to be at school until ten."

"Good, then we won't have to rush." Nicole sat down and poured a cup of coffee. She took a sip, giving them both time to settle their thoughts. "Beth, you asked to talk …"

Beth noted the absence of Nicole's Celtic pendant. With rising trepidation she glanced down to Nicole's hand. The gold band continued to have a place on her ring finger. "I'm sorry about what I said. I didn't mean it."

"I think you did," Nicole countered with conviction.

"I was angry."

"Angry enough to speak the truth."

Beth argued what to her was the senselessness of their separation. "Nicki, you don't leave a relationship because of one angry moment."

Nicole studied Beth, her eyes traveling down to Beth's cross. Nicole had come to believe that she could never reach Beth without understanding the sign. She had not understood the profound consequence living with the cross would have upon her. She found the symbol oppressive. She looked away. "I didn't leave because of one angry moment. Beth … some very important things I believed in have crumbled. I need time to make sense of why and what I'm meant to do about it."

Beth stopped herself from asking the question that pounded at her temples – the question of love. She would not ask if there was another woman, if what Nicole had experienced included the crumbling of her belief in fidelity. Beth would not trivialize Nicole to the level of pedestrian indiscretion.

"Nicki, what aren't you telling me?"

"You've changed," Nicole observed simply.

Beth shook her head, denying the charge.

"Then I have." Nicole turned the responsibility back upon herself. "We could once talk, argue. It was all right for us to disagree. We stopped engaging one another. We set aside the very things that brought us together. I loved your mind. More than that, I loved your heart. Once, I felt invited into your life. I can't tell you how it felt when I sensed the door had closed against me."

"We've never shared a common faith. We never agreed ..." said Beth quietly.

"Except in our fundamental moral values. Except in our search for meaning and truth. Small things, Beth?" Nicole confessed what Beth already knew. "They have never been easy for me to share."

"What you felt wasn't my fault. It isn't my fault the world is mostly Christian ..."

"Depends how wide you cast the net. Chicago. The states. The continent. The globe. Christianity is the minority in the Middle East, in Indonesia, and in China. Spend a lifetime there and you might just begin to understand me."

Beth felt the burden placed on her shoulders. "I will not apologize for my beliefs."

"Do you really think that's what I want?" Nicole asked

"Nicki, I won't take responsibility for the fact you feel displaced. You have felt that way most of your life. One person can't change that for you."

"But you did." Nicole recalled a cherished memory. "That day we spoke about the *vesica piscis*. Remember? That day I felt you finally got it. I can't expect the world to understand me. I always hoped you would. What I believe, what I've staked my life on, has always made me feel as if I'm on the outside looking in to a world I can never belong to."

Beth's compassion towards her partner had never been greater. "We've spoken about that."

"Yes, we have. The loft was my space. It was the one place that I could be me. For the most part, I was able to keep the world at bay. It was a space I was very protective of. When we moved to the apartment you were so careful to respect my wishes that we didn't even have a visible cross. Jacob called me on it. The cross. The chalice. You had every right to have the symbols of your faith in our home. I didn't want to be the one withholding that from you so I gave them to you. I still had the den. I told myself this was what it meant to be in a relationship. Our commitment ceremony was important to you. Pam and I agreed on how it would be done. I'll never regret that I consented. I could see what it meant to you and to be able to declare my love for you, even if it was only before Pam, meant more to me than I ever expected. I thought I had found the balance between your faith and my own.

"This past year has been different. I came to dread the faculty and graduate student events you invited me to. I felt as if I was sport to some of the people there. Not all of them, but enough of them to make me feel uncomfortable. I held my own but that was beside the point."

"You never said anything – not until this August."

"I wanted to be supportive. Going to church, just to pick you up, started to feel the same way. Pam is wonderful. But I began to feel completely out of my element. I watched you with the kids and a part of me ..." Nicole paused, stifling a cheap denouement, she formed a less caustic narrative.

"I watched the kids so open to life, to wonder, and here they were being taught beliefs that went against my vision of the world. They are the new generation. They are our hope. It's hard to see how the cycle continues. The kids ... I could see that they believed with innocent curiosity, asking questions that were already grounded in a very specific point of view. They have the ability to believe with remarkable integrity.

"Those young, beautiful minds are being taught Paul. 'By the grace of God.' There is so much that is wrong with that statement. What does that statement say about me? It's an echo of Jerry's elect, the few to be recognized and given salvation. It's a devastating Catch-22. I can only believe if I have God's grace. Since I don't believe, God has not graced me. I am thus unworthy of God's grace, God's love.

"Day in and day out, I'm reminded of the cruel inference that is the cornerstone of a faith that professes love above all else. I needed to get away.

"Beth, what I've been searching for isn't so different from most seekers. I want certainty, security and community. I've come to understand that given my beliefs, I'll never have any of those three things. Maybe nobody ever has absolute certainty of their God's existence. Maybe nobody ever feels secure, safe from harm. Maybe nobody ever escapes their aloneness within a community, always feeling the ceaseless separation of being a differentiated soul among many souls, but I think that when you are part of a common faith there are moments of respite. There are moments within the church, or temple or mosque or ashram that a believer is able to renew their spirit, taking solace that they don't stand alone. I don't have that option. I never will."

"But you knew this," Beth protested.

"Not as well as I thought I did. Being among the Christians night and day ... "

"I'm one of the Christians." Beth claimed her place in the world.

"You have been one of the most important persons in my life," Nicole said tenderly.

Beth was jarred by Nicole's use of the past tense. "You're not coming back."

"Beth, I feel like I've been torn up from the ground, my roots severed. I can't just plant myself back into the ground and expect to live. I need to find and fuse myself with the roots that I left behind."

Beth understood Nicole more than she wanted to admit.

Nicole continued. "There is no going back to the life we shared. I want to keep the noise at bay. I want silence. I've needed my solitude to reclaim my life and now that I'm getting it slowly back I don't know if I will ever choose to return to a relationship that places me in hostile territory."

"Is that how you think of me – hostile?"

"I don't want any more evangelizing."

"I never ..."

"No, you didn't. But in your world others do."

"Whoever tries ... tell them to go to hell." Beth forcefully re-stated their terms of engagement. "Nicki, you don't have to step foot on campus, you don't have to escort me to church functions."

Nicole dropped her voice to a hush reserved for her most intimate entreaties. "Do you understand what it means to segregate Christianity out of our shared lives? How can we survive when the most important thing in your life is banished from mine? I cannot be Ruth to your Naomi. Your God will never be my God. I will never give you that."

"I haven't asked for it."

"Are you sure?"

"When?" Beth was confident. "Give me one example."

"You assumed our daughter would be raised Christian. You didn't even ask ... you didn't even ask me, Beth."

Beth remained silent as Nicole's statement echoed in her ear, driving the vibrations of the just accusation into the core of her heart. "Nicki ... I didn't ..."

"You did." Nicole would not back down. "You placed our daughter in a Christian schoolroom. You say we are equals, and then you discount me without a second thought. I can take it from the academy. I can take it from members of your church. I cannot, I will not, allow it in my home."

Looking down, Beth clutched the sides of the table. "I need to think."

"I tried to think through this. I couldn't begin to rationalize what I felt then or what I feel now."

Beth looked up. "We can work this out now that I know."

"I fought this day for so long. I didn't ... I don't want to be angry with you. Not you ... anyone but you."

"But you are angry."

"I stopped trying to please you. And when I did, I could see how being with me hurt you. Don't deny that you've been miserable." Nicole returned to Beth's damning declaration. "You will never have to explain me away again.

Deep down inside I always knew that having you in my life was a mistake. I have no excuse. I just wanted to believe that the impossible was possible."

Beth turned her gaze away, looking out the window. She could see St. Ann's steeple. Nicole called her back.

"Beth, look at me." She waited until she had Beth's regard. "I don't regret a day of our life together. Not one."

A veil fell from Beth's eyes. Observing Nicole, she realized that for months she had been living with a different woman Beth wondered when the Nicole she had first met had begun to change. When did Nicole stop fighting? Why did she begin to accept the acts of injustice? Where had Nicole's rage and somewhat dangerous impulses disappeared to? Where was Nicole's uncompromising passion, the passion that showed when she had been hurt or disappointed? Where was the Nicole who had violently kissed her on New Year's Eve, who had regressed to street justice in response to Peter's assault?

The Nicole that Beth fell in love with – the defiant Nicole who fought for her integrity – now sat before her. Behind the stillness was Nicole's strength and willfulness. It did not break out as it once may have. It was self-contained, revealed quietly. Beth knew Nicole well enough to know that her doubt was linked to an object outside of her, and that she was that object.

Beth did not know how to respond. Nicole gave no hope for reconciliation. She had drawn a line and placed them on opposite sides. She had declared their relationship a failed experiment, one that could not ultimately balance their disparate visions. "What do we do now?"

Nicole caught a glimmer of acceptance in Beth's question. "Live our lives."

"Apart?" Beth ventured.

"Yes."

Beth leaned back in her chair. She returned her gaze to the cityscape. As always, life went on indifferently. "Nicki, … our arrangement … it isn't right that you keep covering my living expenses."

Nicole had practiced her arguments for the unavoidable discussion of their finances. "We just renewed the lease."

"I talked to Ben. We can sublease the apartment. I'll find a smaller place."

"I thought you liked the apartment."

Hyde Park was Beth's first true home. "I love the apartment."

"Then stay," said Nicole in a solicitous voice.

"I can't afford it."

"I was wrong to leave you without a word." Nicole reverted to her professional objectivity, hoping reason would serve them both well. "If we had been legally married, you would have deserved half of our community property during the time we were together. Believe me, I'm getting off cheap."

Beth found Nicole's generosity undue. "Aren't we reversing roles? I should be asking you to pay and you should be claiming that I have no right to your money?"

"If you played by the rules you would never have allowed yourself to be with me in the first place."

"Nicki ..." Beth's heart was breaking. She did not deserve to be compensated for risking love.

Nicole wanted their discussion to end. "Beth, please don't make me beg. I believe it's the right thing to do. Let me help you through this school year."

Beth looked down. She dropped her hands onto her lap, out of Nicole's sight. She covered her commitment ring with her right hand. She felt Nicole had left her no recourse but to consent. "We are being terribly mature about this."

Nicole felt they were near closure, miraculously without suffering the harm of accusations and demands for retribution. Neither sought vindication in face of their damaged souls. "Is that wrong?"

"No."

Nicole continued on in spite of Beth's downcast posture. "I still have some things at the apartment. If it's all right, I'll drop by one day when you're at school and pick them up."

Beth nodded.

Nicole's stamina had reached its limit. "Can we wait a little while to take care of separating our assets? I'm not really up to it right now."

Beth raised her eyes. Nicole had, by her request, given Beth a glimpse of the vulnerability that had caused Liza, Jacob and Connor to rally protectively around her. It also struck Beth that this was their good-bye. She stood up. "Nicki, this isn't what I wanted."

Nicole sealed the conversation. "Connor and Liza will always know how to reach me."

Beth withheld her question. She had no right to ask Nicole if she intended to leave Chicago.

CHAPTER 154

November 20, 2003 – Thursday

It was mid-afternoon. Beth sat on a bench outside of The Fields. Liza exited the law office and crossed the street. Beth stood up to greet her. "Liza."

"Beth, it is a lovely afternoon."

Beth smiled nervously. Her anxiousness somewhat allayed by Liza's warmth. "Yes, it is."

"Are you waiting for Nicole?"

"No. I know she's gone to Ann Arbor to see Tess."

"Not just Tess. Little Dion heard her parents talking about Nicole's car accident. She became quite upset. Nicole spoke to her on the phone but the child would not be consoled."

"Tess and Bruce didn't tell Dion about the accident?"

"Dion is very sensitive about Nicole's health."

Beth imagined the child's fear. Dion carried with her the knowledge of Nicole's surgery and temporary paralysis. Beth shifted her thoughts back to the reason she had presented herself outside of The Fields. "Is Jacob in the office?"

"No, he needed to go downtown. I expect him in about an hour."

"I was hoping he might speak to me."

"Beth, he is not ready."

Beth's spirits plummeted.

Liza was curious. "You said you knew Nicole was gone. Have you spoken?"

"We've exchanged emails. Nicki was going to come by and pick up some of her things. She cancelled because of the trip."

"I see."

Beth found Nicole's emails sterile, so unlike the woman she loved. "Liza, how is she?"

Liza sat down. "She seems well to me. I believe the most difficult part of this time in her life is over. Not that she is done. She still must learn to live her new life."

"New life?" Beth wondered again if Nicole had chosen to leave the city. "What did she tell you?"

"That she wants to accept the changes, to see the grace in them."

Beth looked down.

"Nicole has accepted that you have friends in your life. Maybe you would be happier with one of those friends," Liza said judiciously.

Beth understood the inference. She brought it forward into the light of day. "Rachel?"

Liza nodded.

"Damn it!" Beth's frustration surged. "Why does she assume that I could be happy with Rachel?"

"Nicole was wrong to believe this?"

"Rachel is a flicker of a flame to Nicki's fire."

"A fire can burn you in a way that a gentler flame cannot. That is what happened, is it not?"

Beth felt the scorch of her passions. "Why, Liza? Why does it have to be so hard for us?"

"I have asked the same question about Jacob and me. The difficult times have never been because we did not love each other. Because our commitment was strong, we fought for each other. Jacob fought through his depression, and I fought for him to come back to me. I had to convince him that I was more with him than without him. I learned to cherish Jacob and life itself because I could never take him for granted. I sometimes feared that Jacob's depressions were God's reminder to me and to him of the preciousness of life."

Beth was given a rare glimpse into the aged woman's most intimate burden. "Liza …"

"Beth, do not make the same mistake. God is not vindictive. God will not sacrifice Jacob for my sake nor Nicole for yours. Their sacrifices are of their free will and our place in those sacrifices is not meant to harm our souls but to deepen our understanding. Our lives have been blessed with two extraordinary people. Our love for them elevates us in God's esteem."

"I've tried."

"I know you have. Don't give up on Nicole or yourself."

Beth knelt on one knee, placing her hands on Liza's lap. "How can I make Nicki believe in me?"

Liza raised a hand to Beth's cheek. "I think you are mistaken. Nicole never stopped believing in your goodness. She stopped believing that she belonged in your world and the truth is, she's right. She has learned that lesson in the most painful way imaginable. She does not belong. Unfortunately, she has also come to mistakenly believe that only by entering your world does she have the right to embrace you. She assumes that Rachel, and if not Rachel then another of your faith will be the one to have you."

"I've tried to convince her that she's wrong, but she won't listen to me."

"Maybe because she measures you by your actions and not just by your words," said Liza, revealing the painful truth. "She may see your heart more clearly than you do yourself."

Beth leaned back on her heels. "No."

"Then ask yourself, why did you spend so much time with Rachel?"

"Because ..."

Liza interrupted, thwarting an insincere response. "Remember, my dear, our Nicole values the truth above all else."

"She's wrong. Whatever she thought ... I never ..." Beth paused, tallying all the times she had chosen to be with Rachel at Nicole's expense. "Oh, God," she whispered.

Liza guided the troubled young woman to the law office for a cup of tea.

Somewhat settled, Beth turned to the elder. "Liza, how can Nicki hold my Christianity against me?"

"Beth, compared to the masses, not many Christians have stood up and tried to help the Jews. During the *Shoal* there were so few. My generation needed to find a way to see Christians as merciful. Before and after the *Shoal* we have known war at worst and misunderstanding at best. Our experience with the outside world has been consistently one of persecution. What we have that Nicole does not is ourselves. We are a proud people and we will survive." Liza's determination had never been bolder. "More important than my love, what I was able to give Jacob was companionship as he found his way back to God. Never did he have to look into my eyes and see a reflection of those who would harm him; who thought less of him because of his faith, who acknowledged only those within their faith and turned their back on those outside. Never did coming home mean going back to Germany."

Beth was appalled by the analogy. "You can't compare Nicki to Jacob."

"I can and I do," said Liza emphatically. "How does the majority of the Christian faith, and to be fair, the more orthodox and conservative Jews, hold women who love women? How do these faiths and others such as Islam regulate women's lives? How do these faiths address those who believe differently, or who, in their eyes, do not believe at all? Nicole's greatest strengths cause her deepest sorrow. She will bend, but God bless her, she will not be broken."

"Liza, what about me?" Beth felt left at the periphery of Liza's argument. "I'm a woman who loves a woman and I have a place in the Christian world. My life is proof that blatant intolerance isn't as rampant as Nicki seems to believe. There are sanctuaries where compassion and acceptance are the rule."

"Beth, if Nicole were a Jew, would you have given her the pendant, knowing that in our eyes she wore a Christian symbol?"

"We talked about the pendant. Nicki said she knew."

"She knew here." Liza touched her temple with two fingers. "Now she knows here." Liza's hand went to her heart. "What acceptance was there of Nicole's beliefs, what compassion for her feelings when you gave her the pendant? Did you not have other choices?"

Beth was thrown back to her last meeting with Nicole. Nicole had been generous. There had been no recitation of Beth's transgressions. Liza had named a second offense – Rachel, and now a third – the pendant. It was becoming harder for Beth to deny the broad harm done to Nicole, and her role as the perpetrator of that harm.

CHAPTER 155

November 20, 2003 – Thursday

Nicole guided the Jeep to Tess's Cape Cod-style home. In the front yard, Tess knelt beside a flowerbed. Bruce, Dion and five-year old Jack played with a soccer ball on the lawn. Tess set her tools aside and walked towards the vehicle. Nicole stepped out of the Jeep. Tess stopped an arm's length away. She did not know what to expect. Her concerns were tempered by Nicole's smile. She took the taller woman into an embrace. "I'm so sorry."

Nicole relished their closeness. "No 'I told you so?'"

"Not from me."

Nicole felt her leg captured by a sturdy force. She looked down and laughed. "Hey, little man." She raised Jack into her arms.

His father called out, "Hey, Nicki!"

"Bruce." Nicole accepted a kiss.

Bruce looked back to his daughter. "Maybe now she'll believe that you're all right."

Nicole transferred Jack into his father's arms and walked slowly toward Dion. The young girl stood removed from her family, her eyes fixed upon her godmother. Nicole knelt on one knee, leaving a pace between them. "Don't I get a hug?"

Dion stepped forward. She raised her hand to Nicole's forehead, tracing the new scar that marked it.

The child's touch stirred a bittersweet sorrow. "You can see the cut wasn't very bad."

"You okay?" Dion's fearful voice spoke more for the child than her words.

"Yes, sweetheart, I am. Except that I missed you an awful bunch and I was hoping we could spend some time together during my visit. If that's all right with you?"

Dion nodded.

Nicole took Dion's hand and kissed the palm. "I love you, you know."

The child, in a gradual motion, entered Nicole's embrace. Nicole enfolded her godchild with her gentlest strength. She heard the little girl's whisper. "I love you, too." Nicole closed her eyes, knowing love in its purest form, with its power to heal the deepest wounds.

After gently releasing Dion, Nicole accepted Tess's offer to escort her to the guestroom. In the process, Dion had to be restrained by her father. Nicole appeased the unhappy child by promising Dion a private audience prior to dinner. While she unpacked, Nicole recounted the events that had led to her separation from Beth. "I just left and slept in The Fields' office. Liza and Jacob kept an eye on me. Moving into the loft has helped."

Tess sat in a large rocking chair. "How much time are you taking off?"

"I figure I'll outstay my welcome here and then drive back. There's a lot happening with the project. It's keeping me busy. Right now, that's a good thing."

"How are Liza and Jacob doing?"

"Liza is still worried about me. I promised her I'd check in every couple of days. It's hard for Jacob right now." Nicole paused, holding her toiletries case close. "I said some things …"

"What kind of things?" Tess asked with precise diction.

"I told Liza I was afraid he would never be able to really love me because I wasn't a Jew."

"He heard you?"

"Yes." Nicole turned away, entering the adjoining bathroom to store her things.

"Nicki, did you mean it?" Tess called out.

Nicole returned to the room. "At that moment, yes."

"But … Jacob loves you like a father. You know that."

"I was in a bad place."

"Have you talked to Kate since … ?"

"No." Nicole cut her friend short. "Tess, I'm done with her. What she said had little to do with Beth. It was old baggage. I don't need her to remind me of who I was at twenty-two."

"She's been a friend to you."

"I don't deny that, but we've changed, or at least I have. I've been Kate's benchmark. There is a part of me she can always call up and claim superiority over. Then there is another part that she has always wanted to own but couldn't. It's a lose-lose situation. I won't consent to be her foil any longer."

Tess sighed. "Kate will never forgive you for Amelia."

"Amelia?" Nicole was mystified. "What are you talking about?"

"No matter how you cut it, what you did for her was compassionate and selfless."

Nicole felt a press against her chest. She shook her head. "Tess, you can't know …"

Tess struck Nicole's dismissal with a long withheld confession. "Amelia told me."

Nicole fell silent. She traced the chain of knowledge. She feared how far reaching it stretched. "How did Kate find out?"

"I told her."

"Why?" Nicole demanded, mortified at being exposed.

Tess was unrepentant. "She pissed me off at the funeral. She couldn't keep her mouth shut. She said Amelia wouldn't be as frustrated now that she was in heaven. I said at least she slept with the best – you."

Nicole privately granted that Kate had deserved to be taken down a peg. "I know Kate and Amelia never got along. But damn, I gave Kate plenty of other reasons to be angry with me."

"The others were different. Kate resented Amelia because of who she was ... what she was."

Nicole gave Tess a questioning look.

Tess spoke plainly. "She was ugly." Nicole flinched. Tess defended the barefaced assessment. "Don't look at me like that, Nicki. Amelia owned a mirror. She was bright and funny and gentle. None of her virtues could straighten her deformed body. Kate could be second to all your beautiful, superficial conquests. She couldn't fathom why you took Amelia to bed."

"I think everyone, including Amelia, assumed that for me she was a safe, platonic friend because of the way she looked," Nicole mused.

"Wasn't she?"

Nicole recalled their very difficult final night, setting aside any thought that she had acted charitably. "Tess, I'm no saint. It was hard to be with her. It was the most painful sex I've ever had."

"Why did you do it?"

"In all the years we knew each other, she never expected to have me. Our friendship was possible because the thought of sex with her was completely removed from my mind. We were friends enjoying a farewell dinner. When the time came to say goodbye at her apartment door she ... I knew it was my last chance to give her what she had always wanted from me – my physical beauty." Nicole smiled. "You can't put two Classicists together without discussing beauty sooner or later. Early on we had, and she wasn't shy in telling me that she found me beautiful. In that one moment I couldn't reciprocate the sentiment. I wouldn't lie to her. She was beautiful in so many other ways but I saw no beauty in her body. She knew what my silence meant. She took my hand and said, 'Now we can be friends.'"

"So by being with her you gave her your beauty, if only for one night."

"And forgive me for saying it, she gave me her ugliness." Nicole sat on the bed across from Tess. "Amelia's real ugliness was how death hung on her. Her illness was both ennobling and a terrible badge of honor she exploited. Kate always sensed that undercurrent in Amelia. That's one reason they didn't get along. You, my friend, gave Amelia the most latitude of us all."

"I never saw her as manipulative," Tess admitted.

"I know. She stood perfectly in your blind spot. If you had seen her the way Kate and I did, you would have kicked her in the teeth. You've slapped me upside the head enough times that I knew how far your sympathy went before tough love set in."

"Nicki, what are you telling me?"

Nicole presented the complicated patterns of her past with far more clarity than she had ever dared before. "She was dying, Tess. It was easier and less painful to deal with my feelings if I focused on the fact that we could never have a future."

"You were in love with Amelia?"

Nicole was wry as she gave Tess the confirmation her friend had long sought. "Never thought I had it in me?"

"All through school?"

Nicole nodded.

"Amelia knew?"

"I honestly don't know. I don't think so."

Tess was incensed. "Amelia used you."

"I let her. Love makes people do the unthinkable." Nicole owned her responsibility for their final encounter. "That night I drank just enough ..."

"You're telling me you knew what she was doing."

"I knew ... It didn't matter. I wanted to be with her. The drinks got me to Amelia's doorstep. By that time I was sober enough to make a conscious choice whether to go along with her or not. I pretended to still be drunk because that's what she expected of me. I could forgive her because I thought she couldn't have imagined my being with her any other way. But I was wrong. She wasn't who I thought she was. She was so damn artful. As we ... Tess, I wanted to make love to her. She wanted sex. When I realized that she didn't feel ... every kiss, every touch ... I had to stop myself from being repulsed. I wanted to stop but I couldn't. I didn't want to hurt her, in spite of her duplicity. When that night was done she had destroyed everything I felt for her. She had become truly ugly to me. Her illness was supplanted by her betrayal of our friendship."

"Damn ..." Tess turned their conversation back to Nicole's more recent love. "I always hoped Beth wasn't another Amelia to you."

Nicole was visibly angered by the comparison.

Tess was not intimidated. "I didn't know this story, Nicki, so that's not what I'm talking about. Amelia was removed from our world. There was a part of her none of us had access to. We accepted that. We had no choice. Beth is the most religious person I've ever known. It's sometimes easy to forget, because she can be so unassuming. I couldn't help but wonder how much of that private part of her life she would let you see."

"More than you know. Tess, when Beth got sick, as afraid as she was ... as she prepared for the worst possible news, I didn't want to leave her."

Tess said, a challenging note in her voice. "You were angry."

"Because God came first. I don't know if I will ever rise above being jealous of her God. Even during the best of times, there was a kernel of that rivalry in me. What mattered was that I didn't want to lose her. All I wanted was to be with her, to love her. I found beauty in her tears. They came from an honest heart. She had waited most of her life for the day she would face cancer. Beth wasn't obvious like Amelia. It took a long time for me to get a sense of how heavy a burden her family medical history was to her ... it had shaped her life. In some ways it still does. Beth was brave to love me. She was braver still to want a child."

"Nicki ... Beth wasn't brave enough to sustain your relationship. Don't get me wrong, I'm glad to see you like this, but I have to ask. Why aren't you angry with her?"

Nicole looked inside herself. Had she become so expert in hiding her emotions? "Tess, you have no idea."

"Then why don't you show it?" Tess reached out to Nicole. "Nicki, don't deny that you hate what's happened."

"Hate, Tess?" Nicole leaned back, creating a separation between them. "That's not a word I use easily."

"Damn it, I don't want you to hate Beth. I do want her to see the hurt she's caused you."

"She will."

"How do you know that?"

"Because I know Beth."

"And if you're wrong?"

"What good does it do to prove me wrong, except that it'll strip away my belief in her?" Nicole took hold of her friend's hand. "Tess, I still need to believe in Beth's goodness, just like I need to believe in yours."

The following morning, Nicole walked to a nearby park. She sat beside the banks of the Red Cedar River, not as sure as she once had been. Her confidence had slipped away. Acceptance, grace, humility and goodness were no longer to be found in a life with Beth. Nicole's tenets needed to be sustained in her aloneness. The life of her most contented dreams was not the life she was living.

Watching the river waters, Nicole recalled the Jones Avery poem spoken to Beth not only as a vow but also as words of guidance. Beth had failed to heed the voice.

The stream that murmurs by thee – heed its voice,
Nor stop thine ear; 'tis I that bid it flow;
And thou with its glad waters shalt rejoice,
And of the life I live within them know.

And hill, and grove, and flowers, and running stream,
When thou dost live with them shall look more fair;
And thou awake as from a cheating dream,
The life today with me and mine to share.

Miles away from Chicago, Nicole accepted a painful truth. A part of her had died in Hyde Park; the little girl who still dared to dream, who still yearned for unconditional love was forever lost. When she had pulled away from Beth it was an act of self-preservation, no different than when she had pulled away from her mother.

Tess found Nicole by the river. Exchanging silent glances, she sat beside her.

Nicole kept her hands wrapped around a raised knee. Though in her stillness she fit well in the tranquil place, she could not overcome the hint of sadness the constant flow of the waters stirred within her heart.

"I forgot to ask. In spite of everything, how are you?" Tess asked easily.

Tess's paradoxical knack for sharply honed nonchalance never ceased to amaze Nicole. "I have my good days, like today, when I'm more grateful for what Beth gave me than I'm angry for what she took away from me. The bad days I can't imagine ever forgiving her."

"Was there someone else?"

Nicole turned her head towards the questioner. "How long have you been waiting to ask me that?"

"Honestly, I can't imagine Beth being unfaithful, but I was recently told that I had misjudged a friend so I figured it was best not to assume."

"Touché." Nicole patted Tess's leg. "Yes and no. I don't believe there was anything physical between them. Now that I've moved out all bets are off. Rachel is someone Beth knows from the University. She's a logical match."

"Logical?" Tess shuddered at the stoic conclusion.

"Christian." Nicole offered a minimalist's description. "She's involved in social justice."

"Excuse me." Tess took exception to Nicole's self-dismissal. "You've read the New Testament in Greek. You can argue Hebrew and Christian scripture if you put your mind to it. I bet Beth hasn't read Hesiod in English."

"I didn't encourage her."

"Did she encourage your religious reading?"

Nicole marked the chronology of her studies. "I had already read the New Testament by the time I met her."

"Don't make excuses."

"Tess, you and I are Classicists. We live and breathe the Greeks. Most people think of us as eccentrics."

"Nicki, I'm just as much a Christian as Beth is."

Nicole's temper spiked. "It was enough that she loved me!"

"She loved an edited version of you." Tess was unrelenting.

"Is that what you think?"

"Yes! Bruce and I spent half the night debating that very fact. Nicki, I've been thinking about all we've talked about. You held back. You accepted second-class citizenry. You should have guided Beth towards you instead of stepping further and further away from her. You put so much on yourself; of course you couldn't single-handedly hold up your relationship. You never gave Beth a chance to take equal responsibility. That's not the way you two were in the beginning. Maybe you're right. Maybe going back to school changed Beth. But I also think her surgery changed you."

Nicole turned her gaze toward the river.

Tess waited for Nicole's retort. Receiving none she patiently followed the steady journey of the river waters. Nearly a quarter-hour passed in silence. "Nicki."

"Yeah."

"You angry at me?"

"Just thinking."

"About … ?" Tess asked softly.

"The day came when Discord dropped the Golden Apple on the banquet table with an inscription, 'for he who knows the truth' and all the religious leaders stepped up to claim the prize. Centuries have passed and they are still fighting over the apple," Nicole recited.

Tess smiled. "Only you would put such on twist on Homer."

Experience had taught Nicole well. "The truth is hard to know and harder still to accept."

"What truth, Nicki?"

Nicole glanced at her ring. "That we hurt those we love."

CHAPTER 156

November 27, 2003 – Thursday

Beth waited until late morning to call Marie. They had not spoken in months. Beth heard her sister's familiar voice in greeting.

"Happy Thanksgiving."

"Beth." Marie hesitated for a moment. "How are you?"

"Good." Beth projected an upbeat tone. "How are things with you and Joe?"

"We're fine. So what's up?"

"Nothing much. School is school."

"There's nothing you need to tell me?"

Beth hesitated. "What do you mean?"

Marie struck swiftly. "When were you planning on telling me about Nicki? Or did you forget the insignificant fact that you two aren't living together anymore?"

"How did you ..."

"Her birthday, Beth. I called her on her cell. I thought it would be a fun surprise."

"I'm sorry."

"I'm not the one you should be apologizing to. Nicki shouldn't have had to tell me. She didn't know what to say to me and I sure didn't know what to say to her." Marie's tirade was met with silence. Marie calmed her voice. "What happened?"

Beth felt the disappointment that came with knowing that she could not count Marie an ally. She tried to explain, keeping to a neutral perspective. "It's been hard."

"I know Nicki. I know how she feels about you. She didn't just walk out the door. She knows what hard living is all about."

"We've been growing apart."

"Nicki said she didn't belong in your life anymore. What the hell did she mean by that?"

Beth closed her eyes and bowed her head as she tried to focus on the defensible causes. "She hasn't been comfortable with my friends at school."

"And you cared?"

Marie's sarcasm cut deeply. "Yes, I cared," Beth snapped.

"Why?" Marie retorted. "What makes school so special?"

"Marie, school is a big part of my life."

"And your point is? CMT is a big part of Nicki's life. I can't imagine she would divorce you because you didn't get along with Alex and Laura."

"There's more to school than …"

Marie cut Beth off. "You're right, Beth. A bunch of people talking God is more important than Nicki rejuvenating a struggling neighborhood with decent housing and small business development."

Beth was on edge. "I don't want to argue."

"Well I do! Damn it, Beth, we are talking about Nicki." Marie shed a tear. "I'll never forget how she reacted when the doctor told her you were going to be all right. Sis, that's when I realized she was the best thing that ever happened to you. I never questioned your relationship again. Beth, this may sound awful but I always wondered why she chose to be with you. I'm thinking she's asking herself that very same question right now." Marie gentled her voice. "You're wonderful and I love you, but why would Nicki put herself in a position of constantly being put off for her beliefs? Of course she didn't want anything to do with U.C."

Before ending, Beth's conversation with Marie had disintegrated from a challenge to a stinging indictment. After six weeks of separation, Marie's harsh censure lent verisimilitude to the unsalvageable condition of Beth's relationship with Nicole. Beth felt isolated. Her isolation was, in part, of her own making. Given her growing awareness of her role in their separation, and her accompanying guilt, she hesitated in confiding to Cindy and Pam. Within her inner circle, her only explicit conversations regarding Nicole's departure were with Rachel, a confidence she engaged in with mixed emotions.

With the indecisive exception of Kate, of the friends that she and Nicole shared, loyalties were with Nicole. Beth had learned of no charge against her attributed to Nicole, only that Nicole was hurting. The fodder for accusations was inferred from their past history and Nicole's silence.

Beth knew Nicole too well to place much merit on the composed presence that sat across from her during their most recent meeting. Like she had done after 9-11, Nicole had the ability to step up to life's stage and play the role cast no matter how far askew from her nature.

Beth sat in the sunroom. She had found Hyde Park too quiet. Hyde Park had once meant a far different, comforting silence. Beth glanced over to the hallway that led to Nicole's den. Sometimes she swore the apartment's silence had allowed her to hear Nicole breathing a room away.

She missed Nicole's physical presence. She was ashamed to admit that she had failed to affirm their code. Many were the times she had not joined a waiting Nicole on the couch after coming home late from school. Many were the times she had stayed at her desk in the sunroom when she could have easily shifted her reading to the empty couch in invitation.

Their bed was too large for Beth alone. Beth longed to be touched. Her body yearned for Nicole's strong, large hands, hands that swept lightly over her skin. The tenderness of their intimacy had brought more than pleasure; it had brought comfort.

During the past difficult year, with few exceptions, no matter how distant they had felt, in their bed they were able to reconnect. Lying beside Nicole, taken in by her partner's exploring eyes, she would see a glint of approval. When her loneliness had been unbearable, Beth turned to Nicole seeking and receiving assurance as her hands clenched Nicole's nightshirt. Their physical relationship had held the last vestige of their hope.

The doorbell rang. It was past five in the evening. Unsettled by the interruption, Beth went to the intercom. "Yes."

"Beth, it's Rachel. I was in the neighborhood. Thought you might like some company."

Beth buzzed Rachel into the building. She stood by the apartment door, her thoughts still with Nicole. A knock caused her to refocus upon the present moment. She opened the door.

"Hey." Rachel raised a covered plate of food. "I brought leftovers. My Mom outdid herself this year."

"Come in." Beth stepped aside.

Rachel placed the plate on the banister and took off her coat. "I really wished you had come with me."

Beth took the plate and walked toward the kitchen. Rachel followed. "Did you talk to Marie?"

"Yes." Beth set the plate on the counter. She paused, feeling the loneliness that accompanied the renewed estrangement from her sister.

Rachel waited a heartbeat before positioning herself behind Beth. "Hey, I know the holidays can be awful when you're alone." She placed a hand on Beth's waist. "Beth, you're not alone. I'm here ... I want to be here for you."

On this Thanksgiving Day, Rachel's voice sounded the hour with the unbearable announcement of the awfulness of the day for Beth and all like her whose every breath was taken without celebration.

Beth remembered how three years before she had sat at Nicole's bedside praying for both of them, feeling God's compassion enter the stark hospital room. She remembered the year thereafter when she and Nicole had laid upon their couch and discussed the exchange of rings. And finally, Beth remembered the previous year when the couple had hosted their friends at The Garden for a feast. For Beth, the autumn holiday had never been less than warm and tender when spent in Nicole's company.

Beth wanted an end to her isolation. She turned in an uninterrupted motion and embraced Rachel. Feeling Beth's need, Rachel held Beth tenderly. She kissed Beth's cheek. After a moment, she swept Beth's hair aside and explored her neck with her lips. Feeling no resistance, she took possession of Beth's lips. Their kisses deepened. Confident, Rachel gradually led Beth to the bedroom, easing her unto the bed.

Rachel unbuttoned Beth's shirt. Her cool hand swept across Beth's skin. The foreign nature of Rachel's touch jolted Beth back into conscious understanding of what she was consenting to. In spite of her hunger for touch, Beth's body protested. She would retch if the touch continued. The disunity between her carnal greed and her emotional need was suspended. If she had any hope to safeguard her dignity, the moment demanded an exercise of will.

"No," Beth cried in a raspy voice. "Rachel, stop."

Rachel paused, her breaths quick. "What …"

Beth pushed Rachel back. "I don't want this."

"This?" Rachel lay on her side. "You mean me."

Beth stood up and began buttoning her shirt.

Rachel sat up. "Beth?"

"Yes. All right!" Beth howled. "I don't want you. Not now. Not like this."

Beth's forcefulness gave Rachel reason to pause. "Beth, what has Nicole done to you? My God, has she hurt you so badly you won't let another woman touch you?"

"I don't do sex, Rach."

"What do you do?"

"Make love," Beth whispered.

"Beth, you are not just sex to me."

"You would be to me." Beth stepped back feeling the danger inherent in her vulnerability. "Don't you see? I don't want to hurt you."

"You are not thinking of me."

"It's only been six weeks."

"I think it's been longer than that. Hasn't it?"

"No." Beth was emphatic.

The admission took Rachel by surprise. For a moment she said nothing. "I seem to keep apologizing for wanting to be with you."

Beth remained silent, refusing to indulge Rachel for a moment longer than necessary.

Rachel returned to a conciliatory tone. "Do you want me to leave?"

Beth did not trust her voice. She nodded as she tucked her shirt back into her jeans.

Rachel raised herself off the bed and stood before the elusive young woman. She spoke softly. "Beth." She waited until Beth raised her eyes to her. "Maybe we should go out on a date?"

Under the circumstances the concept was bewildering. "I never really dated anyone."

"We'll go slowly, I promise." Rachel approached Beth, kissing her on the cheek. "Good night." She waited. Beth granted her no response. Rachel sighed. She then walked to the front door, retrieved her coat and left the inimical apartment.

Beth walked to the closed den door. She had left the room sealed after Nicole retrieved her things earlier in the week. She was convinced that by entering she would learn whether Nicole saw a future for them. There would be no further delay in seeking her answer. Beth placed a palm on the wood. "Please." She prayed to have the strength to accept what she would find on the other side. She opened the door and turned on the portrait spotlights. The portrait remained untouched. Nicole's prized possession was no longer prized. The image was left behind in Hyde Park, just as Beth had been. She wept, falling into a chair as all strength left her.

Time passed and her tears subsided. She raised her eyes to the portrait. Beth did not understand how a love once so strong could simply end. Without looking down she removed her commitment ring She stood and went to the mantle placing the ring underneath the portrait. She turned away. Upon reaching the threshold she switched the light off and closed the door.

CHAPTER 157

December 9, 2003 — Tuesday

Nicole entered the Levi's apartment. She kissed Liza on the cheek. She was picking up a winter coat the older woman no longer wore. She had been charged to deliver the coat to Yeva.

"Stay a moment and have some tea," said Liza.

"Liza, Tasi doesn't like it when I'm late and you know how Yeva can get. She's harder on me than you and Jacob put together."

"There is someone here to see you." Liza led the way, walking from the foyer to where Beth stood waiting in the living room. "I will be in the kitchen."

"Nicki, how are you?" Beth asked genially.

Nicole turned to watch Liza retreat through a swing door. She shifted an uncertain gaze to her former lover. "I have only a minute."

"There is something I need to tell you."

Nicole nodded.

"I didn't want you to hear this from someone else. Rachel and I ..."

Nicole spoke over Beth. "I need to let Liza know I'm leaving." Nicole entered the kitchen. Liza was sitting at the kitchen table with a cooling cup of tea. Nicole stood directly across from her. She put her hands on each side of the table. Furious, she could have easily flung the table across the room. Nicole leaned down. "You were wrong to do this."

Liza was unapologetic. "Beth did not want to hide the truth from you."

"I already knew the truth." Nicole had never been more impatient with Liza. "You knew I knew. What is the point of this?"

"She needed to tell you."

Nicole bolted up. She removed her commitment ring and slammed in on the table. Her voice was a low growl. "You can give her this."

"It is not for me to do," she said calmly.

Liza's indomitable spirit prevailed. Nicole closed her hand around the ring. She stormed out of the kitchen, towards the front door.

Near the foyer Beth intercepted Nicole, taking her by the arm, arresting her motion. "Don't be angry at Liza."

Nicole looked down, ready to break Beth's hold. Beth did not wear her ring. Nicole looked up. "I'm not angry at Liza ... and I'm not angry at you. I was wrong to hope ..." Nicole moved away. She picked up the coat meant for Yeva and went to the door. She turned back to Beth. "I always wanted the truth. Now I have it. Thank you." Nicole exited.

Stunned, Beth stumbled back to the living room and sat down. Liza entered. "You knew?" asked Beth.

"What, my dear?"

"She still loves me."

"Yes."

"But Jacob said ..."

Liza sat down beside Beth. "Both Nicole and I love my husband, but that does not mean we always agree with him."

Beth was mystified. "What do I do now?"

"You made your choice. That is why you came here today." Liza studied Beth. "Nicole will never be easy to love. Your differences will not go away." With a hint of distaste, Liza reminded Beth that though she no longer had Nicole's flame, she did have another woman's flicker. "You have Rachel."

Beth combed her hands through her hair. "I thought I should try ... We're supposed to be a perfect match. Everyone says so."

Liza was clearly setting her better judgment aside. "You didn't ask me."

Beth could not help smiling. "You're biased."

Liza mirrored Beth's smile. "Yes, I guess I am."

Beth sobered. "It's so hard."

"What is?"

Beth gazed at the front door. "Seeing Nicki ... seeing how much I've hurt her."

"You should never forget."

Beth sadly looked to her hands.

Liza's voice pierced through the silence. "Our memories help us from repeating our mistakes."

"But how do I know?" Beth captured Liza's eyes with her own. "Was I wrong to believe Nicki and I could be together, that our differences wouldn't matter? Am I wrong to believe that she won't, that she can't forgive me? Or am I wrong to believe that I will grow to love Rachel if I just give up all hope of having Nicki back in my life?"

Liza took possession of Beth's hands. "I cannot answer those questions for you."

CHAPTER 158

December 10, 2003 – Wednesday

"I can't imagine how it felt to leave your priesthood and the Church."

Beth's eyes settled warily upon Larry Elliot. The professor had made it a habit to visit Beth during her office hours. Though she enjoyed their talks, she always felt at risk when he touched upon the personal. In spite of her sense of danger, she confided in him.

"From what you've told me about Nicole," said Larry, "I think you share a common need for a spiritual community. The difference is that Nicole has accepted her place outside of any tradition whereas you have known the pain and the harm of being rejected, and you continue to place yourself in jeopardy. Did Nicole understand that though you may stand on hallowed ground it isn't necessarily safe for you?"

Beth purposely closed herself to memories of Nicole's tender mercies. "Politically."

"That's unfortunate. I would have expected her to appreciate the sense of alienation that can come with being a lesbian Christian minister."

"Larry, I think you're exaggerating,'

"And I think you're being naïve." Larry pointed to nowhere in particular. "Are you going to tell me your small Iowan hometown would welcome you with open arms? Chicago distorts reality."

"It doesn't matter." Beth leaned back in her chair, holding her pen firmly in between her fingers. "I won't be looking for a parish after I graduate."

"So you're going to teach?" Larry was unsparing. "Hasn't being on campus taught you anything? At best academia is only a little bit more liberal."

Beth felt the stab. She held the pain under her skin. "I'm not going to teach." She had decided to lessen her long-term exposure to the academy, to remain focused on her calling. "I'll stay with chaplaincy."

"Have you reconsidered CPE Supervision?"

"I'm not sure I want that. Being a chaplain may be enough for me."

"Beth, you should mentor new chaplains. You are one of those rare scholars who also excel in praxis. You can strengthen the ministry at the same time you give pastoral care." Receiving no response, Larry tested Beth, proving he had no concept of the terms diplomacy or meddling. "Well, I hate to say it but I've learned one positive aspect of being single is mobility. Whatever you choose, you now don't have to worry about Nicole's business interests."

Beth did not take the statement well. "All for the better, Larry?" She threw down her pen. "I'll find a safe niche where no one will judge my choice in life partner, or my affectional orientation."

"Someone will always judge you. You could live the life of a celibate nun and someone will indubitably find a reason to criticize you."

Beth's anger surged. "Why does it have to be this way?"

"It doesn't. That's the crime. God didn't ordain intolerance and hatred."

"I think Nicki is right; humanity doesn't learn. After all this time we haven't learned a damn thing."

"You're wrong. There has been change. We've both seen how one person can step in and give us cause to pause and reconsider. Isn't that reason to hope that the next generation will do better? Isn't that what you would want for your child? I pray the day will come when our differences won't keep us apart. Somehow we will find enough common ground."

Beth was disheartened. "But Larry, even when there is common ground there are no guarantees."

"If we've been unsuccessful, it's because we haven't tried hard enough to see below the surface. The answer may not be obvious but it is there, waiting for us to find it."

"Theologians have been searching for centuries."

"Who's talking about theology?" Larry offered a balm for Beth's wounded faith. "But if you insist, I believe the answer can be found in the words of our Christ Jesus. Beth, there is nothing stronger than love."

Beth was not consoled. "Love isn't always wise. Love couldn't make Swift Hall safe for Nicki. Love couldn't stand up against ..."

"Beth, I haven't forgotten how hard it was to get my Ph.D. The academic politics were insane, but I feel in retrospect that part of the stress was of my own making."

"Larry, you're talking about a Christian in a Christian environment."

"That is who you are, isn't it?" Larry pinned Beth with his gaze.

"Yes, but I am not the issue. We are talking about Nicki – a woman who challenges the Christian faith without a second thought."

"Without a second thought? I don't think so." His tone shifted to the scolding. "Let's just pretend that Nicole's interaction with our faith is an act of folly on her part so that we can choose not to take her seriously." Larry returned to his customary voice. "Beth, we're not talking about Nicole. We're talking about you. You were afraid that the University faculty judged you by the fact Nicole was your partner."

Beth defended herself. "The comments were not my imagination."

"I thought you were strong enough to beat back their pettiness. You have to stand up to them; otherwise they won't respect you. Whether it is the fact that you are in love with Nicole or wish to challenge the theology of our times within a Christian framework, one or all, you are going to knowingly and unknowingly touch upon their insecurities. Difference does that. You are a refreshing presence. I hate to see you conform for the sake of a degree, especially one you don't need for your calling."

"My calling doesn't give me all the answers."

"Welcome to the club. I can think of two women who live with the burden of having worldviews that break long set boundaries. What Nicole thrives on scares the hell out of most of us. When we are frightened, we regress to a black and white world, to men and women who tell us they know the answer to the most difficult questions and if we trust them they will lead us to salvation. Nicole, bless her soul, has an uncommon courage. She is able to live with ambiguity. Until recently, Beth, I thought you not only shared her broad vision, you also shared her uncommon courage."

Beth faced her accuser, braving further harm. "You think I'm a coward."

"Yes. You are no more than a tortoise that retracts its head and limbs keeping safe in the shelter of its shell, waiting for the day it can once again lumber safely in the world. For now you peek your head out only long enough to gather what you need to survive."

Beth thought Larry's criticism unwarranted. She reached for a respected authority to justify her actions. "I was reading Bonhoeffer. Sometimes you must wait for the opportunity to fight a good fight and not simply enter a suicide mission."

"Don't you dare compare Nazi Germany to this University." Larry was livid. "Damn it! Living is a suicide mission. We risk small deaths every day. There is a duty to justice. You're not offering a living confession of faith. What you offer is unedifying silence."

"I'm not the only one who is frightened." Beth felt her tears. "Nicki has her reasons to be frightened, too."

"The definition of courage is to act in spite of fear."

"She walked away!"

"Did she? Or did she see the door close and accept that she was no longer invited into the salon."

"Why is Nicki held unaccountable?" Beth demanded.

"What did she do, Beth?" Larry placed everything Beth had told him back on her doorstep. "Did you expect unconditional love? Even if Nicole loved you that selflessly, that does not equate with consent to live life in your faith. You told me yourself, what you needed from her was to have her accept you for who you are. And from what you've told me I think she tried to do that. The question is whether you returned her love equally."

"If she loved me, she would have fought for me," said Beth, echoing Rachel's argument.

Larry was derisive. "You expected her to stand up against God?"

"Why not, when she doesn't believe in God?"

"But you do!"

'Why must it be so hard?' Larry had given Beth answers to her often-asked question, answers she did not want to hear. Feeling battered, she did not have the strength to turn a deaf ear. She heard every word; they pierced through her defenses. They left her humbled. "It's too late. I wouldn't know what to say to her."

Larry proposed a first step. "You could apologize."

CHAPTER 159

December 17, 2003 – Wednesday

Nicole sat on the bench in front of The Fields. She leaned her head back enjoying the warmth of the sun on her face. It was a clear day. The strong winter sunlight reflected off a fresh blanket of snow. The city streets were never more beautiful. The temperature was near freezing. To someone raised in Chicago, it was downright balmy. With winter Solstice approaching, darkness fell too quickly – more reason for Nicole to delight in the day.

By her choice, Thanksgiving had passed with little fanfare. She had made a point of seeing Jacob and Liza the day before. The Fields hosted its annual buffet under the management of the Three Musketeers, as Nicole purposely shunned all contact but two. She had made calls to Tess and Dion, and later to Yeva and Tasi.

Being with Beth had tempered her tendency to isolate herself from Thanksgiving through New Year's. Without Beth, Nicole exercised her prerogative to decline all social invitations. In deference to Nicole, the Musketeers had pulled back on their decoration of The Fields. They maintained an elegant winter wonderland theme, excluding all specific references to the religious holidays.

There was not a day that she did not think of her former partner. On a day such as this day, reason gave her a merciful perspective, one that was kind to both of them. If Beth only understood that their conflict had been a travesty, one equally of Nicole's making.

Nicole had erroneously believed that if Beth could have seen her clearly, without the taint of a grafted faith not her own, the unkind reception of the rest of the world would have been bearable. Nicole had unfairly placed Beth in the position of having to offset every harsh word, every negation, and denigration she had ever experienced and would ever experience.

How she missed Beth. How inevitable that Nicole would return to her lone plateau with the heavens beyond her reach. She knew Beth's place was with the angels, but there were no heavenly angels to lift Nicole up. There never would be. She relied on the mortal angels who had answered her call: Jacob, Liza, and Tess.

Nicole accepted her complicity to the demise of their relationship. As much as she had demanded that Beth not try to change her, she had demanded that Beth change. Nicole had not asked Beth to step away from her faith, but she had expected Beth to stand against the power of her faith's underlying tradition.

Under Nicole's terms, the only way they could have survived would have been if Beth were struck with amnesia, and had forgotten the Church that had made her the woman she is. Nicole granted that if such amnesia had struck, Beth would have become someone other than the woman she loved – thus the travesty, the grotesque tragedy. It was now clear to Nicole that she'd never had a right to expect Beth to fight the Church.

Nicole's gaze fell upon the Levi Law Office door. With the loss of Beth, she shared with Jacob, more than any other, moments of silence. To speak was to intrude upon a purer exchange. Jacob had taken to keeping his gaze still with an uncompromising challenge that she do the same. In those still moments of matched sight, they shared the knowledge of a pain that cut deeper than the heart, and that snuffed all desire to take another breath.

Mercy forgot Nicole during her silent exchanges with Jacob. She yielded to her rage, her shame, her grief. She privately indulged in her darkness, the stream of her essence rose dangerously against the banks of reason. She held the deluge of memories at bay by sheer will. She feared that if she did not, reason would be forever swept away in the ensuing torrent.

Although Jacob exalted love, he also acknowledged the harm of a love annulled. Jacob was angry on Nicole's behalf. As her self-appointed surrogate, he expressed the outrage that she publicly shunned. Seeing the emotion in Jacob reassured Nicole that she was not wrong to feel poorly used.

She thus walked a fine line in thought and feeling. From one day to the next there were no constants. She never knew what the stroke of her internal pendulum would be, but she took comfort in the fact that the pendulum swings were diminishing in arc. She needed time to make peace between the intellect and the heart, and come to a resolution that would allow her to cease her emotional oscillation and stride forward in a new direction.

Jacob stepped out of his office; his brown coat hanging open. Nicole watched him. The previous six weeks had been hard on him. Nicole's efforts to return to a normal routine was partly in response to Jacob's need to see her well, to be reassured that she would weather the loss of her relationship and agree to once again expose herself to the unpredictable elements, living her life completely.

Having taken a few steps into the street, Jacob paused. Nicole's casual gaze fixed on him. He was in obvious discomfort. Nicole quickly glanced to both sides of the street. There was no approaching traffic. With his right hand, Jacob took hold of his left arm. He raised his gaze to Nicole. The silent plea she saw caused her to bolt toward him. "Jacob!"

Feeling Nicole's touch, Jacob stopped fighting the pain and collapsed into her arms. His weight against her, Nicole guided him down to the pavement, using her lap to rest his head. "Old man, please ..."

Jacob grimaced in pain. "Nicole ... my heart."

Nicole struggled to maintain her composure while speaking to the 9-1-1 operator on her cell phone.

A crowd had gathered around the fallen man and the woman caring for him. Liza appeared; she stood frozen as Nicole, following the operator's instructions, gently set Jacob flat on the pavement.

Nicole looked up to Liza; a tear cut a path down her cheek. "I've called an ambulance."

Liza dropped to her knees. "Jacob." Her voice broke. She took her husband's hand.

Jacob opened his eyes and looked at Nicole. "My girl." He turned his gaze to his wife. Faintly, he spoke her name.

Liza was speechless.

Jacob sighed. "God has blessed me." He groaned in pain and once again closed his eyes.

Nicole felt herself catapulted to a distant plane, a parallel universe in space and time, where no emotion was felt, where she was powerless to act as life unfolded before her eyes. She was witness to Jacob drifting toward unconsciousness, to a fearful Liza, and to her helpless self. She knew what she witnessed was the human drama. The players were experiencing the inevitable pain that accompanied love. Once again, Nicole was left to question what kind of god would have conceived of such a stage where loss was so untimely. Just as the need to be loved and consoled was greatest, the best agent was struck down.

Still on the distant plane, Nicole wished for the old man a state of peace where there was no pain or cold. She wished for the old woman the courage to accept her husband's death, if that was what was to come. For herself she wished nothing. She had what she was searching for – the truth. Mercy was finite.

CHAPTER 160

December 18, 2003 – Thursday

Beth received a call from Connor. He informed her of not only Jacob's heart attack but also of Nicole's despairing withdrawal. After the call Beth stood in the sunroom looking out to the day. The sun continued its path, rising above the horizon, crossing the sky. Each day, the breath of life entered the inanimate, creating a new existence, each day the breath of life left the animate, never to return.

She cried for Jacob. Her love for him went beyond their friendship; she loved Jacob equally for his love for Nicole.

Often, when sitting across the dinner table, Nicole had freely shared when she visited with Jacob. If Nicole reached out to Beth, Beth was certain that she had been discussed. An old, male, married Jew and a young, lesbian pantheist talking about the women in their lives had to be a conversation worth hearing. Nicole without Jacob, especially at this time, was a forlorn image.

Woefully, Beth broke free from her reverie. She went to the front closet and retrieved her coat, before leaving for the hospital.

Beth walked along the Mount Sinai hospital corridor. Nicole stood at the far end looking out of a window. Beth remained a handful of paces away, silently waiting to be acknowledged.

Nicole turned to see who neared. Upon recognizing Beth, she spoke dully. "On duty?"

Beth claimed her right to be present as a concerned friend. "No chaplain's jacket, Nicki."

"Have you seen Liza?"

"Yes." It was from the surgical waiting area that Liza directed Beth to Nicole. "She's with friends from Temple."

"I know. Reminds me of sitting *shiva*. I'm not about to rend my coat for Jacob." She scanned the antiseptic barren space. "It's been eighteen months since I've been in an ICU. I'd just about gotten the smell of fear out of my mind."

The reference to her surgery gave Beth hope that Nicole could be consoled. "Jacob is strong."

"He's an old, frail man," Nicole countered harshly.

Beth's response was equally intense. "Who has never stopped fighting to live."

"He has, Beth." Nicole grieved. "We both know he's given up in the past. If it wasn't for Liza he'd have died a long time ago."

"You're his girl. He lives for you, too." Beth shared the heartrending truth. "Nicki, is there anything I can do for you?"

In her misery, Nicole did not have the strength to give Beth a comfortable, innocuous answer. She had only the strength to speak from her desolate soul. "You're the last person in the world who can help me."

Nicole's words were a harsh dismissal, one Beth had not foreseen. Nicole's eyes were pitiless. After a crushing moment, Nicole shifted her gaze toward the window. Beth turned, staggering in her first step. She reached out and braced herself against the corridor wall, and then paused, struggling to compose her fraying emotions Beth closed her eyes. She experienced a void of light and sound. Upon opening her eyes, she walked toward where she knew she would find Liza.

CHAPTER 161

December 20, 2003 — Saturday

Beth entered Jacob's hospital room with Liza by her side.

After angioplasty and placement of a drug-eluting stent, Jacob was faring well. "Young lady. You come to me. Why?"

Beth glanced to Liza for help.

She and Jacob had braved the reasons driving Jacob's anger towards Beth. Liza was sure Beth was in good hands. "Excuse me." She left the room.

Beth was crestfallen to be so unexpectedly forsaken by Liza.

Jacob spoke after the door closed. "Have you see Nicole?"

"I was here Thursday morning," Beth answered softly.

"My Nicole was frightened on that day. She is less frightened now. Still, she could use a friend like you."

"Jacob …" Having the return of his long withdrawn approval, Beth burst into tears.

Jacob reached out a hand. "Come here." He held Beth as she cried. "You and I will talk. It has been a long time, too long since I have had you to myself. Always I share you with Nicole and Liza. Not today. You are mine alone, today. Yes?"

CHAPTER 162

January 10, 2004 – Saturday

Nicole sat across from Jacob at the Levi's dining room table. A chess-board rested between them. She weighed her options, and then raised her rook and positioned it aggressively against Jacob's king. "Check."

Jacob seemed both irritated and impressed. "That is your move?"

"Yes, sir." Nicole knew she had him precariously near checkmate.

"I did not teach you that move."

"No, sir."

"Why did I teach you to play chess?"

"Because you wanted to keep me out of jail."

Jacob pointed a finger at his ward. "I wanted you to learn to think for yourself."

"And look where it got me?" Nicole quipped.

"So I'm responsible?"

"A little." Nicole gave him his due.

Jacob stood and placed his hand on Nicole's shoulder. "I need more coffee. Should I bring the pot?"

Lightheartedly, Nicole exhaled. "Yes, Dad." She paused, surprised by her own jest, which carried far more meaning than she had ever been willing to confess directly to him.

Jacob waited until Nicole looked up to him. He held her gaze. "Be careful, my girl. My heart can only take so much joy in a day."

Nicole smiled. As Jacob ambled to the kitchen, she studied the chess-board, not seeing the pieces. Jacob returned with a coffee decanter and filled his and Nicole's cups.

"Thank you." Nicole sipped her coffee.

"You're a good girl." He returned to his chair. "You have not mentioned Beth."

Jacob last spoke of Beth after her Mt. Sinai visit. Nicole was guarded then. She remained guarded now. "Why would I?"

"Did you receive an invitation to her ordination?"

"Yes."

"Well?"

Nicole tried to close the subject. "I thought you were going to give me a lesson today."

"Don't I get to choose the lesson?" Jacob asked. "Will you consider attending?"

Nicole had been privately debating whether to stand witness to Beth's formal return to the Church as a cleric. Given her regret for how she had received Beth at the hospital, sharing the ritual with Beth might bring them both some measure of healing. "You think I should?"

"Liza and I both do."

"Liza?" Nicole kept a lighthearted tone, concealing her unease. "So if I don't say yes you're going to sic her after me. You two are more dangerous than the world tag team wrestling champions."

"You will attend?"

"I just got the invitation. Can I have some time to think about it?"

"Of course," Jacob said with a mischievous glint in his eyes. "Now, you had a question?"

"Jacob, after all the years ... centuries of persecution, how have the Jews continued to believe in God? There's been so much suffering."

"Not everyone has kept their faith."

Nicole faced a man who had every reason to leave God and yet, somehow had remained steadfast. "You have. Liza has."

"We have both struggled."

"You held on."

Jacob observed Nicole's somber countenance. "My girl, what do you want to understand, suffering or a people's faith in God?"

"If God loved Israel ..."

"God is just and merciful," Jacob declared wholeheartedly. "God does not rejoice in causing suffering. Unfortunately, there are lessons that are not learned without knowing the painful fire of the divine touch."

Nicole returned to a classic example. "What lesson did Job need to learn?"

"We have spoken of this before. Job and all who know his story learned that God is beyond our understanding and that he had a choice to love God or not."

"What about the suffering we cause each other?"

"The price of free will ..." said Jacob. "Too many have fallen away from love."

Nicole pressed further. "What about when we hurt those we love in the name of love?"

Jacob grimaced. "It is not love."

Nicole was stricken. "We have hurt each other. Don't tell me there was no love between us when we did."

"There has always been love, but the hurt wasn't in love: in anger, in confusion, in ignorance, in depression – yes. Not in love."

"Jacob ... you've never made me feel ... you've always listened to me, even when you haven't agreed with me."

"Have you listened to me?"

"Yes, sir."

"Don't you deserve to be heard?"

Nicole looked down to the chessboard. She focused on the most powerful, the queen. Though the black queen possessed great power, the chessboard was still a dangerous place for her. She had a counterpart – the white queen – intent on owning the board for her own purposes. Their reason for existence was to safeguard their respective kings, their sovereigns. "That was the hardest thing about being with my mother. When she was ill, the world revolved around her. Her reality was all that counted and my job was to protect her, to make sure the world would let her be, not to do anything to challenge her truth. What I thought, what I felt, the real truth didn't matter."

Jacob took Nicole's hand. "You always had a place with us."

"I hated going to you and Liza. I felt so weak and helpless. I should have been able to cope on my own."

"My girl, don't you know how much we wanted you with us? You were never a *mitzah*."

"I grew up."

"We are still yours," Jacob reassured.

"I know."

"We are proud of you."

Nicole looked to her life with the Levis, knowing she had disappointed them. "I'm sorry I drifted away from you during college."

"You did not go too far. Liza and I ... we missed you. We also understood that you needed to leave your family for a time. Many young people do. You came back. That is all that matters."

"I came back so you could tutor me." Nicole's need, poignantly felt while Jacob was in the hospital, found easier expression. "I still have a lot to learn."

"Liza would tell you that I'm no rabbi."

"You're more than a rabbi to me."

"Good, because I know you. You are meant to be a teacher. I will be your student."

The thought was beyond Nicole. "Jacob, that will never happen."

He smiled. "My Nicole, it already has."

Liza entered the apartment. Her reproach was immediate. "Jacob Israel Levi, you are supposed to be resting."

Nicole sheepishly smiled as Jacob's demeanor changed. They were both responsible for the infraction. "Sorry, Liza, this chess game has taken longer than usual."

Liza took off her coat and joined them. "That chessboard is not going anywhere. You can finish the game tomorrow."

Nicole glanced at Jacob. "Can't say I didn't try."

Jacob raised himself up grumpily. "I'm banished to an afternoon nap like a child."

Liza raised her hand to his cheek, the most intimate of gestures. He took and kissed the palm of his wife's hand before withdrawing silently to their bedroom. Liza asked Nicole. "How was he?"

"Sharp," Nicole was happy to report. "I think he's going to be all right."

Obviously relieved, Liza took up her role as co-conspirator. "Did Jacob talk to you about Beth?"

Nicole groaned. "Yes."

"And?"

"I haven't decided."

"Forgive her, Nicole."

Nicole verged upon the truth. "I have."

"Be her friend."

"You're not asking much, are you?" Nicole protested.

Liza's tenaciousness was at full force. "I am not asking you to be her partner."

"How do you think Beth and I began our relationship?"

"She has Rachel. There is no risk to you." Liza saw Nicole flinch. She continued, though she was undoubtedly aware that she was no longer being well received. "Nicole, it would mean a great deal to Beth to have your blessing. Come with me and Jacob to her ordination."

Nicole felt subordinated. "Liza, you're setting me aside. What about my feelings?"

"My girl, I have not set you aside. I am thinking of you. You must face Beth. You have stopped denying your anger and your hurt. That is good. You can now go to Beth with an honest heart. This is your chance to do so. Forgive her and set her free to create a new life for herself."

"Without me." Nicole marked the loss she was being asked to bless.

"Yes," Liza said tenderly. "And then you can begin to create a new life for yourself without her. I want you to love again. Will you shut yourself from the world a second time?"

Consoled, Nicole said, "You are a harsh taskmaster, Liza Levi."

"I do so because I love you both. Nicole, keep my love close to your heart. Will you do that for me?"

Nicole stood and embraced Liza. "It's hard not to."

CHAPTER 163

January 16, 2004 – Friday

The time was late afternoon. Nicole sat at The Pub bar drinking seltzer with a lemon slice, reading the Tribune, and exchanging observations with Connor. Paige entered. She was dressed in a leather jacket, a red sweater, and blue jeans. She walked to the bar. Her greeting was cheery. "Connor ... Nicki."

Nicole set down her newspaper. "Paige, long time."

Paige directed herself, now coolly, to Connor. "Do you have some glasses to wash or something?"

"Or something ..." Connor shifted to the opposite end of the bar.

Paige turned to Nicole. "Before we talk ..."

Nicole was in a good mood and went along with her former bedmate. "We're going to talk?"

"Yes, we are. Notice ..." Paige opened her arms, making a show of herself. "I'm sober. No drugs, no alcohol. You can't just ignore what I'm about to say as my being on some kind of binge."

"So noted."

"I hear you're living upstairs ... alone."

"I am."

Paige nodded. "Okay then ... I was wondering if you were in the market for a fuck buddy."

Nicole sat back in her chair.

"Come on ..." Paige protested. "You can't tell me I've shocked you."

"No, no ..." Nicole summoned her wits. "It's just been a long time since anyone has been that blunt with me."

"That a bad thing?"

Nicole smiled. "It's refreshing."

"Good. I know you Nicki. I know your ... appetite." Paige playfully pressed a finger against Nicole's stomach. "You can get real hungry. So can I. If I remember right we could satisfy each other real good."

"True." Nicole had been exercising a satisfactory alternative. "But I can feed myself."

"It's not the same."

"You're right, it's less complicated."

Paige leaned forward seductively, placing her hands on Nicole's thighs. "But you get a bigger kick out of giving than receiving."

Nicole glanced down to Paige's hands. She found the moment quite funny. She answered drolly. "That hasn't changed."

"So?"

"I don't think so."

Disgruntled, Paige identified her competition. "You're not still getting over the priest, are you?"

"Beth," said Nicole with a tight diction. "Her name is Beth."

"You don't look so shook-up. Did you leave her?"

"It was mutual."

Paige renewed her campaign "Look Nicki, I'm not her. We had good times before her and I think we can have good times now. No strings attached."

"Paige, I won't say I'm not tempted. This is not the right time."

Paige sulked. "You've changed."

"Haven't you?"

"I have a few more good years ahead of me before I have to get serious." Paige glided the tip of her tongue across her lips. "Nicki, you still not drinking?"

Nicole raised her glass. The ice cubes clinked.

"I don't get it. Why did you stop? It wasn't like you were out of control, and it was way before you got sick."

Nicole set aside the question indifferently. "I had my reasons."

"You should take up drinking again. You got hooked on the priest ..."

Nicole shot Paige a warning glance.

"Sorry ... Beth," said Paige, her apology unconvincing. "You were never more sober than you were with her, right?"

Nicole had to admit that Paige was right. "Connor!"

The bartender approached. "What's up?"

"Give me a Guinness."

"Nicki ..." Connor challenged.

"It's all right. Really." Nicole saw her friend's unflinching determination. She loved him for it. "Connor, trust me on this."

Paige watched as the two held their positions. Nicole placed her hand over the bartender's. "Don't make me go behind the bar. I am going to have this drink."

Connor cursed Paige. He spoke deliberately. "Cold and dark."

"And bitter." Nicole smiled at the long set aside memory of her regular order. "Pilsner glass ... Paige, what are you having?"

Paige smirked. "Same."

"Make it two."

Nicole and Paige watched silently as Connor drew the tap beer and placed it in front of the women.

Nicole raised her glass and presented it to Paige for a toast. "To living."

"Amen to that."

Nicole laughed easily as the religious reference waved over her. She took a healthy drink from the glass, savoring the full-bodied flavor of the ale.

Nicole stood looking out the loft window. It was past midnight and she could not sleep. She turned her gaze to her bed. It was empty. She had shared the one drink with Paige and then sent her home alone.

Nicole saw Paige in the same light as Kate. At one time they had played a significant role in her life, roles now obsolete. Nicole had moved on and they could not or would not see her differently. The loss of a friendship, especially one that had spanned a number of years, was the loss of a shared history. Nicole valued the longevity of her friendships because she knew many were solidified when she was a far less attractive friend to have, devoid of wealth and community standing, let alone good sense.

She found herself once again attracted to Paige. In spite of her behavior in the past, after leaving Beth, Nicole had not taken the prospect of a casual interlude seriously. She wondered how long she would have found Paige engaging before she began to miss the unique intellectual and emotional challenge of being with Beth or a woman like Beth. That raised the equally intriguing question of whether life without such challenges was not indeed welcomed. Eliminating both extremes of the spectrum, what was left for her?

In the quiet of the night, Nicole slipped into the ease of a life that had become far less complicated. She had consciously removed herself from society, limiting her interaction to an exclusive inner circle of friends. To be social brought her no joy; it was an obligation she endured. Never did she feel the dichotomy of her personality more. When she stepped out of the loft, her public persona ruled. Be it at CMT or downstairs at The Fields, the ever-successful Nicole Thera thrived. Entering the loft she set her work aside, keeping an uncompromising demarcation between her office and her living space. When she entered the loft, bright lights were dimmed. She kept company primarily with her books. She eschewed television, radio, and rarely played her music library. The sounds of the city soothed her, never more than when it rained as it had just begun to.

Of all the changes she had experienced in the previous year, the greatest surprise was Tasi. Their time spent together had become a bittersweet reminder of a foregone dream of a life with Beth – a child to share, and a commitment to the future in a world that did not deserve such optimism. With Tasi, Nicole's public persona had no foothold and her most private, darkest thoughts were never accessed by the child's inquiring mind.

Standing at the window, Nicole felt completely in her element. She had outdistanced the negligent use of another woman. She had also left behind the self-imposed expectation that wholeness came only in the company of a partner. In spite of Plato's assertion, she no longer felt like a severed half seeking her soulmate. She rued the day when that romantic notion had defined her connection to Beth, when her happiness had hinged on embracing Beth as a necessary partner, the one who gave her what she could not give herself.

Nicole looked down at her hand. She still wore her gold band. She had made a conscious assent to accept it. The removal required equal thought. The ring stayed for reasons that were not clear to her. Nicole slipped the band off. She wondered if this symbol, inextricably linked to Beth, would ever have a place in her life again. Nicole admitted that she still wanted Beth. As Paige had proved, the want was not enough to make her act against her better judgment. Nicole closed her hand around the ring. She wished she could imbue it with her lingering emotion, crush it to dust and scatter it on the wind.

She continued to study the night. Images of the past, snapshots of a life she no longer felt connected to, crossed her thoughts. Each image documented the gradual shift in her perspective; each was a testament to how beliefs, even strongly held convictions, could be altered. Prior to Beth, the thought of a commitment was beyond her comprehension. Now she understood how intoxicating the ideal could be. She also understood the devastation that came with the betrayal of the ideal – whether by malice or neglect. She knew both. The outcome was the same.

Standing alone, watching the rainfall strengthen, Nicole came to accept what the Fates had placed before her. She walked to her tall dresser and opened a small oak jewelry box, a gift from Beth. Inside it she stored the gold band.

With the gold band securely stored, no longer carried, no longer touching her, no longer melded to her self image, Nicole returned to the window, within the quiet world of her making. She looked out to the night, over the cityscape in the direction of Hyde Park, to Beth. She would never regret her life with Beth. She accepted the grace of having had Beth in her life. Their shared odyssey had humbled Nicole and quieted her most destructive passions, leaving a stillness she had never thought possible. Having Beth touch the thread of her destiny gave Nicole's life a new, valuable perspective. Having Beth in her life had brought her to this place and time.

Nicole turned her gaze back toward the loft interior. This was her life. Never would she have imagined her path, how she had arrived to her peace, but arrive she believed she had. The space and her place in the space – extraordinary in its simplicity – left her awed.

"Damn," she whispered, a smile etching itself upon her face. She repeated in a louder voice, "Damn." Nicole laughed as a surge of joy found voice.

CHAPTER 164

February 15, 2004 – Sunday

Nicole stood in the back of the church throughout Beth's ordination ceremony. At its conclusion she watched as Jacob took Liza by the arm and together they walked to her.

Upon reaching Nicole, Jacob pointed to her with his finger. "And God has still not struck you dead."

Nicole laughed and made a conscious effort to look up. "Not yet."

"Our Beth has come full circle."

"Yes, she has."

"She stands before God offering the best that she has to give and this time she does not have to leave a part of herself hidden away. That is a good thing," said Liza.

"She's where she belongs," Nicole said.

"Come, give her your blessing," encouraged Liza.

'Blessing.' Nicole did not consider herself to hold such power. "I'll wait. Go ahead without me."

Jacob reached out and cupped Nicole's cheek. "I am proud of you."

Liza embraced Nicole. "You take care of yourself. I know it is not easy for you to be here."

Nicole felt Liza's warmth radiate through her. She closed her eyes and let herself feel the loving cord anchored by the two elders that held her safe. "I love you."

"You are precious to me, Nicole. Remember, you are not just Jacob's. You are my girl, too."

Nicole watched as Liza and Jacob, arm in arm, made their way to the end of the receiving line.

Standing near a church entrance greeting congregants, Beth felt a surge of impatience upon seeing the Levis. She refocused, accepting congratulations from a parishioner and her young son, a boy Beth enjoyed teaching in Sunday school. The boy was uncharacteristically shy. Beth was uncertain whether it was because of the formality of the church or because her vestments marked her renewed identity as a member of the clergy.

Her eyes followed the boy as he took his mother's hand and walked beside her toward the church's community room where refreshments were being served. Beth felt a pang of longing for her own mother. In light of her estrangement from her father, having Marie present for her ordination was a gentle reminder that though her family was limited to one other — her sister — she was not the lone Kelly.

Her thoughts were interrupted by Liza's touch upon her arm. Beth turned to her and for a moment felt the love Liza held for her merge with the memory of her grandmother. She was overwhelmed.

"We are so proud of you." Liza opened her arms.

Beth stepped into Liza's embrace, holding her tightly. Liza felt Beth's need and reciprocated, giving the young woman the security and time she needed. Beth released a sigh. Liza took it as her cue to lessen her embrace. The women looked at one another. Much was shared in silence.

"Are you two going to cry now?" Jacob asked with gentle humor.

Liza looked over her shoulder and chastised her husband. "Old man, leave us be." She captured Beth's gaze anew.

Beth felt tears well in her eyes.

"It was a beautiful ceremony," said Liza.

Beth smiled and shifted towards the elderly man. "Hello, Jacob."

"Hello child, or should I say Reverend?"

"It's wonderful that you came."

Liza squeezed Beth's arm. "We wouldn't have missed this day for the world."

Jacob enjoyed announcing, "You are still the only one I know who can bring my girl under God's roof during a service."

"Nicki is here?" Beth had surveyed the church prior to the ceremony, disappointed that her invitation had not been accepted.

"Standing in the back, watching, listening. She may even have had a tear or two in her eyes."

"Jacob," said Liza, clearly intolerant of any breach of Nicole's confidence.

"Say that it is not true?"

"She will speak to you when you are alone," Liza said.

"I'll go to her. Thank you," said Beth. "Will you stay for the reception?"

"Liza said she will not feed me today so I don't think I have much of a choice."

"There are such things as restaurants, my dear."

"Let's see if they serve kosher," Jacob quipped,

Liza shook her head. "He is in one of his moods. Lord knows what else will pass forth from his lips."

"Only that I love you, woman."

Liza beamed. "Darling, it is what I live for."

Jacob regarded Beth with pride. "Today, we will make a toast to you, young lady."

Beth reached out to Jacob. "Give me a few minutes."

Jacob took hold of and patted Beth's hand. "Take as much time as you need."

Having spoken to the last parishioner waiting to congratulate her, Beth walked toward the far corner of the church. She heard Nicole approach before she could see her form move beyond the shadows.

"Reverend Elizabeth Ann Kelly. It suits you, Beth." Nicole's smile reflected the sincere pride she felt for her former partner.

To Beth, Nicole seemed changed. She held herself confidently, commanding the ground she stood on. There was a casual ease in her voice. Beth touched upon their shared history. "I sometimes doubted this day would come."

"I didn't. It was just a matter of time. And in a couple more years it's going to be the Reverend Doctor. You are destined to leave an indelible mark on the Church and the people whose lives you touch."

Given their last meeting, Nicole's generosity was exquisite. "Nicki …"

Nicole kept to the best the moment offered. She nodded toward the reception. "Reverend, you've got a congregation waiting to toast you with wine and grape juice."

"I don't care."

"Yes, you do," Nicole quietly stressed.

"Don't be so sure, Nicki." Beth breached the distance between them, moving within an arm's length. "Will you stay?"

"I think it's best that I don't."

For whom? Beth silently questioned. She accepted the grace Nicole granted her. She would not press. Beth felt inadequate in expressing her gratitude. "I wouldn't have had this day if it wasn't for you."

Nicole caught sight of Rachel coming toward them. "There's someone looking for you."

Beth glanced back. Upon seeing Rachel, Beth arrested her desire to embrace her former partner. "I should go."

"Say hello to Marie for me."

"I will." Beth was not ready for a farewell. "Nicki, when will I see you again?"

"Why don't we let the Fates decide for us?" Nicole proposed

"A chance meeting while crossing the street?" asked Beth.

"No, the *Moria* are more purposeful than Chance."

"They're not the same?"

The irony of Beth's solicitation of a Classics lesson on this day, in this place, did not escape Nicole. "Some believe they were, others didn't. Chance – *tyche* – explains away what we will never in our lives be able to accept as part of the *Moria's* weavings. All we can do is brace ourselves knowing there is nothing to be done but live on, or not."

Understanding the distinction, Beth wondered, "The first night we met, was that the Fates or Chance?"

Nicole smiled knowingly. "I say the *Moria*."

Beth was heartened. "So do I."

From a distance, Rachel called Beth's name.

Nicole took her leave. "Good bye, Beth."

Beth hesitated. "Be well, Nicki." Not without regret, she turned and walked towards the reception.

Nicole heard Larry call her name as she descended the church steps. Nicole paused. Upon seeing the likable professor, she smiled. "Larry."

Larry stepped down to where Nicole waited. He was as blunt as ever. "I didn't think you would set foot in a church again."

"Never say never, Larry."

"Were those the Levis you were with?"

"Yes."

"I'm looking forward to meeting them. Beth speaks very highly of Jacob and Liza."

From Liza, Nicole had received unsolicited news regarding Beth's studies. "I hear through the grapevine that Beth enjoys working with you."

"It's mutual. When I see a sparkle in her eyes I know she's about to throw another challenge ... she's a post-modernist's dream."

Larry's brief sketch of Beth piqued Nicole's interest. "What do you mean?"

After Larry's challenge, Beth had come to his classroom prepared to engage in the subject at hand. As the first semester progressed, and currently in a second semester class, she had exceeded his expectations. "Her audacious pluralism. Somehow she can hold to her core beliefs while she deconstructs her faith. It has been fascinating to watch, but then I remember she has had you in her life and I'm not so surprised."

"Me?"

"Of course, you. When one of my – let's say less enlightened – students make a questionable statement ..."

"Questionable?" Nicole interrupted. "Larry, do you know that the phrase 'intellectually vacuous' is used to describe your kind of rhetoric?"

Larry laughed. "Fine. When Beth hears a classmate say something judgmental she holds nothing back. I can't help but think that her passion is in some way fueled by her commitment to you. I think her litmus test is whether she can tolerate those statements said in your company."

Nicole rejected Larry's assessment. "Beth's passion for theology has nothing to do with me. She had it long before I met her. And you're wrong to think Beth's sense of justice hinges on me. Jesus has always been her model."

Larry's tone turned critical. "Why is it so hard for you to accept the fact that you've been a positive influence in Beth's life?"

"Because I've learned that she and I don't necessarily speak the same language. There is no influence where there is no understanding."

"Is that how you've decided to move on, by invalidating everything you two have shared?"

He had overstepped his bounds. Nicole was harsh. "Larry, don't presume to understand what I think or what I feel."

Larry was subdued by Nicole's forcefulness. "I'm sorry, Nicole. The truth is that I consider both you and Beth very brave women."

Nicole calmed. "I think you're wrong to say I'm brave."

"It can't be easy to live in a world that is so contrary to your beliefs."

"Depends how you look at the world. Given all the different religions, now and in history, the fact that I believe what I believe doesn't seem so extraordinary."

"Maybe you're a step or two ahead of the rest."

Nicole deflected the inferred superiority. "I don't want to say that, not while Beth is even at the slightest periphery of my life."

"Why not?" Larry asked, with genuine interest.

"Because I want to stand beside her. Not behind her. Not ahead of her."

"Maybe you should talk to Beth a little more. In my class she is exactly what I believe you hope for. Don't let her Christianity taint that truth."

Nicole was not prepared to imagine a renewal of her most intimate conversations with Beth. "I'll keep that in mind if ever the day comes again."

"Nicole ..." Larry's voice drifted to nothing. After a few ticks of time, he declared with exasperation, "All right. You win."

"Larry, this isn't about winning and losing. It's about maintaining our authenticity – mine and Beth's."

"Do you know what I admire most about my best students?"

Nicole smiled, her expectations met. She knew Larry would insist on having the last word. "No, but I'm sure you're going to tell me."

Larry shared the smile. "In my experience the best theological students are not changed by their studies in such a way that they become someone else. The best become more themselves than they have ever been. They shed all the layers of dogma and stand in *emet* to God."

"*Emet?*" Nicole was intrigued by the reference. "Jacob has mentioned it."

"Did he tell you how it relates to the Psalmist?"

"Not specifically."

"How familiar are you with the Psalms?"

Nicole reverted to her usual reticence. "I've read them."

"You've read them?" Larry chuckled. "Am I in for a dose of Socratic irony?"

"This lesson is yours to teach, professor."

"If you've read the Psalms, and I have no doubt you have, then you know that the Psalms are not all praise to God. There are lamentations. There are challenges to God. The Psalms teach us that we can say anything to God The Psalmist stands before God's steadfast love in *emet* – a truth that translates to their abiding faith. What more can God ask from us than we be honest? Anything else would be a sacrilege."

"Even if the student's truth is that she knows nothing but the mystery?"

"That is all anyone of us knows. The rest is faith. What we choose to place our faith in, how our faith informs us and shapes us, what we do because of our faith, that is what I believe is important." Larry acknowledged that Nicole had reason to be suspicious. "I admit not everyone thinks the way I do."

Nicole judged him to be a master of understatement. "Larry, you're in the minority here."

"I disagree, but I won't argue with you. I will say that I am in good company." Larry placed his hand on Nicole's arm to emphasize her inclusion.

"You didn't say how the Psalmist knew he had God's steadfast love? The *hesed*?"

Larry paused, his expression thoughtful. After a moment he posed a reciprocal question. "Do you believe in God's love?"

"I believe in love," Nicole emphasized.

"There, you've answered your own question. Look to your heart, Nicole. It is where you find love and it is also where you find God."

In a church corridor adjacent to the community room, Jacob approached Beth, who sat alone in a quiet alcove. "May I?" He gestured toward the seat beside her.

Beth welcomed him. "Of course."

Jacob sat down. He wasted neither time nor words. "So, were you surprised my girl came?"

Beth wondered if Jacob understood and had come to satisfy her need to discuss Nicole. "I didn't know if she would see me again." Beth still bore the pain of Nicole's rejection. "She was so closed when I saw her at the hospital."

"Don't tell Nicole, but I have always felt she had the essence of a poet. She sees and feels the world in her own unique way and were she bolder, she would tell others instead of keeping to herself."

"She has reason to keep to herself."

Jacob took Beth's hand. "She retreats. She always retreats. Underneath her genius is a shyness few see, for her genius is blinding. I saw it in her when she was young and grew accustomed to it. But for someone who does not know her ... my Nicole can be intimidating." Jacob savored a sip of wine as he revisited his dream for Nicole. "I knew that the woman who would win her heart did not necessarily have to be equal to her genius, although she did need to possess a fine intellect. I knew that more important than intelligence, the woman who would win Nicole would have an insatiable desire to know Nicole's mystery, who to us is God, and that is why I always believed you were that woman."

"I think you're wrong about one thing, Jacob. Nicki did try to share her vision with me. I have never been able to grasp it. I thought I did but I know now it still eludes me."

"If you did not understand, was there then a betrayal?"

"Yes, because understanding is not a pre-requisite to acknowledgement, and I stood by and watched as others placed her in the shadows. I'm ashamed to say that having her at the margins of my school life brought some relief to the endless questions of 'why her?' I can't begin to describe Nicki and do her justice. Either you see her or you don't. When it was just the two of us it wasn't that hard. But when I walked from the apartment to the University everything changed. Nicki was more accommodating than the people at school. I admit I took advantage of her so I wouldn't be inconvenienced. She is the greatest challenge to my faith. You were right when you said that to her."

"She told you?"

"Yes. As much as I love her ... I love her because she challenges me. Sometimes I wish she weren't so damn good at it. It's no longer what she says; it's what she doesn't say. I know what she's thinking. I know she's holding back out of deference to me. But damn it, I've come to hate that she does that for me. I hate myself for letting her do it without a fight."

The community room was near empty as the reception drew to a close. Beth sat alone at a corner table where she had removed herself to be free from the bustle of human society. Rachel joined her. "You've been quiet."

Beth was emotionally spent. "It's been a long day."

Rachel sat down. "I didn't expect to see Nicole." Met with silence, Rachel took a more direct approach. "How is she?"

Beth was dispassionate. "Good, I think."

"What did she say to you?"

"She wished me well."

"That's all?" Rachel asked with undisguised suspicion.

"Yes," Beth assured.

"Why didn't she stay for the reception?"

Beth saw Jacob's poet in her mind's eye. "She wouldn't have felt comfortable."

Rachel's irritation spilled over. "So it wasn't out of respect for us?"

Beth was angered by the intimation. "Her respect goes without question."

"I pity her," Rachel declared curtly.

Beth's ire was compounded by Rachel's cavalier attitude. "Why?"

"Christianity is a common currency that Nicole has no use for. She lives in a state of poverty, bereft to negotiate her life."

Beth stared at Rachel. Never had she been so condescending. "Do you really believe that?"

"Yes."

"Do you believe that all non-Christian religions are in a state of spiritual poverty?"

"You can't compare Nicole's beliefs to the great religions," Rachel said dismissively.

"Nicole's beliefs precede Christianity."

"Fine. She's a materialist with no reverence for the soul."

"That isn't my impression."

"Really?"

Beth ignored Rachel's sarcasm. Her proof would win the argument. "A materialist may live more aware of God's grace than anyone else. Nicki looks to her life for meaning. She values the virtues; there is no forgiveness of sins so she is harder on herself. She is also less prone to self-righteousness." Beth's latter statement was intended as an indictment against Rachel's attitude. "Nicki sees the imperfection of the world with open eyes. Somehow she can reach forgiveness when others wallow in their pain."

"I've never met a materialist that fit your ideal, including Nicole."

"I disagree."

At a disadvantage, Rachel challenged Nicole's authenticity. "She's a good actor."

Beth shot back, "It's no act."

"If she was your ideal, she would never have left you. Beth, how naïve can you be?"

Beth's countenance grew hard. Rachel had yet to learn her lesson. Attacking Nicole would never be a good strategy. That Rachel did attack Nicole only set her poorly against the absent competition.

Rachel's tone grew placatory. "Don't look at me like that. You two are so different. I have never been able to understand how Nicole could meet your needs."

"Rach, you don't know her. You have no right to judge her."

The tether securing Rachel's jealousy snapped. "I know she lives on the fringe. It may not be the lunatic fringe, then again from what you told me about her mother maybe ..."

Beth raged. "Shut up!"

"Forget it."

"No! I don't want to forget it!"

"All right. Tell me. What's Nicole's agenda?" Rachel presented her case with a vengeance. "What kind of person crashes an ordination?"

"I sent her an invitation."

"For the love of God, why?"

Beth took umbrage at having to explain, but nonetheless did. "Nicki has always felt responsible for the fact that I left the priesthood. She shared the pain of my leaving the Church. I wanted her to share my joy in finding a new spiritual home. After everything we've gone through, I owed her that."

"Are you going to keep seeing her?"

Beth hoped Nicole's *Moria* would make it so. "I don't know."

"That's not good enough. I've been patient, Beth. I think it's time you decide whether you want to be with me or with Nicole."

Beth studied Rachel. The woman seethed with indignation, befittingly placed. "You're right. You've waited long enough. You don't have to wait for me any longer."

Beth walked alone, contemplating the milestones of the day, the goal achieved, the relationship ended. She had left the gifts at the church. She would bring them home at another time. She entered the apartment. The streetlight shone through the sunroom, illuminating the living room couch. Rachel had asked how Nicole could meet Beth's needs. Beth lost count of how many times after her surgery, due to symptoms triggered by her surgical menopause, she had found herself on that couch in the middle of a sleepless night, alone, only to have Nicole search her out, wordlessly taking her place behind Beth, coaxing Beth into an embrace, holding her, asking nothing, waiting until Beth fell asleep. Rachel wondered how Nicole could comfort Beth. The answer was that as Nicole did on those lonely nights, as she did on this day in the church, Nicole could and did comfort with a grace that never risked Beth's dignity.

Beth's eye caught sight of a gift-wrapped package on the dinning room table. A card was set on top. No one except Nicole had access to the apartment. She opened the card. Imprinted on the left side:

Wisdom teachers her children
    and gives help to those who
        seek her.
Whoever loves her loves life,
    and those who seek her from
        early morning are filled
    with joy.

Whoever holds her fast inherits
   glory,
and the Lord blesses the place
   she enters.
Those who serve her minister to
   the Holy One;
   the Lord loves those who love
   her.
Sirach 4:11-14.

On the right side of the card she found an inscription in Nicole's script.

Beth,

   May your love of God be a steadfast source of compassion and wisdom in your ministry and in your studies.
Nicki

Beth opened the package. Within lay a white stole. On each side, sewed in gold, a Celtic cross. Beth wept.

CHAPTER 165

March 29, 2004 – Monday

Nicole remained at a distance, intent on Beth and Marie, who sat side by side along their father's gravesite. Joe stood behind Marie. Marie caught sight of Nicole. She slipped out of her chair and whispered in Joe's ear. Joe raised his gaze to Nicole then returned it back to Marie. The younger Kelly stepped away from the service and walked towards her target. Beth's gaze followed Marie's movements. Seeing Nicole, she understood her sister's motives for leaving.

Nicole opened her arms to Beth's sister. Marie embraced Nicole warmly. "Thank you for coming."

"How are you?"

"I want to go home," Marie groused.

Nicole gently released Marie. "Shouldn't you be …?" Nicole nodded her head toward the service.

Marie turned to look at the congregation of people. Nicole followed the younger woman's gaze. The gathering was comprised of members of Fredrick Kelly's church, employees of his hardware store and a few other friends and their spouses. Pam and Cindy flanked Beth. Marie set aside Nicole's remark. "Joe will forgive me."

Nicole noted the exclusion of Beth. She placed her arm over Marie's shoulder. Marie intimately leaned against the taller woman.

The service completed, Marie looked up to Nicole's stately profile. "You're coming to the house, aren't you? We're having the obligatory reception."

"For a little while."

Joe walked to the two women. He offered his hand. "Nicki, it's good to see you."

Nicole greeted the personable young man. "Joe, I wish it was under better circumstances."

Joe maintained an easy demeanor. "Funerals, weddings and christenings. They're all opportunities to do some catching up."

"I'd say family reunions but that just means having Beth and me in the same room," Marie whimpered.

Joe gathered Marie into an embrace. "Irish temperament. Watch out."

Nicole noted how Marie clung to Joe. "You seem to be doing all right."

"I had a feisty Italian grandmother. She broke me in."

Marie raised her gaze up to her lover. "I'll be good. I promise."

Nicole chuckled. "Why do I have my doubts?"

"Hey, we're at a funeral," Marie protested. "Levity is not allowed."

"Then I'd better stay away from your corrupting influence."

Marie gently slapped Nicole's arm. "Look who's calling the kettle black."

Nicole's gaze shifted to the gravesite, where Beth was receiving condolences. The scene exemplified Beth and Marie's relationship. Beth completed the conventional tasks expected of her while Marie took refuge elsewhere. "I should say hello to Beth."

"We'll see you at the house," Joe said as he led Marie to the limousine.

Left alone at the gravesite, Beth's gaze settled upon Nicole's waiting form. She had not expected to see her former partner. She walked towards her. She had no idea what she was going to say.

Nicole stepped forward, meeting Beth on the open expanse of lawn. She kept a pace between them. "I'm sorry."

Beth looked back to her father's casket. "I've had greater losses."

"It still can't be easy."

"I've learned that the hardest losses are the ones I could have prevented. It's harder than those that were out of my control."

"You didn't cause your estrangement."

Beth turned toward Nicole. "Not with my father ..."

A silent moment passed between them. Nicole hesitated in reading too much into Beth's regret. Beth's comment could have easily been a reflection of the current troubled state of her relationship with Marie.

"I'll walk with you," offered Nicole.

Beth looked over to the dispersing procession of automobiles. Marie and Joe stood hand in hand beside the limousine. Beth began to walk towards them. Nicole matched her stride.

"All I've heard since I got here was how much he loved me. I don't know what to say. His love was so terrible."

"The way he treated you and Marie. Beth, that wasn't love."

Beth turned to Nicole. Her voice was strained. "Please don't say that."

Nicole paused. She restrained herself from reaching out to Beth. "I didn't say he didn't love you in his own way. I'm just saying that you can't confuse his ... hardness for love. You told me his beliefs were warped by grief. What he felt and what he showed you were two different things. We are all capable of not living up to our ideal, no matter how good our intentions. All we can hope for is to be forgiven when we fail those we love. I know you never stopped loving him and I know you did your best to forgive him. He's dead, Beth. You need to make peace with him." Nicole could not bring herself to conclude her thought. Once again Beth needed to make peace with her God.

Beth's heart broke anew, for a reason other than the loss of her father. "You do know me."

Nicole felt privileged. "I've tried to."

"Thank you, Nicki."

"I'm parked over there." She pointed in the opposite direction from where they were walking. "Marie asked if I would stop by ..."

Beth welcomed the thought. "Please do."

Nicole cordially excused herself. "I'll see you in a little while."

Nicole purposely delayed her arrival at the Kelly home. She stood outside for a moment in quiet contemplation. If she did not know better, she would have envied a child raised in the Colonial white-framed house. This was where Frederick Kelly had harmed his daughters. This was from where both Beth and Marie escaped to create their own lives.

The front door had been left ajar. Nicole entered. The house was bustling with activity. Pam immediately greeted her. "Nicole, it's good to see you."

Nicole offered her hand. "Pam, thank you for letting me know."

"You obviously had second thoughts."

"I decided to trust your judgment."

"I have faith that what you and Beth shared still has a place and a purpose in your lives."

"Well, I wouldn't want to shake your faith."

"Why not, you play the role so well?" Pam quipped.

Nicole was taken aback. She sobered. "I don't play with other people's faiths."

Pam reached out, her tone shifting to the apologetic. "Nicole, I didn't mean that ... not the way it sounded."

Beth entered the room, distracting Nicole. Pam followed the woman's gaze. She spoke a prayer for both of them. "'All shall be well and all manner of things shall be well.'"

Nicole turned back to Pam. "That's familiar."

"Julian of Norwich."

"There's more, isn't there?"

Pam recited an expanded quote. "'All shall be well and all manner of things shall be well by the purification of the motive in the ground of our beseeching.'"

Nicole distilled the message to one word. "Sincerity?"

"Yes, you could say that."

There were too many people in the room for its size. Beth's presence, coupled with Pam's words, threatened Nicole's equilibrium. Her tolerance for the gathering quickly slipped away. She searched for an exit. "Excuse me. I'm going to get some fresh air."

Nicole stepped through a screened porch into the back yard. She gravitated towards the far edge of the grounds. She sat on a hand-made bench that encircled a large oak tree. Nicole looked up to the bare expansive branches. There was little sign of spring's approach in the dormant arbor.

Within a brief period of time Nicole observed Marie walk toward her. The younger Kelly plopped her body next to Nicole. "It's pretty awful in there, isn't it? If I hear another person say that I should take comfort in knowing that the old man is with Jesus, I'll scream. If it wasn't for Beth I'd kick them all out of the house."

Nicole was sympathetic. "They have the look of a pious group."

"I'm glad you never met him. Then again, it might have been interesting to see him go one-on-one with you."

"From what Beth told me, I don't think your father would have been any different with me than he was with you."

"He had a methodical way of talking. His voice was so cold it could make me shiver in the middle of the summer. He was good at making us give in to him. Beth did her best to protect me. I hated watching what he did to her. She tried to please him and he gave her so little back."

"I know."

"I had to get out. I didn't tell him I was leaving. The morning after my high school graduation I just got on a bus headed east. Beth had no idea. I thought it would be easier for her. She wouldn't have to lie about not knowing where I was going." Marie stood up nervously and fixed her eyes on the house. "The truth is that I was afraid she would choose him over me and tell him. When I finally called her … it was so hard." Marie turned back to Nicole. "Our grandmother couldn't help. I was her only hope and I left her. I never realized … Nicki, how could I tell Beth I didn't trust her?"

Nicole saw Beth's collateral loss reflected in Marie's anguish. "I wish you had given her a chance."

"You did and look what happened."

"Hey … don't compare us."

"Why not?"

"Because you don't know the whole story." Nicole stared Marie down. "If you don't trust Beth, trust me when I tell you that I made my share of mistakes. Do you think I would be here if Beth were completely to blame for our separation?"

Marie set all courtesy aside. "You're here because you still love my sister."

Nicole would not deny the fact. "Pam called me. She invited me drive down for the funeral."

"Yeah, but I notice you drove here alone."

"Funerals can get intense."

Marie's bravado was stifled by the unbridled ferocity in Nicole's glare. "Yes, they can." She attempted to ease the tension. "I'll have to thank Pam. Until I saw you, I felt Joe was my only ally."

Nicole accepted the peace offering and relaxed her taut muscles. "Did I hear right – are you two engaged?"

Marie smiled and returned to her seat. "You're invited to the wedding."

Nicole was pleased. "I'll pencil you in." She casually bumped Marie's shoulder. "So, things are going well."

"He's been so patient with me. When I got the call from Beth about the old man dying … I lost it. I cried like a baby. He held me for hours."

"When my mother died … it was harder than I had imagined … I had to give up hope that one day I would have her love without the taint of her mental illness."

"That's not why. He died of pancreatic cancer. Nicki, I'm starting to feel I'll be lucky to break thirty."

Nicole recognized Marie's fear. "You should talk to Beth."

"How can I? After all these years I still feel our father standing in between us, keeping us apart."

"Maybe now things will get better."

"I don't know. If it wasn't for the old man's dying … Beth and I … it's been tense since Thanksgiving. It's ironic, isn't it? Our father drove a wedge between us and now, like it or not, Beth and I have to stay in contact until his estate is settled."

Nicole was surprised. "He left you both in his will?"

"He gave us everything. I think he was afraid of what people would think if he hadn't. God fearing man that he was, he had a hypocritical need to keep up appearances. I'm grateful for the money, but you know, I really would have rather had his love."

"Isn't that what every kid wants?"

Beth exited the house in the company of an older man. Marie's gaze was intent upon her sister. "I haven't asked Beth the question."

Having followed Marie's gaze, Nicole glanced back to the younger Kelly. "What question?"

"If she believes the old man landed in heaven or hell."

"Heaven," Nicole responded confidently.

"You sure?"

"She has to believe that."

"No, she doesn't."

"She believes your mother and grandmother are waiting for him."

"Damn you!" Marie burst into tears.

Nicole embraced her. Marie was not as immune to Beth's vision of life as she would have herself believe. Consoling Marie gave Nicole an outlet for her desire to ease the self contained pain that radiated from both sisters.

Marie's tears subsided. She rested her head against Nicole's shoulder as she watched the movement of people. Beth reappeared on the back lawn. "She's beautiful, isn't she?"

Not having to ask whom, Nicole answered, "I always thought so. It runs in the family."

"Beth never thought she was beautiful. Our father pressed her down. That's one of the best things you gave her. You made her see herself as beautiful."

"Marie, don't give me credit for loving her."

"You never brought her down."

"I think you're wrong."

Marie sat up and faced Nicole. "If she's had doubts they had nothing to do with you. You were just the scapegoat. She put her doubts on you and sent you into the desert alone."

Nicole yielded the point. "If she did, it was a bloodless sacrifice."

"It wasn't bloodless."

"I was alone before I met Beth. I've just gone back to where I belong."

"It didn't have to be that way."

"Maybe not." Nicole's struggle to accept her fate was far from concluded. "But it happened and nothing is going to change that fact," she said, sounding more certain than she felt.

The time was near midnight. The Kelly house stood quiet in the night. Beth sat in a chair beside the window in her former bedroom. Her gaze was fixed upon the old oak tree, its form visible by the moonlight. She could once again see Marie and Nicole as they sat together, as Marie cried in Nicole's arms. She had wanted to join them. She had wanted to share her tears with both women. Instead, in a familiar, lonely silence, she had cried privately.

Beth heard a soft knock upon her door. After a brief moment, Marie opened the door.

"It's late. Can't sleep?"

Beth shook her head.

Marie stepped inside and sat on the bed across from her sister. "It's over."

"Yes, it is."

"I'm sorry I bailed out on you at the cemetery."

"There was somewhere else you wanted to be," Beth said tolerantly.

"I'm sure you did too."

Beth offered a muted smile. "Isn't that what older sisters are for?"

Marie broached a subject that was paramount in her sister's heart. "It was good to see Nicki."

"You two seemed to have had a nice talk."

"We did. She didn't let me off the hook about things ..."

Beth wondered what 'things' were discussed. She withheld the question. "She's like that."

"I kind of monopolized her time."

"I'm sure she was grateful. When she can't have silence she likes having a safe friend beside her to keep others away."

"I didn't mean to keep her from you."

"You didn't," Beth assured her. "She said what I needed to hear while we were at the cemetery."

Beth was being careful with Marie, in spite of the fact that she wanted to once again have the closeness she had grown accustomed to sharing with her sister.

"What were you thinking about before I came in?" Marie asked.

Beth glanced out the window. "Nicki ... so much about being with her was about being in silence. She has a constant need for it. It would surprise most people to learn that about her. She has the personality to walk into a room and own it. Even today I watched her do it. In the beginning what always, always surprised me was how unconscious she was of her charisma. And then one day we came home from a party Alex had hosted and I realized Nicki hadn't said a word all the way back. She was running on empty. Being with others, even me, drains her. She went to her den and sat alone for a while. I found myself frightened. I wasn't sure why. Maybe because for the first time I realized that I also had that effect on her. I wasn't an exception. I went into the bedroom and changed into my pajamas and then went into the den. I kissed her on the cheek and said goodnight. It wasn't the first time. By then it had gotten to be a routine. But it was the first time I understood what was happening – that I saw Nicki's need to be alone for what it was. How deep it went in her and how she would lose herself if she couldn't have it. The only comfort I could take with me to bed was Nicki's touch. When I kissed her she tended to reach out and cover my hand with hers, giving my hand a gentle squeeze. It was a reassurance I desperately needed. She knew that better than I did.

"There wasn't a day that passed between us that there wasn't that silence in her. And there wasn't a day that passed that she also didn't touch me, that is if I let her. She'd hold my hand or entwined our arms or place her palm against the small of my back when we stood side-by-side." Beth looked at Marie. "Today, Nicki didn't touch me. I watched her hug you. And Marie, I envied you. I envied Joe when she took his hand. I can live with her silence. I haven't learned to live without her touch."

"But Rachel ... you have her, don't you?" Marie asked. "I was wondering why she didn't come here with you."

"We're not ..." Beth chose her words carefully. "We're not friends anymore."

"Why not?" Receiving no answer, Marie railed against her sister's fickleness. "Beth, you didn't want Nicki!"

"I never stopped loving her." A single tear broke free and fell down Beth's cheek. "I told you. It was hard. I made mistakes."

Marie softened her voice. "You see that now?"

"I can't see anything else."

"Tell her."

"You don't understand." Beth considered everything she knew about her former lover. "I crossed a line. On the other side of that line there aren't any second chances – not with Nicki."

"Are you sure?"

"Yes."

"Well, I spent the afternoon with her and I'm not so sure." Marie took Beth's hand. "Beth, for once in your life, listen to your little sister. I know what I'm talking about."

CHAPTER 166

April 6, 2004 – Tuesday

The distance from the Levi Law Office to the Elysian Fields was the length of a four lane Chicago street. It was afternoon when Liza walked the span to reach Beth. "It is Tuesday and as you know, Nicole is with Tasi," Liza said. "Are you waiting for someone in particular?"

Beth smiled. She had longed to speak to one of the Levis and was grateful to see Liza answer her silent call. "Hello, Liza."

"We are beginning our own tradition." The older woman sat down. "For years I've watched Jacob and Nicole sit on a bench together. A part of me has always wanted to join them. I knew it was better that I give them their time alone. Even from across the street I could tell if they were being playful with each other or if their talk had grown serious. I watched Nicole grow up right before my eyes."

"Even when she was a little girl?" Beth asked.

"Even then her mother kept benches outside her tavern." Liza glided her hand across the wood. "These are a family tradition."

"I didn't know."

"Nicole believes in traditions. She keeps memories close to her heart."

Beth took no comfort in unforgotten memories, knowing the damning power they possessed. She wanted to learn how lovers could begin to bridge the fear that separates them. "Liza, I don't know what to say to her."

"When Jacob and I met he would only let me so close. It was true for everyone in his life. I knew I did not want to be outside, always waiting for a glimmer of him to show. He needed time and more patience than I thought I was capable of. With each day I made progress until the day he sent me away."

"He sent you away?" Beth glanced across the street to where the man in question sat working. "Why?"

"Because he loved me and he knew I loved him."

"I don't understand."

"He was afraid … what kept him from me though was more than fear. He did not want me to live with his bouts of depression and he did not want to take the hope of children from me."

Beth had never questioned their childlessness. "You married Jacob knowing you wouldn't have children?"

"Yes."

"Did the Nazis ..."

"No." Liza shook her head sadly. "They starved him and almost worked him to death but they did not experiment on him. Jacob refused to bring a child into the world. He did not trust humanity to prevent another *Shoal.* What was more painful is that he did not trust God."

"That isn't the Jacob I know. Nicki never mentioned why ..."

"She does not know. She came to the same conclusion for very different reasons."

Beth remembered first learning Nicole's decision. "I didn't know how she felt about having a child until after we were living together. It broke my heart. I can't tell you how I felt when she changed her mind."

"When we married I needed to accept Jacob for who he was. Part of my vow was that I would not try to change him." Liza said, imparting a lesson Beth needed to embrace if she hoped to have a future with Nicole.

"Did you ever regret your decision?"

Liza leaned back against the bench, her eyes fixed on the law office façade. "I will not lie to you. In all our years there have been difficult days when I wondered what my life would have been had I walked away. Most days I thank God for giving me the heart to fight for Jacob and for us." Liza turned to Beth. "We have shared a wondrous life."

Beth believed her. "Did you ever disappoint Jacob?"

"Not in the way you disappointed Nicole, no."

Liza's uncompromising statement drew Beth inward. She felt the poverty of a soul unable to reach out for the divine. A soul that failed in obedience to God's dictum, to the challenge to love bravely, to trust in God's grace, to stand as God's instrument against injustice, to willingly risk losing to a stronger human force than oneself in order to realize the ultimate divine initiative. Her failure of obedience was a failure of faith. Nicole was not her adversary; those who claimed to share the fellowship of the Christian faith but who, in fact, turned away from Jesus' teachings of tolerance and acceptance were. She had bent to their insidious will, tainting her heart. She had stood witness to Nicole's downfall because of it. "I want to try ..." Beth hesitated in making her declaration, an uncertain suitor seeking a parent's permission. She prayed the blessing would be given. "I understand my promise now."

"It is not enough. What you are asking is more than forgiveness; it is more than friendship. You are asking her to trust you with her life a second time." Liza was as gentle as she could be. "My dear, Nicole may not have the strength to surrender to you again."

Beth was crushed by Liza's admonition. "I'm not asking her to surrender to me."

"You remember your sermon on *hesed?*" There was no question. Liza was intent on teaching the teacher.

Beth knew that Liza was aware of the importance of that sermon and that it would never leave her memory. "Yes."

"Jacob came home to me after taking Nicole to the service. He shared as much of the sermon with me as he could remember. He was proud of you."

"I don't think Nicki completely understood what I was trying to tell her. Her acceptance of my Christianity wasn't necessary. She had given me so much. Even our first kiss ... she was angry with me. She had a right to be and she was honest in both her anger and her love. I never stopped trembling from that first kiss."

"That was the kiss you mentioned in the sermon?"

"Yes."

"We assumed Nicole is Ruth." Liza took Beth's hand. "Have you ever thought that the analogy should be reversed? Maybe Nicole is not Ruth. Maybe you are. Maybe an act of *hesed* and your redemption are bound together. Maybe your redemption is only possible if you speak Ruth's words, 'Do not press me to leave you or to turn back from following you! Where you go, I will go; where you lodge, I will lodge; your people shall be my people.'"

Beth completed the recitation, "'And your God, my God. Where you die, I will die – there will I be buried. May the LORD do thus and so to me, and more as well, if even death parts me from you!'"

Liza reached up to Beth's tear stained cheek, catching a falling teardrop with her fingertips. "The mistake most of us make is believing we see the obvious when we don't see at all."

Jacob stood by his office door watching the two women speaking. Beth fell into Liza's arms. The younger woman was crying. He could attest that Nicole was finding her way in life, moving cautiously forward toward a new beginning. He wished Beth could do the same. He waited until Beth calmed before he crossed the street.

"Here. Blow you nose."

Beth looked up to where Jacob stood, handkerchief in hand. He wore a tender smile that belied his gruff instruction. She accepted the handkerchief. "Thank you." She blew her nose and wiped her tears from her face.

Jacob bent down and cupped her cheek in his fragile, aged, worn hand. "It is hard to accept."

"What?" Beth was captured by the old man's gravity.

"It is hard to accept that for our Nicole there will always be one thing more important than love. She will sacrifice your love for her truth. That has now been proven to both of us. It breaks her heart. I know this. I also know that she has no choice."

Beth loathed what Nicole was driven to do for the sake of their relationship. "She tried to live a lie for me."

"Not a lie. That is too harsh, too calculated. Nicole has never been insincere." Jacob dropped his hand and glanced up to the loft window. "Before Nicole met you, she would joke that no woman would have her. She felt she would never break free from her aloneness. Then you came into her life and she dared to dream again. She had no understanding how terrible her bargain would be. She thought love worthy at any price."

Beth lowered her eyes.

"My girl, don't look away. You did not act in malice. Loving Nicole is a good thing."

Beth found and held his gaze. "But Jacob, there is one question no one is willing to answer. Is Nicole loving me a good thing? Is it good for her or only for me?"

"What do you believe?" Liza asked.

Beth turned to the woman in her life who lived the one love she most greatly admired, and felt inadequate by comparison. "Right now, I don't know. I can't see what lies behind Nicki's eyes. I don't know how to reach out to her. I don't even know if I should try."

Jacob's answer left no room for doubt. "Try."

CHAPTER 167

April 8, 2004 – Thursday

Liza summoned Nicole for tea. Nicole waited patiently for Liza to reveal her agenda. Liza raised her teacup taking a sip of the warm, milky liquid. "Beth and I had a nice visit."

Nicole braced herself at the mention of her former partner. "Did you?"

"Yes."

Nicole regretted the little time they had shared in Riverton. "How is she?"

"She and Marie had a long talk after her father's funeral. They seem to have resolved their differences."

"Good. They need each other."

Liza took hold of Nicole's hand. "I understand Marie was your defender. She did not like Rachel."

Nicole imagined Beth's scrappy sister standing against Beth in her defense. "What changed Marie's mind?"

"It wasn't Marie who changed. Beth has stopped seeing Rachel."

"Is that why Rachel wasn't at the funeral?"

Liza nodded.

Nicole struggled to control her conflicting emotions. She had reason to dislike Rachel, and to celebrate her failure to earn Beth's love. In turn, she did not wish Beth any further disappointment. "I'm sorry it didn't work out for them."

"Are you?"

Nicole sensed Liza's well meaning, though misguided, intent. "Does Jacob know you're telling me this?"

"You should know better than to interfere in a marriage."

"Advice you should follow."

Liza projected a victor's playful smugness. "So are you telling me there is still a marriage that I should respect?"

Nicole was not to be so easily trumped. "A divorce. Nothing has changed. Beth is still Beth."

"Just as you are the same woman you were before you separated?" Liza patted Nicole's hand. "I know better."

Nicole felt Liza's love as a constant that encircled her protectively, while at the same time it nudged her from the nest, coaxing her to a second leap after a painful failed attempt to spread her wings in flight. "You want me to knock on her door as if nothing happened?"

"That would be a great mistake. If you see Beth you must be brave enough to remember everything, no matter how painful, and decide what you want from her if she is to be in your life."

"I already made that decision."

"Have you?"

"Beth and I were friends before we were lovers. I'm hoping we can be friends again."

Liza was skeptical. "Just friends?"

"Happens all the time."

"I do not think so."

"Liza, you don't know the lesbian community. Trust me. It can be done."

Liza was unsparing. "And what happens if there is another Rachel?"

Nicole looked down to her bare hands. "Not 'if' Liza. It's only a question of when. Nothing will happen except I'll drift into the woodwork. Ex-lovers can be threatening to the new girl – or in Beth's case it might be the new guy on the block."

"Do you think Beth will be as understanding? She has never been part of your community in the same way you have been."

Nicole remembered Beth's reaction to Paige long before they joined. "I can be discreet."

"So you admit that she will care."

"Liza, it's not like we are going to see each other all the time. There aren't that many ordinations and family funerals."

Liza leaned back into her chair, disappointed. "You have no real intention of being her friend."

Nicole anticipated their next encounter. "I'll see her at Marie's wedding."

"When will that be?"

"I don't know."

"Nicole, life has taught me that the preciousness of life is not meant to be set-aside for a fitting moment sometime in the distant future. The present is our only certain opportunity to becoming fully human, to realize God's plan for us. Tell me, do you love Beth?"

"Liza, please."

"Do you?"

Nicole conceded with a nod of her head.

"Beth made a mistake," said Liza. "Yes, it was a terrible mistake and you were hurt. Nicole, you must understand, Beth did not turn away from you. She turned away from God."

"That's not true!"

"It is. She did not trust God. She failed in the prophetic mission of all ministers of God. And she paid a great price. You left her."

Nicole refused to have their separation cast in the light of a religious failure. "What prophetic mission?"

"The prophets were charged by God to speak against the worst of society. In obedience to God they stood alone and challenged the people to heed the divine message. They did so knowing that their fortune was to be exiled or struck down by those to whom they preached. You know as well as I do that Beth stands outside of the conservative Christian community. Her beliefs are liberal and nothing in her life is a greater testament of her beliefs than her love for you. When she failed you, she failed herself. More painful still to Beth, she failed in her calling. She failed God. She knows this and she is inconsolable."

Nicole stilled. Her life with Beth taught her that she could not intercede for Beth in the sight of Beth's God. Beth's faith was too complex, too personal. Beth had had to grapple with the discord in her soul alone. In the past, Nicole had stood witness to Beth's lonely struggle, her heart aching in empathy as Beth navigated the ethical and spiritual uncertainties of the true child of God she aspired to become.

Nicole challenged Liza's role for her. "And the only way she'll find God again is if I ask her back into my life?"

"No. She must find her own way and she cannot make you the proof of God's forgiveness."

Her conclusion confirmed, Nicole wondered what Liza expected of her. "Then what am I supposed to do?"

"Trust in your truth and in your love."

"I'm trying."

"Be brave, my girl. Both of you must have courage. The world is not kind, as you well know."

Nicole stood at the edge of her newly created sanctuary. "Am I to bring an unkind world back into my life, back into The Fields?"

"Make your home in The Fields the place of kindness you have always wanted. Kindness does not exist alone. You must invite another soul to be kind to." Liza made her request. "Nicole, you could invite Beth to the reception."

Nicole considered such an invitation bordering on callousness. "Her father just died."

"It will be good for her to be with others. You can introduce her to Tasi and Yeva. I know Yeva wishes to meet her."

"I should never have introduced you two." Nicole leaned back in her chair. "Liza, I don't think Beth wants to meet Tasi."

"Let her decide."

"I don't want to hurt her anymore."

"What are you trying to protect Beth from? She spends her time with the children of her church."

"This is more personal."

"I think to see you and Tasi together will be good for her."

Nicole relented. "I have never been able to argue with you."

"Then you will invite her to the reception?"

"I'll send her an email."

"Nicole, if she comes, be with her. It will not be easy for Beth to see your friends again."

"Yes, ma'am." Liza had given Nicole much to think about. "May I now be excused?"

"Is being with me such a hardship?" Liza teased.

Nicole stood up and went to the woman who was dear to her. She kissed Liza on the cheek. "I love my time with you and you know it."

CHAPTER 168

April 8, 2004 – Thursday

Larry sat across from Beth in her office. Beth was chronicling the latest notable events in her undergraduate class. "One of my students asked why God must be a personality."

Larry tossed an unopened pack of cigarettes from one hand to another. "What did you say?"

"To me God isn't a personality. Jesus is."

Larry smiled. "What did your student think of your answer?"

"He was fine with it. Hillary took exception," Beth said, referencing her most challenging student. Hillary held very conservative Christian religious beliefs and was outspoken against any interpretation of Christianity contrary to her own. "She said Jesus is God incarnate and therefore God is a personality. I said there are different understandings of Jesus' humanity. The meaning of the incarnation has been a point of contention throughout the centuries. She didn't like that. Most of my students know so little about the tradition. They only know what they learned in Sunday school."

"Don't tell me you were different?" The professor asked.

"I wasn't," Beth admitted. "I wish we taught our children differently. There are so many college students that walk on this campus with only a narrow concept of the Christ."

"What is yours?"

"*Exemplum humilitatis*. When I feel distant from God I look to Jesus." Beth leaned forward, trusting Larry to receive her beliefs without prejudice. "Larry, if Jesus was just a man, only a man, he was still a model of humility toward God. In Gethsemane, in crisis he humbled his will to God. Mark wrote about a man, not the incarnation."

"Mark is not John, Beth. Even your first-year student knows that."

"By the end of the first year." Beth smiled wryly. "In the meantime, it can be tough going."

"Your students aren't the only ones struggling," said Larry. "This has been a tough year for you."

Beth could never anticipate Larry's personal queries. They had the power to slip through her defenses, resulting in a candor she shared with few others. "Losing Nicki …" Beth looked down without completing the thought. Her loss of Nicole was not because of her faith. It was her faith that demanded an accountability she was not yet ready to answer to.

Larry breached the silence. "I believe the human soul is responsible for tending to its faith, to cultivate it, protect if from ill temperate frost and storm. Nature is not generous, it is just as apt to sun and nourish as to freeze and parch. Your faith did not begin with Nicole, nor will it end with her."

"I ..." Beth looked up. "The more I read, the more I'm left questioning. My questions ... some of them sound like an echo of Nicki's."

"Why should that be a surprise? Either you've overestimated yourself or you've underestimated Nicole."

Beth held Larry's gaze for a moment; his words were like a bitter infusion. "The Christian theologians I'm reading ... there's so much disagreement. Sometimes I can't find Christianity in the fray."

"You and I do not deal with a pedestrian understanding of Christianity. We know better. We know the extraordinary complexity of our shared faith. Beth, you know that there has been disagreement from the day Jesus first walked on the scene. Is he man? Is he God? Is he God incarnate? Which of the Gospels carries the greater power in our faith? Mark, because it is the first and the foundation for Matthew and Luke? John, because of his emphasis on the Logos? What about the non-canonical gospels? Thomas? Mary? James? If not the Gospels, what is the keeper of the faith? The Church? Tradition? But wait, should Christianity be limited to the elite, priestly class? No, it is the individual, moving toward the monastic and finally to the recluse. No, again, it is life in community. What is essential? What kindles the heart? What keeps the belief? What survives from one epoch to another?"

Beth smiled. "You ask a lot of questions."

"Yes, I do." Larry stretched out his legs. "And you may also notice I don't give you answers."

"I noticed." Beth felt the best teachers of theology forced their students to struggle to find their own answers. Such teachers did not necessarily share the same motivation for their method. Beth wanted to know Larry's. "Why not?"

"Because I don't have the right. Because I'm afraid of a world inhabited by Dostoyevsky's Grand Inquisitor."

Beth knew the character from *The Brothers Karamazov* well. In Seville, during the Inquisition, the Grand Inquisitor jailed a stranger, taken to be Jesus, and accused him of giving humanity too much freedom.

She kept a steady gaze upon her teacher. She spoke with confidence, certain she had just caught sight of one of the principles that supported the man in his journey toward God. "Some people would say we live in that world."

Larry's eyes glistened. "Have you found me out, Beth?"

Beth had experienced a rare triumph over Larry. "I don't know, Larry. Have I?"

Larry planted his feet firmly on the floor and leaned forward. "The Grand Inquisitor spoke of the three temptations and their corresponding powers:

miracle, mystery, and authority. It isn't enough to believe and worship. There is the need to do so in unity. Humanity will persecute, torture, and kill in order to eliminate doubt. What troubles me is that history has proven how effortlessly humanity will give up freedom. The extreme religious and political leaders prove the point. How can anyone in their right mind follow them? Are their claims of miracles so unassailable? Is their unique salvific knowledge of the mystery so compelling? The answer is easy; reason has little to do with the debate. Insecurity overrules thought. We can be a lazy and superstitious people, setting aside free judgment for an unexamined love. Promised a divine mystery, we resign ourselves and enter the pit blindly. Philosophers and theologians say that humanity needs more than to live; we must have something to live for. How many live for a life without pain, which is no life at all? How many surrender to the first authority that promises them a relief that can truly comes only in death? And die they do. First in mind, then in heart, finally in spirit. The only way you can tell they are still alive is to watch to see if they take a breath, and that they wouldn't do if their bodies didn't demand it."

Beth recalled the ending of the story. It was where her hope for humanity resided. "Remember, when the Inquisitor was done with his accusations, the Prisoner silently went to him and kissed him on the lips. The Inquisitor released the Prisoner and told him to go and never return. The Inquisitor couldn't kill him."

"Beth, the Prisoner went away. Who was right? The Inquisitor or the silent Christ figure?"

"That's a question each one of us must decide for ourselves." She searched her heart and found that her conclusion remained constant. "For me, by freeing the Prisoner, the Inquisitor kept his own feeble hope alive. He wanted to be wrong. He wanted the Prisoner to tell him he was wrong and the Prisoner did by returning love for hate."

CHAPTER 169

April 2004

Beth lay awake in bed. It was near one o'clock in the morning. She held in her mind's eye a drawing her professor placed on the board. A stick person, who knew God, experienced God as a fact. A second stick person, who did not know God, never had a sense of God. God was a belief. The second stick person did not discount the first person's experience of God and the first person did not discount the second person's lack of experience of God. The space that separated them and yet joined them at the edges was the space they were trying to ethically grapple with.

In the nearly four years of knowing one another she had never thought of herself and Nicole in these terms. She should have. She had come to respect Nicole's beliefs. That was true. But in her soul, Beth still believed that she was right. She had never questioned whether their child would be equally Nicole's and yet, she had also never questioned whether her child would be given a Christian upbringing. In one of the most profound ways imaginable, she had segregated their child from Nicole, who had every right not to capitulate to the discounting of her beliefs.

How many times had they navigated their differences? How many times had Nicole allowed Beth's Christianity to dictate? Beth had invited Nicole to situation after situation where Nicole had been forced to choose between a passionate retort against Beth's peers, against Beth herself, or silence. Each time Nicole had chosen silence, not to disrupt Beth's life or compromise her standing at the University. During these moments of truth Beth had said nothing. She had allowed Nicole's regression to occur, grateful for her partner's self-control. Each time, Beth had thanked Nicole by word or by the simple gesture of a comforting hand to calm her tense muscles. Then the day came when they had ceased speaking, never acknowledging the tension – avoiding, so Beth had told herself, placing salt into the wound. Finally, Beth had no longer noticed Nicole's effort, nor the toll Nicole had to pay to tame the waves of discontent.

The following day, Beth found herself on the corner across the street from St. Ann's. She was not sure how she had gotten there. She stood within sight of The Fields, recalling her confused days, when she had found herself torn between both worlds. She had chosen to step away from St. Ann's and the restrictions the Church had placed upon her. She had also made a second choice – Nicole. Her prayers had been answered in Boston when Nicole embraced her.

Beth struggled to reconcile their first year together in Hyde Park with what followed. How could they weather 9-11 and her cancer, knitting a closer, more honest union, only to see it slowly unravel during the quieter time of their second year?

Beth was left to search her memory. She remembered how, during her first semester, she would come home excited, having so much to share with Nicole. She remembered her disappointment when Nicole had engaged her without ever showing an inclination to modify her vision of the world. Nicole had been respectful. She also had been unimpressed by exposition grounded in human speculations of an unknowable world.

Being with her student peers had been far easier. When Beth had been with them, she'd felt as if she were mid-step on Jacob's ladder. They had worked together to find their way up the next rung. When she had been with Nicole, the existence of the ladder came into question. Why had Beth come to expect differently?

She turned her gaze to St. Ann's. She had known joy as well as wretched grief within its walls. Beth crossed the street and walked up the stairs. She entered the vestibule, continuing on to the narthex. She walked slowly down the center aisle toward the nave. She scanned all that was familiar, remembering hours spent in prayer, in worship, meeting quietly with parishioners who had found greater comfort in the church than in her office. She admired anew the stained glass, the solid pews, and the statuary. She paused in the heart of the transept. Her gaze rose and met the Christ. She stood fixed. Beth opened her heart. As if a prayer was answered she felt drawn to her left. She turned her head. There was the pew where she had found Nicole, her hand shaking from the effect of her tumor, in quiet contemplation. It seemed like another lifetime when she went to the enigmatic woman. Finding much to like. Beth remembered Nicole's questioning her interpretation of the Eucharist. Nicole had never stopped questioning her. Beth had stopped answering. She had stopped giving Nicole the opportunity to sit beside her to honestly, simply, exhaustively explore their differences.

Beth returned her gaze back to the Christ. She walked forward toward the chancel. She had forfeited all rights to go beyond to the altar. She knelt at the railing, clasped her hands together and bowed her head. She voiced her own question in a hush. "Why?"

The answer did not come to her in words; it came in a slowly intensifying regret. The answer did not come with a reason beyond her; it came with a reason harbored within her. The merciless answer came and demanded a response. Beth began to cry. Her voice was choked as she begged, "Forgive me." Beth remained in her posture of supplication as she confessed her sin to a knowing God that required no less of her.

It was April 9, 2004 – Good Friday.

CHAPTER 170

April 13, 2004 – Tuesday

Pam entered the church through the office complex. Beth was waiting for her, sitting in a pew midpoint from the altar. They had exchanged emails. The appointment was by Beth's request. Pam chose to sit in the pew in front of Beth, her body turned toward the younger woman.

Beth sat with her hands clasped in front of her. She was solemn. "Thank you for seeing me."

"Of course."

Beth glanced toward the altar. "I was wrong to want a commitment ceremony."

Pam was startled by the declaration. "Why?"

"Nicki wasn't meant to be here."

"Beth, Nicole was happy to do it."

"I'm not so sure."

"I am. I made sure she was doing it for the right reasons before I consented to officiate. It's not wrong to want her here with you." Pam raised her hand, indicating the church.

"I kept making the same mistake. I kept expecting Nicki to bend to me."

"I agree it would be wrong to expect that the responsibility to overcome your differences fell upon her alone. I can't believe that your hearts were so different."

Beth wondered why Pam gave her the benefit of the doubt, why she was assumed to be blameless. "Nicki tried so hard to focus on our similarities and for a while that worked. She had to make herself believe we stood on common ground before she could be with me with any conviction. It had to end. Jacob was right. The only thing Nicki has to hold on to is the truth – her truth. She can't live without it. I didn't see what being with me was doing to her because I didn't want to. Now I have no choice. I can't blame her for wanting someone else …"

"Do you think there was … someone else?" Pam asked cautiously.

Beth did not answer.

Pam tried again. "I've seen how painful infidelity can be."

"There wasn't another woman. I don't believe there could be as long as Nicki wore my ring." Beth grieved that she could not speak for both of them. "There are other ways of leaving. From the beginning of our friendship, Nicki had always put distance between herself and whatever was painful to her. More than once she'd found a reason to leave Chicago because of me."

"She came back. She wanted to come back to you."

"Pam, I want her to come back to me again. I'm afraid she won't."

"What makes you believe she won't?"

"I'm the one who hurt her," said Beth.

"Maybe that makes you the perfect candidate to help her healing. Beth, Nicole may find her answer and it may not be what you're afraid it will be. Didn't you?"

Beth was confused by the turn of the question. "Me?"

"A crisis of faith. Isn't that what we're talking about?"

"I don't know if I would put what Nicki is going through in those terms. This is about what I did. She isn't blaming God. She doesn't see the world that way."

"I know. She places her faith in people. You told me she won't have anything to do with Kate. I wondered how her argument with Kate compares to the break in your relationship. Nicole must make some kind of distinction. She did come to your ordination and your father's funeral."

"Kate and I aren't that different. We both refused to see Nicki for who she is."

Pam noted a critical distinction. "Kate won't apologize."

"I don't think it would matter if she did. Nicki didn't deserve Kate leaving her out in the cold. Kate ignored everything she knew about our relationship. Pam, when I left the Church, I held on to Nicki. Sometimes, she was all I had to hold on to."

"That isn't what you told me. You told me before you left St. Ann's that you were angry Nicole had entered your life and challenged your beliefs."

"She has always been the easier one to blame. Nicki never asked me to leave Christianity. She only asked me to consider a Church that allowed for us to be together."

Pam reversed the subject. "Have you asked Nicole to join the Church?"

"No."

"To accept Christ as her savior?"

"Pam …"

"Will you ask that of her?"

"Of course not. You know better than that."

"Beth, what happened between you two? What went so wrong?"

Beth looked down. Her regret surged as it had done at St. Ann's. She concentrated on trying to steady her breathing. She studied her hands, relaxing her clenched fingers. She willed a fragile calm. Reaching a place of internal quiet she physically stilled. Keeping her gaze lowered, Beth breached the silence in a low, raspy voice. "Will you hear my confession?"

Pam had been given the reason for their meeting. "Yes," she answered, as God's minister.

Beth kept her head bowed as she spoke in an intimately contrite voice. "I sinned against Nicole in word and deed. I broke my vow to honor her. I belittled her beliefs when I assumed our child would be raised in the Church. I kept expecting Nicole to spend time with men and women who didn't acknowledge her intellect and compassion, who did not validate the merit of her beliefs." Beth's self-directed anger continued to drive her to more painful truths. Tears welled in her eyes. "I sacrificed Nicole's dignity because I was afraid my professors disapproved of my relationship with her. I can't remember the last time I let her know how much more her integrity meant to me than having her stand in church with me." Beth covered her face with a trembling hand. "I spent time with Rachel knowing that she had romantic feelings for me. I chose to be with Rachel over Nicole because … God forgive me, I stopped looking to Nicki for …" Beth choked with tears. "I stopped caring … and she knew it."

Pam waited until Beth quieted. She prayed, "God be merciful to you and strengthen your faith. Amen."

"Amen," Beth echoed in a hush.

"Beth, do you believe that the forgiveness I declare is the forgiveness of God?"

Beth heard the question. She fought to reach the answer she knew was required by her faith. Could forgiveness come simply by confession? Was absolution so easily conferred? By giving her answer she did not err and equate divine compassion with that held by humanity – for others and for oneself. "Yes, I do."

Pam closed the confession, completing the sign of the cross as she recited. "Be it done for you as you have believed. According to the command of our Lord Jesus Christ, I forgive you your sins in the name of the Father and of the Son and of the Holy Spirit. Amen. Go in peace."

Pam escorted Beth out of the church. They paused at the top of the exterior steps. It was a beautiful spring evening. The trees flourished, their buds waiting to open – a natural reminder of the transition from winter dormancy to summer's blooms.

Beth embraced Pam. "Thank you."

"You're welcome." The two separated. Pam spoke now as a friend. "Beth, you may be right about one thing. The next step may not be Nicole's to take."

"Nicki sent me an invitation to her new development's grand opening this Saturday."

"She did?" Pam did not hide her surprise. "Are you going?"

The prospect of attending the public affair was daunting. "I'm afraid."

"May I ask you a question?"

Beth nodded.

"It's obvious Nicole wants to keep some kind of connection with you. I know you well enough to believe that every time you see her you will be reminded of your mistakes, of what both of you have lost. Can you live with that? Do you want to?"

Beth was not willing to accept the alternative. "What do you suggest? Am I supposed to walk away?"

"Beth, you can't go to Nicole expecting her to consent to renewing your relationship. Letting go of that possibility may be the kindest thing you can do for both of you."

"Aren't there second chances?"

"There is so much against you. Who is to say history won't repeat itself?"

"I hope it does. I hope Nicki and I can one day live together again."

"After everything that has happened, do you believe she would willingly place herself, for a second time, in such a vulnerable position?"

"I don't know." Beth looked inside herself and examined her motives. "I want to believe her loyalty isn't the only reason why she came to my ordination and my father's funeral. Pam, if she didn't want a second chance, why did she invite me to the reception?"

"The only way to find out is to go and talk to her."

Beth's doubts, stirred by Pam's cautions, once again surged to the fore. "Am I being selfish?"

"I can't answer that question without knowing Nicole's intentions. I can only ask you to please be careful. Don't confuse what you want with what Nicole wants."

"I spoke to Liza. She said to have peace Nicki needs to forgive me."

"So she's advocating a reconciliation?"

"No, she's not."

"And Jacob?"

"He thinks I should try."

"Is there anyone in the world who knows Nicole better than he does?" Pam asked rhetorically.

CHAPTER 171

April 17, 2004 – Saturday

Beth entered the Morales Standard an hour after the festivities had begun. There were a few familiar faces from CMT and the Elysian Fields. She walked a large corridor that one day would connect the residential building with the retail spaces planned for the second phase of the project. Within the corridor, a series of round tables for six were set up with white table linens and flower centerpieces. She spied Liza and Jacob sitting beside a woman. There was no sign of Nicole or a young girl meeting Tasi's description.

"Jacob." Beth extended her hand to him. She then turned to Liza.

The older woman opened her arms and embraced Beth. "I'm happy to see you." Liza made the introductions. "Beth, this is Mrs. Varnasky."

Yeva scrutinized the young woman deliberately. She offered her hand, and spoke in her most acerbic tone. "So you are Nicole's friend."

Beth set aside her tart character. She wished Yeva's statement were true. "It's a pleasure to finally meet you. Nicki has always spoken well of you and your granddaughter."

Yeva's gaze lay heavy upon Beth. "She is not one to speak badly of anyone."

Beth released Yeva's hand, standing up straight. "No, she's not."

From Yeva came a more direct, personal salvo. "I always thought it was unfortunate that your other engagements prevented us from meeting before today. Nicole was very understanding – more understanding than I would have been if I were her."

Beth felt the full force of Yeva's reproach. Though she might deserve Yeva's belligerence, she felt its public nature inappropriate. She responded with aplomb, "Then I count myself lucky that I don't answer to you."

Yeva bit down a smile. "Yes, I would agree."

Liza redirected the conversation. "Tess is here."

"Is she?" Though Beth had doubts of Tess's reception, she felt it could be no colder than what she had just experienced from Yeva. "Did she bring her family?"

"No. And Dion was very upset to be left behind. Nicole had to call her on the phone and promise to visit."

Jacob offered his own jocular observation. "We now have proof that Nicole's greatest weakness is little girls. If you ever need anything Beth, just tell Tasi to ask Nicole and I guarantee you will have it."

"Natasia has never asked for anything from Nicole except to have her love," said Yeva. "It is enough for her. It is obviously not enough for everyone."

Beth was nonplussed. She fell back on the safest sentiment that came to her, maintaining a respectful formality. "I would love to meet Natasia."

Liza attempted to rescue Beth from an unexpectedly cantankerous Yeva. "She is with Nicole. Look in the Children's Center." She tapped Beth on the arm. "Go on."

Beth gratefully excused herself. She walked among the celebrants redoubling her defenses. She was no longer sure she was ready to see Nicole.

She entered the Children's Center. There were about a dozen children playing in the space under the supervision of half as many adults. Nicole sat against the wall with Tasi beside her. Beth paused to watch Nicole with the young girl. She cherished Nicole's masterful approach with children. Nicole had the ability to acknowledge a child's personhood without ever losing sight of their extraordinary vulnerability. Seeing Nicole with Dion had the power to bring Beth to tears. She wanted to place a mirror before Nicole and reflect back her admirable qualities, proof that Nicole was equal to parenthood.

Beth took a deep, calming breath, and then approached. "May I join you?"

"Sure." Nicole smiled. She patted the space next to her. "Tasi, this is Beth."

Tasi looked up. "Hello."

"Hi." Beth sat down. "What are you writing?"

"A poem."

"May I read it?"

Tasi held the poem to her chest. "It's not done yet."

"Maybe after you finish it you can read it to both of us?" Nicole suggested.

"Okay." Tasi looked back and forth from Nicole to Beth. "Can I go play with Jeanie?"

"Sure. I'll be right here," Nicole assured the child.

Tasi looked over to Beth with suspicion and then walked over to the table where her playmate was drawing.

"She's protective of you," said Beth.

"She's not used to sharing me."

Beth wondered how much of her grandmother's character the little girl had inherited. "I met Yeva."

"And you survived?" Nicole quipped.

"Liza and Jacob played interference."

"Don't take it personally. She's tough on everyone."

"Including you?"

"Especially me." Nicole grinned. "So, how are you, Reverend Elizabeth Ann Kelly?"

"Not to you, Nicki. I took the collar off when we became friends."

"That didn't change who you were."

"It changed ..." Beth glanced away.

"What did it change?" Nicole asked gently.

Beth remembered those difficult months in which she had emerged from her self-imposed exile from human intimacy. "I had kept everyone, even Marie, at a distance. For every step you took towards me, I tried to take a step toward you."

Nicole shifted away from the memory of their gradual, at times volatile, union. "I never asked. Who gave you the name 'Beth'?"

Beth recalled her mother's dulcet voice. "My mother. My father always called me by my full name."

"I don't know who Elizabeth was to him, but I know who you are to me."

Nicole's current perception of her was well beyond Beth's ken. She longed to know more. "Who am I to you, Nicki?"

Nicole grasped the opportunity to tend to their wounds. "There is no denying that you are your father's daughter. For better or worse, he made his impression on you. You're also your mother's daughter. It's from her that you learned to be strong in the face of adversity. You have your grandmother's compassion. You're Marie's protective older sister. You buffered her from your father, giving her the ability to stretch her rebellious muscles. You're a chaplain, ministering with a clear knowledge of what it feels like to face the harsh betrayal of one's body, and you are a scholar who searches for the quiet truth amid the dissonance. You're a teacher with the patience to nurture the young and to challenge the emerging identity of an underclassman. Finally, and most importantly, you are a woman who holds a deep, abiding faith in her God. Taken together you are your own woman."

Beth found Nicole's generous sketch difficult to accept. She also painfully noted an omission. "Once, I was your partner, a woman who gave you my vow."

"Beth ..." Nicole tried to preempt Beth's self-incrimination.

"When we spoke our vows, we didn't promise forgiveness."

"You haven't forgiven me?" Nicole asked uneasily.

"You're not the one who broke her vow to honor and respect. Nicki, I know I let you down when we were together at U.C. I felt an emerging cynicism, an intimation that we were destined to fail ... why were they astonished by us?"

"Why wouldn't they be?" The wonder of their union was still very much a part of Nicole. "I was astonished by us. We came together by degrees and that's how we've separated. I'll speak only for myself. Our friendship made me confront my biases. I had to let go of some hard preconceptions in order to be with you. I couldn't do to you what Tess, Amelia and I did to Kate – make a game of our differences. I consented to include in my landscape, what was for me, an arid and barren enclave. I thought that as long as I could have a refuge I'd succeed in mastering the intricate facets of our relationship, keeping them in place so there was always an us and not just a you and me. Beth, I'm not blameless. My mistake was that I lost sight of us. I took the responsibility of our relationship solely on myself. Every time I stepped away from a confrontation, thinking that it was more important to keep the peace, I allowed you to think that we were all right, when we weren't. Maybe after your surgery you did need me to give a little more. Maybe I needed to give you more. There was nothing wrong with that. Beth, I will never forget how I felt after my surgery. You never coddled me. You never stopped challenging me and I loved you for being brave enough to risk my anger. I didn't return the trust. You see ..."

"Nicki, I saw what was happening. I let it happen. It was so much easier to let you back off again and again. I could have stopped you."

Nicole cooled. "What's done is done."

Beth felt Nicole's withdrawal. "Nicki, please ..."

Nicole's distant eyes silenced Beth's entreaty.

Beth was lost. "Who are we to each other? Are we civil ex-lovers? Can we be friends, or are we destined to become strangers?"

Bereaved, Nicole answered honestly, "I don't know."

"What do you want us to be?"

Nicole felt an imminent danger. "What I want is beside the point. I didn't want us to lose what we had, but we did. All I can do is try to see each moment clearly, accept what confronts me, and act with integrity. That's what I'm trying to do right now. There is no 'us'. Not in the way I once believed."

Beth looked away, on the verge of losing her composure.

With the back of her hand, Nicole stealthily wiped a tear from the corner of her eye. She refocused on Beth, and saw a pain-filled look of loss. "I'm sorry ..." Nicole tried to balance their pain with gentler remembrances. "Beth, we shared some extraordinary times in both our lives. It was good to have you waiting for me after my surgery, to encourage me to learn to walk again, to give me reason to return to Chicago and rebuild The Fields, and it meant a great deal to me that I could be some comfort to you when you left the priesthood and when you had your surgery."

"We were happy, weren't we?"

Nicole offered a rueful smile. "Yes, we were."

"Do you still believe I belong in Hyde Park and you belong at The Fields?"

Nicole was convinced that the time had come to speak the most difficult truth. "We weren't supposed to last. One way or another, you or me, you expected us to only have a few years together."

Beth was dismayed by the allegation. "Nicki, that's not true."

"In the beginning, we didn't have anything resembling a normal life. We went from crisis to crisis. You could manage as long as it was just us in our own little world. Once our lives settled, once you began to go out there," said Nicole, pointing toward a window, "and be with others, the harder it was to live with me. Beth, your surgery took a lot from you. It also gave you a future."

Contrary to Nicole's declaration, Beth vividly felt the uncertainty of her well-being. "We don't know that, just like we don't know about your health."

Nicole stayed focused. "Being at U.C. brought you back to your studies. You need the professors to approve of you. Ph.D.'s don't come easy."

"I admit I was wrong. I was insecure and I overreacted. I wanted my fellowship renewed. I tried to be what I believed they would judge the perfect student. There is no such thing. I wasted the opportunity of sharing my work with you. I know better now. I'm looking forward to debating my dissertation with you."

"Rachel," said Nicole, naming her most damning evidence.

Beth shook her head. "Don't."

"Beth ..."

"No, Nicki! I was faithful."

There was no doubt in Nicole's heart. "I believe you. I also believe staying faithful to me was tearing you apart."

Beth trembled with the conviction that upheld her pledge. "I gave you my vow."

"And I gave you mine," Nicole lamented. "What happens when love fails?"

"Nicki, I swear I never stopped loving you."

"You just stopped liking me." The bitter disappointment still cut Nicole deeply. "I honestly can't figure out why. I all but disappeared into myself. I clamped down on every part of me you might object to. It wasn't enough for you."

Without a credible rebuttal, Beth remained silent.

"Beth, you are intelligent and compassionate. You are beautiful. When I met you, you were like a caterpillar living in a cocoon. Now you've broken out of it. Whatever mistakes we made in our relationship, I hope we can learn from them and do better. Beth, I'm not your future."

"You can be." Beth laid her soul bare. "I want you to be."

Nicole was tempted. In response, she clenched hope by the throat and closed her fist. "I can visit your world, but I can't live in it. Beth, you need your world just as much as I need mine. It's knitted into you."

"Nicki …"

"That little girl we imagined. She's lucky we didn't have her. She would have been torn between us. A child shouldn't have to choose between her parents. Children need to feel sure."

Beth whispered, "Tasi loves you."

"Tasi is a Jew. She was born a Jew and Yeva is raising her as a Jew. Tasi belongs with Yeva and if something happens to Yeva, Tasi will live with her uncle. What she feels for me is not the same. I am not her mother."

Beth offered a thoughtfully examined solution. "We won't have children."

Nicole drew in a breath to steady herself. "That could still be the right choice for me. It has never been the right choice for you."

"Maybe my cancer was meant to tell me different. Nicki, in the hospital I wanted to live. I wanted to love you. I didn't have to lose my second ovary. I chose to … it was my choice. I wanted my life with you more than I wanted a child. Please don't tell me I've lost both a child and you."

Why, Nicole raged within herself, did their confrontation have to be so pitiless? "With or without a child, we still live in different worlds."

Beth's stamina was waning. "We merged our lives once. We can do it again. It's enough for me."

Nicole spoke without meaning to hurt. "Until another Rachel reminds you of what I can't give you."

"You can give me your love. Tell me you don't love me!" Beth implored.

Nicole was helpless to deny her love for the rare young woman who so vehemently fought for her. She lowered her voice and slowed her speech. "I remember being ashamed of the fact that I asked Laura to design the loft for me, just in case, so I would always have a place to go to. Leaving Hyde Park and coming back to The Fields felt like such a great failure. But at least I knew that I hadn't done anything disgraceful. I didn't live up to Kate's expectations of me. I'm home, Beth, and I have no intention of ever leaving – not even for you." Nicole reasserted her rigid limits. "I'm sorry but I won't compromise myself again."

"I don't want you to."

"The distance between us has never been greater."

"I think our differences have never been clearer. That doesn't have to translate to distance."

"Aren't you being naïve?"

"After this past year, the one thing I'm not is naïve. Nicki, you can think me a lunatic for wanting to try again. Maybe I am crazy for believing that our differences aren't irreconcilable."

"Beth, I don't want to be academic about us. We are not a field exercise in religious diversity. I have no reason to place myself back in the line of fire."

"You wouldn't be alone, this time. I promise you."

Nicole had accepted that what kept them apart was Beth's infidelity. It took a form far subtler than the common misstep of adultery. Their argument was a diversion, obscuring the truth that Nicole could not bring herself to candidly state. She relied on the most vividly demonstrative image that came to mind. "This coming from the woman who stands with the loaded gun."

"You believe I would hurt you?"

"You did. It's time we both stop lying to each other and to ourselves."

"Nicki, I admit what I did and why. I was trying to protect myself."

"At my expense."

"Yes!" Beth had stopped counting how many times she had confessed her sin. "I didn't realize I was hurting you as badly as I was."

"How could you not?" Nicole demanded. "Do you know me so little?"

"I didn't think you cared. You were so dismissive."

"What choice did I have? Your school friends stood behind a façade of Christian propriety."

"Your beliefs threatened them. They didn't know what to do with you. Not everyone can be a Larry Elliot. Don't you understand, Nicki? You are so far afield that they had no response to you. I know you well enough to know that we stand morally on neighboring planes. I chose to accept the fact that I might not always be able to cross over to you as a consequence of loving you, of being with you, but what motivation did they have?"

"What they preach. Interfaith dialogue."

"With you?" Beth was incredulous. "You don't need a church, dogma, ritual. None of it."

"I needed you!" Nicole closed her eyes and swallowed, harnessing her quickening heartbeat. Calming, Nicole reopened her eyes to the ruin left of Beth. She completed the demolition of whatever dream Beth held to and whispered, "Or at least I thought I did. Life taught me differently." Nicole saw a pall cross over Beth's face. Nicole spoke, hating what she was about to say, though it was the truth. "Beth, I don't know if I can trust you again. Not the way I need to, to let you back into my life."

There was no response Beth could give to Nicole. She was prepared to argue faith. She was prepared to quit if Nicole did not love her. Liza was right to warn her. How could she regain a trust forfeited by indifference? She held Nicole's reluctant gaze, keen and unblinking.

Nicole glanced down to Beth's side. A familiar bulge protruded from Beth's blazer pocket. Nicole reached inside and removed the black velvet pouch where Beth kept her prayer beads. She opened the pouch and let the beads fall into her hand. "Beth, can you pray for yourself?"

Beth kept her gaze fixed upon Nicole's hands. "It's hard."

"Have you been praying for me?"

"As long as I've been able to pray, I found a word for you."

Nicole placed the prayer beads in Beth's hand. "Keep trying."

Tasi watched the two women from a distance. She noticed Nicole wipe a lone tear from her eye. It was soon thereafter that she decided to abandon her friend and to return to Nicole's side.

Nicole welcomed the child. "Hey."

Tasi announced, "I thought you might miss me."

"I did." Nicole opened her arms. "Come here."

Tasi fell happily into Nicole's embrace. She whispered into Nicole's ear, "I love you."

Nicole tightened her hold. She whispered in return, "I love you, too."

Beth regretted not getting to know the child when Nicole had first offered to introduce them. She stood up; her prayer beads remained in her hand. "I should go."

Tasi turned, keeping an arm wrapped around Nicole's neck. Nicole reached up, offering Beth the velvet pouch. "Beth, I'm sorry."

Beth accepted the pouch. "So am I."

Nicole and Tasi watched silently as Beth left. Only after Beth had disappeared behind the Children's Center door did Tasi turn to Nicole. "Is she the one?"

"Yes, what do you think?"

"She doesn't look the way I thought she would."

"She doesn't?"

"No." Tasi shook her head to emphasize.

"I'm curious." Nicole tipped her head to the side. "I wish I could see her through your eyes."

Tasi balked at the idea. "You can't see through my eyes."

"Maybe not," Nicole conceded. "But I can see the way you look when you look at Beth."

"Oh." Tasi's eyes opened wide with undisguised bewilderment.

Nicole laughed.

"What do you see?"

"I'm not sure you liked her."

Tasi was unapologetic. "She made you cry."

Nicole was humbled by the child's sensitivity. "I made her cry."

"She wasn't crying."

"Yes, she was. If you could have seen her through my eyes you would have seen her tears."

"Why were you crying?" Tasi asked timidly.

"Because I was happy to see her. And I was also sad because we can't be together anymore."

Tasi looked toward the entrance door thoughtfully. After a moment she turned back to Nicole. "Why?"

"It's hard to explain. We hurt each other."

Tasi stubbornly pursued a satisfactory answer. "Why?"

Speaking to the child, Nicole reverted to the simplest, truest reasons. "We believe different things and that makes it hard for us to understand each other."

Still uncertain, Tasi said, "Is she a bad person?"

"No." Nicole's belief in Beth's goodness was unmoved. "No Tasi, Beth is not a bad person. She is good. All she wants to do is understand God's ways so she can help others."

"If she's good, why did she hurt you?"

Out of the mouths of babes, Nicole mused silently. "Tasi, you are a Jew, right?"

Tasi nodded.

"You are a good Jew, just like your grandmother and your uncle Aaron. If you had a friend, someone you loved with all your heart, you might want your friend to know God the way you know God. You might want your friend to go to Temple with you."

Tasi nodded again.

"But what if your friend sees the world through different eyes. What if your friend doesn't want to be a Jew?"

Tasi pointed to her playmate. "Jeanie isn't Jewish."

"And you can still be friends?"

"Uh-huh."

"And you wouldn't try to change Jeanie or forget that she doesn't celebrate the same holidays you celebrate?"

"I wouldn't forget."

"Well, in a way Beth forgot. And it was hard for me because I began to feel that for Beth to really love me that I would have to become someone different. And I couldn't ..."

"Does Beth still want you to change?"

"I think a small part of her will always wish that she and I could share her God. But for the most part, I think she loves me for who I am."

"Do you love her?"

Nicole found it far easier to answer Tasi than to answer Beth. "Yes."

"Do you want her to be like you?"

Nicole paused. Tasi's question surprised her. "I honestly never thought about Beth in any other way ... I couldn't imagine her differently."

"Why can't you be friends?"

Nicole responded to the child on an unexpectedly hopeful note. "Maybe we will be friends again." Nicole lifted Tasi in her arms. "Let's go. I have a feeling your grandmother will be looking for us pretty soon."

✝   ✝   ✝

Standing near The Standard's main elevators, Yeva waved Nicole over. "It is time for us to go to our home."

Nicole placed Tasi gently on her feet.

"Nicole, you asked me a question before about seeing Tasi more often."

"Yes, ma'am."

"How long has it been? A year?"

"A little longer."

"Here, I want you to have these." Yeva placed a set of keys to her new apartment into Nicole's hand. "A year of opening the door to you is enough. For now on you let yourself in."

Nicole smiled. "Yeva …"

"Wait, young lady. I am not done. This is also for you." Yeva held up a brightly wrapped package.

"What's this?"

Yeva responded dryly, "I would say it is a gift, but don't trust me – I only went to eighth grade."

Nicole shook her head. It sometimes seemed as if Yeva could not say an unqualified nicety. She took the gift in hand. She unwrapped a book – *Reading Ruth* edited by Judith A. Kates and Gail Twersky Reimer. She opened the front cover. Inside she found an inscription.

My dear Nicole,
> *The stories that speak to us say as much about us as they do about the writer. Here are God's words and the Midrash of thoughtful and devout women. I count you worthy of their company.*
With love and gratitude,
Yeva

Yeva watched Nicole closely, as the young woman grew serious.

Nicole raised her gaze to the older woman. "Thank you."

"You are welcome."

"The Book of Ruth holds a special place in my heart."

"Yes, I know. Liza told me Beth gave a sermon using Ruth's devotion to Naomi as an example of *hesed*. Someday, I hope to see your Beth again."

Nicole raised an eyebrow. "My Beth?"

Yeva would not be contradicted. "Yes, your Beth."

"I don't know. You kind of scared her."

"Yes," said Yeva contritely. "Liza had words with me after Beth left us." Yeva recovered her tempestuousness. "I wanted to see if she had any mettle."

Nicole was not amused. "Test me, Yeva. Not Beth."

Yeva saw a rare disapproval. "So you would champion her?"

"Yes." Nicole's severe response left no room for doubt.

Yeva smiled knowingly. "Well then, I have more reason to get to know her better."

Easing her temper, Nicole placed her hand on top of Tasi's head and looked down to the child. "We'll see."

Beth paused upon hearing Tess's familiar voice call out her name. She would have preferred to have taken her leave unnoticed. She secured the prayer beads into her blazer pocket. To Beth's relief, Tess wore a warm smile. Beth offered her hand. "Tess, how are you?"

Tess hesitated for a moment. "Oh, no, you don't." She embraced Beth.

A shudder travelled through Beth's body.

"Hey." Tess tightened her hold for a moment before gently stepping back.

Beth kept her gaze low as she fought tears. "I'm sorry."

Tess tempered her voice. "Did you see Nicki?"

Beth nodded. She took a deep breath and looked up. "Yes. She was with Tasi."

"Nice kid."

"Yes, she is."

"Nicki is looking good, don't you think?"

Beth granted that Nicole was in far better shape than she was. "She seems happy."

"For the most part, I think she is. You, on the other hand, look like you could use a friend. Why don't we go sit down?"

"No, Tess. Thank you, but I've overstayed my welcome."

"Well, I know everyone here who would matter, so who did the un-pleasantries?"

"No one really." Beth excused Yeva's less-than-warm reception. "I just feel out of place."

"I guess this group can be to you what the U.C. people are to Nicki."

"No." The analogy was unfitting. "If there are hard feelings here, they're with a reason."

"Not if you ask Nicki."

"I'm not so sure."

"She's being careful. Can you blame her?"

"No, I can't." Beth sighed as contrition made her heart quiver. "I don't think she will ever really forgive me."

"Is that what you think is keeping her at a distance?" Tess placed her hands on the younger woman's shoulders. "Beth, what is Nicki most frightened of?" Tess waited a moment before renewing her query. "Come on, after three years you haven't figured that out?"

"She's afraid she'll become like her mother."

Tess's next statement worked the truth with expert precision, like a smith honing a fine weapon. "She's afraid she'll lose herself. She's afraid that all that she is will slip away from her. As intelligent, as talented, and as willful as she is, she's afraid the day will come when, like her mom, she'll find death more attractive than life. Beth, she's afraid that the day will come when she won't be able to bear her interminable aloneness and she'll make a pact with the devil to keep it away. She feels that with you, she got close to making that pact."

"No … Tess, you're proof she's not alone."

"We are all alone to different degrees. You know that. And you also must know that everything that makes Nicki the remarkable woman that she is isolates her. I think that Tasi has given Nicki the pure unconditional love she's only known from my daughter. What separates Tasi from Dion is that Tasi not only loves her, but she also needs her."

"Jacob and Liza …"

"It's not the same. She still feels she has to live up to their expectations. What child doesn't feel that in terms of their parents? The Levis are the closest thing to real parents Nicki's ever had. Look, Nicki never expected to have your love. All she allowed herself to hope for was your friendship. But life played a trick on her and you loved her back. One thing Nicki has always carried inside her is that she is your second love. She can never be your first. What happened between you two only confirmed the danger of not being first in your life. Forgiving you does not change that one crucial fact."

Beth was stricken. "So there is no chance for us."

"I didn't say that you didn't have a chance. Nicki can be as uncompromising about her priorities as you are. She doesn't compromise well, or haven't you noticed?" Tess paused and looked around. "Nicki loves the city. She thrives in an urban setting, but she also loves to walk up into the mountains where there isn't a soul in sight. Anything in-between leaves her empty. She's like that with her relationships. She throws herself into friendships completely. She'll do anything for those few people she loves. Otherwise, she keeps people at a distance. Her business associates and her innumerable acquaintances could all disappear from her life and she wouldn't miss them a bit. Since she left you, Nicki has surprised me in one big way. As far as I know she hasn't taken anyone to bed. The day will come when she'll want to be touched again and she'll find another Paige. I hate seeing her settle for so little."

"She'll find someone to love."

"It took her ten years to meet you."

"She doesn't want me, Tess," Beth said adamantly.

Tess was equally insistent. "Did she say that?"

"She said there was no 'us' in the way we use to be. She said she can't go back. She doesn't know if she can trust me."

"Beth, you'll never get Nicki to forget what happened between you. You would be a fool to think you could. That doesn't mean you can't become something new to each other. If Nicki can't find her way back to you, if only as a friend, I'm afraid she'll never let another woman close to her again."

"How much more are we supposed to go through, Tess? I want the hurting to stop."

"You have to make peace with each other."

Beth pointed to the Children's Center. "We just tried. It didn't happen. I know we can't begin again. I know we can't pretend the last three years didn't happen. Knowing everything I've learned about Nicki and myself, it's better that we don't forget. What I don't know is how to move beyond where we are right now."

"Give her time. She needs to keep some semblance of control. This is her dance to lead and I guarantee you, it's going to be a slow one."

CHAPTER 172

April 18, 2004 – Sunday

The Pub was bustling with patrons. Nicole and Tess shared a booth. Come morning, Tess would return home.

Tess nursed her fourth glass of wine as she redirected their conversation back to the previous day's reception. "Nicki, I was hoping you and Beth might be able to work things out."

"Maybe now that she and I have talked again, the conspiracy to get us back together will end," said Nicole, with wavering conviction as she once again felt the bittersweet emotions that were inseparable from Beth.

Tess leaned over the table and slapped Nicole on the arm. "Hey! Don't pretend that you don't want her back."

"I want her," Nicole admitted. "Tess, I'm afraid. I'm not the hero of this story."

"What are you going to do?"

"I'm waiting for the comic relief." Nicole referenced their common knowledge of the Classics. "Maybe you can usher in a satyr play and put an end to the tetralogy."

"I'm not very good at burlesque."

Nicole smiled sheepishly. "There's always the drag show downstairs – next best thing."

Tess leaned back. "I've listened to you for three days now and I know the answer to your problem."

"You do?"

"Yes, I do," Tess announced triumphantly. "You forgot you are a Greek."

Nicole chuckled. "What?"

"You're a Greek."

"Yes, I am or at least half-Greek."

"No." Tess shook her head for emphasis. "You, Nicole Isabel Thera, are a Greek."

"Remember," said Nicole, going along with her inebriated friend, "I don't know anything about my father."

"I'm not talking about that Greek."

"What other Greek am I?"

"I thought you were smart," Tess said, using her professorial voice to great advantage.

"And I thought you had gotten over being an insulting smart-ass," Nicole sallied back.

"Nicki, you can travel across the world, learn about every living religion, and dead ones too, for what good it would do, and you would still be a Greek. Solan's Greek. Aeschylus' Greek. The Orphic Greek. To first know thyself. That's you."

"I haven't done a very good job of it," Nicole mused

"Not lately, no." After a moment, Tess said, "Actually, yes, you have. You left Beth."

"Tess ..." All humor was lost to Nicole.

Tess did not notice. "Listen. Your tenets: grace, acceptance, goodness and ... ?" She snapped her fingers trying to entice a recollection.

"Humility."

"Where's justice, Nicki?"

A valid question for which Nicole readily held the answer. "In goodness, Tess. Or have you forgotten the four cardinal virtues? A good man must possess courage, temperance, justice and wisdom. When I seek out goodness those are the virtues I look for."

"All right, I knew that." Tess hypnotically tipped her wine glass back and forth on its base. "Damn, you got me off track. Where was I?"

"I'm a Greek."

Tess focused. "Nicki, listen to me. Where are the lessons of your beloved tragedies? The tragedy of life is that there is no escaping our destiny and that there is no destiny devoid of what, Nicki?"

It had been a lifetime since she and Tess peppered each other with questions preparing for an exam. Nicole dutifully answered, "Suffering."

"The Greeks had suffering down long before Jesus came on the scene. The purpose of suffering is what, Nicki?"

"Knowledge."

"That's right. The Jews had Adam and Eve, but what did the Greeks have, Nicki?"

"*Arté.*" Nicole named the inner human force that led to self-destruction.

"So there you go. You are a Greek. You were a Greek before you read the Classics. You can read the Bible and get all involved in its layers and layers of stuff ..."

"Stuff?" Nicole was completely engaged by her learned friend's inability to articulate a complete thought.

Tess ignored Nicole. "I know you. I know the art you like. You've always been a Greek temple – a couple of pillars and an altar. Simple lines. Open spaces. You have never been a Gothic cathedral with ornamentation from one end to the other, with vaults and solitary chapels, each with its own saint with an indirect route to God. What's his name wrote that, remember?"

"I remember."

"What's his name?"

"Yep."

"You are a Greek. I'm not. You are just like Amelia."

"No more wine for you." The mention of Amelia was unwelcome. Nicole retrieved Tess's glass. "When is your flight?"

"One."

"Come on, I'm taking you back to your hotel."

"It's early."

Nicole stood up. There would be no argument. "It's late."

Nicole did not trust Tess to find her hotel room. She parked the Wrangler and escorted the intoxicated professor through the hotel lobby, into an elevator, down a long winding corridor and finally into her room. Tess teetered from side to side, much like the wine glass she had been playing with in The Pub.

"Come on. Stand still," said Nicole.

"What are you doing?" Tess demanded, feeling Nicole's hands on her.

"Do you want to sleep in your clothes?"

Tess slapped Nicole's hand. "Don't treat me like a child. I can undress myself."

Nicole backed off. "Okay, go ahead. Do you have pajamas?"

"Oh come on, PJs? I sleep in Bruce's shirt." Tess pointed to a white shirt hanging over a chair.

Nicole retrieved the garment.

"Nicki ..." Tess called with a hint of distress.

"I'm here."

"Can't get my zipper."

Nicole went to Tess's back and undid the dress zipper. She then carefully guided the dress down.

"God," Tess said lustily, "was this ever a fantasy of mine. To be stripped by a card-carrying lesbian."

"For pity's sake step out of this."

Tess waved Nicole forward. "Come over here."

Nicole stepped in front of Tess. Tess took hold of Nicole's arms and raised her feet out from under the dress. She was compelled to explain. "High heels, you know."

"No, I wouldn't."

Tess scanned Nicole. "You were never butchy. I like that."

"I know. It's always more fun when the dyke doesn't look like a dyke."

Tess feigned shock. "Ms. Thera, don't forget I'm a straight gal."

"Sit down." Nicole gently pushed Tess onto the bed. She knelt on one knee and took off Tess's shoes. "I stopped seducing straight girls a long time ago."

Tess was too far gone into her stupor to care what she said. "What was Beth?"

"Beth wasn't anything."

"What do you mean?"

"She was a virgin."

"Damn, how many virgins have you had? You are a Greek, all right. Virgins coming for you." Tess laughed. "Was there a pun there?"

"Here." Nicole threw Bruce's shirt in Tess's face.

"Bra first."

Nicole sat on the bed behind Tess's back. She removed the bra and covered Tess with the shirt. "Your virtue remains unblemished."

"I wish."

"Under the covers you go."

"Bully."

Nicole used her trump card. "I'm telling Bruce if you don't do as you're told."

The threat hit home. Tess crawled into bed. "I haven't had a girl's night out in a long time."

"Neither have I, but you don't see me getting drunk."

"Sins of the mother ... You always believed that was true. You still do."

"Tess ..."

"Nicki ... this is sober now." Tess sat up against the headboard. "I know what love can do to you. I know what it's done to me. I've changed. I've compromised to be with Bruce. It's hard sometimes but God, I love the man and I love the kids. I don't regret a thing. Not one. But Nicki, Bruce never asked me to change to the point that I wasn't me anymore. Eros is mighty but Eros is not worth selling your soul for. Somewhere deep inside the Greek part of you, you knew you were in trouble. You've let too many people distract you from your vision of what your life should be. Beth, Jacob, Kate. Look in the mirror, my friend. The age of heroes is long gone. You couldn't be the hero. At least not Beth's. She's got Christ. I'm sorry you lost Beth. I really am."

"Tess, it's time you get some rest."

"One more thing. Who was your favorite – Aeschylus, Sophocles or Euripides?"

"You know it's Sophocles."

"Which play?"

"Philoctetes."

"Why?"

"Because Neoptolemus did the honorable thing and confessed to Philoctetes that he and Odysseus were trying to trick him to get him back to Troy so that Greece would fulfill Helenus' prophecy and win the war."

"Neoptolemus was willing to be true to Philoctetes, even if by doing so he went against the gods and sacrificed his future." Tess took Nicole's hand. "Nicki, Beth is no Neoptolemus."

Nicole was exhausted. "It would have been wonderful if she was."

Tess slipped down against her pillow. "You're a Greek."

"Yes, Tess, I'm a Greek."

"You won't forget again?"

"I won't forget."

"Now that you remember, maybe you should tell Beth. Give her a chance to love you again for who you are."

Nicole tucked the covers around the beloved woman. "Can't make up your mind about her, can you?"

Tess's gaze followed Nicole. "I did a long time ago. She's not Neoptolemus to your Philoctetes, but I think she wants to be. And with your help I think she can be."

Nicole paused. After a moment she refocused on her friend. "Sleep." Nicole kissed Tess on the forehead. "I'll call you in the morning."

Tess rolled to her side. "You still taking me to the airport?"

"Wouldn't miss the chance to see your hangover."

"You're mean."

Nicole stood up. She kept watch until Tess closed her eyes and drifted to sleep.

Driving home, Nicole's thoughts lingered on Tess's words. She thought back, trying to remember how many times Beth had asked her 'why the Greeks' and how many times she had given Beth an incomplete, inadequate answer. Tess had given her the answer. Because she was a Greek. She was not a woman who saw the world of infinite complexities. She did not want a theology that required the systematics of an Aquinas. She saw the world with fundamental simplicity. It was a world of mystery and had to be accepted as such. She saw life as a grace, a gift presented without consideration of merit. She saw the greatest threat to humanity as its own *arté* – not a demonic force outside itself, but the human tendency for wanting more – more power, more wealth, more beauty – as if the virtues could be purchased by the highest bidder. And so she struggled to practice humility, to rein in the *arté* that had the force to lead to her self-destruction. In humility, she refrained from drinking. In humility she left her door open to the multiplicity of beliefs so that she would never embrace hubris and arrogantly destroy the faith of others. The counter balance to *arté* was Nicole's belief in goodness. Though difficult, she believed in the goodness in herself. More difficult still, she believed in the goodness of others. And when all her tenets, when acceptance, grace, humility and goodness were not enough to guide her life, she sought out truth – Jacob's *emet*.

Nicole was a Greek. For Nicole, there was no more important search for truth than ones own truth. To 'know thyself' was not only to have a clear vision of her inner landscape. It was to understand her place in the cosmos. She was not one with the gods. Neither did she want to be a maker of gods.

Justice, and she had questioned the place of justice during the previous year, was not to be measured by an individual life in a frozen moment of time. It was not poetic justice where all transgressions and acts of good were respectively punished and rewarded. It was not Solan's inherited justice, where sins from the parent were a stain upon the child for multi-generations. Justice was Simonides' 'rendering to every man his due.' It was human and social, it was to stay within her sphere and respect that of her neighbor.

Where was justice when interwoven with fate? How was justice measured when her mother, Jacob, Liza, Kate, Amelia, Tess, Beth, Yeva, Tasi, and all the others who had touched her life were taken into account? Who lost? Who gained? What could one say when, with time, a loss was experienced as a gain? She had lost Jacob, and when she was able to once again receive him, she learned she shared a common experience with Liza. The shared knowledge of loving someone with a mental illness strengthened her bond to her. She lost Kate, but maybe, just maybe, Kate would finally overcome her unrequited feelings for Nicole. Nicole lost the dream of adoption as she was given the opportunity to touch Tasi's life. She lost herself in the course of securing Beth's love. She lost Beth in her arduous return back to herself. Tess was right. Nicole was a Greek. She would not forget a second time.

CHAPTER 173

April 21, 2004 – Wednesday

Nicole waited outside the Hyde Park apartment. Her keys lay heavy in her coat pocket. She remained standing, chilled by the wind gusts, longing for a once familiar warmth that had nothing to do with brick and mortar, hard wood floors and wool rugs, but all to do with another human being whom she had forced to the margins of her life.

Beth turned the corner. She hugged her raincoat close, keeping her head down in an attempt to save her exposed skin from the bite of the unseasonable cold.

Seeing Beth approach, Nicole shifted off the lamppost to an independent stance. Beth had yet to see her. Nicole watched as Beth removed her hand from her pocket, keys in hand. Beth inserted the key into the lock and opened the door.

Nicole took a silent step forward. She could not find her voice.

Beth caught a glimpse of movement and paused. Seeing Nicole's reflection in the glass, Beth turned around. For a moment the wind calmed.

"Nicki." Beth sensed Nicole's uncertainty. "Would you like to come in?"

Nicole looked up towards the second floor. She gently shook her head. Nicole had waited over an hour for the opportunity to speak. Finding her voice, she wasted no words. "Beth, I was wondering if you would like to have coffee … or dinner with me."

Beth smiled. "I would."

"Friday?"

"Sure."

"6:30."

"Pick me up here?"

Nicole nodded.

Beth waited for another word. None was forthcoming. "Good night, Nicki."

"Beth." Nicole took another step forward. "I'm not sure I know what I'm doing here."

"That's all right. I can wait until you figure things out. Maybe I can help."

"I still think life would be easier for the both of us if we stayed apart."

"You have never done 'easy'."

Nicole noted that Beth did not include herself in the statement. "I can't do this alone."

Beth remembered those same words the night Nicole had left her. "You won't have to. We'll try together."

"I'd like that." Nicole smiled. "Good night, Beth."

Having Nicole so near, Beth was emboldened. "Nicki, are you sure you don't want to come in?"

Nicole's voice carried her regret. "I can't ..."

Beth realized it was the apartment Nicole was avoiding. "I'm kind of in the mood for an espresso."

"Medici's?"

Beth hopped off the stoop. She paused before Nicole. "Ready?"

"Just a minute." Nicole trotted to the Wrangler, which was parked at the curb. She opened the passenger door and retrieved a manila envelope. She returned to Beth, handing her the envelope. "This is for you. Tasi insisted."

Beth retrieved a hand drawn picture. She had difficulty deciphering the image. "I'm afraid to ask what this is."

Nicole placed her hand against the small of Beth's back, leading her toward the restaurant. "I think it's you."

Beth laughed.

CHAPTER 174

May 6, 2004 – Thursday

Beth entered the Morales Standard Children's Center. Nicole sat on the floor beside a low table, working on a jigsaw puzzle with Tasi. Beth was enchanted by Nicole's complete focus on the child and the puzzle. She guided Tasi, encouraging her in her work. Beth would have preferred not to interrupt, however, she was expected. "Hi."

"Hello," Nicole greeted her warmly. "You're right on time. Tasi, you remember Beth?"

"Hi." Tasi looked up from her work.

Beth knelt beside her. "This is a big puzzle."

Tasi continued to work.

Nicole offered Beth an encouraging smile. "We could use some help with the roof." She turned to Tasi. "Would that be a good place for Beth to start?"

"I guess so." Tasi glanced over to Nicole. "Here." Tasi offered Beth a potential piece.

"Thank you." Beth found the piece of little use but she kept it prominently in her hand.

"There you are!" Yeva stood on the playroom threshold. She walked in slowly, leaning on her cane.

Nicole turned to her. With tongue firmly in cheek she declared. "It's Beth's fault. We've been helping her finish the roof and ..."

Yeva bit her lip trying not to smile. "And you lost all track of time."

"Yes, ma'am."

"Would you accept such a reason from Natasia?"

Tasi watched as Nicole got to her feet. "No, I wouldn't. I apologize for not bringing Tasi upstairs on time."

"Very well." Yeva turned to the young minister. "Beth, it is good to see you. What brings you here?"

Beth stood up. "Nicki promised me dinner."

Yeva tapped Nicole with her cane. "Stay for dinner."

Nicole quickly glanced at Beth. A silent private question was posed. Beth nodded imperceptibly. "Do you need anything? I can go to the store."

"A red wine would be good. Beth can help me in the kitchen while we wait for you."

✛   ✛   ✛

The dinner was modest in food, but rich in conversation. Yeva entertained her guests with stories of her life in Russia. Beth was completely engaged. Her questions reflected some knowledge of the religious history of the land. When Yeva touched on the cruelty suffered by her people, Beth expressed a sincere sorrow, condemning religious persecution.

Afterwards, Beth embraced Yeva in farewell. "Thank you for dinner and the stories."

"You must come again." Yeva turned to Nicole. "Come here." Nicole stood in front of the older woman as Beth retrieved her jacket. With her arthritic hands, Yeva closed two buttons on Nicole's coat.

Nicole was grateful for the hospitality Yeva had demonstrated toward Beth. "Thank you for dinner."

"She is lovely."

"Yes, she is."

"She cares for you," Yeva said discreetly. "I can see how you are with her. You welcome her to you as you do Tasi. Your heart cannot help but be opened."

"Yeva ..." Nicole had no answer.

Yeva responded to Nicole's obvious discomfort with a rallying declaration. "Bring her again."

"With her permission."

"She will come." Yeva tapped Nicole's shoulder. "Bend down."

Nicole did as requested. Yeva kissed Nicole on the cheek. "I'm sorry I've been so hard."

Nicole deemed the apology unnecessary. "You had reason to doubt me."

"No, I didn't."

Nicole looked down to her coat. "Am I all dressed now?"

"Yes." Yeva swept her hand over the buttons one final time. "Go now. You're keeping Beth waiting."

With Yeva's final words still lingering in her mind, Nicole walked Beth to her car.

The evening had unfolded unexpectedly. Beth was pleased to have been given a glimpse into Nicole's life with the Varnavskys. "I had a wonderful time. I like Yeva."

"It's mutual." Nicole knew Yeva's warmth was all the proof needed.

"I like seeing you with Tasi." Beth paused in front of her car. "Nicki, what does Tasi know about me?"

What did Tasi know about Beth? What was important to the child? Nicole concluded that for Tasi what she knew, what concerned her, could be summarized by one lone fact. "She knows I once wore your ring."

CHAPTER 175

May 11, 2004 – Monday

Larry entered Beth's office and sat down, not waiting for an invitation. He raised a bound document. "I just finished reading your paper on the Psalms." He then paged through the first few pages. Beth watched her sometimes exasperating professor intently. Larry found what he was looking for. "Here." He glanced up. "You listening?"

Beth smiled. "Yes Larry, I'm listening." Given that she wrote the paper she did not expect any surprises.

Larry recited, "My journey is informed by the relationships between faith and trust, and between the *hesed* – steadfast love of God and the *emet* – truth of humanity ... Creation may be sufficient proof of the existence of God for the Psalmist. This is not true for everyone. For others trust is the precursor to faith. Their lack of trust in God is a function of a model of God given to them in their youth that they have been unable to reason to sustainable life or to satisfactorily replace, given all that goes before their eyes without understanding. Engaging in the Psalms has highlighted what separates them from the Psalmist, and what binds me to the Psalmist. It has reaffirmed that their experience is first and foremost, though not godless in terms of the divine, still one that is marked by the absence of God. My experience is first and foremost marked by the presence of God." Larry looked up from the page. "Has Nicole read this?"

Startled, Beth gave a reflexive answer. "No."

"She should." Larry sat across from Beth's desk.

"I'm not sure she's ready to read my work again."

"Maybe you're right." Larry placed the document on Beth's desk. "Don't hide this away. It's good, Beth. It's better than good. Thank you for sharing it with me."

"You're welcome." Beth had grown fond of her exacting teacher. His praise meant a great deal to her. "It's hard to believe the school year is almost over."

"The time has gone faster than I ever expected."

"I'm going to miss you."

"Beth, I don't do good-byes. You will have to visit me. And bring Nicole with you."

"You can invite her yourself." Beth was pleased to share. "She's coming with me to the end-of-year reception."

Larry patted his chair's arm. "Well, well, that's a good sign."

"I'm trying to take it one step at a time with her."

"I hope things work out for both of you."

Beth summarized their journey in its most essential terms. "We need to find our common ground again."

"Shouldn't be hard." Larry stood up with aplomb. "I'll prove it to you. Where's your Bible?"

"Top shelf."

Larry took possession of the book. "Let's go right to the cornerstone of our faith. I wager Nicole lives by the Ten Commandments." Larry paged through the Bible as he sat down. "Let's see. Exodus 20 ... 'you shall have no other gods before me.' Nicole is faithful to her divine mystery. 'You shall not make for yourself an idol, etc. etc. etc.' No idols for Nicole. 'You shall not make wrongful use of the name of the LORD.' Does Nicole curse God?" Larry brightly answered his own question. "Probably not hers, but who's to say about all the others? 'Remember the Sabbath day, and keep it holy.' Okay, we got her on this one. Nicole doesn't rest on any day of the week, does she? But then how many Christians keep the Sabbath?" Larry did not wait for Beth to answer. 'Honor your mother and father.' I can't comment." He looked to Beth.

"She didn't know her father and her mother died years ago."

"Does she honor her?"

Beth considered the question seriously. In spite of the abuse she suffered, Nicole did honor her mother. "Yes."

"Good. Moving on then. 'You shall not murder, not commit adultery, not steal, bear false witness against your neighbor, covet your neighbor's house, wife, male or female slave, or ox, or donkey, or anything that belongs to your neighbor.' She hasn't killed or stolen. She hasn't coveted a neighbor's donkey has she?"

Beth chuckled. "Not that I know of."

"We're not done yet. Now we go to Matthew 22 and the two great commandments." Larry recited without looking to the page. "'You shall love the LORD your God with all your heart, and with all your soul and with all your mind' and 'You shall love your neighbor as yourself. On these two commandments hang all the law and the prophets.' Beth, as far as I can tell Nicole is one hell of a Christian and except for keeping the Sabbath, not too bad of a Jew."

CHAPTER 176

May 14, 2004 – Friday

Beth knocked on the loft's front door, having eschewed her usual path through The Fields.

Nicole opened the door promptly. "Hi. Come in. Miguel is holding our table."

Beth stepped in. She was pensive. "Nicki, I was wondering if this is a good idea."

Nicole was taken off guard. They had agreed to dine at The Fields before going to the U.C. reception. "What?"

"Eating at The Garden."

"Why wouldn't we?"

"Miguel may not want to see me."

"Beth …"

"The boys have always been protective of you." Beth accepted that sooner or later she would have to face Miguel, Connor and Tony. They were an integral part of Nicole's life in The Fields and The Fields was an integral part of Nicole. She feared how the men judged the nascent reemergence of their relationship. She did not want to subject herself or Nicole to their disapproval. "I'm sorry. I'm being stupid."

Nicole gave credence to Beth's concern. "We can eat somewhere else."

Beth gathered her courage. If Nicole could face U.C., she could face The Fields. "I think I can manage … that is if you can?"

"If Miguel gets out of line, I'll fire him." Nicole quipped.

Beth smiled. It had been a long time since she had felt Nicole's protectiveness.

Surrounded by many familiar faces, the two women enjoyed a leisurely dinner. Nicole reached over and placed her hand over Beth's. "Come on, we don't want to be late."

The sensation of Nicole's touch took Beth by surprise. She tried not to elude any sense that what was once an easy gesture had taken on far greater meaning. The sensation reaffirmed how profoundly she felt the absence of touch. "I'm parked in the back, by the Jeep."

"I'll follow you to the apartment." Nicole stood and offered her hand to Beth. Beth accepted and walked beside Nicole.

Miguel stepped out of the kitchen. He called out. "Hey! Hey! Hey! Were you going to leave without seeing me?"

Beth gazed disbelievingly at the flamboyant man. Nicole smiled in appreciation.

"Where's my hug?" Miguel demanded

Beth looked at Nicole. "Is this a new work practice?"

"I think he's looking for a tip."

Miguel was playfully indignant. "Don't go on like I'm not here!"

Beth laughed lightly. "Miguel, that would be impossible."

"I should hope so."

Beth gave the Latino a heartfelt embrace. "Dinner was wonderful."

"Hey boss, did you hear the compliment?"

"Remember who it's coming from."

"I noticed you didn't leave any food on your plate."

"I hate to break up this reunion but we are expected somewhere else."

Miguel proved he had mastered the art form of attitude. "Fine. Be that way. You explain to Connor and Tony why you didn't stay."

Beth looked to Nicole. She wondered what Nicole had told them that would usher such a welcome. "We've got time. Maybe we could stop by The Pub?"

Nicole was pleased. "Sure."

"Tell Tony I'm sorry I missed him."

Miguel crossed his arms. "Only if you promise to come back."

Beth would not make the promise. A return to The Fields was only by Nicole's invitation. She kissed Miguel on the cheek. "Thank you."

Nicole kept by Beth's side for the better part of the evening. Those they spoke to at the reception were congenial. Relief for the end of another school year was palpable. A few present had achieved their degrees and looked forward to commencement. Nicole sighted the one man she wanted to speak to. She whispered in Beth's ear, "I see Larry. I'll be back."

Beth watched as Nicole stepped away. She felt secure that no harm would come to Nicole in Larry's company.

Larry responded to Nicole's greeting. "I was hoping to see you tonight. Come on, let's take a walk."

"Are you ready to go home?"

"Yes, I am."

"Any regrets?"

"None. It's been a good experience. Far better than I expected last September. I should have given my colleagues more of the benefit of the doubt."

"Beth is going to miss you."

"I'm going to miss her. She is a gifted theologian. I respect the fact that she lives in the world the way she does. It's not clean and neat and that's reflected in her very gritty theology."

Nicole glanced over to where the subject at hand stood speaking to a fellow student.

Larry stepped out into the hall. "Beth mentioned that you were dating."

Nicole followed. "Dating?" She was amused by the representation. "I guess we are."

"She seems happier. You know you two will always be an example to me."

"How so?"

"You share God, even though to you God is concealed while to Beth God is a revelation."

Nicole paused by a large window, leaning against the sill. "You're wrong to generalize. Beth knows how it feels to have God beyond her reach. It is terrible for her. And I know how it feels to stand in awe of creation. It's a rare feeling but I have known it. What makes us so different is our capacity for love. Hers reaches beyond anything I could conceive. I stand objectively and observe life. She immerses herself in it. She feels and there is no stopping it. I don't and there is no pretending."

"You underestimate yourself."

"No, sir, you presume."

Larry paused, clearly weighing all that he had learned about Nicole. "If you stand at a distance, Nicole, it is because of your capacity to feel."

"Maybe." Nicole accepted her nature. "It doesn't really matter why if the end result is that I can't shed a tear for my neighbor."

"You don't?"

"Rarely."

"When you do ..."

Nicole was resolute. "I've been reminded that I do see the world for what it is."

"I didn't get the impression that you thought the world was a terrible place."

"It can be. It can also be beautiful. Tears come for both reasons ... the locus of the beautiful and the terrible is sometimes found in the heart of the same creation. As much as I wish I could, I can't segregate one from the other. There is no escaping the risk, only minimizing one's exposure."

"Which is what you choose to do. Don't you think in her own way Beth does the same thing?"

Nicole marveled at Beth's growth. "In the past she had reason to. I think those reasons have slowly been stripped away from her, making her the gritty theologian you now see."

÷   ÷   ÷

At the conclusion of their conversation, Nicole bid a final warm farewell to Larry. She chose to remain in the quiet space as he returned to the reception. Larry had a knack for stirring her thoughts. She gazed through the window out into a courtyard, retracing their conversation's more animated exchanges.

Rachel approached. "If I didn't know better I'd say you were praying. Looking for your deliverance, Nicole?"

Nicole met and held Rachel's eyes with her own. She said nothing.

Rachel twitched uncomfortably. "These academic receptions can be a bit much."

Nicole returned her gaze to the courtyard.

Rachel took a deep breath as she looked down to the wine glass she was holding. After a moment she stepped forward. "You've changed your mind about Beth." Another step. "I don't blame you, she's a special person."

Nicole could see Rachel's reflection in the glass pane. She felt sympathy for the younger woman who, by her agitated gestures, seemed very much out of place, more so than Nicole thought herself to be.

"You must despise me."

Nicole faced her antagonist. "No. Under different circumstances I would probably like you."

"Don't be so sure. I haven't been very nice."

"You fell in love with Beth. I do understand what that feels like."

"Why didn't you fight for her? I did," Rachel confessed. "I wish you had fought for Beth instead of stepping aside and inviting me to take your place."

No matter how true, Nicole would not give Rachel the satisfaction of concurring with her assessment. "Is that what I did?"

"God, yes."

"Do you really think that's what she wanted, to be fought over?"

"I know it is."

"Rachel, I didn't have the right to expect anything from Beth. I left her."

"You just gave up."

"No. I kept on living."

Rachel took a gulp of her wine. "I have no one to blame but myself. It was obvious Beth never stopped loving you but that didn't stop me from trying to win her over. I'm ashamed of some of the things I said to her."

"That's between the two of you."

Rachel glanced back at the reception hall. "She won't even look at me."

"Give her time."

"I don't want to be your friend. If I could I would take Beth from you tonight," Rachel said bitterly.

"Who said Beth is anyone's to take? She doesn't belong to me."

"No, she looks to a higher authority." Rachel knew what arrows to sling.

Nicole had always known the terms of engagement. She set the fact nakedly before Rachel. "That's who she is."

"I can't figure out how she can be happy with someone whose beliefs are so incompatible with hers."

Nicole promised herself never to fall again under the thumb of the likes of Rachel. "Maybe they aren't as incompatible as you think."

Rachel drank the last of her wine. She grimaced. "This tastes awful. God, I'm glad that there are plenty of things in life that taste better than this."

Nicole held a steady gaze upon Rachel, keeping to her silence.

"Speaking of … how did you ever get Beth into bed?" asked Rachel.

Nicole checked her outrage. "I think you've had too much to drink."

"You're right." Rachel raised up the glass, making a show of it. "I started drinking the moment you walked through the door." She looked back again towards the reception. "From what I can tell, Beth didn't give anyone a hint that she was seeing you again. Damn, I envy you. To make love to a woman knowing that you are the only lover she's ever had or ever wanted. How often can you say that anymore?"

The disclosure was staggering. Nicole showed no emotion. "Are you driving?"

"Don't worry. I've got a ride." Rachel would not be put off. "There's another reason why I envy you."

Nicole was on the verge of losing control. "Rachel, stop this."

"No, really. You'll appreciate what I have to say." Rachel's tone shifted to the conciliatory. "You see, you still have your ideals. All I've got is the memory that I couldn't live up to mine."

"I made my share of mistakes."

"And Beth, she was perfect. Right?" Rachel laughed contemptuously. "Maybe I was wrong. Maybe I shouldn't envy you. Maybe you deserve my pity."

Nicole's anger left no room for reciprocating pity. "I don't have to look any further than the human mind to find evil. I don't have to look beyond nature to find the debilitating kill or be killed competition for living. I'm told an intelligent, loving God created this world. Fine! Rachel, between the two of us, I'm not the one to be pitied. Maybe to you, someone with my beliefs is heartless and soulless. I'm not either. I'm telling you to live in the world. If you do, you will be more practical and far less idealistic. And just in case you think I live in a dark merciless void, I'll say one last thing. We are also the source of love. To be alive, to really be alive is to understand that in life there is both good and evil, joy and sorrow, love and hate." Nicole looked down, reining in her anger. The night had been remarkably easy until this moment and she could not blame anyone but Rachel for an assault that was rooted in a disappointment Nicole knew too well.

"Nicki?" Beth's soft, trembling voice cut through Nicole's thoughts. Nicole raised her gaze.

Beth had entered the hall seeking reassurance of Nicole's well being. Her gut clenched at the tableau vivant of Nicole and Rachel. Nicole's fierce gaze, a gaze that reflected no vulnerability, did nothing to assuage Beth's concern. Confused, she turned to Rachel.

Rachel withdrew. "I'd better get back to my date."

Nicole watched Rachel depart, and then turned to Beth.

Beth stepped forward. "What did Rachel say to you?"

"She misses your friendship." Nicole's bearing gentled.

Beth sensed no lie. She also sensed that Nicole was not completely forthcoming and would not be if she pursued the subject. "I'm tired, Nicki. I'd like to go home."

Nicole heard defeat in Beth's faint request. "I'll get our coats."

Having retrieved their coats, Nicole held Beth's for her. Beth donned the garment. From behind, Nicole briefly placed her hands reassuringly on Beth's arms. Beth was not comforted.

Silently walking back to the apartment, Beth withdrew her hands to her coat pockets, precluding any gesture on Nicole's part to console.

It had been raining. Puddles of water bordered the curb. Nicole leaped over a pool and turned back, reaching out her hand to Beth. Beth paused. After a moment's hesitation, she took the offered hand, allowing herself to be guided over the water. Nicole did not release Beth and Beth did nothing to free herself. They walked hand in hand for the few remaining blocks. Upon reaching the apartment, Beth stood on the stoop, which made her equal to Nicole's height. "Thank you for coming."

"Thank you for inviting me." Nicole tried to end the evening on a positive note. "It was good to have a chance to say good-bye to Larry. There's nothing like a post-modern Christian, although I still think the concept is an oxymoron."

Beth smiled. "I could debate that."

Nicole was relieved to see Beth's tone lighten. "I'm sure you could."

"Would you like to come up?"

"Not tonight." Nicole continued to consciously avoid the scene of their separation. "A rain check on the post-modern?"

"Call me." Beth reached out and touched Nicole's shoulder. Their shows of affection remained muted.

"I will." Nicole stepped away.

Beth called out Nicole's name. Nicole turned once again toward Beth.

"I'm sorry about Rachel. I didn't know she would be at the reception."

"No harm done. Beth? Rachel said something about you two ... about your intimate relationship ... why didn't you ..."

Beth had not known how to tell Nicole. She had never expected Rachel to do her the favor. "Because she wasn't you."

Nicole smiled wryly. "Must have been a bitch for her."

Beth offered a smile of her own. "She had a lot of frustrated energy."

Nicole chuckled. "Good night, Beth."

"Good night, Nicki. Drive safely."

Nicole walked toward the Wrangler. She raised her hand and blindly waved back to Beth.

CHAPTER 177

May 20, 2004 – Thursday

The Hyde Park apartment door opened. Beth stood dressed in her robe, black sweatpants and a white tank top. She looked miserable.

"Hi." Nicole raised a ceramic crock in her hands. "Thought you would like some of Miguel's chicken soup."

The soup was not the only gift Nicole bore.

"What's under your arm?" asked Beth.

"French bread. Still warm."

Beth stepped aside. "Come in." She sneezed. "Excuse me."

Nicole crossed the threshold. She was not accustomed to the apartment. She felt a stranger among the familiar. She glanced to the closed den door, mourning the comfort that room once had granted her. Nicole noticed a rumpled blanket on the couch. "Why don't you lie down?"

"No argument here." Beth shuffled back to her resting place.

"Are you hungry?"

"Maybe later."

In the kitchen, Nicole placed the soup container in the refrigerator and set the bread on the counter. Returning her attention to Beth, she raised the blanket and gently draped it over her patient. She sat down on the coffee table. "Anything else I can do?"

Beth reached out and rested her hand on Nicole's arm. "Keep me company for a while."

Nicole covered Beth's hand with her own. "How are you doing?"

"May I ask you something?"

Nicole nodded.

"Since your surgery, have you experienced being sick differently?"

"You know how hard I fight letting anyone take care of me. I felt that way before the surgery and I still feel that way now. After the surgery, having you in my life, I had to rein in my temper … I'm not sure you knew me well enough to notice."

Beth stifled her laugh. "I noticed."

Nicole admired the hint of humor in Beth's eyes. "I was frightened that if I didn't behave, you wouldn't come back to see me. That was before I realized that when it came to be being stubborn, I had met my match."

"I bet if I look hard enough I'll find a compliment in that statement," Beth quipped.

Nicole grew serious. "My surgery and what happened in Shenandoah did affect how I experience my health. I'm more grateful for being able to take care of myself."

"But, Nicki, why do you still believe that you're left to your own devices? Didn't that time prove you could count on others?"

"It's not that I don't believe I can't reach out for help. I have, and my closest friends haven't disappointed me. I don't like being helpless. I don't want to be a burden to others. I know how it feels to take care of someone who is ill."

"Your mother was an extraordinary situation."

Her mother. Amelia. Beth. Jacob. They had all taught her differently. "Everyone is an extraordinary situation."

Beth found Nicole's propensity to give of herself without expecting reciprocation both admirable and frustrating. "You didn't shy away from taking care of me or with being with Jacob when he got sick. I don't know how I would have coped with my cancer if I had been alone."

"Did your cancer change how you experience being ill?"

"When I was growing up, I took care of Marie and my father. I had to be self-sufficient. Now, I get to the point where … there are times when I just want someone to take care of me."

"I'm here."

Beth's illness had drawn down her defenses. "For how long, Nicki?"

For all they shared. For all she felt, Nicole would not turn away from Beth. "Whatever happens, I've learned one thing. I don't want to live without your friendship. I'll be here."

Beth quieted. Another friendship came to mind. She looked away.

"Beth?"

"Kate sent me an email. I called her. We talked." Kate had grown to miss her connection with The Fields. Without specifically apologizing, she had voiced remorse for her brutishness. "Nicki, I know you value your friends. I'm grateful you can still think of me as a friend. You've proven to me that you can forgive those you love. It doesn't seem right that you and I can be friends and …"

"It's different," Nicole interrupted sharply.

"Kate's been your friend since college."

"Beth, please …"

Beth questioned whether she truly understood how great a crime had been committed. "What did Kate say to you after you left me?"

"You know what she said. She accused me of being unfaithful to you. Not a surprise, considering what she thinks of me."

Though painful, Beth felt her own transgression was far greater. "You love Tess. You've never been shy in expressing your feelings for her. Kate has always been different. I can't remember one time when you've told her you loved her. How can you have been such close friends and ..."

Nicole touched the truth. "There's history between us that we have both refused to face. Until we do, there can't be a friendship."

"Who is supposed to make the first move?"

"Not you." Nicole's severe gaze demanded an ending.

Beth endured the reprimand. "You wanted Kate and I to be friends. Were you afraid that if I had known she was in love with you that would never have happened?"

Nicole knew better than to be surprised by Beth's ability to see in the hearts of others. "No."

"Nicki, what happened?"

With Kate's feeling exposed, there was little reason to withhold the past. "Early in my first year of grad school I was at Kate's. We'd both had too much to drink. Kate ... I knew I needed to stop her from ever trying to seduce me again. I was cruel. I told her she would never be good enough for me. The next day she left me a message on my answering machine. She said she didn't remember the night before. She joked that we must have had a hell of a good time." Nicole was rueful. "Saving face by amnesia. I went along with her. We kept on going out. I kept on picking up new girls and leaving her behind."

Beth wondered who Kate would have been if she'd had Nicole's love. Would the harsher, resentful side of her been tempered? "Why wouldn't you be with her?"

"Honestly, I wasn't attracted to her. No chemistry. She was also my friend. I didn't want to lose our friendship."

"You couldn't tell her that?"

"I tried."

"Before or after that night?"

"Before. After ... I had said all I needed to." Now that the subject had been raised Nicole wanted all questions posed and answered so they would never have to discuss Kate again. "Anything else?"

Beth remembered Tess's chronology. Nicole did not stop drinking until the end of graduate school. "You didn't stop drinking because of what happened with Kate. Why did you?"

"Beth, it's in the past. Let it go."

"It's not in the past. Whatever it is, it's obviously here, right now."

Would Beth command, on this day, a reckoning of all her past mistakes? "Do you want me to tell you about every woman I took to bed ... every woman I've hurt? You never asked before. Why ask me now?" She stood to leave.

Beth's hold on Nicole's arm slipped to her wrist. Beth tightened her grip as she raised herself up on her elbow. "I didn't ask you about the women in your life. I asked why you stopped drinking."

Nicole had inadvertently opened the door to an episode in her past she had purposely kept from Beth. She attempted to close the door in one quick stroke. "At the end of grad school I did something I still regret. I promised myself never to take the risk of losing control again."

Beth gentled her hold, her voice compassionate. "What happened?"

With a jerk of her arm, Nicole released herself from Beth. "I'm going home."

"Nicki …" Beth sat up.

"No, Beth!" Nicole shouted. "That one night is mine alone. I won't share it with you."

Beth kept her composure. "Who did you hurt?"

"I didn't hurt anyone!" For the whole of their relationship, Nicole had withheld that one moment of time at bay. The lesson from it, had she heeded it, would have stopped her from pursuing Beth at the footsteps of St. Ann's or for a second time, at the doorstep of Hyde Park. Only Tess knew the truth and Nicole was not the one who had spoken. Why did she have to speak its name now? Why did Beth demand this from her? What grace could come from the telling? She was not seeking absolution. She wanted peace. Nicole's voice was even. Her words carried her anguish. "I didn't … I let myself be used. I let a woman manipulate me into bed against my better judgment. When we were done I wanted to rip my skin off. Standing in the shower didn't begin to remove how dirty I felt."

The reason was unexpected. "I'm sorry."

"So am I. I've tried for years to put a good spin on that night."

Given whom Nicole admitted to being during those years, Beth could not begin to imagine, let alone name the woman that'd had the power to hurt her. "Who was she?"

Nicole steeled. "A friend."

Having come so close to the truth, Beth was unwilling to shy away. "Who, Nicki?"

"Amelia."

Beth was speechless.

"You see, Beth. One thing I learned a long time ago is that love arising from friendship can't always be trusted." Nicole left the apartment without another word spoken.

CHAPTER 178

May 26, 2004 – Wednesday

Beth sat with her office desk chair turned toward the large arched window; her prayer beads were draped over her right palm. Her prayers complete, she sat for a few minutes in silent repose. She had found Nicole's final words to her a haunting reminder of her former partner's ability to isolate shards of her broken heart and keep them from sight.

Beth turned her chair forward. She stood up, swung her briefcase strap over her shoulder and took hold of a medium sized box, three-quarters full with her belongings. She walked the length of the hall and down the two flights of stairs that led out into the late spring evening. She passed through the heart of the courtyard. A feeling of nostalgia touched her. Beth stopped and turned her gaze back to Swift Hall. Her second year of school was done. Having passed her qualifying exams, the following school years would be devoted to her dissertation. She felt a new freedom. It was accompanied by the knowledge that the future promised a different student life, one accountable to her dissertation committee. She would not have the daily interaction with professors and students. Except for her meetings with her dissertation advisor, she was very much on her own.

Academia filled a need in her. She cherished the dialogue, the communal search for meaning, the quiet hours of private study and introspection – all within a Christian context. She could share the love of academia with Nicole. What she could not share was her enthusiasm for the Christian context in which her work took place, a context that Nicole found limiting. Beth's heart ached. She had wanted to believe that somehow academia would be a bridge, in a way the Church could not be, to their greater understanding of one another. The fact remained that spiritually, their worlds were different. Attending the University did not change that fact. It only accentuated their differences.

Beth understood that she was, and yet was not, whom she saw reflected in Nicole's eyes. Nicole was unceasing in recognizing Beth in the light of the cross. Whatever love Nicole still felt for her was separate, stood apart from Beth's faith. Beth found the separation difficult to accept. Without the cross she did not believe she was the same woman. If she did not live as the woman she believed herself to be, if she did not stride to become the woman God intended, how could she trust Nicole's love to be for her and not a false shell, a fraud? In turn, she wondered what would have happened to her love of

Nicole if Nicole had converted to Christianity and stood under the light of
the same cross. Beth took stock of how Nicole judged, measured, defined the
world, considering Nicole in light of Nicole's faith and then shifting it to a
Christian foundation. For Beth, a Christian Nicole was unimaginable.

Beth tried to see Swift Hall in light of Nicole's faith. The school's origins, its foundational beliefs were contrary to Nicole's worldview. Where the
Divinity School was a source of sustenance to Beth, Nicole went hungry, if
not starved. Given Nicole's nature, it could not be otherwise.

Beth feared that as a consequence of her actions, she would live a life
removed from Nicole's greatest intimacies. She longed to renew her role as a
co-creator of a safe haven they could share. Beth felt an overwhelming surge
of remorse. There was nothing she could do to stop herself from breaking
apart. She dropped the box. She looked down at the scattered contents. She
knelt on one knee. Her hands trembled as she repacked the box. The last book
in place, she stared at her hands. She could not still them. She raised her hands
up to her face, unable to keep her tears at bay.

Within the hour Beth found herself standing at Nicole's office threshold.
The office was empty. The adjacent loft door was open. Beth walked the span
from one threshold to another. She slowly opened the door and scanned the
loft. The sound of a steaming teakettle directed her attention to the kitchen.
Nicole stood with her back to Beth. She poured hot water into a mug. Beth
knocked lightly on the door. Nicole looked over to her. She reset the teakettle
as she offered Beth a cautious greeting. "Hello."

Beth entered the loft, her step quickened. She ran directly into Nicole's
arms and clung to her.

"Hey." Nicole was startled. She recovered her wits sufficiently to take
Beth into a protective hold, gentle yet firm. She waited for Beth to speak, to
no avail. Nicole whispered into Beth's ear. "Tell me."

"Don't." Beth's voice was muffled.

"Don't what?"

"Don't ask me to leave you."

Nicole released her embrace and held Beth at arms length. "Beth."

Beth pleaded. "What do I have to do for you to trust me?"

"I can't answer that."

"Give me a chance to prove myself to you. Nicki, please ... I'm begging
you."

"No. You don't beg me for anything." Nicole asked herself how trust
was formed. The answers came simply: with time, with testing, and with small
signifiers that reinforced promises. "Beth, I'm afraid that no matter how careful I am ... how careful we are ... we'll fall back and repeat our mistakes ... I

don't want to lose myself again. And I don't want you to ever have to defend the partner you've chosen."

"Chosen, Nicki. It's my choice to make. Don't ask me to accept the Church in place of you. Don't ask me to fall into the arms of a good Christian. I know you believe what you're doing is for my own good, but you're wrong, Nicki." Beth's voice lowered to a whisper. "You're wrong."

"Are you sure? Are you sure you shouldn't have someone in your life who'll support you in your faith."

"When haven't you supported me in my faith?"

"Beth, I'm not the same person you met three years ago."

"Do you want me to stop my studies?"

"No."

"Do you want me to leave the Church?"

"No, but right now I don't have any reason to step into a church again."

"Then don't."

"I don't want to feel obligated to attend your University functions."

"Will you see me graduate?"

Nicole was being bested in their unexpected negotiations. She wanted to be bested. "I make exceptions for ordinations and graduations."

"Then we're fine. What else?"

Nicole's gaze fell upon Beth's cross. She would not ask Beth for the symbolic gesture. She shifted away. "Beth, I can't."

Beth mirrored Nicole's motion. "No, I won't let you close the door on us without telling me what is stopping you from trying. Tell me. I deserve to know."

"I won't do to you what …" Nicole felt a surge of anger. She arrested it before it was completely voiced.

Beth knowingly completed the thought. She spoke in a hush. "You won't do to me what I did to you." Beth had followed Nicole's gaze. She knew where it had fallen. She reached back and unclasped her chain, removing the chain and the cross. "You don't need to see this all the time."

"Damn it! Don't!" Nicole felt she was witness to a desecration performed on her behalf.

Beth stepped forward, mollifying Nicole's outrage with a gentle touch of her hand. "Liza helped me understand. Maybe the day will come again when you can see the cross on me without it hurting. Until then I'll wear it when I'm not with you."

Nicole restrained the temptation to pull away.

Beth was determined to work through Nicole's objections. "Anything else?"

Nicole remained silent. She averted her eyes.

Beth studied her partner. She feared Nicole was slipping away from her. In desperation she spoke the two words she intimately used to call Nicole to her. "Nicki, please ..."

Nicole mined for reasons not to respond. There were many, but reason did not rule her. Try as she might, reason had failed to stop her from pursuing her heart's desire. Reason had failed to stop her from seeking Beth while under the shadow of St. Ann's. What power had reason in the light of the loft? She wanted Beth's love. She wanted to love Beth. Harder still, she wanted to trust her. Nicole found and held Beth's gaze. "Would you like some tea?"

Beth would never cease to be surprised by Nicole's dramatic shifts. Nicole's casual invitation assured her that she would not be sent away. "Yes. Thank you."

Nicole retrieved a second mug and prepared the tea. She gestured Beth toward one of the stools by the kitchen island. "When Tess was here for the reception, she came to the brilliant conclusion that I'm a Greek."

"Really?" Beth found the obvious observation funny. She suspected there was more to Tess's comment than Nicole's genealogy.

"Here you go." Nicole sat down across from Beth, setting a tea mug before her. "We were talking about the four cardinal virtues. Do you know them?"

"No, I don't think you've ever told me."

"Interested?"

"Sure."

Nicole was hungry. "I was about to raid The Garden and bring back a tray. If you haven't eaten ... would you like to have dinner with me?"

"I'd like that."

"Good." Nicole stood. "Any requests?"

"You know what I like."

"Make yourself at home. I'll be back in a minute."

Left alone in the loft, Beth was transported back in time. It was true she had never dated Nicole, but she had spent countless hours in the old Fields and in Nicole's previous loft. When she had visited she had felt the privilege of her access to Nicole's inner circle. Scanning the new loft Beth marveled at the beauty of the space. Nicole remained true to her unpretentious signature aesthetic. She exercised patience. Completely furnished, only half the wall space was adorned. Beth wondered if there were more gallery walks in their future.

Nicole reappeared. She set the food tray on the kitchen island.

Beth inspected their meal selection. It was some of Miguel's best Cuban. Beth got to her feet. "Where do you keep the silverware?"

Nicole pointed to a drawer.

"Napkins."

"To the left."

"How about spices? I know you like extra cumin on your black beans."

"You'd better not tell Miguel that!" Nicole warned.

"And get a dose of his Latino wrath? I don't think so."

Nicole secured the spice in question from a top cabinet.

Beth examined the table setting. Only one thing was missing. "What do you want to drink?"

"Mineral water."

Beth went to the refrigerator. "Could you get the glasses?"

Nicole gladly fulfilled the request, placing two pilsner glasses on the island. She sat on one of the stools. Beth returned and sat opposite Nicole.

For Beth, the moment of normalcy was a stark reminder of its loss, of the months of lonely dinners. Humbly, she bowed her head and closed her eyes, saying a brief 'thank you' as grace. With difficulty she took hold of her fork. She was unable to lead it to the plate of food. The shared silence drew Beth further inward, where there was no solace, where echoes of accusations reverberated in a chamber of dark solitude.

Nicole's eyes lay tenderly upon Beth. She saw the younger woman's composure seep away. Nicole tilted her head to better see Beth. She marked the quiet tears.

Beth felt a physical presence approach; the touch of Nicole's gentle hands pulled her from the stool into an embrace.

"I'm here," Nicole whispered.

Beth's hands clutched Nicole's shirt as she released a deep sob. "I'm sorry … I've missed you. I've been so afraid."

Nicole soothingly stroked Beth's back. She could not find it within herself to understate the import of her own hurt. She struggled to find the words that would honor her truth and console Beth. She waited for Beth's tears to subside. With a muted smile, Nicole offered Beth her napkin to use as a handkerchief. "Here …"

Calming, Beth blew her nose.

"We can sit by the window after dinner," said Nicole. "We'll talk."

Beth nodded.

"You have to eat something, otherwise Miguel will give me hell."

Beth appreciated the diversion. "You don't have to tell him."

"He'll ask. I'll lie. He'll know the truth anyway."

"You're not that transparent."

"Aren't I?"

Beth placed her hand over Nicole's heart. "No, you're not."

Their meal completed, Nicole sat on the window seat. She invited Beth to rest against her. Holding Beth, Nicole's eyes fell upon her partner's reflection. It was a lonely image. Nicole felt Beth's trembling form. "Hey, you're shivering."

"Just a chill." Beth curled closer, seeking Nicole's warmth.

Nicole had told Beth they would talk. She took the lead. "From the beginning of our friendship, I believed you and I had to build a bridge to each other. I believed the reason we were together was because somehow we did find a way to build that bridge. I was wrong to think that way. A bridge is stationary and promises safety. The assumption is that you and I stand on our respective sides, unchanged, even as the waters of life flow on past us. I've come to believe that you and I will always belong on our respective sides of the river. We are always walking downstream, along with the waters. As we do, we keep our eyes open for points in the river that we can ford. Sometimes we cross over completely to the other side and we touch one another in surprising ways. Sometimes we both ford the river meeting in the middle. At times the waters are calm and it's easy and peaceful. At other times, the river waters are higher and moving faster and our effort is harder. And then there are times when our need for each other is so great that either one or both of us decide to ford the waters at deep rapids. We're compelled to reach out to one another in spite of the danger. It's frightening because our lifelines are thin, and we risk their breaking and being swept away. Right now, on my side, the river is deep and running wild and I'm not half as frightened for myself as I am for you because I see in you a need to cross over to me, and it may be safer to wait until we get further downstream and the waters are calmer."

"What if I ask you to cross and come to me?"

"I've tried, Beth. I really have. The currents have been pulling me down for a long time now. I had to come back to my side of the shore. It's where I've been since I left Hyde Park."

Beth turned to face Nicole. "Come to me for a different reason. Just to be with me. Not because I ask you to but because you want to."

"It's not that simple. Not anymore."

"It can be again. Nicki, I missed you even before you left Hyde Park. We may be on two separate shores and life may be changing us, but there is a part of you that I don't believe will ever change." Beth sat up. "You are still the angry woman who kissed me on our first New Year's Eve. You were angry because you felt your integrity was being compromised and that was one thing you couldn't allow – not even by me. I think especially by me."

Nicole agreed that she was still the angry woman. "Tell me you don't wish I'd change."

"You have changed. We both have. I would never forgive myself if you lived a lie because of me. Some things in our lives might be easier, but we would both be the poorer for it."

"Do you really believe that?"

"Yes. I know you will never love the cross. I also know that you respect it. If you didn't, you would never have let me into your life."

Beth rested back against Nicole. Time passed unmarked, except for the sensation of Beth's thumb stroking Nicole's arm. "Nicki?"

Nicole tightened her hold.

Beth, her confidence compromised, appreciated the tactile reassurance. "I love you. And unless you tell me differently, I believe you love me. We may not be together in the future. If we're not, it's because we weren't meant to be. Your *Moria.*"

"You once believed we would always be together ... our commitment ceremony," Nicole said softly.

"If I have to, I'll accept that I was wrong. I still believe I'm right."

"You do?"

"Yes, I do."

Nicole watched their reflection in the glass. Chicago, specifically Hyde Park, remained beyond the pane. Nicole refused to repeat her mistake. "Beth, this is my home."

Lying in Nicole's arms, Beth accepted that her home would be unlike the one she had first imagined. Home was no longer defined by a shared space. "I know."

Beth drifted into a light slumber. With Beth sleeping in her arms, Nicole held a woman who no longer denied her transgression. Nicole felt she held a woman who shared her awful pain and was transformed by it. She had never wished the unfathomable depth of pain upon Beth. She did not want Beth to feel what she had felt. More importantly, finding a modicum of peace, Nicole did not want to ever look in a mirror and witness the return of that pain etched on her own face. To turn away the possibility, to eliminate the pain from her horizon, she had distanced herself from the source. With Beth's return, the source lay in her arms. A question lingered. Could she trust Beth again? How to begin? Had she just begun?

Nicole shifted causing Beth to stir.

The time was past midnight. Nicole whispered tenderly, "Come to bed."

"Nicki ..." Beth's voice was small, confused.

"It's late. Sleep here tonight."

Beth looked up into Nicole's eyes, finding a sincere concern.

"Please stay."

Beth nodded. "Okay."

"Good. Come on." Nicole helped Beth to her feet and led her to the bed. She retrieved an oversized sleep shirt from her chest of drawers and offered it to Beth. "Why don't you change into this while I close up my office."

Yawning, Beth accepted the garment. "Thank you."

"I'll be back in a few minutes."

Nicole found Beth sleeping soundly. She changed into her night clothes and slipped into bed. She could not sleep beside Beth without touching her. Nicole moved behind Beth, gently embracing the smaller woman, as was once her custom. The sensation of their bodies molded to the other was familiar, comforting; the sensation provoked a sense of sated hunger.

CHAPTER 179

June 18, 2004 – Friday

Larissa Willard escorted Nicole out of her law office. "I'll have the contract delivered to your office by the end of the week."

Nicole shook her hand. "Thank you." Walking down the corridor, Nicole paused. Continuing straight ahead would take her to the main entrance. To her left was Kate's office. She decided to take the detour.

Kate's administrative assistant announced Nicole. Nicole was promptly given entrance.

Kate remained stiffly behind her desk. "What brings you here?"

Nicole remained at a distance, seeking an abbreviated interview. "Beth."

"Is she all right?" Kate's concern was evident.

"She's having a hard time forgiving herself. I know the feeling." Nicole took a step forward. "Kate, that one day in your dorm ... I never apologized. I'm sorry it happened."

Kate was blind-sided. "I don't know what you're talking about."

Nicole was done with denials. "It was easier to go along with you and pretend it never happened."

Nicole sensed Kate's acute discomfort. Nicole stood waiting, by her very presence demanding an answer.

"Why, Nicki? Why did you have to be such a bitch?" Kate asked.

"Kate ..." Nicole hardened. "I didn't want you. You knew that but you pushed me anyway. Getting me drunk didn't change how I felt about you."

Kate had no defense against Nicole's recrimination. "Anything else?"

Nicole was determined to close every open wound. "Tess told me that you know about Amelia."

"Were you drunk when you were with her?" Kate asked sharply.

"No excuses. I knew exactly what I was doing." Nicole granted that Kate and Amelia had one thing in common. "If it's any consolation it wasn't beneath Amelia to take advantage of me."

"What could she give you that I couldn't?"

"Until that last night we had an understanding ..."

"You're wrong if you think Amelia accepted your bloody terms of engagement."

Nicole was unyielding. "If she didn't, she was never obvious about her feelings. She was never pathetic. She was a lot of things, but never that."

"And I was?"

"Yes. You hung onto my coattails. You degraded yourself." Nicole gentled her voice. "Kate, you had so much more than Amelia and you were throwing all of it away for me."

"Nicki, you have something to learn about apologies."

"The truth hurts."

"The truth? Tell me, Nicki, if I was throwing away my life, what do you call what you were doing?"

"I was in love with Amelia. Tess knew it. As close as you and I were ... I could never figure out whether you knew and that was why you disliked Amelia, or it you were so blinded by her physical appearance that you couldn't imagine my loving her."

Kate was flabbergasted by the admission. "You loved her?"

"Love isn't qualified, Kate. At least not the kind of love I feel most deeply. Love can make you accept the ugly and even the hateful. I know you know that. Kate, you and I ... no one has the power to segregate parts of herself from being exposed. Sooner or later we're found out. That night I found Amelia out and she knew it."

"You're telling me that Amelia hurt you?"

"When I fell in love with Beth ... I thought, 'how appropriate'. I was destined to always love a woman I couldn't have."

"You could have had Amelia."

"For how long? I'm not as brave as you think I am. I watched my mother slowly die in front of my eyes. Do you really think I would have knowingly consented to go through that again?"

"That's why ..." Kate's demeanor altered, calming. She invoked the one woman in Nicole's life akin to Amelia in circumstance. "Beth ... does she know?"

"Not everything." Nicole could not avow what the knowledge of Beth's probable illness would have meant to her. "By the time I found out about Beth's family history, it was too late. When she told me about her cancer ... her illness dwarfed all our differences. She was so fragile after the surgery. I was determined to give her the best life I could. I subordinated all my needs to meet hers. That was my second mistake. I gave up so much of myself I forgot who I was. Beth lost respect for me in the process."

"She never stopped respecting you," said Kate unequivocally.

"Let's agree to disagree on this one." Nicole wore an amused smile. "Funny how you've always defended me ... even to Beth. That changed with time, didn't it? Beth raised the bar with us. I'm not complaining. I was grateful you didn't resent her. It made a difference to Beth and it made a difference to me."

"Why didn't you tell me why you left Beth?" asked Kate with a hint of grief.

"I tried. You were convinced that our separation was my fault. That day at CMT you weren't in the mood to hear anything I had to say to you. You had already made up your mind. Or have you forgotten?"

Kate hesitated before speaking. "What now?"

Nicole heard a door open in Kate's question. The gesture was subtle. Before Nicole laid the last vestige of one of her most enduring friendships. She needed to decide whether to recognize the effort, whether to do so was in her best interest, whether a return was in both of their best interests. "I'm tired, Kate. I can't ... I won't be your friend. I also won't interfere with your friendship with Beth."

Kate grew cold. "That's what you came here to tell me?"

Nicole hurt for Kate. "Yes."

"You think that's good enough?"

Nicole's hurt broadened. "Good enough for whom? Beth? No. She wants to see us friends again. Me? Damn straight. You? That's for you to decide."

Nicole left Kate no room for hope. "Nicki, you've just proven to me that there's one thing about you that hasn't changed," Kate said resentfully. "You still insist on unilaterally dictating your relationships. Right now I have no idea what I ever saw in you."

"I was your friend. I loved you."

"You never loved me," she snapped.

"Oh, yes, I did!" Nicole no longer doubted her decision. "My friendship was enough for Tess. It was never enough for you. You wanted to own me. That was your mistake. I'm done pretending. There's nothing between us left worth salvaging." Nicole turned away.

Kate stood up. "Nicki."

Nicole paused at the door.

"Don't leave thinking ..." Kate drew back. After taking a breath she continued. "Nicki, I cared ... I did want to see you happy."

"I know," Nicole whispered.

"How are you and Beth doing?"

Nicole debated whether to answer. "She thinks we have a chance of making a life together."

"What do you think?"

"I'm trying my damnedest to believe her."

"Believe her," Kate said with a rare, ardent sincerity.

Nicole responded in equal spirit. "Take care of yourself, Kate."

CHAPTER 180

July 6, 2004 – Tuesday

Beth sat in the sunroom. She set her reading aside, her gaze resting on the telephone. Marie had called her earlier in the day. Their conversation had been warm and easy. Beth was thankful for her sibling's jovial teasing. It had been a fine way to open her birthday. She had lunched with Pam and Cindy. Not only did she welcome their companionship, she had sought out their counsel.

Beth's inheritance was generous, giving her the freedom to complete her graduate studies without financial concern. She had spent the summer days working part-time at Memorial. She also spent time alone taking inventory of her professional as well as her personal life. Voices rose and ebbed in her inner ear. Her father's voice had lost its righteous fervor. Larry's voice presented challenges that refused to be set aside. Marie's voice continued to encourage the gradual renewal of her sister's relationship with Nicole. She had reminded Beth that she, too, had hesitated in love, and yet was conquered by Joe's patience and ardor.

Pam and Cindy's voices brought further insights. They knew her in the context of her chaplaincy. Though much in her life had changed, one constant was the import of her ministry. As heartbreaking as a chaplain's day could be, she continued seeking out those moments when solace touched the heart of a patient, a family member, a friend or a hospital staff person, moments her presence facilitated.

She intended to address issues of suffering in her dissertation. She had found lessons of merit in her praxis that overshadowed those learned in her scholarship, leaving Beth to wonder if the pursuit of her Ph.D. best served her calling. Pam had offered her a permanent position at Memorial beginning in September, and had also encouraged Beth to consider pursuing CPE Supervision in the future. The probability of leaving the Ph.D. program was becoming more and more salient in Beth's vision for her future. Full-time chaplaincy would allow her to further discern her calling.

The one voice that Beth longed to hear was Nicole's. She had yet to share her thoughts about leaving the University. Beth feared Nicole would take the decision as a concession. The issue of her vocation's impact on their shared life still hung precariously between them. They had yet to renew their theological and philosophical conversations. That terrain was treacherous and she continued to tread carefully.

Nicole's silence on this one day was a reminder that they were only beginning to mend their relationship. There was no repetition of Beth's night at The Fields. Nicole had reverted back to maintaining her physical distance. Her shows of affection were limited to casual touches and offering her hand as they walked. Today was Nicole's day with Tasi. Beth understood without being told that Nicole's time with the child was sacrosanct.

The telephone rang. Beth took up the handset. "Hello."

"Hi. Where are you in the apartment?" asked Nicole brightly.

"The sunroom. Why?"

"Look out the window."

Beth did as asked. Across the street stood Nicole and Tasi. Tasi held a string of three balloons. The center balloon carried a 'Happy Birthday' message. Beth laughed.

Hearing Beth's reaction, Nicole said, "Hold on. There's someone here who wants to speak to you."

Nicole crouched down to Tasi, taking possession of the balloons as she handed her cell phone to the little girl. "Here you go."

Tasi took the phone in hand. "Hello."

"Hi, Tasi."

"Happy Birthday, Beth."

"Thank you, sweetheart. Those balloons are wonderful."

"You like them?"

"I sure do."

Tasi turned to Nicole. "Beth likes the balloons."

"You picked out good ones."

"Should I ask her now?"

Nicole nodded.

Beth listened to the exchange with great pleasure.

"Beth?"

"I'm here."

"Would you like to go for some ice cream and cake? Nicki said Medi …"

"Medici's," said Nicole.

Tasi tried again. "Me-di-ci's has real good food."

"I'd love to. Tell Nicki I'll be down in a minute."

"Okay." Tasi handed the cell phone to Nicole. "Beth is coming."

The birthday celebration was a success. The restaurant staff surprised Beth with a robust rendition of *Happy Birthday*. Nicole's smile was broad as Beth blushed through the song. Tasi had never been more animated with Beth, sharing news of her activities in a neighborhood children's day camp that she was attending, compliments of Nicole's generosity. Nicole had promised to have Tasi home by 8:30 p.m., thus the evening drew to an early close.

The threesome walked back to Beth's apartment. Nicole held the balloons in one hand and Tasi's hand with her other. Tasi reached up and claimed Beth's hand completing their link.

Reaching the apartment, Beth knelt down and hugged Tasi warmly. "I had a wonderful time. I'm so happy you decided to share my birthday with me."

The child returned the affection enthusiastically. "I had a good time, too."

Beth stood up. Nicole offered her the balloons. "These are yours."

Beth took the strings. She quieted, looking at Nicole with a gaze that conveyed her deeply felt gratitude. "Thank you, Nicki."

"You're welcome."

Beth hesitated before turning and walking up on the apartment stairs. Nicole called her name. She turned around. Nicole stepped forward and opened her arms. Beth fell into Nicole's embrace. Beth's body's bleeding emotion conveyed everything Beth withheld in deference to Nicole's feelings. In this one moment Nicole could not ask anything more of Beth. She kissed her on the cheek and whispered, "Elizabeth, I love you."

Beth heard Nicole's renewed vow. She was overwhelmed. She began to cry. Nicole soothingly stroked Beth's back. Waiting a few moments until Beth's tears quieted, Nicole gently said, "Remember, we have an audience." In response, Beth shook her head against Nicole's shoulder. "Oh, yes, we do. And she's going to tell Yeva I made you cry. I'm in trouble now." Beth laughed lightly. Nicole continued. "You're going to have to write a note to Yeva saying that I really was on my best behavior. Before we left she was only worried about Tasi. Goes to show you, you just never know with the two of us."

Beth released Nicole. Nicole reached up and wiped a few tears from Beth's face with her thumb. Beth took hold of Nicole's hand and kissed the palm. The gesture was very much part of their foreplay. Nicole waited until she had Beth's regard. A moment of shared silence led them to each other in a tender kiss. The kiss ended easily. Nicole greeted her lover. "Hi."

Beth smiled. "Hi."

Tasi was fascinated by the exchange. Her apparent fascination turned to confusion when the two adults greeted each other. "Why are you saying 'hi'? Aren't you supposed to be saying good-bye?"

The women looked at the child in amusement. Nicole bent down and took Tasi into her arms. "You! I'll explain on the way home."

Having her place in Nicole's embrace righted Tasi's uncertainty. "Okay."

Nicole and Tasi turned to Beth. Beth was witness to Nicole's unabashed happiness. She reveled in the vision. Nicole directed her young ward, "Say good-night to Beth."

Tasi leaned her head on Nicole's shoulder. "Good-night."

Beth reached out and touched Tasi's arm. "Good-night, sweetheart." She returned her gaze to Nicole. "Nicki ..." Words failed her.

"I know." Nicole leaned forward and kissed Beth on the cheek. "Good-night, Reverend." She shifted Tasi on her arms and walked toward the Jeep.

Beth watched Nicole's departure with a mixture of emotion: love, gratitude, joy and humility. She closed her eyes and prayed. "Thank you."

CHAPTER 181

July 22, 2004 – Friday

Nicole and Beth walked hand in hand. They had shared dinner at Salonika's. Beth stepped up onto the stoop. She was eye to eye with Nicole. "Tomorrow is Saturday."

"That's because today is Friday."

Beth kept to the jovial mood that they had shared throughout the evening. "I have nowhere I have to be in the morning."

"So you can be lazy and sleep in."

"Uh-huh."

"I'll make sure and not call you until later in the day."

Beth was hopeful the banter was only a delay tactic to what would be an acquiescence. "If you stay the night you can save the call."

Nicole saw Beth's eyes glisten. She did not want to cause the light within them to fade. Together they had reached this moment. An invitation given; all she needed to do was accept. "I'm sorry …"

Beth searched Nicole's face. She saw an honest regret. "Nicki, we are doing better, aren't we?"

Nicole placed her hand on Beth's waist. She had wanted so much to touch her. "Yes, we are."

"If there is anything I can do …"

"I'll let you know."

Beth leaned forward and passionately kissed Nicole. The kiss was returned. They separated gently. "Good night."

"Good night."

Beth went to the door, removing her keys from her pocket. Nicole stood and watched.

"Beth …" Nicole waited until Beth heeded her call. "I can't face the apartment. Not for the night. Not just yet. Would you like to stay over at the loft?"

Beth did her best to keep the magnitude of Nicole's reciprocal invitation from her response. "Breakfast in bed?"

Nicole found the request irresistible. "I'll raid The Garden. Scones with English cream and fresh ground coffee."

"I need to throw together a few things."

"I'll wait here."

Beth ran upstairs. Nicole smiled. The truth had served her well.

Nicole traded her street clothes for a sleep shirt while Beth entered the bathroom to change and put away her toiletries. Nicole retreated to the kitchen, sitting on one of the island stools in wait. Their mutual modesty reflected the uncertainty of what Nicole's invitation meant to them. Would they share more than the comforting presence of one another in bed? Would they make love?

Beth exited the bathroom, dressed in a white silk sleep shirt. It was Nicole's favorite. She set her folded clothes on a nearby chair and placed her shoes on the floor. She looked across the room, beyond the bed to where Nicole remained quietly at a distance. Beth took heed of Tess's guidance. Their return was a slow dance, and if she and Nicole were to make love on this night, their lovemaking would require a constant attentiveness to her partner's nuanced gestures and words.

Nicole waited for her. Beth recalled moments previously shared when Nicole's assertiveness was arrested by her uncertainty. Many such moments had come as their relationship was unraveling. Nicole, obviously confused, questioning whether her sexual overtures were welcomed, had waited for Beth as she did now. She had waited for an invitation clearly offered; one that left no room for doubt that she was desired.

Beth approached and stood silently before Nicole. There was no place for words. Speech would shatter the fragile balance that kept the two women bravely bound to one another. Beth undid the buttons of her sleep shirt, starting from the top and working her way down. She held her gaze gently to Nicole's. She saw in Nicole a hesitant desire, a wanting tempered by caution. With the last button undone, Beth allowed her shirt to drape open, exposing portions of her breast and abdomen.

Nicole lowered her gaze. She knew Beth's body. She wondered if Beth would feel as soft to her touch as she remembered. Nicole reached out, resting her hand on Beth's waist. Nicole closed her eyes as the sensation of Beth's warmth radiated through her fingertips and palm.

Beth slowly stepped closer, encouraging Nicole's embrace. She felt Nicole's hand travel to her back, the reassurance Beth needed if she was to continue to lead. She rested her cheek against Nicole's, shutting her eyes as she said a silent prayer, seeking a blessing to their reunion.

Beth understood Nicole's silence to be neither consent nor denial. She sought consent. She whispered in Nicole's ear so softly that if Nicole chose not to respond they could both pretend she had not been heard. "Nicki, please."

Nicole was ready to give pleasure. She was not so sure she could accept Beth's most intimate touch. She felt Beth tense in their mutual silence. Seeking to reassure, Nicole tenderly kissed Beth on the cheek. She slowly separated herself from her partner. She found and held Beth's fearful gaze. Nicole took Beth's hands and guided them to the top button of her shirt.

Caring for Nicole, Beth longed to make love, to return to the sensual, a sharing Nicole had first introduced her to and that she had only experienced with her one partner. Rachel had stirred Beth's loneliness more than her passion; Rachel had offered a temporary distraction from the emptiness Beth had felt. Rachel could not awaken the deep yearning that commanded Beth in the presence of Nicole's strength and vulnerability alike.

In Nicole's strength, Beth surrendered. Beth arched her back as she followed Nicole's unwavering guidance towards a state of mind where the world was forgotten and she could drown in a tense, near painful pleasure.

In silence, through touch, Beth loved Nicole uniquely. Beth never gave of herself as nakedly; stripped of her own defenses. She felt Nicole's heartbeat as her own as they breathed in unison. With each breath she felt the further devastation of her fears. So searing was Nicole's touch that Beth was engulfed in a long-lost stilling of her doubts. She cried out as she climaxed. The powerful release overwhelmed. She reached for and clung to Nicole.

Nicole gently ceased her intimate strokes and offered Beth a comforting caress. She could feel Beth's trembling body underneath her. She soothed with a light steady rhythmic sweep of her hand against Beth's back. With time, Beth's body quieted and her hold lessened, a signal to Nicole to guide her lover back to rest against the pillow. She released Beth and leaned back.

Nicole watched a tear fall from the corner of Beth's eye. She smiled, and spoke softly, keeping to a beguiling murmur. "St. John Chrysostom?"

The unexpected reference acknowledging Beth's essential merging of her love for Nicole with her love for God broke Beth's heart. Nicole had invited God into their bed. Her generosity would never cease to humble Beth. She once again raised herself up, her genuine need for Nicole supplanting all other thoughts.

In embracing and safeguarding Nicole's vulnerability, Beth knew and relished her own hard-won strength. She treasured her ability to assure Nicole that the tenderness she offered was freely given, reserved for her, only her. Nicole's needs did not diminish her dignity or her humanity, valued for its capacity to bruise and bleed.

Nicole hesitated. Beth felt Nicole's tentative response to her touch. Beth soothed, she encouraged with her caresses, striving to earn Nicole's trust, to lead Nicole to a place where she would once again willingly allow her passion to ignite. Beth extended her awareness, immersing herself in their essential connection, knowing it once again. She was mystified that she had allowed its forfeiture, and questioned if, of all her transgressions, had her physical withdrawal from Nicole been the greatest wrong. In their incomplete union, Nicole would have known the betrayal of an unspoken promise.

During the formative months of their physical relationship, through innumerable days and nights of touch enveloped in silence, Beth had promised never to betray Nicole's trust. Beth had coaxed Nicole's greatest intimacies to the surface by her patient lovemaking. Her silent mercies were rewarded by Nicole's cautious, voluntary relinquishment of control Beth trembled. How, she wondered, had Nicole found the courage to invite her back to this raw emotional realm? Was it that Nicole had no choice? Had her need overwhelmed her reason? Was it madness or resilience? Could she be at once both a woman of great courage and great dependence? Had Nicole so great a faith? Beth felt Nicole's weight upon her belly, the crucial posture in their intimate life where Nicole wordlessly requested comfort. For the second time during their evening, Nicole left Beth humbled.

Beth looked up through the skylight to the few visible stars. She felt the unique peace that came to her only when in Nicole's embrace. She fought sleep for as long as she could, not wanting to surrender the moment. With time sleep did come; her dreams equaled her tender night.

Nicole woke with Beth's body draped over her. She had missed how Beth's light weight secured her in their bed. Extricating herself without disturbing her partner was a skill perfected after many trials, as Beth tended to tighten, not relax her hold whenever Nicole attempted to inch away. The key was to offer a reassuring touch as she murmured words of love. This morning she made her escape with minor resistance.

Nicole picked up their discarded sleep clothes. As she placed Beth's shirt with her other clothes, Nicole noticed a gold chain dangling out from a front pocket of Beth's jeans. She reached into the pocket, taking Beth's cross into her hand. As much as she wished otherwise for Beth's sake, Nicole did not want to see the cross. She returned the cross to the pocket and reset the jeans. She left the bedroom after allowing her gaze to linger one final moment on Beth's sleeping form.

Beth stirred. She lay alone. She turned her body toward the heart of the loft. Nicole was in the kitchen setting breakfast. Beth wrapped herself with a bed sheet and crossed the open space. "I thought I was getting breakfast in bed?"

At the sight of Beth, with her bright green eyes, cream completion, and disheveled hair, Nicole knew happiness. "Jump back in and I'll serve you."

Beth kissed Nicole. "I'm fine right here. Hand me a scone."

After breakfast the two women found themselves back in bed. Nicole lay reflecting upon their journey. The forgiveness they needed was possible only through mutual agency. Nicole needed to accept that harm had been done. It was only after she allowed herself to feel the pain that she could begin to work through her grief. With each passing day she re-embraced her humility. She was imperfect, so too, was Beth. To hold either one of them to a standard of perfection was to sentence their respective souls to perpetual agony. There was never any doubt of Beth's goodness, but Nicole needed to once again recognize it, hold to it, and rely on it. Of her tenets, Nicole struggled to find grace in their estrangement. What of value had come from it? How could she mine meaning? She remained uncertain. For her, what she had gained was a better understanding of the price she was willing to pay for love. She also learned that she had mistakenly deferred her needs to her harm, and to the harm of their relationship.

She studied Beth. Contrite, broken hearted, Beth owned the impact of her acts and her failure to act. Would Beth now be a more equal partner? Would Beth be a better scholar, teacher, minister? Had Beth come closer to her own ideal, reflective of the model of Jesus of Nazareth – Christ? Was this the grace? Jacob had shown Nicole where in the Talmud it stated that the innocent would bear the judgment of God for the sake of the transgressors. Nicole was far from innocent. She was not Tasi and yet was the lesson the same? If humanity learned from its mistakes, that inevitably meant that the harm of the mistake would be felt – by definition undeserved. Was this then where forgiveness finds its foothold? To understand that it must be this way, that a price must be paid. This time, between them, Nicole had to pay the price so that Beth would experience the insight of her own bias. They were not done. Forgiveness did not guarantee reconciliation; it did not guarantee a renewal of their commitment. The necessary leap of faith required more than love; it required the renewal of trust, a renewal Nicole had begun to embrace.

Nicole felt Beth's thumb stroke her abdomen. "What are you thinking?" she asked softly.

Beth recited her vow. "'I am my beloved's/and her desire is for me/ Come, my beloved/let us go forth into the fields/and lodge in the villages … There I will give you my love.'"

Nicole looked up at the skylight. "I've gone back to those words a hundred times since you first said them to me. I've got a permanent crease in my Bible." She recalled her own vow. "I've been haunted by my words to you. 'I call to thee from every leafy bough/But thou are far away and canst not hear.'"

Beth closed her eyes, regretting her part in Nicole's loneliness. "I remember how the poem ends. 'And though awake as from a cheating dream/The life today with me and mine to share?' It's a question not a statement of fact. You weren't sure."

"No, I wasn't."

Beth raised herself up. She chose to end her silence. "Nicki, I want you in my life. I want to hear about your days and I want to tell you about mine. I don't want to feel as if there are parts of your life you can't share with me. If I can't come home to you every night, I want to be invited to sleep in your arms from time to time." She took Nicole's hand. "And Nicki, I want you to help me find a way that I can be with you without hurting you or reminding you of those who have and continue to hurt you."

CHAPTER 182

August 5, 2004 – Thursday

Arriving at the loft, Nicole chuckled, unable to erase the memory of Tasi's violin recital from her mind. The students were as awful in music making as they were earnest in the trying. The humor of their effort had reduced Nicole to tears within the first thirty minutes. Beth, far more accustomed to the efforts of children, had maintained her composure with ease, and had nudged Nicole more than once to show her half-hearted disapproval.

Beth had, in fact, enjoyed Nicole's complete loss of decorum. Their movement back to one another was cautious and temperate. Mirth's complete possession of Nicole was a gift to both of them. Beth had given Tasi a warm hug and encouraged the child on with her music if only to have more such recitals in their future.

Beth backhanded Nicole lightly on the belly as they removed their jackets. "You're going to strain a muscle with all your laughing."

Nicole was shameless. "How could you keep a straight face?"

Beth walked to the kitchen seeking a cup of tea. She called over her shoulder, "Remember, the first chair of the Chicago Symphony started the same way."

Nicole stood in the center of the loft. "Did you see Tasi? She was beaming."

"Of course. She had you and Yeva there." Beth turned back toward Nicole. "She likes showing you off to her friends." Once Beth had been as obvious as Tasi in her public admiration of Nicole. She recalled Nicole's first introduction to the chaplains at Memorial, how they had assessed the tall, intelligent beauty, and how she had embraced Nicole without apology. Beth had allowed her unqualified pride in Nicole to slip away.

Nicole met and held Beth's gaze. Beth wondered if Nicole could read her mind and feel her regret. "You're quite impressive."

After a heartbeat, Nicole turned toward the bedroom to change. "To little kids who don't know better."

Beth watched Nicole retreat, seeing the wounded child that had yet to learn to accept praise. "No, love. To little kids who know best," Beth whispered.

Beth's body rested against Nicole's. The sun fell below the horizon, casting twilight through the large windows. With the renewal of their physical intimacy, Beth felt a resurgence of her longing for their most intimate conversations, those that touched upon their respective beliefs. To once again discuss philosophy and theology was to test the farthest most reach of their healing.

"I read a letter written by Simone Weil. I thought of you. There were things she wrote that were so familiar."

Nicole wondered what she could have in common with the modern mystic. "Such as?"

"She wrote about silence found in the infinite that isn't an absence of sound. She experienced it as a positive sensation."

"Positive as in tangible?"

"I think so."

Nicole was acquainted with the heaviness of silence. "What else did she write?"

Beth was pleased with Nicole's engagement. She sat up, modestly wrapping the bed sheet around her body. She eagerly anticipated Nicole's reaction to another of Weil's observations. "She said one can never wrestle enough with God if one does so out of the pure regard for the truth."

"She would have us all be enlightened." Nicole brought forth one of her favorite Hebrew Bible images. "Jacob's wrestling with the angel?"

"No. She equated Christ with truth."

Nicole remained silent. Her silence fell uncomfortably between them. Beth knew she had to push through her hesitancy to speak of theology in Christian terms. She continued. "At one time, Weil believed that pure truth came at the moment of death."

Nicole raised herself up and rested her back against the headboard. Given Beth's renewal of her physical modesty, Nicole mimicked her lover and pulled the bed sheet up, covering her breasts. Nicole had long lived with a particularly absurd notion. She stated an oft-repeated observance. "Ironically, if I'm right, I won't know it. I'll only know if I'm wrong."

Beth prayed that when the time came, Nicole would humbly accept the knowledge of her error.

"Hey!" Nicole hurled a playful accusation, "What's that smile for?"

"Nothing …" Caught in her reverie, Beth returned to the subject at hand. "Weil mentioned Marcus Aurelius and the Stoics when she wrote of our duty of acceptance in all that concerns the will of God. 'The *amor fati*.'"

"'Love of fate.'" Nicole mused. "That's more than I can give. Acceptance is hard enough."

"When Weil was a teenager, she decided that the problem of God didn't have a solution so she chose to leave it alone."

Given Weil's reputation as a seeker Nicole believed otherwise. "But did she really?"

"Did you?"

"What do you think?"

Beth took care to respond in terms Nicole used to define her vision of life. "You've never stopped wrestling with the truth." Nicole's smile and slight nod of her head reassured Beth.

The loft was dark except for the city lights and moonlight cast through the skylight. Beth woke alone. Sitting up, she scanned the loft. Nicole sat on the window seat. "Nicki ... can't sleep?"

"Hey ... I think I'm still buzzed from the recital. I can't get Tasi and the rest of the kids out of my mind."

Beth eased out of bed, donning her robe. She stood before Nicole. "Tasi is enough for you, isn't she?"

Nicole was at a loss how to answer. "Beth ..."

"Nicki, it's all right. I want you to know that I won't ask more from you."

Their reconciliation was too new to broach the subject of a child. "I'm sorry."

"Don't apologize." Beth slipped into Nicole's arms.

Nicole held Beth close. Though it was true that Beth had grown fond of Tasi, Nicole still believed that terrible was a future that denied Beth a child. The risks of adoption remained. At the best of times, they no longer seemed insurmountable.

The two women sat together in silence. After a while Nicole felt Beth's thumb rhythmically stroking her hand. She glanced down. Beth rested against her, eyes closed. Other than in their lovemaking, Nicole knew no greater intimacy.

Beth stilled and she looked at her lover, a wondrous glint in her eyes. Nicole marveled at Beth's quiet contentment. An insight struck Nicole. Had the obvious escaped her for so long? Beth's movement mimicked her hand motion when she prayed with her prayer beads. She wondered if Beth realized how her body spoke for her.

Nicole chose her words carefully. If she was wrong, no harm would be done. "A good prayer?"

Beth smiled and laid her head back over Nicole's heart. "Yes." Her prayer had come easily in Nicole's arms. After months of struggle, she relished the sheer joy of prayer, of being with God. Her prayer was a meeting made possible in equal measure by God's invitation and by Beth's sense of worthiness to receive God's blessing. She felt the grace of forgiveness. She renewed her vow to bring Nicole into her mother's house and to honor her. How she loved Nicole, how equally determined she was to deserve Nicole's renewed trust.

She continued to be cautious. What once came without forethought was now charged with the power to derail their journey toward parallel paths.

"Nicki."

"I'm here."

"I love you." Beth closed her eyes and waited, knowing she could not buttress her heart from the disappointment that was companion to Nicole's reticence.

Nicole tightened her embrace. "I love you, too."

Beth knew an inexpressible joy.

CHAPTER 183

August 20, 2004 – Friday

Their evening was spent sitting together on the couch reading. Nicole chose a biography of the poet John Donne. Beth read from Isaiah. An uncharacteristically quiet Beth signaled she was ready for bed by closing her Bible and resting her ear over Nicole's heart. Nicole withheld her question, hoping Beth would volunteer what troubled her.

Lying in bed, Beth lay beside Nicole, holding to Nicole's arm, not moving nearer. She drifted into a fitful sleep. Nicole pulled Beth to her, comforting her partner with her touch.

With the break of day Nicole sat on a stool in the kitchen watching Beth from a distance. Beth took a book in her hand. She paused soberly, examining the volume before storing it in her backpack. "Who are your reading?" Nicole asked.

"Bonhoeffer." Beth stepped to Nicole. "Have you read him?"

"Snippets."

"I don't meet his criteria of discipleship."

Nicole clamped down on her indignation. She reached out to her partner. "Why not?"

Beth took Nicole's hand and entered an embrace. "A few reasons."

Nicole kissed Beth's cheek. "Name one."

"Prayer."

Nicole was dumbfounded. She pulled Beth away. Her lover was serious. She was also grief-stricken. "Beth, you have a prayerful life," Nicole said forcefully.

Beth touched Nicole's lips, calming the surging outrage felt on her behalf. "Do you know I don't pray to Jesus? I pray to God. It doesn't matter what words I say, I don't believe I need Jesus as a mediator to God. Bonhoeffer was very christocentric."

"Isn't this just another example of form over content?"

"He believes Christian prayer is always petitionary."

Nicole tried to lead with her questions. "And for you it's more?"

When Beth petitioned God, she asked for wisdom, acceptance, patience, for all the virtues that would help her to live a life of goodness. Beth's prayer included praise, thanksgiving, and professions of trust. When most troubled, Beth voiced her grief and regret in prayer. "Much more."

"What else?"

"I agree with him that Christians have no right to impose our faith upon others. The Gospel shouldn't be forced. What I don't like is his belief that unbelievers are in need of salvation."

Nicole was unmoved. She had lived with that damning declaration for all of her adult life. Bonhoeffer's German Protestant Confessing Church was far from unique. "But don't Christians believe that they need salvation? Isn't he putting you and me on the same plane?"

Beth was not consoled. "I understand him to believe in the divine elect. Confession and good works isn't enough. Jesus will judge us. Those that are saved are those that Jesus can say he has known. If Jesus is so harsh with the imperfection we carry in us by God's own design, what chance do I have? What chance do you have?"

Nicole understood that Beth conceived the timelessness of eternity as an experience they would share together, otherwise, for Beth, there would be no heaven. Nicole focused first on what she deemed to be a more manageable problem. "Beth, I understand and agree in the denial of the value of good works when the focus is kept to the earthly. There is no justice, at least not the way we conceive justice as an ideal. Life is capricious, equally able to harm the good as it is to harm the evil. Even the Bible lays down the fact that God cannot be understood by the measure of just rewards and punishment. But when it comes to heaven ..." Here Nicole confessed, what was to her, always an amusing scenario, presenting it with a sincerity meant to both honor and console Beth. "If I'm wrong, I always thought I would wait at the gates of heaven for you to advocate my case before St. Peter. Either you would be waiting for me or I would wait, however long it would take, for you to leave your life here and join me. I've never doubted your place in heaven. Don't let Bonhoeffer or anyone else make you think differently."

"I said I didn't meet his standard ..."

Nicole wondered what the men and women who professed to speak for God thought of their peers who held differing opinions. Did they ever doubt that the voice, or impulse, or whatever it was that they pointed to as their authority, was not God but their own will recast subconsciously as the divine? "You don't meet the Catholic or Anglican standard either. Bonhoeffer was an extraordinary man willing to destroy his country for the sake of having a Christian world. Under the mantle of Nazi Germany, it's hard to argue against his cause until you remember the persecution Christians imposed against others in Germany before the rise of Social Nationalism."

Beth poked Nicole's shoulder with her index finger. "I thought I was the one reading the book."

"Better you than me. Beth, you're a scholar and a Christian searcher. You're willing to do the hard work that I don't have the patience for, like reading Bonhoeffer's writings. I can respect him as a man of faith and still disagree with him. He was part of a plot to kill Hitler. I can only hope that I would have been standing with him as he tried. Neither he nor I rise to the heights of Gandhi or Martin Luther King. In spite of the fact that his theology condemns me, I will not condemn him. I also won't let him shake my confidence. My vision of the universe is equal to, though quite different from, his."

Nicole's unrestrained assertion of the legitimacy of her beliefs caused Beth to smile. "Nicki, we use to talk like this all the time."

Nicole kept a serious cast. "And I usually could tell when you were struggling."

"I've never stopped struggling. Some days are just better than others."

"This isn't a good day."

"No, I guess it's not." Beth took Nicole's hand and gave it a gentle squeeze. "Thanks for noticing."

Nicole raised their joined hands. They were bound to one another. Beth's pain did not go unfelt by Nicole. "Beth, what's bothering you?"

Beth's doubts converged. "I don't know what I can give you ... what part of me has any meaning for you."

Beth had Bonhoeffer. Nicole chose her source from the same generation. "After WWII, Albert Camus was invited by an order of Dominican monks to speak on the subject of what he and others like him expected from Christians. He was very clear and brief in his message. He wanted that never again in the world would there be any doubt of Christianity's condemnation of evil. He asked that Christianity step away from abstraction and enter history. Beth, your faith is not an abstraction. It is painfully real and that is what I admire most about it. You stumble, you fall, you pick yourself up, and you keep trying to live up to the elusive ideal. It's what I try to do in my own way."

"And that's what I admire most about your faith."

Validation. Could what Nicole sought from Beth be so easily given? Could she with equal ease receive? "Thank you." Nicole refocused. "Now ... there's something you're not telling me."

Beth had run out of time. She delivered her practiced speech in a quick clip, leaving Nicole no room to interrupt. "I've quit school. I don't need a Ph.D. for my calling. I'm perfectly happy in chaplaincy and occasionally standing in a pulpit as a guest celebrant." Nicole's stoic mien caused Beth to falter. "I think I wanted to be the best ... to have all the credentials ... Dr. Reverend ... maybe then my father would have accepted me. And if he didn't ... my professors were the next best thing."

Nicole released Beth's hand. She stood and took a few steps away; creating a distance that would allow her to wade through what she heard without thrashing against any obstacles, such as Beth's questioning eyes.

Beth felt Nicole's retreat as a painful severing. "Nicki?"

Nicole turned to Beth. "No one achieves your kind of scholarship if they're not passionate about learning. You have always thrived on your studies."

Beth had not given up on her studies, only the formality of the University. "That hasn't changed."

"By teaching, you can open so many hearts and minds."

"And I will when the hearts and minds are young and most impressionable. I want the children in my church to have a chance to grow up seeing the world as a family of diverse peoples, beliefs and traditions."

Nicole continued systematically down her mental list. "Your dissertation?"

"Two ... three years I'd rather spend doing my ministry. I don't need the degree."

"One day you'll look back ..."

Beth stepped forward, claiming her place before God and Nicole. "And be grateful I was honest enough to follow my calling."

Nicole looked out the window towards St. Ann's.

Beth followed her gaze. "If it wasn't for you, I would still be living a life based on other people's expectations of me. Because of you, I've spent the last four years trying to find an honest way to God. There have been times I've been lost. And there have been times I've been sure. Most of the time I'm somewhere in between. Right now ... right this moment, I feel God's mercy."

Nicole turned to Beth. "So, you're here in this moment by the grace of God?"

Beth reached out and took Nicole's hand with her own. "I'm alive by God's grace. I'm here because we, you and I, have free will."

CHAPTER 184

October 31, 2004 — Sunday

In September, Beth had learned of an available one-bedroom apartment on the same floor of her apartment building. She had arranged to lease the smaller apartment and sublet her own. It was the least disruptive move she could have imagined for herself, resulting in a prudent decrease in her monthly expenses.

She had shared her decision with Nicole, presenting her with a reasoned case. Nicole had listened with her characteristic reserve. After a moment's hesitation, Nicole had offered to assist in anyway she could. Beth had limited her request to storage space in The Fields' basement for the den furniture. All her other belongings could be easily transferred to the new apartment. Nicole consented.

The day of the move arrived. It was spent with an assembly of helpful friends. The short journey from one end of the building floor to the other resulted in a quick, relatively painless transition. By Beth's request, Nicole was not among the recruited labor. Nicole continued to reluctantly enter the apartment. Beth did not want to expose her to the harsh reminder of the changes necessitated by the turmoil in their relationship.

Beth entered the den. All its furniture had been packed into a truck. The driver waited for her on the street. Beth walked to the portrait. She had never considered the portrait hers. It belonged to Nicole. Throughout their separation, the subject of the portrait had never been broached. Beside the portrait rested her ring, dust covered. She opened her left hand. Within it, she held the *vesica piscis*. She had found the Celtic pendant the day before, while cleaning the fireplace; the mystery of the pendant's whereabouts had been answered. Nicole had left it behind, just as she had left the portrait.

Each of the symbolic possessions reflected Beth's life with Nicole. Time and events had the power to change their meaning. The *vesica piscis*, once worn proudly by Nicole, would now always be burdened with a harsh indictment against Beth. The portrait maintained its power to remind Beth of Nicole's generosity and impeccable ability to gift her with a patient, constant love. As in the portrait, Beth wore her cross. The cross was a symbol that stood alone; unlike the *vesica piscis*, the cross was free of all pretenses to merge the pagan with the Christian. The cross was a symbol that Nicole still refused to invite into her home. That truth caused Beth pause as she contemplated the future of the portrait.

Beth held the ring between her finger and thumb and studied the universal symbol of eternity. She placed the ring in the palm of her left hand, beside the pendant, closing her fist over them both. Beth bowed her head in prayer. From the pendant rose her feelings of remorse. From the ring rose a renewal of her hope, reflecting her gradually rebuilt confidence in her union with Nicole. "Please LORD." She felt her emotion rise. She felt a profound need to wear the ring again. She feared Nicole's disapproval. Regardless of her fear she decided to try. She placed the ring on her finger, still holding the pendant as a reminder of the risk in her act. She prepared herself, for if she must, by Nicole's insistence, she would once again remove the symbol of Nicole's vow. Unlike the cross, like the pendant, the ring had no meaning apart from Nicole.

CHAPTER 185

November 1, 2004 – Monday

Nicole stood before the Holy Hill Shrine, debating whether to enter. The previous week she had informed Beth that she would be spending her birthday away from the city. Beth did not question her. Without any further words exchanged, seeing her lover's pained expression, Nicole was sure Beth knew her destination. She was also sure Beth would have welcomed an invitation to join her. However, after setting her stringent terms regarding everything associated with the Church and the cross, Nicole did not want to try to explain why, once again, after foregoing her annual pilgrimage the previous year, she felt compelled to honor her mother's memory in this particular sanctuary.

On this day, Nicole's mother had given birth to her. Nicole had never been told whether she was welcomed. Deeply, she wanted to believe that her mother loved her, wanted her. Nicole had never been the kind of child who escaped into fantasy. She had never filled her emptiness with bright visions assuring her that all was well, and all would be well. Her interior emptiness was a place that remained dark, the emotions stirred because of it, murky.

Nicole felt a familiar vague sorrow and regret. Her mourning of what could have been was not limited to her mother. Her heart was as sensitive as exposed nerve endings after a fire. The slightest sensation: the touch of the sweeping breeze, the sounds of the church bells, the smells of the moist foliage coupled with her presence on the Hill, was sufficient to sear her composure, leaving a mark emblematic of her most difficult memories of Beth.

The church bells sounded for 11:00 a.m. mass. In her mind's eye she saw her mother beckoning her to enter the spiritual edifice, to join her in the worship of all that was greater than humanity. It was not enough to remain outside. With the hour nearing, Nicole entered. Unlike her visits to the Hill with Beth, she sat in a back corner of the church. The interior remained unchanged in the two years since she had last visited. The act of return did not change the fact that she was on foreign soil. Never had she felt more a stranger.

The mass proceeded to the Sign of Peace. To Nicole, it seemed apropos that she stood far away from the worshipers. She observed the exchange of greeting with a longing for Beth. She wanted to wish Beth peace, a state of soul that her partner continued to seek.

"Peace be with you."

Nicole turned toward the gentle low male voice. A priest offered his hand. Nicole met his humble gaze and held it. She took his hand. "Peace be with you, Father."

The priest smiled. He released her hand and walked away.

Driving home, Nicole's thoughts shifted away from her mother to Jacob and Liza. They had always been her true parents. It had taken her a lifetime to acknowledge them as such. Their adoption of her had been covert, a necessary strategy to prevent her mother from taking any actions to stifle the transfer of Nicole's love. Nicole's commitment to the Levis had always carried the stigma of betrayal. She had chosen them over her mother. The beatings at her mother's hand were a reasonable punishment for her failure to love as completely as was expected of her, or so she had once believed.

From the Levis, her thoughts swept to memories of Carrie. She still missed her friend, especially on this day. She relived her last night with Amelia. The hurt was as fine as a thread, barely noticeable. She mourned the loss of her problematic friendship with Kate. She smiled, feeling a strongly rooted gratitude for Tess, who was capable of touching her heart with a unique blend of compassion and exacting expectation, who gave her the gift of a godchild – Dion. From one child Nicole's thoughts turned to another – Tasi, and her grandmother, Yeva, appreciating the richness both young and old had brought to her life. And most of all, Nicole's thoughts tenderly regarded Beth – the woman who loved her with a knowing appreciation of their friendship and their intimate union. Her love for Beth had grown in its ferocity, proving Jacob right; the depths of love were truly unfathomable.

Nicole returned home late in the evening. Waiting for her inside the loft, near the front door, was a large wrapped package. Taped to it an envelope with her name written in Beth's recognizable script. The size and shape of the package betrayed its contents. Nicole opened the envelope and read the card.

Nicki,

> *I give you what has and will always be yours.*
> *I pray that you accept my love.*

Happy Birthday,
Beth

Nicole's fingertips fell lightly over the script. She knelt before the package and tore the wrapping away, revealing the portrait. Over the glass, she traced Beth's face with her finger, gliding it down Beth's neck to her cross. She leaned back taking in the image of Beth complete. The truth was blissful. "I love you, Elizabeth Ann Kelly."

CHAPTER 186

November 11, 2004 – Thursday

Nicole toweled her hair dry as she walked from the bathroom to the ringing telephone. "Good morning."

"Hi," Beth said brightly.

Nicole could not help smiling. "Hello to you, too. What's up?"

"Can't I want to hear your voice before I start my day?"

"No objection here."

"Glad to hear it. How about dinner tonight? I'll play chef."

Nicole looked about the loft. She had had every intention of spending a quiet evening alone. She hesitated. "This isn't the best day."

"Oh … okay." Beth was disappointed. More so, she felt she had reason to be concerned.

Nicole counter-offered. "How about tomorrow, here?"

"Sure …" Beth debated whether to question Nicole further. Challenging Nicole was still hard for her. "Nicki, is everything all right?"

Telling Beth made the gravity of her day palpable. "I'm having tests at the hospital."

Beth reminded herself that Nicole had an annual checkup near the anniversary of her surgery. Her fear was not completely appeased. "Is there something I should know?"

"The usual drill," Nicole responded casually.

Beth's desire to see Nicole became a need. "I can come over for a late dinner."

Nicole thought to protest. Knowing how it felt to be in Beth's position, she made her decision. "Let yourself in. Connor will have keys at the bar."

Beth entered The Pub, where Happy Hour was in full swing. She waved to Connor. He responded in kind. She raised her wrist and touched her watch, indicating she was running late.

Connor tossed Beth the keys to the loft. He called out over the din of the crowd. "They're yours to keep. Drop by on the way out."

Beth ran up the stairs to Nicole's office. Beth's elation to hold in her hand another sign of her return to The Fields momentarily displaced the soberness of the day. She passed through the office to the loft door. She used the keys to enter the loft. The space was dark except for the light over the kitchen island

and another emanating near the bed. Beth spied Nicole dressed in her white robe, resting by the window, her head leaning against the plane. Seeing Nicole sleeping was to see her vulnerable.

On this day, as Nicole had been given a battery of tests, all that was considered the normality of life was set aside. Death shifted from the periphery to the forefront of their minds. They stood together in the void of not knowing.

Beth shared with Nicole a tacit understanding of the paradox that, as their respective illnesses brought them closer to one another, those same illnesses also prompted cautious consideration of their future as a couple. Death was an intimate companion, rarely spoken of but uniquely acknowledged in their lovemaking. Trace evidence of death's dominion remained in the surgical scar on Beth's flesh, a scar Nicole reverently kissed. Nicole's scars were hidden under the growth of her hair. They were tactility revealed to Beth whenever she physically explored her lover. Beth anticipated that on this night there would be no lovemaking to celebrate their lives and their love. The reality of cancer offered an opportunity to reassure simply by standing before Nicole alive.

Beth caught sight of the source of the second light. A new pair of spotlights illuminated the portrait, which was suspended over the bed headboard from the ceiling by a fine wire. Beth smiled. She had learned early in their friendship that Nicole's gestures often preceded the spoken word. She had also learned to trust Nicole's silence when intimately shared, a far different silence in tone than Nicole's silence in withdrawal. After Nicole's birthday, Beth had been gifted with both Nicole's gestures and her penetrating silence. Seeing the portrait, never discussed, Beth realized that Nicole was not done giving.

Beth chose to leave Nicole undisturbed. She secured a tray of food from Miguel. After eating lightly, she stored the remainder, and made herself comfortable in Nicole's leather lounge chair, reading by lamplight.

The city sounds wafted into Nicole's consciousness. She felt the cool glass pane against her forehead. She opened her eyes to the intermittent streetlights and Beth's reflection in the glass. The younger woman was focused on her reading. It was an image Nicole had missed. She enjoyed the privilege of observing Beth unguarded. Though the young scholar was intent, she also had a relaxed air. Beth was in her element. Nicole debated whether the effect came from Beth's immersion in her book or if the loft touched Beth's disposition. Had the loft become a home to Beth?

Rachel's words echoed in Nicole's mind, 'Why didn't you fight for her?' What Rachel did not understand was the brutal impact of self-recognition presented, not in strokes of demand, but in the still, silent space of nothingness.

When circumstances are made by one's own hand and the outcome is discernibly unjust, the greatest incursion can be achieved by exposing the disavowed.

Nicole could not go back and change their past. She could never erase the memories of their painful divergence. She could and did accept that they had both done their best.

Beth looked up from her book. "Hey."

"Hi."

"How long have your been awake?"

"Just a little while. What time is it?"

Beth glanced at her watch. "8:15." She set her book down and went to sit beside Nicole. She tugged Nicole's robe belt. "Shower did you in?"

"Not my favorite day of the year. I don't like MRIs."

Beth sympathetically winced. "Worse than lumbar punctures?"

"I wish I had a choice of neither."

"How long before you get the results?"

"A few days, maybe a week. First glimpse, everything looked okay."

"That's good news." Beth felt the fearful press of the day ease. "Miguel threw together a tray. Hungry?"

"Not right now."

Beth entwined her hand with Nicole's. Her gaze held Nicole's, attempting to breach her lover's reticence. "How are you, really?"

"I ..." Nicole looked out into the night. "There are moments when the world doesn't seem real to me. I guess that's how I've felt most of the day."

"Tell me."

Nicole looked back toward the interior of the loft. She found and held Beth's gaze. "I feel like I'm an observer, watching life like a heartless tourist. I don't have any sense of compassion or pity, joy or disgust. What I see just is. There is nothing ordinary or extraordinary. I don't feel the weight of my body. I breathe easily, so easily my breath makes the least possible impression. I don't belong. I don't not belong. I'm me and the world isn't me. The separation doesn't matter. I lose sight of those I love: Jacob, Liza, Tess ..." Nicole paused. "You," she emphasized with a low, vibrant voice. "There is no such thing as being alone. I couldn't describe what loneliness is. I've forgotten. It's slipped away. Forgetting brings a halcyon life." Nicole turned back to the night. "Why is it that whenever death is so close that I can see it shimmer in front of my eyes, I see life in its simplest form? What more does anyone need to know to be awed by the very chance of life, and when the time comes, what greater gift can we be given then the release death grants us?"

Beth listened, entranced by her partner's description of what she understood to be a mystical experience. "I didn't know you felt life like that."

Nicole looked at Beth. "Telling you I'm heartless has never struck me as a good idea."

"Nicki, you're not heartless. That's not what I heard." Beth tightened her hold on Nicole's hand. "Remember, I know you. When you get cut, you bleed. Hiding your wounds from me doesn't change the fact that you're hurting."

"For myself. Not for others."

"That's not true ..." Beth arrested her protest. She chose to honor Nicole's statement. "Nicki, why tell me now?"

"Sometimes I'm afraid that the price I've paid for surviving is that I've become jaded."

Human resilience could be so misunderstood. Beth offered the insight garnered from her experience. "When I did my first three month's of CPE while I was still in seminary, I came home almost every day and cried ..."

"You still cry for the patients."

"Not like I did then. To be surrounded by that kind of physical and emotional pain.... sitting with death on a daily basis ... that was all new to me. And then the day came when the truth got below my skin; it cut through my heart and touched my soul. What I was witness to was life. I couldn't be any good to anyone if I was constantly falling apart. I set aside my sentimentality. And when I did I came to a place much like what you described. I thought there was something wrong with me. How could I hear fear and not be moved? How could I touch ugliness without being repulsed? How could I embrace hopelessness and be at peace?"

"How can you?" Nicole sincerely wondered where Beth found the strength to follow her calling.

"You know how." Beth chose to use Nicole's own terms. "Because in that moment life itself, no matter how terrible it might seem, was reason to be awed. Because I knew that when the time comes, death does not harm us. Death grants us relief."

"You don't always feel that way."

"Once in a blue moon," Beth admitted. "Nicki, once they knew it, the greatest mystics in history spent their lives trying to recapture that elusive feeling of unity. I don't believe you can make it come to you. I think it is a grace."

Nicole firmly planted her tongue in cheek. "Greek or Christian?"

Beth laughed lightly. "You know the answer to that question, too."

"Doesn't hurt to make sure."

"Hey ..." Beth glanced over to the portrait. "I noticed the new addition to your personal gallery."

Nicole enjoyed seeing the glimmer in Beth's eyes. "You always wanted me to hang the portrait over our bed."

"Do I still have visiting rights?"

"Anytime."

Beth felt her very being quake. Having Nicole before her, she felt a surge of her love. She knew the feeling; she was falling deeper in love with her partner. "You know what I realized? I was so busy being the preeminent doctoral student that I forgot how much more my life had been and could still be. I've missed coming to The Fields to see you. I've missed our lunches and our dinners in The Garden, and our Sunday afternoons in The Pub with the brunch crowd. And I've missed seeing you sitting outside with Jacob. That was how we began."

Nicole looked down. Only the week before, after seeing Beth wearing her ring, had she removed the gold band – the symbol of Beth's promise to her – from its safe house and returned it to her hand. She had been waiting to see if their promise had merit. Beth, by wearing her ring, had tacitly renewed her vow, offering an unabashed declaration of her commitment. Nicole wanted the same. She did not realize how much until that unexpected moment. Nicole was frightened. She also felt an exhilaration long forgotten. She struggled with her conflicting emotions. Living separately and yet considering themselves in union was not Beth's dream. "Visiting rights aren't the only thing I promised you."

"No, you promised me much more. You promised to love me and you have never broken that promise."

Having Beth in the loft brought a comforting visual fusion of Nicole's safe havens: the loft and Beth. "I'm glad you're here."

Beth kissed Nicole. "So am I."

CHAPTER 187

November 27, 2004 – Saturday

Cindy and Beth enjoyed their after dinner coffee while sitting at The Garden's best table. The restaurant was nearly empty; all but a few patrons had left for The Pub or The Fields.

"We've talked about everything and everybody except Nicki. How is she?" asked Cindy.

Beth beamed. "Wonderful. Her medical test results couldn't have been better."

"That's great, Beth. I would say, judging from that look on your face, that more than Nicki's health is good."

Beth blushed. She glanced down shyly. "Yeah."

Cindy laughed. "I'm happy for both of you."

Beth raised her gaze. She realized it was Cindy's sincerely voiced inclusion of Nicole in her concern that distinguished her from many of her U.C. friends. She understood that this was the subtle difference that Nicole had perceived and appreciated. "Thank you."

"So, am I going to see her tonight?"

"She's planning to come up from The Fields after the charity event finishes. She promised me a slow dance."

"You know, Beth, after the first time you brought me here, I could never separate Nicki from The Fields. She needed to come back here, didn't she?"

"Hyde Park will never be her home again."

"I remember what you told me a long time ago. You said that you and Nicki fell in love somewhere between St. Ann's and The Fields. Now it seems as if you are going to live somewhere between Hyde Park and here."

Beth looked out the window. "Sometimes it feels like we're standing together in a wilderness."

"Isn't that where many of us go to find God?"

"And more." Beth leaned back in her chair. She considered the gradual change she enjoyed in Nicole. Not sharing Hyde Park with Nicole was a reasonable price to keep their relationship on its current path. She tried to explain by touching upon a history she feared she would never be able to revisit without a broken heart. "When Nicki and I were in Ireland we stopped at a cove with a small lighthouse. We walked a path leading to a wooden staircase that weaved down the cliff. When we reached the shoreline we discovered that it was blanketed by stones naturally cut into large plates." Beth extended her hands to illustrate. "The cliff walls had the same jagged patterns. Nicki hopped on a large stone and quietly looked around. Slowly a smile came to her. She has this magnificent smile that tells me that everything is right and good. I didn't realize how much I missed that particular smile until I saw it again. I hadn't seen it since my surgery. Nicki started taking pictures focusing the telephoto down to the rock bed and up to the cliffs. I asked her what she was seeing. She gave me the camera and told me what to look for. She had been framing the geometric patterns of the stones with the camera lens creating compositions of form and texture that reminded me of the abstract art she likes best. I said so. She agreed." Beth paused. She had Cindy's complete attention. "In that moment, not only did I see what Nicki saw, I understood how she found art in nature and nature in art, and how the beauty of both awed her and gave her joy." Beth felt her unshed tears of Ireland return. "I've seen that smile again and I can't tell you how it makes me feel."

Cindy smiled knowingly. "Was she looking at you when she did?"

Beth nodded, unable to raise a word from her emotionally bound throat. Gathering her composure, Beth held up her left hand. "She gave me that smile the night she saw that I was wearing my ring again. The next morning she was wearing hers."

"You know, you two have never been a conventional couple. It may be that living a conventional life will never be right for either of you."

"It's ironic because I think deep down, Nicki wanted a conventional life. She wanted a partnership and a child. She just never trusted that she deserved love and she feared she would hurt her child the way she had been hurt. I was so close to giving her both."

"I would say you have given her the love she's been searching for."

"I pray that I never disappoint her again."

Cindy took Beth's hand. "Beth, no relationship is free from hurt ..."

"Irish!" Connor called out across the restaurant.

Startled, Beth called back, "Connor, is something wrong?"

The bar manager advanced towards his target. "No. You have to come with me. You too, Cindy."

Cindy got to her feet. "Where are we going?"

"The Fields. This is too good. Just wait, I've got to get Miguel." Connor ran into the kitchen.

Beth laughed. "Come on, we might as well see what's going on."

Connor and Miguel exited the kitchen. "*Chica*, come." Miguel took Beth's hand, leading her out of the restaurant.

Entering The Fields, Connor directed them into the elevated DJ booth where Tony was holding court. There was standing room only on the dance floor. The patrons were focused on the stage where an elegantly dressed Nicole stood seductively beside a handsome tuxedoed man equal to her in age. Nicole had just begun to lip-synch Etta James' rendition of "At Last".

"*Dios mio*" Miguel laughed.

Connor slapped Tony on the shoulder. "How did you get her to do it?"

Tony was triumphant. "Charity. Gets her every time."

"Not like this," said Connor. "She always writes a check."

"Italian charm goes a long way," bragged Tony.

Beth was mesmerized. Nicole was clearly enjoying the song, flirting with her partner, taking in the hoots and hollers. This was another part of Nicole that had been lost to Beth. Nicole's joyful exuberance had always been contained, and Beth took solace in the rare release, often reserved for their private exchanges. Nicole Isabel Thera was happy.

Beth listened to the lyrics. Nicole would not have chosen the song indiscriminately. The song spoke of the end of loneliness, of a dream realized. Beth's heart burst open when she heard the reference to the two lovers together in heaven. She did not want the song to end.

The song did end. The performers took a bow. Nicole kissed her partner on the cheek and continued to exchange words, laughing as she did. She took possession of an oversized cognac glass and jumped off stage coaxing donations, accepting compliments and hugs. Beth's gaze remained fixed on her partner's delight.

"She was wonderful," Cindy offered.

Beth's smile was shared. "Yes, she was."

Nicole looked at the production booth and waved. Beth knew Nicole could not see her behind the tinted glass. Nicole completed making a round of the dance floor, and returned to the stage, handing the cognac glass to her partner who was hosting the event. She trotted to the side of the production booth, calling out to Tony, "Fifty bucks!"

Connor quipped, "Italian charm, right?"

Nicole caught sight of Beth and Cindy. "Hey."

Beth went to her and leaned down. "You can still take my breath away."

Charmed, Nicole offered her most intimate expression of love. "Elizabeth."

Beth was enraptured. "Nicki, what made you change your mind?"

"I remembered something Jacob said when we were talking about Simchat Torah. Can you imagine Jacob dancing with the Torah?"

"I wish I could see that."

"If he can dance, I can pretend I can sing. How was dinner?"

"Miguel outdid himself."

Nicole looked over to Beth's companion. "Cindy, long time."

Cindy was appreciative. "I didn't know you were such a show-woman."

"Some things are worth making a fool out of yourself for. Right, Tony?"

Tony agreed. "Worth every penny."

Nicole returned her attention to Beth. "Who drove?"

"I did, why?"

"I thought you might like to spend the night."

"I can always drive Cindy home and come back."

"You could, but it's getting late."

Beth offered her own invitation; one Nicole had yet to accept. "Meet me at Hyde Park."

Nicole wanted to spend the night with Beth. The location was inconsequential. "This could be our life, you know."

"What do you mean?"

"Two homes. One more yours. The other more mine."

"I'm happy," Beth confessed.

Nicole searched her partner's eyes. "Are you?"

"Yes." Beth felt the truth of her answer.

Nicole kissed Beth. She smiled. It was the smile that told Beth all was right and good. "Remind me to pack a few things before we leave tonight."

CHAPTER 188

December 14, 2004 – Tuesday

Beth sat on the street bench, her gaze cast down to her clasped hands. A shadow crossed over and stayed stationary. Beth looked up. Jacob stood before her. Their eyes met and held for a few heartbeats before Jacob moved to the side taking a seat next to the young woman. They sat in silence, watching the city traffic.

After a handful of minutes Jacob asked, not unkindly, "Would you prefer a different companion? Maybe I should send Liza here to you."

Jacob had misunderstood Beth's silence. She returned to the present moment from her contemplative state. "I'm sorry. It's not …" She placed a comforting hand on Jacob's arm. "When Nicki and I lived together at Hyde Park, I would go to her den whenever I missed her. I may have seen her that morning but it didn't matter. I'd just wanted to be someplace that meant her to me."

"You miss her today?"

Beth nodded.

"You could have visited Tasi with Nicole."

"I do, but never on Tuesdays." Having Jacob beside her, Beth longed to keep to the subject of Nicole. "Jacob, I promise you I will try never to take Nicki for granted again."

Beth's promise was clearly unexpected. Nonetheless, Jacob appeared grateful to have it. "Her wounds are healing. Her deepest hurt will not heal easily. My girl puts on a brave face. You must be careful with her."

"I am."

Jacob offered Beth a consolation in return. "You know she never stopped loving you."

"I know."

"I have sat here with Nicole many times, speaking of women." Jacob took Beth's hand. "It has been a difficult journey for her. There was the first one, the one whose name she will not speak, who seduced her. When Nicole learned she had been used because of her beauty, she stopped believing any woman could love her. And then Amelia came into her life and compounded the lesson proving to her that her love would only bring her heartbreak."

Beth knew better than to be surprised by the confidences Nicole share with Jacob. "You know about Amelia?"

"I know Nicole confessed to you that she had loved Amelia. Amelia did not attend the University seeking a future. She studied to fill the otherwise empty, limited hours in her life. Nicole knew this. She could not allow herself to admit to a love that had no future. After her mother, she would not risk losing love to an illness again."

Beth was overwhelmed by the revelation. Nicole had only spoken of her sense of betrayal, never what Amelia's imminent death had meant to her. "Jacob, when I became sick ..." Beth faltered.

Jacob nodded. "That is why our Nicole changed. You were proof, once again, that she was not to have a lasting love. My Beth, Nicole could not bear it; she still cannot bear the thought of losing you to death. She can give you up to God or to another lover, but not to death. Her mistake, and she knows this, is that she allowed her fear to stop her from being an equal partner to you. She made allowances she should not have because she did not want to hurt you. Because being with you, in spite of the hardship, was a blessing to her."

Jacob's insight had troubling implications. Beth would consider them at a later time. For now she was pleased to report, "Nicki's fighting back the way she used to."

"Good. I do not want her to make allowances for the hurt done to her by others in the name of God."

Beth noted a change in Jacob. "This isn't the way ..." She touched upon a favorite memory, juxtaposing the past with the present. "I will never forget the first time I saw you and Nicki together. You teased her mercilessly."

"God has taught me to be tender with my girl." Jacob gently squeezed Beth's hand. "And with you. Beth, I never told you why I was so angry with you. I saw myself in you. It was hard accepting that we had both made the same mistake."

"I understand." Beth was grateful for Jacob's confession. Jacob in turn was grateful for Beth's acceptance and compassion.

The two friends drifted into silence, their thoughts directed toward a common love. Beth imagined her future would take her to visiting The Fields, including the bench she sat on, much more often. "Nicki and I won't be living together, at least not for a while."

"Nicole's choice?"

"Yes. And if we do live together we won't be adopting a child."

Jacob was dismayed. "Has she said this?"

Beth could not swear that Nicole spoke those very words since their tual return. She could say that the subject of a child was painful to them . "She has Tasi."

And before Tasi, there was Dion. Nicole needs time to overcome the mother set into her heart. Unless she tells me in her own words, I will ve she has chosen to forgo the dream of a child."

Beth was determined to face her future honestly. "There are other reasons."

"Your medical histories? You have less than three years to wait."

Beth looked at Jacob sadly. "That was before I hurt her. I can't blame Nicki. Raising a child together takes trust. I don't think she can trust me in that way anymore."

"It is true that you hurt Nicole when you assumed that the child you would raise together would learn to abide by your beliefs and not her own. Give her time."

"Jacob, I accept the consequences of my actions."

The elder turned to the younger woman. His counsel was uncompromising. "You are repeating your mistake. You are judging Nicole by your beliefs. See the world through her heart. If she did not trust you, she would never have returned to you."

Beth wanted to believe him. "How can she?"

"Because she has learned her hardest lessons by her mistakes. Haven't we all?"

Beth rested her head against Jacob's shoulder as she took hold of his arm, seeking his comfort.

"What about you?" Jacob asked gently.

Beth's voice was a hush. "I've made my choice." It was a simple definitive statement.

Jacob took Beth's hand and kissed it. "Remember Beth, so, too, has Nicole."

THE END

Also from Cavalier Press

Words Heard in Silence by T. Novan and Taylor Rickard
North and South unite in this sweeping novel set in the Civil War. The love of Charlie and Rebecca defies social convention and overcomes the brutality of war, as they come together to found a new dynasty in this, the first volume of The Redmond Chronicles.

Madam President by T. Novan and Blayne Cooper
Life in the White House with Devlyn Marlowe, the first woman President of the United States, and her official biographer, soon-to-be-lover, Lauren Strayer. Politics and pug dogs, drama and devilment run through the pages of this entertaining romantic novel.

First Lady by T. Novan and Blayne Cooper
Devlyn and Lauren prepare for their wedding in this sequel to *Madam President*. Their relationship deepens as the couple struggles to balance the tensions of a public life with the private business of getting married and establishing a family life.

Adeptus Major by Alex Mykals
Princess Evelynne deMolay, heir to the modern-day Kingdom of Atlantis, is saved from assassination by Alleandre Tretiak, a mysterious woman with paranormal abilities. As their friendship grows into love, Evelynne and Ally are forced to question some long-held assumptions about themselves and about their places in society.

In the Blood of the Greeks by Mary D. Brooks
The first of a series that follows the lives of two women who meet in occupied Greece during the Second World War and subsequently make a new life for themselves in Australia.

Where Shadows Linger by Mary D. Brooks
The sequel to *In the Blood of the Greeks* - Coming May 2006

Black by Gaslight by Nene Adams
Black by Gaslight is the first book in a series following the adventures of Lady Evangeline St. Clair, an unconventional and wealthy Victorian woman, and her companion, Rhiannon Moore, throughout England and Europe. Lady St. Clair is a consulting detective, and the eccentric aristocrat's avocation takes her into strange and sometimes dangerous places.

The Madonna of the Sorrows by Nene Adams
The Madonna of the Sorrows is the second book in the *Gaslight* series. Lady Evangeline St. Clair and Rhiannon Moore travel to the World's Fair in Paris in pursuit of the solution to a mystery almost a century old, and as they do, come up against danger which threatens their lives and their love.

Seasons by Anne Azel
Seasons follows the lives and trials of successful and wild film star/director Robbie Williams and her partner Janet, widow of Robbie's deceased brother, from their first highly stressfu meeting through a most unusual courtship and finally, to the adventures of raising a collc tion of highly intelligent and sometimes willful children.

Facing Evil by CL Hart

A serial killer stalks the police officer who almost brought him to justice. Haunted by her failure, Detective Abby Stanfield retreats to a mountain resort where she becomes involved with Sarah, the beautiful woman in the cabin next door. And in so doing, she puts into motion a string of events that will have both women fighting for their love and their very survival.

Penetrate by Kathleen Kelly

Two women on separate journeys up the Amazon. Kali, a ruthless pirate, on an assassination mission for a powerful criminal cartel; Maddie, a sheltered academic, studying the fragile rainforest environment. Inexplicably drawn to each other from their first meeting, the women find themselves together on a perilous passage through the steamy Brazilian jungle. - Coming April 2006

*Purchase online at www.cavalierpress.com
or at your local GLBT bookstore.*

About the Author

Cuban-born Maytee Aspuro y Gonzalez currently resides in Madison, Wisconsin. She holds a Masters in Management and a Masters in Religious Studies. She is a career Executive with the State of Wisconsin. Hesed is her first novel.